THE NUMBER of the BEAST

Books by Robert A. Heinlein

THE NUMBER
of the
BEAST

Robert A. Heinlein

FAWCETT GOLD MEDAL • NEW YORK

A Fawcett Gold Medal Book

Published by Ballantine Books

Copyright © 1980 by Robert A. Heinlein

ISBN 0-449-14476-3

Manufactured in the United States of America

First Fawcett Columbine printing: August 1980
First Ballantine Books Edition: July 1982
10 9 8 7 6 5 4 3 2 1

For Walter and Marion Minton

Contents

PART ONE

The Mandarin's Butterfly

PART TWO

The Butterfly's Mandarin

PART THREE

Death and Resurrection

L'Envoi

The Mandarin's Butterfly

I   "—*it is better to marry than to burn.*"
—Saul of Tarsus

"He's a Mad Scientist and I'm his Beautiful Daughter."

That's what she said: the oldest cliché in pulp fiction. She wasn't old enough to remember the pulps.

The thing to do with a silly remark is to fail to hear it. I went on waltzing while taking another look down her evening formal. Nice view. Not foam rubber.

She waltzed well. Today most girls who even attempt ballroom dancing drape themselves around your neck and expect you to shove them around the floor. She kept her weight on her own feet, danced close without snuggling, and knew what I was going to do a split second before I led it. A perfect partner—as long as she didn't talk.

"Well?" she persisted.

My paternal grandfather—an unsavory old reactionary; the FemLibbers would have lynched him—used to say, "Zebadiah, the mistake we made was not in putting shoes on them or in teaching them to read—we should *never* have taught them to talk!"

I signaled a twirl by pressure; she floated into it and back into my arms right on the beat. I inspected her hands and the outer corners of her eyes. Yes, she really was young—minimum eighteen (Hilda Corners never permitted legal "infants" at her parties), maximum twenty-five, first approximation twenty-two. Yet she danced like her grandmother's generation.

"Well?" she repeated more firmly.

This time I openly stared. "Is that cantilevering natural? Or is

11

there an invisible bra, you being in fact the sole support of two dependents?"

She glanced down, looked up and grinned. "They do stick out, don't they? Your comment is rude, crude, unrefined, and designed to change the subject."

"What subject? I made a polite inquiry; you parried it with amphigory."

"'Amphigory' my tired feet! I answered precisely."

"'Amphigory,'" I repeated. "The operative symbols were 'mad,' 'scientist,' 'beautiful,' and 'daughter.' The first has several meanings—the others denote opinions. Semantic content: zero."

She looked thoughtful rather than angry. "Pop isn't rabid . . . although I did use 'mad' in ambivalent mode. 'Scientist' and 'beautiful' each contain descriptive opinions, I stipulate. But are you in doubt as to my sex? If so, are you qualified to check my twenty-third chromosome pair? With transsexual surgery so common I assume that anything less would not satisfy you."

"I prefer a field test."

"On the *dance floor?*"

"No, the bushes back of the pool. Yes, I'm qualified—laboratory or field. But it was not your sex that lay in the area of opinion; that is a fact that can be established . . . although the gross evidence is convincing. I—"

"Ninety-five centimeters isn't gross! Not for my height. One hundred seventy bare-footed, one eighty in these heels. It's just that I'm wasp-waisted for my mass—forty-eight centimeters versus fifty-nine kilos."

"And your teeth are your own and you don't have dandruff. Take it easy, Deedee; I didn't mean to shake your aplomb"—or those twin glands that are not gross but delicious. I have an infantile bias and have known it since I was six—six months, that is. "But the symbol 'daughter' encompasses two statements, one factual— sex—and the other a matter of opinion even when stated by a forensic genetohematologist."

"Gosh, what big words you know, Mister. I mean 'Doctor.'"

"'Mister' is correct. On this campus it is swank to assume that everyone holds a doctorate. Even I have one, Ph.D. Do you know what that stands for?"

"Doesn't everybody? I have a Ph.D., too. 'Piled Higher and Deeper.'"

I raised that maximum to twenty-six and assigned it as second approximation. "Phys. ed.?"

"Mister Doctor, you are trying to get my goat. Won't work.

I had an undergraduate double major, one being phys. ed. with teacher's credentials in case I needed a job. But my real major was math—which I continued in graduate school."

"And here I had been assuming that 'Deedee' meant 'Doctor of Divinity.'"

"Go wash out your mouth with soap. My nickname is my initials—Dee Tee. Or Deety. Doctor D. T. Burroughs if being formal, as I can't be 'Mister' and refuse to be 'Miz' or 'Miss.' See here, Mister; I'm supposed to be luring you with my radiant beauty, then hooking you with my feminine charm . . . and not getting anywhere. Let's try another tack. Tell me what you piled higher and deeper."

"Let me think. Flycasting? Or was it basketweaving? It was one of those transdisciplinary things in which the committee simply weighs the dissertation. Tell you what. I've got a copy around my digs. I'll find it and see what title the researcher who wrote it put on it."

"Don't bother. The title is 'Some Implications of a Six-Dimensional Non-Newtonian Continuum.' Pop wants to discuss it." ·

I stopped waltzing. "Huh? He'd better discuss *that* paper with the bloke who wrote it."

"Nonsense; I saw you blink—I've hooked you. Pop wants to discuss it, then offer you a job."

"'*Job*'! I just slipped off the hook."

"Oh, dear! Pop will be *really* mad. Please? Please, sir!"

"You said that you had used 'mad' in ambivalent mode. How?"

"Oh. Mad-angry because his colleagues won't listen to him. Mad-psychotic in the opinions of some colleagues. They say his papers don't make sense."

"Do they make sense?"

"I'm not that good a mathematician, sir. My work is usually simplifying software. Child's play compared with n-dimensional spaces."

I wasn't required to express an opinion; the trio started *Blue Tango,* Deety melted into my arms. You don't talk if you know tango.

Deety knew. After an eternity of sensual bliss, I swung her out into position precisely on coda; she answered my bow and scrape with a deep curtsy. "Thank you, sir."

"Whew! After a tango like that the couple ought to get married."

"All right. I'll find our hostess and tell Pop. Five minutes? Front door, or side?"

She looked serenely happy. I said, "Deety, do you mean what you appear to mean? That you intend to marry *me?* A total stranger?"

Her face remained calm but the light went out—and her nipples went down. She answered steadily. "After that tango we are no longer strangers. I construed your statement as a proposal—no, a willingness—to marry me. Was I mistaken?"

My mind went into emergency, reviewing the past years the way a drowning man's life is supposed to flash before his eyes (how could anyone know that?): a rainy afternoon when my chum's older sister had initiated me into the mysteries; the curious effect caused by the first time strangers had shot back at me; a twelve-month cohabitation contract that had started with a bang and had ended without a whimper; countless events which had left me determined never to marry.

I answered instantly, "I meant what I implied—marriage, in its older meaning. I'm willing. But why are *you* willing? I'm no prize."

She took a deep breath, straining the fabric, and—thank Allah!—her nipples came up. "Sir, you are the prize I was sent to fetch, and, when you said that we really ought to get married—hyperbole and I knew it—I suddenly realized, with a deep burst of happiness, that *this* was the means of fetching you that I wanted above all!"

She went on, "But I will not trap you through misconstruing a gallantry. If you wish, you may take me into those bushes back of the pool . . . and *not* marry me." She went on firmly, "But for that . . . whoring . . . my fee is for you to talk with my father and to let him show you something."

"Deety, you're an idiot! You would ruin that pretty gown."

"Mussing a dress is irrelevant but I can take it off. I will. There's nothing under it."

"There's a great deal under it!"

That fetched a grin, instantly wiped away. "Thank you. Shall we head for the bushes?"

"Wait a half! I'm about to be noble and regret it the rest of my life. You've made a mistake. Your father doesn't want to talk to *me;* I don't know anything about *n*-dimensional geometry." (Why do I get these attacks of honesty? I've never done anything to deserve them.)

"Pop thinks you do; that is sufficient. Shall we go? I want to get Pop out of here before he busts somebody in the mouth."

"Don't rush me; I didn't ask you to rassle on the grass; I said

I wanted to *marry* you—but wanted to know why you were willing to marry *me*. Your answer concerned what your father wants. I'm not trying to marry your father; he's not my type. Speak for yourself, Deety. Or drop it." (Am I a masochist? There's a sunbathing couch back of those bushes.)

Solemnly she looked me over, from my formal tights to my crooked bow tie and on up to my thinning brush cut—a hundred and ninety-four centimeters of big ugly galoot. "I like your firm lead in dancing. I like the way you look. I like the way your voice rumbles. I like your hair-splitting games with words—you sound like Whorf debating Korzybski with Shannon as referee." She took another deep breath, finished almost sadly: "Most of all, I like the way you smell."

It would have taken a sharp nose to whiff me. I had been squeaky clean ninety minutes earlier, and it takes more than one waltz and a tango to make me sweat. But her remark had that skid in it that Deety put into almost anything. Most girls, when they want to ruin a man's judgment, squeeze his biceps and say, "Goodness, you're strong!"

I grinned down at her. "You smell good too. Your perfume could rouse a corpse."

"I'm not wearing perfume."

"Oh. Correction: your natural pheromone. Enchanting. Get your wrap. Side door. Five minutes."

"Yes, sir."

"Tell your father we're getting married. He gets that talk, free. I decided that before you started to argue. It won't take him long to decide that I'm not Lobachevski."

"That's Pop's problem," she answered, moving. "Will you let him show you this thing he's built in our basement?"

"Sure, why not? What is it?"

"A time machine."

II "This Universe never did make sense—"

Zeb:

Tomorrow I will seven eagles see, a great comet will appear, and voices will speak from whirlwinds foretelling monstrous and fearful things— This Universe never did make sense; I suspect that it was built on government contract.

"Big basement?"

"Medium. Nine by twelve. But cluttered. Work benches and power tools."

A hundred and eight square meters— Ceiling height probably two and a half— Had Pop made the mistake of the man who built a boat in his basement?

My musing was interrupted by a male voice in a high scream: "You overeducated, obstipated, pedantic ignoramus! Your mathematical intuition froze solid the day you matriculated!"

I didn't recognize the screamer but did know the stuffed shirt he addressed: Professor Neil O'Heret Brain, head of the department of mathematics—and God help the student who addressed a note to "Professor N. O. Brain" or even "N. O'H. Brain." "Brainy" had spent his life in a search for The Truth—intending to place it under house arrest.

He was puffed up like a pouter pigeon with his professional pontifical pomposity reeling. His expression suggested that he was giving birth to a porcupine.

Deety gasped, "It's started," and dashed toward the row. Me, I stay out of rows; I'm a coward by trade and wear fake zero-prescription glasses as a buffer—when some oaf snarls, "Take off your glasses!" that gives me time to retreat.

I headed straight for the row.

Deety had placed herself between the two, facing the screamer, and was saying in a low but forceful voice, "Pop, don't you dare!—I won't bail you out!" She was reaching for his glasses

16

with evident intent to put them back on his face. It was clear that he had taken them off for combat; he was holding them out of her reach.

I reached over their heads, plucked them out of his hand, gave them to Deety. She flashed me a smile and put them back on her father. He gave up and let her. She then took his arm firmly. "Aunt Hilda!"

Our hostess converged on the row. "Yes, Deety? Why did you stop them, darling? You didn't give us time to get bets down." Fights were no novelty at "Sharp" Corners' parties. Her food and liquor were lavish, the music always live; her guests were often eccentric but never dull—I had been surprised at the presence of N. O. Brain.

I now felt that I understood it: a planned hypergolic mixture.

Deety ignored her questions. "Will you excuse Pop and me and Mr. Carter? Something urgent has come up."

"You and Jake may leave if you must. But you can't drag Zebbie away. Deety, that's cheating."

Deety looked at me. "May I tell?"

"Eh? *Certainly!*"

That bliffy "Brainy" picked this moment to interrupt. "Mrs. Corners, Doctor Burroughs can't leave until he apologizes! I insist. My privilege!"

Our hostess looked at him with scorn. "Merde, Professor. I'm not one of your teaching fellows. Shout right back at Jake Burroughs if you like. If your command of invective equals his, we'll enjoy hearing it. But just *one more word* that sounds like an order to me or to one of my guests—and out you go! Then you had best go straight home; the Chancellor will be trying to reach you." She turned her back on him. "Deety, you started to add something?"

"Sharp" Corners can intimidate Internal Revenue agents. She hadn't cut loose on "Brainy"—just a warning shot across his bow. But from his face one would have thought she had hulled him. However, her remark to Deety left me no time to see whether he would have a stroke.

"Not Deety, Hilda. Me. Zeb."

"Quiet, Zebbie. Whatever it is, the answer is No. Deety? Go ahead, dear."

Hilda Corners is related to that famous mule. I did not use a baseball bat because she comes only up to my armpits and grosses forty-odd kilos. I picked her up by her elbows and turned her around, facing me. "Hilda, we're going to get married."

"Zebbie darling! I thought you would *never* ask."

"Not you, you old harridan. Deety. I proposed, she accepted; I'm going to nail it down before the anesthetic wears off."

Hilda looked thoughtfully interested. "That's reasonable." She craned her neck to look at Deety. "Did he mention his wife in Boston, Deety? Or the twins?"

I set her back on her feet. "Pipe down, Sharpie; this is serious. Doctor Burroughs, I am unmarried, in good health, solvent, and able to support a family. I hope this meets with your approval."

"Pop says Yes," Deety answered. "I hold his power of attorney."

"You pipe down, too. My name is Carter, sir—Zeb Carter. I'm on campus; you can check my record. But I intend to marry Deety at once, if she will have me."

"I know your name and record, sir. It doesn't require my approval; Deety is of age. But you have it anyhow." He looked thoughtful. "If you two are getting married at once, you'll be too busy for shop talk. Or would you be?"

"Pop—let it be; it's all set."

"So? Thank you, Hilda, for a pleasant evening. I'll call you tomorrow."

"You'll do no such thing; you'll come straight back and give me a full report. Jake, you are *not* going on their honeymoon— I heard you."

"Aunt Hilda—please! I'll manage everything."

We were out the side door close on schedule. At the parking lot there was a bobble: which heap, mine or theirs. Mine is intended for two but can take four. The rear seats are okay for two for short trips. Theirs was a four-passenger family saloon, not fast but roomy—and their luggage was in it. "How much luggage?" I asked Deety, while I visualized two overnight bags strapped into one back seat with my prospective father-in-law stashed in the other.

"I don't have much, but Pop has two big bags and a fat briefcase. I had better show you."

(Damn.) "Perhaps you had better." I like my own rig, I don't like to drive other people's cars, and, while Deety probably handled controls as smoothly as she danced, I did not *know* that she did—and I'm chicken. I didn't figure her father into the equation; trusting my skin to his temper did not appeal. Maybe Deety would settle for letting him trail us—but my bride-to-be was going to ride with *me!* "Where?"

"Over in the far corner. I'll unlock it and turn on the lights."

She reached into her father's inside jacket pocket, took out a Magic Wand.

"Wait for baby!"

The shout was from our hostess. Hilda was running down the path from her house, purse clutched in one hand and about eight thousand newdollars of sunset mink flying like a flag from the other.

So the discussion started over. Seems Sharpie had decided to come along to make certain that Jake behaved himself and had taken just long enough to tell Max (her bouncer-butler-driver) when to throw the drunks out or cover them with blankets, as needed.

She listened to Deety's summary, then nodded. "Got it. I can handle yours, Deety; Jake and I will go in it. You ride with Zebbie, dear." She turned to me. "Hold down the speed, Zebbie, so that I can follow. No tricks, Buster. Don't try to lose us or you'll have cops busting out of your ears."

I turned my sweet innocent eyes toward her. "Why, Sharpie darling, you know I wouldn't do anything like that."

"You'd steal city hall if you could figure a way to carry it. Who dumped that load of lime Jello into my swimming pool?"

"I was in Africa at that time, as you know."

"So you say. Deety darling, keep him on a short leash and don't feed him meat. But marry him; he's loaded. Now where's that radio link? And your car."

"Here," said Deety, pointed the Magic Wand and pressed the switch.

I gathered all three into my arms and dived. We hit the ground as the blast hit everything else. But not us. The blast shadow of other cars protected us.

III *"—Professor Moriarty isn't fooled—"*

Zeb:

Don't ask me how. Ask a trapeze artist how he does a triple 'sault. Ask a crapshooter how he knows when he's "hot." But don't ask me how I know it's going to happen just before it hits the fan.

It doesn't tell me anything I don't need to know. I don't know what's in a letter until I open it (except the time it was a letter bomb). I have no precognition for harmless events. But this split-second knowledge when I need it has kept me alive and relatively unscarred in an era when homicide kills more people than does cancer and the favorite form of suicide is to take a rifle up some tower and keep shooting until the riot squad settles it.

I don't *see* the car around the curve on the wrong side; I automatically hit the ditch. When the San Andreas Fault cut loose, I jumped out a window and was in the open when the shock arrived—and didn't know why I had jumped.

Aside from this, my E.S.P. is erratic; I bought it cheap from a war-surplus outlet.

I sprawled with three under me. I got up fast, trying to avoid crushing them. I gave a hand to each woman, then dragged Pop to his feet. No one seemed damaged. Deety stared at the fire blazing where their car had been, face impassive. Her father was looking at the ground, searching. Deety stopped him. "Here, Pop." She put his glasses back on him.

"Thank you, my dear." He started toward the fire.

I grabbed his shoulder. *"No!* Into my car—*fast!"*

"Eh? My briefcase—could have blown clear."

"Shut up and move! All of you!"

"Do it, Pop!" Deety grabbed Hilda's arm. We stuffed the older ones into the after space; I shoved Deety into the front passenger

20

seat and snapped: "Seat belts!" as I slammed the door—then was around to the left so fast that I should have caused a sonic boom. "Seat belts fastened?" I demanded as I fastened my own and locked the door.

"Jake's is fastened and so is mine, Zebbie dear," Hilda said cheerfully.

"Belt tight, door locked," Deety reported.

The heap was hot; I had left it on trickle—what use is a fast car that won't go *scat*? I switched from trickle to full, did not turn on lights, glanced at the board and released the brake.

It says here that duos must stay grounded inside city limits—so I was lifting her nose before she had rolled a meter and she was pointed straight up as we were clearing the parking lot.

Half a klick straight up while the gee meter climbed—two, three, four—I let it reach five and held it, not being sure what Pop's heart would take. When the altimeter read four klicks, I cut everything—power, transponder, the works—while hitting a button that dropped chaff, and let her go ballistic. I didn't *know* that anyone was tracking us—I didn't want to find out.

When the altimeter showed that we had topped out, I let the wings open a trifle. When I felt them bite air, I snap-rolled onto her belly, let wings crawl out to subsonic aspect and let her glide. "Everybody okay?"

Hilda giggled. "Whoops, dearie! Do that again! This time, somebody kiss me."

"Pipe down, you shameless old strumpet. Pop?"

"I'm okay, son."

"Deety?"

"Okay here."

"Did that fall in the parking lot hurt you?"

"No, sir. I twisted in the air and took it on one buttock while getting Pop's glasses. But next time put a bed under me, please. Or a wrestling mat."

"I'll remember." I switched on radio but not transponder, tried all police frequencies. If anyone had noticed our didoes, they weren't discussing it on the air. We were down to two klicks; I made an abrupt wingover to the right, then switched on power. "Deety, where do you and your Pop live?"

"Logan, Utah."

"How long does it take to get married there?"

"Zebbie," Hilda cut in, "Utah has no waiting time—"

"So we go to Logan."

"—but does require blood test. Deety, do you know Zebbie's

nickname around campus? The Wasp. For 'Wassermann Positive.' Zebbie, everybody knows that Nevada is the only state that offers twenty-four-hour service, no waiting time, no blood test. So point this bomb at Reno and sign off."

"Sharpie darling," I said gently, "would you like to walk home from two thousand meters?"

"I don't know; I've never tried it."

"That's an ejection seat . . . but no parachutes."

"Oh, how romantic! Jake darling, we'll sing the *Liebestod* on the way down—you sing tenor, I'll force a soprano and we'll die in each other's arms. Zebbie, could we have more altitude? For the timing."

"Doctor Burroughs, gag that hitchhiker. Sharpie, *Liebestod* is a solo."

"Picky, picky! Isn't dead-on-arrival enough? Jealous because you can't carry a tune? I *told* Dicky Boy that should be a duet and Cosima agreed with me—"

"Sharpie, button your frimpin' lip while I explain. One: Everybody at your party knows why we left and will assume that we headed for Reno. You probably called out something to that effect as you left—"

"I believe I did. Yes, I did."

"Shut up. Somebody made a professional effort to kill Doctor Burroughs. Not just kill but overkill; that combo of high explosive and Thermit was intended to leave nothing to analyze. But it is possible that no one saw us lift. We were into this go-wagon and I was goosing it less than thirty seconds after that booby trap exploded. Innocent bystanders would look at the fire, not at us. *Guilty* bystanders— There wouldn't be any. A professional who booby-traps a car either holes up or crosses a state line and gets lost. The party or parties who paid for the contract may be nearby, but if they are, Hilda, they're in your house."

"One of my *guests?*"

"Oh, shut it, Sharpie; you are never interested in the morals of your guests. If they can be depended on to throw custard pies or do impromptu strips or some other prank that will keep your party from growing dull, that qualifies them. However, I am *not* assuming that the boss villain was at your party; I am saying that he would not be lurking where the Man might put the arm on him. Your house would be the best place to hide and watch the plot develop.

"But, guest or not, he was someone who *knew* that Doctor

Burroughs would be at your party. Hilda, who knew that key fact?"

She answered with uncustomary seriousness. "I don't know, Zebbie. I would have to think."

"Think hard."

"Mmm, not many. Several were invited because Jake was coming—you, for example—"

"I became aware of that."

"—but you weren't told that Jake would be present. Some were told—'No Brain,' for example—but I can't imagine that old fool booby-trapping a car."

"I can't either, but killers don't look like killers; they look like people. How *long* before the party did you tell 'Brainy' that Pop would be present?"

"I told him when I invited him. Mmm, eight days ago."

I sighed. "The possibles include not only the campus but the entire globe. So we must try to figure probables. Doctor Burroughs, can you think of anyone who would like to see you dead?"

"Several!"

"Let me rephrase it. Who hates your guts so bitterly that he would not hesitate to kill your daughter as long as he got *you?* And also bystanders such as Hilda and me. Not that we figure, save to show that he didn't give a hoot who caught it. A deficient personality. Amoral. *Who is he?*"

Pop Burroughs hesitated. "Doctor Carter, disagreement between mathematicians can be extremely heated . . . and I am not without fault." (You're telling *me*, Pop!) "But these quarrels rarely result in violence. Even the death of Archimedes was only indirectly related to his—our—profession. To encompass my daughter as well—no, even Doctor Brain, much as I despise him, does not fit the picture."

Deety said, "Zeb, could it have been *me* they were shooting at?"

"*You* tell *me*. Whose dolly have you busted?"

"Hmm—I can't think of anyone who dislikes me even enough to snub me. Sounds silly but it's true."

"It's the truth," put in Sharpie. "Deety is just like her mother was. When Jane—Deety's mother, and my best friend until we lost her—when Jane and I were roommates in college, I was always getting into jams and Jane was always getting me out—and never got into one herself. A peacemaker. So is Deety."

"Okay, Deety, you're out of it. So is Hilda and so am I, as whoever placed that booby trap could not predict that either Hilda or I would be in blast range. So it's Pop they're gunning for. Who we don't know, why we don't know. When we figure out why, we'll know who. Meantime we've got to keep Pop out of range. I'm going to marry you as fast as possible, not only because you smell good but to give me a legitimate interest in this fight."

"So we go first to Reno."

"Shut up, Sharpie. We've been on course for Reno since we leveled off." I flipped on the transponder, but to the left, not right. It would now answer with a registered, legal signal . . . but not one registered to my name. This cost me some shekels I did not need but were appreciated by a tight-lipped family man in Indio. Sometimes it is convenient not to be identified by sky cops every time one crosses a state line.

"But we aren't going to Reno. Those cowboy maneuvers were intended to deceive the eye, radar, and heat seekers. The evasion against the heat seekers—that rough turn while we were still in glide—either worked or was not needed, as we haven't had a missile up the tail. Probably wasn't needed; people who booby-trap cars aren't likely to be prepared to shoot a duo out of the sky. But I couldn't be certain, so I ducked. We may be assumed to be dead in the blast and fire, and that assumption may stand up until the mess has cooled down and there is daylight to work by. Even later it may stand up, as the cops may not tell anyone that they were unable to find organic remains. But I *must* assume that Professor Moriarty isn't fooled, that he is watching by repeater scope in his secret HQ, that he knows we are headed for Reno, and that hostiles will greet us there. So we won't go there. Now quiet, please; I must tell this baby what to do."

The computer-pilot of my car can't cook but what she can do, she does well. I called for display map, changed scale to include Utah, used the light pen to trace route—complex as it curved around Reno to the south, back north again, made easting over some very empty country, and passed north of Hill Air Force Range in approaching Logan. I fed in height-above-ground while giving her leeway to smooth out bumps, and added one change in speed-over-ground once we were clear of Reno radar. "Got it, girl?" I asked her.

"Got it, Zeb."

"Ten-minute call, please."

"Call you ten minutes before end of routing—right!"

"You're a smart girl, Gay."

"Boss, I bet you tell that to all the girls. Over."

"Roger and out, Gay." The display faded.

Certainly I could have programmed my autopilot to accept a plan in response to a punched "Execute." But isn't it pleasanter to be answered by a warm contralto? But the "smart girl" aspect lay in the fact that it took *my* voice to make a flight plan operative. A skilled electron pusher might find a way to override my lock, then drive her manually. But the first time he attempted to use autopilot, the car would not only not accept the program but would scream for help on all police frequencies. This causes car thieves to feel maladjusted.

I looked up and saw that Deety had been following this intently. I waited for some question. Instead Deety said, "She has a very pleasant voice, Zeb."

"Gay Deceiver is a very nice girl, Deety."

"And talented. Zeb, I have never before been in a Ford that can do the things this car—Gay Deceiver?—can do."

"After we're married I'll introduce you to her more formally. It will require reprogramming."

"I look forward to knowing her better."

"You will. Gay is not exactly all Ford. Her external appearance was made by Ford of Canada. Most of the rest of her once belonged to Australian Defense Forces. But I added a few doodads. The bowling alley. The powder room. The veranda. Little homey touches."

"I'm sure she appreciates them, Zeb. I know I do. I suspect that, had she not had them, we would all be as dead as canasta."

"You may be right. If so, it would not be the first time Gay has kept me alive. You have not seen all her talents."

"I'm beyond being surprised. So far as I could see you didn't tell her to land at Logan."

"Logan seems to be the next most likely place for a reception committee. Who in Logan knows that you and your father were going to visit Hilda?"

"No one, through me."

"Mail? Milk cartons? Newspapers?"

"No deliveries to the house, Zeb." She turned her head, "Pop, does anyone in Logan know where we went?"

"Doctor Carter, to the best of my knowledge, no one in Logan knows that we left. Having lived many years in the buzzing gossip of Academe, I have learned to keep my life as private as possible."

"Then I suggest that you all ease your belts and sleep. Until ten minutes before reaching Logan there is little to do."

"Doctor Carter—"

"Better call me Zeb, Pop. Get used to it."

"'Zeb' it is, son. On page eighty-seven of your monograph, after the equation numbered one-twenty-one in your discussion of the rotation of six-dimensional spaces of positive curvature, you said, 'From this it is evident that—' and immediately write your equation one-twenty-two. How did you do it? I'm not disagreeing, sir—on the contrary! But in an unpublished paper of my own I used a dozen pages to arrive at the same transformation. Did you have a direct intuition? Or did you simply omit publishing details? No criticism, I am impressed either way. Sheer curiosity."

"Doctor, *I* did not write that paper. I told Deety so."

"That *is* what he claimed, Pop."

"Oh, come now! *Two* Doctors Zebulon E. Carter on one campus?"

"No. But that's not my name. I'm Zebadiah J. Carter. Zebulon E.-for-Edward Carter and called 'Ed' is my cousin. While he is probably listed as being on campus, in fact he is doing an exchange year in Singapore. It's not as improbable as it sounds; *all* male members of my family have first names starting with 'Z.' It has to do with money and a will and a trust fund and the fact that my grandfather and his father were somewhat eccentric."

"Whereas *you* aren't," Hilda said sweetly.

"Quiet, dear." I turned toward Deety. "Deety, do you want to be released from our engagement? I *did* try to tell you that you had trapped the wrong bird."

"Zebadiah—"

"Yes, Deety?"

"I intend to marry you before this night is over. But you haven't kissed me. I want to be kissed."

I unfastened my seat belt, started to unfasten hers, found that she had done so.

Deety kisses even better than she tangos.

During a break for oxygen, I asked her in a whisper: "Deety, what do your initials stand for?"

"Well . . . please don't laugh."

"I won't. But I have to know them for the ceremony."

"I know. All right, Dee Tee stands for Dejah Thoris."

Dejah Thoris— Dejah Thoris Burroughs— Dejah Thoris *Carter!* I cracked up.

I got it under control after two whoops. Too many. Deety said sadly, "You said you wouldn't laugh."

"Deety darling, I wasn't laughing at *your* name; I was laughing at *mine.*"

"I don't think 'Zebadiah' is a funny name. I like it."

"So do I. It keeps me from being mixed up with the endless Bobs and Eds and Toms. But I didn't tell my middle name. What's a funny name starting with 'J'?"

"I won't guess."

"Let me lead up to it. I was born near the campus of the university Thomas Jefferson founded. The day I graduated from college I was commissioned a second looie Aerospace Reserve. I've been promoted twice. My middle initial stands for 'John.'"

It took not quite a second for her to add it up. "Captain . . . John . . . Carter—of Virginia."

"'A clean-limbed fighting man,'" I agreed. "Kaor, Dejah Thoris. At your service, my princess. Now and forever!"

"Kaor, Captain John Carter. Helium is proud to accept."

We fell on each other's shoulders, howling. After a bit the howling died down and turned into another kiss.

When we came up for air, Hilda tapped me on a shoulder. "Would you let us in on the joke?"

"Do we tell her, Deety?"

"I'm not sure. Aunt Hilda talks."

"Oh, nonsense! I know your full name and I've never told anyone—I held you at your christening. You were wet, too. At both ends. Now give!"

"All right. We don't have to get married—we already *are*. For years. More than a century."

Pop spoke up. "Eh? What's this?" I explained to him. He looked thoughtful, then nodded. "Logical." He went back to figuring he was doing in a notebook, then looked up. "Your cousin Zebulon— Is he on the telephone?"

"Probably not but he lives at the New Raffles."

"Excellent. I'll try both the hotel and the university. Doctor— Son—Zeb, would you be so kind as to place the call? My comcredit code is Nero Aleph eight zero one dash seven five two dash three nine three two Zed Star Zed." (Zed Star Zed credit rating— I was not going to have to support my prospective father-in-law.)

Deety cut in. "Pop, you must *not* call Professor Carter—Zebulon Carter—at this hour."

"But, my dear daughter, it is not late at night in—"

"Of course it isn't; I can count. You want a favor from him, so don't interrupt his after-lunch nap. 'Mad dogs and Englishmen.'"

"It isn't noon in Singapore; it's—"

"—siesta time, even hotter than noon. So wait."

"Deety is right, Pop," I interrupted, "but for the wrong reasons.

It doesn't seem to be a matter of life and death to call him this minute. Whereas it might be a matter of life and death—ours, I mean—to make a call from this car . . . especially with your credit code. Until we find out who the Boys in the Black Hats are, I advise that you place calls from the ground and from public phones that you can feed with newdollars instead of your code. Say a phone in Peoria. Or Paducah. Can it wait?"

"Since you put it that way, sir—yes, it can wait. Although I have trouble believing that anyone wishes to kill me."

"Available data indicate it."

"Agreed. But I have not yet grasped it emotionally."

"Takes a baseball bat," said Hilda. "I had to sit on him while Jane proposed to him."

"Why, Hilda my dear, that is utterly unfactual. I wrote my late beloved a polite note saying—"

I let them argue while I tried to add to available data. "Gay Deceiver."

"Yes, Boss?"

"News, dear."

"Ready, Boss."

"Retrieval parameters. Time—since twenty-one hundred. Area—California, Nevada, Utah. Persons—your kindly boss, dear. Doctor Jacob Burroughs, Doctor D. T. Burroughs, Miz Hilda Corners—" I hesitated. "Professor Neil O'Heret Brain." I felt silly adding "Brainy"—but there had been a row between Pop and him, and years earlier my best teacher had said, "Never neglect the so-called 'trivial' roots of an equation," and had pointed out that two Nobel prizes had derived from "trivial" roots.

"Parameters complete, Boss?"

Doctor Burroughs touched my shoulder. "Can your computer check the news if any on your cousin?"

"Mmm, maybe. She stores sixty million bytes, then wipes last-in-last-out everything not placed on permanent. But her news storage is weighted sixty-forty in favor of North America. I'll try. Smart Girl."

"Holding, Boss."

"Addendum. First retrieve by parameters given. Then retrieve by new program. Time—backwards from now to wipe time. Area—Singapore. Person—Zebulon Edward Carter aka Ed Carter aka Doctor Z. E. Carter aka Professor Z. E. Carter aka Professor or Doctor Carter of Raffles University."

"Two retrieval programs in succession. Got it, Zeb."

"You're a smart girl, Gay."

"Boss, I bet you tell that to all the girls. Over."

"Roger, Gay. Execute!"

"AP San Francisco. A mysterious explosion disturbed the academic quiet of—" A story ending with the usual claim about an arrest being expected "momentarily" settled several points: All of us were believed dead. Our village top cop claimed to have a theory but was keeping it mum—meaning that he knew even less than we did. Since we were reported as "presumed dead" and since the news said nothing about an illegal lift-off and other capers that annoy sky cops, I assumed tentatively that police radar had not been looking at us until after we had become just one more blip behaving legally. The lack of mention of the absence of Gay Deceiver did not surprise me, as I had roaded in and had been last or nearly last to park—and could have arrived by taxi, public capsule, or on foot. Doctor Brain was not mentioned, nothing about the row. Guests had been questioned and released. Five cars parked near the explosion had been damaged.

"Nevada—null retrieval. Utah—UPI Salt Lake City. A fire near Utah State University campus in Logan destroyed—" "Blokes in Black Hats" again and Deety and her Pop were dead twice over, as they were presumed to have been overcome by smoke, unable to escape. No one else hurt or missing. Fire attributed to faulty wiring. "End of first retrieval, Zeb. Second retrieval starting." Gay shut up.

I said soberly, "Pop, somebody doesn't like you."

He groaned, "Gone! All gone!"

"No copies of your papers elsewhere? And your...gadget?"

"Eh? No, no!—*much* worse! My irreplaceable collection of pulp magazines. Weird Tales, Argosy, All-Story, the early Gernsbachs, The Shadow, Black Mask—*Ooooooh!*"

"Pop really does feel bad," Deety whispered, "and I could manage tears myself. I taught myself to read from that collection. War Aces, Air Wonder, the complete Clayton Astoundings— It was appraised at two hundred and thirteen thousand newdollars. Grandpop started it, Pop continued it—I grew up reading them."

"I'm sorry, Deety." I hugged her. "They should have been microfiched."

"They were. But that's not having the magazines in your hands."

"I agree. Uh, how about the...thing in the basement?"

"What 'Thing in the Basement'?" demanded Sharpie. "Zebbie, you sound like H. P. Lovecraft."

"Later, Sharpie. Comfort Jake; we're busy. Gay!"

"Here, Zeb. Where's the riot?"

"Display map, please." We were midway over northern Nevada. "Cancel routing and cruise random. Report nearest county seat."

"Winnemucca and Elko are equidistant to one percent. Elko closer by ETA as I am now vectored eleven degrees north of Elko bearing."

"Deety, would you like to be married in Elko?"

"Zebadiah, I would love to be married in Elko."

"Elko it is, but loving may have to wait. Gay, vector for Elko and ground us, normal private cruising speed. Report ETA in elapsed minutes."

"Roger Wilco, Elko. Nine minutes seventeen seconds."

Hilda said soothingly, "There, there, Jake darling; Mama is here"—then added in her top sergeant voice, "Quit stalling, Zebbie! What 'Thing' in which basement?"

"Sharpie, you're nosy. It belonged to Pop and now it's destroyed and that's all you need to know."

"Oh, but it wasn't," Doctor Burroughs said. "Zeb is speaking of my continua craft, Hilda. It's safe. Not in Logan."

"What in the Name of the Dog is a 'continua craft'?"

"Pop means," Deety explained, "his time machine."

"Then why didn't he say so? Everybody savvies 'Time Machine.' George Pal's 'Time Machine'—a classic goodie. I've caught it on the late-late-early show more than once."

"Sharpie," I asked, "can you read?"

"Certainly I can read! 'Run, Spot, run. See Spot run.' Smarty."

"Have you ever heard of H. G. Wells?"

"Heard of him? I've *had* him."

"You are a boastful old tart, but not that old. When Mr. Wells died, you were still a virgin."

"Slanderer! Hit him, Jake—he insulted me."

"Zeb didn't mean to insult you, I feel sure. Deety won't permit me to hit people, even when they need it."

"We'll change that."

"Second retrieval complete," Gay Deceiver reported. "Holding."

"Report second retrieval, please."

"Reuters, Singapore. The Marston expedition in Sumatra is still unreported according to authorities at Palembang. The party is thirteen days overdue. Besides Professor Marston and native guides and assistants, the party included Doctor Z.E. Carter, Doctor Cecil Yang, and Mr. Giles Smythe-Belisha. The Minister of

Tourism and Culture stated that the search will be pursued assiduously. End of retrieval."

Poor Ed. We had never been close but he had never caused me grief. I hoped that he was shacked up with something soft and sultry—rather than losing his head to a jungle machete, which seemed more likely. "Pop, a few minutes ago I said that somebody doesn't like you. I now suspect that somebody doesn't like *n*-dimensional geometers."

"It would seem so, Zeb. I do hope your cousin is safe—a most brilliant mind! He would be a great loss to all mankind."

(And to himself, I added mentally. And me, since family duty required that I do something about it. When what I had in mind was a honeymoon.) "Gay."

"Here, Zeb."

"Addendum. Third news retrieval program. Use all parameters second program. Add Sumatra to area. Add all proper names and titles found in second retrieval. Run until canceled. Place retrievals in permanent memory. Report new items soonest. Start."

"Running, Boss."

"You're a good girl, Gay."

"Thank you, Zeb. Grounding Elko two minutes seven seconds."

Deety squeezed my hand harder. "Pop, as soon as I'm legally Mrs. John Carter I think we should all go to Snug Harbor."

"Eh? Obviously."

"You, too, Aunt Hilda. It might not be safe for you to go home."

"Change in plans, dear. It's going to be a double wedding. Jake. Me."

Deety looked alert but not displeased. "Pop?"

"Hilda has at last consented to marry me, dear."

"Rats," said Sharpie. "Jake has never asked me in the past and didn't this time; I simply told him. Hit him with it while he was upset over losing his comic books and unable to defend himself. It's necessary, Deety—I promised Jane I would take care of Jake and I have—through you, up to now. But from here on you'll be taking care of Zebbie, keeping him out of trouble, wiping his nose . . . so I've got to hogtie Jake into marriage to keep my promise to Jane. Instead of sneaking into his bed from time to time as in the past."

"Why, Hilda dear, you have never been in my bed!"

"Don't shame me in front of the children, Jake. I gave you a test run before I let Jane marry you and you don't dare deny it."

Jake shrugged helplessly. "As you wish, dear Hilda."

"Aunt Hilda . . . do you love Pop?"

"Would I marry him if I didn't? I could carry out my promise to Jane more simply by having him committed to a shrink factory. Deety, I've loved Jake longer than you have. *Much!* But he loved Jane . . . which shows that he is basically rational despite his weird ways. I shan't try to change him, Deety; I'm simply going to see to it that he wears his overshoes and takes his vitamins—as you've been doing. I'll still be 'Aunt Hilda,' not 'Mother.' Jane was and *is* your mother."

"Thank you, Aunt Hilda. I thought I was happy as a woman can be, getting Zebadiah. But you've made me still happier. No worries."

(*I* had worries. Blokes with Black Hats and no faces. But I didn't say so, as Deety was snuggling closer and assuring me that it was all right because Aunt Hilda wouldn't fib about loving Pop . . . but I should ignore that guff about her sneaking into Pop's bed—on which I had no opinion and less interest.) "Deety, where and what is 'Snug Harbor'?"

"It's . . . a nowhere place. A hideout. Land Pop leased from the government when he decided to build his time twister instead of just writing equations. But we may have to wait for daylight. Unless— Can Gay Deceiver home on a given latitude and longitude?"

"She certainly can! Precisely."

"Then it's all right. I can give it to you in degrees, minutes, and fractions of a second."

"Grounding," Gay warned us.

The Elko County Clerk did not object to getting out of bed and seemed pleased with the century note I slipped him. The County Judge was just as accommodating and pocketed her honorarium without glancing at it. I stammered but managed to say, "I, Zebadiah John, take thee, Dejah Thoris—" Deety went through it as solemnly and perfectly as if she had rehearsed it . . . while Hilda sniffled throughout.

A good thing that Gay can home on a pin point; I was in no shape to drive even in daylight. I had her plan her route, too, a dogleg for minimum radar and no coverage at all for the last hundred-odd kilometers to this place in the Arizona Strip north of the Grand Canyon. But I had her hover before grounding—I being scared silly until I was certain there was not a third fire there.

A cabin, fireproof, with underground parking for Gay—I relaxed.

We split a bottle of chablis. Pop seemed about to head for the basement. Sharpie tromped on it and Deety ignored it.

I carried Deety over the threshold into her bedroom, put her gently down, faced her. "Dejah Thoris—"

"Yes, John Carter?"

"I did not have time to buy you a wedding present—"

"I need no present from my captain."

"Hear me out, my princess. My Uncle Zamir did not have as fine a collection as your father had . . . but may I gift you with a complete set of Clayton Astoundings—"

She suddenly smiled.

"—and first editions of the first six Oz books, quite worn but with the original color plates? And a first in almost mint condition of 'A Princess of Mars'?"

The smile became a grin and she looked nine years old. *"Yes!"*

"Would your father accept a complete set of Weird Tales?"

"Would he! Northwest Smith and Jirel of Joiry? I'm going to borrow them—or he can't look at my Oz books. I'm stubborn, I am. And selfish. And *mean!*"

"'Stubborn' stipulated. The others denied."

Deety stuck out her tongue. "You'll find out." Suddenly her face was solemn. "But I sorrow, my prince, that I have no present for my husband."

"But you have!"

"I do?"

"Yes. Beautifully wrapped and making me dizzy with heavenly fragrance."

"Oh." She looked solemn but serenely happy. "Will my husband unwrap me? Please?"

I did.

That is all anyone is ever going to know about our wedding night.

IV Because two things equal to the same thing are never equal to each other.

Deety:

I woke early as I always do at Snug Harbor, wondered why I was ecstatically happy—then remembered, and turned my head. My husband—*"husband!"*—what a heart-filling word—my husband was sprawled face down beside me, snoring softly and drooling onto his pillow. I held still, thinking how beautiful he was, how gently strong and gallantly tender.

I was tempted to wake him but I knew that my darling needed rest. So I eased out of bed and snuck noiselessly into my bath—*our* bath!—and quietly took care of this and that. I did not risk drawing a tub—although I needed one. I have a strong body odor that calls for at least one sudsy bath a day, two if I am going out that evening—and this morning I was certainly whiff as a polecat.

I made do with a stand-up bath by letting water run in a noiseless trickle into the basin—I would grab that proper bath after my Captain was awake; meanwhile I would stay downwind.

I pulled on briefs, started to tie on a halter—stopped and looked in the mirror. I have a face-shaped face and a muscular body that I keep in top condition. I would never reach semifinals in a beauty contest but my teats are shapely, exceptionally firm, stand out without sagging and look larger than they are because my waist is small for my height, shoulders and hips. I've known this since I was twelve, from mirror and from comments by others.

Now I was acutely aware of them from what Zebadiah calls his "infantile bias." I was awfully glad I had them; my husband liked them so much and had told me so again and again, making me feel warm and tingly inside. Teats get in the way, and I once found out painfully why Amazons are alleged to have removed their starboard ones to make archery easier.

Today I was most pleased that Mama had required me to wear

34

a bra for tennis and horseback and such—no stretch marks, no "Cooper's droop," no sag, and my husband called them "wedding presents"! *Hooray!*

Doubtless they would become baby-chewed and soft—but by then I planned to have Zebadiah steadfastly in love with me for better reasons. You hear that, Deety? Don't be stubborn, don't be bossy, don't be difficult—and above all don't sulk! Mama never sulked, although Pop wasn't and isn't easy to live with. For example he dislikes the word "teat" even though I spell it correctly and pronounce it correctly (as if spelled "tit"). Pop insists that teats are on cows, not women.

After I started symbolic logic and information theory I became acutely conscious of precise nomenclature, and tried to argue with Pop, pointing out that "breast" denoted the upper frontal torso of male and female alike, that "mammary gland" was medical argot, but "teat" was correct English.

He had slammed down a book. "I don't give a damn what The Oxford English Dictionary says! As long as I am head of this house, language used in it will conform to my notions of propriety!"

I never argued such points with Pop again. Mama and I went on calling them "teats" between ourselves and did not use such words in Pop's presence. Mama told me gently that logic had little to do with keeping a husband happy and that anyone who "won" a family argument had in fact lost it. Mama never argued and Pop always did what she wanted—if she really wanted it. When at seventeen I had to grow up and try to replace her, I tried to emulate her—not always successfully. I inherited some of Pop's temper, some of Mama's calm. I try to suppress the former and cultivate the latter. But I'm not Jane, I'm Deety.

Suddenly I wondered why I was putting on a halter. The day was going to be hot. While Pop is so cubical about some things that he turns up at the corners, skin is not one of them. (Possibly he had been, then Mama had gently gotten her own way.) I like to be naked and usually am at Snug Harbor, weather permitting. Pop is almost as casual. Aunt Hilda was family-by-choice; we had often used her pool and never with suits—screened for the purpose.

That left just my lovely new husband, and if there was a square centimeter of me he had not examined (and praised), I could not recall it. Zebadiah is easy to be with, in bed or out. After our hasty wedding I was slightly tense lest he ask me when and how I had mislaid my virginity . . . but when the subject could have come up I forgot it and he apparently never thought about it. I was the lusty wench I have always been and he seemed pleased— I *know* he was.

So why was I tying on this teat hammock? I was—but *why?*

Because two things equal to the same thing are never equal to each other. Basic mathematics if you select the proper sheaf of postulates. People are not abstract symbols. I could be naked with any one of them but not all three.

I felt a twinge that Pop and Aunt Hilda might be in the way on my honeymoon . . . then realized that Zebadiah and I were just as much in the way on theirs—and stopped worrying; it would work out.

Took one last look in the mirror, saw that my scrap of halter, like a good evening gown, made me nakeder than skin would. My nipples popped out; I grinned and stuck out my tongue at them. They stayed up; I was happy.

I started to cat-foot through our bedroom when I noticed Zebadiah's clothes—and stopped. The darling would not want to wear evening dress to breakfast. Deety, you are not being wifely— figure this out. Are any of Pop's clothes where I can get them without waking the others?

Yep! An old shirt that I had liberated as a house coat, khaki shorts I had been darning the last time we had been down—both in my wardrobe in my—*our!*—bathroom. I crept back, got them, laid them over my darling's evening clothes so that he could not miss them.

I went through and closed after me two soundproof doors, then no longer had to keep quiet. Pop does not tolerate anything shoddy—if it doesn't work properly, he fixes it. Pop's B.S. was in mechanical engineering, his M.S. in physics, his Ph.D. in mathematics; there isn't *anything* he can't design and build. A second Leonardo da Vinci—or a Paul Dirac.

No one in the everything room. I decided not to head for the kitchen end yet; if the others slept a bit longer I could get in my morning tone-up. No violent exercise this morning, mustn't get more whiff than I am—just controlled limbering. Stretch high, then palms to the floor without bending knees—ten is enough. Vertical splits, both legs, then the same to the floor with my forehead to my shin, first right, then left.

I was doing a back bend when I heard, "Ghastly. The battered bride. Deety, stop that."

I continued into a backwards walkover and stood up facing

Pop's bride. "Good morning, Aunt Hillbilly." I kissed and hugged her. "Not battered. Bartered, maybe."

"'Battered,'" she repeated, yawning. "Who gave you those bruises? What's-his-name?—your husband."

"Not a bruise on me and you've known his name longer than I have. What causes those circles under the bags under the rings under your eyes?"

"Worry, Deety. Your father is very ill."

"*What?* How?"

"Satyriasis. Incurable—I hope."

I let out my breath. "Aunt Hillbilly, you're a bitchie, bitchie tease."

"Not a bitch this morning, dear. A nanny goat—who has been topped all night by the most amazing billy goat on the ranch. And him past fifty and me only twenty-nine. Astounding."

"Pop's forty-nine, you're forty-two. You're complaining?"

"Oh, no! Had I known twenty-four years ago what I know now, I would never have let Jane lay eyes on him."

"—what you know now—Last night you were claiming to have sneaked into Pop's bed, over and over again. Doesn't jibe, Aunt Nanny Goat."

"Those were quickies. Not a real test." She yawned again.

"Auntie, you lie in your teeth. You were never in his bed until last night."

"How do you know, dear? Unless you were in it yourself? Were you? Incest?"

"What have you got against incest, you bawdy old nanny goat? Don't knock it if you haven't tried it."

"Oh, so you *have?* How fascinating—tell Auntie!"

"I'll tell you the truth, Aunt Hilda. Pop has never laid a hand on me. But if he had...I would not have refused. I love him."

Hilda stopped to kiss me more warmly than before. "So do I, dear one. I honor you for what you just told me. He could have had me, too. But never did. Until last night. Now I'm the happiest woman in America."

"Nope. Second happiest. You're looking at the happiest."

"Mmm, a futile discussion. So my problem child is adequate?"

"Well...he's not a member of the Ku Klux Klan—"

"I never thought he was! Zebbie isn't that sort."

"—but he's a wizard under a sheet!"

Aunt Hilda looked startled, then guffawed. "I surrender. We're both the happiest woman in the world."

"And the luckiest. Aunt Nanny Goat, that robe of Pop's is too hot. I'll get something of mine. How about a tie-on fit-anybody bikini?"

"Thanks, dear, but you might wake Zebbie." Aunt Hilda opened Pop's robe and held it wide, fanning it. I looked at her with new eyes. She's had three or four term contracts, no children. At forty-two her face looks thirty-five, but from her collarbones down she could pass for eighteen. Little bitty teats—I had more at twelve. Flat belly and lovely legs. A china doll—makes me feel like a giant.

She added, "If it weren't for your husband, I would simply wear this old hide. It *is* hot."

"If it weren't for *your* husband, so would I."

"Jacob? Deety, he's changed your diapers. I know how Jane reared you. True modesty, no false modesty."

"It's not the same, Aunt Hilda. Not today."

"No, it's not. You always did have a wise head, Deety. Women are tough-minded, men are not; we have to protect them . . . while pretending to be fragile ourselves, to build up their fragile egos. But I've never been good at it—I like to play with matches."

"Aunt Hilda, you are *very* good at it, in your own way. I'm certain Mama knows what you've done for Pop and blesses it and is happy for Pop. For all of us—all five of us."

"Don't make me cry, Deety. Let's break out the orange juice; our men will wake any time. First secret of living with a man: Feed him as soon as he wakes."

"So I know."

"Yes, of course you know. Ever since we lost Jane. Does Zebbie know how lucky he is?"

"He says so. I'm going to try hard not to disillusion him."

V "—a wedding ring is not a ring in my nose—"

Jake:

I woke in drowsy euphoria, became aware that I was in bed in our cabin that my daughter calls "Snug Harbor"—then woke completely and looked at the other pillow—the dent in it. Not a dream! Euphoric for the best of reasons!

Hilda was not in sight. I closed my eyes and simulated sleep as I had something to do. "Jane?" I said in my mind.

"I hear you, dearest one. It has my blessing. Now we are all happy together."

"We couldn't expect Deety to become a sour old maid, just to take care of her crotchety old father. This young man, he's okay, to the nth power. I felt it at once, and Hilda is certain of it."

"He is. Don't worry, Jacob. Our Deety can never be sour and you will never be old. This is exactly as Hilda and I planned it, more than five of your years ago. Predestined. She told you so, last night."

"Okay, darling."

"Get up and brush your teeth and take a quick shower. Don't dawdle, breakfast is waiting. Call me when you need me. Kiss."

So I got up, feeling like a boy on Christmas morning. Everything was jake with Jake; Jane had put her stamp of approval on it. Let me tell you, you nonexistent reader sitting there with a tolerant sneer: Don't be smug. Jane is more real than *you* are.

The spirit of a good woman cannot be coded by nucleic acids arranged in a double helix, and only an overeducated fool could think so. I could prove that mathematically save that mathematics can never prove anything. No mathematics has any content. All any mathematics can do is—sometimes—turn out to be useful in describing some aspects of our so-called "physical universe."

39

That is a bonus; most forms of mathematics are as meaning-free as chess.

I don't know *any* final answers. I'm an all-around mechanic and a competent mathematician . . . and neither is of any use in unscrewing the inscrutable.

Some people go to church to talk to God, Whoever He is. When I have something on my mind, I talk to Jane. I don't hear "voices," but the answers that come into my mind have as much claim to infallibility, it seems to me, as any handed down by any Pope speaking *ex cathedra*. If this be blasphemy, make the most of it; I won't budge. Jane is, was, and ever shall be, worlds without end. I had the priceless privilege of living with her for eighteen years and I can never lose her.

Hilda was not in the bath but my toothbrush was damp. I smiled at this. Logical, as any germs I was harboring, Hilda now had—and Hilda, for all her playfulness, is no-nonsense practical. She faces danger without a qualm (had done so last night) but she would say "Gesundheit!" to an erupting volcano even as she fled from it. Jane is equally brave but would omit the quip. They are alike only in—no, not that way, either. Different but equal. Let it stand that I have been blessed in marriage by two superb women. (And blessed by a daughter whose Pop thinks she is perfect.)

I showered, shaved, and brushed my teeth in nine minutes and dressed in under nine seconds as I simply wrapped around my waist a terry-cloth sarong Deety had bought for me—the day promised to be a scorcher. Even that hip wrap was a concession to propriety, i.e., I did not know my new son-in-law well enough to subject him abruptly to our casual ways; it might offend Deety.

I was last up, and saw that all had made much the same decision. Deety was wearing what amounted to a bikini minimum (indecently "decent"!) and my bride was "dressed" in a tie-on job belonging to Deety. The tie-ties had unusually large bows; Hilda is tiny, my daughter is not. Zeb was the only one fully dressed: an old pair of working shorts, a worn-out denim shirt Deety had confiscated, and his evening shoes. He was dressed for the street in any western town save for one thing: I'm built like a pear, Zeb is built like the Gray Lensman.

My shorts fitted him well enough—a bit loose—but his shoulders were splitting the shirt's seams. He looked uncomfortable.

I took care of amenities—a good-morning to all, a kiss for my bride, one for my daughter, a handshake for my son-in-law—good hands, calloused. Then I said, "Zeb, take that shirt off. It's hot and getting hotter. Relax. This is your home."

"Thanks, Pop." Zeb peeled off my shirt.

Hilda stood up on her chair, making her about as tall as Zeb. "I'm a militant women's-rights gal," she announced, "and a wedding ring is not a ring in my nose—a ring that you have not yet given me, you old goat."

"When have I had time? You'll get one, dear—first chance."

"Excuses, excuses! Don't interrupt when I'm orating. Sauce for the gander is no excuse for goosing the goose. If you male chauvinist pigs—I mean 'goats'—can dress comfortably, Deety and I have the same privilege." Whereupon my lovely little bride untied that bikini top and threw it aside like a stripper.

"'"What's for breakfast?" asked Pooh,'" I misquoted.

I was not answered. Deety made me proud of her for the *n*th time. For years she had consulted me, at least with her eyes, on "policy decisions." Now she looked not at me but at her husband. Zeb was doing Old Stone Face, refusing assent or dissent. Deety stared at him, gave a tiny shrug, reached behind her and untied or unsnapped something and discarded her own top.

"I said, 'What's for breakfast?'" I repeated.

"Greedy gut," my daughter answered. "You men have had baths, while Aunt Hilda and I haven't had a chance to get clean for fear of waking you slugabeds."

"Is that what it is? I thought a skunk had wandered past. 'What's for breakfast?'"

"Aunt Hilda, in only hours Pop has lost all the training I've given him for five years. Pop, it's laid out and ready to go. How about cooking while Hilda and I grab a tub?"

Zeb stood up. "I'll cook, Deety; I've been getting my own breakfast for years."

"Hold it, Buster!" my bride interrupted. "Sit down, Zebbie. Deety, never encourage a man to cook breakfast; it causes him to wonder if women are necessary. If you always get his breakfast and don't raise controversial issues until after his second cup of coffee, you can get away with murder the rest of the time. They don't notice other odors when they smell bacon. I'm going to have to coach you."

My daughter reversed the field, fast. She turned to her husband and said meekly, "What does my Captain wish for breakfast?"

"My Princess, whatever your lovely hands offer me."

What we were offered, as fast as Deety could pour batter and Hilda could serve, was a gourmet specialty that would enrage a *Cordon Bleu* but which, for my taste, is ambrosia: A one-eyed Texas stack—a tall stack of thin, tender buttermilk pancakes to

Jane's recipe, supporting one large egg, up and easy, surrounded by hot sausage, and the edifice drowned in melting butter and hot maple syrup, with a big glass of orange juice and a big mug of coffee on the side.

Zeb ate two stacks. I concluded that my daughter would have a happy marriage.

VI   *Are men and women one race?*

Hilda:

Deety and I washed dishes, then soaked in her tub and talked about husbands. We giggled, and talked with the frankness of women who trust each other and are sure that no men can overhear. Do men talk that openly in parallel circumstances? From all I have been able to learn in after-midnight horizontal conversations, all passion spent, men do *not*. Or not men I would take to bed. Whereas a "perfect lady" (which Jane was, Deety is, and I can simulate) will talk with another "perfect lady" she trusts in a way that would cause her father, husband, or son to faint.

I had better leave out our conversation; this memoir might fall into the hands of one of the weaker sex and I would not want his death on my conscience.

Are men and women one race? I know what biologists say— but history is loaded with "scientists" jumping to conclusions from superficial evidence. It seems to me far more likely that they are symbiotes. I am not speaking from ignorance; I was one trimester short of a B.S. in biology (and a straight-A student) when a "biology experiment" blew up in my face and caused me to leave school abruptly.

Not that I need that degree— I've papered my private bath with honorary degrees, mostly doctorates. I hear that there are things no whore will do for money but I have yet to find *anything* that a university chancellor faced with a deficit will boggle at. The secret is never to set up a permanent fund but to dole it out when need is sharpest, once every academic year. Done that way, you not only own a campus but also the town cops learn that it's a waste of time to hassle you. A univer$ity alway$ $tand$ $taunchly by it$ $olvent a$$ociate$; that'$ the ba$ic $ecret of $chola$tic $ucce$$.

Forgive my digre$$ion; we were speaking of men and women. I am strong for women's rights but was never taken in by unisex nonsense. I don't yearn to be equal; Sharpie is as *un*equal as possible, with all the perks and bonuses and special privileges that come from being one of the superior sex. If a man fails to hold a door for me, I fail to see him and step on his instep. I feel no shame in making lavish use of the strongest muscles, namely male ones (but my own strongest muscle is dedicated to the service of men—*noblesse oblige*). I don't begrudge men one whit of their natural advantages as long as they respect mine. I am not an unhappy pseudomale; I am *female* and like it that way.

I borrowed makeup that Deety rarely uses, but I carry my own perfume in my purse and used it in the twenty-two classic places. Deety uses only the basic aphrodisiac: soap and water. Perfume on her would be gilding the lily; fresh out of a hot tub she smells like a harem. If I had her natural fragrance, I could have saved at least ten thousand newdollars over the years as well as many hours spent dabbing bait here and there.

She offered me a dress and I told her not to be silly; any dress of hers would fit me like a tent. "You put something bridal and frilly around your hips and lend me your boldest G-string job. Dear, I surprised you when I jockeyed you into taking off your halter, after telling you that you were wise not to rush it. But the chance showed up and I grabbed the ring on the fly. We've got our men gentled to nearly naked and we'll hold that gain. At first opportunity we'll get pants off all of us, too, without anything as childish as strip poker. Deety, I want us to be a solid family, and relaxed about it. So that skin doesn't mean sex, it just means we are home, en famille."

"Your skin is pretty sexy, Nanny Goat."

"Deety, do you think I'm trying to make a pass at Zebbie?"

"Heavens, no, Aunt Hilda. You would never do that."

"Piffle, dear. I don't have morals, just customs. I don't wait for a man to make a pass; they fumble around and waste time. But when I met him I picked Zebbie for a chum—so I gave him an opening; he made a polite pass, I carefully failed to see it, and that ended it. I'm sure he's as much fun on the workbench as you tell me he is—but bedmates are easy to find, while worthwhile male friends are scarce. Zebbie is one to whom I can holler for help in the middle of the night and be certain he'll rally around. I'm not going to let that change merely because a weird concatenation now makes him my son-in-law. Besides, Deety, although your old Aunt Sharpie may seem undignified, I refuse to be the campus widow who seduces younger men. Save for minor exceptions close to my age, I always have bedded older men. When I was your age, I tripped several three times my age. Educational."

"It certainly is! Aunt Hilda, I got ninety percent of my instruction two years ago—a widower three times my age. I was programming for him and we took shared time when we could get it, often after midnight. I didn't think anything of it until one night I was startled to find that I was helping him to take off my panties. Then I was still more surprised to learn how *little* I had learned in seven years. He gave me a tutored seminar, usually three times a week—all the time he was willing to spare me—for the next six months. I'm glad I got tutoring from an expert before last night rolled around—or Zebadiah would have found me a dead arse, willing but clumsy. I didn't tell this to my darling; I let him think he was teaching me."

"That's right, dear. Never tell a man anything he doesn't need to know, and lie with a straight face rather than hurt his feelings or diminish his pride."

"Aunt Nanny Goat, I just plain love you."

We quit yakking and looked for our men. Deety said that they were certain to be in the basement. "Aunt Hilda, I don't go there without invitation. It's Pop's sanctum sanctorum."

"You're warning me not to risk a faux pas?"

"I'm his daughter, you're his wife. Not the same."

"Well . . . he hasn't told me not to—and today he'll forgive me, if ever. Where do you hide the stairs?"

"That bookcase swings out."

"Be darned! For a so-called cabin this place is loaded with surprises. A bidet in each bath didn't startle me; Jane would have required them. Your walk-in freezer startled me only by being big enough for a restaurant. But a bookcase concealing a priest's hole—as Great-Aunt Nettie used to say, 'I do declare!' "

"You should see our septic tank—yours, now."

"I've seen septic tanks. Pesky things—always need pumping at the most inconvenient time."

"This one won't have to be pumped. Over three hundred meters deep. An even thousand feet."

"For the love of— *Why?*"

"It's an abandoned mine shaft below us that some optimist dug a hundred years back. Here was this big hole, so Pop used it. There is a spring farther up the mountain. Pop cleaned that out, covered it, concealed it, put pipe underground, and we have lavish pure water under pressure. The rest of Snug Harbor Pop designed mostly from prefab catalogs, fireproof and solid and heavily insulated. We have—you have, I mean—this big fireplace and the little ones in the bedrooms, but you won't need them, other than for homeyness. Radiant heat makes it skin-comfortable even in a blizzard."

"Where do you get your power? From the nearest town?"

"Oh, no! Snug Harbor is a hideout, nobody but Pop and me—and now you and Zebadiah—knows it's here. Power packs, Aunt Hilda, and an inverter in a space behind the back wall of the garage. We bring in power packs ourselves, and take them out the same way. Private. Oh, the leasehold record is buried in a computer in Washington or Denver, and the Federal rangers know the leaseholds. But they don't see us if we see or hear them first. Mostly they cruise on past. Once one came by on horseback. Pop fed him beer out under the trees—and from outside this is just a prefab, a living room and two shedroof bedrooms. Nothing to show that important parts are underground."

"Deety, I'm beginning to think that this place—this *cabin*—cost more than my townhouse."

"Uh . . . probably."

"I think I'm disappointed. Sugar Pie, I married your papa because I love him and want to take care of him and promised Jane that I would. I've been thinking happily that my wedding present to my bridegroom would be his weight in bullion, so that dear man need never work again."

"Don't be disappointed, Aunt Hilda. Pop has to work; it's his nature. Me, too. Work is necessary to us. Without it, we're lost."

"Well . . . yes. But working because you want to is the best sort of play."

"Correct!"

"That's what I thought I could give Jacob. I don't understand it. Jane wasn't rich, she was on a scholarship. Jacob had no money—still a teaching fellow, a few months shy of his doctorate. Deety, Jacob's suit that he wore to be married in was threadbare. I know that he pulled up from that; he made full professor awfully fast. I thought it was that and Jane's good management."

"It was both."

"That doesn't account for *this*. Forgive me, Deety, but Utah State doesn't pay what Harvard pays."

"Pop doesn't lack offers. We like Logan. Both the town and the civilized behavior of Mormons. But— Aunt Hilda, I must tell you some things."

The child looked worried. I said, "Deety, if Jacob wants me to know something he'll tell me."

"Oh, but he won't and I must!"

"*No*, Deety!"

"Listen, please! When I said, 'I do,' I resigned as Pop's manager. When you said, 'I do,' the load landed on you. It *has* to be that way, Aunt Hilda. Pop won't do it; he has other things to think about, things that take genius. Mama did it for years, then I learned how, and now it's your job. Because it can't be farmed out. Do you understand accountancy?"

"Well, I *understand* it, I took a course in it. Have to understand it, or the government will skin you alive. But I don't *do* it, I have accountants for that—and smart shysters to keep it inside the law."

"Would it bother you to be outside the law? On taxes?"

"What? Heavens, no! But Sharpie wants to stay outside of jail—I detest an institutional diet."

"You'll stay out of jail. Don't worry, Aunt Hilda—I'll teach you double-entry bookkeeping they don't teach in school. *Very* double. One set for the revenooers and another set for you and Jake."

"It's that second set that worries me. That one puts you in the pokey. Fresh air alternate Wednesdays."

"Nope. The second set is not on paper; it's in the campus computer at Logan—"

"Worse!"

"Aunt Hilda, *please!* Certainly my computer address code is in the department's vault and an I.R.S. agent could get a court order. It wouldn't do him any good. It would spill out our first set of books while wiping every trace of the second set. Inconvenient but not disastrous. Aunt Hillbilly, I'm not a champion at anything else but I'm the best software artist in the business. I can make a computer sit up and beg. Or roll over and play dead. And I'll be at your elbow until you are sure of yourself.

"Now about how Pop got rich— All the time he's been teaching he's also been inventing gadgets—as automatically as a hen lays eggs. A better can opener. A lawn irrigation system that does a better job, costs less, uses less water. Lots of things. But none has his name on it and royalties trickle back in devious ways.

"But we aren't freeloaders. Every year Pop and I study the Federal Budget and decide what is useful and what is sheer waste by fat-arsed chairwarmers and pork-barrel raiders. Even before Mama died we were paying *more* income tax than the total of Pop's salary, and we've paid more each year while I've been running it. It *does* take a bundle to run this country. We don't begrudge money spent on roads and public health and national defense and truly useful things. But we've quit paying for parasites wherever we can identify them.

"It's your job now, Aunt Hilda. If you decide that it's dishonest or too risky, I can cause the computer to make it all open and legal so smoothly that hanky-panky would never show. It would take me maybe three years, and Pop would pay high capital gains. But *you* are in charge of Pop now."

"Deety, don't talk dirty."

"Dirty, how? I didn't even say 'spit.'"

"Suggesting that I would *willingly* pay what those clowns in Washington want to squeeze out of us. I would not be supporting so many accountants and shysters if I didn't think we were being robbed blind. Deety, how about being manager for all of us?"

"No, ma'am! I'm in charge of Zebadiah. I have my own interests to manage, too. Mama wasn't as poor as you thought. When I was a little girl, she came into a chunk from a trust her grandmother had set up. She and Pop gradually moved it over into my name and again avoided inheritance and estate taxes, all legal as Sunday School. When I was eighteen, I converted it into cash, then caused it to disappear. Besides that, I've been paying me a whopping salary as Pop's manager. I'm not as rich as you are, Aunt Hilda, and certainly not as rich as Pop. But I ain't hurtin'."

"Zebbie may be richer than all of us."

"You said last night that he was loaded but I didn't pay attention because I had already decided to marry him. But after experiencing what sort of car he drives I realize that you weren't kidding. Not that it matters. Yes, it *did* matter—it took both Zebadiah's courage and Gay Deceiver's unusual talents to save our lives."

"You may never find out how loaded Zebbie is, dear. Some people don't let their left hands know what their right hands are doing. Zebbie doesn't let his thumb know what his fingers are doing."

Deety shrugged. "I don't care. He's kind and gentle and he's a storybook hero who saved my life and Pop's and yours . . . and last night he proved to me that life is worth living when I've been uncertain about it since Mama had to leave us. Let's go find our men, Aunt Nanny Goat. I'll risk Pop's Holy of Holies if you'll go first."

"Suits. Lay on your duff and cursed be he who first cries, 'Nay, enough.'"

"I don't think they're interested in that now, Nanny Goat."

"Spoilsport. How do you swing back this bookcase?"

"Switch on the cove lights, then turn on the cold water at the sink. Then switch off the cove lights, then turn off the water—in that order."

"'Curiouser and curiouser,' said Alice."

The bookcase closed behind us and was a door with a knob on the upper landing side. The staircase was wide, treads were broad and nonskid, risers gentle, guard rails on both sides—not the legbreaker most houses have as cellar stairs. Deety went down beside me, holding my hand like a child needing reassurance.

The room was beautifully lighted, well ventilated, and did not seem like a basement. Our men were at the far end, bent over a table, and did not appear to notice us. I looked around for a time machine, could not spot it—at least not anything like George Pal's or any I had ever read about. All around was machinery. A drill press looks the same anywhere and so does a lathe, but others were strange—except that they reminded me of machine shops.

My husband caught sight of us, stood up, and said, "Welcome, ladies!"

Zebbie turned his head and said sharply, "Late to class! Find seats, no whispering during the lecture, take notes; there will be a quiz at eight o'clock tomorrow morning. If you have questions, raise your hands and wait to be called on. Anyone who misbehaves will remain after class and wash the chalk boards."

Deety stuck out her tongue, sat down quietly. I rubbed his brush cut and whispered an indecency into his ear. Then I kissed my husband and sat down.

My husband resumed talking to Zebbie. "I lost more gyroscopes that way."

I held up my hand. My husband said, "Yes, Hilda dear?"

"Monkey Ward's sells gyro tops—I'll buy you a gross."

"Thank you, dearest, but these weren't that sort. They were made by Sperry Division of General Foods."

"So I'll get them from Sperry."

"Sharpie," put in Zeb, "you're honing to clean the erasers, too."

"Just a moment, Son. Hilda may be the perfect case to find out whether or not what I have tried to convey to you—and which really can't be conveyed save in the equations your cousin Zebulon used, a mathematics you say is unfamiliar to you—"

"It is!"

"—but which you appear to grasp as mechanics. Would you explain the concept to Hilda? If she understands it, we may hypothesize that a continua craft can be designed to be operated by a nontechnical person."

"Sure," I said scornfully, "poor little me, with a button for a head. I don't have to know where the electrons go to use television or holovision. I just twist knobs. Go ahead, Zebbie. Take a swing at it, I dare you."

"I'll try," Zebbie agreed. "But, Sharpie, don't chatter and keep your comments to the point. Or I'll ask Pop to give you a fat lip."

"He wouldn't dast!"

"So? I'm going to give him a horsewhip for a wedding present—besides the Weird Tales, Jake; you get those too. But you need a whip. Attention, Sharpie."

"Yes, Zebbie. And the same to you doubled."

"Do you know what 'precess' means?"

"Certainly. Precession of the equinoxes. Means that Vega will be the North Star when I'm a great-grandmother. Thirty thousand years or some such."

"Correct in essence. But you're not even a mother yet."

"You don't know what happened last night. I'm an expectant mother. Jacob doesn't dare use a whip on me."

My husband looked startled but pleased—and I felt relieved. Zebbie looked at his own bride. Deety said solemnly, "It is possible, Zebadiah. Neither of us was protected, each was on or close on ovulation. Hilda is blood type B Rhesus positive and my father is AB positive. I am A Rh positive. May I inquire yours, sir?"

"I'm an O positive. Uh . . . I may have shot you down the first salvo."

"It would seem likely. But—does this meet with your approval?"

"'Approval'!" Zebbie stood up, knocking over his chair. "Princess, you could not make me happier! Jake! This calls for a toast!"

My husband stopped kissing me. "Unanimous! Daughter, is there champagne chilled?"

"Yes, Pop."

"Hold it!" I said. "Let's not get excited over a normal biological function. Deety and I don't *know* that we caught; we just hope so. And—"

"So we try again," Zebbie interrupted. "What's your calendar?"

"Twenty-eight and a half days, Zebadiah. My rhythm is pendulum steady."

"Mine's twenty-seven; Deety and I just happen to be in step. But I want that toast at dinner and a luau afterwards; it might be the last for a long time. Deety, do you get morning sick?"

"I don't know; I've never been pregnant . . . before."

"I have and I do and it's miserable. Then I lost the naked little grub after trying hard to keep it. But I'm not going to lose this one! Fresh air and proper exercise and careful diet and nothing but champagne for me tonight, then not another drop until I know. In the meantime— Professors, may I point out that class is in session? I want to know about time machines and I'm not sure I could understand with champagne buzzing my buttonhead."

"Sharpie, sometimes you astound me."

"Zebbie, sometimes I astound myself. Since my husband builds time machines, I want to know what makes them tick. Or at least which knobs to turn. He might be clawed by the Bandersnatch and I would have to pilot him home. Get on with your lecture."

"I read you loud and clear."

But we wasted *("wasted?")* a few moments because everybody had to kiss everybody else—even Zebbie and my husband pounded each other on the back and kissed both cheeks Latin style. Zebbie tried to kiss me as if I were truly his mother-in-law but I haven't kissed that way since junior high. Once I was firm with him he gave in and kissed me better than he ever had before—whew! I'm certain Deety is right but I won't risk worrying my older husband over a younger man and I'd be an idiot to risk competing with Deety's teats et cetera when all I have is fried eggs and my wonderful old goat seems so pleased with my et cetera.

Class resumed. "Sharpie, can you explain precession in gyroscopes?"

"Well, maybe. Physics One was required but that was a long time ago. Push a gyroscope and it doesn't go the way you expect, but ninety degrees from that direction so that the push lines up with the spin. Like this—" I pointed a forefinger like a little boy going: "*Bang!*—you're dead!"

"My thumb is the axis, my forefinger represents the push, the other fingers show the rotation."

"Go to the head of the class. Now—think hard!—suppose we put a gyroscope in a frame, then impress equal forces at *all three* spatial coordinates at once; what would it do?"

I tried to visualize it. "I think it would either faint or drop dead."

"A good first hypothesis. According to Jake, it disappears."

"They *do* disappear, Aunt Hilda. I watched it happen several times."

"But where do they go?"

"I can't follow Jake's math; I have to accept his transformations without proof. But it is based on the notion of six space-time coordinates, three of space, the usual three that we see—marked x, y, and z—and three time coordinates: one marked 't' like this—' (t) "—and one marked 'tau,' Greek alphabet—" (τ) "—and the third from the Cyrillic alphabet, 'teh'—" ($\overline{m}$)

"Looks like an 'm' with a macron over it."

"So it does, but it's what the Russians use for 't.'"

"No, the Russians use 'chai' for tea. In thick glasses with strawberry jam."

"Stow it, Sharpie. So we have x, y, and z; t, tau, and teh, six dimensions. It is basic to the theory that all are at right angles to each other, and that any one may be swapped for any of the others by rotation—or that a new coordinate may be found (not a seventh but replacing any of the six) by translation—say 'tau' to 'tau prime' by displacement along 'x.'"

"Zebbie, I think I fell off about four coordinates back."

My husband suggested, "Show her the caltrop, Zeb."

"Good idea." Zeb accepted a widget from my husband, placed it in front of me. It looked like jacks I used to play with as a little girl but not enough things sticking out—four instead of six. Three touched the table, a tripod; the fourth stuck straight up.

Zeb said, "This is a weapon, invented centuries ago. The points should be sharp but these have been filed down." He flipped it, let it fall to the table. "No matter how it falls, one prong is vertical. Scatter them in front of cavalry; the horses go down—discouraging. They came into use again in Wars One and Two against anything with pneumatic tires—bicycles, motorcycles, lorries, and so forth. Big enough, they disable tanks and tracked vehicles. A small sort can be whittled from thorn bushes for guerrilla warfare—usually poisoned and quite nasty.

"But here this lethal toy is a geometrical projection, a drawing of the coordinates of a four-dimensional space-time continuum. Each spike is exactly ninety degrees from every other spike."

"But they aren't," I objected. "Each angle is more than a right angle."

"I said it was a *projection*. Sharpie, it's an isometric projection of four-dimensional coordinates in three-dimensional space. That distorts the angles...and the human eye is even more limited. Cover one eye and hold still and you see only two dimensions. The illusion of depth is a construct of the brain."

"I'm not very good at holding still—"

"No, she isn't," agreed my bridegroom whom I love dearly and at that instant could have choked.

"But I can close both eyes and *feel* three dimensions with my hands."

"A good point. Close your eyes and pick this up and think of the prongs as the four directions of a four-dimensional space. Does the word tesseract mean anything to you?"

"My high school geometry teacher showed us how to construct them—projections—with modeling wax and toothpicks. Fun. I found other four-dimensional figures that were easy to project. And a number of ways to project them."

"Sharpie, you must have had an exceptional geometry teacher."

"In an exceptional geometry class. Don't faint, Zebbie, but I was grouped with what they called 'overachievers' after it became 'undemocratic' to call them 'gifted children.'"

"Be durned! Why do you always behave like a fritterhead?"

"Why don't you ever look beneath the surface, young man! I laugh because I dare not cry. This is a crazy world and the only way to enjoy it is to treat it as a joke. That doesn't mean I don't read and can't think. I read everything from Giblett to Hoyle, from Sartre to Pauling. I read in the tub, I read on the john, I read in bed, I read when I eat alone, and I would read in my sleep if I could keep my eyes open. Deety, this is proof that Zebbie has never been in my bed: the books downstairs are display; the stuff I read is stacked in my bedroom."

"Deety, did you think I had been sleeping with Sharpie?"

"No, Zebadiah."

"And you never will! Deety told me what a sex maniac you are! You lay your lecherous hands on me and I'll scream for Jacob and he'll beat you to a pulp."

"Don't count on it, dear one," my husband said mildly. "Zeb is bigger and younger and stronger than I...and if I found it needful to try, Deety would cry and beat *me* to a pulp. Son, I should have warned you: my daughter is *vicious* at karate. The killer instinct."

"Thanks. Forewarned, forearmed. I'll use a kitchen chair in one hand, a revolver in the second, and a whip in the other, just as I used to do in handling the big cats for Ringling, Barnum, and Bailey."

"That's three hands," said Deety.

"I'm four-dimensional, darling. Professor, we can speed up this seminar; we've been underrating our overachiever. Hilda is a brain."

"Zebbie, can we kiss and make up?"

"Class is in session."

"Zebadiah, there is always time for that. Right, Pop?"

"Kiss her, Son, or she'll sulk."

"I don't sulk, I bite."

"I think you're cute, too," Zebbie answered, grabbed me by both shoulders, dragged me over the table, and kissed me hard. Our teeth grated and my nipples went *spung!* Sometimes I wish I weren't so noble.

He dropped me abruptly and said, "Attention, class. The two prongs of the caltrop painted blue represent our three-dimensional space of experience. The third prong painted yellow is the t-time we are used to. The red fourth prong simulates both *Tau*-time and *Teh*-time, the unexplored time dimensions necessary to Jake's theory. Sharpie, we have condensed six dimensions into four, then we either work by analogy into six, or we have to use math that apparently nobody but Jake and my cousin Ed understands. Unless you can think of some way to project six dimensions into three— you seem to be smart at such projections."

I closed my eyes and thought hard. "Zebbie, I don't think it can be done. Maybe Escher could have done it."

"It can be done, my dearest," answered my dearest, "but it is unsatisfactory. Even with a display computer with capacity to subtract one or more dimensions at a time. A superhypertesseract—a to the sixth power—has too many lines and corners and planes and solids and hypersolids for the eye to grasp. Cause the computer to subtract dimensions and what you have left is what you already knew. I fear it is an innate incapacity of visual conception in the human brain."

"I think Pop is right," agreed Deety. "I worked hard on that program. I don't think the late great Dr. Marvin Minsky could have done it better in flat projection. Holovision? I don't know.

I would like to try if I ever get my hands on a computer with holovideo display and the capacity to add, subtract, and rotate six coordinates."

"But why six dimensions?" I asked. "Why not five? Or even four, since you speak of rotating them interchangeably."

"Jake?" said Zeb.

My darling looked fussed. "It bothered me that a space-time continuum seemed to require three space dimensions but only one time dimension. Granted that the universe is what it is, nevertheless nature is filled with symmetries. Even after the destruction of the parity principle, scientists kept finding new ones. Philosophers stay wedded to symmetry—but I don't count philosophers."

"Of course not," agreed Zeb. "No philosopher allows his opinions to be swayed by facts—he would be kicked out of his guild. Theologians, the lot of them."

"I concur. Hilda my darling, after I found a way to experiment, it turned out that six dimensions existed. Possibly more—but I see no way to reach them."

"Let me see," I said. "If I understood earlier, each dimension can be swapped for any other."

"By ninety-degree rotation, yes."

"Wouldn't that be the combinations taken four at a time out of a set of six? How many is that?"

"Fifteen," Zebbie answered.

"Goodness! Fifteen whole universes? And we use only *one?*"

"No, no, my darling! That would be ninety-degree rotations of one Euclidean universe. But our universe, or universes, has been known to be non-Euclidean at least since 1919. Or 1886 if you prefer. I stipulate that cosmology is an imperfect discipline, nevertheless, for considerations that I cannot state in nonmathematical terms, I was forced to assume a curved space of positive radius—that is to say, a closed space. That makes the universes possibly accessible to use either by rotation or by translation of *this* number." My husband rapidly wrote three sixes.

"Six sixty-six," I said wonderingly. "'The Number of the Beast.'"

"Eh? *Oh!* The Revelation of Saint John the Divine. But I scrawled it sloppily. You took it that I wrote *this:* '666.'" But what I intended to write was this:" "6^{6^6}" "Six raised to its sixth power, and the result in turn raised to its sixth power. That number is *this:*" $1.03144+ \times 10^{28}$ "—or written in full:" 10,314,424,-

798,490,535,546,171,949,056 "—or more than ten million sextillion universes in our group."

What can one say to that? Jacob went on, "Those universes are our nextdoor neighbors, one rotation or one translation away. But if one includes *combinations* of rotation *and* translation—think of a hyperplane slicing through superhypercontinua not at the point of here-now—the total becomes indenumerable. Not infinity—infinity has no meaning. Uncountable. Not subject to manipulation by mathematics thus far invented. Accessible to continua craft but no known way to count them."

"Pop—"

"Yes, Deety?"

"Maybe Aunt Hilda hit on something. Agnostic as you are, you nevertheless keep the Bible around as history and poetry and myth."

"Who said I was agnostic, my daughter?"

"Sorry, sir. I long ago reached that conclusion because you won't talk about it. Wrong of me. Lack of data never justifies a conclusion. But this key number—one-point-oh-three-one-four-four-plus times ten to its twenty-eighth power—perhaps that *is* the 'Number of the Beast.'"

"What do you mean, Deety?"

"That Revelation isn't history, it's not good poetry, and it's not myth. There must have been *some* reason for a large number of learned men to include it—while chucking out several dozen gospels. Why not make a first hypothesis with Occam's Razor and read it as what it purports to be? Prophecy."

"Hmm. The shelves under the stairs, next to Shakespeare. The King James version, never mind the other three."

Deety was back in a moment with a well-worn black book—which surprised me. I read the Bible for my own reasons but it never occurred to me that Jacob would. We always marry strangers.

"Here," said Deety. "Chapter thirteen, verse eighteen: 'Here is wisdom. Let him that hath understanding count the number of the beast: for it is the number of a man; and his number *is* Six hundred threescore *and* six.'"

"That can't be read as exponents, Deety."

"But this is a *translation,* Pop. Wasn't the original in Greek? I don't remember when exponents were invented but the Greek mathematicians of that time certainly understood powers. Suppose the original read 'Zeta, Zeta, **Zeta!**'—and those scholars, who weren't mathematicians, mistranslated it as six hundred and sixty-six?"

"Uh . . . moondrift, Daughter."

"Who taught me that the world is not only stranger than we imagine but stranger than we *can* imagine? Who has already taken me into two universes that are *not* this one . . . and brought me safely home?"

"Wait a half!" Zebbie said. "You and Pop have already tried the time-space machine?"

"Didn't Pop tell you? We made one minimum translation. We didn't seem to have gone anywhere and Pop thought he had failed. Until I tried to look up a number in the phone book. No 'J' in the book. No 'J' in the Britannica. No 'J' in any dictionary. So we popped back in, and Pop returned the verniers to zero, and we got out, and the alphabet was back the way it ought to be and I stopped shaking. But our rotation was even more scary and we almost died. Out in space with blazing stars—but air was leaking out and Pop just barely put it back to zero before we passed out . . . and came to, back here in Snug Harbor."

"Jake," Zebbie said seriously, "that gadget has got to have more fail-safes, in series with deadman switches for homing." He frowned. "I'm going to keep my eye open for both numbers, six sixty-six and the long one. I trust Deety's hunches. Deety, where is the verse with the description of the Beast? It's somewhere in the middle of the chapter."

"Here. 'And I beheld another beast coming up out of the earth; and he had two horns like a lamb, and he spake as a dragon.'"

"Hmm— I don't know how dragons speak. But if something comes up out of the earth and has two horns . . . and I see or hear either number—I'm going to assume that he has a 'Black Hat' and try to do unto him before he does unto us. Deety, I'm peaceable by policy . . . but two near misses is too many. Next time I shoot first."

I would as lief Zebbie hadn't mentioned "Black Hats." Hard to believe that someone was trying to kill anyone as sweet and innocent and harmless as my darling Jacob. But they *were*—and we knew it.

I said, "Where is this time machine? All I've seen is a claptrap."

"'Caltrop,' Aunt Hilda. You're looking at the space-time machine."

"Huh? Where? Why aren't we in it and going somewhere *fast*? I don't want my husband killed; he's practically brand-new. I expect to get years of wear out of him."

"Sharpie, stop the chatter," Zebbie put in. "It's on that bench, across the table from you."

"All I see is a portable sewing machine."

"That's it."

"What? How do you get inside? Or do you ride it like a broom?"

"Neither. You mount it rigidly in a vehicle—one airtight and watertight by strong preference. Pop had it mounted in their car—not quite airtight and now kaputt. Pop and I are going to mount it in Gay Deceiver, which *is* airtight. With better fail-safes."

"*Much* better fail-safes, Zebbie," I agreed.

"They will be. I find that being married makes a difference. I used to worry about my own skin. Now I'm worried about Deety's. And yours. And Pop's. All four of us."

"Hear, hear!" I agreed. "All for one, and one for all!"

"Yup," Zebbie answered. "Us four, no more. Deety, when's lunch?"

VII   *"Avete, alieni, nos morituri vos spernimus!"*

Deety:

While Aunt Hilda and I assembled lunch, our men disappeared. They returned just in time to sit down. Zebadiah carried an intercom unit; Pop had a wire that he plugged into a jack in the wall, then hooked to the intercom.

"Gentlemen, your timing is perfect; the work is all done," Aunt Hilda greeted them. "What is that?"

"A guest for lunch, my dearest," Pop answered. "Miss Gay Deceiver."

"Plenty for all," Aunt Hilda agreed. "I'll set another place." She did so; Zebadiah placed the intercom on the fifth plate. "Does she take coffee or tea?"

"She's not programmed for either, Hilda," Zebadiah answered, "but I thank you on her behalf. Ladies, I got itchy about news from Singapore and Sumatra. So I asked my autopilot to report. Jake came along, then pointed out that he had spare cold circuits here and there, just in case—and this was a just-in-case. Gay is plugged to the garage end of that jack, and this is a voice-switched master-master intercom at this end. I can call Gay and she can call me if anything new comes in—and I increased her programming by reinstating the earlier programs, Logan and back home, for running retrieval of new data."

"I'll add an outlet in the basement," agreed Pop. "But, Son, *this* is your home—not California."

"Well—"

"Don't fight it, Zebbie. This is *my* home since Jacob legalized me . . . and any step-son-in-law of mine is at home here; you heard Jacob say so. Right, Deety?"

"Of course," I agreed. "Aunt Hilda is housewife and I'm scullery maid. But Snug Harbor is *my* home, too, until Pop and Aunt Hilda kick me out into the snow—and that includes my husband."

"Not into snow, Deety," Aunt Hilda corrected me. "Jacob would insist on a sunny day; he's kind and gentle. But that would not leave you with no roof over your head. My California home—mine and Jacob's—has long been your home-from-home, and Zebbie has been dropping in for years, whenever he was hungry."

"I had better put my bachelor flat into the pot."

"Zebbie, you *can't* put Deety on your day bed. It's lumpy, Deety. Broken springs. Bruises. Zebbie, break your lease and send your furniture back to Good Will."

"Sharpie, you're at it again. Deety, there is no day bed in my digs. An emperor-size bed big enough for three—six if they are well acquainted."

"My Captain, do you go in for orgies?" I asked.

"No. But you can't tell what may turn up in the future."

"You always look ahead, Zebadiah," I said approvingly. "Am I invited?"

"At any orgy of mine, my wife will pick the guests and send the invitations."

"Thank you, sir. I'll wait until you seem to be bored, then look over the crop and pick out choice specimens for you. Assorted flavors and colors."

"My Princess, I will not spank a pregnant woman. But I can think about it. Pop, Snug Harbor continues to impress me. Did you use an architect?"

"Hrrumph! 'Architect' is a dirty word. I studied *engineering*. Architects copy each other's mistakes and call it 'Art.' Even Frank

Lloyd Wright never understood what the Gilbreths were doing. His houses looked great from the outside—inside they were hideously inefficient. Dust collectors. Gloomy. Psych lab rat mazes. Pfui!"

"How about Neutra?"

"If he hadn't been hamstrung by building codes and union rules and zoning laws, Neutra could have been great. But people don't want efficient machines for living; they prefer to crouch in medieval hovels, as their flea-bitten forebears did. Cold, drafty, unsanitary, poor lighting, and no need for any of it."

"I respect your opinion, sir. Pop—three fireplaces . . . no chimneys. How? Why?"

"Zeb, I like fireplaces—and a few cords of wood can save your life in the mountains. But I see no reason to warm the outdoors or to call attention to the fact that we are in residence or to place trust in spark arresters in forest-fire country. Lighting a fire in a fireplace here automatically starts its exhaust fan. Smoke and particles are electrostatically precipitated. The precipitators are autoscrubbed when stack temperature passes twenty-five Celsius, dropping. Hot air goes through labyrinths under bathtubs and floors, then under other floors, thence into a rock heat-sink under the garage, a sink that drives the heat pump that serves the house. When flue gas finally escapes, at points distant from the house, it is so close to ambient temperature that only the most sensitive heat-seeker could sniff it. Thermal efficiency plus the security of being inconspicuous."

"But suppose you are snowed in so long that your power packs play out?"

"Franklin stoves in storage, stove pipe to match, stops in the walls removable from inside to receive thimbles for flue pipes."

"Pop," I inquired, "is this covered by Rule One? Or was Rule One abolished last night in Elko?"

"Eh? The chair must rule that it is suspended until Hilda ratifies or cancels it. Hilda my love, years back Jane instituted Rule One—"

"I ratify it!"

"Thank you. But listen first. It applies to meals. No news broadcasts—"

"Pop," I again interrupted, "while Rule One is still in limbo—*did Gay Deceiver have any news?* I worry, I do!"

"Null retrievals, dear. With the amusing conclusion that you and I are still presumed to have died *twice*, but the news services do not appear to have noticed the discrepancy. However, Miss

Gay Deceiver will interrupt if a bulletin comes in; Rule One is never invoked during emergencies. Zeb, do you want this rig in your bedroom at night?"

"I don't want it but should have it. Prompt notice might save our skins."

"We'll leave this here and parallel another into there, with gain stepped to wake you. Back to Rule One: No news broadcasts at meals, no newspapers. No shop talk, no business or financial matters, no discussion of ailments. No political discussion, no mention of taxes, or of foreign or domestic policy. Reading of fiction permitted en famille—not with guests present. Conversation limited to cheerful subjects—"

"No scandal, no gossip?" demanded Aunt Hilda.

"A matter of your judgment, dear. Cheerful gossip about friends and acquaintances, juicy scandal about people we do not like—fine! Now—do you wish to ratify, abolish, amend, or take under advisement?"

"I ratify it unchanged. Who knows some juicy scandal about someone we don't like?"

"I know an item about 'No Brain'—Doctor Neil Brain," Zebadiah offered.

"Give!"

"I got this from a reliable source but can't prove it."

"Irrelevant as long as it's juicy. Go ahead, Zebbie."

"Well, a certain zaftig coed told this on herself. She tried to give her all to 'Brainy' in exchange for a passing grade in the general math course necessary to *any* degree on our campus. It is rigged to permit prominent but stupid athletes to graduate. Miss Zaftig was flunking it, which takes exceptional talent.

"So she arranged an appointment with the department head—'Brainy'—and made her quid-pro-quo clear. He could give her horizontal tutoring then and there or in her apartment or his apartment or in a motel and she would pay for it or whenever and wherever he chose. But she *had* to pass."

"Happens on every campus, Son," Pop told him.

"I haven't reached the point. She blabbed the story—not angry but puzzled. She says that she was unable to get her intention over to him (which seems impossible, I've seen this young woman). 'Brainy' didn't accept, didn't refuse, wasn't offended, didn't seem to understand. He told her that she had better talk to her instructor about getting tutoring and a re-exam. Now Miss Zaftig is circulating the story that Prof 'No Brain' must be a eunuch or a robot. Not even a homo. Totally sexless."

"He's undoubtedly stupid," Aunt Hilda commented. "But I've never met a man I couldn't get that point across to, if I tried. Even if he was uninterested in my fair virginal carcass. I've never tried with Professor Brain because I'm not interested in *his* carcass. Even barbecued."

"Then, Hilda my darling, why did you invite him to your party?"

"*What?* Because of your note, Jacob. I don't refuse you favors."

"But, Hilda, I don't understand. When I talked to you by telephone, I asked you to invite Zeb—under the impression that he was his cousin Zebulon—and I did say that two or three others from the department of mathematics might make it less conspicuously an arranged meeting. But I didn't mention Doctor Brain. And I did *not* write."

"Jacob—I *have* your note. In California. On your University stationery with your name printed on it."

Professor Burroughs shook his head, looked sad. Zebadiah Carter said, "Sharpie—handwritten or typed?"

"Typed. But it was signed! Wait a moment, let me think. It has my name and address down in the lower left. Jacob's name was typed, too, but it was signed 'Jake.' Uh . . . 'My dear Hilda, A hasty P.S. to my phone call of yesterday—Would you be so kind as to include Doctor Neil O. Brain, chairman of mathematics? I don't know what possessed me that I forgot to mention him. Probably the pleasure of hearing your dear voice.

"'Deety sends her love, as do I. Ever yours, Jacob J. Burroughs' with 'Jake' signed above the typed name."

Zebadiah said to me, "'Watson, you know my methods.'"

"Certainly, my dear Holmes. A 'Black Hat.' In Logan."

"We knew that. What *new* data?"

"Well . . . Pop made that call from the house; I remember it. So somebody has a tap on our phone. Had, I mean; the fire probably destroyed it."

"A recording tap. The purpose of that fire may have been to destroy it and other evidence. For now we know that the 'Blokes in the Black Hats' *knew* that your father—and you, but it's Pop they are after—was in California last evening. After 'killing' him in California, they destroyed all they could in Utah. Professor, I predict that we will learn that your office was robbed last night—any papers on six-dimensional spaces."

Pop shrugged. "They wouldn't find much. I had postponed my final paper after the—humiliating—reception my preliminary paper received. I worked on it only at home, or here, and moved notes made in Logan to our basement here each time we came down."

"Any missing here?"

"I am certain this place has not been entered. Not that papers would matter; I have it in my head. The continua apparatus has not been touched."

"Zebadiah, is Doctor Brain a 'Black Hat'?" I asked.

"I don't know, Deety. He may be a stooge in their hire. But he's part of their plot, or they would not have risked forging a letter to put him into Hilda's house. Jake, how difficult is it to steal your professional stationery?"

"Not difficult. I don't keep a secretary; I send for a stenographer when I need one. I seldom lock my office when I'm on campus."

"Deety, can you scrounge pen and paper? I want to see how Jake signs 'Jake.'"

"Sure." I fetched them. "Pop's signature is easy; I often sign it. I hold his power of attorney."

"It's the simple signatures that are hardest to forge well enough to fool a handwriting expert. But their scheme did not require fooling an expert—phrasing the note was more difficult . . . since Hilda accepted it as ringing true."

"It does ring true, Son; it is very like what I would have said had I written such a note to Hilda."

"The forger probably has read many of your letters and listened to many of your conversations. Jake, will you write 'Jake' four or five times, the way you sign a note to a friend?"

Pop did so, my husband studied the specimens. "Normal variations." Zebadiah then signed "Jake" about a dozen times, looked at his work, took a fresh sheet, signed "Jake" once, passed it to Aunt Hilda. "Well, Sharpie?"

Aunt Hilda studied it. "It wouldn't occur to me to question it—on Jacob's stationary under a note that sounded like his phrasing. Where do we stand now?"

"Stuck in the mud. But we have added data. At least three are involved, two 'Black Hats' and Doctor Brain, who may or may not be a 'Black Hat.' He is, at minimum, a hired hand, an unwitting stooge, or a puppet they can move around like a chessman.

"While two plus 'Brainy' is minimum, it is not the most probable number. This scheme was not whipped up overnight. It involves arson, forgery, booby-trapping a car, wiretapping, theft, and secret communications between points widely separated, with coordinated criminal actions at each end—and it may involve doing in my cousin Zebulon. We can assume that the 'Black Hats' know that *I* am not the Zeb Carter who is the *n*-dimensional geometer; I'm written off as a bystander who got himself killed.

"Which doesn't bother them. These playful darlings would swat a fly with a sledgehammer, or cure a cough with a guillotine. They are smart, organized, efficient, and vicious—and the only clue is an interest in six-dimensional non-Euclidean geometry.

"We don't have a glimmer as to 'who'—other than Doctor Brain, whose role is unclear. But, Jake, I think I know 'why'—and that will lead us to 'who.'"

"*Why,* Zebadiah?" I demanded.

"Princess, your father could have worked on endless other branches of mathematics and they would not have bothered him. But he happened—I don't mean chance; I don't believe in 'chance' in this sense—he worked on the *one* variety of the endless possible number of geometries—the *only* one that *correctly* describes how space-time is put together. Having found it, because he is a genius in both theory and practice, he saw that it was a means by which to build a simple craft—amazingly simple, the greatest invention since the wheel—a space-time craft that offers access to all universes to the full Number of the Beast. Plus undenumerable variations of each of those many universes.

"We have one advantage."

"I don't see any advantage! They're shooting at my Jacob!"

"One strong advantage, Sharpie. The 'Black Hats' know that Jake has worked out this mathematics. They *don't* know that he has built his space-time tail-twister; they think he has just put symbols on paper. They tried to discredit his work and were successful. They tried to kill him and barely missed. They probably think Jake is dead—and it seems likely that they have killed Ed. But they *don't* know about Snug Harbor."

"Why do you say that, Zeb? Oh, I hope they do not!—but why do you feel sure?"

"Because these blokes aren't fooling. They blew up your car and burned your flat; what would they do here?—if they knew. An A-bomb?"

"Son, do you think that criminals can lay hands on atomic weapons?"

"Jake, these aren't *criminals*. A 'criminal' is a member of the subset of the larger set 'human beings.' These creatures are not human."

"*Eh?* Zeb, your reasoning escapes me."

"Deety. Run it through the computer. The one between your ears."

I did not answer; I just sat and thought. After several minutes of unpleasant thoughts I said, "Zebadiah, the 'Black Hats' don't know about the apparatus in our basement."

"Conclusive assumption," my husband agreed, "because we are still alive."

"They are determined to destroy a new work in mathematics . . . and to kill the brain that produced it."

"A probability approaching unity," Zebadiah again agreed.

"Because it can be used to travel among the universes."

"Conclusive corollary," my husband noted.

"For this purpose, human beings fall into three groups. Those not interested in mathematics more complex than that needed to handle money, those who know a bit about other mathematics, and a quite small third group who could understand the possibilities."

"Yes."

"But our race does not know *anything* of other universes so far as I know."

"They don't. Necessary assumption."

"But that third group would not try to stop an attempt to travel among the universes. They would wait with intellectual interest to see how it turned out. They might believe or disbelieve or suspend judgment. But they would *not* oppose; they would be delighted if my father succeeded. The joy of intellectual discovery—the mark of a true scientist."

I sighed and added, "I see no other grouping. Save for a few sick people, psychotic, these three subsets complete the set. Our opponents are not psychotic; they are intelligent, crafty, and organized."

"As we all know too well," Zebadiah echoed.

"Therefore our opponents are not human beings. They are alien intelligences from elsewhere." I sighed again and shut up. Being an oracle is a no-good profession!

"Or elsewhen. Sharpie, can you kill?"

"Kill whom, Zebbie? Or what?"

"Can you kill to protect Jake?"

"You bet your frimpin' life I'll kill to protect Jacob!"

"I won't ask you, Princess; I know Dejah Thoris." Zebadiah went on, "That's the situation, ladies. We have the most valuable man on this planet to protect. We don't know from what. Jake, your bodyguard musters two Amazons, one small, one medium large, both probably knocked up, and one Cowardly Lion. I'd hire the Dorsai if I knew their P.O. Box. Or the Gray Lensman and all his pals. But we are all there are and we'll try! *Avete, alieni, nos morituri vos spernimus!* Let's break out that champagne."

"My Captain, do you think we should?" I asked. "I'm frightened."

"We should. I'm no good for more work today, and neither is Jake. Tomorrow we'll start installing the gadget in Gay Deceiver, do rewiring and reprogramming so that she will work for any of us. Meanwhile we need a couple of laughs and a night's sleep. What better time to drink life to the dregs than when we know that any hour may be our last?"

Aunt Hilda punched Zebadiah in the ribs. "Yer dern tootin', Buster! I'm going to get giggle happy and make a fool of myself and then take my man and put him to sleep with Old Mother Sharpie's Time-Tested Nostrum. Deety, I prescribe the same for you."

I suddenly felt better. "Check, Aunt Hilda! Captain John Carter always wins. 'Cowardly Lion' my foot! Who is Pop? The Little Wizard?"

"I think he is."

"Could be. Pop, will you open the bubbly? I always hurt my thumbs."

"Right away, Deety. I mean 'Dejah Thoris, royal consort of the Warlord.'"

"No need to be formal, Pop. This is going to be an informal party. Very! Pop! Do I have to keep my pants on?"

"Ask your husband. You're *his* problem now."

VIII *"Let us all preserve our illusions—"*

Hilda:

In my old age, sucking my gums in front of the fire and living over my misdeeds, I'll remember the next few days as the happiest in my life. I'd had three honeymoons earlier, one with each of my term-contract husbands; two had been good, one had been okay and (eventually) very lucrative. But my honeymoon with Jacob was heavenly.

The whiff of danger sharpened the joy. Jacob seemed unworried, and Zebbie has hunches, like a horseplayer. Seeing that Zebbie was relaxed, Deety got over being jumpy—and I never was, as I hope to end like a firecracker, not linger on, ugly, helpless, useless....

A spice of danger adds zest to life. Even during a honeymoon—especially during a honeymoon.

An odd honeymoon— We worked hard but our husbands seemed never too busy for pat fanny, squeeze titty, and unhurried kisses. Not a group marriage but two twosomes that were one family, comfortable each with the others. I dropped most of my own sparky-bitch ways, and Zebbie sometimes called me "Hilda" rather than "Sharpie."

Jacob and I moved into marriage like ham and eggs. Jacob is not tall (178 centimeters) (but tall compared with my scant one fifty-two) and his hairline recedes and he has a paunch from years at a desk—but he looks just right to me. If I wanted to look at male beauty, I could always look at Deety's giant—appreciate him without lusting; my own loving goat kept Sharpie quite blunted.

I did not decide, when Zebbie came on campus, to make a pet of him for his looks but for his veering sense of humor. But if there was ever a man who could have played the role of John

Carter, Warlord of Mars, it was Zebadiah Carter whose middle name just happens to be "John." Indoors with clothes and wearing his fake horn-rims he looks awkward, too big, clumsy. I did not realize that he was beautiful and graceful until the first time he used my pool. (That afternoon I was tempted to seduce him. But, as little dignity as I have, I had resolved to stick to older men, so I shut off the thought.)

Outdoors at Snug Harbor, wearing little or no clothes, Zebbie looked at home—a mountain lion in grace and muscle. An incident one later afternoon showed me how much he was like the Warlord of Mars. A sword— Those old stories were familiar to me. My father had acquired the Ballantine Del Rey paperback reissues; they were around the house when I was a little girl. Once I learned to read, I read everything, and vastly preferred Barsoom stories to "girls" books given to me for birthdays and Christmas. Thuvia was the heroine I identified with—"toy" of the cruel priests of Issus, then with virginity miraculously restored in the next book: *Thuvia, Maid of Mars*. I resolved to change my name to Thuvia when I was old enough. When I was eighteen, I did not consider it; I had always been "Hilda," a new name held no attraction.

I was responsible in part for Deety's name, one that embarrassed her until she discovered that her husband liked it. Jacob had wanted to name his daughter "Dejah Thoris" (Jacob looks like and *is* a professor, but he is incurably romantic). Jane had misgivings. I told her, "Don't be a chump, Janie. If your man wants something, and you can accommodate him with no grief, give it to him! Do you want him to love this child or to resent her?" Jane looked thoughtful and "Doris Anne" became "Dejah Thoris" at christening, then "Deety" before she could talk—which satisfied everyone.

We settled into a routine: Up early every day; our men worked on instruments and wires and things and installing the time-space widget into Gay Deceiver's gizzard—while Deety and I gave the housework a lick and a promise (our mountain home needed little attention—more of Jacob's genius), then Deety and I got busy on a technical matter that Deety could do with some help from me.

I'm not much use for technical work, biology being the only thing I studied in depth and never finished my degree. This was amplified by almost six thousand hours as volunteer nurse's aid in our campus medical center and I took courses that make me an uncertified nurse or medical tech or even jackleg paramedic— I don't shriek at the sight of blood and can clean up vomit without a qualm and would not hesitate to fill in as scrub nurse. Being a campus widow with too much money is fun but not soul filling. I like to feel that I've paid rent on the piece of earth I'm using.

Besides that, I have a smattering of everything from addiction to the printed page, plus attending campus lectures that sound intriguing . . . then sometimes auditing a related course. I audited descriptive astronomy, took the final as if for credit—got an "A." I had even figured a cometary orbit correctly, to my surprise (and the professor's).

I can wire a doorbell or clean out a stopped-up soil pipe with a plumber's "snake"—but if it's really technical, I hire specialists. So Hilda can help but usually can't do the job alone. Gay Deceiver had to be reprogrammed—and Deety, who does not *look* like a genius, *is* one. Jacob's daughter *should* be a genius and her mother had an I.Q. that startled even me, her closest friend. I ran across it while helping poor grief-stricken Jacob to decide what to save, what to burn. (I burned unflattering pictures, useless papers, and clothes. A dead person's clothes should be given away or burned; *nothing* should be kept that does not inspire happy memories. I cried a bit and that saved Jacob and Deety from having to cry later.)

We all held private duo licenses; Zebbie, as Captain Z. J. Carter, U.S.A.-S.R., held "command" rating as well—he told us that his space rating was largely honorary, just some free-fall time and one landing of a shuttle. Zebbie is mendacious, untruthful, and tells fibs; I got a chance to sneak a look at his aerospace log and shamelessly took it. He had logged more than he claimed in one exchange tour with Australia. Someday I'm going to sit on his chest and make him tell Mama Hilda the truth. Should be interesting . . . if I can sort out fact from fiction. I do *not* believe his story about intimate relations with a female kangaroo.

Zebbie and Jacob decided that we all must be able to control Gay Deceiver all four ways, on the road, in the air, in trajectory (she's not a spaceship but can make high-trajectory jumps), and in space-time, i.e. among the universes to the Number of the Beast, plus variants impossible to count.

I had fingers crossed about being able to learn that, but both men assured me that they had worked out a fail-safe that would get me out of a crunch if I ever had to do it alone.

Part of the problem lay in the fact that Gay Deceiver was a one-man girl; her doors unlocked only to her master's voice or to his thumbprint, or to a tapping code if he were shy both voice and right thumb; Zeb tended to plan ahead—"Outwitting Murphy's

Law," he called it, "'Anything that can go wrong, *will* go wrong.'" (Grandma called it "The Butter-Side Down Rule.")

First priority was to introduce us to Gay Deceiver—teach her that all four voices and right thumbprints were acceptable.

That took a couple of hours, with Deety helping Zebbie. The tapping code took even less, it being based on an old military cadence—its trickiness being that a thief would be unlikely to guess that this car would open if tapped a certain way and in guessing the correct cadence. Zebbie called the cadence "Drunken Soldier." Jacob said that it was "Bumboat." Deety claimed that its title was "Pay Day," because she had heard it from Jane's grandfather.

Our men conceded that she must be right, as she had words for it. Her words included "Drunken Sailor" instead of "Drunken Soldier"—plus both "Pay Day" and "Bumboat."

Introductions taken care of, Zeb dug out Gay's anatomy, one volume her body, one her brain. He handed the latter to Deety, took the other into our basement. The next two days were easy for me, hard for Deety. I held lights and made notes on a clip board while she studied that book and frowned and got smudged and sweaty getting herself into impossible positions and once she cursed in a fashion that would have caused Jane to scold. She added, "Aunt Nanny Goat, your step-son-in-law has done things to this mass of spaghetti that no decent computer should put up with! It's a bastard hybrid."

"You shouldn't call Gay 'it,' Deety. And she's not a bastard."

"She can't hear us; I've got her ears unhooked—except that piece that is monitoring news retrieval programs—and that goes through this wire to that jack in the wall; she can talk with Zebadiah only in the basement now. Oh, I'm sure she was a nice girl until that big ape of mine raped her. Aunt Hilda, don't worry about hurting Gay's feelings; she hasn't any. This is an idiot as computers go. Any one-horse college and most high schools own or share time in computers much more complex. This one is primarily cybernetics, an autopilot plus limited digital capacity and limited storage. But the mods Zebadiah has tacked on make it more than an autopilot but not a general-purpose computer. A misbegotten hybrid. It has far more random-number options than it needs and it has extra functions that IBM never dreamed of."

"Deety, why are you taking off cover plates? I thought you were strictly a programmer? Software. Not a mechanic."

"I *am* strictly a software mathematician. I wouldn't attempt to modify this monster even on written orders from my lovable but sneaky husband. But how in the name of Allah can a software hack think about simplification analysis for program if she doesn't know the circuitry? The first half of this book shows what this autopilot was manufactured to do . . . and the second half, the Xeroxed pages, show the follies Zebadiah has seduced her into. This bleedin' bundle of chips now speaks three logic languages, interfaced—when it was built to use only one. But it won't accept *any* of them until it has been wheedled with Zebadiah's double talk. Even then it rarely answers a code phrase with the same answer twice in a row. What does it say in answer to: 'You're a smart girl, Gay.'?"

"I remember. 'Boss, I bet you tell that to all the girls. Over.'"

"Sometimes. Oftenest, as that answer is weighted to come up three times as often as any of the others. But listen to this:

"'Zeb, I'm so smart I scare myself.'

"'Then why did you turn me down for that raise?'

"'Never mind the compliments! Take your hand off my knee!'

"'Not so loud, dear. I don't want my boyfriend to hear.'

"—and there are more. There are at least four answers to any of Zebadiah's code phrases. *He* uses just one list, but the autopilot answers several ways for each of his phrases—and all any of them mean is either 'Roger' or 'Null program; rephrase.'"

"I like the idea. Fun."

"Well . . . I do myself. I animize a computer; I think of them as people . . . and this semirandom answer list makes Gay Deceiver feel much more alive . . . when she isn't. Not even versatile compared with a ground-based computer. But—" Deety gave a quick smile. "I'm going to hand my husband some surprises."

"How, Deety?"

"You know how he says, 'Good morning, Gay. How are you?' when we sit down for breakfast."

"Yes. I like it. Friendly. She usually answers, 'I'm fine, Zeb.'"

"Yes. It's a test code. It orders the autopilot to run a self-check throughout and to report any running instruction. Which takes less than a millisecond. If he didn't get that or an equivalent answer, he would rush straight here to find out what's wrong. But I'm going to add another answer. Or more."

"I thought you refused to modify anything."

"Aunt Hillbilly, this is *software*, not hardware. I'm authorized and directed to amplify the answers to include all of us, by name for each of our voices. That is programming, elementary. You say good morning to this gadget and it will—when I'm finished—answer you and call you either 'Hilda' or 'Mrs. Burroughs.'"

"Oh, let her call me 'Hilda.'"

"All right, but let her call you 'Mrs. Burroughs' now and then for variety."

"Well . . . all right. Keep her a personality."

"I could even have her call you—low weighting!—'Nanny Goat.'"

I guffawed. "Do, Deety, please do. But I want to be around to see Jacob's face."

"You will be; it won't be programmed to answer that way to any voice but yours. Just don't say, 'Good morning, Gay' unless Pop *is* listening. But here's one for my husband: Zebadiah says, 'Good morning, Gay. How are you?'—and the speaker answers, 'I'm fine, Zeb. But your fly is unzipped and your eyes are bloodshot. Are you hung over *again*?'"

Deety is so solemn and yet playful. "Do it, dear! Poor Zebbie—who drinks least of any of us. But he might not be wearing anything zippered."

"Zebadiah always wears something at meals. Even his underwear shorts are zippered. He dislikes elastic."

"But he'll recognize your voice, Deety."

"Nope. Because it will be *your* voice—modified."

And it was. I'm contralto about the range of the actress—or girl friend—who recorded Gay Deceiver's voice originally. I don't think my voice has her sultry, bedroom quality but I'm a natural mimic. Deety borrowed a wigglescope—oscilloscope?—from her father, my Jacob, and I practiced until my patterns for Gay Deceiver's original repertoire matched hers well enough—Deety said she could not tell them apart without close checking.

I got into the spirit of it, such as having Deety cause Gay Deceiver occasionally to say to my husband, "Fine—except for my back ache, you wicked old Billy Goat!"—and Jacob tripped that reply one morning when I *did* have a back ache, and I feel sure he had one, too.

We didn't put in answers that Deety felt might be too bawdy for Jacob's "innocent" mind—I didn't even hint how her father actually talked, to me in private. Let us all preserve our illusions; it lubricates social relations. Possibly Deety and Zebbie talked the same way to each other in private—and regarded us "old folks" as hopelessly square.

IX   *Most males have an unhealthy tendency to obey laws.*

Deety:

Aunt Hilda and I finished reprogramming in the time it took Zebadiah and Pop to design and make the fail-safes and other mods needed to turn Gay Deceiver, with the time-space widget installed, into a continua traveler—which included placing the back seats twenty centimeters farther back (for leg room) after they had been pulled out to place the widget abaft the bulkhead and weld it to the shell. The precessing controls and triple verniers were remoted to the driver's instrument board—with one voice control for the widget, all others manual:

If any of our voices said, "Gay Deceiver, take us home!" car and passengers would instantly return to Snug Harbor.

I don't know but I trust my Pop. He brought us home safe twice, doing it with *no* fail-safes and no dead-man switch. The latter paralleled the "Take us home!" voice order, was normally clamped closed and covered—but could be uncovered and held in a fist, closed. There were other fail-safes for temperature, pressure, air, radar collision course, and other dangers. If we wound up inside a star or planet, none of this could save us, but it is easy to prove that the chances of falling downstairs and breaking your neck are enormously higher than the chance of co-occupying space with other matter in our native universe—space is plentiful, mass is scarce. We hoped that this would be true of other universes.

No way ahead of time to check on the Number-of-the-Beast spaces—but "The cowards never started and the weaklings died on the way." None of us ever mentioned *not* trying to travel the universes. Besides, our home planet had turned unfriendly. We didn't discuss "Black Hats" but we all knew that they were still here, and that we remained alive by lying doggo and letting the world think we were dead.

We ate breakfast better each morning after hearing Gay Deceiver offer "null report" on news retrievals. Zebadiah, I am fairly certain, had given up his cousin for dead. I feel sure Zebadiah would have gone to Sumatra to follow a lost hope, were it not that he had acquired a wife and a prospective child. I missed my next period, so did Hilda. Our men toasted our not-yet bulging bellies; Hilda and I smugly resolved to be good girls, yes, sir!— and careful. Hilda joined my morning toning up, and the men joined us the first time they caught us at it.

Zebadiah did not need it but seemed to enjoy it. Pop brought his waistline down five centimeters in one week.

Shortly after that toast Zebadiah pressure-tested Gay Deceiver's shell—four atmospheres inside her and a pressure gauge sticking out through a fitting in her shell.

There being little we could do while our space-time rover was sealed, we knocked off early. "Swim, anybody?" I asked. Snug Harbor doesn't have a city-type pool, and a mountain stream is too *cooold*. Pop had fixed that when he concealed our spring. Overflow was piped underground to a clump of bushes and thereby created a "natural" mountain rivulet that passed near the house; then Pop had made use of a huge fallen boulder, plus biggish ones, to create a pool, one that filled and spilled. He had done work with pigments in concrete to make this look like an accident of water flow.

This makes Pop sound like Paul Bunyan. Pop *could* have built Snug Harbor with his own hands. But Spanish-speaking labor from Nogales built the underground and assembled the prefab shell of the cabin. An air crane fetched parts and materials from an Albuquerque engineering company Jane had bought for Pop through a front—lawyers in Dallas. The company's manager drove the air crane himself, having had it impressed on him that this was for a rich client of the law firm, and that it would be prudent to do the job and forget it. Pop bossed the work in TexMex, with help from his secretary—me—Spanish being one language I had picked for my doctorate.

Laborers and mechanics never got a chance to pinpoint where they were, but they were well paid, well fed, comfortably housed in prefabs brought in by crane, and the backbreaking labor was done by power—who cares what "locos gringos" do? Two pilots had to know where we were building, but they homed in on a radar beacon that is no longer there.

"Blokes in Black Hats" had nothing to do with this secrecy; it was jungle caution I had learned from Mama: Never let the revenooers know anything. Pay cash, keep your lips closed, put nothing through banks that does not appear later in tax returns— pay taxes greater than your apparent standard of living and declare income accordingly. We had been audited three times since Mama died; each time the government returned a small "overpayment"— I was building a reputation of being stupid and honest.

My inquiry of "Swim, anybody?" was greeted with silence. Then Pop said, "Zeb, your wife is too energetic. Deety, later the water will be warmer and the trees will give us shade. Then we can walk slowly down to the pool. Zeb?"

"I agree, Jake. I need to conserve ergs."

"Nap?"

"I don't have the energy to take one. What were you saying this morning about reengineering the system?"

Aunt Hilda looked startled. "I thought Miss Gay Deceiver was already engineered? Are you thinking of changing everything?"

"Take it easy, Sharpie darlin'. Gay Deceiver *is* finished. A few things to stow that have been weighed and their moment arms calculated."

I could have told her. In the course of figuring what could be stowed in every nook and cranny and what that would do to Gay's balance, I had discovered that my husband had a highly illegal laser cannon. I said nothing, merely included its mass and distance from optimum center of weight in my calculations. I sometimes wonder which of us is the outlaw: Zebadiah or I? Most males have an unhealthy tendency to obey laws. But that concealed L-cannon made me wonder.

"Why not leave well enough alone?" Aunt Hilda demanded. "Jacob and God know I'm happy here . . . But You All Know Why We Should Not Stay Here Longer Than We Must."

"We weren't talking about Gay Deceiver; Jake and I were discussing reengineering the Solar System."

"The *Solar System!* What's wrong with it the way it is?"

"Lots of things," Zebadiah told Aunt Hilda. "It's untidy. Real estate going to waste. This tired old planet is crowded and sort o' worn in spots. True, industry in orbit and power from orbit have helped, and both Lagrange-Four and -Five have self-supporting populations; anybody who invested in space stations early enough made a pile." (Including Pop, Zebadiah!) "But these are minor compared with what *can* be done—and this planet is in worse shape each year. Jake's six-dimensional principle can change that."

"Move people into another universe? Would they go?"

"We weren't thinking of that, Hilda. We're trying to apply Clarke's Law."

"I don't recall it. Maybe it was while I was out with mumps."

"Arthur C. Clarke," Pop told her. "Great man—too bad he was liquidated in The Purge. Clarke defined how to make a great discovery or create a key invention. Study what the most respected authorities agree can *not* be done—then do it. My continua craft is a godchild of Clarke via his Law. His insight inspired my treatment of six-dimensional continua. But this morning Zeb added corollaries."

"Jake, don't kid the ladies. I asked a question; you grabbed the ball and ran."

"Uh, we heterodyned. Hilda, you know that the time-space traveler doesn't require power."

"I'm afraid I don't know, darling man. Why were you installing power packs in Gay Deceiver?"

"Auxiliary uses. So that you won't have to cook over an open fire, for example."

"But the pretzel bender doesn't use power," agreed Zebadiah. "Don't ask why. I did, and Jake started writing equations in Sanskrit and I got a headache."

"It doesn't use power, Aunt Hilda," I agreed. "Just parasitic power. A few microwatts so that the gyros never slow down, milliwatts for instrument readouts and for controls—but the widget itself uses none."

"What happened to the law of conservation of energy?"

"Sharpie," my husband answered, "as a fairish mechanic, an amateur electron pusher, and as a bloke who has herded unlikely junk through the sky, I never worry about theory as long as machinery does what it is supposed to do. I worry when a machine turns and bites me. That's why I specialize in fail-safes and back-ups and triple redundancy. I try *never* to get a machine sore at me. There's no theory for that but every engineer knows it."

"Hilda my beloved, the law of conservation of mass-energy is not broken by our continua craft; it is simply not relevant to it. Once Zeb understood that—"

"I didn't say I understood it."

"Well . . . once Zeb stipulated that, he raised interesting questions. For example: Jupiter doesn't need Ganymede—"

"Whereas Venus does. Although Titan might be better."

"Mmm . . . possible."

"Yes. Make an inhabitable base more quickly. But the urgent problem, Jake, is to seed Venus, move atmosphere to Mars, put both of them through forced aging. Then respot them. Earth-Sol Trojan points?"

"Certainly. We've had millions of years of evolution this distance from the Sun. We had best plan on living neither closer nor farther. With careful attention to stratospheric protection. But I still have doubts about anchoring in the Venerian crust. We wouldn't want to lose the planet on *Tau* axis."

"Mere R. & D., Jake. Calculate pressures and temperatures; beef up the vehicle accordingly—spherical, save for exterior anchors—then apply a jigger factor of four. With automatic controls quintuply redundant. Catch it when it comes out and steady it down in Earth's orbit, sixty degrees trailing—and start selling subdivisions the size of old Spanish Land Grants. Jake, we should gather enough mass to create new earths at *all* Trojan points, a hexagon around the Sun. Five brand-new earths would give the race room enough to breed. On this maiden voyage let's keep our eyes open."

Aunt Hilda looked at Zebadiah with horror. "Zebbie! Creating planets indeed! Who do you think you are? Jesus Christ?"

"I'm not that junior. That's the Holy Ghost over there, scratching his belly. The Supreme Inseminator. I'm the other one, the Maker and Shaper. But in setting up a pantheon for the Celestial Age, we're going to respect women's rights, Hilda. Deety is Earth Mother; she's perfect for the job. You are Moon Goddess, Selene. Good job, dear—more moons than earths. It fits you. You're little and silvery and you wax and wane and you're beautiful in all your phases. How about it? Us four and no more."

"Quit pulling my leg!"

My husband answered, "I haven't been pulling your leg. Come closer and I will; you have pretty legs, Step-Mother-in-Law. These things Jake and I have been discussing are practical—once we thought about the fact that the space-time twister uses no power. Move anything anywhere—all spaces, all times. I add the plural because at first I could not see what Jake had in mind when he spoke of forced aging of a planet. Rotate Venus into the *Tau* axis, fetch it back along *Teh* axis, reinsert it centuries—or millennia—older at this point in 't' axis. Perhaps translate it a year or so into the future—*our* future—so as to be ready for it when it returns, all sweet and green and beautiful and ready to grow children and puppies and butterflies. Terraformed but virginal."

Aunt Hilda looked frightened. "Jacob? Would one highball do any harm to this peanut inside me? I need a bracer."

"I don't think so. Jane often had a drink with me while she was pregnant. Her doctor did not have her stop until her third trimester. Can't see that it hurt Deety. Deety was so healthy she drove Jane home from the hospital."

"Pop, that's a fib. I didn't learn to drive until I was three months old. But I need one, too," I added. "Zebadiah?"

"Certainly, Princess. A medicinal drink should be by body mass. That's half a jigger for you, Sharpie dear, a jigger for Deety, a jigger and a half for Jake—two jiggers for me."

"Oh, how unfair!"

"It certainly is," I agreed. "I outweigh Pop—he's been losing, I've been gaining. Pick us up and see!"

My husband took us each around the waist, crouched, then straightened and lifted us.

"Close to a standoff," he announced. "Pop may be a trifle heavier, but you're more cuddly"—kissed me and put us down.

"There is *no* one more cuddly than Jacob!"

"Hilda, you're prejudiced. Let's each mix our own drinks, at the strength required for our emotional and physical conditions."

So we did—it wound up with Hilda and me each taking a jigger with soda, Pop taking a jigger and a half over ice—and Zebadiah taking a half jigger of vodka and drowning it with Coke.

While we were sipping our "medicine," Zebadiah, sprawled out, looked up over the fireplace. "Pop, you were in the Navy?"

"No—Army. If you count 'chair-borne infantry.' They handed me a commission for having a doctorate in mathematics, told me they needed me for ballistics. Then I spent my whole tour as a personnel officer, signing papers."

"Standard Operating Procedure. That's a Navy sword and belt up there. Thought it might be yours."

"It's Deety's—belonged to Jane's Grandfather Rodgers. I have a dress saber. Belonged to my Dad, who gave it to me when the Army took me. Dress blues, too. I took them with me, never had occasion to wear either." Pop got up and went into his-their bedroom, calling back, "I'll show you the saber."

My husband said to me, "Deety, would you mind my handling your sword?"

"My Captain, that sword is yours."

"Heavens, dear, I can't accept an heirloom."

"If my warlord will not permit his princess to gift him with a sword, he can leave it where it is! I've been wanting to give you a wedding present—and did not realize that I had the perfect gift for Captain John Carter."

"My apologies, Dejah Thoris. I accept and will keep it bright. I will defend my princess with it against all enemies."

"Helium is proud to accept. If you make a cradle of your hands, I can stand in them and reach it down."

Zebadiah grasped me, a hand above each knee, and I was suddenly three meters tall. Sword and belt were on hooks; I lifted them down, and myself was placed down. My husband stood straight while I buckled it around him—then he dropped to one knee and kissed my hand.

My husband is mad north-northwest but his madness suits me. I got tears in my eyes which Deety doesn't do much but Dejah Thoris seems prone to, since John Carter made her his.

Pop and Aunt Hilda watched—then imitated, including (I saw!) tears in Hilda's eyes after she buckled on Pop's saber, when he knelt and kissed her hand.

Zebadiah drew sword, tried its balance, sighted along its blade. "Handmade and balanced close to the hilt. Deety, your great-grandfather paid a pretty penny for this. It's an honest weapon."

"I don't think he knew what it cost. It was presented to him."

"For good reason, I feel certain." Zebadiah stood back, went into hanging guard, made fast moulinets vertically, left and right, then horizontally clockwise and counterclockwise—suddenly dropped into swordsman's guard—lunged and recovered, fast as a striking cat.

I said softly to Pop, "Did you notice?"

Pop answered quietly. "Know saber. Sword, too."

Hilda said loudly, "Zebbie! You never told me you went to Heidelberg."

"You never asked, Sharpie. Around the Red Ox they called me 'The Scourge of the Neckar.'"

"What happened to your scars?"

"Never got any, dear. I hung around an extra year, hoping for one. But no one got through my guard—ever. Hate to think about how many German faces I carved into checkerboards."

"Zebadiah, was that where you took your doctorate?"

My husband grinned and sat down, still wearing sword. "No, another school."

"M.I.T.?" inquired Pop.

"Hardly. Pop, this should stay in the family. I undertook to prove that a man can get a doctorate from a major university without knowing anything and without adding anything whatever to human knowledge."

"*I* think you have a degree in aerospace engineering," Pop said flatly.

"I'll concede that I have the requisite hours. I hold two degrees—a baccalaureate in humane arts . . . meaning I squeaked through . . . and a doctorate from an old and prestigious school— a Ph.D. in education."

"Zebadiah! You *wouldn't!*" (I was horrified.)

"But I did, Deety. To prove that degrees *per se* are worthless. Often they are honorifics of true scientists or learned scholars or inspired teachers. Much more frequently they are false faces for overeducated jackasses."

Pop said, "You'll get no argument from me, Zeb. A doctorate is a union card to get a tenured job. It does *not* mean that the holder thereof is wise or learned."

"Yes, sir. I was taught it at my grandfather's knee—my Grandfather Zachariah, the man responsible for the intial 'Z' in the names of his male descendants. Deety, his influence on me was so strong that I must explain him—no that's impossible; I must tell about him in order to explain *me* . . . and how I happened to take a worthless degree."

Hilda said, "Deety, he's pulling a long bow again."

"Quiet, woman. 'Get thee to a nunnery, go!'"

"I don't take orders from my step-son-in-law. Make that a monastery and I'll consider it."

I kept my blinkin' mouf shut. My husband's fibs entertain me. (If they *are* fibs.)

"Grandpa Zach was as cantankerous an old coot as you'll ever meet. Hated government, hated lawyers, hated civil servants, hated preachers, hated automobiles, public schools, and telephones, was contemptuous of most editors, most writers, most professors, most of almost anything. But he overtipped waitresses and porters and would go out of his way to avoid stepping on an insect.

"Grandpa had three doctorates: biochemistry, medicine, and law—and he regarded anyone who couldn't read Latin, Greek, Hebrew, French, and German as illiterate."

"Zebbie, can you read all those?"

"Fortunately for me, my grandfather had a stroke while filling out a tax form before he could ask me that question. I don't know Hebrew. I can read Latin, puzzle out Greek, speak and read French, read technical German, understand it in some accents, swear in Russian—very useful!—and speak an ungrammatical smattering of Spanish picked up in cantinas and from horizontal dictionaries.

"Grandpa would have classed me as subliterate as I don't do any of these well—and I sometimes split infinitives which would have infuriated him. He practiced forensic medicine, medical jurisprudence, was an expert witness in toxicology, pathology, and traumatology, bullied judges, terrorized lawyers, medical students, and law students. He once threw a tax assessor out of his office and required him to return with a search warrant setting forth in detail its constitutional limitations. He regarded the income tax and the Seventeenth Amendment and the direct primary as signs of the decay of the Republic."

"How did he feel about the Nineteenth?"

"Hilda, Grandpa Zach supported female suffrage. I remember hearing him say that if women were so dad-burned foolish as to *want* to assume the burden, they should be allowed to—they couldn't do the country more harm than men had. 'Votes for Women' didn't annoy him but nine thousand other things did. He lived at a slow simmer, always ready to break into a rolling boil.

"He had one hobby: collecting steel engravings."

"'Steel engravings'?" I repeated.

"Of dead presidents, my Princess. Especially of McKinley, Cleveland, and Madison—but he didn't scorn those of Washington. He had that instinct for timing so necessary to a collector. In 1929 on Black Thursday he held not one share of common stock; instead he had sold short. When the 1933 Bank Holiday came along every old-dollar he owned, except current cash, was in Zurich in Swiss money. Eventually U.S. citizens were forbidden by 'emergency' decree to own gold even abroad.

"Grandpa Zach ducked into Canada, applied for Swiss citizenship, got it, and thereafter split his time between Europe and America, immune to inflation and the confiscatory laws that eventually caused us to knock three zeros off the old-dollar in creating the newdollar.

"So he died rich, in Locarno—beautiful place; I stayed with him two summers as a boy. His will was probated in Switzerland and the U.S. Revenue Service could not touch it.

"Most of it was a trust with its nature known to his offspring before his death or I would not have been named Zebadiah.

"Female descendants got pro-rata shares of income with no strings attached but males had to have first names starting with 'Z'—and even that got them not one Swiss franc; there was a 'Root, hog, or die!' clause. Zachariah believed in taking care of daughters, but sons and grandsons had to go out and scratch, with no help from their fathers, until they had earned and saved on their own—or accumulated without going to jail—assets equal to one pro-rata share of the capital sum of the trust before they shared in the trust's income."

"Sexism," said Aunt Hilda. "Raw, unadulterated sexism. Any FemLib gal would sneer at his dirty old money, on those terms."

"Would you have refused it, Sharpie?"

"*Me?* Zebbie dear, are you feverish? I would have both greedy hands out. I'm strong for women's rights but no fanatic. Sharpie wants to be pampered and that's what men are best at—their natural function."

"Pop, do you need help in coping with her?"

"No, Son. I *like* pampering Hilda. I don't see you abusing my daughter."

"I don't dare; you told me she's vicious at karate." (I *am* good at karate; Pop made sure that I learned all the dirty fighting possible. But not against Zebadiah! If I ever do—Heaven forbid!—find myself opposed to my husband, I'll quiver my chin and cry.)

"On my graduation from high school my father had a talk with me. 'Zeb,' he told me. 'The time has come. I'll put you through any school you choose. Or you can take what you have saved, strike out on your own, and try to qualify for a share in your grandfather's will. Suit yourself, I shan't influence you.'

"Folks, I had to think. My father's younger brother was past forty and *still* hadn't qualified. The size of the trust made a pro-rata of its assets amount to a requirement that a male descendant had to get rich on his own—well-to-do at least—whereupon he was suddenly twice as rich. But with over half of this country's population living on the taxes of the lesser number it is not as easy to get rich as it was in Grandpa's day.

"Turn down a paid-for education at Princeton, or M.I.T.? Or go out and try to get rich with nothing but a high school education?—I hadn't learned much in high school; I had majored in girls.

"So I had to think hard and long. Almost ten seconds. I left home next day with one suitcase and a pitiful sum of money.

"Wound up on campus that had two things to recommend it: an Aerospace R.O.T.C. that would pick up part of my expenses, and a phys. ed. department willing to award me a jockstrap scholarship in exchange for daily bruises and contusions, plus all-out effort whenever we played. I took the deal."

"What did you play?" asked my father.

"Football, basketball, and track—they would have demanded more had they been able to figure a way to do it."

"I had thought you were going to mention fencing."

"No, that's another story. These did not quite close the gap. So I also waited tables for meals—food so bad the cockroaches ate out. But that closed the gap, and I added to it by tutoring in mathematics. That gave me my start toward piling up money to qualify."

I asked, "Did tutoring math pay enough to matter? I tutored math before Mama died; the hourly rate was low."

"Not *that* sort of tutoring, Princess. I taught prosperous young optimists not to draw to inside straights, and that stud poker is not a game of chance, but that craps *is*, controlled by mathematical laws that cannot be flouted with impunity. To quote Grandfather Zachariah, 'A man who bets on greed and dishonesty won't be wrong too often.' There is an amazingly high percentage of greedy people and it is even easier to win from a dishonest gambler than it is from an honest one... and neither is likely to know the odds at craps, especially side bets, or *all* of the odds in poker, in particular how odds change according to the number of players, where one is seated in relation to the dealer, and how to calculate changes as cards are exposed in stud.

"That was also how I quit drinking, my darling, except for special celebrations. In every 'friendly' game some players contribute, some take a profit; a player determined to take a profit must be neither drunk nor tired. Pop, the shadows are growing long—I don't think anybody wants to know how I got a worthless doctorate."

"I do!" I put in. "Me, too!" echoed Aunt Hilda.

"Son, you're outvoted."

"Okay. Two years active duty after I graduated. Sky jockeys are even more optimistic than students and have more money—meanwhile I learned more math and engineering. Was sent inactive just in time to be called up again for the Spasm War. Didn't get hurt, I was safer than civilians. But that kept me on another year even though fighting was mostly over before I reported in. That made me a veteran, with benefits. I went to Manhattan and signed up for school again. Doctoral candidate. School of Education. Not serious at first, simply intending to use my veteran's benefits while enjoying the benefits of being a student—and devote most of my time to piling up cash to qualify for the trust.

"I knew that the stupidest students, the silliest professors, and the worst bull courses are concentrated in schools of education.

By signing for large-class evening lectures and the unpopular eight a.m. classes I figured I could spend most of my time finding out how the stock market ticked. I did, by working there, before I risked a dime.

"Eventually I had to pick a research problem or give up the advantages of being a student. I was sick of a school in which the pie was all meringue and no filling but I stuck as I knew how to cope with courses in which the answers are matters of opinion and the opinion that counts is that of the professor. And how to cope with those large-class evening lectures: Buy the lecture notes. Read everything that professor ever published. Don't cut too often and when you do show up, get there early, sit front row center, be certain the prof catches your eye every time he looks your way—by never taking your eyes off him. Ask *one* question you know he can answer because you've picked it out of his published papers—and state your name in asking a question. Luckily 'Zebadiah Carter' is a name easy to remember. Family, I got straight 'A's in both required courses and seminars . . . because I did *not* study 'education,' I studied professors of education.

"But I still had to make that 'original contribution to human knowledge' without which a candidate may not be awarded a doctor's degree in most so-called disciplines . . . and the few that don't require it are a tough row to hoe.

"I studied my faculty committee before letting myself be tied down to a research problem . . . not only reading everything each had published but also buying their publications or paying the library to make copies of out-of-print papers."

My husband took me by my shoulders. "Dejah Thoris, here follows the title of my dissertation. You can have your divorce on your own terms."

"Zebadiah, don't talk that way!"

"Then brace yourself. 'An Ad-Hoc Inquiry Concerning the Optimization of the Infrastructure of Primary Educational Institutions at the Interface Between Administration and Instruction, with Special Attention to Group Dynamics Desiderata.'"

"Zebbie! What does that mean?"

"It means nothing, Hilda."

"Zeb, quit kidding our ladies. Such a title would never be accepted."

"Jake, it seems certain that you have never taken a course in a school of education."

"Well . . . no. Teaching credentials are not required at university level but—"

"But me no 'buts,' Pop. I have a copy of my dissertation; you can check its authenticity. While that paper totally lacks meaning it is a literary gem in the sense in which a successful forging of an 'old master' is itself a work of art. It is loaded with buzz words. The average length of sentences is eighty-one words. The average word length, discounting 'of,' 'a,' 'the,' and other syntactical particles, is eleven-plus letters in slightly under four syllables. The bibliography is longer than the dissertation and cites three papers of each member of my committee and four of the chairman, and those citations are quoted in part—while avoiding any mention of matters on which I knew that members of the committee held divergent (but equally stupid) opinions.

"But the best touch was to get permission to do field work in Europe and have it count toward time on campus; half the citations were in foreign languages, ranging from Finnish to Croatian—and the translated bits invariably agreed with the prejudices of my committee. It took careful quoting out of context to achieve this, but it had the advantage that the papers were unlikely to be on campus and my committee were not likely to go to the trouble of looking them up even if they were. Most of them weren't at home in other languages, even easy ones like French, German, and Spanish.

"But I did not waste time on phony field work; I simply wanted a trip to Europe at student air fares and the use of student hostels—dirt cheap way to travel. *And* a visit to the trustees of Grandpa's fund.

"Good news! The fund was blue chips and triple-A bonds and, at that time, speculative stocks were rising. So the current cash value of the fund was down, even though income was up. And two more of my cousins and one uncle had qualified, again reducing the pro-rata . . . so, Glory Be!—I was within reaching distance. I had brought with me all that I had saved, swore before a notary that it was all mine, nothing borrowed, nothing from my father—and left it on deposit in Zurich, using the trustees as a front. And I told them about my stamp and coin collection.

"Good stamps and coins never go down, always up. I had nothing but proof sets, first-day covers, and unbroken sheets, all in perfect condition—and had a notarized inventory and appraisal with me. The trustees got me to swear that the items I had collected before I left home had come from earned money—true, the earliest items represented mowed lawns and such—and agreed to hold the pro-rata at that day's cash value—lower if the trend continued—

if I would sell my collection and send a draft to Zurich, with businesslike speed as soon as I returned to the States.

"I agreed. One trustee took me to lunch, tried to get me liquored up—then offered me ten percent over appraisal if I would sell that very afternoon, then send it to him by courier at his expense (bonded couriers go back and forth between Europe and America every week).

"We shook hands on it, went back and consulted the other trustees. I signed papers transferring title, the trustee buying signed his draft to me, I endorsed it to the trustees to add to the cash I was leaving in their custody. Three weeks later I got a cable certifying that the collection matched the inventory. I had qualified.

"Five months later I was awarded the degree of doctor of philosophy, summa cum laude. And that, dear ones, is the shameful story of my life. Anyone have the energy to go swimming?"

"Son, if there is a word of truth in that, it is indeed a shameful story."

"Pop! That's not fair! Zebadiah used *their* rules—and out-smarted them!"

"I didn't say that *Zeb* had anything to be ashamed of. It is a commentary on American higher education. What Zeb claims to have written is no worse than trash I *know* is accepted as dissertations these days. His case is the only one I have encountered wherein an intelligent and able scholar—*you*, Zeb—set out to show that an 'earned' Ph.D. could be obtained from a famous institution—I know which one!—in exchange for deliberately meaningless pseudoresearch. The cases I have encountered have involved button-counting by stupid and humorless young persons under the supervision of stupid and humorless old fools. I see no way to stop it; the rot is too deep. The *only* answer is to chuck the system and start over." My father shrugged. "Impossible."

"Zebbie," Aunt Hilda asked, "what do you do on campus? I've never asked."

My husband grinned. "Oh, much what you do, Sharpie."

"I don't do anything. Enjoy myself."

"Me, too. If you look, you will find me listed as 'research professor in residence.' An examination of the university's books would show that I am paid a stipend to match my rank. Further search would show that slightly more than that amount is paid by some trustees in Zurich to the university's general fund . . . as long as I remain on campus, a condition not written down. I like being on campus, Sharpie; it gives me privileges not granted the bar-

barians outside the pale. I teach a course occasionally, as supply for someone on sabbatical or ill."

"Huh? What courses? What departments?"

"Any department but education. Engineering mathematics. Physics One-Oh-One. Thermogoddamics. Machine elements. Saber and dueling sword. Swimming. And—don't laugh—English poetry from Chaucer through the Elizabethans. I enjoy teaching something worth teaching. I don't charge for courses I teach; the Chancellor and I understand each other."

"I'm not sure I understand you," I said, "but I love you anyhow. Let's go swimming."

X   "'—and he had two horns like a lamb, and he spake as a dragon'!"

Zeb:
Before heading for the pool our wives argued over how Barsoomian warriors dress—a debate complicated by the fact that I was the only one fairly sober. While I was telling my "shameful story," Jake had refreshed his Scotch-on-rocks and was genially argumentative. Our brides had stuck to one highball each but, while one jigger gave Deety a happy glow, Sharpie's mass is so slight that the same dosage made her squiffed.

Jake and I agreed to wear side arms. Our princesses had buckled them on; we would wear them. But Deety wanted me to take off the greasestained shorts I had worn while working. "Captain John Carter never wears clothes. He arrived on Barsoom naked, and from then on never wore anything but the leather and weapons of a fighting man. Jeweled leather for state occasions, plain leather for fighting—and sleeping silks at night. Barsoomians don't wear clothes. When John Carter first laid eyes on Dejah Thoris," Deety closed her eyes and recited: "'She was as destitute of clothes as the Green Martians . . . save for her highly wrought ornaments she was entirely naked . . .'" Deety opened her eyes, stared solemnly. "The women never wear clothes, just jewelry."

"Purty shilly," said her father, with a belch. "Scuse me!"

"When they were chilly, they wrapped furs around them, Pop. I mean 'Mors Kajak, my revered father.'"

Jake answered with slow precision. "Not . . . 'chilly.' *Silly!* With a clash of blades and flash of steel, man doesn't want family treasures swinging in the breeze 'n' banging his knees. Distracts him. Might get 'em sliced off. Correc', Captain John Carter?"

"Logical," I agreed.

"Besides, illustrations showed men wearing breech clouts. Pro'ly steel jockstrap underneath. *I* would."

"Those pictures were painted early in the twentieth century, Pop. Censored. But the stories make it clear. Weapons for men, jewelry for women—furs for cold weather."

"I know how I should dress," put in Sharpie. "Thuvia wears jewels on bits of gauze—I remember the book cover. Not clothes. Just something to fasten jewels to. Deety—Dejah Thoris, I mean—do you have a gauze scarf I can use? Fortunately I was wearing pearls when Mors Kajak kidnapped me."

"Sharpie," I objected, "you can't be Thuvia. She married Carthoris. Mors Kajak—or Mors Ka*jake,* might be a misspelling—is your husband."

"Cer'nly Mors Jake is my husband! But I'm his *second* wife; that explains everything. But it ill becomes the Warlord to address a princess of the House of Ptarth as 'Sharpie.'" Mrs. Burroughs drew herself up to her full 152 centimeters and tried to look offended.

"My humble apologies, Your Highness."

Sharpie giggled. "Can't stay mad at our Warlord. Dejah Thoris hon— Green tulle? Blue? Anything but white."

"I'll go look."

"Ladies," I objected, "if we don't get moving, the pool will cool off. You can sew on pearls this evening. Anyhow, where do pearls come from on Barsoom? Dead sea bottoms—no oysters."

"From Korus, the Lost Sea of Dor," Deety explained.

"They've got you, Son. But I either go swimming right now— or I have another drink . . . and then another, and then another. Working too hard. Too tense. Too much worry."

"Okay, Pop; we swim. Aunt H— Aunt Thuvia?"

"All right, Dejah Thoris. To save Mors Jacob from himself.

But I *won't* wear earthling clothes. You can have my mink cape; may be chilly coming back."

Jake wrapped his sarong into a breech clout, strapped it in place with his saber belt. I replaced those grimy shorts with swim briefs which Deety conceded were "almost Barsoomian." I was no longer dependent on Jake's clothes; my travel kit, always in my car, once I got at it, supplied necessities from passport to poncho. Sharpie wore pearls and rings she had been wearing at her party, plus a scarf around her waist to which she attached all the costume jewelry Deety could dig up. Deety carried Hilda's mink cape—then wrapped it around her. "My Captain, someday I want one like this."

"I'll skin the minks personally," I promised her.

"Oh, dear! I think this is synthetic."

"I don't. Ask Hilda."

"I will most carefully *not* ask her. But I'll settle for synthetic."

I said, "My beloved Princess, you eat meat. Minks are vicious carnivores and the ones used for fur are raised for no other purpose—*not* trapped. They are well treated, then killed humanely. If your ancestors had not killed for meat and fur as the last glaciation retreated, *you* would not be here. Illogical sentiment leads to the sort of tragedy you find in India and Bangladesh."

Deety was silent some moments as we followed Jake and Hilda down toward the pool. "My Captain—"

"Yes, Princess?"

"I stand corrected. But your brain works so much like a computer that you scare me."

"I don't ever want to scare you. I'm not bloodthirsty—not with minks, not with steers, not with anything. But I'll kill without hesitation . . . for you."

"Zebadiah—"

"Yes, Deety?"

"I am proud that you made me your wife. I will try to be a good wife . . . and your princess."

"You do. You have. You always will. Dejah Thoris, my princess and only love, until I met you, I was a boy playing with oversized toys. Today I am a man. With a wife to protect and cherish . . . a child to plan for. I'm truly alive, at last! Hey! What are you sniffling about? Stop it!"

"I'll cry if I feel like it!"

"Well . . . don't get it on Hilda's cape."

"Gimme a hanky."

"I don't even have a Kleenex." I brushed away her tears with my fingers. "Sniff hard. You can cry on me tonight. In bed."

"Let's go to bed early."

"Right after dinner. Sniffles all gone?"

"I think so. Do pregnant women always cry?"

"So I hear."

"Well . . . I'm not going to do it again. No excuse for it; I'm terribly happy."

"The Polynesians do something they call 'Crying happy.' Maybe that's what you do."

"I guess so. But I'll save it for private." Deety started to shrug the cape off. "Too hot, lovely as it feels." She stopped with the cape off her shoulders, suddenly pulled it around her again. "Who's coming up the hill?"

I looked up, saw that Jake and Hilda had reached the pool—and a figure was appearing from below, beyond the boulder that dammed it.

"I don't know. Stay behind me." I hurried toward the pool.

The stranger was dressed as a Federal Ranger. As I closed in, I heard the stranger say to Jake, "Are you Jacob Burroughs?"

"Why do you ask?"

"Are you or aren't you? If you are, I have business with you. If you're not, you're trespassing. Federal land, restricted access."

"Jake!" I called out. "Who is he?"

The newcomer turned his head. "Who are *you*?"

"Wrong sequence," I told him. "You haven't identified yourself."

"Don't be funny," the stranger said. "You know this uniform. I'm Bennie Hibol, the Ranger hereabouts."

I answered most carefully, "Mr. Highball, you are a man in a uniform, wearing a gun belt and a shield. That doesn't make you a Federal officer. Show your credentials and state your business."

The uniformed character sighed. "I got no time to listen to smart talk." He rested his hand on the butt of his gun. "If one of you is Burroughs, speak up. I'm going to search this site and cabin. There's stuff coming up from Sonora; this sure as hell is the transfer point."

Deety suddenly came out from behind me, moved quickly and placed herself beside her father. "Where's your search warrant? Show your authority!" She had the cape clutched around her; her face quivered with indignation.

"Another joker!" This clown snapped open his holster. "Federal land—here's my authority!"

Deety suddenly dropped the cape, stood naked in front of him. I drew, lunged, and cut down in one motion—slashed the wrist, recovered, thrust upward from low line into the belly above the gun belt.

As my point entered, Jake's saber cut the side of the neck almost to decapitation. Our target collapsed like a puppet with cut strings, lay by the pool, bleeding at three wounds.

"Zebadiah, I'm sorry!"

"About what, Princess?" I asked as I wiped my blade on the alleged ranger's uniform. I noticed the color of the blood with distaste.

"He didn't react! I thought my strip act would give you more time."

"You did distract him," I reassured her. "He watched *you* and didn't watch *me*. Jake, what kind of a creature has bluish green blood?"

"I don't know."

Sharpie came forward, squatted down, dabbed a finger in the blood, sniffed it. "Hemocyanin. I think," she said calmly. "Deety, you were right. Alien. The largest terrestrial fauna with that method of oxygen transport is a lobster. But this *thing* is no lobster, it's a 'Black Hat.' *How did you know?*"

"I didn't. But he didn't sound right. Rangers are polite. And they never fuss about showing their I.D.'s."

"I didn't know," I admitted. "I wasn't suspicious, just annoyed."

"You moved mighty fast," Jake approved.

"I never know why till it's over. You didn't waste time yourself, tovarishch. Drawing saber while he was pulling a gun—that takes guts and speed. But let's not talk now—*where are his pals?* We may be picked off getting back to the house."

"Look at his pants," Hilda suggested. "He hasn't been on horseback. Hasn't climbed far, either. Jacob, is there a jeep trail?"

"No. This isn't accessible by jeep—just barely by horse."

"Hasn't been anything overhead," I added. "No chopper, no air car."

"Continua craft," said Deety.

"Huh?"

"Zebadiah, the 'Black Hats' are aliens who don't want Pop to build a time-space machine. We *know* that. So it follows that *they* have continua craft. Q.E.D."

I thought about it. "Deety, I'm going to bring you breakfast in bed. Jake, how do we spot an alien continua craft? It doesn't have to look like Gay Deceiver."

Jake frowned. "No. *Any* shape. But a one-passenger craft might not be much larger than a phone booth."

"If it's a one-man—one-alien—job, it should be parked down in that scrub," I said, pointing. "We can find it."

"Zebadiah," protested Deety, "we don't have *time* to search. We ought to get *out* of here! *Fast!*"

Jake said, "My daughter is right but not for that reason. Its craft is not necessarily waiting. It could be parked an infinitesimal interval away along any of six axes, and either return automatically, preprogrammed, or by some method of signaling that we can postulate but not describe. The alien craft would not be here-now... but *will* be here-later. For pickup."

"In that case, Jake, you and I and the gals should scram out of here-now to there-then. Be missing. How long has our pressure test been running? What time is it?"

"Seventeen-seventeen," Deety answered instantly.

I looked at my wife. "Naked as a frog. Where do you hide your watch, dearest? Surely, not *there*."

She stuck out her tongue. "Smarty. I have a clock in my head. I never mention it because people give me funny looks."

"Deety does have innate time sense," agreed her father, "accurate to thirteen seconds plus or minus about four seconds; I've measured it."

"I'm sorry, Zebadiah—I don't *mean* to be a freak."

"Sorry about what, Princess? I'm impressed. What do you do about time zones?"

"Same as you do. Add or subtract as necessary. Darling, *everyone* has a built-in circadian. Mine is merely more nearly exact than most people's. Like having absolute pitch—some do, some don't."

"Are you a lightning calculator?"

"Yes... but computers are so much faster that I no longer do it much. Except one thing— I can sense a glitch—spot a wrong answer. Then I look for garbage in the program. If I don't find it, I send for a hardware specialist. Look, sweetheart, discuss my oddities later. Pop, let's dump that *thing* down the septic tank and *go*. I'm nervous, I am."

"Not so fast, Deety." Hilda was still squatting by the corpse. "Zebbie. Consult your hunches. Are we in danger?"

"Well... not this instant."

"Good. I want to dissect this creature."

"Aunt Hilda!"

"Take a Miltown, Deety. Gentlemen, the Bible or somebody said, 'Know thy enemy.' This is the only 'Black Hat' we've seen . . . and he's not human and not born on earth. There is a wealth of knowledge lying here and it ought not to be shoved down a septic tank until we know more about it. Jacob, feel this."

Hilda's husband got down on his knees, let her guide his hand through the "ranger's" hair. "Feel those bumps, dearest?"

"Yes!"

"Much like the budding horns of a lamb, are they not?"

"Oh— 'And I beheld another beast coming up out of the earth; and he had two horns like a lamb, and he spake as a dragon'!"

I squatted down, felt for horn buds. "Be damned! He did come up out of the earth—up this slope anyhow—and he spake as a dragon. Talked unfriendly, and all the dragons I've ever heard of talked mean or belched fire. Hilda, when you field-strip this critter, keep an eye out for the Number of the Beast."

"I shall! Who's going to help me get this specimen up to the house? I want three volunteers."

Deety gave a deep sigh. "I volunteer. Aunt Hilda . . . *must* you do this?"

"Deety, it ought to be done at Johns Hopkins, with x-ray and proper tools and color holovision. But I'm the best biologist for it because I'm the only biologist. Honey child, you don't have to watch. Aunt Sharpie has helped in an emergency room after a five-car crash; to me, blood is just a mess to clean up. Green blood doesn't bother me even that much."

Deety gulped. "I'll help carry. I *said* I would!"

"Dejah Thoris!"

"Sir? Yes, my Captain?"

"Back away from that. Take this. And this." I unbuckled sword and belt, shoved down my swimming briefs, handed all of it to Deety. "Jake, help me get him up into fireman's carry."

"I'll help carry, Son."

"No, I can tote him easier than two could. Sharpie, where do you want to work?"

"It will have to be the dining table."

"Aunt Hilda, I don't want that thing on my—! I beg your pardon; it's *your* dining table."

"You're forgiven only if you'll concede that it is *our* dining table. Deety, how many times must I repeat that I am *not* crowding you out of your home? We are co-housewives—my only seniority lies in being twenty years older. To my regret."

"Hilda my dear one, what would you say to a workbench in the garage with a drop cloth on it and flood lights over it?"

"I say, 'Swell!' I don't think a dining table is the place for a dissection, either. But I couldn't think of anywhere else."

With help from Jake, I got that damned carcass draped across my shoulders in fireman's carry. Deety started up the path with me, carrying my belt and sword and my briefs in one arm so that she could hold my free hand—despite my warning that she might be splashed with alien blood. "No, Zebadiah, I got overtaken by childishness. I won't let it happen again. I must conquer all squeamishness—I'll be changing diapers soon." She was silent a moment. "That is the first time I've seen death. In a person, I mean. An alien humanoid person I should say . . . but I thought he was a man. I once saw a puppy run over—I threw up. Even though it was not my puppy and I didn't go close." She added, "An adult should face up to death, should she not?"

"Face up to it, yes," I agreed. "But not grow calloused. Deety, I've seen too many men die. I've never grown inured to it. One must accept death, learn not to fear it, then never worry about it. 'Make Today Count!' as a friend whose days are numbered told me. Live in that spirit and when death comes, it will come as a welcome friend."

"You say much what my mother told me before she died."

"Your mother must have been an extraordinary woman. Deety, in the two weeks I've known you, I've heard so much about her from all three of you that I feel as if I knew her. A friend I hadn't seen lately. She sounds like a wise woman."

"I think she was, Zebadiah. Certainly she was good. Sometimes, when I have a hard choice, I ask myself, 'What would Mama do?'—and everything falls into place."

"Both good *and* wise . . . and her daughter shows it. Uh, how old are you, Deety?"

"Does it matter, sir?"

"No. Curiosity."

"I wrote my birth date on our marriage license application."

"Beloved, my head was spinning so hard that I had trouble remembering my own. But I should not have asked—women have birthdays, men have ages. I want to know your birthday; I have no need to know the year."

"April twenty-second, Zebadiah—one day older than Shakespeare."

"'Age could not wither her—' Woman, you carry your years well."

"Thank you, sir."

"That snoopy question came from having concluded in my mind that you were twenty-six . . . figuring from the fact that you have a doctor's degree. Although you look younger."

"I think twenty-six is a satisfactory age."

"I wasn't asking," I said hastily. "I got confused from knowing Hilda's age . . . then hearing her say that she is—or claims to be— twenty years older than you. It did not jibe with my earlier estimate, based on your probable age on graduating from high school plus your two degrees."

Jake and Hilda had lingered at the pool while Jake washed his hands and rinsed from his body smears of alien ichor. Being less burdened, they climbed the path faster than we and came up behind us just as Deety answered,

"Zebadiah, I never graduated from high school."

"Oh."

"That's right," agreed her father. "Deety matriculated by taking College Boards. At fourteen. No problem since she stayed home and didn't have to live in a dorm. Got her B.S. in three years . . . and that was a happy thing, as Jane lived to see Deety move the tassel from one side of her mortar board to the other. Jane in a wheelchair and happy as a child—her doctor said it couldn't hurt her . . . meaning she was dying anyhow." He added, "Had her mother been granted only three more years she could have seen Deety's doctorate conferred, two years ago."

"Pop . . . sometimes you chatter."

"Did I say something out of line?"

"No, Jake," I assured him. "But I've just learned that I robbed the cradle. I knew I had but hadn't realized how much. Deety darling, you are twenty-two."

"Is twenty-two an unsatisfactory age?"

"No, my Princess. Just right."

"My Captain said that women have birthdays while men have ages. Is it permitted to inquire your age, sir? I didn't pay close attention to that form we had to fill out, either."

I answered solemnly, "But Dejah Thoris knows that Captain John Carter is centuries old, cannot recall his childhood, and has always looked thirty years old."

"Zebadiah, if that is your age, you've had a busy thirty years. You said you left home when you graduated from high school, worked your way through college, spent three years on active duty, then worked your way through a doctor's degree—"

"A phony one!"

"That doesn't reduce required residence. Aunt Hilda says you've been a professor four years."

"Uh . . . will you settle for nine years older than you are?"

"I'll settle for whatever you say."

"He's at it again," put in Sharpie. "He was run off two other campuses. Co-ed scandals. Then he found that in California nobody cared, so he moved west."

I tried to look hurt. "Sharpie darling, I *always* married them. One gal turned out already to be married and in the other case the child wasn't mine; she slipped one over on me."

"The truth isn't in him, Deety. But he's brave and he bathes every day and he's rich—and we love him anyhow."

"The truth isn't in you either, Aunt Hilda. But we love you anyhow. It says in 'Little Women' that a bride should be half her husband's age plus seven years. Zebadiah and I hit close to that."

"A rule that makes an old hag out of me. Jacob, I'm just Zebbie's age—thirty-one. But we've both been thirty-one for ages."

"I'll bet he does feel aged after carrying that thing uphill. Atlas, can you support your burden while I get the garage open, a bench dragged out and covered? Or shall I help you put it down?"

"I'd just have to pick it up again. But don't dally."

XI "—citizens must protect themselves."

Zeb:

I felt better after I got that "ranger's" corpse dumped and the garage door closed, everyone indoors. I had told Hilda that I felt no "immediate" danger—but my wild talent does *not* warn me until the Moment of Truth. The "Blokes in the Black Hats" had us located. Or possibly had never lost us; what applies to human gangsters has little to do with aliens whose powers and motives and plans we had no way to guess.

We might be as naive as a kitten who thinks he is hidden because his head is, unaware that his little rump sticks out.

They were alien, they were powerful, they were multiple (three thousand? three million?—we didn't know the Number of the Beast)—and they knew where we were. True, we had killed one— by luck, not by planning. That "ranger" would be missed; we could expect more to call in force.

Foolhardiness has never appealed to me. Given a chance to run, I run. I don't mean I'll bug out on wing mate when the unfriendlies show up, and certainly not on a wife and unborn child. But I wanted us *all* to run—me, my wife, my blood brother who was also my father-in-law, and his wife, my chum Sharpie who was brave, practical, smart, and unsqueamish (that she would joke in the jaws of Moloch was not a fault but a source of esprit).

I wanted us to *go!*—*Tau* axis, *Teh* axis, rotate, translate, whatever—anywhere not infested by gruesomes with green gore.

I checked the gauge and felt better; Gay's inner pressure had not dropped. Too much to expect Gay to be a spaceship—not equipped to scavenge and replenish air. But it was pleasant to know that she would hold pressure much longer than it would take us to scram for home if we had to—assuming that unfriendlies had not shot holes in her graceful shell.

I went by the inside passageway into the cabin, used soap and hot water, rinsed off and did it again, dried down and felt clean enough to kiss my wife, which I did. Deety held onto me and reported.

"Your kit is packed, sir. I'm finishing mine, the planned weight and space, and nothing but practical clothes—"

"Sweetheart."

"Yes, Zebadiah?"

"Take the clothes you were married in and mine too. Same for Jake and Hilda. And your father's dress uniform. Or was it burned in Logan?"

"But, Zebadiah, you emphasized rugged clothes."

"So I did. To keep your mind on the fact that we can't guess the conditions we'll encounter and don't know how long we'll be gone or if we'll be back. So I listed everything that might be useful in pioneering a virgin planet—since we might be stranded and *never* get home. Everything from Jake's microscope and water-testing gear to technical manuals and tools. And weapons—and flea powder. But it's possible that we will have to play the roles of ambassadors for humanity at the court of His Extreme Majesty, Overlord of Galactic Empires in thousandth-and-third continuum. We may need the gaudiest clothes we can whip up. We *don't* know, we *can't* guess."

"I'd rather pioneer."

"We may not have a choice. When you were figuring weights, do you recall spaces marked 'Assigned mass such and such—list to come'?"

"Certainly. Total exactly one hundred kilos, which seemed odd. Space slightly less than one cubic meter split into crannies."

"Those are yours, snubnose. And Pop or Hilda. Mass can be up to fifty percent over; I'll tell Gay to trim to match. Got an old doll? A security blanket? A favorite book of poems? Scrapbook? Family photographs? Bring 'em all!"

"Golly!" (I never enjoy looking at my wife quite so much as when she lights up and is suddenly a little girl.)

"Don't leave space for me. I have only what I arrived with. What about shoes for Hilda?"

"She claims she doesn't need any, Zebadiah—that her calluses are getting calluses on them. But I've worked out expedients. I got Pop some Dr. Scholl's shoe liners when we were building; I have three pairs left and can trim them. Liners and enough bobby sox make her size three-and-half feet fit my clodhoppers pretty well. And I have a sentimental keepsake; Keds Pop bought me when I first went to summer camp, at ten. They fit Aunt Hilda."

"Good girl!" I added, "You seem to have everything in hand. How about food? Not stores we are carrying, I mean *now*. Has anybody thought about dinner? Killing aliens makes me hungry."

"Buffet style, Zebadiah. Sandwiches and stuff on the kitchen counter, and I thawed and heated an apple pie. I fed one sandwich to Hilda, holding it for her; she says she's going to finish working, then scrub before she eats anything more."

"Sharpie munched a sandwich while she carved that *thing?*"

"Aunt Hilda is rugged, Zebadiah—almost as rugged as you are."

"*More* rugged than I am. I could do an autopsy if I had to—but not while eating. I think I speak for Jake, too."

"I know you speak for Pop. He saw me feeding her, turned green and went elsewhere. Go look at what she's been doing, Zebadiah; Hilda has found interesting things."

"Hmmm— Are you the little girl who had a tizzy at the idea of dissecting a dead alien?"

"No, sir, I am not. I've decided to stay grown up. It's not easy.

But it's more satisfying. An adult doesn't panic at a snake; she just checks to see if it's got rattles. I'll never squeal again. I'm grown up at last...a wife instead of a pampered princess."

"You will always be my Princess!"

"I hope so, my Chieftain. But to merit that, I must learn to be a pioneer mother—wring the neck of a rooster, butcher a hog, load while my husband shoots, take his place and his rifle when he is wounded. I'll learn—I'm stubborn, I am. Grab a hunk of pie and go see Hilda. I know just what to do with the extra hundred kilos: books, photographs, Pop's microfilm files and portable viewer, Pop's rifle and a case of ammo that the weight schedule didn't allow for—"

"Didn't know he had it—*what calibre?*"

"Seven point six two millimeters, long cartridge."

"Glory be! Pop and I use the same ammo!"

"Didn't know you carried a rifle, Zebadiah."

"I don't advertise it, it's unlicensed. I must show all of you how to get at it."

"Got any use for a lady's purse gun? A needle gun, Skoda fléchettes. Not much range but either they poison or they break up and expand...and it fires ninety times on one magazine."

"What are you, Deety? Honorable Hatchet Man?"

"No, sir. Pop got it for me—black market—when I started working nights. He said he would rather hire shysters to get me acquitted—or maybe probation—than to have to go down to the morgue to identify my body. Haven't had to use it; in Logan I hardly need it. Zebadiah, Pop has gone to a great deal of trouble to get me the best possible training in self-defense. He's just as highly trained—that's why I keep him out of fist fights. Because it would be a massacre. He and Mama decided this when I was a baby. Pop says cops and courts no longer protect citizens, so citizens must protect themselves."

"I'm afraid he's right."

"My husband, I can't evaluate my opinions of right and wrong because I learned them from my parents and haven't lived long enough to have formed opinions in disagreement with theirs."

"Deety, your parents did okay."

"I think so...but that's subjective. As may be, I was kept out of blackboard jungles—public schools—until we moved to Utah. And I was trained to fight—armed or unarmed. Pop and I noticed how you handled a sword. Your moulinets are like clockwork. And when you drop into point guard, your forearm is perfectly covered."

"Jake is no slouch. He drew so fast I never saw it, and cut precisely above the collar."

"Pop says you are better at it."

"Mmm— Longer reach. He's probably faster. Deety, the best swordmaster I ever had was your height and reach. I couldn't even cross blades with him unless he allowed me to."

"You never did say where you had taken up swordsmanship."

I grinned down at her. "Y.M.C.A. in downtown Manhattan. I had foil in high school. I fiddled with saber and épée in college. But I never encountered *swordsmen* until I moved to Manhattan. Took it up because I was getting soft. Then during that so-called 'research trip' in Europe I met swordsmen with family tradition— sons and grandsons and great-grandsons of maîtres d'armes. Learned that it was a way of life—and I had started too late. Deety, I fibbed to Hilda; I've never fought a student duel. But I did train in saber in Heidelberg under the Säbelmeister reputed to coach one underground Korps. He was the little guy I couldn't cross steel with. *Fast!* Up to then I had thought *I* was fast. But I got faster under his tutelage. The day I was leaving he told me that he wished he had had me twenty years sooner; he might have made a swordsman of me."

"You were fast enough this afternoon!"

"No, Deety. You had his eye, I attacked from the flank. *You* won that fight—not me, not Pop. Although what Pop did was far more dangerous than what I did."

"My Captain, I will not let you disparage yourself! I cannot hear you!"

Women, bless their warm hearts and strange minds—Deety had appointed me her hero; that settled it. I would have to try to measure up. I cut a piece of apple pie, ate it quickly while I walked slowly through the passage into the garage—didn't want to reach the "morgue" still eating.

The "ranger" was on its back with clothes cut away, open from chin to crotch, and spread. Nameless chunks of gizzard were here and there around the cadaver. It gave off a fetid odor.

Hilda was still carving, ice tongs in left hand, knife in her right, greenish goo up over her wrists. As I approached she put down the knife, picked up a razor blade—did not look up until I spoke. "Learning things, Sharpie?"

She put down her tools, wiped her hands on a towel, pushed back her hair with her forearm. "Zebbie, you wouldn't believe it."

"Try me."

"Well . . . look at this." She touched the corpse's right leg, and spoke to the corpse itself. "What's a nice joint like this doing in a girl like you?"

I saw what she meant: a long, gaunt leg with an extra knee lower than the human knee; it bent backwards. Looking higher, I saw that its arms had similar extra articulation. "Did you say 'girl'?"

"I said 'girl.' Zebbie, this monster is either female or hermaphroditic. A fully developed uterus, two-horned like a cat, one ovary above each horn. But there appear to be testes lower down and a dingus that may be a retractable phallus. Female—but probably male as well. Bisexual but does not impregnate itself; the plumbing wouldn't hook up. I think these critters can both pitch and catch."

"Taking turns? Or simultaneously?"

"Wouldn't that be sump'n? No, for mechanical reasons I think they take turns. Whether ten minutes apart or ten years, deponent sayeth not. But I'd give a pretty to see two of 'em going to it!"

"Sharpie, you've got a one-track mind."

"It's the main track. Reproduction *is* the main track; the methods and mores of sexual copulation are the central feature of all higher developments of life."

"You're ignoring money and television."

"Piffle! All human activities including scientific research are either mating dances and care of the young, or the dismal sublimations of born losers in the only game in town. Don't try to kid Sharpie. Took me forty-two years to grab a real man and get myself knocked up—but I made it! Everything I've done up to the last two weeks has been 'vamp till ready.' How about you, you shameless stud? Am I not right? Careful how you answer; I'll tell Deety."

"I'll take the Fifth."

"Make mine a quart. Zebbie, I *hate* these monsters; they interfere with my plans—a rose-covered cottage, a baby in the crib, a pot roast in the oven, me in a gingham dress, and my man coming down the lane after a hard day flunking freshmen—me with his slippers and his pipe and a dry martini waiting for him. Heaven! All else is vanity and vexation. Four fully developed mammary glands but lacking the redundant fat characteristic of the human female—'cept me, damn it. A double stomach, a single intestine. A two-compartment heart that seems to pump by peristalsis rather than by beating. Cordate. I haven't examined the brain; I don't have a proper saw—but it must be as well developed as ours. Definitely humanoid, outrageously nonhuman. Don't knock over those bottles; they are specimens of body fluids."

"What are these things?"

"Splints to conceal the unhuman articulation. Plastic surgery on the face, too, I'm pretty sure, and cheaters to reshape the skull. The hair is fake; these Boojums don't have hair. Something like tattooing—or maybe masking I haven't been able to peel off—to make the face and other exposed skin look human instead of blue-green. Zeb, seven-to-two a large number of missing persons have been used as guinea pigs before they worked out methods for this masquerade. *Swoop!* A flying saucer dips down and two more guinea pigs wind up in their laboratories."

"There hasn't been a flying saucer scare in years."

"Poetic license, dear. If they have space-time twisters, they can pop up anywhere, steal what they want—or replace a real human with a convincing fake—and be gone like switching off a light."

"This one couldn't get by very long. Rangers have to take physical examinations."

"This one may be a rush job, prepared just for us. A permanent substitution might fool anything but an x-ray—and might fool even x-ray if the doctor giving the examination was one of *Them* . . . a theory you might think about. Zebbie, I must get to work. There is so *much* to learn and so little time. I can't learn a fraction of what this carcass could tell a real comparative biologist."

"Can I help?" (I was not anxious to.)

"Well—"

"I haven't much to do until Jake and Deety finish assembling the last of what they are going to take. So what can I do to help?"

"I could work twice as fast if you would take pictures. I have to stop to wipe my hands before I touch the camera."

"I'm your boy, Sharpie. Just say what angle, distance, and when."

Hilda looked relieved. "Zebbie, have I told you that I love you despite your gorilla appearance and idiot grin? Underneath you have the soul of a cherub. I want a bath so badly I can taste it—could be the last hot bath in a long time. And the bidet—the acme of civilized decadence. I've been afraid I would still be carving strange meat when Jacob said it was time to leave."

"Carve away, dear; you'll get your bath." I picked up the camera, the one Jake used for record-keeping: a Polaroid Stereo-Instamatic—self-focusing, automatic irising, automatic processing, the perfect camera for engineer or scientist who needs a running record.

I took endless pictures while Hilda sweated away. "Sharpie, doesn't it worry you to work with bare hands? You might catch the Never-Get-Overs."

"Zebbie, if these critters could be killed by our bugs, they would have arrived here with no immunities and died quickly. They didn't. Therefore it seems likely that we can't by hurt by *their* bugs. Radically different biochemistries."

It sounded logical—but I could not forget Kettering's Law: "Logic is an organized way of going wrong with confidence."

Deety appeared, set down a loaded hamper. "That's the last." She had her hair up in a bath knot and was dressed solely in rubber gloves. "Hi, dearest. Aunt Hilda, I'm ready to help."

"Not much you can do, Deety hon—unless you want to relieve Zebbie."

Deety was staring at the corpse and did not look happy—her nipples were down flat. "Go take a bath!" I told her. "Scram."

"Do I stink that badly?"

"You stink swell, honey girl. But Sharpie pointed out that this may be our last chance at soap and hot water in quite a while. I've promised her that we won't leave for Canopus and points east until she has her bath. So get yours out of the way, then you can help me stow while she gets sanitary."

"All right." Deety backed off and her nipples showed faintly— not rigid but she was feeling better. My darling keeps her feelings out of her face, mostly—but those pretty pink spigots are barometers of her morale.

"Just a sec, Deety," Hilda added. "This afternoon you said, 'He didn't react!' What did you mean?"

"What I said. Strip in front of a man and he reacts, one way or another. Even if he tries to ignore it, his eyes give him away. But he *didn't*. Of course he's not a man—but I didn't know that when I tried to distract him."

I said, "But he did notice you, Deety—and that gave me my chance."

"But only the way a dog, or a horse, or any animal, will notice any movement. He noticed but ignored it. No reaction."

"Zebbie, does that remind you of anything?"

"Should it?"

"The first day we were here you told us a story about a 'zaftig co-ed.'"

"I did?"

"She was flunking math."

"*Oh!* 'Brainy.'"

"Yes, Professor N. O'Heret Brain. See any parallel?"

"But 'No Brain' has been on campus for years. Furthermore he turns red in the face. Not a tattoo job."

"I said this one might be a rush job. Would anyone be in a better position to discredit a mathematical theory than the head of the department of mathematics at a very prominent university? Especially if he was familiar with that theory and *knew* that it was correct?"

"Hey, wait a minute!" put in Deety. "Are you talking about that professor who argued with Pop? The one with the phony invitation? I thought he was just a stooge? Pop says he's a fool."

"He behaves like a pompous old fool," agreed Hilda. "I can't stand him. I plan to do an autopsy on him."

"But he's not dead."

"That can be corrected!" Sharpie said sharply.

XII   *"They might fumigate this planet and take it."*

Hilda:

By the time I was out of my bath, Jacob, Deety, and Zebbie had Gay Deceiver stowed and lists checked (can opener, cameras, et cetera)—even samples of fluids and tissues from the cadaver, as Zebbie's miracle car had a small refrigerator. Deety wasn't happy about my specimens being in the refrigerator but they were *very* well packed, layer on layer of plastic wrap, then sealed into a freezer box. Besides, that refrigerator contained mostly camera film, dynamite caps, and other noneatables. Food was mostly freeze-dried and sealed in nitrogen, except foods that won't spoil.

We were dog tired. Jacob moved that we sleep, then leave. "Zeb, unless you expect a new attack in the next eight hours, we should rest. I need to be clear-headed in handling verniers. This house is almost a fortress, will be pitch black, and does not radiate any part of the spectrum. They may conclude that we ran for it right after we got their boy—hermaphrodite, I mean; the fake 'ranger'—what do you think?"

"Jake, I wouldn't have been surprised had we been clobbered at any moment. Since they didn't— Well, I don't like to handle Gay when I'm not sharp. More mistakes are made in battle through fatigue than from any other cause. Let's sack in. Anybody need a sleeping pill?"

"All I need is a bed. Hilda my love, tonight I sleep on my own side."

I said, "Can't I even cuddle up your back?"

"Promise not to tickle?"

I made a face at my darling. "I promise."

"Zebadiah," Deety said. "I don't want to cuddle; I want to be *held* . . . so I'll know I'm safe. For the first time since my twelfth birthday I don't feel sexy."

"Princess, it's settled; we sleep. But I suggest that we be up before daylight. Let's not crowd our luck."

"Sensible," agreed Jacob.

I shrugged. "You men have to pilot; Deety and I are cargo. We can nap in the back seats—if we miss a few universes, what of it? If you've seen one universe, you've seen 'em all. Deety?"

"If it were up to me, I would lam out of here so fast my shoes would be left standing. But Zebadiah has to pilot and Pop has to set verniers . . . and both are tired and don't want to chance it. But, Zebadiah . . . don't fret if I rest with my eyes and ears open."

"Huh? Deety—*why?*"

"Somebody ought to be on watch. It might give us that split-second advantage—split seconds have saved us at least twice. Don't worry, darling; I often skip a night to work a long program under shared time. Doesn't hurt me; a nap next day and I'm ready to bite rattlesnakes. Tell him, Pop."

"That's correct, Zeb, but—"

Zebbie cut him off. "Maybe you gals can split watches and have breakfast ready. Right now I've got to hook up Gay Deceiver so that she can reach me in our bedroom. Deety, I can add a program so that she can listen around the cabin, too. Properly programmed, Gay's the best watch dog of any of us. Will that satisfy you duty-struck little broads?"

Deety said nothing so I kept quiet. Zebbie, frowning, turned back to his car, opened a door and prepared to hook Gay's voice and ears to the three house intercoms. "Want to shift the basement talky-talk to your bedroom, Jake?"

"Good idea," Jacob agreed.

"Wait a half while I ask Gay what she has. Hello, Gay."

"Howdy, Zeb. Wipe off your chin."

"Program. Running new retrievals. Report new items since last report."

"Null report, Boss."

"Thank you, Gay."

"You're welcome, Zeb."

"Program, Gay. Add running news retrieval. Area, Arizona Strip north of Grand Canyon plus Utah. Persons: all persons listed in current running news retrieval programs plus rangers, Federal rangers, forest rangers, park rangers, state rangers. End of added program."

"New program running, Boss."

"Program. Add running acoustic report, maximum gain."

"New program running, Zeb."

"You're a smart girl, Gay."

"Isn't it time you married me?"

"Good night, Gay."

"Good night, Zeb. Sleep with your hands outside the covers."

"Deety, you've corrupted Gay. I'll run a lead outdoors for a microphone while Jake moves the basement intercom to the master bedroom. But maximum gain will put a coyote yapping ten miles away right into bed with you. Jake, I can tell Gay to subtract acoustic report from the news retrieval for your bedroom."

"Hilda my love, do you want the acoustic subtracted?"

I didn't but didn't say so; Gay interrupted:

"Running news retrieval, Boss."

"Report!"

"Reuters, Straits Times, Singapore. Tragic News of Marston Expedition. Indonesian News Service, Palembang. Two bodies identified as Dr. Cecil Yang and Dr. Z. Edward Carter were brought by jungle buggy to National Militia Headquarters, Teluk-betung. The district commandant stated that they will be transferred by air to Palembang for further transport to Singapore when the commandant-in-chief releases them to the Minister of Tourism and Culture. Professor Marston and Mr. Smythe-Belisha are still unreported. Commandants of both districts concede that hopes of finding them alive have diminished. However, a spokesman for the Minister of Tourism and Culture assured a press conference that the Indonesian government would pursue the search more assiduously than ever."

Zebbie whistled tunelessly. Finally, he said, "Opinions, anyone?"

"He was a brilliant man, Son," my husband said soberly. "An irreplaceable loss. Tragic."

"Ed was a good Joe, Jake. But that's not what I mean. Our tactical situation. *Now. Here.*"

My husband paused before answering, "Zeb, whatever happened in Sumatra apparently happened about a month ago. Emotionally I feel great turmoil. Logically I am forced to state that I cannot see that our situation has changed."

"Hilda? Deety?"

"News retrieval report," announced Gay.

"Report!"

"AP San Francisco via satellite from Saipan, Marianas. TWA hypersonic-semiballistic liner *Winged Victory* out of San Francisco International at twenty o'clock this evening Pacific Coast Time was seen by eye and radar to implode on reentry. AP Honolulu US Navy Official. USS Submersible Carrier *Flying Fish* operating near Wake Island has been ordered to proceed flank speed toward site of *Winged Victory* reentry. She will surface and launch search craft at optimum point. Navy PIO spokesman, when asked what was 'optimum,' replied 'No comment.' Associated Press's military editor noted that submerged speed of *Flying Fish* class, and type and characteristics of craft carried, are classified information. AP-UPI add San Francisco, *Winged Victory* disaster. TWA public relations released a statement quote if reports received concerning *Winged Victory* are correct it must be tentatively assumed that no survivors can be expected. But our engineering department denies that implosion could be cause. Collision with orbital debris decaying into atmosphere or even a strike by a meteor could repeat could endrep cause disaster by mischance so unlikely that it can only be described as an Act of God endquote TWA spokesmen released passenger list by order of the Civil Aerospace Board. List follows: California—"

The list was longish. I did not recognize any names until Gay reached: "Doctor Neil O. Brain—"

I gasped. But no one said a word until Gay announced: "End running news retrieval."

"Thank you, Gay."

"A pleasure, Zeb."

Zebbie said, "Proféssor?"

"You're in command, Captain!"

"Very well, sir! All of you—lifeboat rules! I expect fast action and no back talk. Estimated departure—five minutes! First everybody take a pee! Second, put on the clothes you'll travel in. Jake, switch off, lock up—whatever you do to secure your house for long absence. Deety—follow Jake, make sure he hasn't missed anything—then *you*, not Jake, switch out lights and close doors. Hilda, bundle what's left of that Dutch lunch and fetch it—fast, not fussy. Check the refrigerator for solid foods—no liquids—and cram what you can into Gay's refrigerator. Don't dither over choices. Questions, anyone? Move!"

I gave Jacob first crack at our bathroom because the poor dear tenses up; I used the time to slide sandwiches into a freezer sack and half a pie into another. Potato salad? Scrape it into a third and stick in one plastic picnic spoon; germs were now community property. I stuffed this and some pickles into the biggest freezer sack Deety stocked, and closed it.

Jake came out of our bedroom; I threw him a kiss *en passant*, ducked into our john, turned on water in the basin, sat down, and recited mantras—that often works when I'm jumpy—then used the bidet—patted it and told it good-bye without stopping. My travel clothes were Deety's baby tennis shoes with a green-and-gold denim miniskirt dress of hers that came to my knees but wasn't too dreadful with a scarf to belt it. Panties? I had none. Deety had put a pair of hers out for me—but her size would fall off me. Then I saw that the dear baby had gotten at the elastic and knotted it. Yup! pretty good fit—and, with no telling when our next baths would be, panties were practical even though a nuisance.

I spread my cape in front of the refrigerator, dumped my purse and our picnic lunch into it, started salvaging—half a boned ham, quite a bit of cheese, a loaf and a half of bread, two pounds of butter (freezer sacks, and the same for the ham—if Deety hadn't had a lavish supply of freezer sacks I could not have salvaged much—as it was, I didn't even get spots on my cape). I decided that jams and jellies and catsup were liquid within Zebbie's meaning—except some in squeeze tubes. Half a chocolate cake, and the cupboard was bare.

By using my cape as a Santa Claus pack, I carried food into the garage and put it down by Gay—and was delighted to find that I was first.

Zebbie strode in behind me, dressed in a coverall with thigh pockets, a pilot suit. He looked at the pile on my cape. "Where's the elephant, Sharpie?"

"Cap'n Zebbie, you didn't say how *much*, you just said *what*. What won't go *she* can have." I hooked a thumb at the chopped-up corpse.

"Sorry, Hilda; you are correct." Zebbie glanced at his wrist watch, the multiple-dial sort they call a "navigator's watch."

"Cap'n, this house has loads of gimmicks and gadgets and bells and whistles. You gave them an impossible schedule."

"On purpose, dear. Let's see how much food we can stow."

Gay's cold chest is set flush in the deck of the driver's compartment. Zebbie told Gay to open up, then with his shoulders sideways, reached down and unlocked it. "Hand me stuff."

I tapped his butt. "Out of there, you overgrown midget, and let Sharpie pack. I'll let you know when it's tight as a girdle."

Space that makes Zebbie twist and grunt is roomy for me. He passed things in, I fitted them for maximum stowage. The third item he handed me was the leavings of our buffet dinner. "That's our picnic lunch," I told him, putting it on his seat.

"Can't leave it loose in the cabin."

"Cap'n, we'll eat it before it can spoil. I will be strapped down; is it okay if I clutch it to my bosom?"

"Sharpie, have I ever won an argument with you?"

"Only by brute force, dear. Can the chatter and pass the chow."

With the help of God and a shoehorn it all went in. I was in a back seat with our lunch in my lap and my cape under me before our spouses showed up. "Cap'n Zebbie? Why did the news of Brainy's death cause your change of mind?"

"Do you disapprove, Sharpie?"

"On the contrary, Skipper. Do you want my guess?"

"Yes."

"*Winged Victory* was booby-trapped. And dear Doctor Brain, who isn't the fool I thought he was, was not aboard. Those poor people were killed so that he could disappear."

"Go to the head of the class, Sharpie. Too many coincidences ... and they—the 'Blokes in the Black Hats'—know where we are."

"Meaning that Professor No Brain, instead of being dead in the Pacific, might show up any second."

"He and a gang of green-blooded aliens who don't like geometers."

"Zebbie, what do you figure their plans are?"

"Can't guess. They might fumigate this planet and take it. Or conquer us as cattle or as slaves. The only data we have is that they are alien, that they are powerful—and that they have no compunction about killing us. So I have no compunction about killing them. To my regret, I don't know how. So I'm running— running scared—and taking the three I'm certain are in danger with me."

"Will we *ever* be able to find them and kill them?"

Zebbie didn't answer because Deety and my Jacob arrived, breathless. Father and daughter were in jump suits. Deety looked chesty and cute; my darling looked trim—but worried. "We're late. Sorry!"

"You're not late," Zeb told them. "But into your seats on the bounce."

"As quick as I open the garage door and switch out the lights."

"Jake, Jake—Gay is now programmed to do those things herself. In you go, Princess, and strap down. Seat belts, Sharpie. Copilot, after you lock the starboard door, check its seal all the way around by touch before you strap down."

"Wilco, Cap'n." It tickled me to hear my darling boning military. He had told me privately that he was a reserve colonel of ordnance—but that Deety had promised not to tell this to our smart young captain and that he wanted the same promise from me—because the T.O. was as it should be; Zeb should command while Jacob handled space-time controls—to each his own. Jacob had asked me to please take orders from Zeb with no back talk . . . which had miffed me a little. I was an unskilled crew member; I am not stupid, I knew this. In direst emergency I would try to get us home. But even Deety was better qualified than I.

Checkoffs completed, Gay switched off lights, opened the garage door, and backed out onto the landing flat.

"Copilot, can you read your verniers?"

"Captain, I had better loosen my chest belt."

"Do so if you wish. But your seat adjusts forward twenty centimeters—here, I'll get it." Zeb reached down, did something between their seats. "Say when."

"There—that's about right. I can read 'em and reach 'em, with chest strap in place. Orders, sir?"

"Where was your car when you and Deety went to the space-time that lacked the letter 'J'?"

"About where we are now."

"Can you send us there?"

"I think so. Minimum translation, positive—entropy increasing—along *Tau* axis."

"Please move us there, sir."

My husband touched the controls. "That's it, Captain."

I couldn't see any change. Our house was still a silhouette against the sky, with the garage a black maw in front of us. The stars hadn't even flickered.

Zebbie said, "Let's check," and switched on Gay's roading lights, brightly lighting our garage. Empty and looked normal.

Zebbie said, *"Hey! Look at that!"*

"Look at *what?*" I demanded, and tried to see around Jacob.

"At nothing, rather. Sharpie, where's your alien?"

Then I understood. No corpse. No green-blood mess. Work-bench against the wall and flood lights not rigged.

Zebbie said, "Gay Deceiver, take us home!"

Instantly the same scene...but with carved-up corpse. I gulped.

Zebbie switched out the lights. I felt better but not much.

"Captain?"

"Copilot."

"Wouldn't it have been well to have checked for that letter 'J'? It would have given me a check on calibration."

"I did check, Jake."

"Eh?"

"You have bins on the back of your garage neatly stenciled. The one at left center reads 'Junk Metal.'"

"Oh!"

"Yes, and your analog in that space—your twin, Jake-prime, or what you will—has your neat habits. The left-corner bin read 'Iunk Metal' spelled with an 'I.' A cupboard above and to the right contained 'Iugs & Iars.' So I told Gay to take us home. I was afraid they might catch us. Embarrassing."

Deety said, "Zebadiah—I mean 'Captain'—embarrassing how, sir? Oh, that missing letter in the alphabet scared me but it no longer does. Now I'm nervous about aliens. 'Black Hats.'"

"Deety, you were lucky that first time. Because Deety-prime was not at home. But she may be, tonight. Possibly in bed with her husband, named Zebadiah-prime. Unstable cuss. Likely to shoot at a strange car shining lights into his father-in-law's garage. A violent character."

"You're teasing me."

"No, Princess; it did worry me. A parallel space, with so small a difference as the lack of one unnecessary letter, but with house and grounds you mistook for your own, seems to imply a father and daughter named 'Iacob' and 'Deiah Thoris.'" (Captain Zebbie pronounced the names 'Yacob' and 'Deyah Thoris.')

"Zebadiah, that scares me almost as much as aliens."

"Aliens scare me far more. Hello, Gay."

"Howdy, Zeb. Your nose is runny."

"Smart Girl, one gee vertically to one klick. Hover."

"Roger dodger, you old codger."

We rested on our backs and head rests for a few moments, then with the stomach-surging swoosh of a fast lift, we leveled off and hovered. Zebbie said, "Deety, can the autopilot accept a change in that homing program by voice? Or does it take an offset in the verniers?"

"What do you want to do?"

"Same ell-and-ell two klicks above ground."

"I think so. Shall I? Or do you want to do it, Captain?"

"You try it, Deety."

"Yes, sir. Hello, Gay."

"Hi, Deety!"

"Program check. Define 'Home.'"

"'Home.' Cancel any-all inertials transitions translations rotations. Return to preprogrammed zero latitude longitude, ground level."

"Report present location."

"One klick vertically above 'Home.'"

"Gay. Program revision."

"Waiting, Deety."

"Home program. Cancel 'Ground level.' Substitute 'Two klicks above ground level, hovering.'"

"Program revision recorded."

"Gay Deceiver, take us home!"

Instantly, with no feeling of motion, we were much higher.

Zeb said, "Two klicks on the nose! Deety, you're a smart girl!"

"Zebadiah, I bet you tell that to all the girls."

"No, just to some. Gay, you're a smart girl."

"Then why are you shacked up with that strawberry blonde with the fat knockers?"

Zebbie craned his neck and looked at me. "Sharpie, that's your voice."

I ignored him with dignity. Zebbie drove south to the Grand Canyon, eerie in starlight. Without slowing, he said, "Gay Deceiver, take us home!"—and again we were hovering over our cabin. No jar, no shock, no nothing.

Zebbie said, "Jake, once I figure the angles, I'm going to quit spending money on juice. How does she do it when we haven't been anywhere?—no rotation, no translation."

"I may have given insufficient thought to a trivial root in equation ninety-seven. But it is analogous to what we were considering doing with planets. A five-dimensional transform simplified to three."

"'I dunno, I just work here,'" Captain Zebbie admitted. "But it looks like we will be peddling gravity and transport, as well as real estate and time. Burroughs and Company, Space Warps Unlimited—'No job too large, no job too small.' Send one newdollar for our free brochure."

"Captain," suggested Jacob, "would it not be prudent to translate into another space before experimenting further? The alien danger is still with us—is it not?"

Zebbie sobered at once. "Copilot, you are right and it is your duty to advise me when I goof off. However, before we leave, we have one duty we *must* carry out."

"Something more urgent than getting our wives to safety?" my Jacob asked—and I felt humble and proud.

"'Something more urgent.' Jake, I've bounced her around not only to test but to make it hard to track us. Because we must break radio silence. To warn our fellow humans."

"Oh. Yes, Captain. My apologies, sir. I sometimes forget the broader picture."

"Don't we all! I've wanted to run and hide ever since this rumpus started. But that took preparation and the delay gave me time to think. Point number one: We don't know how to fight these critters so we *must* take cover. Point number two: We are duty-bound to tell the world what we know about aliens. While that little isn't much—we've stayed alive by the skin of our teeth—if five billion people are watching for them, they can be caught. I hope."

"Captain," asked Deety, "may I speak?"

"Of course! Anyone with ideas about how to cope with these monsters *must* speak."

"I'm sorry but I don't have such ideas. You must warn the world, sir—of course! But you won't be believed."

"I'm afraid you're right, Deety. But they don't have to believe *me*. That monster in the garage speaks for itself. I'm going to call rangers—real rangers!—to pick it up."

I said, "So that was why you told me just to leave it! I thought it was lack of time."

"Both, Hilda. We didn't have time to sack that cadaver and

store it in the freezer room. But, if I can get rangers—*real*
rangers—to that garage before 'Black Hats' get there, that corpse
tells its own story: an undeniable alien lying in its goo on a ranger's
uniform that has been cut away from it. Not a 'close encounter'
UFO that can be explained away, but a creature more startling
than the duckbill platypus ever was. But we have to hook it in
with other factors to show them what to look for. Your booby-
trapped car, an arson case in Logan, Professor Brain's convenient
disappearance, my cousin's death in Sumatra—and your six-dimensional non-Euclidean geometry."

I said, "Excuse me, gentlemen. Can't we move somewhere
away from right over our cabin before you break silence? I'm
jumpy—'Black Hats' are hunting us."

"You're right, Sharpie; I'm about to move us. The story isn't
long—all but the math—so I taped a summary while the rest of
you were getting ready. Gay will speed-zip it, a hundred to one."
Zebbie reached for the controls. "All secure?"

"Captain Zebadiah!"

"Trouble, Princess?"

"May I attempt a novel program? It may save time."

"Programming is your pidgin. Certainly."

"Hello, Gay."

"Hi, Deety!"

"Retrieve last program. Report execute code."

"Reporting, Deety. 'Gay Deceiver, take us home!'"

"Negative erase permanent program controlled by execute-code
Gay Deceiver take us home. Report confirm."

"Confirmation report. Permanent program execute-coded Gay
Deceiver take us home negative erase. I tell you three times."

"Deety," said Zeb, "a neg scrub to Gay tells her to place item
in perms three places. Redundancy safety factor."

"Don't bother me, dear! She and I sling the same lingo. Hello,
Gay."

"Hello, Deety!"

"Analyze latest program execute-coded Gay Deceiver take us
home. Report."

"Analysis complete."

"Invert analysis."

"Null program."

Deety sighed. "Typing a program is easier. New program."

"Waiting, Deety."

"Execute-code new permanent program. Gay Deceiver, countermarch! At new execute-code, repeat reversed in real time latest

sequence inertials transitions translations rotations before last use of program execute-code Gay Deceiver take us home."

"New permanent program accepted."

"Gay, I tell you three times."

"Deety, I hear you three times."

"Gay Deceiver—countermarch!"

Instantly we were over the Grand Canyon, cruising south. I saw Zeb reach for the manual controls. "Deety, that was slick."

"I didn't save time, sir—I goofed. Gay, you're a smart girl."

"Deety, don't make me blush."

"You're both smart girls," said Captain Zebbie. "If anyone had us on radar, he must think he's getting cataracts. Vice versa, if anyone picked us up here, he's wondering how we popped up. Smart dodge, dear. You've got Gay Deceiver so deceptive that nobody can home on us. We'll be elsewhere."

"Yes—but I had something else in mind, too, my Captain."

"Princess, I like your ideas. Spill it."

"Suppose we used that homing preprogram and went from frying pan into fire. It might be useful to have a preprogram that would take us back into the frying pan, then do something else quickly. Should I try to think up a third escape-maneuver preprogram?"

"Sure—but discuss it with the court magician, your esteemed father—not me. I'm just a sky jockey."

"Zebadiah, I will not listen to you disparage yours—"

"Deety! Lifeboat rules. Jake, are your professional papers aboard? Both theoretical and drawings?"

"Why, no, Zeb—Captain. Too bulky. Microfilms I brought. Originals are in the basement vault. Have I erred?"

"Not a bit! Is there *any* geometer who gave your published paper on this six-way system a friendly reception?"

"Captain, there aren't more than a handful of geometers capable of judging my postulate system without long and intensive study. It's too unorthodox. Your late cousin was one—a truly brilliant mind! Uh...I now suspect that Doctor Brain understood it and sabotaged it for his own purposes."

"Jake, is there *anyone* friendly to you and able to understand the stuff in your vault? I'm trying to figure out how to warn our fellow humans. A fantastic story of apparently unrelated incidents is not enough. Not even with the corpse of an extra-terrestrial to back it up. You should leave mathematical theory and engineering drawings to someone able to understand them and whom you trust. *We* can't handle it; every time we stick our heads up, somebody takes a shot at us and we have *no* way to fight back. It's a job that may require our whole race. Well? Is there a man you can trust as your professional executor?"

"Well . . . one, perhaps. Not my field of geometry but brilliant. He did write me a most encouraging letter when I published my first paper—the paper that was so sneered at by almost everyone except your cousin and this one other. Professor Seppo Räikannonen. Turku. Finland."

"Are you certain *he's* not an alien?"

"What? He's been on the faculty at Turku for years! Over fifteen."

I said, "Jacob . . . that is about how long Professor Brain was around."

"But—" My husband looked around at me and suddenly smiled. "Hilda my love, have you ever taken sauna?"

"Once."

"Then tell our Captain why I am sure that my friend Seppo is not an alien in disguise. I—Deety and I—attended a professional meeting in Helsinki last year. After the meeting we visited their summer place in the Lake Country . . . and took sauna with them."

"Papa, Mama, and three kids." agreed Deety. "Unmistakably human."

"'Brainy' was a bachelor," I added thoughtfully. "Cap'n Zebbie, wouldn't disguised aliens have to be bachelors?"

"Or single women. Or pseudo-married couples. No kids, the masquerade wouldn't hold up. Jake, let's try to phone your friend. Mmm, nearly breakfast time in Finland—or we may wake him. That's better than missing him."

"Good! My comcredit number is Nero Aleph—"

"Let's try mine. Yours might trigger something . . . if 'Black Hats' are as smart as I think they are. Smart Girl."

"Yes, Boss."

"Don Ameche."

"To hear is to obey, O Mighty One."

"Deety, you've been giving Gay bad habits."

Shortly a flat male voice answered, "The communications credit number you have cited is not a valid number. Please refer to your card and try again. This is a recording."

Zebbie made a highly unlikely suggestion. "Gay *can't* send out my comcredit code incorrectly; she has it tell-me-three-times. The glitch is in *their* system. Pop, we have to use yours."

I said, "Try mine, Zebbie. My comcredit is good; I predeposit."

A female voice this time: "—not a valid number. Puh-lease refer to your card and try again. This is a recording."

Then my husband got a second female voice: "—try again. This is a recording."

Deety said, "I don't have one. Pop and I use the same number."

"It doesn't matter," Cap'n Zebbie said bitterly. "These aren't glitches. We've been scrubbed. Unpersons. We're all dead."

I didn't argue. I had suspected that we were dead since the morning two weeks earlier when I woke up in bed with my cuddly new husband. But how *long* had we been dead? Since my party? Or more recently?

I didn't care. This was a better grade of heaven than a Sunday School in Terre Haute had taught me to expect. While I don't think I've been outstandingly wicked, I haven't been very good either. Of the Ten Commandments I've broken six and bent some others. But Moses apparently had not had the last Word from on High—being dead was weird and wonderful and I was enjoying every minute . . . or eon, as the case may be.

XIII   *Being too close to a fireball can worry a man—*

Zeb:

Not being able to phone from my car was my most frustrating experience since a night I spent in jail through mistake (*I* made the mistake). I considered grounding to phone—but the ground did not seem healthy. Even if all of us were presumed dead, nullifying our comcredit cards so quickly seemed unfriendly; all of us had high credit ratings.

Canceling Sharpie's comcredit without proof of death was more than unfriendly; it was outrageous as she used the predeposit method.

I was forced to the decision that it was my duty to make a military report; I radioed NORAD, stated name, rank, reserve commission serial number, and asked for scramble for a crash priority report.

—and ran into "correct" procedure that causes instant ulcers. What was my clearance? What led me to think that I had crash priority intelligence? By what authority did I demand a scramble code? Do you know how many screwball calls come in here every day? Get off this frequency; it's for official traffic only. One more word out of you and I shall alert the civil sky patrol to pick you up.

I said one more word after I chopped off. Deety and her father ignored it; Hilda said, "My sentiments exactly!"

I tried the Federal Rangers Kaibab Barracks at Jacob Lake, then the office at Littlefield—and back to Kaibab. Littlefield didn't answer; Jacob Lake answered: "This is a recording. Routine messages may be recorded during beep tone. Emergency reports should be transmitted to Flagstaff HQ. Stand by for beep tone . . . Beep! . . . Beep! . . . Beep! . . ."

I was about to tell Gay to zip my tape—when the whole world was lighted by the brightest light imaginable.

Luckily we were cruising south with that light behind us. I goosed Gay to flank speed while telling her to tuck in her wings. Not one of my partners asked a foolish question, although I suspect that none had ever seen a fireball or mushroom cloud.

"Smart Girl."

"Here, Boss."

"DR problem. Record true bearing light beacon relative bearing astern. Record radar range and bearing same beacon. Solve latitude longitude beacon. Compare solution with fixes in perms. Confirm."

"Program confirmed."

"Execute."

"Roger Wilco, Zeb. Heard any new ones lately?" She added at once, "Solution. True bearing identical with fix execute-coded 'Gay Deceiver take us home.' True range identical plus-minus zero point six klicks."

"You're a smart girl, Gay."

"Flattery will get you anywhere, Zeb. Over."

"Roger and out. Hang onto your hats, folks; we're going straight up." I had outraced the shock wave but we were close to the Mexican border; either side might send sprint birds homing on us. "Copilot!"

"Captain."

"Move us! Out of this space!"

"Where, Captain?"

"Anywhere! *Fast!*"

"Uh, can you ease the acceleration? I can't lift my arms."

Cursing myself, I cut power, let Gay Deceiver climb free. Those vernier controls should have been mounted on arm rests. (Designs that look perfect on the drawing board can kill test pilots.)

"Translation complete, Captain."

"Roger, Copilot. Thank you." I glanced at the board: six-plus klicks height-above-ground and rising—thin but enough air to bite. "Hang onto our lunch, Sharpie!" I leaned us backwards while doing an Immelman into level flight, course north, power still off. I told Gay to stretch the glide, then tell me when we had dropped to three klicks H-above-G.

What should be Phoenix was off to the right; another city—Flagstaff?—farther away, north and a bit east; we appeared to be headed home. There was no glowing cloud on the horizon. "Jake, where are we?"

"Captain, I've never been in this universe. We translated ten quanta positive *Tau* axis. So we should be in analogous space close to ours—ten minimum intervals or quanta."

"This looks like Arizona."

"I would expect it to, Captain. You recall that one-quantum translation on this axis was so very like our own world that Deety and I confused it with our own, until she picked up a dictionary."

"Phone book, Pop."

"Irrelevant, dear. Until she missed the letter 'J' in an alphabetical list. Ten quanta should not change geological features appreciably and placement of cities is largely controlled by geography."

"Approaching three klicks, Boss."

"Thanks, Gay. Hold course and H-above-G. Correction! Hold course and absolute altitude. Confirm and execute."

"Roger Wilco, Zeb."

I had forgotten that the Grand Canyon lay ahead—or should. "Smart Girl" *is* smart, but she's literal-minded. She would have held height-above-ground precisely and given us the wildest roller-coaster ride in history. She is *very* flexible but the "garbage-in-garbage-out" law applies. She had many extra fail-safes—because *I* make mistakes. Gay *can't;* anything she does wrong is *my* mistake. Since I've been making mistakes all my life, I surrounded her with all the safeguards I could think of. But she had no program against wild rides—she was beefed up to accept them. Violent evasive tactics had saved our lives two weeks ago, and tonight as well. Being too close to a fireball can worry a man—to death.

"Gay, display map, please."

The map showed Arizona—*our* Arizona; Gay does not have in her gizzards any strange universes. I changed course to cause us to pass over our cabin site—its analog for this space-time. (Didn't dare tell her: "Gay, take us home!"—for reasons left as an exercise for the class.) "Deety, how long ago did that bomb go off?"

"Six minutes twenty-three seconds. Zebadiah, was that *really* an A-bomb?"

"Pony bomb, perhaps. Maybe two kilotons. Gay Deceiver."

"I'm all ears, Zeb."

"Report time interval since radar-ranging beacon."

"Five minutes forty-four seconds, Zeb."

Deety gasped. "Was I that far off?"

"No, darling. You reported time since flash. I didn't ask Gay to range until *after* we were hypersonic."

"Oh. I feel better."

"Captain," inquired Jake, "how did Gay range an atomic explosion? I would expect radiation to make it impossible. Does she have instrumentation of which I am not aware?"

"Copilot, she has several gadgets I have not shown you. I have not been holding out—any more than you held out in not telling me about guns and ammo you—"

"My apologies, sir!"

"Oh, stuff it, Jake. Neither of us held out; we've been running under the whip. Deety, how long has it been since we killed that fake ranger?"

"That was seventeen fourteen. It is now twenty-two twenty. Five hours six minutes."

I glanced at the board; Deety's "circadian clock" apparently couldn't be jarred by anything; Gay's clock showed 0520 (Greenwich) with "ZONE PLUS SEVEN" display. "Call it five hours—feels like five weeks. We need a vacation."

"Loud cheers!" agreed Sharpie.

"Check. Jake, I didn't *know* that Gay could range an atomic blast. Light 'beacon' means a visible light to her just as 'radar beacon' means to her a navigational radar beacon. I told her to get a bearing on the light beacon directly aft; she selected the brightest light with that bearing. Then I told her to take radar range and bearing on it—spun my prayer wheel and prayed.

"There was 'white noise' possibly blanketing her radar frequency. But her own radar bursts are tagged; it would take a *very* high noise level at the same frequency to keep her from recognizing echoes with her signature. Clearly she had trouble for she reported 'plus-minus' of six hundred meters. Nevertheless range and bearing matched a fix in her permanents and told us our cabin had been bombed. Bad news. But the aliens got there too late to bomb *us*. Good news."

"Captain, I decline to grieve over material loss. We are *alive*."

"I agree—although I'll remember Snug Harbor as the happiest home I've ever had. But there is no point in trying to warn Earth— *our* Earth—about aliens. That blast destroyed the clincher: that alien's cadaver. And papers and drawings you were going to turn over to your Finnish friend. I'm not sure we *can* go home again."

"Oh, that's no problem, Captain. Two seconds to set the verniers. Not to mention the 'deadman switch' and the program in Gay's permanents."

"Jake, I wish you would knock off 'Captain' other than for command conditions."

"Zeb, I like calling you 'Captain.' "

"So do I!—my Captain."

"Me, too, Cap'n Zebbie!"

"Don't overdo it. Jake, I didn't mean that you can't pilot us home; I mean we should not risk it. We've lost our last lead on the aliens. But *they* know who *we* are and have shown dismaying skill in tracking us down. I'd like to live to see two babies born and grown up."

"Amen!" said Sharpie. "This might be the place for it. Out of a million billion zillion earths this one may be vermin-free. Highly likely."

"Hilda my dear, there are no data on which to base *any* assumption."

"Jacob, there is *one* datum."

"Eh? What did I miss, dear?"

"That we *do* know that our native planet *is* infested. So I don't want to raise kids on it. If this isn't the place we're looking for, let's keep looking."

"Mmm, logical. Yes. Cap— Zeb?"

"I agree. But we can't tell much before morning. Jake, I'm unclear on a key point. If we translated back to our own earth now, where would we find ourselves? And *when?*"

"Pop, may I answer that?"

"Go ahead, Deety."

"The time Pop and I translated to the place with no 'J' we thought we had failed. Pop stayed in our car, trying to figure it out. I went inside, intending to fix lunch. Everything looked normal. But the phone book was on the kitchen counter and doesn't belong there. That book had a toll area map on its back cover. My eye happened to land on 'Juab County'—and it was spelled 'Iuab'—and I thought, 'What a funny misprint!' Then I looked inside and couldn't find any 'J's' and dropped the book and went running for Pop."

"I thought Deety was hysterical. But when I checked a dictionary and the Britannica we got out in a hurry."

"This is the point, Zebadiah. When we flipped back, I dashed into the house. The phone book was where it belonged. The alphabet was back the way it ought to be. The clock in my head said that we had been gone twenty-seven minutes. The kitchen clock confirmed it and it agreed with the clock in the car. Does that answer you, sir?"

"I think so. In a translation, duration just keeps chugging along. I wondered because I'd like to check that crater after it has had time to cool down. What about that one rotation?"

"Harder to figure, Zebadiah. We weren't in that other spacetime but a few seconds and we both passed out. Indeterminate."

"I'm convinced. But, Jake, what about Earth's proper motions? Rotation, revolution around the Sun, sidereal motion, and so forth."

"A theoretical answer calls for mathematics you tell me are outside your scope of study, uh—Zeb."

"Beyond my capacity, you mean."

"As you will, sir. An excursion elsewhere-and-else*when* . . . and *return* . . . brings you back *to where you would have been* had you experienced that duration *on earth*. But '*when*' requires further definition. As we were discussing, uh . . . earlier this afternoon but it seems longer, we can adjust the controls to reenter *any* axis at *any* point *with permanent change of interval*. For planetary engineering. Or other purposes. Including reentry reversed against the entropy arrow. But I suspect that would cause death."

"Why, Pop? Why wouldn't it just reverse your memory?"

"Memory is tied to entropy increase, my darling daughter. Death might be preferable to amnesia combined with prophetic knowledge. Uncertainty may be the factor that makes life tolerable. Hope is what keeps us going. Captain!"

"Copilot."

"We have just passed over North Rim."

"Thank you, Copilot." I placed my hands lightly on the controls.

"Pop, our cabin is still there. Lights in it, too."

"So I see. They've added a wing on the west."

"Yes. Where we discussed adding a library."

I said, "Family, I'm not going closer. Your analogs in this world seem to be holding a party. Flood lights show four cars on the grounding flat." I started Gay into a wide circle. "I'm not going to hover; it could draw attention. A call to their sky cops—Hell's bells, I don't even know that they speak English."

"Captain, we've seen all we need. It's not *our* cabin."

"Recommendation?"

"Sir, I suggest maximum altitude. Discuss what to do while we get there."

"Gay Deceiver."

"On deck, Captain Ahab."

"One gee, vertical."

"Aye aye, sir." (How many answers had Deety taped?)

"Anybody want a sandwich?" asked Sharpie. "I do—I'm a pregnant mother."

I suddenly realized that I had had nothing but a piece of pie since noon. As we climbed we finished what was left of supper.

"Zat Marsh?"

"Don't talk with your mouth full, Sharpie."

"Zebbie you brute, I said, 'Is that Mars?' Over there."

"That's Antares. Mars is— Look left about thirty degrees. See it? Same color as Antares but brighter."

"Got it. Jacob darling, let's take that vacation on Barsoom!"

"Hilda dearest, Mars is uninhabitable. The Mars Expedition used pressure suits. We have no pressure suits."

I added, "Even if we did, they would get in the way of a honeymoon."

Hilda answered, "I read a jingle about 'A Space Suit Built for Two.' Anyhow, let's go to Barsoom! Jacob, you did tell me we could go anywhere in *Zip*—nothing flat."

"Quite true."

"So let's go to Barsoom."

I decided to flank her. "Hilda, we can't go to Barsoom. Mors Kajak and John Carter don't have their swords."

"Want to bet?" Deety said sweetly.

"Huh?"

"Sir, you left it to me to pick baggage for that unassigned space. If you'll check that long, narrow stowage under the instrument board, you'll find the sword and saber, with belts. With socks and underwear crammed in to keep them from rattling."

I said soberly, "My Princess, I couldn't moan about my sword when your father took the loss of his house so calmly—but thank you, with all my heart."

"Let me add my thanks, Deety. I set much store by that old saber, unnecessary as it is."

"Father, it was *quite* necessary this afternoon."

"Hi *ho!* Hi *ho!* It's to Barsoom we go!"

"Captain, we *could* use the hours till dawn for a quick jaunt to Mars. Uh— Oh, dear, I have to know its present distance—I don't."

"No problem," I said. "Gay gobbles the Aerospace Almanac each year."

"Indeed! I'm impressed."

"Gay Deceiver."

"You again? I was thinking."

"So think about this. Calculation program. Data address, Aerospace Almanac. Running calculation, line-of-sight distance to planet Mars. Report current answers on demand. Execute."

"Program running."

"Report."

"Klicks two-two-four-zero-nine-zero-eight-two-seven point plus-minus nine-eight-zero."

"Display running report."

Gay did so. "You're a smart girl, Gay."

"I can do card tricks, too. Program continuing."

"Jake, how do we this?"

"Align 'L' axis with your gun sight. Isn't that easiest?"

"By far!" I aimed at Mars as if to shoot her out of the sky—then got cold feet. "Jake? A little Tennessee windage? I think those figures are from center-of-gravity to center-of-gravity. Half a mil would place us a safe distance away. Over a hundred thousand klicks."

"A hundred and twelve thousand," Jake agreed, watching the display.

I offset one half mil. "Copilot."

"Captain."

"Transit when ready. Execute."

Mars in half phase, big and round and ruddy and beautiful, was swimming off our starboard side.

"Quit worrying and enjoy the ride."

Deety:

Aunt Hilda said softly, "Barsoom. Dead sea bottoms. Green giants." I just gulped.

"Mars, Hilda darling," Pop gently corrected her. "Barsoom is a myth."

"Barsoom," she repeated firmly. "It's not a myth, it's *there*. Who says its name is Mars? A bunch of long-dead Romans. Aren't the natives entitled to name it? Barsoom."

"My dearest, there *are* no natives. Names are assigned by an international committee sponsored by Harvard Observatory. They confirmed the traditional name."

"Pooh! They don't have any more right to name it than I have. Deety, isn't that right?"

I think Aunt Hilda had the best argument but I don't argue with Pop unless necessary; he gets emotional. My husband saved me.

"Copilot, astrogation problem. How are we going to figure distance and vector? I would like to put this wagon into orbit. But Gay is no spaceship; I don't have instruments. Not even a sextant!"

"Mmm, suppose we try it one piece at a time, Captain. We don't seem to be falling fast and—*ulp!*"

"What's the trouble, Jake!"

Pop turned pale, sweat broke out, he clenched his jaws, swallowed and reswallowed. Then his lips barely opened. "M'sheashick."

"No, you're space sick. *Deety!*"

"Yessir!"

"Emergency kit, back of my seat. Unzip it, get Lomine. One pill—don't let the others get loose."

I got at the first-aid kit, found a tube marked Lomine. A second pill did get loose but I snatched it out of the air. Free fall is funny—you don't know whether you are standing on your head or floating sideways. "Here, Captain."

Pop said, "Mall righ' now. Jus' took all over queer a moment."

"Sure, you're all right. You can take this pill—or you can have it pushed down your throat with my dirty, calloused finger. Which?"

"Uh, Captain, I'd have to have water to swallow it—and I don't think I *can*."

"Doesn't take water, pal. Chew it. Tastes good, raspberry flavor. Then keep gulping your saliva. Here." Zebadiah pinched Pop's nostrils. "Open up."

I became aware of a strangled sound beside me. Aunt Hilda had a hanky pressed to her mouth and her eyes were streaming tears—she was split seconds from adding potato salad and used sandwich to the cabin air.

Good thing I was still clutching that wayward pill. Aunt Hilda struggled but she's a little bitty. I treated her the way my husband had treated her husband, then clamped my hand over her mouth. I don't understand seasickness (or free-fall nausea); I can walk on bulkheads with a sandwich in one hand and a drink in the other and enjoy it.

But the victims really are sick and somewhat out of their heads. So I held her mouth closed and whispered into her ear. "Chew it, Aunty darling, and swallow it, or I'm going to spank you with a club."

Shortly I could feel her chewing. After several minutes she relaxed. I asked her, "Is it safe for me to ungag you?"

She nodded. I took my hand away. She smiled wanly and patted my hand. "Thanks, Deety." She added, "You wouldn't really beat Aunt Sharpie."

"I sure would, darling. I'd cry and cry and wallop you and wallop you. I'm glad I don't have to."

"I'm glad, too. Can we kiss and make up—or is my breath sour?"

It wasn't but I wouldn't have let that stop me. I loosened my chest strap and hers, and put both arms around her. I have two ways of kissing: one is suitable for faculty teas; the other way I mean it. I never got a chance to pick; Aunt Hilda apparently never found out about the faculty-tea sort. No, her breath wasn't sour—just a slight taste of raspberry.

Me, I'm the wholesome type; if it weren't for those advertisements on my chest, men wouldn't give me a second glance. Hilda is a miniature Messalina, pure sex in a small package. Funny how a person can grow up never really believing that the adults you grow up with have sex—just gender. Now my saintly father turns out to be an insatiable goat, and Aunt Hilda, who had babied me and changed my diapers, is sexy enough for a platoon of Marines.

I let her go while thinking pleasant thoughts about teaching my husband technique I had learned—unless Hilda had taught him in the past. No, or he would have taught *me*—and he hadn't shown her style of virtuosity. Zebadiah, just wait till I get you alone!

Which might not be too soon. Gay Deceiver is wonderful but no honeymoon cottage. There was space back of the bulkhead behind my head—like a big phone booth on its side—where Zebadiah kept a sleeping bag and (he says) sometimes sacked out. But it had the space-time twister in it and nineteen dozen other things. Hilda and I were going to have to repress our primary imperative until our men found us a pied-à-terre on some planet in some universe, somewhere, somewhen.

Mars-Barsoom seemed to have grown while I was curing Aunt Hilda's space sickness. Our men were talking astrogation. My husband was saying, "Sorry, but at extreme range Gay's radar can see a thousand kilos. You tell me our distance is about a hundred times that."

"About. We're falling toward Mars. Captain, we must do it by triangulation."

"Not even a protractor where I can get at it. *How?*"

"Hmmmm— If the Captain pleases, recall how you worked that 'Tennessee windage.'"

My darling looked like a school boy caught making a silly answer. "Jake, if you don't quit being polite when I'm stupid, I'm going to space you and put Deety in the copilot's seat. No, we need you to get us home. I'd better resign and you take over."

"Zeb, a captain *can't* resign while his ship is underway. That's universal."

"This is another universe."

"Transuniversal. As long as you are alive, you are stuck with it. Let's attempt that triangulation."

"Stand by to record." Zebadiah settled into his seat, pressed his head against its rest. "Copilot."

"Ready to record, sir."

"Damn!"

"Trouble, Captain?"

"Some. This reflectosight is scaled fifteen mils on a side, concentric circles crossed at center point horizontally and vertically. Normal to deck and parallel to deck, I mean. When I center the fifteen-mil ring on Mars, I have a border around it. I'm going to have to guesstimate. Uh, the border looks to be about eighteen mils wide. So double that and add thirty."

"Sixty-six mils."

"And a mil is one-to-one-thousand. One-to-one-thousand-and-eighteen and a whisker, actually—but one-to-a-thousand is good enough. Wait a half! I've got two sharp high lights near the meridian—if the polar caps mark the meridian. Le'me tilt this buggy and put a line crossing them—then I'll yaw and what we can't measure in one jump, we'll catch in three."

I saw the larger "upper" polar cap (north? south? well, it *felt* north) roll gently about eighty degrees, while my husband fiddled with Gay's manual controls. "Twenty-nine point five, maybe . . . plus eighteen point seven . . . plus sixteen point three. Add."

My father answered, "Sixty-four and a half" while I said, six four point five in my mind and kept quiet.

"Who knows the diameter of Mars? Or shall I ask Gay?"

Hilda answered, "Six thousand seven hundred fifty kilometers, near enough."

Plenty near enough for Zebadiah's estimates. Zebadiah said, "Sharpie! How did you happen to know *that?*"

"I read comic books. You know—'Zap! Polaris is missing.'"

"I don't read comic books."

"Lots of interesting things in comic books, Zebbie. I thought the Aerospace Force used comic-book instruction manuals."

My darling's ears turned red. "Some are," he admitted, "but they are edited for technical accuracy. Hmm— Maybe I had better check that figure with Gay."

I love my husband but sometimes women must stick together. "Don't bother, Zebadiah," I said in chilly tones. "Aunt Hilda is correct. The polar diameter of Mars is six seven five two point eight plus. But surely three significant figures is enough for your data."

Zebadiah did not answer . . . but did *not* ask his computer. Instead he said, "Copilot, will you run it off on your pocket calculator? We can treat it as a tangent at this distance."

This time I didn't even try to keep still. Zebadiah's surprise that Hilda knew anything about astronomy caused me pique. "Our height above surface is one hundred four thousand six hundred and seventy-two kilometers plus or minus the error of the data supplied. That assumes that Mars is spherical and ignores the edge effect or horizon bulge . . . negligible for the quality of your data."

Zebadiah answered so gently that I was sorry that I had shown off: "Thank you, Deety. Would you care to calculate the time to fall to surface from rest at this point?"

"That's an unsmooth integral, sir. I can approximate it but Gay can do it faster and more accurately. Why not ask *her?* But it will be many hours."

"I had hoped to take a better look. Jake, Gay has enough juice to put us into a tight orbit, I think . . . but I don't know where or when I'll be able to juice her again. If we simply fall, the air will get stale and we'll need the panic button—or *some* maneuver—without ever seeing the surface close up."

"Captain, would it suit you to read the diameter again? I don't think we've simply been falling."

Pop and Zebadiah got busy again. I let them alone, and they ran even the simplest computations through Gay. Presently, Pop said, "Over twenty-four kilometers per second! Captain, at that rate we'll be there in a little over an hour."

"Except that we'll scram before that. But, ladies, you'll get your closer look. Dead sea bottoms and green giants. If any."

"Zebadiah, twenty-four kilometers per second is Mars' orbital speed."

My father answered, "Eh? Why, so it is!" He looked very puzzled, then said, "Captain—I confess to a foolish mistake."

"Not one that will keep us from getting home, I hope."

"No, sir. I'm still learning what our continua craft can do. Captain, we did not aim for Mars."

"I know. I was chicken."

"No, sir, you were properly cautious. *We aimed for a specific point in empty space.* We transited to that point . . . but *not* with Mars' proper motion. With that of the Solar System, yes. With Earth's motions subtracted; that is in the program. But we are a short distance ahead of Mars in its orbit . . . so it is rushing toward us."

"Does that mean we can never land on any planet but Earth?"

"Not at all. *Any* vector can be included in the program—either before or after transition, translation or rotation. Any subsequent change in motion is taken into account by the inertial integrator. But I am learning that we still have things to learn."

"Jake, that is true even of a bicycle. Quit worrying and enjoy the ride. Brother, what a view!"

"Jake, that doesn't look like the photographs the Mars Expedition brought back."

"Of course not," said Aunt Hilda. "I *said* it was Barsoom."

I kept my mouth shut. Ever since Dr. Sagan's photographs anyone who reads *The National Geographic*—or anything— knows what Mars looks like. But when it involves changing male minds, it is better to let men reach their own decisions; they become somewhat less pig-headed. That planet rushing toward us was *not* the Mars of our native sky. White clouds at the caps, big green areas that had to be forest or crops, one deep blue area that almost certainly was water—all this against ruddy shades that dominated much of the planet.

What was lacking were the rugged mountains and craters and canyons of "our" planet Mars. There were mountains—but nothing like the Devil's Junkyard known to science.

I heard Zebadiah say, "Copilot, are you certain you took us to Mars?"

"Captain, I took us to Mars-*ten*, via plus on *Tau* axis. Either that or I'm a patient in a locked ward."

"Take it easy, Jake. It doesn't resemble Mars as much as Earth-ten resembles Earth."

"Uh, may I point out that we saw just a bit of Earth-ten, on a moonless night?"

"Meaning we didn't see it. Conceded."

Aunt Hilda said, "I *told* you it was Barsoom. You wouldn't listen."

"Hilda, I apologize. 'Barsoom.' Copilot, log it. New planet, 'Barsoom,' named by right of discovery by Hilda Corners Burroughs, Science Officer of Continua Craft Gay Deceiver. We'll all witness: Z. J. Carter, Commanding—Jacob J. Burroughs, Chief Officer—D. T. B. Carter, uh, Astrogator. I'll send certified copies to Harvard Observatory as soon as possible."

"I'm not astrogator, Zebadiah!"

"Mutiny. Who reprogrammed this cloud buster into a continua craft? I'm pilot until I can train all of you in Gay's little quirks. Jake is copilot until he can train more copilots in setting the verniers. You are astrogator because nobody else can acquire your special knowledge of programming and skill at calculation. None of your lip, young woman, and don't fight the Law of Space. Sharpie is chief of science because of her breadth of knowledge. She not only recognized a new planet as *not* being Mars quicker than anyone else but carved up that double-joined alien with the skill of a born butcher. Right, Jake?"

"Sure thing!" agreed Pop.

"Cap'n Zebbie," Aunt Hilda drawled, "I'm science officer if you say so. But I had better be ship's cook, too. And cabin boy."

"Certainly, we all have to wear more than one hat. Log it, Copilot. 'Here's to our jolly cabin girl, the plucky little nipper—'"

"Don't finish it, Zebbie," Aunt Hilda cut in, "I don't like the way the plot develops."

> " '—she carves fake ranger,
> 'Dubs planet stranger,
> 'And dazzles crew and skipper.' "

Aunt Hilda looked thoughtful. "That's not the classic version. I like the sentiment better . . . though the scansion limps."

"Sharpie darling, you are a floccinaucinihilipilificatrix."

"Is that a compliment?"

"Certainly! Means you're so sharp you spot the slightest flaw."

I kept quiet. It was possible that Zebadiah meant it as a compliment. Just barely—

"Maybe I'd better check it in a dictionary."

"By all means, dear—after you are off watch." (I dismissed the matter. Merriam Microfilm was all we had aboard and Aunt Hilda would not find *that* word in anything less than the O.E.D.)

"Copilot, got it logged?"

"Captain, I didn't know we *had* a log."

"No *log?* Even Vanderdecken keeps a log. Deety, the log falls in your department. Take your father's notes, get what you need from Gay, and let's have a taut ship. First time we pass a Woolworth's we'll pick up a journal and you can transcribe it—notes taken now are your rough log."

"Aye aye, sir. Tyrant."

" 'Tyrant,' *sir,* please. Meanwhile let's share the binoculars and see if we can spot any colorful exotic natives in colorful exotic costumes singing colorful exotic songs with their colorful exotic hands out for baksheesh. First one to spot evidence of intelligent life gets to wash the dishes."

XV "We'll hit so hard we'll hardly notice it."

Hilda:

I was so flattered by Cap'n Zebbie's crediting me with "discovering" Barsoom that I pretended not to understand the jibe he added. It was unlikely that Deety would know such a useless word, or my beloved Jacob. It was gallant of Zeb to give in all the way, once he realized that this planet was unlike its analog in "our" universe. Zebbie is a funny one—he wears rudeness like a Hallowe'en mask, afraid that someone will discover the Galahad underneath.

I knew that "my" Barsoom was not the planet of the classic romances. But there are precedents: The first nuclear submarine was named for an imaginary undersea vessel made famous by Jules Verne; an aircraft carrier of the Second Global War had been named "Shangri La" for a land as nonexistent as "Erewhon"; the first space freighter had been named for a starship that existed only in the hearts of its millions of fans—the list is endless. Nature copies art.

Or as Deety put it: "Truth is more fantastic than reality."

During that hour Barsoom *rushed* at us. It began to swell and swell, so rapidly that binoculars were a nuisance—and my heart swelled with it, in childlike joy. Deety and I unstrapped so that we could see better, floating just "above" and behind our husbands while steadying ourselves on their headrests.

We were seeing it in half phase, one half dark, the other in sunlight—ocher and umber and olive green and brown and all of it beautiful.

Our pilot and copilot did not sightsee; Zebbie kept taking sights, kept Jacob busy calculating. At last he said, "Copilot, if our approximations are correct, at the height at which we will get our

131

first radar range, we will be only a bit over half a minute from crashing. Check?"

"To the accuracy of our data, Captain."

"Too close. I don't fancy arriving like a meteor. Is it time to hit the panic button? Advise, please—but bear in mind that puts us—*should* put us—two klicks over a hot, new crater . . . possibly in the middle of a radioactive cloud. Ideas?"

"Captain, we can do that just before crashing—and it either works or it doesn't. If it works, that radioactive cloud will have had more time to blow away. If it doesn't work—"

"We'll hit so hard we'll hardly notice it. Gay Deceiver isn't built to reenter at twenty-four klicks per second. She's beefed up—but she's still a Ford, not a reentry vehicle."

"Captain, I can try to subtract the planet's orbital speed. We've time to make the attempt."

"Fasten seat belts and report! *Move it, gals!*"

Free fall is funny stuff. I was over that deathly sickness—was enjoying weightlessness, but didn't know how to move in it. Nor did Deety. We floundered the way one does the first time on ice skates—only worse.

"Report, damn it!"

Deety got a hand on something, grabbed me. We started getting into seats—she in mine, I in hers. "Strapping down, Captain!" she called out, while frantically trying to loosen my belts to fit her. (I was doing the same in reverse.)

"Speed it up!"

Deety reported, "Seat belts fastened," while still getting her chest belt buckled—by squeezing out all her breath. I reached over and helped her loosen it.

"Copilot."

"Captain!"

"Along 'L' axis, subtract vector twenty-four klicks per second—and for God's sake don't get the signs reversed."

"I won't!"

"Execute."

Seconds later Jacob reported, "That does it, Captain. I hope."

"Let's check. Two readings, ten seconds apart. I'll call the first, you call the end of ten seconds. *Mark!*"

Zeb added, "One point two. Record."

After what seemed a terribly long time Jacob said, "Seven seconds . . . eight seconds . . . nine seconds . . . *mark!*"

Our men conferred, then Jacob said, "Captain, we are still falling too fast."

"Of course," said Deety. "We've been accelerating from gravity. Escape speed for Mars is five klicks per second. If Barsoom has the same mass as Mars—"

"Thank you, Astrogator. Jake, can you trim off, uh, four klicks per second?"

"Sure!"

"Do it."

"Uh . . . done! How does she look?"

"Uh . . . distance slowly closing. Hello, Gay."

"Howdy, Zeb."

"Program. Radar. Target dead ahead. Range."

"No reading."

"Continue ranging. Report first reading. Add program. Display running radar ranges to target."

"Program running. Who blacked your eye?"

"You're a Smart Girl, Gay."

"I'm sexy, too. Over."

"Continue program." Zeb sighed, then said, "Copilot, there's atmosphere down there. I plan to attempt to ground. Comment? Advice?"

"Captain, those are words I hoped to hear. Let's go!"

"Barsoom—here we come!"

XVI —a maiden knight, eager to break a lance—

Jake:

My beloved bride was no more eager than I to visit "Barsoom." I had been afraid that our captain would do the sensible thing: establish orbit, take pictures, then return to our own space-time before our air was stale. We were not prepared to explore strange planets. Gay Deceiver was a bachelor's sports car. We had a little water, less food, enough air for about three hours. Our craft re-freshed its air by the scoop method. If she made a "high jump," her scoop valves sealed from internal pressure just as did com-mercial ballistic-hypersonic intercontinental liners—but "high jump" is not space travel.

True, we could go from point to point in our own or any universe in null time, but how many heavenly bodies have breath-able atmospheres? Countless billions—but a small fraction of one percent from a practical viewpoint—and no publication lists their whereabouts. We had no spectroscope, no star catalogs, no at-mosphere testing equipment, no radiation instruments, no means of detecting dangerous organisms. Columbus with his cockleshells was better equipped than we.

None of this worried me.

Reckless? Do you pause to shop for an elephant gun while an elephant is chasing you?

Three times we had escaped death by seconds. We had evaded our killers by going to earth—and that safety had not lasted. So again we fled like rabbits.

At least once every human should have to run for his life, to teach him that milk does not come from supermarkets, that safety does not come from policemen, that "news" is not something that happens to other people. He might learn how his ancestors lived and that he himself is no different—in the crunch his life depends on his agility, alertness, and personal resourcefulness.

I was not distressed. I felt more alive than I had felt since the death of my first wife.

Underneath the *persona* each shows the world lies a being different from the masque. My own *persona* was a professorial archetype. Underneath? Would you believe a maiden knight, eager to break a lance? I could have avoided military service—married, a father, protected profession. But I spent three weeks in basic training, sweating with the rest, cursing drill instructors—and loving it! Then they took my rifle, told me I was an officer, gave me a swivel chair and a useless job. I never forgave them for that.

Hilda, until we married, I knew not at all. I had valued her as a link to my lost love but I had thought her a lightweight, a social butterfly. Then I found myself married to her and learned that I had unnecessarily suffered lonely years. Hilda was what I needed, I was what she needed—Jane had known it and blessed us when at last *we* knew it. But I *still* did not realize the diamond-hard quality of my tiny darling until I saw her dissecting that pseudo "ranger." Killing that alien was easy. But what Hilda did—I almost lost my supper.

Hilda is small and weak; I'll protect her with my life. But I won't underrate her again!

Zeb is the only one of us who *looks* the part of intrepid explorer—tall, broad-shouldered, strongly muscled, skilled with machines and with weapons, and (sine qua non!) cool-headed in crisis and gifted with the "voice of command."

One night I had been forced to reason with my darling; Hilda felt that *I* should lead our little band. I was oldest, I was inventor of the time-space "distorter"—it was all right for Zeb to pilot—but *I* must command. In her eyes Zeb was somewhere between an overage adolescent and an affectionate Saint Bernard. She pointed out that Zeb claimed to be a "coward by trade" and did not *want* responsibility.

I told her that no born leader seeks command; the mantle descends on him, he wears the burden because he must. Hilda could not see it—she was willing to take orders from *me* but *not* from her pet youngster "Zebbie."

I had to be firm: Either accept Zeb as commander or tomorrow Zeb and I would dismount my apparatus from Zeb's car so that Mr. and Mrs. Carter could go elsewhere. Where? Not my business or yours, Hilda. I turned over and pretended to sleep.

When I heard sobs, I turned again and held her. But I did not budge. No need to record what was said; Hilda promised to take any orders Zeb might give—once we left.

But her capitulation was merely coerced until the gory incident at the pool. Zeb's instantaneous attack changed her attitude. From then on my darling carried out Zeb's orders without argument—and between times kidded and ragged him as always. Hilda's spirit wasn't broken; instead she placed her indomitable spirit subject to the decisions of our captain. Discipline—self-discipline; there is no other sort.

Zeb is indeed a "coward by trade"—he avoids trouble whenever possible—a most commendable trait in a leader. If a captain worries about the safety of his command, those under him need not worry.

Barsoom continued to swell. At last Gay's voice said, "Ranging, Boss" as she displayed "1000 km," and flicked at once to "999 km." I started timing when Zeb made it unnecessary: "Smart Girl!"

"Here, Zeb."

"Continue range display. Show as H-above-G. Add dive rate."

"Null program."

"Correction. Add program. Display dive rate soonest."

"New program dive rate stored. Display starts H-above-G six hundred klicks."

"You're a smart girl, Gay."

"'Smartest little girl in the County, Oh! Daddy and Mommy told me so!' Over."

"Continue programs."

Height-above-ground seemed to drop both quickly and with stomach-tensing slowness. No one said a word; I barely breathed. As "600 km" appeared the figures were suddenly backed by a grid; on it was a steep curve, height-against-time, and a new figure flashed underneath the H-above-G figure: **1968 km/hr.** As the figure changed, a bright abscissa lowered down on the grid.

Our captain let out a sigh. "We can handle that. But I'd give fifty cents and a double-dip ice-cream cone for a parachute brake."

"What flavor?"

"Your choice, Sharpie. Don't worry, folks; I can stand her on her tail and blast. But it's an expensive way to slow up. Gay Deceiver."

"Busy, Boss."

"I keep forgetting that I can't ask her to display too many data at once. Anybody know the sea level—I mean 'surface' atmospheric pressure of Mars? Don't all speak at once."

My darling said hesitantly, "It averages about five millibars. But, Captain—this isn't Mars."

"Huh? So it isn't—and from the looks of that green stuff, Barsoom must have lots more atmosphere than Mars." Zeb took the controls, overrode the computer, cautiously waggled her elevons. "Can't feel bite. Sharpie, how come you bone astronomy? Girl Scout?"

"Never got past tenderfoot. I audited a course, then subscribed to 'Astronomy' and 'Sky and Telescope.' It's sort o' fun."

"Chief of Science, you have again justified my faith in you. Copilot, as soon as I have air bite, I'm going to ease to the east. We're headed too close to the terminator. I want to ground in daylight. Keep an eye out for level ground. I'll hover at the last—but I don't want to ground in forest. Or in badlands."

"Aye aye, sir."

"Astrogator."

"Yessir!"

"Deety darling, search to port—and forward, as much as you can see around me. Jake can favor the starboard side."

"Captain—I'm on the starboard side. Behind Pop."

"Huh? How did you gals get swapped around?"

"Well . . . you hurried us, sir—any old seat in a storm."

"Two demerits for wrong seat—and no syrup on the hot cakes we're going to have for breakfast as soon as we're grounded."

"Uh, I don't believe hot cakes are possible."

"I can dream, can't I? Chief Science Officer, watch my side."

"Yes, Cap'n."

"While Deety backs up Jake. Any cow pasture."

"Hey! I feel air! She bites!"

I held my breath while Zeb slowly brought the ship out of dive, easing her east. "Gay Deceiver."

"How now, Brown Cow?"

"Cancel display programs. Execute."

"Inshallâh, ya sayyid."

The displays faded. Zeb held her just short of stalling. We were still high, about six klicks, still hypersonic.

Zeb slowly started spreading her wings as air speed and altitude dropped. After we dropped below speed of sound, he opened her wings full for maximum lift. "Did anyone remember to bring a canary?"

"A *canary!*" said Deety. "What for, Boss Man?"

"My gentle way of reminding everyone that we have no way to test atmosphere. Copilot."

"Captain," I acknowledged.

"Uncover deadman switch. Hold it closed while you remove clamp. Hold it high where we all can see it. Once you report switch ready to operate, I'm going to crack the air scoops. If you pass out, your hand will relax and the switch will get us home. I hope. But—All hands!—if anyone feels dizzy or woozy or faint . . . or sees any of us start to slump, don't wait! Give the order orally. Deety, spell the order I mean. Don't say it—spell it."

"G, A, Y, D, E, C, I, E, V, E, R, T, A, K, E, U, S, H, O, M, E."

"You misspelled it."

"I did not!"

"You did so; '"i" before "e" except after "c." ' You reversed 'em."

"Well . . . maybe I did. That diphthong has always given me trouble. Floccinaucinihilipilificator!"

"So you understood it? From now on, on Barsoom, 'i' comes before 'e' at all times. By order of John Carter, Warlord. I have spoken. Copilot?"

"Deadman switch ready, Captain," I answered.

"You gals hold your breaths or breathe, as you wish. Pilot and copilot will breathe. I am about to open air scoops."

I tried to breathe normally and wondered if my hand would relax if I passed out.

The cabin got suddenly chilly, then the heaters picked up. I felt normal. Cabin pressure slightly higher, I thought, under ram effect.

"Everybody feel right? Does everybody *look* right? Copilot?"

"I feel fine. You look okay. So does Hilda. I can't see Deety."

"Science Officer?"

"Deety looks normal. I feel fine."

"Deety. Speak up."

"Golly, I had forgotten what fresh air smells like!"

"Copilot, carefully—*most* carefully!—put the clamp back on the switch, then rack and cover it. Report completion."

A few seconds later I reported, "Deadman switch secured, Captain."

"Good. I see a golf course; we'll ground." Zeb switched to powered flight; Gay responded, felt alive. We spiraled, hovered briefly, grounded with a gentle bump. "Grounded on Barsoom. Log it, Astrogator. Time and date."

"Huh?"

"On the instrument board."

"But that says oh-eight-oh-three and it's just after dawn here."

"Log it Greenwich. With it, log estimated local time and Barsoom day one." Zeb yawned. "I wish they wouldn't hold mornings so early."

"Too sleepy for hot cakes?" my wife inquired.

"Never that sleepy."

"Aunt Hilda!"

"Deety, I stowed Aunt Jemima mix. And powdered milk. And butter. Zebbie, no syrup—sorry. But there is grape jelly in a tube. And freeze-dried coffee. If one of you will undog this bulkhead door, we'll have breakfast in a few minutes."

"Chief Science Officer, you have a duty to perform."

"I do? But— Yes, Captain?"

"Put your dainty toe to the ground. It's your planet, your privilege. Starboard side of the car, under the wing, is the ladies' powder room—portside is the men's jakes. Ladies may have armed escort on request."

I was glad Zeb remembered that. The car had a "honey bucket" under the cushion of the port rear seat, and, with it, plastic liners. I did not ever want to have to use it.

Gay Deceiver was wonderful but, as a spaceship, she left much to be desired. However, she had brought us safely to Barsoom.

Barsoom! Visions of thoats and beautiful princesses—

XVII   *The world wobbled—*

Deety:
We spent our first hour on "Barsoom" getting oriented. Aunt Hilda stepped outside, then stayed out. "Isn't cold," she told us. "Going to be hot later."

"Watch where you step!" my husband warned her. "Might be snakes or anything." He hurried after her—and went head over heels.

Zebadiah was not hurt; the ground was padded, a greenish-yellow mat somewhat like "ice plant" but looking more like clover. He got up carefully, then swayed as if walking on a rubber mattress. "I don't understand it," he complained. "This gravity ought to be twice that of Luna. But I feel lighter."

Aunt Hillbilly sat down on the turf. "On the Moon you were carrying pressure suit and tanks and equipment." She unfastened her shoes. "Here you aren't."

"Yeah, so I was," agreed my husband. "What are you doing?"

"Taking off my shoes. When were you on the Moon? Cap'n Zebbie, you're a fraud."

"Don't take off your shoes! You don't know what's in this grass."

The Hillbilly stopped, one shoe off. "If they bite me, I bite 'em back. Captain, in Gay Deceiver you are absolute boss. But doesn't your crew have *any* free will? I'll play it either way: free citizen . . . or your thrall who dassn't even take off a shoe without permission. Just tell me."

"Uh—"

"If you try to make all decisions, all the time, you're going to get as hysterical as a hen raising ducklings. Even Deety can be notional. But *I* won't even pee without permission. Shall I put this back on? Or take the other off?"

"Aunt Hilda, quit teasing my husband!" (I was annoyed!)

"Dejah Thoris, I am not teasing your husband; I am asking our captain for instructions."

Zebadiah sighed. "Sometimes I wish I'd stayed in Australia."

I said, "Is it all right for Pop and me to come out?"

"Oh. Certainly. Watch your step; it's tricky."

I jumped down, then jumped high and wide, with *entrechats* as I floated—landed *sur les pointes*. "Oh, boy! What a wonderful place for ballet!" I added, "Shouldn't do that on a full bladder. Aunt Hilda, let's see if that powder room is unoccupied."

"I was about to, dear, but I must get a ruling from our captain."

"You're teasing him."

"No, Deety; Hilda is right; doctrine has to be clear. Jake? How about taking charge on the ground?"

"No, Captain. Druther be a Balkan general, given my druthers."

Aunt Hilda stood up, shoe in hand, reached high with her other hand, patted my husband's cheek. "Zebbie, you are a dear. You worry about us all—me especially, because you think I'm a featherhead. Remember how we did at Snug Harbor? Each one did what she could do best and there was no friction. If that worked there, it ought to work here."

"Well . . . all right. But will you gals *please* be careful?"

"We'll be careful. How's your E.S.P.? Any feeling?"

Zebadiah wrinkled his forehead. "No. But I don't get advance warning. Just barely enough."

"'Just barely' is enough. Before we had to leave, you were about to program Gay to listen at high gain. Would that change 'just barely' to 'ample'?"

"Yes! Sharpie, I'll put you in charge, on the ground."

"In your hat, Buster. Ole Massa done freed us slaves. Zebbie, the quicker you quit dodging, the sooner you get those hot cakes. Spread my cape down and put the hot plate on the step."

We ate breakfast in basic Barsoomian dress: skin. Aunt Hilda pointed out that laundries seemed scarce, and the car's water tanks had to be saved for drinking and cooking. "Deety, I have just this dress you gave me; I'll air it and let the wrinkles hang out. Panties, too. An air bath is better than no bath. I know you'll divvy with me but you are no closer to a laundry than I am."

My jump suit joined Hilda's dress. "Aunt Hilda, you could skip bathing a week. Me, right after a bath I have a body odor but not too bad. In twenty-four hours I'm whiff. Forty-eight and I smell like a skunk. An air bath may help."

The same reasoning caused our men to spread their used clothing on the port wing, and caused Zebadiah to pick up Hilda's cape. "Sharpie, you can't get fur Hollanderized in this universe. Jake, you stowed some tarps?"

After dishes were "washed" (scoured with turf, placed in the sun) we were sleepy. Zebadiah wanted us to sleep inside, doors locked. Aunt Hilda and I wanted to nap on a tarpaulin in the shade of the car. I pointed out that moving rear seats aft in refitting had made it impossible to recline them.

Zebadiah offered to give up his seat to either of us women. I snapped, "Don't be silly, dear! You barely fit into a rear seat and it brings your knees so far forward that the seat in front *can't* be reclined."

Pop intervened. "Hold it! Daughter, I'm disappointed—snapping at your husband. But, Zeb, we've *got* to rest. If I sleep sitting up, I get swollen ankles, half crippled, not good for much."

"I was trying to keep us safe," Zebadiah said plaintively.

"I know, Son; you've been doing so—and a smart job, or we all would be dead three times over. Deety knows it, I know it, Hilda knows it—"

"I sure do, Zebbie!"

"My Captain, I'm sorry I snapped at you."

"We'll need you later. Flesh has its limits—even yours. If necessary, we would bed you down and stand guard over you—"

"No!"

"We sure would, Zebbie!"

"We *will*, my Captain."

"But I doubt that it's necessary. When we sat on the ground to eat, did anyone get chigger bites or anything?"

My husband shook his head.

"Not me," Aunt Hilda agreed.

I added, "I saw some little beasties but they didn't bother me."

"Apparently," Pop went on, "they don't like our taste. A ferocious-looking dingus sniffed at my ankle--but it scurried away. Zeb, Gay can hear better than we can?"

"Oh, *much* better!"

"Can her radar be programmed to warn us?"

Zebadiah looked thoughtful. "Uh . . . anti-collision alarm would wake the dead. If I pulled it in to minimum range, then— No, the display would be cluttered with 'grass.' We're on the ground. False returns."

I said, "Subtract static display, Zebadiah."

"Eh? How, Deety?"

"Gay can do it. Shall I try?"

"Deety, if you switch on radar, we *have* to sleep inside. Microwaves cook your brains."

"I know, sir. Gay has sidelookers, eyes fore and aft, belly, and umbrella—has she not?"

"Yes. That's why—"

"Switch off her belly eye. Can sidelookers hurt us if we sleep *under* her?"

His eyes widened. "Astrogator, you know more about my car than I do. I'd better sign her over to you."

"My Captain, you have already endowed me with all your worldly goods. I don't know more about Gay; I know more about *programming.*"

We made a bed under the car by opening Zebadiah's sleeping bag out flat, a tarpaulin on each side. Aunt Hilda dug out sheets: "In case anyone gets chilly."

"Unlikely," Pop told her. "Hot now, not a cloud and no breeze."

"Keep it by you, dearest. Here's one for Zebbie." She dropped two more on the sleeping bag, lay down on it. "Down flat, gentlemen"—waited for them to comply, then called to me: *"Deety!* Everybody's down."

From inside I called back, *"Right with you!"*—then said, "Hello, Gay."

"Hi, Deety!"

"Retrieve newest program. Execute."

Five scopes lighted, faded to dimness; the belly eye remained blank. I told her, "You're a good girl, Gay."

"I like you, too, Deety. Over."

"Roger and out, sister." I scrunched down, got at the stowage under the instrument board, pulled out padding and removed saber and sword, each with belt. These I placed at the door by a pie tin used at breakfast. I slithered head first out the door, turned without rising, got swords and pie plate, and crawled toward the pallet, left arm cluttered with hardware.

I stopped. "Your sword, Captain."

"Deety! Do I need a sword to nap?"

"No, sir. *I* shall sleep soundly knowing that my captain has his sword."

"Hmm—" Zebadiah withdrew it a span, returned it with a click. "Silly . . . but *I* feel comforted by it, too."

"I see nothing silly, sir. Ten hours ago you killed a *thing* with it that would have killed me."

"I stand—sprawl—corrected, my Princess. Dejah Thoris is always correct."

"I hope my Chieftain will always think so."

"He will. Give me a big kiss. What's the pie pan for?"

"Radar alarm test."

Having delivered the kiss, I crawled past Hilda and handed Pop his saber. He grinned at me. "Deety hon, you're a one! Just the security blanket I need. How did you know?"

"Because Aunt Hilda and I need it. With our warriors armed, we will sleep soundly." I kissed Pop, crawled out from under. "Cover your ears!"

I got to my knees, sailed that pan far and high, dropped flat and covered my ears. As the pan sailed into the zone of microwave radiation, a horrid clamor sounded inside the car, kept up until the pan struck the ground and stopped rolling—chopped off. "Somebody remind me to recover that. Good night, all!"

I crawled back, stretched out by Hilda, kissed her goodnight, set the clock in my head for six hours, went to sleep.

The sun was saying that it was fourteen instead of fourteen-fifteen and I decided that my circadian did not fit Barsoom. Would the clock in my head "slow" to match a day forty minutes longer? Would it give me trouble? Not likely—I've always been able to sleep anytime. I felt grand and ready for anything.

I crept off the pallet, snaked up into the car's cabin, and stretched. Felt good!

I crawled through the bulkhead door back of the rear seats, got some scarves and my jewelry case, went forward into the space between seats and instrument board.

I tried tying a filmy green scarf as a bikini bottom, but it looked like a diaper. I took it off, folded it corner to corner, pinned it at my left hip with a jeweled brooch. Lots better! "Indecently decent" Pop would say.

I looped a rope of imitation pearls around my hips, arranged strands to drape with the cloth, fastened them at the brooch. I hung around my neck a pendant of pearls and cabochon emeralds—from my father the day I received the title doctor of philosophy.

I was adding bracelets and rings when I heard *"Psst!"*—looked down and saw the Hillbilly's head and hands at the doorsill. Hilda put a finger to her lips. I nodded, gave her a hand up, whispered, "Still asleep?"

"Like babies."

"Let's get you dressed . . . 'Princess Thuvia.'"

Aunt Hilda giggled. "Thank you . . . 'Princess' Dejah Thoris."

"Want anything but jewelry?"

"Just something to anchor it. That old-gold scarf if you can spare it."

"Course I can! Nothing's too good for my Aunt Thuvia and that scarf is durn near nothing. Baby doll, we're going to deck you out for the auction block. Will you do my hair?"

"And you mine. Deety—I mean 'Dejah Thoris'—I miss a three-way mirror."

"We'll be mirrors for each other," I told her. "I don't mind camping out. My great-great-great-grandmother had two babies in a sod house. Except"—I ducked my head, sniffed my armpit—"we'd better find a stream." I added, "Hold still. Or shall I pin it through your skin?"

"Either way, dear. We'll find water—all this ground cover."

"Ground cover doesn't prove running water. This place may *be* a 'dead sea bottom of Barsoom.'"

"Doesn't look dead," Aunt Hilda countered. "It's pretty."

"Yes, but this looks like a dead sea bottom. Which gave me an idea. Hold up your hair; I want to arrange your necklaces."

"What idea?" Aunt Hilda demanded.

"Zebadiah told me to figure a third escape program. The first two—I'll paraphrase, Gay is awake. One tells her to take us back to a height over Snug Harbor; the other tells her to scoot back to where she was before she was last given the first order."

"I thought that one told her to place us over the Grand Canyon?"

"It does, at present. But if she got the first order *now,* that would change the second order. Instead of over the Grand Canyon, we would be back here quicker'n a frog could wink its eye."

"Okay if you say so."

"She's programmed that way. Hit the panic button and we are over our cabin site. Suppose we arrive there and find trouble, then use the 'C' order. She takes us *back to wherever she last got the 'T' order.* Dangerous or we would not have left in a rush. So we need a *third* escape program, to take us to a safe place. This looks safe."

"It's peaceful."

"Seems so. There!—more doodads than a Christmas tree and you look nakeder than ever."

"That's the effect we want, isn't it? Sit down in the copilot's seat; I'll do your hair."

"Want shoes?" I asked.

"On *Barsoom?* Dejah Thoris, thank you for your little-girl shoes. But they pinch my toes. You're going to wear *shoes?*"

"Not bleedin' likely, Aunt Nanny Goat. I toughened my feet for karate—I can break a four-by-nine with my feet and get nary a bruise. Or run on sharp gravel. What's a good escape phrase? I plan to store in Gay an emergency signal for every spot we visit that looks like a safe hidey-hole. So give me a phrase."

"Your mudder chaws terbacker!"

"Nanny Goat! A code-phrase should have a built-in mnemonic."

"'Bug Out'?"

"A horrid expression and just what we need. 'Bug Out' will mean to take us to this exact spot. I'll program it. And post it and others on the instrument board so that, if anyone forgets, she can read it."

"And so could any outsider, if she got in."

"Fat lot of good it would do her! Gay ignores an order not in our voices. Hello, Gay."

"Hello, Deety!"

"Retrieve present location. Report."

"Null program."

"Are we *lost?*"

"Not at all, Aunt Hilda. I was sloppy. Gay, program check. Define 'Home.'"

"Cancel any-all transitions translations rotations inertials. Return to zero-designated latitude longitude two klicks above ground level hovering."

"Search memory reversed-real-time for last order execute-coded Gay Deceiver take us home."

"Retrieved."

"From time of retrieved order integrate to time-present all transitions translations rotations inertials."

"Integrated."

"Test check. Report summary of integration."

"Origin 'Home.' Countermarch program executed. Complex

maneuver inertials. Translation Tau axis ten minimals positive. Complex maneuver inertials. Translation Ell axis two-two-four-zero-nine-zero-eight-two-seven point zero klicks. Negative vector Ell axis twenty-four klicks per sec. Negative vector Ell axis four klicks per sec. Complex manuever inertials. Grounded here-then oh-eight-oh-two-forty-nine. Grounded inertials continuing eight hours three minutes nineteen seconds *mark!* Grounded inertials continue running real-time."

"New program. Here-now grounded inertial location real-time running to real-time new execute order equals code-phrase bug-out. Report new program."

Gay answered: "New program code-phrase bug-out: Definition: Here-now grounded inertials running real-time to future-time execute order code-phrase bug-out."

"Gay, I tell you three times."

"Deety, I hear you three times."

"New program. Execute-coded Gay Deceiver Bug Out. At execute-code move to location coded 'bug-out.' I tell you three times."

"I hear you three times."

"Gay Deceiver, you're a smart girl."

"Deety, why don't you leave that big ape and live with me? Over."

"Good night, Gay. Roger and out. Hillbilly, I didn't give you that answer." I tried to look fierce.

"Why, Deety, how could you say such a thing?"

"I know I didn't. Well?"

"I 'fess up, Deetikins. A few days ago while you and I were working, you were called away. While I waited, I stuck that in. Want it erased?"

I don't know how to look fierce; I snickered. "No. Maybe Zebadiah will be around the next time it pops up. I wish our men would wake, I do."

"They need rest, dear."

"I know. But I want to check that new program."

"It sounded complex."

"Can be, by voice. I'd rather work on paper. A computer doesn't accept excuses. A mistake can be anything from 'null program' to disaster. This one has features I've never tried. I don't really *understand* what Pop does. Non-Euclidean *n*-dimensional geometry is way out in left field."

"To me it's not in the ball park."

"So I'm itchy."

"Let's talk about something else."

"Did I show you our micro walky-talkies?"

"Jacob gave me one."

"There's one for each. Tiny but amazingly long-ranged. Uses less power than a hand calculator and weighs less—under two hundred grams. Mass, I mean—weight here is much less. Today I thought of a new use. Gay can accept their frequency."

"That's nice. How do you plan to use this?"

"This car can be remote-controlled."

"Deety, who would you want to do *that?*"

I admitted that I did not know. "But Gay can be preprogrammed to do almost anything. For example, we could go outside and tell Gay, via walky-talky, to carry out two programs in succession: H,O,M,E, followed by B,U,G,O,U,T. Imagine Zebadiah's face when he wakes up from sun in his eyes—because his car has vanished—then his expression two hours later when it pops back into existence."

"Deety, go stand in the corner for *thinking* such an unfunny joke!" Then Aunt Hilda looked thoughtful. "Why would it take two hours? I thought Gay could go *anywhere* in *no* time."

"Depends on your postulates, Princess Thuvia. We took a couple of hours to get here because we fiddled. Gay would have to follow that route in reverse because it's the only one she knows. Then—" I stopped, suddenly confused. "Or would it be *four* hours? No, vectors would cancel and— But that would make it instantaneous; we would never know that she had left. Or would we? Aunt Hilda, I don't *know!* Oh, I wish our men would wake up, I do!" The world wobbled and I felt scared.

"I'm awake," Pop answered, his head just showing above the doorsill. "What's this debate?" He gave Aunt Hilda a lecherous leer. "Little girl, if you'll come up to my room, I'll give you some candy."

"Get away from me, you old wolf!"

"Hilda my love, I could sell you down to Rio and retire on the proceeds. You look like expensive stuff."

"I'm *very* expensive stuff, darling wolf. All I want is every cent a man has and constant pampering—then a fat estate when he dies."

"I'll try to die with plenty of money in the bank, dearest."

"Instead we're both dead and our bank accounts have gone Heaven knows where and I haven't a rag to my back—and I'm wonderfully happy. Come inside—mind the radar!—and kiss me, you old wolf; you don't have to buy me candy."

"Pop," I asked, "is Zebadiah asleep?"

"Just woke up."

I spoke to Gay, then to Pop: "Will you tell Zebadiah radar is off? He can stand up without getting his ears fried."

"Sure." Pop ducked down and yelled, "Zeb, it's safe; her husband left."

"Coming!" Zebadiah's voice rumbled back. "Tell Deety to put the steaks on." My darling appeared wearing sword, carrying pie pan and sheets. "Are the steaks ready?" he asked, then kissed me.

"Not quite, sir," I told him. "First, go shoot a thoat. Or will you settle for peanut butter sandwiches?"

"Don't talk dirty. Did you say 'thoat'?"

"Yes. This is Barsoom."

"I thoat that was what you said."

"If that's a pun, you can eat it for supper. With peanut butter." Zebadiah shuddered. "I'd rather cut my thoat."

Pop said, "Don't do it, Zeb. A man can't eat with his thoat cut. He can't even talk clearly."

Aunt Hilda said mildly, "If you three will cease those atrocities, I'll see what I can scrape up for dinner."

"I'll help," I told her, "but can we run my test first? I'm itchy."

"Certainly, Deety. It will be a scratch meal."

Pop looked at Aunt Hilda reproachfully. "And *you* told *us* to stop."

"What test?" demanded my husband.

I explained the Bug-Out program. "I *think* I programmed it correctly. But here is a test. Road the car a hundred meters. If my program works—fine! If it tests null, no harm done but you and Pop will have to teach me more about the twister before I'll risk new programming."

"I don't want to road the car, Deety; I'm stingy with every erg until I know when and where I can juice Gay. However— Jake, what's your minimum transition?"

"Ten kilometers. Can't use spatial quanta for transitions—too small. But the scale goes up fast—logarithmic. That's short range. Middle range is in light-years—logarithmic again."

"What's long range, Jake?"

"Gravitic radiation versus time. We won't use *that* one."

"Why not, Jacob?" asked Aunt Hilda.

Pop looked sheepish. "I'm scared of it, dearest. There are three major theories concerning gravitic propagation. At the time I machined those controls, one theory seemed proved. Since then other physicists have reported not being able to reproduce the data. So

I blocked off long range." Pop smiled sourly. "I know the gun is loaded but not what it will do. So I spiked it."

"Sensible," agreed my husband. "Russian roulette lacks appeal. Jake, do you have any guess as to what options you shut off?"

"Better than a guess, Zeb. It reduces the number of universes accessible to us on this axis from the sixth power of six-to-the-sixth-power to a mere six to the sixth power. Forty-six thousand, six hundred, fifty-six."

"Gee, that's tough!"

"I didn't mean it as a joke, Zeb."

"Jake, I was laughing at *me*. I've been looking forward to a lifetime exploring universes—and now I learn that I'm limited to a fiddlin' forty-six thousand and some. Suppose I have a half century of exploration left in me. Assume that I take off no time for eating, sleeping, or teasing the cat, how much time can I spend in each universe?"

"About nine hours twenty minutes per universe," I told him. "Nine hours, twenty-three minutes, thirty-eight point seven-two-two seconds, plus, to be more nearly accurate."

"Deety, let's do be accurate," Zebadiah said solemnly. "If we stayed a minute too long in each universe, we would miss nearly a hundred universes."

I was getting into the spirit. "Let's hurry instead. If we work at it, we can do three universes a day for fifty years—one of us on watch, one on standby, two off duty—and still squeeze in maintenance, plus a few hours on the ground, once a year. If we hurry."

"We haven't a second to lose!" Zebadiah answered. "All hands!—places! Stand by to lift! *Move!*"

I was startled but hurried to my seat. Pop's chin dropped but he took his place. Aunt Hilda hesitated a split second before diving for her seat, but, as she strapped herself in, wailed, "Captain? Are we *really* leaving Barsoom?"

"Quiet, please. Gay Deceiver, close doors! Report seat belts. Copilot, check starboard door seal."

"Seat belt fastened," I reported with no expression.

"Mine's fastened. *Oh, dear!*"

"Copilot, by low range, 'H' axis upward, minimum transition."

"Set, Captain."

"Execute."

Sky outside was dark, the ground far below. "Ten klicks exactly," my husband approved. "Astrogator, take the conn, test your new program. Science Officer observe."

"Yessir. Gay Deceiver—*Bug Out!*"

We were parked on the ground.

"Science Officer—report," Zebadiah ordered.

"Report what?" Aunt Hilda demanded.

"We tested a new program. Did it pass test?"

"Uh, we seem to be back where we were. We were weightless maybe ten seconds. I guess the test was okay. Except—"

"'Except' what?"

"Captain Zebbie, you're the worst tease on Earth! And Barsoom! You did so put lime Jello in my pool!"

"I was in Africa."

"Then you arranged it!"

"Hilda—please! I *never* said we were leaving Barsoom. I said that we haven't a second to waste. We don't, with so much to explore."

"Excuses. *What about my clothes?* All on the starboard wing. Where are they now? Floating up in the stratosphere? Coming down *where?* I'll *never* find them."

"I thought you preferred to dress Barsoomian style?"

"Doesn't mean I want to be *forced* to! Besides, Deety lent them to me. I'm sorry, Deety."

I patted her hand. "'S'all right, Aunt Hilda. I'll lend you more. Give them, I mean." I hesitated, then said firmly, "Zebadiah, you should apologize to Aunt Hilda."

"Oh, for the love of— Sharpie? Sharpie darling."

"Yes, Zebbie?"

"I'm sorry I let you think that we were leaving Barsoom. I'll buy you clothes that fit. We'll make a quick trip back to Earth—"

"Don't want to go back to Earth! *Aliens!* They scare me."

"They scare me, too. I started to say: 'Earth-without-a-J.' It's so much like our own that I can probably use U.S. money. If not, I have gold. Or I can barter. For you, Sharpie, I'll *steal* clothes. We'll go to Phoenix-without-a-J—tomorrow—today we take a walk and see some of this planet—*your* planet—and we'll stay on your planet until *you* get tired of it. Is that enough? Or must I confess putting Jello into your pool when I *didn't?*"

"You really didn't?"

"Cross my heart."

"Be darned. Actually I thought it was funny. I wonder who did it? Aliens, maybe?"

"They play rougher than that. Sharpie darling, I'm not the only weirdo in your stable—not by dozens."

"Guess maybe. Zebbie? Will you kiss Sharpie and make up?"

On the ground, under the starboard wing, we found our travel clothes, and under the port wing, those of our husbands. Zebadiah looked bemused. "Jake? I thought Hilda was right. It had slipped my mind that we had clothing on the wings."

"Use your head, Son."

"I'm not sure I have one."

"I don't understand it either, darling," Aunt Hilda added.

"Daughter?" Pop said.

"Pop, I *think* I know. But— I pass!"

"Zeb, the car never moved. Instead—"

Aunt Hilda interrupted, "Jacob, are you saying that we did *not* go straight up? We were *there*—five minutes ago."

"Yes, my darling. But we didn't *move* there. Motion has a definable meaning: A duration of changing locations. But no duration was involved. We did *not* successively occupy loci between here-then and there-then."

Aunt Hilda shook her head. "I don't understand. We went *whoosh!* up into the sky . . . then *whoosh!* back where we started."

"My darling, we didn't *whoosh!* Deety! Don't be reticent."

I sighed. "Pop, I'm not sure there exists a symbol for the referent. Aunt Hilda. Zebadiah. A discontinuity. The car—"

"Got it!" said Zebadiah.

"*I* didn't," Aunt Hilda persisted.

"Like this, Sharpie," my husband went on. "My car is *here*. *Spung!*—it vanishes. Our clothes fall to the ground. Ten seconds later—*flip!*—we're back where we started. But our clothes are on the ground. Get it now?"

"I— I guess so. Yes."

"I'm glad you do . . . because *I* don't. To me, it's magic." Zebadiah shrugged. "'Magic.'"

"'Magic,'" I stated, "is a symbol for any process not understood."

"That's what I said, Deety. 'Magic.' Jake, would it have mattered if the car had been indoors?"

"Well . . . that fretted me the first time Deety and I translated to Earth-without-the-letter-J. So I moved our car outdoors. But now I think that only the destination matters. It should be empty— I *think*. But I'm too timid to experiment."

"Might be interesting. Unmanned vehicle. Worthless target. A small asteroid. A baby sun?"

"I don't *know*, Zeb. Nor do I have apparatus to spare. It took me three years to build this one."

"So we wait a few years. Jake? Air has mass."

"That worried me also. But any mass, other than degenerate mass, is mostly empty space. Air—Earth sea-level air—has about a thousandth the density of the human body. The body is mostly water and water accepts air readily. I can't say that it has *no* effect—twice I've thought that my temperature went up a trifle at transition or translation in atmosphere but it could have been excitement. I've never experienced caisson disease from it. Has any of us felt discomfort?"

"Not me, Jake."

"I've felt all right, Pop," I agreed.

"I got space sick. Till Deety cured it," Aunt Hilda added.

"So did I, my darling. But that was into vacuo and could not involve the phenomenon."

"Pop," I said earnestly, "we weren't hurt; we don't have to know *why*. A basic proposition of epistemology, bedrock both for the three basic statements of semantics and for information theory, is that an observed fact requires no proof. It simply *is*, self-demonstrating. Let philosophers worry about it; they haven't anything better to do."

"Suits me!" agreed Hilda. "You big brains had Sharpie panting. I thought we were going to take a walk?"

"We are, dear," agreed my husband. "Right after those steaks."

XVIII   *"—the whole world is alive."*

Zebadiah:

Four Dagwoods later we were ready to start walkabout. Deety delayed by wanting to repeat her test by remote control. I put my foot down. "No!"

"Why not, my Captain? I've taught Gay a program to take her straight up ten klicks. It's G, A, Y, B, O, U, N, C, E—a new fast-escape with no execution word necessary. Then I'll recall her by B, U, G, O, U, T. If one works via walky-talky, so will the second. It can save our lives, it can!"

"Uh—" I went on folding tarps and stowing my sleeping bag. The female mind is too fast for me. I often can reach the same conclusion; a woman gets there first and *never* by the route I have to follow. Besides that, Deety is a genius.

"You were saying, my Captain?"

"I was thinking. Deety, do it with me aboard. I won't touch the controls. Check pilot, nothing more."

"Then it won't be a test."

"Yes, it will. I promise, Cub Scout honor, to let it fall sixty seconds. Or to three klicks H-above-G, whichever comes first."

"These walky-talkies have more range than ten kilometers even between themselves. Gay's reception is *much* better."

"Deety, you trust machinery; I don't. If Gay doesn't pick up your second command—sun spots, interference, open circuit, anything—I'll keep her from crashing."

"But if something else goes wrong and you *did* crash, I would have *killed* you!" She started to cry.

So we compromised. Her way. The exact test she had originally proposed. I wasted juice by roading Gay Deceiver a hundred meters, got out, and we all backed off. Deety said into her walky-talky, "Gay Deceiver . . . Bug Out!"

It's more startling to watch than it is to be inside. There was Gay Deceiver off to our right, then she was off to our left. No noise—not even an implosion *splat!* Magic.

"Well, Deety? Are you satisfied?"

"Yes, Zebadiah. Thank you, darling. But it had to be a real test. You see that—don't you?"

I agreed, while harboring a suspicion that my test had been more stringent. "Deety, could you reverse that? Go somewhere else and tell Gay to come to you?"

"Somewhere she's never been?"

"Yes."

Deety switched off her walky-talky and made sure that mine was off. "I don't want her to hear this. Zebadiah, I always feel animistic about a computer. The Pathetic Fallacy—I know. But Gay is a person to me."

Deety sighed. "I know it's a machine. It doesn't have ears; it can't see; it doesn't have a concept of space-time. What it *can* do is manipulate circuitry in complex ways—complexities limited by its grammar and vocabulary. But those limits are exact. If I don't stay precisely with its grammar and vocabulary, it reports 'Null program.' I can tell it anything by radio that I can tell it by voice inside the cabin—and so can you. But I *can't* tell it to come look for me in a meadow beyond a canyon about twelve or thirteen klicks approximately southwest of here-now. That's a null program—five undefined terms."

"Because you made it null. You fed 'garbage in' and expect me to be surprised at 'garbage out'—when you did it a-purpose."

"I did not either, I didn't!"

I kissed the end of her nose. "Deety darling, you should trust your instincts. Here's one way to tell Gay to do that without defining even one new term into her vocabulary. Tell her to expect a three-part program. First part: bounce one minimum, ten klicks. Second part: transit twelve point five klicks true course two-two-five. Third part: drop to one klick H-over-G and hover. At that point, if what you described as your location is roughly correct, you will see her and can coach her to a landing without using Jake's twister."

"Uh . . . twelve and a half kilometers can't be done in units of ten kilometers. Powered flight?"

"*Waste juice?* Hon, you just flunked high school geometry. Using Euclid's tools, compass and straight edge, lay out that course and distance, then lay out how to get there in ten-klick units—no fractions."

My wife stared. Then her eyes cleared. "Transit one minimum true course one-seven-three and two thirds, then transit one minimum true course two-seven-six and one third. The mirror image solution uses the same courses in reverse. Plus endless trivial solutions using more than two minima."

"Go to the head of the class. If you don't spot her, have her do a retreating search curve—in her perms, in an Aussie accent. Honey girl, did you actually do that Euclid style?"

"I *approximated* it Euclid style—but you didn't supply compass and straight edge! Scribe circle radius twelve point five. Bisect circle horizontally by straight edge through origin; quarter it by dropping a vertical. Bisect lower left quadrant—that gives true course two-two-five or southwest. Then set compass at ten units and scribe arcs from origin and from southwest point of circle; the intersections give courses and vertices for both major roots to the accuracy of your straight edge and compass. But simply to *visualize* that construction—well, I got *visualized* angles of two-seven-five and one-seven-five. Pretty sloppy.

"So I did it accurately by Pythagorean proposition by splitting the isosceles triangle into two right triangles. Hypotenuse is ten, one side is six and a quarter—and that gives the missing side as seven point eight-zero-six-two-four-seven plus—which gives you one course and you read off the other by the scandalous Fifth Axiom. But I did check by trig. Arc sine point seven-eight-zero-six-two-four-seven—"

"Hold it! I believe you. What other ways can you program Gay to find you, using her present vocabulary?"

"Uh . . . burn juice?"

"If necessary."

"I would have her bounce a minimum, then maximize my signal. Home on me."

"Certainly. Now do the same thing *without* using juice. Just Jake's twister."

Deety looked thoughtful and about twelve years old, then suddenly said, "'Drunkard's Walk'!"—added at once, "But I would place a locus around the Walk just large enough to be certain that I'm inside it. Gay should plot signal level at each vertex. Such a plot would pinpoint the signal source."

"Which way is faster? Home straight in under power? Or Drunkard's Walk?"

Deety answered, "Why, the—"—looked startled. "Those are solid-state relays."

"Jake sets verniers by hand—but when Gay is directing herself there are no moving parts. Solid state."

"Zebadiah, am I thinking straight? Using power, at that distance—call it twelve kilometers—Gay should be able to home on me in three or four minutes. But—Zebadiah, this can't be right!—using *no* power and relying on random numbers and pure chance in a Drunkard's Walk, Gay should find me in less than a second. Where did I go wrong?"

"On the high side, Deety girl. Lost your nerve. The first fifty milliseconds should show the hot spot; in less than the second fifty she'll part your hair. All over in a tenth of a second—or less. But, honey, we *still* haven't talked about the best way. I said that *you should trust your instincts.* Gay is *not* an 'it.' She's a *person.* You'll never know how relieved I was when it turned out that you two were going to be friends. If she had been jealous of you— May the gods deliver us from a vindictive machine! But she's not; she thinks you're swell."

"Zebadiah, you believe that?"

"Dejah Thoris, I *know* that."

Deety looked relieved. "I know it, too—despite what I said earlier."

"Deety, to me the whole world is alive. Some parts are sleeping and some are dozing and some are awake but yawning . . . and some are bright-eyed and bushy-tailed and always ready to go. Gay is one of those."

"Yes, she is. I'm sorry I called her an 'it.' But what is this 'best way'?"

"Isn't it obvious? Don't tell her *how*—just *tell* her. Say to her, 'Gay, come find me!' All four words are in her vocabulary; the sentence is compatible with her grammar. She'll find you."

"But how? Drunkard's Walk?"

"A tenth of a second might strike her as too long—she *likes* you, hon. She'll look through her registers and pick the optimum solution. She might not be able to tell you how she did it, since she wipes anything she's not told to remember. I *think* she does; I've never been certain."

Jake and Hilda had wandered off while Deety and I had been talking. They had turned back, so we started toward them. Sharpie called out, "Zebbie, what happened to that hike?"

"Right away," I agreed. "Jake, we have about three hours. We ought to be buttoned up before sundown. Check?"

"I agree. The temperature will drop rapidly at sundown."

"Yup. We can't do real exploring today. So let's treat it as drill. Fully armed, patrol formation, radio discipline, and always alert, as if there were a 'Black Hat' behind every bush."

"No bushes," objected Hilda.

I pretended not to hear. "But what constitutes 'fully armed,' Jake? We each have rifles. You have that oldstyle Army automatic that will knock down anything if you're close enough but—how good a shot are you?"

"Good enough."

"How good is 'Good enough'?" (Most people are as accurate with a baseball as with a pistol.)

"Skipper, I won't attempt a target more than fifty meters away. But if I intend to hit, the target will be within range and I will hit it."

I opened my mouth . . . closed it. Fifty meters is a *long* range for that weapon. But hint that my father-in-law was boasting?

Deety caught my hesitation. "Zebadiah—Pop taught me pistol in the campus R.O.T.C. range. I've seen him practice bobbing targets at thirty meters. I saw him miss one. *Once.*"

Jake harrumphed. "My daughter omitted to mention that I skip most surprise targets."

"Father! 'Most' means 'more than fifty percent.' Not true!''

"Near enough."

"Six occasions. Four strings, twenty-eight targets on three—"

"Hold it, honey! Jake, it's silly to argue figures with your daughter. With my police special I won't attempt anything over twenty meters—except covering fire. But I hand-load my ammo and pour my own dumdums; the result is almost as lethal as that howitzer of yours. But if it comes to trouble, or hunting for meat, we'll use rifles, backed by Deety's shotgun. Deety, can you shoot?"

"Throw your hat into the air."

"I don't like the sound of that. Sharpie, we have five firearms, four people—is there one that fits you?"

"Cap'n Zebbie, the one time I fired a gun, I went backwards, the bullet went that-a-way, and I had a sore shoulder. Better have me walk in front to trip land mines."

"Zebadiah, she could carry my fléchette gun."

"Sharpie, we'll put you in the middle and you carry the first-aid kit; you're medical officer—armed with Deety's purse gun for defense. Jake, it's time we stowed these swords and quit pretending to be Barsoomian warriors. Field boots. I'm going to wear that same sweaty pilot suit, about equivalent to jump suits you and Deety wore—which I suggest you wear now. We should carry water canteens and iron rations. I can't think of anything that would serve as a canteen. Damn! Jake, we aren't doing this by the book."

"What book?" demanded Hilda.

"Those romances about interstellar exploration. There's always a giant mother ship in orbit, loaded with everything from catheters to Coca-Cola, and scouting is by landing craft, in touch with the mother ship. Somehow, we aren't doing it that way."

(All the more reason to conduct drill as realistically as possible. Jake or I, one of us, is honor bound to stay alive to take care of two women and unborn children; exterminating 'Black-Hat' vermin holds a poor second to that.)

"Zebbie, why are you staring at me?"

I hadn't known that I was. "Trying to figure how to dress you, dear. Sharpie, you look cute in jewelry and perfume. But it's not enough for a sortie in the bush. Take 'em off and put 'em away.

You, too, Deety. Deety, do you have another jump suit that can be pinned up or stitched up for Hilda?"

"A something, sure. But it would take hours to do a good job. My sewing kit isn't much."

"'Hours' will have to be another day. Today we'll make do with safety pins. But take time to do a careful job of padding her feet into your stoutest shoes. Confound it, she should have field boots. Sharpie, remind me when we make that shopping trip to Earth-without-a-J."

"To hear is to obey, Exalted One. Is it permitted to make a parliamentary inquiry?"

She startled me. "Hilda, what did I do to cause that frosty tone?"

"It was what you didn't do." Suddenly she smiled, reached high and patted my cheek. "You mean well, Zebbie. But you slipped. While Gay Deceiver is on the ground, we're equal. But you've been giving orders right and left."

I started to answer; Jake cut in. "Hilda my love, for a scouting expedition the situation becomes equivalent to a craft in motion. Again we require a captain."

Sharpie turned toward her husband. "Conceded, sir. But may I point out that we are *not yet* on that hike? Zebbie has consulted you; he has not consulted Deety and me. He asked us for information—darned seldom! Aside from that he has simply laid down the law. What are we, Zebbie? Poor little female critters whose opinions are worthless?"

Caught with your hand in the cooky jar, throw yourself on the mercy of the court.

"Sharpie, you're right and I'm dead wrong. But before you pass sentence I claim extenuating circumstances: Youth and in-experience, plus long and faithful service."

"You can't," put in my helpful wife. "You can plead one or the other but not both. They can't overlap."

Sharpie stood on tiptoes and kissed my chin. "In Zebbie's case they *do* overlap. Do you still want to know what to use as water canteens?"

"Certainly!"

"Then why didn't you ask?"

"But I did!"

"No, Cap'n Zebbie; you did not ask and did not even give us time to volunteer the answer."

"I'm sorry, Hilda. Too many things on my mind."

"I know, dear; Sharpie does not mean to scold. But I *had* to get your attention."

"That baseball bat?"

"Almost. For an ersatz canteen—— A hot-water bottle?"

Again she startled me. "In the danger we were in when we left, you worried about cold feet in bed? And packed a hot-water bottle?"

"Two," answered Deety. "Aunt Hilda fetched one. So did I."

"Deety, you don't have cold feet and neither do I."

Sharpie said, "Deety, is he actually that naïve?"

"I'm afraid he is, Aunt Hilda. But he's sweet."

"And brave," added Hilda. "But retarded in spots. They *do* overlap in Zebbie's case. He's unique."

"What," I demanded, "are you talking about?"

"Aunt Hilda means that, when you refitted Gay, you neglected to install a bidet."

"Oh." That was the wittiest I could manage. "It's not a subject I give much thought to."

"No reason you should, Zebbie. Although men use them, too."

"Zebadiah does. Pop, too. Bidets, I mean. Not hot-water bottles."

"I meant hot-water bottles, dear. As medical officer I may find it necessary to administer an enema to the Captain."

"Oh, no!" I objected. "You're not equipped."

"But she is, Zebadiah. We fetched both sorts of nozzles."

"But you didn't fetch four husky orderlies to hold me down. Let's move on. Sharpie, what was the advice you would have given if I had been bright enough to consult you?"

"Some is not advice but a statement of fact. I'm not going for a hike on a hot day swaddled in a pinned-up jump suit eight sizes too big. While you all play Cowboys-and-Indians, I'm going to curl up in my seat and read 'The Oxford Book of English Verse.' Thank you for fetching it, Jacob."

"Hilda beloved, I will worry."

"No need to worry about *me*, Jacob. I can always tell Gay to lock her doors. But, were I to go with you, I would be a handicap. You three are trained to fight; I'm not." Sharpie turned toward me. "Captain, since I'm not going, that's all I have to say."

What was there for me to say? "Thank you, Hilda. Deety, do you have things on your mind?"

"Yes, sir. I go along with field boots and jump suits and so forth even though they'll be beastly hot. But I wish you would change your mind about your sword and Pop's saber. Maybe they aren't much compared with rifles but they're good for my morale."

Hilda interjected, "Had I decided to go, Captain, I would have said the same. Possibly it is an emotional effect from what happened, uh—was it only yesterday?—but perhaps it is subconscious logic. Just yesterday bare blades defeated a man—a thing, an alien—armed with a firearm and ready to use it."

Jake spoke up. "Captain, I didn't want to take off my saber."

"We'll wear them." *Any* excuse is a good excuse to wear a sword. "Are we through? We've lost an hour and the Sun is dropping. Deety?"

"One more thing, Zebadiah—and I expect to be outvoted. I say to cancel the hike."

"So? Princess, you've said too much or not enough."

"If we do this, we spend the night here—sitting up. If we chase the Sun instead— There were lights on the night side that looked like cities. There was blue on the day side that looked like a sea. I think I saw canals. But whether we find something or not, at worst we'll catch up with sunrise and be able to sleep outdoors in daylight, just as we did today."

"Deety! Gay can overtake the Sun. Once. You want to use all her remaining juice just to sleep outdoors?"

"Zebadiah, I wasn't planning on using *any* power."

"Huh? It sounded like it."

"Oh, no! Do transitions of three minima or more, bearing west. Aim us out of the atmosphere; we fall back in while looking for places of interest. As we reenter, we glide, but where depends on what you want to look at. When you have stretched the glide to the limit, unless you decide to ground, you do another transition. There is great flexibility, Zebadiah. You can reach sunrise line in the next few minutes. Or you could elect to stay on the day side for weeks, never land, never use any juice, and inspect the entire planet from pole to pole."

"Maybe Gay can stay up for weeks—but not me. I'm good for several more hours. With that limitation, it sounds good. How about it? Hilda? Jake?"

"You mean that female suffrage is *permanent?* I vote Yes!"

Jake said, "You have a majority; no need for a male vote."

"Jacob!" his wife said reproachfully.

"Joking, my dear. It's unanimous."

I said, "Somebody just cancelled the election. Look there." We all looked. Deety said, "What is it? A pterodactyl?"

"No, an ornithopter. A big one."

PART TWO

The Butterfly's Mandarin

XIX *Something is gained in translation—*

Hilda:

Jacob tightened his arm around me. "Zeb," he said softly, "I don't believe it." He was staring (we all were) at this mechaniwockle pteranodon coming at us over the hills in the west.

"Neither do I," Zebbie answered. "Wrong wing loading. Impossible articulation. There's a second one. A third! All hands! Grab your clothes! Man the ship! Prepare to lift! *Move!* Jake, unbuckle your saber and into your jump suit, *fast!*"

Cap'n Zebbie was unhooking his sword belt and grabbing his coveralls as he yelped. I was inside first as I didn't stop to dress— grabbed Deety's baby shoes with one hand, my dress and panties with the other.

I wiggled into panties, slid the dress over my head, slipped on Deety's Keds.

I anticipated the order to fasten seat belts—stopped suddenly and eased my belt. I had not stopped to take off the doodads that proclaimed me a Barsoomian "princess." Now it seemed that every item of frippery was about to imprint me for life.

Deety was cursing softly over the same problem. Deety's jump suit was harder to reach into, even when she unbelted and opened the zipper all the way. I helped readjust the hardware but cautioned her not to remove it and to close the zipper clear to her chin. "Deety, if you get holes in your hide, you'll get well. But if something loose catches our captain in the eye, the culprit will be broken on the wheel."

I clucked-clucked at her answer but big ones do get in the way. Meanwhile our men were having problems. That space under the

163

instrument board could not be seen by a full-sized male. The best position to reach it was impossible for Jacob, ridiculously impossible for Zebbie.

Zebbie's profanity was louder than Deety's but not as colorful. My own darling was keeping quiet which meant that he was *really* in trouble. I said, "Gentlemen—"

Zebbie grunted, "Shut up, Sharpie; we've got problems! Deety! How did you get these toadstickers into this compartment?"

"I didn't. Aunt Hilda did."

"Sharpie, can I apologize later? Those Martians are circling us *now!*"

So they were, at least a dozen flapping monstrosities. One appeared about to ground. "Captain, I'll do it—but there is a faster way."

"How?"

"Unhook your scabbards, put on your sword belts. Saber and sword in scabbards fit easily if you point one right, the other left. They will rattle unless you stuff clothing around them."

"They can bloody well rattle!" In seconds, our gallants had blades and scabbards stowed. As Cap'n Zebbie resumed sword belt and started on his seat belt he called out, "Fasten belts, prepare to lift! Sharpie, have I told you today that in addition to loving you, I admire you?"

"I think not, Captain."

"I do. Enormously. Report! Science Officer?"

"Seat belt fastened. Thank you, Zebbie."

"Seat belt fastened," reported Deety. "Bulkhead door dogged."

"Seat belt fastened, starboard door seal checked, copilot ready, sir!"

"Port door seal checked, pilot strapped down; we're ready— and none too soon! One has grounded and somebody is getting out. Hey! They're human!"

"Or disguised aliens," said my darling.

"Well . . . yes, there's that. I may lift any second. Deety—that new program: Just G, A, Y, B, O, U, N, C, E? No 'do-it' word?"

"Check."

"Good. I won't use it unless forced to. This may be that 'first contact' the world has been expecting."

"Cap'n Zebbie, why would aliens disguise themselves when they outnumber us? I think they are human."

"I hope you're right. Copilot, should I open the door? Advice, please."

"Captain, you can open the door anytime. But if it *is* open, it takes a few seconds to close it and the ship won't lift with a door open."

"Too right. Gay Deceiver."

"Hi, Boss. Where did you pick up the tarts?"

"Gay, check and report."

"All circuits checked, all systems go, juice point seven-eight—and I'm in the mood."

"Cast loose L-gun. Prepare to burn."

"Done!"

"Captain," my husband said worriedly, "are you planning to blast them?"

"I hope not. I'd rather run than fight. I'd rather stay and get help than either. But they grounded where I *can* burn them—using offset."

"Captain, don't do it!"

"Copilot, I don't plan to. Now drop it!"

The grounded flappy bird was about two hundred meters and a few degrees left of dead ahead. Two men—they looked like men—had disembarked and headed toward us. They were dressed alike—uniforms? They seemed vaguely familiar—but all uniforms seem vaguely familiar, do they not?

They were less than a hundred meters from us. Cap'n Zebbie did something at his instrument board and suddenly their voices were inside, blastingly loud. He adjusted the setting and we could hear clearly. Zebbie said, "That's Russian! Isn't it, Jake?"

"Captain, I *think* so. A Slavic language, in any case." Jacob added, "Do you understand it?"

"*Me?* Jake, I said that I can swear in Russian; I didn't say I could speak it. I can say 'thank you' and 'please' and 'da' and 'nyet'—maybe six more. How about you?"

"I can puzzle out a paper about mathematics with the aid of a dictionary. But speak it? Understand it? No."

I tried to remember whether or not I had ever told Zebbie that I know Russian. My husband and Deety I had not told. Well, if Zebbie knew, he would call on me. It is not something I mention as it does not fit my *persona*. I started it out of curiosity; I wanted to read those great Russian novelists—Dostoievsky, Tolstoy, and so forth—in the original in order to find out why they were so celebrated. Why I had never been able to read one of those classic novels all the way through? (They had cured me of sleeping pills.)

So I set out to learn Russian. Soon I was wearing earphones to bed, listening to Russian in my sleep, working with a tutor in the daytime. I never mastered a good accent; those six-consonantsin-a-row words tie knots in my tongue. But one cannot read a language easily unless one can "hear" the words. So I learned the spoken language along with the written.

(Oh, yes, those "classic novels": Having invested so much effort I carried out my purpose: *War and Peace, The Idiot, The Brothers Karamazov, Anna Karenina,* and so forth. Would you believe it? Something is *gained* in translation; the originals are even more depressing and soporific than translations. I'm not sure what purpose Russian fiction has, but it *can't* be entertainment.)

I decided to wait. I was not eager to be interpreter and it would not be necessary if it turned out that Zebbie or Jacob had a language in common with our visitors—and I rationalized my decision by telling myself that it might turn out to be an advantage if the strangers thought that no one of us understood Russian.

(At that point I realized that I had been thinking in Russian. It's a wonderful language for paranoid thoughts.)

When Zebbie switched on the outside mikes, the older was telling the younger: "—not let Fyodor Ivanovitch get wind of such thoughts, Yevgeny. He does not believe that (no good? stupid?) Britishers can excel us in anything. So don't refer to that curious craft as 'advanced engineering.' A 'weird assemblage of poorly organized experiments' would be better."

"I will remember. Shall I loosen my holster and take off the safety? To guard you, sir?"

The older man laughed. "You haven't dealt with the damned British as long as I have. Never let them suspect that you are even mildly nervous. And always be sure to insult him first. Bear in mind that the lowliest serf in Ykraina is better than their so-called King-Emperor. That serf—"

—when Zebbie interrupted: *"Arrêtez-là!"*

The younger hesitated but the older never broke stride. Instead he answered in French: "You are telling *me* to halt, you British swine? An officer of the Tsar on Russian soil! I spit on your mother. And your father if your mother can remember who he was. Why are you speaking French, you soiled British spy? You fool no one. Speak Russian—or, if you are uncultured, speak English."

Zebbie thumbed a button. "What about it, Jake? Switch to English when he's so hipped on the subject of Englishmen? Or bull it through in French? My accent is better than his."

"Maybe you can get away with it, Captain. I can't."

Zebbie nodded and opened the mike, spoke in English: "We are not British, not spies. We are American tourists and—"

"'American'? What nonsense is this?" (He had shifted to English.) "A British colonial is still British—and a spy."

My husband reached over, shut off the microphone. "Captain, I advise lifting. He won't listen to reason."

"Copilot, not till I *must*. We don't even have enough water. I must try to parley." Zebbie thumbed the switch. "I am not a British colonial. I am Zeb Carter of California, a citizen of the United States of America; I have my passport. If we have trespassed, we regret it and apologize."

"Spy, that is the most bold-faced bluff I have ever heard. There is no such country as the United States of America. I am placing you under arrest. In the name of His Imperial Majesty the Tsar of All the Russias, by authority delegated to me by His Viceroy for New Russia Grand Duke Fyodor Ivanovitch Romanov, I arrest you and your party for the crime of espionage. Open up!"

By now they had reached Gay Deceiver and were at the portside door.

Zebbie answered, "You haven't told me your name, much less identified yourself as a Russian officer. Or shown any authority over what is clearly unoccupied land."

"What? Preposterous! I am Colonel the Count Morinosky of Novy Kiev, of the Viceroy's Imperial Guard. As for my authority, look at the sky around you!" The self-proclaimed colonel drew his pistol, reversed it, and used the butt to pound on the door. "'Open up!' I said."

Zebbie has good temper and calm judgment. Both are likely to slip if anyone abuses Gay Deceiver.

He said softly, "Colonel, your craft on the ground ahead—is there anyone in it?"

"Eh? Of course not. It's a two-seater, as anyone can see. My private scoutabout. Never mind that. Keep quiet and open up."

Zebbie again switched off his microphone. "Gay Deceiver, at command 'Execute' burn one tenth of a second at point of aim, intensity four."

"Gotcha, Boss."

"Colonel, how can you take four prisoners in a two-seater?"

"Simple. You and I will ride in your vehicle. The other members of your party will be hostage for your good behavior and will ride where assigned. You won't see which craft lest you get foolish ideas. My pilot will fly my craft."

"Execute."

The grounded ornithopter began to burn fiercely—but the colonel did not see it. We saw it—but he was looking at Zebbie.

Zebbie said, "Colonel, please stand clear of the door so that I can open it."

"Oh. Very well."

"Colonel! *Look!*" The younger officer, in stepping back, caught sight of the fire—and I have rarely heard such anguish.

Or, an instant later in the colonel's face, such astonishment switching to rage. He attempted to shoot Zebbie—with his hand still gripping the barrel of his pistol. In a moment he realized what he was doing and flipped it to catch it by the grip.

I never saw whether or not he made the catch; Cap'n Zebbie commanded, "Gay Bounce!" and the scene blacked out while the colonel's hand was open for the catch.

Zebbie was saying, "Jake, I lost my temper. I should not have done it; it ruined our last chance to deal with those Russians. But I hope it taught the ruddy snarf not to go around hammering dents into other people's cars."

"Captain, you did *not* ruin our 'last chance'; we never *had* one. You ran into classic Russian xenophobia. The Commies didn't invent that attitude; it goes back at least a thousand years. Read your history." Jacob added, "I'm not sorry you burned his kite. I wish he had to walk home. Regrettably one of his craft will pick him up."

"Jake, if I could afford to—in juice, in time—I would go back and *keep* him from being picked up. Harry them, not let them land. I won't. Hmm— Shall we fall a bit farther and see what they are doing? Before we get on with our interrupted schedule?"

"Uh . . . Captain, may I have a Lomine pill?"

I squealed, "Me, too!"

"Deety, take care of 'em. I'll put her in dive and we'll look."

"Captain, why not use the B, U, G, program?"

"Deety, somebody might be on that spot. Wups! I'm biting air." Cap'n Zebbie leaned us over, placed Barsoom—I mean "Mars"—Mars-10 or whatever—dead ahead. "Should spot flappy birds in few minutes. Jake, how about binoculars?"

Zebbie didn't want them himself while piloting. We passed them around and I spotted an ornithopter, then two more, and passed the glasses to Deety.

"Zebadiah, there is no one where we were parked."

"You're certain?"

"Yessir. The colonel's scoutabout is still burning; there are people near it, nowhere else. That's why I'm certain there is no one where we were. B, U, G, O, U, T is safe."

Zebbie was slow to answer. "How about it, folks? It would be an unnecessary risk. Just one squawk and I'll skip it."

I kept quiet and hoped the others would, too. I don't worry; I'm going to live as long as Atropos permits—meanwhile I intend to enjoy every minute. Zebbie waited, then said, "Here we go. Gay—*Bug Out!*"

XX —*right theory, wrong universe.*

Zeb:

Deety is going to force me to look like a hero because I don't have the guts to let her down. I thought my copilot would veto going back to the scene of the crime; Jake is level-headed about safety precautions. I didn't count on Sharpie; she's unpredictable. But I thought Jake would object.

He didn't. I waited until I was certain that no one was going to get me off the spot...then waited some more...then said sadly, "Here we go," and told Gay to "BUG OUT!"

I expected to be a mushroom cloud. Instead we were parked where we had been and the colonel's craft was burning briskly. (Someday I am going to run that experiment: a transition to attempt to cause two masses to occupy the same space. But I won't be part of the experiment. The Bug-Out program scared me, and I liked the Take-Us-Home program a lot better after we made it two klicks H-above-G instead of parked. Could the Bug-Out program be modified so that Gay sneaked up on her target, checked it by radar, before accepting it? Take it up with Deety, Zeb—stick to what you know!)

The Russians appeared to be slow to notice our return. One ornithopter had grounded not far from the fire; there were several bystanders. I could not see whether or not my erstwhile arresting officer, Colonel Somethingsky, was in the group. I assumed that he was.

Then I was sure: A figure broke loose and headed toward us,

waving a pistol. I said briskly, "Shipmates, is there any reason to hang around?"

I waited a short beat. "Hearing no objection—*Gay Bounce!*"

That black sky looked good. I wondered how Bumpsky was going to explain to the Grand Duke. Brass Hats are notoriously reluctant to believe unlikely stories.

"Did I bounce too quickly? Have you all seen what you wanted to see?"

Only Deety answered. "I was checking that program. I think I see a way to avoid two masses conflicting."

"Keep talking."

"Gay could sneak up on the target, inspect it by radar, accept it and ground, or refuse it and bounce—with no loss of time and with the same execute code. That spot could be knee-deep in Russians and Gay would simply whoosh us to where we are now."

(I *said* to leave it to Deety. You heard me.) "Good idea. Do it. Can't have too many fail-safes."

"I'll reprogram when we stop."

"Correction. I want that fail-safe programmed *now*. I might need your revised program any moment."

"Aye, aye, Captain."

"'Captain *darling*,' if you please. If you must call me 'Captain.' Then review *all* preprograms and debug them, if necessary, with analogous fail-safes. And any new ones in the future. Now— Just put her into glide, headed west, and transit three minima?"

"Or more. Or less. I thought that a spot check every thirty kilometers would be about right for a rapid survey."

"What altitude will we wind up? Assuming I simply aim her at the horizon and transit tangent to the curve."

"Oh. What altitude do you want, Captain—Captain darling? A tangent does little in three minima, just a touch over a hundred meters. Is ten kilometers about right?"

"Ten klicks is fine. I could aim at the horizon, make transition, then at once give the B, O, U, N, C, E order."

"So you could, Zebadiah, but if you will use the horizon as reference and aim eighteen and a half degrees above it— Will your gunsight depress that far?"

"No, but I'll tell Gay. No problem."

"Three minima on that upward slant will place you ten klicks H-above-G and a couple of klicks short of three minima on the curve."

"Plus my present altitude."

"No, no! Visualize the triangle, Zebadiah. It makes no real

difference whether you do this from ten klicks H-above-G, or parked on the ground. Do you want exact figures?"

"You visualize triangles, Deety; that's your department. I've got air bite now; I'm going to head west; I want to see where those ornithopters came from. Meantime work out that new fail-safe." Did it really make no difference whether I started from ten thousand meters or right on deck? Didn't I have to add in— No, of course not . . . but one way was sine and the other way was tan. But which one? Hell, it *didn't* matter; Deety was right. She always is, on figures—but someday I'm going to work it carefully, on paper, with diagrams and tables. "Copilot."

"Captain."

"L axis, transit, three minima."

"Transition, L axis, thirty kilometers—set!"

"Gay Deceiver."

"I'm not at home but you may record a message."

"Change attitude to climb eighteen point five degrees and report."

"Roger Wilco. Climbing. Ten. Twelve. Fourteen. Sixteen. Eighteen. Mark!"

"Execute!"

We were somewhere else with black sky. "Gay, vertical dive. Execute."

"No trouble, Clyde; enjoy the ride."

"Zebadiah, may I talk with Gay while you look over the terrain? To reprogram that fail-safe."

"Sure, go ahead. Jake, want to scan with binox while I eyeball it? I'll warn before transition."

"Zebadiah, I could give her a scouting program, automatic. Skip the verniers, skip the climb order; just an 'execute' code word. Place her on course . . . or I could include course."

"I'll head her manually; the rest is swell—after that fail-safe. What's the code word?"

"'Scout'?"

"Good. Include the 'execute' idea in the code word. Deety, I've decided that I love you for your brain. Not those irrelevant physical attributes."

"Zebadiah, once I've had a bath you may change your mind. I've had a sudden attack of brain fever. You had better program her yourself."

"Mutiny again. I retract and apologize. You smell yummy and should marinate another week. It's not your cortex or your character I love but your carcass—delectable! If it weren't for these seat belts, it would be rape, rape, rape, all the way to the ground. Actually you're sort o' stupid—but *what* a chassis!"

"That's better. Although I'm not stupid."

"You married me. Res ipsa loquitur! Jake, are you spotting anything?"

"Dry hills, Captain. Might as well move on."

"Zebadiah, will you place her in glide and hold a few minutes?"

"Sure. See something you want to check?"

"No, sir. But when we emerged here, we had seventy-three seconds to impact. We've used twenty-one seconds. I'd like a few moments to insert those preprograms."

I overrode manually and started Gay into a stretched glide while I extended her wings. Then I let Deety and Gay talk to each other. Deety had both changes fully worked out; not once did Gay answer, "Null program."

I was about to warn Deety that Gay was not a sailplane when she reported, "All done, Captain. For the 'S' program I added in an alarm for two klicks H-above-G."

"Good idea. So now I head west again and give her that 'S' code word—no 'Execute'?"

"Yessir. 'Cept I'd like to try the revised B, U, G, O, U, T program. It has been less than four minutes since we left. Someone may be in that exact spot."

"Deety, I share your curiosity. But it's like testing a parachute the hard way. Can't we save it until we need it? Then, if there is a glitch, we'll be dead so fast we'll hardly notice it."

Deety said nothing. I waited, then said, "Comment, please."

"No comment, Captain." Deety's answer was toneless.

"Hmm— Science Officer . . . comment, please."

"I have no comment to offer, Captain." (A slight chill?)

"Copilot, I require your advice."

"Uh, if the Captain please. Am I privileged to ask for written orders?"

"Well, I'll be dipped in— Gay Bounce! Is there such a thing as a 'space lawyer'? Like 'sea lawyer'? Jake, in general, anyone, save in the face of the enemy, may demand written orders . . . if he'll risk his career to perpetuate evidence for the court-martial he knows will follow. Did it myself once and saved my neck and cost my temporary boss fifty numbers—and I wound up senior to him and he resigned.

"But a second-in-command is in a special position; it is his *duty* to advise his C.O., even if the C.O. doesn't ask for advice. So I don't see how you can demand written orders on a point already one of your duties. But I won't make an issue of it. I'll direct the Astrogator to log your request, then I can dictate my reply into the log. Then I am going to ground this go-buggy and turn command over to you. Maybe you'll have more luck chairing this debating society than I have had. I wish you luck—you'll need it!"

"But, Captain, I did not ask for written orders."

"Eh?" I thought back. He hadn't, quite. "It sounded as if you were about to."

"I was stalling. I *must* advise you to follow the prudent course. Unofficially, I prefer to risk the test. But I should not have stalled. I'm sorry that my intransigence caused you to consider relinquishing command."

"I didn't just consider it; I *have*. Resignation effective the first time we ground. You've bought it, Jake."

"Captain—"

"Yes, Deety?"

"You are correct; the test I suggested is useless, and could be fatal. I should *not* have asked for it. I'm sorry . . . sir."

"Me, too! I felt you were being too strict with Deety. But you weren't; you were taking care of us, as you always do, Zebbie. *Captain* Zebbie. Of *course* you shouldn't make a risky test we don't need."

I said, "Anyone anything to add?" No one spoke up, so I added, "I'm heading west," and did so. "Gay Deceiver—*Bug Out!*"

Black sky above us; that "dead sea bottom" far below. . . . I remarked, "Looks as if a Russian, or one of their flappy craft, is in our parking spot. Deety, your revised program worked perfectly."

"But, Zebadiah—*why did you risk it?*" She sounded terribly distressed.

"Because all of you wanted to, despite what you said later. Because it's my last chance to make such a decision." I added, "Jake, I'm going to tilt her over. Grab the binox and see if you can identify where we were parked. If that fire is smoking, you can use it for reference."

"But, Captain, I'm *not* taking command. I won't accept it."

"Pipe down and carry out your orders! It's this damned yack-yack and endless argument that's giving me ulcers. If you won't accept command, then it's up for grabs. But *not* me! Oh, I'll pilot as the new C.O. orders. But I won't *command*. Deety, how long did Gay pause to make that radar check? At what height?"

"H-above-G was half a klick. Duration I don't know but I can retrieve it. Darling—Captain! You're not *really* going to quit commanding us?"

"Deety, I don't make threats. Pipe down and retrieve that duration. Jake, what do you see?"

"I've located the fire. Several ornithopters are on the ground. My guess places one of them about where we were parked. Captain, I advise not dropping lower."

"Advice noted. Deety, how about that duration?" I didn't know how to ask for it myself, not having written the program.

Deety retrieved it smoothly: 0.071 seconds—call it a fifteenth of a second. Radar is not instantaneous; Gay had to stop and sweep that spot long enough for a "picture" to form in her gizzards, to tell her whether or not she could park there. A fifteenth of a second is loads of time for the human eye. I hoped that Colonel Frimpsky had been watching when Gay popped up and blinked out.

"Five klicks H-above-G, Captain."

"Thanks, Jake." The board showed dive rate—straight down!— of over seven hundred kilometers per hour, and increasing so fast that the units figure was an unreadable blur, and the tens place next to it was blinking one higher almost by the second.

Most carefully I eased her out of dive, and gently, slowly opened her wings part way for more lift as she slowed, while making a wide clockwise sweep to the east—slowed her *dive*, that is, not her speed through the air. When I had completed that sweep, and straightened out headed for that column of smoke on course west, I was making over eight hundred kilometers per hour in unpowered glide and *still* had almost a klick H-above-G I could turn into greater speed.

Not that I needed it— I had satisfied myself by eye of what I had been certain of by theory: an ornithopter is slow.

Jake said worriedly, "May I ask the Captain his plans?"

"I'm going to give Colonel Pistolsky something to remember us by! Gay Deceiver."

"Still aboard, Boss."

I kept my eye on the flappy birds still in the air while I let Gay fly herself. Those silly contraptions could not catch us but there was always a chance that a pilot might dodge the wrong way.

Most of them seemed anxious to be elsewhere; they were lumbering aside right and left. I looked at the smoke—dead ahead— and saw what I had not noticed before: an ornithopter beyond the smoke.

Jake gasped but said nothing. We were on collision course

closing at about 900 kms/hr, most of it ours. Suicide pilot? Idiot? Panicked and frozen?

I let him get within one klick of us, which brought us almost to the smoke and near the deck, about 200 meters H-above-G—and I yelped, "Scout!"

Yes, Deety is a careful programmer; the sky was black, we were ten klicks H-above-G, and so far as I could tell, the same barren hills under us that we had left five minutes earlier—and I was feeling cocky. My sole regret was that I would not hear Colonel Snarfsky try to explain to the Grand Duke the "ghost" craft now used by "British spies."

Did Russian nobility practice "honorable hara-kiri"? Perhaps the loaded-pistol symbol? You know that one: The officer in disgrace returns to his quarters and finds that someone has thoughtfully loaded his pistol and placed it on his desk . . . thereby saving the regiment the scandal of a court.

I didn't want the bliffy dead but busted to buck private. With time to reflect on politeness and international protocol while he cleaned stables.

I checked our heading, found that we were still pointed west. "Gay Deceiver, *Scout!*"

Black sky again, the same depressing landscape— "Copilot, is it worthwhile to tilt down for a better look? That either takes juice—not much but some—or it takes time to drop far enough to bite air and do it with elevons. We can't afford to waste either time or juice."

"Captain, I don't think this area is worth scouting."

"Careful of that participle; better say 'exploring.'"

"Captain, may I say something?"

"Deety, if you are speaking as Astrogator, you not only may but must."

"I could reprogram to put us lower if I knew what altitude was just high enough to let you use elevons. Conserve both time and juice, I mean."

"It seems to be about eight klicks H-above-G, usually. Hard to say since we don't have a sea-level."

"Shall I change angle to arrive at eight <u>klicks</u> H-above-G?"

"How long does it take us to fall two klicks when we arrive?"

She barely hesitated. "Thirty-two and a half seconds."

"Only half a minute? Seems longer."

"Three-two point six seconds, Captain, if this planet has the same surface gravity as Mars in our own universe—three-seven-six centimeters per second squared. I've been using it and haven't run into discrepancies. But I don't see how this planet holds so much atmosphere when Mars—*our* Mars—has so little."

"This universe may not have the same laws as ours. Ask your father. He's in charge of universes."

"Yes, sir. Shall I revise the program?"

"Deety, never monkey with a system that is working well enough—First Corollary of Murphy's Law. If it is an area as unattractive as this, we'll simply get out. If it has possibilities, half a minute isn't too long to wait, and the additional height will give us a better idea of the whole area. Gay Deceiver, *Scout!*"

We all gasped. Thirty kilometers and those barren hills were gone; the ground was green and fairly level—and a *river* was in sight. Or a canal.

"Oh, boy! Copilot, don't let me waste juice—be firm with me. Deety, count seconds. Everybody eyeball his sector, report anything interesting."

Deety started chanting ". . . thirteen . . . . . fourteen . . . . . fifteen—" and each second felt like ten. I took my hands off the controls to keep from temptation. That was either a canal or a stream that had been straightened, revetted, and maintained for years, maybe eons. Professor Lowell had been right—right theory, wrong universe.

"Deety, how far is the horizon?"

"—seventeen—about two hundred fifty klicks—twenty—"

I placed my hands gently on the controls. "Hon, that's the first time you've ever used the word 'about' with reference to a number."

"—twenty-four—insufficient data!—twenty-six—"

"You can stop counting; I felt a quiver." I put a soft nose-down pressure on the elevons and decided to leave her wings spread; we might want to stretch this one. "Insufficient data?"

"Zebadiah, it was changing steadily and you had me counting seconds. Horizon distance at ten klicks height above ground should be within one percent of two hundred and seventy kilometers. That assumes that this planet is a perfect sphere and that it is exactly like Mars in our universe—neither is true. It ignores refraction effects, tricky even at home—and unknown to me here. I treated it as geometry, length of tangent for an angle of four degrees thirty-seven minutes."

"Four and half degrees? Where in the world did you get that figure?"

"Oh! Sorry, dear, I skipped about six steps. On Earth one nautical mile is one minute of arc—check?"

"Yes. Subject to minor reservations. With a sextant, or in dead reckoning, or on a chart, a mile is a minute, a minute is a mile. Makes it simple. Otherwise we would be saying a minute is one thousand eight hundred fifty-three meters and the arithmetic would get hairy."

"One-eight-five-three point one-eight-seven-seven-oh-five plus," she corrected me. "*Very* hairy. Best not convert to MKS until the last step. But, Zebadiah, there is a simpler relation here. One minute of arc equals one kilometer, near enough not to matter. So I treated H-above-G, ten klicks, as a versine, applied the haversine rule and got four degrees thirty-seven minutes or two hundred seventy-seven kilometers to the theoretical horizon. You see?"

"I see everything but how you hide haversine tables in a jump suit. Me, I hide 'em in Gay . . . and make her do the work." Yes, I could nose her over now—easy does it, boy.

"Well, I didn't, exactly. I calculated it, but I did it the easy way: Naperian logarithms and angles in radians, then converted back to degrees to show the relationship to kilometers on the ground."

"That's 'the easy way'?"

"It is for *me*, sir!"

"If you're quivering your chin, stop it. I told you it was your luscious body, not your brain. Most *idiots-savants* are homely and can't do anything but their one trick. But you're an adequate cook, as well."

That got me a stony silence. I kept easing her nose down. "Time for binox, Jake."

"Aye aye, sir. Captain, I am required to advise you. With that last remark to the Astrogator you risked your life."

"Are you implying that Deety is an *in*adequate cook? Why, Jake!"

Hilda interrupted. "She's a gourmet cook!"

"I know she is, Sharpie . . . but I don't like to say it where Gay can hear—Gay can't cook. Nor has she Deety's other talent which 'tis death to hide. Jake, that's a settlement below."

"Of sorts: A one-church village."

"Do you see ornithopters? Anything that could give us trouble?"

"Depends. Are you interested in church architecture?"

"Jake, this is no time for a cultural chat."

"I'm required to advise you, sir. This church has towers, something like minarets topped off with onion-shaped structures."

"Russian Orthodox!"

Hilda said that. I said nothing. I eased Gay's nose up to level flight, lined her up with what I thought was downstream, and snapped, "Gay, *Scout!*"

The canal was still in sight, almost under us and stretching over the horizon. I was almost lined up with it. "Gay, *Scout!*

"Anybody see that settlement that was almost ahead before this last transition? Report."

"Captain Zebbie, it's much closer now but on this side."

"I see. Or don't. Jake isn't transparent."

"Captain, the city—quite large—is about a forty-five-degree slant down to starboard, not in sight from your seat."

"If forty-five degrees is a close guess, a minimum transition on that bearing should place us over the city."

"Captain, I advise against it," Jake told me.

"Reasons, please."

"This is a large city that might be well defended. Their orni-thopters look odd and ineffective but we must assume they have spaceships as good or better than ours or the Tsar could not have a colony here. This causes me to suspect that they may have smart missiles. Or weapons utterly strange. I would rather check for onion towers from a distance. And not stay long in one place— I think we've been here too long. I'm jumpy."

"I'm not"—my sixth sense was not jabbing me—"but set ver-niers for a minimum transition along L axis, then execute at will. No need to be a slow fat target."

"One minimum, L axis—*set!*"

Suddenly my guardian angel goosed me. "Execute!"

I noticed the transition principally because Gay was now live under my hand—air bite. Perhaps she had not been quite level. I turned her nose down to gather maneuvering speed unpowered, then did a skew turn—and yelped, "Gay *Bounce!*" having seen all that I wanted to see: an expanding cloud. Atomic? I think not. Lethal? *You* test it; I'm satisfied.

I told Gay to bounce three more times, placing us a bit less than fifty klicks above ground. Then I spent a trifle of power to nose her over. "Jake, use the binox to see how far this valley runs, whether it is all cultivated, whether it has more settlements. We are *not* going to get close enough to look for onion spires; that last shot was unfriendly. Rude. Impetuous. Or am I prejudiced? Science Officer? Le mot juste, s'il vous plait."

"Nye kultoorni."

"I remember that one! Makes Russians turn green. What does it mean? How did you happen to know it, Sharpie?"

"Means what it sounds like: 'uncultured.' I didn't just 'happen,' Cap'n Zebbie; I know Russian."

I was flabbergasted. "Why didn't you *say* so?"

"You didn't ask me."

"Sharpie, if you handled the negotiations, we might not have had trouble."

"Zebbie, if you'll believe that, you'll believe anything. He was calling you a spy and insulting you while the palaver was still in French. I thought it might be advantageous if they thought none of us knew Russian. They might spill something."

"Did they?"

"No. The colonel was coaching his pilot in how to be arrogant. Then you told them to halt, in French, and no more Russian was spoken save for meaningless side remarks. Zebbie, when they tried to shoot us down just now, would they have refrained had they known that I had studied Russian?"

"Mmm— Sharpie, I should know better than to argue with you. I'm going to vote for you for captain."

"Oh, *No!*"

"Oh, Yes. Copilot, I'm going to assume that everything this side of the hills and involved with this watercourse—courses—twin canals—is New Russia and that honorary Englishmen—us!—aren't safe here. So I'm going to look for the British colony. It may turn out that they won't like us, either. But the British are strong on protocol; we'll have a chance to speak our piece. They may hang us but they'll give us a trial, with wigs and robes and rules of evidence and counsel who will fight for us." I hesitated. "One hitch. Colonel Snotsky said there was no such country as the United States of America and I had the impression that he believed it."

Sharpie said, "He *did* believe it, Cap'n Zebbie. I caught some side chatter. I think we must assume that, in this universe, there was no American Revolution."

"So I concluded. Should we all be from the East Coast? I have a hunch that the West Coast may be part Russian, part Spanish—but not British. Where are we from? Baltimore, maybe? Philadelphia? Suggestions?"

Sharpie said, "I have a suggestion, Cap'n Zebbie."

"Science Officer, I like your suggestions."

"You won't like this one. When all else fails, tell the truth."

XXI —three seconds is a long time—

Deety:
Zebadiah is convinced that I can program anything. Usually
I can, given a large and flexible computer—but my husband
expects me to manage it with Gay Deceiver and Gay is not big.
She started life as an autopilot and is one, mostly.

But Gay is sweet-tempered and we both want to please him.

While he and my father were looking over the area that we
thought of as "Russian Valley" or "New Russia," he asked me to
work up a program to locate the British colony in minimum time,
if it were in daylight. If not, then we would sleep near the sunrise
line, and find it on the new daylight side.

I thought of bouncing out about a thousand kilometers and
searching for probable areas by color. Then I realized that I didn't
know that much about this planet. "Dead sea bottoms" from space
looked like farm land.

At last I recalled something Zebadiah had suggested yesterday—no, *today!* less than two hours ago. (So much had happened
that my sense of time played tricks. It was still accurate—but I
had to *think* instead of just knowing.)

Random numbers— Gay had plenty of them. Random numbers
are to a computer what free will is to a human being.

I defined a locus for Gay: nothing east of where we were,
nothing in "Russian Valley," nothing on the dark side, nothing
north of 45°, nothing south of 45° south. Yesterday I could not
have told her the latter; but Mars has a good spin, one a gyrocompass can read. While we slept, Gay had noted that her gyrocompass did not have its axis parallel to that of this strange planet
and had precessed it until it did.

Inside that locus I told Gay to take a Drunkard's Walk, any
jumps that suited her, a three-second pause at each vertex, and,

if one of us yelled *"Bingo!"* display latitude, longitude, and Greenwich, and log all three, so we could find it again.

Oh, yes—she was to pause that three seconds exactly one minimum H-above-G at each vertex.

I told her to run the program for one hour . . . but that any of us could yell "Stop!" and then say "Continue" and that would be time-out, not part of the hour. But I warned my shipmates that yelling *"Stop!"* not only slowed things but also gave Russians (or British or anybody) a chance to shoot at us. I emphasized that three seconds is a *long* time (most people don't know it).

One hour—

Three seconds for each check—

Twelve hundred random spot checks—

This is not a "space-filling" curve. But it should locate where the British were most thickly settled. If one hour did not do it, ten hours certainly would.

Without Gay, without her ability to do a Drunkard's Walk, we could have searched that planet for a lifetime, and never found either colony. It took the entire human race (of our universe) thirty centuries to search Terra . . . and many spots were missing until they could be photographed from space.

My husband said, "Let's get this straight." He bounced us four minima. "These subprograms— Gay, are you listening?"

"Of course. Are you?"

"Gay, go to sleep."

"Roger and out, Boss."

"Deety, I want to make sure of these subprograms but couldn't use code words while she was awake. I—"

"Excuse me, Zebadiah, but you can. She will ignore code words for subprograms except while the general program is running. The code for the general program is unusual and requires the execution command, so it can't be started by accident. You can wake Gay. We need her on some points."

"You're a smart girl, Deety."

"I'll bet you tell that to all adequate cooks, Boss."

"Ouch!"

"Captain, it is not difficult to program a computer to supervise cooking machines. The software sold under the trademark 'Cordon Bleu' is reputed to be excellent. Before you wake Gay, would you answer a hypothetical question concerning computers and cooking?"

"Captain!"

"Copilot?"

"I advise against permitting the Astrogator to discuss side issues—such as cooking—while we have this problem facing us."

"Thank you, Copilot. Astrogator, what was your hypothetical question?"

Pop had been careful not to interfere between Zebadiah and me. But his advice from copilot to captain was intended for *my* ears—he was telling me to *shut up,* and I suddenly heard Jane saying, "Deety, anytime a wife thinks she has won an argument, she has lost it."

I'm not Jane, I'm Deety. I get my temper from my father. I'm not as quick to flare up as he is, but I do have his tendency to nurse a grievance. Zebadiah is sometimes a tease and knows how to get my goat.

But Pop was telling me: *"Drop it, Deety!"*

Maybe Zebadiah was right—too much argument, too much discussion, too much "sewing circle & debating society." We were all intensely interested as we were all in the same peril . . . *but how much tougher is it to be captain rather than one of the crew?* Twice? Ten times?

I didn't know. Was my husband cracking under the pressure? "Getting ulcers"?

Was *I* adding to his burden?

I didn't have to stop to think this through; it was preprogrammed below the conscious level; Pop pushed the "execute" button and the answers spilled out. I answered my husband at once,

"What hypocritical question, sir?"

"You said, 'hypothetical.' Something about computers and cooking."

"Captain, my mind has gone blank. Perhaps we had better get on with the job before I forget how it works."

"Deety, you wouldn't fib to your poor old broken-down husband?"

"Sir, when my husband is poor and old and broken-down, I will not fib to him."

"Hmm— If I hadn't already promised my support to Hilda, I would vote for you for captain."

Aunt Hilda cut in: "Zebbie, I release you! I'm not a candidate."

"No, Sharpie, once having promised political support an honorable man *never* welches. So it's all right for Gay to listen in?"

"Certainly, sir. For display I must have her. Hello, Gay."

"Hi, Deety."

"Display dayside, globe." At once Gay's largest screen showed the western hemisphere of Earth, *our* Earth in *our* universe—

Terra. Early afternoon at Snug Harbor? Yes, the clock in my head said so and GMT on the instrument board read 20:23:07. Good heavens, it had been only twenty hours since my husband and my father had killed the fake "ranger." How can a lifetime be crowded into less than a day? Despite the clock in my head it seemed *years* since I had walked down to our pool, a touch tiddly and hanging onto my bridegroom for support.

"Display meridians parallels. Subtract geographical features." Gay did so. "From program coded 'A Tramp Abroad' display locus."

Gay used orthographic projection, so the 45th parallels were straight lines. Since I had told her to display dayside, these two bright lines ran to the left edge of the display, that being the sunrise line. But the right edge of the locus was an irregular line running southwest. "Add display Russian Valley."

To the right of the locus and touching it, Gay displayed as solid brightness a very long and quite wide blotch. "Subtract Russian Valley." The area we had sketchily explored disappeared.

"Deety," my husband asked, "how is Gay doing this? Her perms have no reference points for Mars—not even Mars of our own universe."

"Oh. Gay, display 'Touchdown.'"

"Null program."

"Mmm, yes, that's right; the Sun has just set where we were parked. Zebadiah, shall I have her rotate the globe enough to show it? All she would show would be a bright spot almost on the equator. I have defined the spot where we grounded as Zero meridian—Greenwich for Mars. *This* Mars."

"And zero parallel? An arbitrary equator?"

"Oh, no, no! While we slept Gay adjusted her gyrocompass to match this planet. Which gave her true north and latitude. She already knows the radius and curvature of Mars—I started to tell her and found she had retrieved it from her perms. Aerospace Almanac?"

"I suppose so. But we discussed Mars' diameter last night while Gay was awake. Both you and Hilda knew it; Jake and I did not."

As I remembered it, Aunt Hilda spoke up—then Pop kept quiet. If Pop wanted to sit back and be proud of Aunt Hilda's encyclopedic memory that was all right with me. If my husband has a flaw, it is that he has trouble believing that females have brains . . . probably because he is so intensely interested in the other end. I went on with my lecture:

"Once I start Gay, she will say and record nothing unless ordered. She will make random transitions inside that locus until someone yells 'Bingo!' She won't slow down even then. She will place a bright point on the map at that latitude and longitude, record both latitude and longitude, and the exact time. She will display the Bingo time, too, for one second. If you want to retrieve that Bingo, you had better jot down that time—to the second. Because she'll be doing twenty jumps each minute. Don't worry about the hour, just the minute and the second. Oh, you could still retrieve it if you had the minute right, as I can ask her to run through all Bingoes in a given minute. Can't be more than twenty and your Bingo might be the only one.

"When we've done one hour of this, that map could, at most, have twelve hundred dots on it—but may have only a few—or none. If they are clustered, I'll reduce the locus and we'll run it again. If not, we can sleep and eat and do it for the other day side, the one twelve hours away. Either way, Gay will find the British—and we'll be safe."

"I hope you're right. Ever heard of the Opium Wars, Deety?"

"Yes, Captain. Sir, every nation is capable of atrocities, including our own. But the British have a tradition of decent behavior no matter what blemishes there are."

"Sorry. Why a one-hour program?"

"We may have to shorten it. A decision every three seconds for sixty minutes may be too tiring. If we start showing a marked hot spot sooner than that, we can shorten the first run and reduce the locus. We'll have to try it and see. But I feel certain that a one-hour run, a short rest, then another one-hour run, will locate the British if they are now on the day side."

"Deety, what do you define as 'Bingo'?"

"Anything that suggests human settlement. Buildings. Roads. Cultivated fields. Walls, fences, dams, aircraft, vehicles— But it is not 'Bingo' just because it looks interesting. Although it might be 'Stop!'"

"What's the difference?"

"'Stop' does *not* tell Gay to record or to display. For that you must add 'Bingo.' 'Stop' is for anything you want to look at more than three seconds. Maybe it looks promising and a few seconds more will let you decide. But please, everyone! There should not be more than a dozen calls for 'Stop!' in the hour. Any more questions?"

We started. Hilda gave the first Bingo. I saw it, too—farm buildings. Aunt Hilda is faster than I. I almost broke my own injunction; I had to bite down on "Stop!" The temptation to take a longer look was almost overpowering.

All of us made mistakes—but none serious. Hilda racked up the most Bingoes and Zebadiah the fewest—but I'm fairly certain that my husband was "cheating" by waiting to give Pop or me first crack at it. (He would not be competing with Aunt Hilda; port-forward and starboard-after seats have little overlapping coverage.)

I thought it would be tedious; instead it was exciting—but dreadfully tiring. Slowly, less than one a minute, bright dots appeared on the display. I saw with disappointment that most Bingoes were clustered adjacent to the irregular margin marking Russian territory. It seemed probable that these marked Russian territory, so very probable that it hardly seemed worthwhile to check for onion spires.

Once my husband called "Stop" and then "Bingo" at a point north and far west, at least fifteen hundred kilometers from the nearest Bingo light. I noted the time—Greenwich 21:16:51—then tried to figure out why Zebadiah had stopped us. It was pretty country, green hills and lightly wooded and I spotted a wild stream, not a canal. But I saw no buildings or anything suggesting settlement.

Zebadiah wrote something on his knee pad, then said, "Continue." I was itching to ask why he had stopped, but when a decision must be made every three seconds there is no time to chat.

When the hour was nearly up, a single Bingo light in the far west that had been shining since the first five minutes was joined by another when Hilda scored another Bingo and two minutes later Pop said "Bingo!" and we had an equilateral triangle twenty kilometers on a side. I noted the time most carefully—then told myself not to be disappointed if inspection showed onion towers; we still had a hemisphere to go.

I decided to believe in that British colony the way one has to believe *hard* in fairies to save Tinker Bell's life. If there were no British colony, we might have to risk Earth-without-a-J. Gay Deceiver was a lovely car but as a spaceship she had shortcomings. No plumbing. Air for about four hours and no way to recycle. No plumbing. Limited food storage. No plumbing. No comfortable way to sleep in her. No plumbing.

But she had talents no other spaceship had. Her shortcomings (according to my father and husband) could be corrected at any modern machine shop. But in the meantime we did not have even an outhouse behind the barn.

At last Gay stopped, continued to display, and announced, "One hour of 'A Tramp Abroad' completed. Instructions, please."

"Gay, Bounce," said Zebadiah. "Deety, I don't think we've nailed down the piece The Sun Never Sets On. But this dense cluster here to the right— Too close to the Little Father's little children. Eh?"

"Yes, Zebadiah, I should tell Gay to trim the locus on the east to eliminate the clustered lights, and now we can add almost nine hundred kilometers on the west, to the present sunrise line. Gay can rotate the display to show the added area. I suspect that one more hour will fill in the picture sufficiently."

"Maybe even less. You were right; three seconds is not only a long time; it is excessively long. Isn't two seconds enough? Can you change that without starting from scratch?"

"Yes to both, Captain."

"Good. You can add thirty degrees on the west instead of fifteen. Because we are going to kill an hour—stretch our legs, eat a snack . . . and I for one want to find a bush. How do I tell Gay to return to a particular Bingo? Or will that mess up your program?"

"Not a bit. Tell her to return to Bingo such-and-such, stating the time."

I was unsurprised when he said, "Gay, return to Bingo Greenwich twenty-one sixteen fifty-one."

It was indeed a pretty stream. Zebadiah said happily, "That beats burning juice. Who sees a clearing close to that creek, big enough for Gay? Hover and squat, I mean; I don't dare make a glide landing, dead stick—the old girl is loaded."

"Zebbie, I'm sober as you are!"

"Don't boast about it, Sharpie. I think I see a spot. Close your eyes; I'm going to."

I almost wish I had.

Zebadiah came in on a long glide, everything set for maximum lift—but no power. I kept waiting for that vibration that meant that Gay was alive and roaring . . . and waited . . . and waited—

He said, "Gay—" and I thought that he was going to tell her to turn herself on. No. We actually dropped below the level of that bank.

Then he suddenly switched on power by hand but in *reverse*—flipped us up on that bank; we stalled, and dropped perhaps a meter—we just *barely* missed that bank.

I didn't say anything. Aunt Hilda was whispering, "Hail Mary Mother of God Om Mani Padme Hum There is No God but God and Mahomet is His Prophet—" then some language I did not know but it sounded very sincere.

Pop said, "Son, do you always cut it that fine?"

"I saw a man do it that way when he had to; I've always wondered if I could. But what you didn't know was—Gay, are you listening?"

"Sure thing, Boss. You alerted me. Where's the riot?"

"You're a smart girl, Gay."

"Then why am I pushing this baby carriage?"

"Gay, go to sleep."

"Sleepy time. Roger and out, Boss."

"Jake, what you didn't know was that I had my cheeks puffed to say B, O, U, N, C, E, explosively. Your gadget has made Gay's reflexes so fast that I knew I could come within a split second of disaster and she would get us out. I wasn't cutting didoes. Look at that meter. Seventy-four percent of capacity. I don't know how many landings I'm going to have to make on that much juice."

"Captain, it was brilliant. Even though it almost scared it out of me."

"Wrong honorific, *Captain*. I'm the pilot going off duty. We're landed; my resignation is effective; you're holding the sack."

"Zeb, I told you that I would *not* be captain."

"You can't help it; you *are*. The second-in-command takes command when the captain dies, or goes over the hill—or quits. Jake, you can cut your throat, or desert, or go on the binnacle list, or take other actions—but you can't say you are not captain, when you *are*—Captain!"

"If you can resign, I can resign!"

"Obviously. To the Astrogator, she being next in line of command."

"Deety, I resign! Captain Deety, I mean."

"Pop, you can't do this to me! I'll— I'll—" I shut up because I didn't know what to do. Then I did. "*I* resign . . . Captain Hilda."

"What? Why, that's silly, Deety. A medical officer is not in line of command. But if 'medical officer' is a joke and 'science officer,' too, then I'm a passenger and still not in line of command."

My husband said, "Sharpie, you have the qualifications the rest of us have. You can drive a duo—"

"Suddenly I've forgotten how."

"—but that's not necessary. Mature judgment and the support of your crew are the only requirements, as we are millions of miles and several universes from licenses and such. You have my support; I think you have it from the rest. Jake?"

"Me? Of course!"

"Deety?"

"Captain Hilda knows she has my support," I agreed. "I was first to call her 'Captain.'"

Aunt Hilda said, "Deety, I've just resigned."

"Oh, no, you haven't anybody to resign to!" I'm afraid I was shrill.

"I resign to the Great Spirit Manitou. Or to you, Zebbie, and it comes around in a circle and you are captain again . . . as you should be."

"Oh, no, Sharpie. I've stood my watch; it's somebody else's turn. Now that you have resigned, we have no organization. If you think you've stuck me with it, think again. You have simply picked an unusual way to homestead on this spot. In the meantime, while nobody is in charge, I hope that you all are getting both ears and a belly full of what got me disgusted. Yack yack yack; argue, fuss, and jabber—a cross between a Hyde Park open forum and a high school debating society."

Aunt Hilda said, in sober surprise, "Why, Zebbie, you almost sound vindictive."

"Mrs. Burroughs, it is possible that you have hit upon the right word. I have taken a lot of guff . . . and quite a bit of it has been from you."

I haven't seen Aunt Hilda look so distressed since Mama Jane died. "I am *very* sorry, Zebbie. I had not realized that my conduct had displeased you so. I did not intend it so, ever. I am aware— constantly!—that you have saved our—*my*—life five distinct times . . . as well as continuously by your leadership. I'm as grateful as my nature permits—a giant amount, even though you consider me a shallow person. But one can't show deepest gratitude every instant, just as one cannot remain in orgasm continuously; some emotions are too strong to stay always at peak."

She sighed, and tears rolled down her face. "Zebbie, will you let me try again? I'll quit being a Smart Aleck. It will be a hard habit to break; I've been one for years—my defense mechanism. But I *will* break it."

"Don't be so tragic, Hilda," Zebadiah said gently. "You know I love you . . . despite your little ways."

"Oh, I know you do!—you big ugly giant. Will you come back to us? Be our captain again?"

"Hilda, I've never left. I'll go right on doing the things I know how to do or can learn. And as I'm told. But I *won't* be captain."

"Oh, dear!"

"It's not tragic. We simply elect a new C.O."

My father picked this moment to get hairy. "Zeb, you're being pretty damned stiff-necked and self-righteous with Hilda. *I* don't think she has misbehaved."

"Jake, you are in no position to judge. First, because she's your bride. Second, because *you* haven't been sitting in the worry seat; *I* have. And *you* have supplied some of the worst guff yourself."

"I was not aware of it . . . Captain."

"You're doing it now . . . by calling me 'Captain' when I'm not. But do you recall a couple of hours ago when I asked my second-in-command for advice—and got some back chat about 'written orders'?"

"Mmm . . . I was out of line. Yes, sir."

"Do you want other examples?"

"No. No, I stipulate that there are others. I understand your point, sir." Pop gave a wry smile. "Well, I'm glad Deety hasn't given you trouble."

"On the contrary, she has given me the most."

I had been upset—I had never really believed that Zebadiah would resign. But now I was shocked and bewildered and hurt. "Zebadiah, what have I *done?*"

"The same sort of nonsense as the other two . . . but harder for me because I'm married to you."

"But— But *what?*"

"I'll tell you in private."

"It's all right for Pop and Aunt Hilda to hear."

"Not with *me*. We can share our joys with others but difficulties between us we settle in private."

My nose was stuffy and I was blinking back tears. "But I must *know.*"

"Dejah Thoris, you can list the incidents if you choose to be honest with yourself. You have perfect memory and it all took place in the last twenty-four hours."

He turned his face away from me. "One thing I must urge *before* we choose a captain. I let myself be wheedled and bullied into surrendering authority on the ground. That was a *bad* mistake. A sea captain is still captain when his ship is anchored. Whoever becomes captain should profit by my mistake and not relinquish *any* authority merely because Gay is grounded. She can relax the rules according to the situation. But *the captain* must decide. The situation can be *more* dangerous on the ground than in air or in space. As it was today when the Russians showed up. Simply grounding must not be: 'School's out! Now we can play!'"

"I'm sorry, Zebbie."

"Hilda, I was more at fault than you. I wanted to be free of responsibility. I let myself be talked into it, then my brain went on vacation. Take that 'practice hike.' I don't recall who suggested it—"

"I did," said my father.

"Maybe you did, Jake; but we all climbed on the bandwagon. We were about to run off like a bunch of Scouts with no Scoutmaster. If we had started as quickly as we had expected to, where would we be now? In a Russian jail? Or dead? Oh, I'm not giving myself high marks; one reason I've resigned is that I haven't handled it well. Planning to leave Gay Deceiver and everything we own unguarded while we made walkabout—good God! If I had felt the weight of command I would never have considered it."

Zebadiah made a sour face, then looked at my father. "Jake, you're eldest. Why don't you take the gavel while we pick a new C.O.? I so move."

"Second!"

"Question!"

"White ballot!"

"*What* gavel? I'll bet there isn't a gavel on this planet." In a moment Father quit stalling. We all voted, using a page from Zebadiah's notebook torn in four. They were folded and handed to me and I was required to declare the vote. So I did:

Zeb
Zebadiah
Zebbie
Sharpie

Zebadiah reached back, got the ballots from me, handed back the one that meant "Aunt Hilda," took the other three and tore them into small pieces. "Apparently you did not understand me. I've *stood* my watch; someone else must take it—or we'll park on this bank until we die of old age. Sharpie seems to have an overwhelming lead—is she elected? Or do we ballot again?"

We balloted again:

Sharpie
Jacob

Jacob

Hilda

"A tie," Father said. "Shall we invite Gay to vote?"

"Shut up and deal the cards."

Sharpie

Deety

Deety

Hilda

"Hey!" I protested. "Who switched?" (I certainly didn't vote for *me*.)

Sharpie

Hilda

Zebbie

Hilda

"One spoiled ballot," said my husband. "A non-candidate. Will you confirm that, Mr. Chairman?"

"Yes," Pop agreed. "My dear...Captain Hilda. You are elected without a dissenting vote."

Aunt Hilda looked as if she might cry again. "You're a bunch of stinkers!"

"So we are," agreed my husband, "But we are *your* stinkers, Captain Hilda."

That got him a wan smile. "Guess maybe. Well, I'll *try*."

"We'll all try," said Pop.

"And we'll all help," said my husband.

"Sure we will!" I said, and meant it.

Pop said, "If you will excuse me? I've been anxious to find a handy bush since before this started." He started to get out.

"Just a moment!"

"Eh? Yes, my dear? Captain."

"No one is to seek out a bush without an armed guard. Not more—and not less—than two people are to leave the car's vicinity at one time. Jacob, if your need is urgent, you must ask Zebbie to hurry—I want the guard to carry both rifle and pistol."

I think it worked out that Pop got the use of a bush last—and must have been about to burst his bladder. Later I overheard Pop say, "Son, you've read Aesop's Fables?"

"Certainly."

"Does anything remind you of King Log and King Stork?"

XXII "'From each according to his ability, to each according to his needs.'"

Hilda:

I could tell from the first ballot that Zebbie was determined to make me take a turn as captain. Once I realized that, I decided to be captain—let them get sick of me and anxious to have Zebbie back.

Then suddenly I *was* captain—and it's different. I did not ever again think of trying to make them sick of me; I just started to worry. And *try*.

First my husband wanted to find a bush for the obvious reason—and I suddenly realized that a banth might get him. Not a Barsoomian banth but whatever this planet held in dangerous carnivores.

So I ordered armed guards. With rules about not getting separated. It was a nuisance but I was firm . . . and knew at last what a crushing load there had been on Zebbie.

But one thing I could improve: Arrange for us to sleep inside the car.

The space back of the bulkhead behind the rear seats was not organized. We had about six hours till sundown (having gained on the Sun in going west), so I had *everything* in that space pulled out.

Space enough for Zebbie and Deety, on his sleeping bag opened out, blankets over them. Jacob and I? The piloting chairs we moved forward all the set screws would allow, laid them back almost flat and padded the cracks with pillows, and, to support our legs, the cushions from the rear seats were placed on boxes we would otherwise discard once I had the car organized. It wasn't

the best bed but low gravity and my cuddlesome husband made
it a most attractive one.

Baths— In the stream and *cold!* Same rules as for bushes:
armed guards. Soap thoroughly on the bank, get in and rinse *fast,*
bounce out and towel till you glowed. Primitive? *Luxurious!*

This did not go smoothly. Take the "handy bush" problem. I
did not have to be told that a latrine should be downstream or that
our shovel should be carried every time without fail—rules for
a clean camp are as old as the Old Testament.

But my first order called for no more than two and no less than
two to leave the car at any time, and one must be armed—the
other rifle and pistol must guard Gay.

I blurted out that order when the truth landed on me like a load
of bricks that *I*, the runt who had never grown up, was now
responsible for the lives of four people. At the time my orders
seemed not only logical but necessary and feasible: Jacob would
guard me, Zebbie would guard Deety, our men would guard each
other.

There was a flaw. I did not realize that my edict required: a)
one rifleman always to be at the car; b) *both* men to be away from
the car from time to time.

Since this is not possible I amended it: When the men had to
answer calls of nature, we women would lock ourselves in. I
didn't *know* that this planet had anything more dangerous than
Alice's Bread-and-Butter Fly. But that was the point: I didn't *know*
and until I *did*, I must assume that something as dangerous as a
tiger lurked behind every bush.

Heavens! the *bush* might be carnivorous.

I was learning, with breath-snatching speed, something that
most people never learn: A commanding officer's "unlimited"
authority isn't freedom; it's a straitjacket. She can't do as *she*
pleases; she *never* can—because every minute, awake and asleep,
she must protect those under her command.

She can't take any avoidable risk herself; her life does not
belong to her; it belongs to her command.

When the captaincy was thrust on me, I decided that we would
stay where we were until Gay Deceiver was reorganized so that
all four of us could sleep comfortably and safely—no swollen
ankles.

Sharpie hadn't thought of this; *Captain Hilda Burroughs*
thought of it *at once*. Captain Zebbie had thought of it when we
first grounded, then had let himself be overruled.

I knew that I could rearrange the car to let us all sleep behind locked doors. But it would take time, sweat, and muscles, and I had just proclaimed an order that would take one or both sets of big muscles off the job for . . . how many times a day? Four people? Such needs can't be hurried. I had a horrid suspicion that having someone standing over you with a rifle, even your nearest and dearest, might cause a healthy reflex to fail.

What to do?

Cancel the order?

No!

Cancel if a better scheme turned up. But *don't* cancel without finding something better. This was a pretty spot, but there still might be that "banth." Or bandersnatch. Or boojum. Especially a boojum. What if Zebbie should wander off that distance dictated by modesty and/or relaxation of nerves . . . and "softly and silently vanish away"?

And it was *Zebbie* I was having trouble with—*Zebbie*, who wasn't going to give the new captain any back talk whatsoever. "Cap'n Hilda honey, I don't need a chaperon, honest. I'll carry my rifle and guard myself. No problem. Safety off and a cartridge under the firing pin. Promise."

"Zebbie, I am not asking you, I am *telling* you."

"But I don't like to leave you girls unguarded!"

"Chief Pilot."

"Ma'am. Captain."

"I am not a girl. I am eleven years your senior."

"I simply meant—"

"Pipe down!"

The poor dear's ears turned red but he shut up. I said, "Astrogator!"

"Huh? Yes, Captain Auntie."

"Can you use a rifle?"

"Oh, sure, Pop made me learn. But I don't like a rifle; I like my shotgun."

"Take the Chief Pilot's rifle and guard the camp—"

"Look, I can do it better with my shotgun."

"Pipe down and carry out your orders."

Deety looked startled, trotted over to Zebbie, who surrendered his rifle without comment, face frozen. "Copilot," I said to my husband, "arm yourself with rifle and pistol, go with the Chief Pilot, guard him while he does what he has to do."

Deety looked startled, trotted over to Zebbie, who surrendered his rifle without comment, face frozen. "Copilot," I said to my husband, "arm yourself with rifle and pistol, go with the Chief Pilot, guard him while he does what he has to do."

Zebbie swallowed. "Sharpie—I mean '*Captain* Sharpie.' It won't be necessary. The golden moment has passed. All this talk."

"Chief Pilot, please refrain from using my nickname while I am your commanding officer. Copilot, carry out your orders. Remain with the Chief Pilot and guard him continuously *as long as necessary* to accomplish the purpose of the trip." (If Zebbie meant "constipation"—an emotional to-do can have that effect— I would act later in my capacity as "medical officer"—and it would not take four husky orderlies to make Zebbie hold still. The authority of a commanding officer almost never requires force. Odd but true—I wondered how I knew that.)

Once our men were out of earshot, I said, "Deety, could I learn to shoot that rifle?"

"I'm not sure I'm speaking to you. You humiliated my husband . . . when we all owe him so much."

"Astrogator!"

Deety's eyes got wide. "Good God—it's gone to your head!"

"Astrogator."

"Uh . . . yes, Captain."

"You will refrain from personal remarks to me or about me during my tenure as commanding officer. Acknowledge that order, then log it."

Deety's face assumed the expression that means that she has shut out the world. "Aye aye, Captain. Gay Deceiver!"

"Hello, Deety!"

"Log mode. The Captain has ordered the Astrogator to refrain from personal remarks to her or about her during her tenure as commanding officer. I acknowledge receipt of order and will comply. Log date, time, and Bingo code. I tell you three times."

"Deety, I hear you three times."

"Back to sleep, Gay."

"Roger and out."

Deety turned to me, face and voice normal again. "Captain, I can teach you to shoot in such a way that you won't get a sore shoulder or be knocked down. But to become a *good* shot with a rifle takes a long time. My shotgun doesn't kick as hard . . . and you won't need skill."

"I thought a shotgun was more difficult."

"Depends. A shotgun is usually for surprise targets in the air. That takes skill. But for a stationary target—within range—it's about like a garden hose. The shot spreads in a cone. So easy that it's not sporting."

"'Not sporting' suits me. Will you show me how? What kind of target do we need?"

"It ought to be a large sheet of paper to show how the shot spreads. But, Captain, you know what will happen if I fire a gun?"

"What?"

"We will have two men back here at a dead run—one of them trying to dress as he runs. I don't think he'll be pleased."

"Meaning I shouldn't get Zebbie angry twice in ten minutes."

"It might be *your* husband. Stands to reason that they'll both take care of needs before returning. If I fire a shot, I'd better have a dead body to show for it, or one or the other will blow his top. Or both."

"Both! Thanks, Deety—I didn't think it through."

"But also, the Captain will recall that she ordered me to guard camp. I can't teach shooting at the same time."

(Sharpie, can't you do *anything* right?) "No, of course you can't! Deety, I'm off to a bad start. All of you annoyed at me and one, maybe two, really angry."

"Does the Captain expect me to comment?"

"Deety, *can't* you call me 'Aunt Hilda'?" I wasn't crying— I've trained myself not to. But I *needed* to. "Yes, I want your comment."

"Captain Aunt Hilda, I need to call you by your title to keep myself reminded that you *are* captain. Since you ordered me to refrain from personal remarks to you or about you, I needed a second order before I *could* comment."

"As bad as that? Don't spare me but make it quick."

"The Captain hasn't done badly."

"I *haven't?* Deety, don't fib to Hilda; you never used to."

"And I'm not going to now. Captain, *I* think you are off to a good start."

"But you said it had gone to my head!"

"I was wrong. I realized how wrong when I was logging your order to me. What I said was worse than anything I said to Zebadiah while he was captain—he required me to review in my mind all the things I've said . . . and at least twice he should have given me a fat lip"—Deety smiled grimly—"'cept that Zebadiah couldn't bring himself to strike a woman even if she weren't pregnant. Captain—Captain Aunt Hilda honey—Zebadiah didn't crack down on us when he should have. He turned over to you a gang of rugged individualists, not one with any concept of discipline. I certainly had none. But I do now."

"I'm not sure that I do," I said miserably.

"It means obeying orders you don't like and strongly disagree with—with no back talk. 'Into the jaws of death rode the six hundred.' Zebadiah would not do *that* to us . . . but he did let us annoy him into testing my new Bug-Out program. He had told me that the test was a useless risk; I should have agreed because it *was* useless. Instead I gave him a snooty 'No comment,' and you were as bad and Pop was worse. Mmm . . . I don't think Zebadiah has had much experience as a commanding officer."

"Why so, Deety? He *is* a captain."

"That doesn't mean that he has ever been a commanding officer. He has soloed quite a lot, in fighters. He has logged control time in larger craft or he wouldn't hold a command pilot rating. But has he ever actually commanded? Nothing he has said to me indicated it . . . but he did tell me that before the last war a major was often captain of an air-and-space craft but now it almost always took a lieutenant colonel while majors wound up as co-pilots. He was explaining why he liked one-man fighters so well. Aunt Hilda—Captain—I think commanding was as new to Zebadiah as it is to you. Like sex, or having a baby, you can't understand it till you've tried it." She suddenly grinned. "So don't hold Zebadiah's mistakes against him."

"*What* mistakes? He's saved our lives again and again. I don't blame him—now—for wanting a rest from commanding. Deety, it's the hardest work possible even if you don't lift a finger. I never suspected it. I don't expect to sleep a wink tonight."

"We'll guard you!"

"No."

"Yes, we will!"

"Pipe down."

"Sorry, Ma'am."

"What mistakes did Zebbie make?"

"Well . . . he didn't crack down. You wasted no time in letting us know who is boss. You didn't let us argue; you slapped us down at once. I hate to say this but I think you have more talent for command than Zebadiah has."

"Deety, that's silly!"

"Is it? Napoleon wasn't tall."

"So I have a Napoleonic complex. Humph!"

"Captain, I'm going to ignore that because, under that order you made me log, I'm damned if I do and damned if I don't."

"Well . . . I know how not to get a Napoleonic complex. Deety, you're my second-in-command."

"But *Pop* is second-in-command."

"Wrong tense. 'Was'—he is no longer. As astrogator you mày have inherited it anyhow; you can ask Zebbie—but in private; my decision is not subject to debate. Simply acknowledge it."

"I— Aye aye, Captain."

"You are now required to advise me whenever you think that I am about to make a serious mistake. You are also required to advise me on request."

"My advice isn't worth much. Look how I goofed a few minutes ago."

"That was *before* you were appointed second-in-command. Deety, actually holding an office makes a big difference."

Deety blinked and looked solemn, then said soberly, "Yes, I think it does. Yes, it does. I feel it, I do! Weird."

"Wait till you're captain. Eight times as weird."

"Never. Pop wouldn't go for it, Zebadiah wouldn't, I won't— that's three votes."

"I said No right up to the point where I could not avoid it. Don't worry about it now. I'll boss and you'll advise me."

"In that case, Captain, I advise you to reconsider letting us guard you. After we eat and start scouting again, I advise that, even if we find the British quickly, instead of making contact, we should find a spot as deserted as this at the sunrise line and get a long day's sleep. We crew can get eight hours—I'll take the middle watch; the men can get eight hours solid each . . . and the Captain can get anything up to twelve."

"Advice noted. It's good advice. But that's not the program; we're going to sleep *here.*" I told Deety what I had in mind. "When the car is restowed, we'll eat. If there is daylight left, we'll bathe before we eat. Otherwise in the morning."

"I'd rather hurry through eating and get a bath . . . since you tell me I'm going to be able to sleep with my husband. When I'm frightened I stink worse . . . and I've been *much* more scared than I've tried to let on."

"Into cold water after eating? Deety, you know better."

"Oh. I'll skip eating, if necessary, to bathe."

"Astrogator, we'll do it my way."

"Yes, Captain. But I stink, I do."

"We'll all stink by the time we restow this car and may wind up eating sandwiches in the dark because everything that we don't throw away is going to be inside with us and Gay locked and not a light showing by sundown." I cocked my head. "Hear something, Deety?"

Our men came back looking cheerful, with Zebbie carrying Jacob's rifle and wearing Jacob's pistol. Zebbie gave me a big grin. "Cap'n, there wasn't a durn thing wrong with me that Carter's Little Liver Pills couldn't have fixed. Now I'm right."

"Good."

"But just barely," agreed my husband. "Hilda—Captain Hilda my beloved—your complex schedule almost caused me to have a childish accident."

"I think that unnecessary discussion wasted more time than did my schedule. As may be, Jacob, I would rather have to clean up a 'childish accident' than have to bury you."

"But—"

"Drop the matter!"

"Pop, you had better believe it!" sang out Deety.

Jacob looked startled (and hurt, and I felt the hurt). Zebbie looked sharply at me, no longer grinning. He said nothing, went to Deety, reached for his rifle. "I'll take that, hon."

Deety held it away from him. "The Captain has not relieved me."

"Oh. Okay, we'll do it by the book." Zebbie looked at me. "Captain, I thoroughly approve of your doctrine of a continuous guard; I was too slack. It was my intention to relieve the watch. I volunteer to stand guard while you three eat—"

"—then I'll guard while Zeb eats," added Jacob. "We already worked it out. When do we eat? I could eat an ostrich with the feathers left on." He added, "Hilda my love, you're captain . . . but you're still cook, aren't you? Or is Deety the cook?"

(Decisions! How does the captain of a *big* ship cope?) "I've made changes. Deety remains astrogator but is now second-in-command and my executive officer. In my absence she commands. When I'm present, Deety's orders are my orders; she will be giving them to implement what I want done. Neither she nor I will cook. Uh, medical officer—" (Damn it, Sharpie, all those hours in the emergency room make *you* the only candidate. Or does it? Mmm—) "Zebbie, does 'command pilot' include paramedical training?"

"Yes. Pretty sketchy. What to do to keep the bloke alive until the surgeon sees him."

"You're medical officer. I am assistant medical officer when you need me—if I don't have something else that *must* be done."

"Captain, may I put in a word?"

"Please do, Chief Pilot."

"Sometimes you have to let the bloke die because there is something else that *has* to be done." Zebbie looked bleak. "Saw it happen. Does no good to worry ahead of time or grieve about it afterwards. You do what you must."

"So I am learning, Zebbie. Cook— Gentlemen, I've never eaten your cooking. You must assess yourselves. Which one of you is 'adequate'—"

"Ouch."

"Your wording, Zebbie. —and which one is inadequate?"

They backed and filled and deferred to each other, so I put a stop to it. "You will alternate as first and second cook until evidence shows that one is chief cook and the other assistant. Jacob, today you are first cook—"

"Good! I'll get busy at once!"

"No, Jacob." I explained what we were going to do. "While you two get *everything* out of the car, Deety will teach me the rudiments of shotgun. Then I will take over guard duty and she can help unload. But keep your rifles loaded and handy, 'cause if I shoot, I'll need help in a hurry. Then, when we restow, I'll do it because I'm smallest and can stand up, mostly, behind the bulkhead. While Zebbie stands guard, and Deety and Jacob pass things in to me."

Jacob wasn't smiling—and I suddenly recognized his expression. I once had a dog who (theoretically) was never fed at the table. He would sit near my knee and look at me with that same expression. Why, my poor darling was hungry! Gut-rumble hungry. I had such a galloping case of nerves from becoming captain that I had no appetite.

"Deety, in the pantry back at Snug Harbor I noticed a carton of Milky Way bars. Did that get packed?"

"Certainly did! Those are Pop's—his vice and eventual downfall."

"Really? I don't recall seeing him eat one."

My husband said, "I haven't been eating them lately. All things considered, my dear—my dear Captain—I prefer you to candy bars."

"Why, thank you, Jacob! Will you share those candy bars? We understand that they are your personal property."

"They are not my personal property; they belong to all of us. Share and share alike."

"Yup," agreed Zebbie. "A perfect communism. 'From each

according to his ability, to each according to his needs.' With the usual communist dictator on top."

"Zebbie, I've been called everything from a black reactionary to a promiscuous old whore—but never before a communist dictator. Very well, you may address me as 'Comrade Captain.' When we come across those candy bars, everybody grab one for quick energy—unless somebody remembers where they were packed?"

"Gay knows!" said Deety, and backed toward the car's open door while still keeping her eyes swinging the arc away from the river—perfect sentry and looking cute at it. "Gay Deceiver!"

"Hi, Deety! Getting any?"

"Inventory. Food supplies. Candy. Milky Way bars. Report location."

"Frame twenty. Starboard. Closed storage seven-Ess-high. Bottom shelf."

Five hours later everything was back inside except a heap of wrapping, packaging, and such—yet the increase in space was far greater than that pile. This was because storage did not have to be logical. Just tell Gay. A left shoe could fill an odd space in with the swords while the right shoe from the same pair was a space filler in a tool storage far to the rear—yet the only inconvenience lay in having to go to two places to get them.

I did the stowing; Deety stayed in the cabin, received items handed from outside, described the item to Gay, then described to Gay where the item was stowed, as I reported it. Gay was under instruction to hear only Deety's voice—and what Deety told Gay was so logical that no one need remember it. Like this: "Gay Deceiver."

"Boss, when will you learn to say 'Please'?"

"Clothing. Zeb. Shoes. Field boots."

"Right boot. Abaft bulkhead. Starboard. Frame forty. Under deckplate. Outboard compartment. Left boot. Abaft bulkhead. Portside. Frame sixty. Under deckplate, middle compartment. Warning: Both boots filled with rifle ammo padded with socks."

You see? If you got categories in the wrong order, Gay would restring them. Give her the basic category and the identification, leaving out the other steps, and Gay would search the "tree" (Deety's words) and get the "twig" you identified. You could even fail to give category and she would search until she found it.

But hardest was to build up the decking of the rear compartment about twenty centimeters with chattels or stores that would not crush, fasten it down to keep it from floating in free fall, and make it smooth enough that it would not be unbearably lumpy as a bed—while making *some* effort neither to build into this platform nor to store in compartments under it things needed frequently or quickly.

I had to lower my standards. It is impossible to store so many things in such limited space and have *all* readily at hand.

I studied things outside, admitted that I could not do it, then asked for advice. Zebbie solved it: "Captain, do a dry run."

"Uh . . . go on, Zebbie."

"Take my sleeping bag inside, open it out. It is too wide for the space, especially at the rear. So keep it as far forward as you can and still miss Jake's twister and the bulkhead door. Mark the amount you have to lap it. Mark on the deck the foot of the opened-out bag. You'll find space abaft that, frustum of a cone, sort of. Drag the sleeping bag outside, mark the tuck-in, build your platform on it. Then fill that rear space and build a bulkhead. Better get Jake; he's a born mechanic."

"Zebbie, would you prefer to build this bed yourself?"

"Nope."

"Why not? I'm not speaking as captain; I'm inquiring as your old friend Sharpie."

"Because I'm twice as big as you, which makes that space half as big for me. Tell you what, Cap'n Sharpie—*excuse me!*—Captain Hilda—do the measuring. Meanwhile we'll pick out plunder that might be bricks in that platform. Then drag the sleeping bag outside. If you'll let Jake relieve me, Deety and I can piece together the platform in jig time."

It changed "impossible" to "possible." The cubbyhole was filled, contents held in place with opened-out cartons tied with wire to hold-downs—"padeyes" Jacob called them. The platform was built, chinked with this and that, covered with more flattened-out cartons, and topped off with sleeping bag and blankets.

It was still light. Deety assured me that there was one hour and forty-three minutes till sundown. "Time enough if we hurry. Jacob, first bath. Deety, guard him. Both come back so Jacob can start dinner—then Zebbie and Deety go down—goodness, this sounds like the farmer and the rowboat with the fox and the geese—and bathe, taking turns guarding. Both come back; Deety relieves me; Zebbie takes me down to bathe while he guards. But please hurry; I want a bath, too. Forty minutes before sundown bathing stops and we eat—at sundown we are inside, dirty dishes and all, locked in till sunrise. If that does me out of a bath, we still hold to it.

Jacob, how far is this 'easy way' down? I mean, 'How many minutes?'"

"Maybe five. Hilda my love, if you weren't insisting on always-two-together there would be no hurry. All go down together; I hurry through my bath, grab my rifle and trot back. The rest needn't hurry. You've got us going down and up, down and up, four times—forty minutes. Which squeezes four baths into twenty minutes, five minutes to undress, soap, squat down and rinse off, towel dry, and dress. Hardly worth the trip."

"Jacob, who guards you while you're getting supper? No. I can bathe in the morning." (Damn! I *wanted* that bath. I'm used to a shower in the morning, a tub at night, a bidet at any excuse. Decadent—that's me.)

"Beloved, this place is *safe*. While we were out earlier, Zeb and I scouted for sign. None. That's when we found this way down to the creek. It would be a natural watering place. No sign. I don't think there are any large fauna here."

I was wavering when Deety spoke up. "Pop, that's *three* down-and-ups, not four, as Zebadiah and I get baths on one. But, Captain Hilda, if we all go down and come back together, there *can't* be danger. Put that stuff back inside and lock up, of course." She pointed at Jacob's preparations. While Jacob had been handing stuff to Deety, he had set aside a hot plate, cooking and eating utensils, a tarpaulin, comestibles for supper and breakfast, and had passed word for me *please* to store food so that it could be reached easily.

Jacob said hastily, "Deety, I've got it planned for minimum therbligs. Dried apricots soaking in that pan, soup mix in that one. There's no level deck space left inside."

Deety started to say, "But, Pop, if we—" when I cut in with, "Quiet, please"—not shouted.

They kept quiet—"Captain Bligh" was being listened to. "Gay Deceiver will *not* be left unguarded. My orders will not be discussed further. One modification: Supper is cut from forty minutes to twenty-five. Astrogator adjust schedule accordingly. Sound a blast on the siren five minutes before suppertime. We lock up on the dot. I placed the honey bucket just beyond the swing of the bulkhead door as the car will not be unlocked for *any* reason until sunrise. Questions?"

"Yes, Captain. Where are the towels?"

An hour later I was squatting in the stream, rinsing off and hurrying—covered with goose bumps. As I stepped out, Zebbie put down his rifle and had a big, fluffy towel, long as I am tall, waiting to wrap me. I should have required him to behave as a guard should.

But I told myself that he was still wearing his revolver and, anyhow, he has this sixth sense about danger—lying in my teeth. *Nothing* makes a woman feel more cherished than to have a man wrap her in a big towel the instant she's out of the water. I lack character, that's all. Every woman has her price, and a big, fluffy towel at the right time comes close to being mine.

Zebbie was rubbing firmly, getting me not only dry but warm. "Feels good, Captain?"

"'Captain Hilda' never came down the bank, Zebbie. Feels *swell!*"

"Remember the first time I gave you a rubdown?"

"Sure do! Dressing room at my pool."

"Yup. I tried to lay you. I've never been turned down so smoothly."

"You tried to lay me, Zebbie? Truly?" I looked up at him, my best innocent look.

"Sharpie darling, you lie as easily as I do. A man does *this*"—and he did—"even with a towel, a woman is certain what he means. But you refused to notice it, turned me down, without hurting my pride."

"I'm refusing to notice it now and find it just as difficult as I did that afternoon. Stop it, *please!*" He did. "Thanks, dear. You got me all shaky. Zebbie, do you think Deety thinks I rigged this to get you alone? I would not willingly upset her."

"On the contrary. She gave me a hunting license concerning you—*you*, not females in general—ten days back. *In writing.*"

"*Really?*"

"In writing so that she could limit it. I am required not to run any risk of hurting Jake."

"You haven't tried to use that license."

"I took it as a compliment to you and to me, kissed Deety and thanked her. You settled this four years ago. But I've sometimes wondered why. I'm young, healthy, take care of my teeth, and keep my nails clean—mostly—and you seemed to like me. What made me ineligible? Not complaining, dear, just asking."

I tried to explain the difference between a male friend and a bedmate—the scarcity of the first, the boring plethora of applicants for the other.

He listened, then shook his head. "Masochism."

"Hasn't it worked out better this way? I do love you, Zebbie."

"I know you do, Sharpie." Zebbie turned me around and looked down into my eyes. "And I love you and you know that, too"—and he kissed me.

That kiss went on and neither of us seemed inclined to stop. My towel slipped to the ground. I noticed because it felt better to be closer and ever so much nicer to have his hands on me. Zebbie hadn't given me a sexy kiss since the day I had invited a pass and then ignored it.

I began to wonder why I had decided to ignore it. Then I was wondering how much time we had left in our schedule. Then I knew the exact time . . . for that infernal, earsplitting siren sounded. God watches over Hilda Mae and that's why I keep Him on my payroll. But sometimes He is rough about it.

We let go. I put on Deety's Keds, slid my borrowed dress over my head, hung the towel over my arm—elapsed time: nine seconds. Zebbie was again carrying his rifle at the ready (is that correct?—both hands, I mean).

"Captain, shall we go?"

"Yes, Chief Pilot. Zebbie, when did I become 'captain' again? Just from putting on clothes? You've seen this old hide before."

"Skin has nothing to do with it, Captain. Quoting Deety quoting the Japanese: 'Nakedness is often seen but never noticed.' Except that sometimes I *do* notice, hot diggity dog and other comments. You have superior skin, Captain. You went back to being Captain when I picked up my rifle. But I was never off duty. Did you notice, when I dried you, that I picked you up and swung you around, so that *I* faced the bank? I kept alert even while I was nuzzling you . . . and you make fine nuzzle, Captain Step-Mother-in-Law Hilda."

"So do you, Zebbie. I'm still Sharpie till we get to your car." We reached the top of the bank. "Ten seconds to catch my breath. Zebbie—"

"Yes, Sharpie?"

"Four years ago— I'm sorry I turned away your pass."

He patted my bottom. "So am I, dear. But it has worked out quite well. And"—he grinned that irresistible, ugly grin—"who knows?—we aren't dead yet."

When we arrived, Jacob was slurping soup. "You're late," he stated. "So we waited."

"So I see."

"Don't listen to Pop, Captain Auntie; you are two minutes seventeen seconds ahead of time. Are you sure you stayed in long enough to get clean?"

"I stayed in long enough to get freezing cold. Aren't you chilly?" Deety had worn skin most of the day and so had I; we had been doing sweaty work. But she had been dressed when I last saw her. "Jacob, is there no soup for Zebbie and me?"

"A smidgen. You get this pan as soon as I'm through—now!—and that means one less dish to wash."

"And Zebadiah gets mine—also now—and I took that jump suit off because it's dirty and I'm clean. I still haven't figured out how to do a laundry. Nothing for a tub, no way to heat water. What's that other way? Pound them on a rock the way it shows in *National Geographic?* I don't believe it!"

We were in bed by sundown, Gay's doors locked—pitch dark in minutes. According to Deety and Gay sunrise was ten hours and forty-three minutes away. "Deety, please tell Gay to wake us at sunrise."

"Aye aye, Captain Auntie."

"Zebbie, you told us that the air in the car was good for about four hours."

"In space. The scoops are open now."

"But do you get air back there? Should the bulkhead door be open?"

"Oh. Top scoop serves this space. The cabin is ventilated by the chin scoop. Scoops stay open unless internal pressure closes them."

"Can anything get in through them? Snakes or such?"

"Hilda my dear, you worry too much."

"My very own darling Copilot, will you please pipe down while I'm speaking to the Chief Pilot? There are many things about this car that I do not know—yet I am responsible."

Zebbie answered, "Each scoop has a grid inside and a fine screen at the inner end; nothing can get in. Have to clean 'em occasionally. Remind me, Deety."

"I'll tell Gay." She did—and almost at once there was a crash of metal. I sat up abruptly. "What's that?"

"Hilda, I am afraid that I have kicked over the supper dishes." My husband added, "Zeb, how do I find the cabin light?"

"No, no! Jacob, don't try to find it. No light *at all* until sunrise. Don't fret about dishes. But what happened? I thought they were under the instrument board."

"I couldn't quite reach with this bed made up. But the carton that supports my feet sticks out beyond the seat cushion on it. So I stacked them there."

"No harm done. We can expect bobbles as we shake down."

"I suppose so."

"We can cope. Jacob, that was an excellent dinner."

Deety called out, "Good night, chatterboxes! We want to sleep." She closed the bulkhead door, dogged it.

XXIII   *"The farce is over."*

Jake:

For me, the best soporific is to hold Hilda in my arms. I slept ten hours.

I might have slept longer had I not been blasted by a bugle call: *Reveille.*

I thought I was back in basic, tried to rouse out fast—banged my head. That slowed me; I reoriented, saw my lovely bride beside me, yawning prettily—realized that we were on Mars.

Mars! Not even our own Mars but another universe.

That hateful tune started to repeat, louder.

I banged on the bulkhead. "How do you shut this thing off?"

Shortly I saw dogs of the bulkhead door turning, then the door swung—as the call went into its third time around still louder. Zeb showed, blinking. *"Do you have a problem?"*

I couldn't hear but I could piece out what he meant.

"HOW DO YOU SHUT OFF THIS RACKET?"

"No problem." (I think that's what he said.) "Good morning, Gay."

The bugle faded into the distance. "Good morning, Boss."

"I'm awake."

"Ah, but will you stay awake?"

"I won't go back to bed. Promise."

"I've dealt with your sort before, me bucko. If you aren't out of here before my landlady wakes up, I'll lose this room. Then another hassle with the cops. It's not worth it . . . you cheapskate!"

"You're a smart girl, Gay."

"So smart I'm looking for another job."

"Back to sleep, Gay. Over."

"Roger and out, Boss"—and blessed silence.

I said to my daughter, "Deety, how could you do this to us?"

Her husband answered. "Deety didn't, Jake. She was told to place a call for sunrise. But didn't know what a morning call means to Gay."

I grumped, and opened the starboard door. Hilda's rearrangements had given me the best rest I had had in days. But two double beds in a sports car left no room on arising to do anything but get out.

So I slid out the door, groped for the step, paused to ask Hilda for shoes and coverall—caught sight of something and said quietly, "Hilda. My rifle. Quickly!"

My little treasure is always reliable in emergency; her clowning is simply *persona*. (A most pleasant one; the worst aspect of the jest of making her "captain" was that she lost her smile—I hoped that Zeb would soon resume command. We had needed the lesson—but no need to go on.)

I digress— I asked for my rifle; she whispered, "Roger," and had it in my hand at once with the quiet report: "Locked, one in the chamber. Wait—I'm getting Zeb."

That made sense. By staying on the step in the corner formed by door and car, my rear was safe and I need cover only a small sector. I prefer a bolt action—correction: I have a bolt-action rifle I inherited from my father's eldest brother, who had "liberated" it on leaving the Marine Corps.

I unlocked it, opened the bolt slightly, saw that a cartridge was in the chamber, closed the bolt, left the piece unlocked.

Zeb said at my ear, softly, "What's the excitement?"

"Over there." I pulled my head out of the way, saw Hilda and Deety almost on top of Zeb—Hilda with Deety's shotgun, Deety with her husband's police special.

Zeb said, "Pixies. They may still be around; let's check. Cover me from here?"

"No, Zeb. You to the right, me to the left, we check the port side, meet back at the dump. Make it fast."

"Say the word." Zeb said over his shoulder, "You girls stay in the car. Jake?"

"Now!" We came bursting out like greyhounds, guns at high port. The reason for my disquiet was simple: The dump of wrappings and cartons was no longer a heap. Something had spread it over many meters, and the litter was not nearly enough to account for the pile. Wind? Zeb had left the wings extended; the

slightest wind would wake him, warn him of change in weather. The car had not rocked in the night; ergo, no wind. Ergo, nocturnal visitors. Nor were they small.

I rounded the car to the left, seeing nothing until I spotted Zeb—waved at him, started back around to join him at the dump.

He arrived before I did. "I told you girls to stay in the car!" He was quite angry, and the cause, both of them, were also at the dump.

My darling answered, "Chief Pilot."

Zeb said, "Huh? Sharpie, there's no time for that; there's something dangerous around! You girls get inside before I—"

"Pipe *DOWN!*"

One would not believe that so small a body could produce such a blast. It caught Zeb mouth open and jammed his words down his throat.

Hilda did not give him opportunity to answer. She continued, forcefully: "Chief Pilot, there are *no* 'girls' here; there are four adult humans. One of them is my second-in-command and executive officer. *My* executive officer; I am in command." Hilda looked at my daughter. "Astrogator, did you tell anyone to remain in the car?"

"No, Captain." Deety was wearing her "Name, rank, and serial number" face.

"Nor did I." Hilda looked at Zeb. "There is no need to discuss it." She stirred litter with a toe. "I had hoped that we could find salvage. But three fourths of it has been eaten. By large animals from those tooth marks. I would have trouble visualizing a large animal that eats cellulose but is nevertheless carnivorous—save that I know one. So we will get as much done as possible while keeping a tight guard. I have the program planned but I'm open to advice."

"*Hilda!*" I let my tone get a bit sharp.

My wife looked around with features as impassive as those of my daughter. "Copilot, are you addressing me officially or socially?"

"Uh . . . as your husband! I must put my foot down! Hilda, you don't realize the situation. We'll lift as soon as possible—and Zeb will be in command. The farce is over."

I hated to speak to my beloved that way but sometimes one must. I braced myself for a blast.

None came. Hilda turned to Zeb and said quietly, "Chief Pilot, was my election a farce?"

"No, Captain."

"Astrogator, did you think of it as farce?"

"Me? Heavens, no, Captain Auntie!"

Hilda looked at me. "Jacob, from the balloting you voted for me at least once, possibly three times. Were you joking?"

I could not remember how I had felt when it dawned on me that Zeb really did intend to resign—panic, I think, that I was about to be stuck with the job. That was now irrelevant as I knew that I was not more than one micron from again being a bachelor . . . so I resorted to Higher Truth.

"No, no, my darling—my darling Captain! I was dead serious!"

"Did you find some malfeasance?"

"What? No! I— I made a mistake. Jumped to conclusions. I assumed that we would be leaving at once . . . and that Zeb would command once we lifted. After all, it's his car."

Hilda gave me the briefest smile. "There is something to that last argument. Zebbie, did you intend—"

"Wait a half! Cap'n, that car belongs to *all* of us just like Jake's Milky Way bars; we pooled resources."

"So I have heard you all say. Since I had nothing to pool but a fur cape, I took it with a grain of salt. Zebbie, do you intend to resume command when we lift?"

"Captain, the only way you can quit is by resigning . . . whereupon Deety would be captain."

"No, sir*ree!*" (My daughter is not often that shrill.)

"Then Jake would wind up holding the sack. Captain, I'll pilot when ordered, chop wood and carry water between times. But I didn't sign up to boss a madhouse. I think you're finding out what I mean."

"I think so, too, Zebbie. You thought there was an emergency and started giving orders. I would not want that to happen in a *real* emergency—"

"It won't! Captain."

"And I find to my chagrin that my husband considers me to be a play captain. I think I must ask for a vote of confidence. Will you please find something to use as white and black balls?"

"Captain Auntie!"

"Yes, dear?"

"I am required to advise you. A commanding officer *commands;* she doesn't ask for votes. You can resign—or—die—or lose to a mutiny and get hanged from your own yardarm. But if you take a vote, you're not a captain; you're a politician."

"Deety's right, Captain," Zeb told my wife. "Had a case-law case in R.O.T.C. Naval vessel. Department told the skipper to pick one of two ports for holidays. He let his crew vote on it. Word got back to Washington and he was relieved at sea by his second-in-command and never again ordered to sea. C.O.'s don't *ask;* they *tell* 'em. However, if it matters to you, I'm sorry I goofed, and you *do* enjoy my confidence."

"Mine, too!"

"And mine, Hilda my dear Captain!" (In truth I wanted Zeb and *only* Zeb to command when the car was off the ground. But I made myself a solemn vow never again to say or do anything that might cause Hilda to suspect it. We would crash and die together rather than let her suspect that I thought her other than the ideal commanding officer.)

Hilda said, "The incident is closed. Who can't wait? Speak up."

I hesitated—my bladder is not used to bedtime right after dinner. When no one else spoke, I said, "Perhaps I had better be first; I have breakfast to prepare."

"Dear, you are not First Cook today; Zebbie is. Deety, grab a rifle and take your father to his 'handy bush'—and do make it handy; that giant termite might be lurking. Then hand Jacob the rifle and it's your turn. Don't dally."

It was a busy day. Water tanks had to be topped off. Zeb and I used two collapsible buckets, taking turns (that hill got steeper every trip, even at 0.38 gee), while Deety guarded us. Endless trips—

That afternoon I was a ladies' tailor. Hilda had something for Deety to do; Zeb had a job to complete. The space behind the bulkhead has padeyes every 30 cms or so. No one wants the center of gravity to shift when one is in the air. Zeb's arrangements were Samson cord in many lengths with snap hooks. Zeb told Hilda he wanted to secure the bed aft for air or space, and to store items used in rigging the forward bed so that they would be secure but available—and where were his Samson ties?—Gay didn't know. He had to explain to Hilda what they looked like—whereupon Hilda said, "Oh! Thingammies! Gay Deceiver. Inventory. Incidentals. Small. Thingammies." Zeb spent the afternoon making certain that the "bed" could not slide, then built a net of Samson cord to hold the items for turning seats into a bed, then, finding that he had Samson ties left, Zeb removed the wires with which I had secured the aftermost storage, and replaced them with ties. When he was through, he relieved me as guard, and I wound up as seamstress.

Our wives had decided that one of Deety's jump suits should be altered for Hilda until we reached some place where clothes could be purchased. Hilda had vetoed Earth-without-a-J. "Jacob, as captain I look at things from another perspective. It is better to be a lively frump than a stylish corpse. Wups! You pinned Sharpie."

"Thorry," I said, around a mouthful of pins. Hilda was wearing the suit inside out; I was pinning excess material. Once this caused it to fit, lines held by pins would be tacked, pins removed, tacked lines sewed in short stitches (by hand; Deety's sewing machine was ashes in another universe), and excess cloth trimmed away.

Such was theory.

I tackled reducing the waist line by pinning darts on both sides. Then I folded up the trousers so that the crease came at the instep—but had to pin them up 17 cms!

Seventeen centimeters! I had taken in the waist first, knowing that doing so would, in effect, shorten the trousers. It did—one centimeter.

The appearance was as if I were trying to fit her with a chimpanzee suit for a masquerade. Lift it at the shoulders? I tried, almost cutting off circulation. Still a horrid case of droopy drawers—

Take a tuck all the way around the waist? That suit closed with one zipper. Have you ever tried to take a tuck in a zipper?

I stepped back and looked at my creative artistry.

Ghastly.

"Hilda my love, Deety was better at this by the age of ten. Shall I fetch her?"

"No, no!"

"Yes, yes. If at first you don't succeed, find the mistake. I'm the mistake. You need Deety."

"No, Jacob. It would be better for me to get along without clothes than to interrupt the work I have assigned to the Astrogator. With you at the verniers and Zebbie at the controls, Gay can do almost anything and quickly. Yes?"

"I wouldn't phrase it that way. But I understand you."

"If she's been preprogrammed, she can do it even faster?"

"Certainly. Why the quiz, dear?"

"How much faster?"

"Without preprogramming, it takes a few seconds to acknowledge and set it, about as long to check what I've done, then I report 'Set!' Zeb says 'Execute!' I punch the button. Five to fifteen seconds. With a preprogram—is it debugged in all ways, no conflicts, no ambiguities, no sounds easy to confuse?"

"Darling, that is why I won't let Deety be disturbed. Yes."

"So. Maximum time would be with Gay asleep. Wake her, she acknowledges, you state the preprogram in the exact words in her memory, then say 'Execute!' Call it three seconds. Minimum— That would be an emergency preprogram with 'Execute' included in the code word. My dear, we saw minimum time yesterday. When that Russian tried to shoot Zeb."

"Jacob, that is what caused me to put Deety to work. I saw his pistol in the air. His fingers were curled to catch it. Then we were in the sky. How long?"

"I saw him start to reverse his weapon, and bent over my verniers to bounce us by switch . . . then stopped. Not needed. Mmm— A tenth of a second? A fifth?"

"Whichever, it is the fastest we can manage. While you dears were carrying water, I was preparing a list of preprograms. Some are to save juice or time or to carry out something we do frequently; those require 'Execute!' Some are intended to save our lives and don't require 'Execute.' Like 'Bounce' and 'Bug Out' and 'Take us home!' But more. Jacob, I did *not* tell Deety how to phrase these; that's *her* specialty. I wrote out what I thought we ought to be able to do and told her to add any she wished."

"Did you consult Zeb?"

"Copilot, the Captain did not consult the Chief Pilot."

"Whew! I beg your pardon—Captain."

"Only if I get a kiss—mind the pins! Deety will post a copy on the instrument board. After you and Zebbie read them, I want your advice and his."

I gave up on that jump suit. I took out eighty-five or a thousand pins. Hilda was covered with sweat so I invited her to order me to take her down to bathe. She hesitated.

I said, "Does the Captain have duties of which I am unaware?"

"No. But everyone else is working, Jacob."

"Captain, Rank Hath Its Privileges. You are on duty twenty-four hours a day—twenty-four and a half here—"

"Twenty-four hours, thirty-nine minutes, thirty-five seconds— local day, not sidereal."

"Did you measure it? Or remember what some professor said?"

"Neither, Jacob. It's the figure Gay uses. I suppose she got it from the Aerospace Almanac."

"Are you going to believe an almanac? Or your husband?"

"Excuse me, Jacob, while I tell Gay the correct figure."

"Hand back my leg, beloved. Captain, since you are on duty all the time, you are entitled to bathe, rest, or relax, at any time."

"Well . . . two seconds while I grab a towel—and tell Zebbie that I will start dinner while he is down bathing."

"Captain, *I* am number-two cook today. You said so."

"You will guard, Jacob, which you do better than I. While the Carters are guarding each other."

Hilda came trotting back with a towel. I said, "Cap'n, I've figured out clothes for you."

"Goody. Yes, dear?" We headed for the path down.

"Were my Hawaiian shirts packed?" I had her fall in behind me.

"'Inventory. Clothing. Jacob. Shirts. Aloha.'"

"Do you recall a blue one with white flowers?"

"Yes."

"I take 'medium' but can get into a 'small' and Andrade's didn't have this in 'medium.' But this one is so small I haven't been wearing it. Hilda, you'll like it—and it will be easy to cut down." (A steep pitch—no place to lose your footing while carrying a gun.)

"I won't cut it down. Jacob, your shirt is my first maternity smock."

"A happy thought! Did Deety fetch sailor pants? White."

"I recall white duck slacks." Hilda kicked off her Keds, stepped into the water.

"That's the pair. She wore them one summer while maturing. The following summer they were too tight. She was always about to alter them but never did."

"Jacob, if Deety likes those pants so well that she saved them and fetched them along, I won't ask her to give them to me."

"*I* will ask her. Hilda, you worry about the wrong things. We pooled resources. I chucked in my candy bars, Zeb chucked in his car, Deety chucks in her sailor pants."

"And what did I chuck in? Nothing!"

"Your mink cape. If you offered it to Deety in exchange for a pair of old white—"

"It's a deal!"

"It is like hell, Mistress Mine. That cape is valuta. Only days ago each of us was wealthy. Now we are unpersons who can't go home. What happens to our bank accounts I do not know but it seems certain that we will never realize anything from them, or from stocks, bonds, and other securities. Any paper money we have is worthless. As you know, I have bullion and gold coins and Jake has, also; we each like money that clinks and we don't trust governments. Gay *must* be juiced from time to time; that calls for valuta. Such as gold. Such as mink coats. Come out of there before you freeze! I would rub you dry but that giant termite worries me."

"Last night Zebbie rubbed me dry."

(Why do women have this compulsion to confess? It is not a typical male vice.) "He did? I should speak to him."

"Jacob, you are angry."

"Only somewhat, as yesterday we didn't know about the giant termite, and Zeb and I considered your guard rules silly. Nevertheless Zeb neglected his duty."

"I meant 'angry with *me*'!"

"For what? Did you force it on him?"

"No. He offered it—towel open and ready, just as you do. I went straight into it, let him wrap me and rub me down."

"Feel good?"

"Golly, yes! I'm a bad girl, Jacob—but I loved it."

"Don't give yourself airs, my darling; you are not a bad girl. Yesterday was not the first time Zeb has rubbed you dry."

"Well . . . no." (They have to confess, they have to be shrived.)

"Do you any harm, then or now?"

"I don't think so."

"I'm sure it didn't. Listen, beloved—you are twenty-nine going on forty-two. You've had three term contracts and now have a traditional marriage. In college you were a scandal to the jaybirds. Zeb has been your chum for years. Both of you horny as goats. My darling, I assumed what is called 'the worst' and is often the best."

"But, Jacob, we didn't, we didn't! And we *haven't!*"

"So? People who pass up temptations have only themselves to blame. Just one thing, my only love, if you and Zeb ever pick up the matter, try not to look guilty."

"But we aren't going to, ever!"

"Should it come to pass, warn Zeb not to hurt Deety. She loves him deeply. Not surprising as Zeb is a lovable man. Get your shoes on, dearest one, and we'll let someone else have the community bathtub."

"Jacob? You *still* think we have. Zebbie and I."

"Hilda, I married you convinced that Zeb was, at that time and for some years, your lover. Or one of them. Today you have convinced me that the matter is unproven . . . assuming that one or both of you have rocks in your head. But I can't see that it makes a tinker's dam either way. Jane taught me that the only important rule is not to hurt people ... which very often—Jane's words!—consists in not talking unnecessarily."

"Jane told *me* that, too. Jacob? Will you kiss me?"

"Madame—what did you say your name was?—that is the toll I charge before a client starts up this bank."

As we climbed, I asked Hilda, "Darling, what is the animal that eats cellulose but is carnivorous?"

"Oh. Two. H. sapiens and Rattus."

"Men? Cellulose?"

"Sawdust is often processed as food. Have you ever eaten in a fast food joint?"

My daughter had done a wonderful job on preprograms; we all were eager to learn them. We placed guards, Zeb and me, at the doors, while Deety took Zeb's seat and talked, and Hilda sat in mine.

"Captain Auntie had two ideas," Deety told us. "To optimize emergency escapes and to work out ways to use as near to no juice as possible. The latter involves figuring ways to ground us in strange places *without* the skill Zebadiah has in dead-stick grounding."

"I don't depend on skill," put in my son-in-law. "I won't risk a dead-stick grounding other than on a hard-surfaced strip. You've seen me avoid it twice—by power-on just before grounding. Yesterday I cut it a bit fine."

I shuddered.

My daughter continued, "We have this new program. Set it, by voice, for bearing and as many minima as you please. Our Smart Girl goes there and attempts to ground. She uses radar twice, once in range-finder mode, second time in precautionary mode as in 'Bug Out.' If her target is not clear, she does a Drunkard's Walk in locus ten klicks radius, sampling spots two per second. When she finds a good spot, she grounds. Unless we don't like it and order her to try again.

"Study that and you will see that you can cruise all over this or any planet, land anywhere, and not use juice.

"Escape programs— We must be most careful in saying G, A, Y. Refer to her as 'smart girl' or 'the car' or anything not starting with that syllable. That syllable will now wake her. If it is followed by her last name, she goes into 'awaiting orders' mode. But if G, A, Y, alone is followed by any of eight code words, she executes that escape instantly. I have tried to select monosyllables that ordinarily do not follow her first name. Gay Deceiver."

"Hi, Deety!"

"Dictionary. G, A, Y. Read."

"Gayety, gayfeather, Gayle, Gaylord, Gay-Pay-Oo, gay-wings—"

XXIV *Captains aren't supposed to cry.*

Hilda:

I ordered an early dinner by starting it when Zebbie and Deety went down to bathe. I had ready a public reason but my motive was personal: I didn't want a pillow talk with Jacob.

Annoyed at him? At *me!* I had had a perfect chance to keep my lip zipped—and muffed it! Was I boasting? Or confessing? Or trying to hurt Jacob? (Oh, no!—can the id be *that* idiotic!)

Don't rationalize it, Sharpie! Had not your husband been kind, tolerant, and far more sophisticated than you ever dreamed, you would be in trouble.

When dinner was over, Zebbie said lazily, "I'll do the dishes in the morning."

I said, "I prefer that they be done tonight, please."

Zebbie sat up and looked at me. His thoughts were coming through so strongly that I was getting them as words. I never allow myself to be close with a person whose thoughts I can't sense at all; I distrust a blank wall. But now I could "hear" such names as "Queeg" and "Bligh" and "Vanderdecken" and "Ahab"—and suddenly Captain Ahab was harpooning the White Whale and I was the whale!

Zebbie bounced to his feet with a grin that made me uneasy. "Sure thing, Cap'n! Deety, grab a rifle and hold it on me to make sure I get 'em clean."

I cut in quickly, "I'm sorry, Chief Pilot, but I need the Astrogator. Jacob is your assistant."

When they were gone, Deety said, "Will my shotgun do? I don't think the cardboard eater comes out in daylight."

"Bring the guns inside; we're going to close the doors."

I waited until we were settled. "Deety, will you make me a copy of your new programs before our men come back?"

"If they take time to wash them properly. Men and dishes— you know."

"I hope they stall—"

"—and get over their mad," Deety finished.

"That, too. But I intend to write a sequential program and I want you to check me. After you make that copy."

They did stay down—"man talk," no doubt. Men need us but can just barely stand us; every now and then they have to discuss our faults. I *think* that is why they shut us out.

Deety made a copy while I wrote what I planned to do. Deety looked it over, corrected some wording. Looked it over again— and said nothing pointedly.

"Deety, can you handle your father's lab camera?"

"Certainly."

"Will you check its load and shoot when I ask for it?"

"Of course."

"If I goof on an order, correct me at once."

"You don't intend to hand this to Zebadiah to carry out?"

"No. I prefer that you not mention that I prepared it ahead of time. Deety, the Chief Pilot assured me that any of us could command in aerospace. I am about to make a test run. The Chief Pilot is in a position to override. If he does, I shan't fight it; I have said all along that he should be captain."

We had time to dig out that shirt with the white flowers. Deety's sailor pants were long; we turned up cuffs. The lacing at the back made them small enough in the waist. She gave me a blue belt to pull in the shirt, which I wore outside—then she added a blue hair ribbon.

"Captain Auntie, you look *good*. Better than I will in this jump suit I am reluctantly pulling on. Gosh, I'm glad Zebadiah isn't square about skin!"

"He was when I adopted him. Fetched swim briefs the first time I invited him over to swim. But I was firm. There they come! Open the doors."

They appeared to be over their mad. Zebbie looked at me and said, "How fancy! Are we going to church?"—and my husband added, "You look pretty, my dear."

"Thank you, sir. All hands, prepare for space. Secure loose gear. Lock firearms. Anyone requiring a bush stop say so. Dress for space. Before manning car, take a turn around the car, searching for gear on the ground."

"What is this?" demanded Zebbie.

"Prepare for space. *Move!*"

He hesitated a split second. "Aye aye, Captain."

In two minutes and thirteen seconds (I checked Gay's clock) I was squeezing past my husband into the starboard rear seat. I said, "In reporting, include status of firearms. Astrogator."

"Belted down. Bulkhead door dogged. Shotgun loaded and locked. I slid it under the sleeping bag."

"Fléchette gun?"

"Wups! In my purse. Loaded and locked. Purse clipped to my seat, outboard."

"Copilot."

"Belt fastened. Door locked, seal checked. Continua device ready. Rifle loaded and locked, secure under sleeping bag. I'm wearing my pistol loaded and locked."

"Chief Pilot."

"Belt fastened, door locked, seal checked. Rifle loaded, locked, under sleeping bag. Wearing revolver, loaded and locked. No loose gear. Water tanks topped off. Load trimmed. Two reserve power packs, two zeroed. Juice zero point seven-two capacity. Wings spread full. Wheels down, unlocked to retract. All systems go. Ready."

"Chief Pilot, after first maneuver, execute vertical dive fastest without power and without retracting wheels. Relock wheel-retracting gear. Leave wings spread max."

"Wheel retractors locked. After first maneuver fastest, no-power vertical dive, wings full subsonic, wheels down."

I glanced at Deety; she held up the camera and mouthed, "Ready."

"Gay *Home!*"

In Arizona it was shortly before sunset, as Deety had predicted. My husband repressed a gasp. I snapped, "Copilot, report H-above-G."

"Uh . . . two klicks minus, falling." Zebbie had bite now; the horizon ahead tilted slowly up, then faster. As we leaned over, Deety stretched high, catlike, to shoot between our pilots. We steadied with Snug Harbor dead ahead—*a crater!* I felt a burst of anger, a wish to *kill!*

"Picture!"

"Gay *B'gout!*"

Instead of being stationary at "Touchdown" we were in free fall on the night side of some planet. I could see stars, with blackness below the "horizon"—if horizon it were. Deety said, "Looks like the Russians left something on our parking space."

"Perhaps. Jacob, H-above-G, please."

"Under ten klicks, decreasing slowly."

"So far, so good. But we aren't sure that we have the right planet and universe."

"Captain, that's Antares ahead."

"Thanks, Zebbie. I assume that at least we are in one of the analogs of our native universe. Deety, can you get from Gay the acceleration and check it against Mars-ten?"

"'Bout four ways, Cap'n."

"Go ahead."

"Gay Deceiver."

"Hi, Deety!"

"Hi, Gay. H-above-G, closing rate running, solve first differential, report answer."

Instantly Gay answered, "Three-seven-six centimeters per second squared."

"You're a smart girl, Gay."

So it was either Mars-ten or an unreasonable facsimile. "Gay B'gout!"

We were stationary, with what we had come to feel as "proper weight." Deety said, "Maybe an animal wandered across our spot. How about lights, Captain? This snapshot ought to be colors by now."

"Not yet. Chief Pilot, when I alert the autopilot by G, A, Y, please switch on forward landing lights."

"Roger Wilco."

"Gay—"

Blinding light—men in its path were blinded, not us. *"Bounce!* Kill the light, Zebbie. The Little Father left sentries in case we came back—and we did."

"Captain Auntie, may I have cabin light now?"

"Please be patient, dear. I saw two men. Jacob?"

"Three men, dear . . . dear Captain. Russian soldiers in uniform. Weapons, but no details."

"Deety?"

"Looked like bazookas."

"Chief Pilot?"

"Bazookas. A good thing you were on the bounce with Bounce, Skipper. Gay can take a lot...but a bazooka would make her unhappy." He added, "Speed saved me yesterday. Deety, let that be a lesson: Never lose your temper."

"Look who's talking!"

"I quit being C.O., didn't I? Cap'n Sharpie doesn't do foolish stunts. If *I* were skipper, we would chase 'em all over that sea bottom. Never be in one place long enough for them to aim and they would think there were thirty of us. If Colonel Snotsky is there—I think he's afraid to go home—"

We were over Arizona.

I snapped, "Gay *Termite!*"

—and were parked by our stream. Zebbie said, "What the devil? Who did *that?*"

"*You* did, Zebadiah," Deety answered.

"*Me?* I did no such thing. I was—"

"*Silence!*" (That was I, Captain Bligh.)

I went on, "Gay Deceiver, go to sleep. Over."

"Sleepy time, Hilda. Roger and out."

"Chief Pilot, is there a way to shut off the autopilot so completely that she cannot possibly be activated by voice?"

"Oh, certainly." Zebbie reached up, threw a switch.

"Thanks, Zebbie. Deety, your new escape programs are swell...but I missed how that happened. But first— Did anyone else see our giant termite?"

"Huh?"—"I did."—"Where?"

I said, "I was looking out to starboard as we transited. The creature was feeding on packing debris—and took off uphill at high speed. Looked like a very big, fat, white dog with too many legs. Six, I think."

"'Six,'" agreed my husband. "Put me in mind of a polar bear. Hilda, I think it *is* carnivorous."

"We are not going to find out. Deety, tell Zebbie—all of us—what happened."

Deety shrugged. "Zebadiah said 'bounce' twice when he should not have, but Gay wasn't triggered. Then he said 'Gay can take a lot—' and she *was* triggered. More chitchat and Zebadiah said '—I think he's afraid to go home—' That did it. Our smart girl hears what she has been taught. She heard: 'Gay Home' and that is the short form that used to be: 'Gay Deceiver Take Us Home.'"

Zebbie shook his head. "A gun should never be that hair-trigger."

"Chief Pilot, yesterday you used the first of these clipped programs to avoid a bullet in your face. First 'Gay'—then after more words—'bounce!' It saved you."

"But—"

"I'm not through. Astrogator, study the escape programs. Search for possibility of danger if triggered accidentally. Zebbie, escape programs can't be compared to a hair trigger on a gun; they are to *escape*, not to kill."

"Captain Auntie, I've spent *all day* making *certain* that programs can't put us out of the frying pan into the fire. That's why I killed 'countermarch.' The nearest thing to danger is the 'Home' program because our home planet is unfriendly." Deety sounded sad. "I hate to cut our last link with home."

"It needn't be cut," I said. "Just stretched. Put it back into long form and add 'Execute.'"

Deety answered, "Captain, I will do as you say. But we might be a billion klicks from nowhere and hit by a meteor. If anyone can gasp, 'GayHome,' then we are two klicks over our cabin site in air, not vacuum. Even if we've passed out, Gay won't crash us; she's built not to. If I'm gasping my last, I don't want to have to say, 'Gay Deceiver, take us home. Execute.' That's ten syllables against two . . . with air whooshing out."

I said, "That settles it. The 'Gay Home' program stands unless my successor changes it."

"You're not talking to me, Captain Sharpie darling—I mean, Captain Hilda—because I'm *not* your successor. But Deety convinced me. I will *not* admit that those vermin have run me *permanently* off my own planet. At least I can return to it to die."

"Son, let's not speak of dying. We are going to stay alive and raise kids and enjoy it."

"That's my Pop! Say, doesn't *anybody* want to see this picture?"

We made it a rest stop, worrying more about giant termites than about bushes . . . and Jacob found a can opener. *The* can opener. I put a stop to an attempt to fix the blame. Advice to all explorers: Do not roam the universes without a spare can opener.

Then it was "Prepare for lift!" and a new program. "Chief Pilot, switch on autopilot. Gay Deceiver. Explore. True bearing two-six-five. Unit jump five minima. Use bingo stop continue. End program short of sunrise line. Ground. Acknowledge by paraphrase."

"Explore west five degrees south fifty-klick units. Two-second check each jump. Ground myself no power Greenwich time oh-three-seventeen."

"Deety, is that time right?"

"For that program."

"Gay Deceiver. Program revision. Cancel grounding. From program coded 'A Tramp Abroad' display locus. Display Bingoes."

She displayed Mars at once, but gibbous. I scrawled a note to Deety: *"How do I rotate to show day side only?"*

Dear Deety! She wrote her answer. Passed it over—I doubt that our men saw it: "Program revision. Display locus real-time day side."

Gay accommodated. It took several steps to define new locus as sunset line (right edge - east) to sunrise line (left edge - west), and between 50°N and 50°S (some Russian area had been close to 45°S, so I widened the search)—then let the locus move with the terminators. (Gay can "see" in the dark but *I* can't.)

I told her to end "Explore" at Greenwich oh-three-seventeen and start "A Tramp Abroad," continue until directed otherwise, and had Gay repeat back in her phrasing.

I touched Zebbie's shoulder, pointed to the switch that cut out Gay's ears, drew a finger across my throat. He nodded and shut her out. I said, "Questions, gentlemen? Deety?"

"I do, Captain," said our Chief Pilot. "Do you plan on sleeping tonight?"

"Certainly, Zebbie. An ideal sleeping spot would be one far from the Russians but close to the present sunset line. Or did *you* want to work all night?"

"If you wish. I noticed that you gave Gay a program that could keep her going for days or weeks—and that you had reduced H-above-G to six klicks. Breathable air. By rotating duties, with one or two always stretched out aft, we can stay up a week, easily, and still give Jake's ankles a break."

"I can skip a night's sleep," said Deety. "Captain Auntie honey, with enough random samples and a defined locus, sampling soon approaches a grid a fly couldn't get through. Do you want the formula?"

"Heavens, no! As long as it works."

"It works. Let's make a *long* run, get a *big* sampling. But I'd like to add something. Let's parallel the display onto a sidelooker screen, and light every vertex—while the main display shows Bingoes. You'll see how tight a screen you're building."

"Sharpie, don't let her do it!" Zebbie added, "'Scuse, please!

Captain, the Astrogator is correct on software but I know more about *this* hardware. You can crowd a computer into a nervous breakdown. I have safeguards around Smart Girl; if I give her too much to do, she tells me to go to hell. But she *likes* Deety. Like a willing horse, she'll try hard for Deety even when it's too much."

Deety said soberly, "Captain, I gave you bad advice."

Her husband said, "Don't be so humble, Deety. You're smarter than I am and we all know it. But we are dependent on Smart Girl and can't let her break down. Captain, I don't know how much strain the time-space twister puts on her but she has unnecessary programs. At the Captain's convenience, I would like to review everything in her perms and wipe those we can do without."

"My *very* early convenience, sir. Is the schedule okay?"

"Oh, sure. Just don't add that side display."

"Thank you, Chief Pilot. Anyone else? Copilot?"

"My dear . . . my dear Captain, is there some reason to find a spot near the sunset line? If you intend to work all night?"

"Oh! But, Jacob, I do *not* plan to work all night. It is now about twenty hundred by our personal circadians, as established by when we got up. I think we can search for three to four hours. I hope that we can find a spot of sleep near the sunset line, scout it in daylight, let Gay land herself on it for her perms—then return to it in the dark when we get tired."

"I see, in part. My dear, unless I misunderstood you, you are heading *west*. But you said that you wanted to find us a place to sleep near the present sunset line. *East*. Or did I misunderstood you?"

"It's very simply explained, Jacob."

"Yes, dear Captain?"

"I made a horrible mistake in navigation."

"Oh."

"Chief Pilot, did you spot it?"

"Yup. Yes, Captain."

"Why didn't you speak up?"

"Not my business, Ma'am. Nothing you planned to do was any danger."

"Zebbie, I'm not sure whether to thank you for keeping quiet, or to complain because you did. Deety, you spotted the mistake, I am certain. You are supposed to advise me."

"Captain, I'm supposed to speak up to stop a *bad* mistake. This was not. I wasn't certain that it was a mistake until you told on yourself. But you spotted the mistake when Gay predicted the time to end the 'Explore' program, then you corrected it by telling her to shift to 'A Tramp Abroad.' So there was never a reason to advise you."

I let out a sigh. "You're covering for me and I love you all and I'm no good as captain. I've served as many hours as Zebbie and we are on the ground, so now it's time to elect someone who can do it *right*. You, Zebbie."

"Not me. Jake and Deety must each do a stint before I'd admit that it might be my turn."

"Captain—"

"Deety, I'm not captain; I resigned!"

"No, Aunt Hilda, you didn't actually do it. It is my duty to advise you when you seem about to make a bad mistake. You made a minor mistake and corrected it. In my business we call that 'debugging'—and spend more time on it than we do on writing programs. Because *everybody* makes mistakes."

Jane's little girl managed to sound the way Jane used to. I resolved to listen—because all too often I hadn't listened to Jane. "Captain Auntie, if you were resigning because of the way your crew treated you—as Zebadiah did—I wouldn't say a word. But that's not your reason. Or is it?"

"What? Oh, no! You've all helped—you've been angels. Uh, well, mostly."

"'Angels'—hummph! I can't use the correct words; I'd shock our men. Aunt Hilda, I gave you far worse lip than I ever gave Zebadiah. You slapped me down *hard*—and I've been your strongest supporter ever since. Zebadiah, what *you* did was worse—"

"I know."

"—but you admitted that you were wrong. Nevertheless you've been chewing the bit. Demanding explanations. Zebadiah, the captain of a ship doesn't have to explain why she gives an order. Or does she?"

"Of course not. Oh, a captain sometimes does explain. But she shouldn't do it often or the crew will start thinking they are entitled to explanations. In a crunch this can kill you. Waste that split second." Zebbie brooded. "Captain says 'Frog,' you *hop*. Couple of times I failed to hop. Captain, I'm sorry."

"Zebbie, we get along all right."

He reached back and patted my knee. "Pretty well in the past. Better from now on."

My darling Jacob said worriedly, "I'm afraid I have been remiss, too."

I was about to reassure him when Deety cut in: "'Remiss'! Pop, you're the worst of all! If *I* had been your wife, I would have tossed you back and rebaited my hook. 'Farce' is worse than mutinous; it's *insulting*. Be glad Jane didn't hear you!"

"I know, I know!"

I touched Deety's arm and whispered, "That's enough, dear."

Zebbie said soberly, "Captain, as I analyze it, you made a mistake in sign. Every navigator makes mistakes—and has some routine by which to check his work. If you're going to get upset because recheck shows that you wrote down 'plus' when the declination is 'south,' you're going to have ulcers. You're just under strain from being C.O. We've all made the strain worse. But we want to do better. I'd *hate* to have you resign over a minor error . . . when *we* caused your upset. I hope you'll give us another chance."

Captains aren't supposed to cry. I blinked 'em back, got my voice under control, and said, "All hands! Still ready for lift? Report."

"Aye, Captain!"—"Affirmative!"—"Yes, my dear Hilda."

"Zebbie, switch on Gay's ears." He did.

"Execute!"—Termite Creek was gone and we were fifty klicks west and a touch south. Pretty and green but no Bingo. It would take us about seven minutes to overtake the Sun and approach sunrise line, plus any holds we made. Then I would go east to the sunset line in nothing flat (have Zebbie and Jacob do it); then bounce & glide, bounce & glide, while looking for a place to sleep in a spot suitable for Gay to try her new unpowered auto-grounding program—in daylight with the hottest pilot in two worlds ready to override any error.

If Gay could do this, we would be almost independent of juice—and have a new "bug-out" sanctuary each time she landed herself. Power packs—Zebbie had a hand-cranked D.C. generator—but heavy work for husky men for endless hours. (40 hrs from zero to full charge; you see why Zebbie would rather buy fresh charges.)

We had been skipping along nearly three minutes, over four thousand klicks, before spotting a Bingo (by Zebbie). I called a "Hold" and added, "Where, Zebbie?"

He nosed us down. Farm buildings and cultivated fields—a happy contrast to the terrain—barren, green, flat, rugged—all lacking any sign of humans, in the stops we had made. "Astrogator, record time. Continue."

Then over three minutes with no Bingoes— At elapsed time 6^{m}4^s Jacob called out, "Bingo! A town."

"Hold! Onion towers?"

"I think not, dear. I see a flag—dare we go nearer?"

"Yes! But anyone use a scram at will. Jacob, may I have the binoculars, please?"

The Stars and Stripes are engraved on my heart, but in the next moments the Cross of Saint Andrew and the Cross of Saint George were added. It was an ensign with a blue field and some white shapes—three half moons in three sizes.

"Gay Deceiver."

"I'm all ears, Hilda."

"Move current program to standby."

"Roger Wilco Done."

"Gay Bounce. Zebbie, let's sweep this area for a bigger settlement."

Zebbie placed a locus around the town, radius five hundred klicks, and started "A Tramp Abroad" with vertex time cut to one second. Thirty-one minutes later we had a city. I guessed it at a hundred thousand plus.

"Captain," Zebbie said, "may I suggest that we bounce and try to raise them by radio? This place is big enough for A.A. guns or missiles—"

"Gay Bounce!"

"—and we know that their Slavic neighbors have aircraft."

"Is your guardian angel warning you?"

"Well . . . 'tain't polite to ground without clearance; such rudeness can make one suddenly dead."

"Gay Bounce, Gay Bounce. Are we out of reach of missiles?"

"Captain, British and Russians of this universe are ahead of us in spaceships or they wouldn't be here. That requires us to assume that their missiles and lasers and X-weapons are better than ours."

"What's an 'X-weapon'? And what do you advise?"

"I advise evasive tactics. An X-weapon is a 'Nobody-Knows.'"

"Evasive tactics, your choice. I assume you won't waste juice."

"No juice. Jake, gallop in all directions. Up, down, and sideways. Don't wait for 'Execute'; jump as fast as you can. That's it! Keep moving!"

"Captain Auntie, may I suggest an easier way?"

"Speak up, Deety."

"Zebadiah, how big is that city? Kilometers."

"That's indefinite. Oh, call it eight klicks in diameter."

"You've got that one-second 'Tramp' program on hold. Change locus. Center on that biggest building, make the radius six klicks. Then start program and Pop can rest."

"Uh . . . Deety, I'm stupid. Six klicks radius, ten klicks is a minimum— A bit tight?"

"Meant to be. Shall I draw a picture?"

"Maybe you'd better."

(Deety had defined an annulus two kilometers wide, outer radius six, inner radius four. We would "circle" the city six klicks above ground, random jumps, sixty per minute. I doubted that even robot weapons could find us, range us, hit us, in one second.)

Deety loosened her belt, slithered forward, and sketched. Suddenly Zebbie said, "Gotcha! Deety, you're a smart girl."

"'Boss, I'll bet you tell that to all the girls.'"

"Nope, just smart ones. Gay Deceiver!"

"Less noise, please."

"Program revision. A Tramp Abroad. Locus a circle radius six klicks. Center defined by next Bingo. Acknowledge paraphrase."

"Revised program A Tramp Abroad. Circle twelve klicks diameter center next real-time Bingo."

"Jake, put us over that big building downtown. If necessary, make several tries but don't hang around. Once I like the position I'll say the magic word, then scram."

"Aye aye, Chief."

Jacob made a dozen jumps before Zebbie said, "Bingo Gay Bounce" and a light appeared on the display. He started the program and told Gay to increase scale; the light spread out into a circle with a lighted dot in the center. "Captain, watch this. I've told Gay that every stop is a Bingo. You may be surprised."

"Thanks, Zebbie." The circle was becoming freckled inside its perimeter. With no feeling of motion, the scene flicked every second. It was mid-morning; each scene was sharp. That big building would be dead ahead—blink your eye and you're staring at fields—then again at the city but with that building off to starboard. It put me in mind of holovideo tape spliced to create confusion.

Zebbie had on his phones and was ignoring everything else. Jacob was watching the flickering scenery, as was I, as was Deety—when Jacob suddenly turned his head, said, "Deety-please-the-Lo—" and clapped his hand over his mouth.

I said, "Two Lomines, Deety—quickly!"

Deety was reaching for them. "You, too, Auntie Cap'n?"

"It's this flickering." I gave one to Jacob, made certain that he saw me take one. I had not been motion-sick since I had been made Captain. But any time my husband must take one, I will keep him company.

Today I should have taken one as soon as I spotted that British flag; Lomine tranquilizes the nerves as well as the tummy . . . and soon I must act as—ambassador? Something of the sort; I intended to go straight to the top. Dealing with underlings is frustrating. In college I would not have lasted almost four years had it been up to the dean of women. But I always managed to take it over her head to the president; the top boss can bend the rules.

(But my senior year the president was female and as tough a bitch as I am. She listened to my best Clarence-Darrow defense, congratulated me, told me I should have studied law, then said, "Go pack. I want you off campus by noon.")

Zebbie pushed the phone off his right ear. "Captain, I've got this loud enough to put on the horn. Want to talk to them?"

"No. I've never grounded outside the States. You know how, you do it. But, Chief Pilot—"

"Yes, Ma'am?"

"And Copilot and Astrogator. Stick to the truth at all times. *But do not unnecessarily give information.* Answer questions uninformatively—but truthfully. If pressed, tell them, 'See the Captain.'"

"My dear," Jacob said worriedly, "I've been meaning to speak about this. Zeb has had diplomatic experience. Wouldn't it be wise for us to place him in charge on the ground? Please understand, I'm not criticizing your performance as captain. But with his experience and in view of the fact that our principal purpose is to obtain certain things for his car—"

"Gay Bounce Gay Bounce Gay Bounce! Astrogator."

"Yes, Captain."

"Place us in a parking orbit. Soonest."

"Aye aye, Ma'am! Copilot, don't touch the verniers. Chief Pilot, check that the car is level. Gay Deceiver."

"On deck, Deety."

"Program. L axis add speed vector three point six klicks per second. Paraphrase acknowledge."

"Increase forward speed three and six tenths kilometers per second."

"Chief Pilot?"

"Level."

"Execute." Deety glanced at the board. "Gay Deceiver, H-above-G will soon stop decreasing, then increase very slowly. In about fifty minutes it will maximize. Program. When H-above-G is maximum, alert me."

"Roger Wilco."

"If-when one hundred klicks H-above-G, alert me."

"Roger Wilco."

"If-when air drag exceeds zero, alert me."

"Roger Wilco."

"Remain in piloting mode. Ignore voices including program code words until you are called by your full name. Acknowledge by reporting your full name."

"'Gay Deceiver,'" answered Gay Deceiver.

"Is that okay, Captain? Smart Girl can't hear the short-form programs now, until she hears her full name *first*. Then you would still have to say 'Gay' to alert her, and 'Home' or whatever to scram. But there should be loads of time, as she'll tell me if anything starts to go wrong. You heard her."

"That's fine, Astrogator."

"I turned her ears off because there may be discussion in which you might not want to have to be careful to use code words . . . but still be able to put her ears back fast if you need them. Faster than the switch and besides the switch can be reached only from the left front seat."

Deety had a touch of nervous chattering; I understood the reasons for each step. And I understood why she was chattering.

"Well done. Thank you. Remain at the conn. Chief Pilot, Copilot, the Second-in-Command has the conn. I am going aft and do not wish to be disturbed." I lowered my voice, spoke directly to Deety. *"You* are free to call me. You *only."*

"Aye aye, Captain," Deety acknowledged quietly. "I must remind you: air for four hours only."

"If I fall asleep, call me in three hours." I kissed her quickly, floated out of my chair and started to undog the bulkhead door— got nowhere; Deety had to help me. Deety flipped a light switch for me. She closed me in and dogged one dog.

I got a blanket out of the cradle, took off my clothes, tried to wrap myself in the blanket. It kept slithering away.

No seat belts— But the web straps used to make a bedroll of Zebbie's sleeping bag were attached through loops and tucked under thingammies. Soon I had a belt across my waist and the blanket around me.

Being a runt, the only way I can fight is with words. But best for me is to walk away. Fight with *Jacob?* I was so angry I wanted to slap him! But I *never* slap anyone; a woman who takes advantage of her size and sex to slap a man is herself no gentleman. So I walked away—got out of there before I said something that would tear it—lose me my lovable, cuddly, thoughtful—and sometimes *unbearable!*—husband.

I wept in my pillow—no pillow and no Kleenex. After a while I slept.

XXV   *"—leave bad enough alone!"*

Deety:
After I helped Aunt Hilda with the bulkhead door, I got back into my seat—and said nothing. If I opened my mouth, I would say too much. I love Pop a heap, and respect him as a mathematician.

Pop is also one of the most selfish people I've ever known.

Doesn't mean he's tight with money; he isn't. Doesn't mean he wouldn't share his last crust of bread—he would. With a stranger.

But if he doesn't want to do something, he won't. When Jane died, I had to take over money management at once. At seventeen. Because Pop ignored it. It was all I could do to get him to sign his name.

I was bucking for my doctorate. Pop seemed to think that I should cook, clean house, shop, keep financial records, manage our businesses, cope with taxes—and earn my doctorate simultaneously.

Once I let dishes stack to see how long it would take him to notice. About two weeks later he said, "Deety, aren't you ever going to do the dishes?"

I answered, "No, sir."

"Eh? Why not?"

"I don't have time."

He looked puzzled. "Jane didn't seem to find keeping house difficult. Is something wrong, dear?"

"Pop, Mama wasn't bucking for a doctorate against a committee of dunderheads. My research subject was approved two years ago...but I've got men judging me—four out of seven—who can't tell Fortran from Serutan, hate computers, and have dark fears that computer scientists are going to take their jobs away from them. They make me do work over because *they* don't understand it. And besides— Well, Mama Jane always had help, mine, and a housekeeper toward the end."

Pop is okay. He hired a housekeeper who stuck with us till I got my Ph.D. He investigated, discovered that the head of the department had put men on my committee who knew nothing about computers—not on purpose; the department head did not know computers. I wound up with an even tougher committee but *they knew computers*. Fair enough.

Pop means to be good to me and he adores Aunt Hilda and means to pamper her. Pop is one of those men who sincerely believe in Women's Lib, always support it—but so deep down that they aren't aware of it, their emotions tell them that women never get over being children.

A mistake easy to make with Aunt Hilda— There are twelve-year-old girls bigger than she is and with more curves.

For a horrid time, we three said nothing. Zebadiah watched his instruments; Pop stared straight ahead.

At last my husband gave my father the chewing out that Pop would never have taken from me. "Jake. Tell me how you do it."

"Eh?"

"You're a genius. You aren't the absent-minded sort who needs a boy to lead him around. You can hammer a nail with the best of them and can use power tools without chopping your fingers. You're good company and you managed to attract one of the three finest women I've ever known so much that she married you. Yet you have publicly insulted her twice in one day. *Twice.* Tell me: Do you have to *study* to be that stupid? Or is it a gift, like your genius for mathematics?"

Pop covered his face with his hands. Zebadiah shut up.

I could see Pop's shoulders shake. Presently his sobbing stopped. He wiped his eyes, unfastened his seat belt. When I realized he was heading for the bulkhead door, I unstrapped fast and placed myself in his way. He said, "Please move out of my way, Deety."

"Copilot, return to your seat."

"But, Daughter, you *can't* come between husband and wife!"

"Address me as 'Astrogator.' The Captain does not wish to be disturbed. Gay Deceiver!"

"Here, Deety!"

"Log mode. Copilot, I will not permit you to disobey the Captain's orders. Return to your seat, strap down—and *stay there!*"

"Or would you rather be placed in it?" Zebadiah growled. "With your arms strapped under the belts, and the buckles where you can't reach them."

"Chief Pilot, do not intervene unless I call on you. Copilot, *move!*"

Pop turned in the air, almost kicking me in the face and unaware of it. He was speaking through sobs. "But I *must* apologize to Hilda! Can't you understand that?" But he was getting back into his seat.

"Jake, you'll be a worse damn' fool if you do."

"What? Zeb, you can't mean that."

"I do mean it. You apologized once today. Hypocrisy, as Sharpie realizes. Jake, your *only* chance of staying married is to shut up and soldier; your word is no longer worth a fiat dollar. But if you behave yourself for four or five years, she might forget it. Correction: forgive it. She'll *never* forget it. Establish a long record of good behavior and she might allow you some minor faults. But don't *ever* hint that she is not as competent as any man. Sure, she'd be picked last for a tug-o'-war team, and she has to stand on a stool to reach a high shelf—*does that affect her brain?* Hell's bells, if size mattered, *I* would be the supergenius around here—not *you*. Or perhaps you think being able to grow a beard confers wisdom? Jake, leave bad enough alone! Mess with it, you'll make it worse."

Time for a diversion: Pop must *not* be given a chance to answer. If Pop started defending himself, he would wind up self-righteous. The ability of the male mind to rationalize its deeds—and misdeeds—cannot be measured.

(And some female minds. But we females have more wild animal in us; mostly we don't feel any need to justify ourselves. We just do it, whatever it is, because we want to. Is there ever any other reason?)

"Gentlemen," I added, close on Zebadiah's last remark before Pop could attempt rebuttal, "speaking of beards, you each have a three-day growth. If we are about to ask sanctuary, shouldn't we be neat? I'm going to comb my hair and dig the dirt out from under my nails, and—Glory be!—I've got one spandy-clean jump suit. In light green, Zebadiah; matches your pilot suits. Got a clean one, dear?"

"I believe so."

"I know so; I packed it when Aunt Hilda and I rearranged inventory. Pop, your light green jump suit is clean. That one you are wearing has wrinkles in the wrinkles and a big soup spot. We three will look as if we were in uniform. Aunt Hilda won't but the captain-and-owner of a yacht doesn't dress like her crew."

"'Owner'?" said Pop.

"'"Owner,"'" Zebadiah said firmly. "We pooled our resources. Sharpie is captain; she'll stand as owner for all of us. Simpler."

"She cautioned us not to tell lies, Zeb." (Pop sounded normal—his usual argumentative self.)

"No lie. But if *she* finds it necessary to lie for us, we back her up. Come on, Jake, let's put on our squeakin' shoes; the Captain might decide to land any orbit. How long are these orbits, Deety?"

"One hundred minutes, plus a bit. But Gay could ground us from the far side in five minutes if the Captain asked for it."

"So let's get shipshape and Bristol style. Deety, will you keep an eye on the board while Jake and I shave?"

Pop said, "I'm sorry but I can't shave until the Captain joins us. My gear is aft."

"Jake, use mine. Glove compartment. Remington okay?" My husband added, "You first; I want to read the news."

"The 'news'?"

"Smart Girl has been sampling all frequencies, AM and FM, twice a second. If there is pattern, she copies."

"But Deet— The Astrogator switched off the autopilot's ears."

"Jake, you just flunked Physics One-Oh-One. Deety told S.G. to shut off *audio*. I had in mind the electromagnetic spectrum. You've heard of it?"

Pop chuckled. *"Touché!* That makes us even for the one you pulled while we were calibrating."

(I heaved a sigh of relief. I had not been trying to save Pop's marriage—that's *his* problem. Even my own marriage was secondary; I was trying to save *the team,* and so was Zebadiah. We were two marriages and that is important—but most important we were a survival team and either we worked together smoothly or none would live through it.)

While Pop shaved and Zebadiah read the news, I cleaned my nails. If I clean them before each meal and again at bedtime, they are dirty only in between—dirt likes me. Mama Jane told me that centuries ago, while ouching my hair for school—not a criticism; a statement of fact.

The men swapped headset for shaver and I combed my hair and pinned it into place—no longer an "ouch" job as I keep it short, ringlets rather than curls. Men like it long—but caring for long hair is a career in itself, and I've been pushed for time since I was twelve.

Zebadiah stopped to feel his chin—so I deduced as the buzzing stopped. I asked, "What did Smart Girl have to say?"

"Not much. Le'me finish this. BBC Third Program mostly."

"From *London?*" He had resumed shaving and couldn't hear me.

Zebadiah finished shaving and passed his shaver to Pop, who stowed it, then took off the headset and handed it back. Zebadiah racked and secured it. I was about to ask for it, when I heard Aunt Hilda's sweet voice:

"Hello, everyone! What did I miss?"

"Halley's Comet."

"Halley's— Zebbie, you're a tease. Jacob— *Oh!* You shaved! How very nice! Hold still, my darling; you're going to be kissed, ready or not."

A kiss in free fall is interesting to watch when one participant is safety-belted and the other half is floating free. Hilda held Pop's cheeks, he had her head in his hands, and Aunt Hilda drifted like a flag in a breeze. She was dressed but barefooted; I was intrigued when she curled her toes, hard. Was Pop that good?—my cubical father, so I had thought until recently. Did Jane teach him? Or— Shut up, Deety, you're a voyeuse with a nasty curiosity.

They broke and Hilda floated between the pilot seats, a hand on each, and looked at the board. My husband said—to her, not to me—"Don't I get a kiss? It was *my* razor."

Aunt Hilda hesitated. Pop said, "Kiss him, beloved, or he'll sulk." So she did. It occurs to me that Aunt Hilda may have taught Zebadiah and that Mama Jane and Aunt Hilda may have been trained by the same coach before Pop came along—if so, who was my Unknown Benefactor?

"Not a whole lot," Zebadiah was saying. "Mostly tapes from BBC. Five minutes of news from Windsor City—which may be the city we bingoed—as exciting as local news from any town you've never been in. Chatter in Russian. The Smart Girl saved that for you."

"I'll listen to it. But I must learn something. I was tempery a while ago, but a nap fixed me up and now I am filled with sweetness and light. I must have a report from each of you. We all have had cumulative fatigue. It is now bedtime at Termite Terrace but about lunchtime in Windsor City if that is its name. We can go back to our stream or we can tackle the British. I am not taking a vote; I shall decide and I have a way to take care of anyone who is tired. But I insist on honest data. Deety?"

"Captain Auntie, sleep is never my problem."

"Zebbie?"

"I was a zombie. Until you recharged me. Now I'm rarin' to go!"

She mussed his hair. "Zebbie, quit teasing."

"Captain, on an earlier occasion I told you the facts: My alert time exceeds twenty-four hours. Forty-eight if I must. If that kiss did not stimulate you as much as it did me, let's try it again and find out what went wrong."

Aunt Hilda turned away abruptly. "Jacob dear, how do you feel? With the time difference this may be equivalent to staying up all night, possibly under great tension."

"Hilda my love, were we to return to our streamside, I would not sleep, knowing that this contact was coming. A night without sleep does not strain me."

"Pop's not exaggerating, Captain Auntie. I get my night-owl capacity from Pop."

"Very well. But I have a method of taking care of anyone who may have exaggerated. I can leave one person aboard as guard."

"Captain, this wagon does not need a guard."

"Chief Pilot, I was offering *sleep*—under pretext of guarding. Car locked and sleep where I just napped—outsiders would not know. Anyone? Speak up."

(I wouldn't have missed it for a Persian kitten! Did Hilda expect anyone to stay behind? I don't think so.)

"Very well. No firearms. Gentlemen, please hide your pistols and belts with the guns, aft. Zebbie, is there a way to lock that door in addition to dogging it?"

"Sure. Tell Gay. May I ask why? No one can break into the cabin without damaging the old girl so much that she won't lift."

"Conceded, Zebbie. But I will be bringing visitors into this space. If anyone is brash enough to ask to be shown beyond the bulkhead door, I shall tell him that is my private compartment." Aunt Hilda grinned wickedly. "If he persists, I'll freeze his ears. What's the program for locking and unlocking it?"

"*Very* complicated. Tell her, 'Lock the bulkhead door,' or 'Unlock the bulkhead door.' Concealed solenoids. If the car is cold, the bolts drop back."

"Goodness, you were thorough."

"No, Ma'am. The Aussies were. But it turns out to be convenient for things we wouldn't like to lose. Cap'n, I don't trust banks any more than I trust governments, so I carry my safety deposit vault with me."

"If you cut the trickle charge, it unlocks?" Pop asked.

"Jake, I knew you would spot that. An accumulator across the solenoids, floating. Shut down the car and the solenoids work for another month...*unless* you open a switch in an odd location. Anyone want to know where it is?—what you don't know, you can't tell."

He got no takers. Instead I said, "Captain, is a fléchette gun a 'firearm'?"

"Hmm—Will it fit into a zippered compartment in your purse?"

"It fits into a *concealed* zipper compartment."

"Keep it with you. No swords, gentlemen, as well as no firearms; we are a civilian party. One thing we should carry: those miniature walky-talkies, Deety and I in our purses, you gentlemen in your pockets. If they are noticed, tell the truth: a means of keeping our party in touch."

Aunt Hilda suddenly looked stern. "This next order should be in writing. Please understand that there are *no* exceptions, *no* special circumstances, *no* variations left to individual judgment. I require Roger-Wilcoes from each of you or *we do not ground*. This party does *not* separate. Not for thirty seconds. Not for ten seconds. Not at all."

"Will the Captain entertain a question?"

"Certainly, Zebbie."

"Washrooms. Restrooms. Bathrooms. If these British behave like their analogs, such facilities are segregated."

"Zebbie, all I can say to that is that I will look for a way to cope. But we stay together until I—until *I*, the Captain—decide that it is safe to ease the rule. In the meantime— We should use that unpopular honey bucket before we ground...then, if necessary, return to the car, together, to use it later. That's not subject to discussion. Once we are on the ground, you three, acting unanimously, can hold a bloodless mutiny over this order or any"— Aunt Hilda looked directly at her husband—"and I will let myself be kicked out without a word...out of office as captain, out of the car, out of the party. Remain here, on Mars-ten, with the British if they will have me. No more questions. No further discussion by me or among yourselves. Astrogator."

"Roger Wilco!"

"Thank you. Please state it in the long form."

"I understand the Captain's order and will comply exactly with no mental reservations."

"Chief Pilot."

"I understand—"

"Short form. Deety defined it."

"Roger Wilco, Captain!"

Aunt Hilda turned in the air toward Pop—and I held my breath, three endless seconds. "Jacob?"

"Roger Wilco, Captain."

"Very well. We will ground as soon as we get clearance but will not ask for clearance until I've heard the news and translated that Russian." Whereupon I told her that we all intended to put on our best bib and tucker; the time should come out about right— and could we be relieved one by one? As I intended to use that darned thunder mug—when you must, you must.

Aunt Hilda frowned slightly. "I do wish that I had a jump suit in my size. This outfit—"

"Aunt Hilda! Your crew is in uniform but *you* are wearing the latest Hollywood style. That model was created by Ferrara himself and he charged you more than you paid for that mink cape. You are the Captain and dress to please yourself. I tell you three times!"

Aunt Hilda smiled. "Should I acknowledge in paraphrase?"

"By all means."

"Deety, I require my crew to wear uniforms. But *I* dress to suit myself, and when I saw what the world-famous couturier Mario Ferrara was doing to change the trend in women's sports clothes, I sent for him and worked him silly until he got *just* what I wanted. Including repeated washings of the trousers to give them that not-quite-new look so favored by the smart set for yachting. When you come back will you fetch your little shoes—my Keds— and the hair ribbon you gave me? They are part of Signor Ferrara's creation."

"Aunt Hilda honey, you make it sound true!"

"It *is* true. You told me three times. I don't even regret the thousand newdollar bonus I gave him. That man is a genius! Get along dear—git. Chief Pilot, you have the conn; I want the earphones."

I was back in ten minutes with jump suits for self and Pop and clean pilot suit for my husband.

I sailed their clothes toward Pop and Zebadiah. Aunt Hilda was handing phones back to Zebadiah; his suit caught both of them. "Wups, sorry but not very. What do the Russians say?"

"We're baddies," said my husband.

"We are? The suit I took off is loose back aft. Wrap it around your pistol and belt and shove them under the sleeping bag—pretty please?"

"With sugar on it?"

"At *today's* prices? Yes. Beat it. Cap'n, what sort of baddies?"

"Spies and agents-saboteurs and other things and indemnity is demanded in the name of the Tsar and the surrender of our persons, all twelve of us—"

"Twelve?"

"So they claim. —for trial before they hang us. Or else. The 'or-else' amounts to a threat of war."

"Heavens! Are we going to ground?"

"Yes. The British comment was that a source close to the Governor reports that the Russians have made another of their periodic claims of territorial violation and espionage and the note was routinely rejected. I intend to be cautious. We won't leave the car unless I am convinced that we will receive decent treatment."

Shortly we were again doing one-second jumps in a circle around Windsor City. Had Pop not pulled another blunder in handling Aunt Hilda we would have been on the ground two hours ago. "Blunder," rather than "insult"—but I'm not Hilda, I'm Deety. My ego is not easily bruised. Before I married, if a man patronized me and it mattered, I used to invite him to go skeet shooting. Even if he beat me (happened once), he *never* patronized me again.

If it's an unsocial encounter— I'm big, I'm strong, I fight dirty. A male has to be bigger, stronger, and just as well trained or I can take him. Haven't had to use the fléchette gun yet. But twice I've broken arms and once I kicked a mugger in the crotch and said he fainted.

Zebadiah was having trouble with traffic control. "—request permission to ground. This is private yacht Gay Deceiver, U.S. registry, Chief Pilot Carter speaking. All we want is clearance to ground. You're behaving like those you-know-what-I-mean Russians. I didn't expect this from Englishmen."

"Now, now! Where are you? You sound close by . . . but we can't get a fix on you."

"We are circling your city at a height above ground of five kilometers."

"How much is that in feet? Or miles?"

I touched my husband's shoulder. "Tell him sixteen thousand feet."

"Sixteen thousand feet."

"What bearing?"

"We're circling."

"Yes, but— See Imperial House at City Center? What bearing?"

"We are much too fast for you to take a bearing. While you speak one sentence, we've gone around twice."

"Oh, tell that to the Jollies; old sailors will never believe it."

Aunt Hilda tapped Zebadiah; he passed the microphone to her. Aunt Hilda said crisply, "This is Captain Burroughs, commanding. State your name, rating, and organization number."

I heard a groan, then silence. Twenty-three seconds later another voice came on. *"This is the officer of the watch, Leftenant Bean. Is there a spot of trouble?"*

"No, Lieutenant, merely stupidity. My chief pilot has been trying for fifteen minutes for clearance to ground. Is this a closed port? We were not told so by your embassy on Earth. We were warned that the Russians discouraged visitors, and indeed, they tried to shoot us out of the sky. What is your full name and your regiment, Lieutenant; I intend to make a formal report when I return home."

"Please, Madam! This is Leftenant Brian Bean, Devonshire Royal Fusiliers. May I ask to whom I am speaking?"

"Very well. I will speak slowly; please record. I am Captain Hilda Burroughs, commanding space yacht Gay Deceiver, out of Snug Harbor in the Americas."

"Captain, let me get this clear. Are you commanding both a spaceship in orbit and a landing craft from your ship? Either way, please let me have the elements of your ship's orbit for my log, and tell me the present position of your landing craft. Then I can assign you a berth to ground."

"Do I have your word as a British officer and gentleman that you will not shoot us out of the sky as those Russian vandals attempted to do?"

"Madam—Captain—you have my word."

"Gay Bounce. We are now approximately forty-nine thousand feet above your city."

"But— We understood you to say 'Sixteen thousand'?"

"That was five minutes ago; this craft is fast." Aunt Hilda released the button. "Deety, get rid of the special 'Tramp' program."

I told Gay to return "Tramp" to her perms and to wipe the temporary mods. "Done."

Aunt Hilda pressed the mike button. "Do you see us now?" She released the button. "Deety, I want us over that big building— 'Imperial House,' probably—in one transition. Can you tell Zebbie and Jacob what it takes?"

I looked it over. We should be at the edge of the city—but were we? Get a range and triangulate? No time! Guess at the answer, double it and divide by two. Arc tan four tenths. "Pop, can you transit twenty-one degrees from vertical toward city hall?"

"Twenty-one degrees. Sixty-nine degrees of dive toward the big barn in the park, relative bearing broad on the port bow, approx—set! One unit transition, ten klicks—set!"

"I can see you now, I do believe," came Mr. Bean's voice. *"Barely."*

"We'll come lower." Aunt Hilda chopped off the lieutenant. "Zebbie, put her into glide as soon as you execute. Deety, watch H-above-G and scram if necessary—don't wait to be told. Zebbie, execute at will."

"Jake, execute!"—and we were down so fast I got goose bumps...especially as Zebadiah then dived vertically to gain glide speed and that's mushy, slow, *slow,* on Mars.

But soon Aunt Hilda was saying tranquilly, "We are over Imperial House. You see us?"

"Yes, yes! My word! Bloody!"

"Leftenant, watch your language!" Aunt Hilda winked at me and snickered silently.

"Madam, I apologize."

"'Captain,' if you please," she said, smiling while her voice dripped icicles.

"Captain, I apologize."

"Accepted. Where am I to ground?"

"Ah, figured from Imperial House, there is a landing field due south of it twelve miles. I will tell them to expect you."

Hilda let up on the button, said, "Gay Bounce" and racked the microphone. "How unfortunate that the lieutenant's radio cut out before he could tell us how far away that field is. Or was it our radio?"

I said, "Captain, you know durn well both radios worked okay."

"Mercy, I must be getting old. Was Smart Girl in recording mode?"

I said, "She always is, during maneuvers. She wipes it in a ten-hour cycle."

"Then my bad hearing doesn't matter. Please ask her to repeat the lieutenant's last speech." I did, and Gay did. "Deety, can you have her wipe it right after the word 'it'?"

"Auntie, you ain't goin' to Heaven." I had Gay wipe twelve-miles-I-will-tell-them-to-expect-you. "But you wouldn't know anybody there."

"Probably not, dear. Zebbie, how does one have Smart Girl ground herself without juice?"

"Deety had better go over it again. Unless—Jake, will you explain it?"

"It's Deety's caper. I could use another drill."

"All right," I agreed. "Switch off Gay's ears, Zebadiah. Gay can make *any* transition *exactly* if she knows precisely where her target is. Even a jump of less than one minimum. I found that out the day we got here when we were testing remote control. The rest came from perfecting the 'Bug-Out' routine by having her pause and sweep the target and if it's obstructed, she bounces. Aunt Hilda, if you intend to ground, we had better not be much under five klicks or we'll have to bounce and start over."

"I've got air bite, Captain. I'll stretch it."

"Thanks, Zebbie. Deety, you do it. Let us all learn."

"Okay. I need both pilots. You haven't said where to ground."

"Wasn't that clear? Due south of Imperial House. I think it is a parade ground. Nothing on it but a flagpole on the north side. Put her down in front of the building but miss that flagpole."

"It would take override to hit that flagpole. Zebadiah, gunsight the spot you want to park on. I'll talk to Gay. Then put her in level flight in the orientation you want, and give 'Execute.' Pop, Gay should pause at exactly one-half klick, to see that her parking spot is clear and to recheck distance. That stop won't be long—a fraction of a second—but, if she fails to make it, try to bounce. Probably you can't; if I missed in debugging, maybe we'll all be radioactive. Been nice knowing you all. Okay, switch on her ears." My husband did so.

"Gay Deceiver."

"Hello, Deety. I've missed you."

"Unpowered autogrounding mode."

"Gonna ground by myself without a drop of juice! Where?"

"New target. Code word: 'Parade Ground.' Point of aim and range-finder method."

"Show him to me. I can lick him!"

I touched my husband's shoulder. "Let her know."

"On target, Gay. Steady on target."

"Range three-seven-two-nine, three-seven-naughty-nought, three-five-nine-nine—got him, Deety!"

Zebadiah leveled us out, headed us north. "Execute!"

We were parked facing the big front steps. That flagpole was ten meters from Gay's nose.

Pop said, "Deety, I could *see* the check stop but it was too short for me to act. But your programs always work."

"Until the day one blows up. Aunt Hilda, what do we do now?"

"We wait."

XXVI *The Keys to the City*

Jake:

I do not believe that I am wrong in insisting that Zeb should lead us. I am forced to conclude that being right has little to do with holding a woman's affections. I *never* intend to hurt Hilda's feelings. I now plan to make a career of keeping my mouth shut.

But I do not think it was diplomatic to spat with that radio operator or proper to be—well, yes, *rude*—rude to his officer. As for grounding twelve miles, nineteen klicks, from where we were told to—is *this* the behavior of guests!

But we did ground where we should not have. I started to open the door to get out, then help Hilda to disembark, when I heard her say: "We wait."

Hilda added, "Leave doors locked and belts fastened. Gay Deceiver, remain in maneuvering mode. Lock the bulkhead door."

"Hot and rarin' to go, Hilda. Bulkhead door locked."

"You're a smart girl, Gay."

"That makes two of us, Hilda."

"Chief Pilot, in this mode does she record outside as well as inside?"

"She does if I switch on outside speakers and mikes, Captain."

"Please do."

"What volume, Captain? Outside, and inside."

"I didn't know they were separate. Straight-line gain?"

"Logarithmic, Ma'am. From a gnat's whisper to a small earthquake."

"I would like outside pickup to amplify enough that we won't miss anything. What I send out should be a bit forceful."

"Captain, I'll give you a decibel advantage. You want it louder, squeeze my shoulder. I won't turn it higher than seven—unless you want to use it as a weapon. But to talk privately inside I have to keep switching off, then on. As with the Russians—remember?"

"Oh, yes. All hands, I will speak for all of us. If anyone needs to speak to me, attract Zebbie's attention—"

"Slap my shoulder."

"—and he'll give us privacy and confirm it with thumbs-up. Don't ask for it unnecessarily."

"Hilda, why these complex arrangements? Here comes someone now; it would be polite to go meet them. In any case, we can open the door to talk—these are not Russians." I simply could not bear to watch my darling handle this delicate matter with such—well, *rudeness!*

Was I thanked? "Copilot, pipe down. All hands, we may go upstairs any instant; report readiness for space. Astrogator."

"Ready, Captain."

"Chief Pilot."

"Still ready. Outside audio hot."

"Copilot."

"I'm checking this door seal again. Earlier I started to open it. There! Ready for space. Hilda, I don't think—"

"Correct! But the Chief Pilot *did* think, and gave me thumbs-up as soon as you started to talk. Pipe down! Chief Pilot, cut in our sender as soon as one of them speaks. Copilot, call me 'Captain' as the others do. Protocol applies; I'll explain family relationships later, when appropriate."

I resolved not to open my mouth for any reason, feeling quite disgruntled. Disgruntled? I found myself giving serious thought to whether or not Hilda's temporary and inappropriate authority could do permanent harm to her personality.

But the top of my mind was observing the Lord High Executioner, approaching us flanked by two henchmen. He was wearing a uniform more suited to musical comedy than to the field. Fierce moustaches, sunburn-pink complexion, service ribbons, and a swagger cane completed the effect.

His henchmen were younger, not so fancy, fewer ribbons, and

appeared to be sergeants. I could not read the officer's shoulder straps. A crown, I thought, but was there a pip beside it?

He strode toward us and was ten meters from my door when Hilda said firmly, "That's close enough. Please tell the Governor General that Captain Burroughs has grounded as directed and awaits his pleasure."

He stopped briefly and bellowed, "You were *not* directed to land *here!* You're supposed to be at the field! Customs, immigration, health inspection, visas, tourist cards, intelligence—"

I saw Hilda squeeze Zeb's shoulder. *"Quiet!"* Her voice came more loudly from outside than from her despite Gay's sound-proofing. Zeb reduced gain as she continued, "My good man, send one of your ratings to the Governor General to deliver my message. While we wait, state your name, rank, and regiment; I shall make formal report of your behavior."

"Preee*pos*terous!"

"Behavior 'unbecoming an officer and a gentleman,'" Hilda said with gentle sweetness, "since you insist. While you won't tell your name, like a naughty boy, others know it. The Paymaster. The Governor General. Others." She squeezed Zeb's shoulder. "Deliver my message!"

"I'm Colonel Brumby, Chief Constable of the Imperial House-hold, and *not* your messenger boy! Open up! I'm going to parade you before the Governor General—under arrest!"

Hilda said quietly to Zeb, "Seven"—allowed the Chief Constable to stride two more steps before saying, *"STOP!"*

My ears hurt.

All three stopped. The old fool braced himself and started again. Hilda must have poked Zeb; he answered with thumbs-up. "Back to normal volume but be ready with that earthquake."

He nodded; she went on, *"Leftenant* Colonel, is it not? I don't see that extra pip. Leftenant Colonel, I warn you for your own safety not to come closer."

He did not answer, kept coming, took his cane from under his arm. His sergeants followed—slowly, at a respectful distance. Hilda let him reach my door—I could see a network of broken veins on his nose—and for the second time in two days someone started to pound on Gay's door. He raised his cane—

"Stop that!"

I was deafened. The Chief Constable was missing. The sergeants were a long way back. They stopped running, turned and faced us. I looked down through my door's port, saw a pair of legs and a swagger cane—inferred a torso.

I turned my head, saw that Zeb had his thumb up. "Captain," he said, "I disobeyed you."

"How, Zebbie?"

"I gave him an eight; I wasn't sure his heart could take a ten. He looks like an old bottle-a-day man."

"An eight may have been too much," I commented. "He's on the ground. Dead, maybe."

"Oh, I hope not!"

"Unlikely, Captain," Zeb told her. "Shall I tell his noncoms to come get him?"

"I'll tell them, Zebbie. Normal level." Hilda waited until he signalled, then called out, "Sergeants! Colonel Brumby needs help. There will be no more loud noises."

The sergeants hesitated, then hurried. Shortly they were dragging him away. Presently he came to life, fought them off—sent one chasing back for his cane. The man caught my eye—and winked. I concluded that Brumby was not popular.

There was now a man standing on the entrance stairs. (Perhaps there had been people nearby earlier—but not after the noise started.) Imperial House had its ground floor with no doors on the front side. The first floor was the main floor and was reached by wide, sweeping stairs. The man near the top was small, dapper, dressed in mufti. As Brumby reached him, Brumby saluted, stopped, and they talked. Brumby's ramrod stiffness spoke for itself.

Shortly the smaller man trotted down the long steps, moved quickly toward us, stopped about thirty meters away, and called out, "In the landing craft! Is it safe to come closer?"

"Certainly," agreed Hilda.

"Thank you, Ma'am." He approached, talking as he walked. "I dare say we should introduce ourselves. I'm Lieutenant General Smythe-Carstairs, the Governor hereabouts. I take it you are Captain Burroughs?"

"That is correct, Excellency."

"Thank you. Although I can't tell, really, to whom I am speaking. Awkward, is it not, chatting via an announcing system? An open door would be pleasanter, don't you think? More friendly."

"You are right, Excellency. But the Russians gave us so unpleasant, so *dangerous,* a reception that I am nervous."

"Those bounders. They have been making a bit of fuss over you, on the wireless. That was how I recognized your craft—smaller than they claimed but an accurate description—for a Rus-

sian. But surely you don't think that we British wear our shirt tails
out? You will receive decent treatment here."

"That is pleasing to hear, Excellency. I was tempted to leave.
That policeman chap is most unpleasant."

"Sorry about that. Sheer mischance that he was first to greet
you. Important as this colony is to the Empire, no doubt you have
heard that being posted to it is not welcome to some. Not my own
case, I asked for it. But some ranks and ratings. Now let's have
that door open, shall we? I dislike to insist but I *am* in charge
here."

Hilda looked thoughtful. "Governor General, I can either open
the doors or leave. I prefer to stay. But the shocking treatment
by the Russians followed by the totally unexpected behavior of
your chief constable causes me to worry. I need a guarantee that
our party will be permitted to remain together at all times, and a
written safe-conduct for us, signed and sealed by you on behalf
of H.I.M."

"My dear Captain, a captain does not bargain with one who
stands in place of and holds the authority of His Imperial Majesty.
As a man, and you being a delightful lady, I would be happy to
bargain with you endlessly just for the pleasure of your company.
But I can't."

"I was not bargaining, Excellency; I was hoping for a boon.
Since you will not grant it, I must leave at once."

He shook his head. "I cannot permit you to leave as yet."

"Gay Bounce. Zebbie, will you try to reach that nice Mr.
Bean?"

Zeb had him shortly. *"Leftenant Bean heah."*

"Captain Burroughs, Leftenant. Our radio chopped off while
you were talking. No harm done; the important part got through.
We grounded where you told us to, due south of Imperial House."

"So that's what happened? I must admit to feeling relieved."

"Is your post of duty in Imperial House?"

*"Yes, Ma'am. On it, rather. We have a small housing on the
roof."*

"Good. I have a message for the Governor General. Will you
record?"

"Oh, certainly."

"This is Hilda Burroughs speaking, Master of Spacecraft Gay
Deceiver out of Snug Harbor. I am sorry that I had to leave without
saying good-bye. But your last statement forced me to take meas-
ures to protect my craft and crew." My darling Hilda cut the mike.
"Zebbie, when you have air, glide away from the city." She con-

tinued, "In a small way my responsibilities parallel yours; I cannot bargain concerning the safety of my crew and my craft. I hope that you will reconsider, as I have no stomach for dealing with the Russians—even though they have more to offer us in exchange. I still ask for safe-conduct but now must ask for a still third item in such a document: that all four of us be allowed to leave at will. You have my name. My second-in-command is Doctor D. T. Burroughs Carter, my chief pilot is Doctor Z. J. Carter, my copilot is Doctor Jacob Burroughs. You will have noticed surnames. Doctor Jacob is my husband; the other two are our daughter and her husband. I am Doctor Hilda Corners but I am much prouder of being Mrs. Jacob Burroughs—although at present I must use 'Captain Hilda Burroughs' since I am commanding. Sir, while dictating this I have made a decision. I will *not* make a second attempt to negotiate with Russians. We will wait thirty minutes in the warm hope of hearing from you . . . then return to Earth, report to our own government, send a detailed complaint to the Tsar of All the Russias, and make a formal report of our attempt here to His Imperial Majesty. Signed Respectfully yours, H. C. Burroughs, Commanding. Leftenant, what are the full names and titles of the Governor General?"

"Ah, His Excellency Lieutenant General the Right Honourable Herbert Evelyn James Smythe-Carstairs, K.G., V.C., C.B.E., Governor General of the Imperial Realms Beyond the Sky."

"Preface it formally, please, and I will wait until oh-nine-hundred hours Greenwich time or thirty-six minutes from now. *Mark!*"

"I will add the heading, Captain, and deliver it by hand."

After Hilda signed off she said, "I'm going to try to sleep thirty of those thirty-six minutes. Can anyone think of a program that will let all of us nap? This contact is more tiring than I had expected. Jacob, Deety, Zeb—don't all speak at once."

"I can, my dear," I answered.

"Yes, Jacob?"

"Gay Termite."

To my mild surprise it was night at our creek bank. To my pleasure my first attempt to maneuver by voice was smoothly successful. My daughter's ingenuity in constructing voiced programs had left me little to do. While I did not resent it (I'm proud of Deety), nevertheless while sitting as copilot, I sometimes wondered whether anyone remembered that it was *my* brainchild that moved this chariot. Ah, vanity!

To my greater pleasure Hilda clapped her hands and looked

delighted. "Jacob! How clever of you! How stupid of *me!* All right, everyone off duty for a half hour 'cept the rule about always two and always a rifle. Gay, alert us in thirty minutes. And please unlock the bulkhead door."

"Aunt Hillbilly, are you going to sleep back there?"

"I had thought of stretching out and inviting Jacob to join me. But the space belongs to you and Zebbie; I was thoughtless."

"We aren't going to sleep. But we had better drag those rifles out of that sack or *you* won't sleep. I want to empty the oubliette and stow that pesky plastic potty under the cushion of my seat. Durned if I'll use it when I have the whole outdoors at hand."

"Most certainly—but stay inside Gay's lights—and do please remind me before we leave. Deety, I've so much on my mind that I forget housekeeping details."

"Hillbilly, you're doing swell. I'll handle housekeeping; you worry about the big picture."

Hilda cuddled up to me in the after compartment and my nerves began to relax. Would the Governor General relent? Where would we go next? We had a myriad universes to choose from, a myriad myriad planets—but only one was home and we didn't dare go *there*. What about juice for Zeb's car and a thousand other things? Perhaps we should risk Earth-without-a-J. What about the time bomb, ticking away in my darling's belly?

Hilda sniffed into my shoulder. I patted her head. "Relax, dearest."

"I *can't*. Jacob, I don't *like* this job. I snap at you, you argue with me, we both get upset. It's not good for us—we *never* behaved this way at Snug Harbor."

"Then give it up."

"I'm going to. After I finish the job I started. Jacob, when we lift from this planet, *you* will be captain."

"Oh, no! *Zeb*." (Hilda my only love, you should turn it over to him *now*.)

"Zebbie won't take it. It's you or Deety, Jacob. If Deety is our next captain, you will back-seat drive even more than you have with me. No, Jacob, you *must* be captain *before* Deety is, so that you will understand what she is up against."

I felt that I had been scolded enough. I started to tell Hilda when that pejorative epithet played back in my mind: "—back-seat drive—"

I trust that I am honest with myself. I know that I am not very sociable and I expect to go on being so; a man capable of creative work has no time to spare for fools who would like to visit. But a "back-seat driver"?

Some facts: Jane learned to drive before I did—her father's duo. Our first car, a roadable, coincided with her pregnancy; I got instruction so that I could drive for Jane. She resumed driving after Deety was born but when both of us were in the car, I always drove. She drove with me as passenger once or twice before the custom became established—but she never complained that I had been back-seat driving.

But Jane never complained.

Deety laid it on the line. I don't know who taught Deety to drive but I recall that she was driving, on roads as well as in the air, when she was twelve or thirteen. She had no occasion to drive for me until Jane's illness. There was a time after we lost Jane that Deety often drove for me. After a while we alternated. Then came a day when she was driving and I pointed out that her H-above-G was, oh, some figure less than a thousand meters, with a town ahead.

She said, "Thanks, Pop"—and grounded at that town, an un-planned stop. She switched off, got out, walked around and said, "Shove over, Pop. From now on, I'll enjoy the scenery while you herd us through the sky."

I didn't shove over, so Deety got into the back seat. Deety gets her stubbornness from both parents. Jane's was covered with marshmallow that concealed chrome steel; mine is covered with a coat of sullen anger if frustrated. But Deety's stubbornness isn't concealed. She has a sweet disposition but Torquemada could not force Deety to do that which she decided against.

For four hours we ignored each other. Then I turned around (intending to start an argument, I suppose—I was in the mood for one)—and Deety was asleep, curled up in the back seat.

I wrote a note, stuck it to the wind screen, left the keys, got quietly out, made sure all doors were locked, hired another car and drove home—by air; I was too angry to risk roading.

Instead of going straight home I went to the Commons to eat, and found Deety already eating. So I took my tray and joined her. She looked up, smiled, and greeted me: "Hello, Pop! How nice we ran into each other!" She opened her purse. "Here are your keys."

I took them. "Where is our car?"

"*Your* car, Pop. Where you left it."

"*I* left it?"

"You had the keys; you were in the front seat; you hold title.

You left a passenger asleep in the back seat. Good thing she's over eighteen, isn't it?" She added, "There is an Opel duo I have my eye on. Tried it once; it's in good shape."

"We don't need two cars!"

"A matter of taste. Yours. And mine."

"We can't afford two cars."

"How would you know, Pop? I handle the money."

She did not buy the Opel. But she never again drove when we both were in our car.

Three data are not a statistical universe. But it appears that the three women I have loved most all consider me to be a back-seat driver. Jane never said so . . . but I realize today that she agreed with Deety and Hilda.

I don't consider myself to be a back-seat driver! I don't yell "Look out!" or "Watch what you're doing!" But four eyes are better than two: Should not a passenger offer, simply as data, something the driver may not have seen? Criticism? Constructive criticism only and most sparingly and only to close friends.

But I try to be self-honest; *my* opinion is not important in this. I must convince Hilda and Deety, by deeds, not words. Long habit is not changed by mere good resolution; I must keep the matter at the top of my mind.

There was banging at the bulkhead; I realized that I had been asleep. The door opened a crack. "Lift in five minutes."

"Okay, Deety," Hilda answered. "Nice nap, beloved?"

"Yes indeed. Did you?"

As we crawled out, Deety said, "Starboard door is open; Pop's rifle is leaning against it, locked. Captain, you asked to be reminded. Shall I take the conn?"

"Yes, thank you."

We lost no time as Deety used two preprograms: Bingo Windsor, plus Gay Bounce. Zeb had the communication watch officer almost at once. "—very well. I will see if the Captain will take the message. No over. Hold."

Zeb looked around, ostentatiously counted ten seconds, then pointed at Hilda.

"Captain Burroughs speaking. Leftenant Bean?"

"Yes, yes! Oh, my word, I've been trying to reach you the past twenty minutes."

"It is still a few seconds short of the time I gave you."

"Nevertheless I am enormously relieved to hear your voice, Captain. I have a message from the Governor General. Are you ready to record?"

Zeb nodded; Hilda answered Yes; the lieutenant continued: "'From the Governor General to H. C. Burroughs, Master Gay Deceiver: Hurry home, the children are crying. We all miss you. The fatted calf is turning on the spit. That document is signed and sealed, including the additional clause. Signed: "Bertie"' —— — Captain, that is the Governor's way of signing a message to an intimate friend. A signal honor, if I may say so."

"Gracious of him. Please tell the Governor General that I am ready to ground and will do so as soon as you tell me that the spot in which we were parked—the *exact* spot—is free of any obstruction whatever."

Bean was back in about three minutes saying that our spot was clear and would be kept so. Hilda nodded to Deety, who said, "Gay Parade Ground."

I had a flash of buildings fairly close, then we were back in the sky. Hilda snapped, "Chief Pilot, get Leftenant Bean!"

Then—"Mr. Bean! Our spot was *not* clear."

"It is now, Captain; I have just come from the parapet. The Governor's poodle got loose and ran out. The Governor chased him and brought him back. Could that have been it?"

"It decidedly *was* it. You may tell the Governor—privately—that never in battle has he been so close to death. Astrogator, take her down!"

"GayParadeGround!"

Bean must have heard the gasp, then cheers, while Hilda's words were still echoing in his radio shack. We were exactly as before, save that the wide, showy steps to the King-Emperor's residence on Mars were jammed with people: officers, soldiers, civil servants with that slightly dusty look, women with children, and a few dogs, all under restraint.

I didn't spot the Right Honourable "Bertie" until he moved toward us. He was no longer in mufti but in what I could call "service dress" or "undress"—not a dress uniform—but dressy. Ribbons, piping, wound stripes, etc.—sword when appropriate. Since he was not wearing sword I interpreted our status as "honored guests" rather than "official visitors"—he was ready to jump either way.

He had his wife on his arm—another smart move, our captain being female. His aide (?—left shoulder "chicken guts" but possibly a unit decoration) was with him, too—no one else. The crowd stayed back.

Hilda said, "Chief Pilot—" then pointed to the mikes, drew

her finger across her throat. Zeb said, "Outside audio is cold, Cap'n."

"Thank you, Gay, lock the bulkhead door, open your doors."

I jumped down and handed Hilda out, offered her my arm, while Zeb was doing the same with Deety portside. We met, four abreast at Gay's nose, continued moving forward a few paces and halted facing the Governor's party as they halted. It looked rehearsed but we had not even discussed it. This placed our ladies between us, with my tiny darling standing tall, opposite the Governor.

The aide boomed, "His Excellency Governor General the Lieutenant General the Right Honourable Herbert Evelyn James Smythe-Carstairs and Lady Herbert Evelyn James!"

The Governor grinned. "Dreadful," he said quietly, "but worse with ruffles, flourishes, and the Viceroy's March—I spared you that." He raised his voice, did not shout but it projected—and saluted Hilda. "Captain Burroughs! We bid you welcome!"

Hilda bowed, returning the salute. "Excellency . . . Lady Herbert . . . thank you! We are happy to be here."

Lady Herbert smiled at being included, and bobbed about two centimeters—a minimum curtsy, I suppose, but can't swear to it, as she was swathed in one of those dreadful garden-party-formal things—big hat, long skirt, long gloves. Hilda answered with a smile and a minimum bow.

"Permit me to present my companions," Hilda continued. "My family and also my crew. On my left my astrogator and second-in-command, our daughter Doctor D. T. Burroughs Carter, and on her left is her husband our son-in-law, my chief pilot, Doctor Zebadiah John Carter, Captain U.S. Aerospace Reserve." Deety dropped a curtsy as her name was mentioned, a 6-cm job, with spine straight. Zeb acknowledged his name with a slight bow.

Hilda turned her head and shoulders toward me. "It gives me more pride than I can express," she sang, her eyes and mouth smiling, her whole being speaking such serene happiness that it made me choke up, "to present our copilot, my husband Doctor Jacob Jeremiah Burroughs, Colonel of Ordnance A.U.S."

The Governor stepped forward quickly and held out his hand. "Doctor, we are honored!" His handshake was firm.

I returned it in kind, saying in a nonprojecting voice, "Hilda should not have done that to me. Off campus, I'm 'Mister' to strangers and 'Jake' to my friends."

"I'm Bertie, Jake," he answered in his intimate voice, "other than on occasions when I can't avoid that string of goods wagons. Or I'll call you 'Doctor.'"

"You do and it's fifty lines." That made him laugh again.

"And I'm Betty, Jake," Lady Herbert said, in closing in. "Captain Burroughs, may I call you 'Hilda'?" (Was that a hiccup?)

"Call her 'Doctor,'" I suggested. "She told on the rest of us. How many doctorates do you hold, dear? Seven? Or eight?"

"After the first one, it no longer matters. Of course I'm 'Hilda,' Betty. But, Bertie, we have yet to meet the Brigadier."

I glanced at the tabs of the officer with the aiguillette and booming voice. Yes, A crown inboard and three pips— But when had Hilda learned British insignia? Many Americans can't read their own. I am ceasing to be surprised at how many facts can be stuffed into so small a space.

"Sorry. Friends, this is Brigadier Iver Hird-Jones. Squeaky finds things I lose and remembers things I forget."

"Ladies. Gentlemen. Charmed. Here is something you told me to remember, General." The Brigadier handed a sealed envelope to his boss.

"Ah, yes!" Smythe-Carstairs handed it to my wife. "The Keys to the City, Ma'am. Phrased as you specified, each of you named, and that third factor included. Signed by me for the Sovereign and carrying the Imperial seal."

"Your Excellency is most gracious," Hilda said formally, and turned toward Deety. "Astrogator."

"Aye, Captain." Deety placed it in her purse.

Our host looked surprised. "Jake, doesn't your wife have normal curiosity? She seems to have forgot my name, too."

Hilda protested, "I haven't forgotten your name, Bertie. It's an official matter; I treated it formally. I shall read it when I have leisure to open that envelope without damaging the flap seal. To you this is one of thousands of papers; to *me* it is a once-in-a-lifetime souvenir. If I sound impressed, it's because I *am.*"

Lady Herbert said, "Don't flatter him, my deah." (Yes, she had had a couple.) "You'll turn his head, quite." She added, "Bertie, you're causing our guests to stand when we could be inside, sitting down."

"You're right, m'dear." Bertie looked longingly at Zeb's car.

Hilda played a trump. "Care to look inside, Bertie? Betty, you can sit down here; the captain's chair is comfortable. Will you do me the honor? Someday I'll tell my grandchildren that Lady Herbert sat in that very seat."

"What a charming thought!"

Hilda tried to catch my eye but I was a jump ahead of her, handing Lady Herbert in, making certain that she didn't miss the step, getting her turned around, making sure that she didn't sit down on belts. "If we were about to lift," I told her, while fastening the seat belt loosely (first, moving the buckle—she's Hilda's height but my thickness), "this safety belt would be fastened firmly."

"Oh, I wouldn't dare!"

"Gangway, Pop! Another customer." I got out of the way, and Deety installed Brigadier Hird-Jones in her seat. Deety said, "Pop, if you'll put the Governor in your seat, Zebadiah will take his own and give his two-hour lecture on the care and feeding of spacecraft, while you and I and Hilda hang in the doorways and correct his errors."

"I'm only up to chapter four," Zeb said defensively. "Jake, make her quit picking on me."

"You're her husband; I'm merely her father. Bertie, I must ask one thing. *Don't* touch *anything*. This car is *not* shut down; it is ready to go, instantly."

"I'll be careful, Jake. But we're leaving the ladies standing. The Captain herself! This is not right."

Deety said, "Bertie, I don't want to sit down. This trip doesn't give me nearly the exercise I need."

"But I *can't* permit Captain Hilda to stand. Sit here and I'll stand." (I appreciated his gallantry but I could see an impasse coming: two people, each aware of her/his prerogatives and they conflicted.)

Hilda avoided it by something she had discovered in working out how to rig a double bed in the control compartment. Although pilots have separate seats, the passenger's seats are really one, built all the way across but separated by armrests . . . which could be removed with screwdriver and sweat.

I had eliminated sweat and screwdriver; a natural mechanic, such as Zeb, accumulates miscellaneous hardware. Those armrests could now be removed and clamped out of the way with butterfly nuts. Hilda started to do so; the Brigadier dismounted them once he saw what she was doing.

It was a snug fit, but Hird-Jones has trim hips and Hilda has the slimmest bottom in town (any town).

"An important feature," said Zeb, "of this design is a voice-controlled autopilot—"

XXVII   *"Are you open to a bribe?"*

Deety:

Zebadiah, for seventeen dull minutes, said nothing and said it very well. During that plethora of polysyllabic nullities, I was beginning to think that I would have to take Pop to a quiet spot and reason with him with a club—when Captain Auntie showed that she needed no help.

Pop had interrupted with: "Let me put it simply. What Zeb said is—"

"Copilot." Cap'n Hilda did not speak loudly but Pop should know that when she says "Copilot," she does *not* mean: "Jacob darling, this is your little wifey." Pop is a slow learner. But he *can* learn. Just drop an anvil on him.

"Yes, Hilda?" Aunt Hilda let the seconds creep past, never took her eyes off Pop. I was embarrassed; Pop isn't usually that slow—then the anvil hit. "Yes, Captain?"

"Please do not interrupt the Chief Pilot's presentation." Her tone was warm and sweet: I don't think our guests realized that Pop had just been court-martialed, convicted, keelhauled, and restored to duty—on probation. But I knew it, Zeb knew it—Pop knew it. "Aye aye, Captain!"

I concluded that Captain Auntie never intended to stand outside. She had told me to offer my seat to Squeaky and had added, "Why don't you suggest to your father that he offer his to the Governor?" I don't need an anvil.

It was a foregone conclusion that Bertie would object to ladies having to stand while he sat. But if he had not, I feel certain that the Hillbilly would have held up proceedings until she was seated where she could watch everyone but our visitors could not watch her.

How tall was Machiavelli?

As they were climbing out the Brigadier was telling me that he understood how she was controlled—but how did she flap her wings?—and I answered that technical questions were best put to the Captain—I was unsurprised to hear Cap'n Auntie say, "Certainly, Bertie . . . if you don't mind being squeezed between Deety and me."

"'Mind'? I should pay for the privilege!"

"Certainly you should," I agreed—the Hillbilly's eyes widened but she let me talk. "What am I offered to scrunch over?" I slapped myself where I'm widest. "Squeaky is a snake's hips—not me!"

"Are you open to a bribe?"

"How big a bribe?"

"A purse of gold and half the county? Or cream tarts at tea?"

"Oh, much more! A bath. A bath in a tub, with loads of hot water and lots of suds. The last time I bathed was in a stream and it was *coooold*!" I shivered for him.

The Governor appeared to think. "Squeaky, do we have a bathtub?"

Lady Herbert interrupted. "Bertie, I was thinking of the Princess Suite. My deah, since you are all one family, it popped into mind. Two bedrooms, two bathrooms, two bathtubs. The drawing room is gloomy, rather."

I answered, "Bertie, you didn't talk fast enough; Betty gets the first ride."

"Oh, no, no, no! I don't fly even in our own flying carriage."

"Hah*rooomph!*" Squeaky boomed. "Are you still open to a bribe?"

"You might try our captain; she's as corruptible as I am."

Aunt Hilda picked it up. "Now that I've heard that two bathtubs go with the suite, my cup runneth over. But my husband and my son-in-law have matters to discuss with the Governor's technical staff. I don't have to be bribed to offer a few joy rides, Brigadier— one passenger at a time and, as Deety implies, not too wide a passenger." Aunt Hilda added, "Betty, I must confess my own weakness. Clothes. What I am wearing, for example. A Ferrara original. An exclusive—Mario himself created it for me. While it is intended for salt-water yachting, it is just as practical for space yachting—and I couldn't resist it. Do you have nice shops here?"

Bertie answered for his wife. "Hilda, there are shops—but Windsor City is not London. However, Betty has a seamstress who is clever at copying styles from pictures in periodicals from home—old but new to us." He added, "She'll show you what we have. Now concerning this ride you so kindly offered me—does it suit you to give me an appointment?"

"Is right now soon enough?"

"Report readiness for space. Astrogator."

"Ready!" I snapped, trying to sound efficient. "Belt tight."

"Chief Pilot."

"Belt fastened. Portside door locked, seal checked. Juice zero point seven-one. Wings subsonic full. Wheels down and locked. Car trimmed assuming passenger at six-six kilos."

"General, is that your mass?"

"Dear me! I think in pounds. The factor is—"

I interrupted. "I'll take it in pounds here or pounds London."

"I weigh myself each morning and I have had the scale recalibrated. Eh, with these boots, one hundred forty-five pounds I dare say."

"Correct to three significant figures, Zebadiah." (I did not mention that weight bearing on each wheel shows on the instrument board. Let Bertie think my husband a magician; he's a wizard to me.)

"Thank you, Astrogator. Car is trimmed, Captain."

"Copilot."

"Belt fastened. Door seal checked. Continua device ready."

"Passenger," said Cap'n Auntie.

"Eh? What should a passenger report?"

"Principally that your belt is secure, but I saw to that myself." (By using a web belt from our sleeping bag to link Hilda's seat belt to mine.) "I must ask one question," Aunt Hilda went on: "Are you subject to motion sickness? The Channel can be rough and so can the Straits of Dover. Did mal de mer ever hit you?"

"Oh, I'll be right. Short flight and all that."

"One Lomine, Deety. General, Admiral Lord Nelson was seasick all his life. My husband and I are susceptible; we took our pills earlier today. Deety and Zebbie are the horrid sort who eat greasy sandwiches during a typhoon and laugh at the dying—"

"I don't laugh!" I protested.

"But these pills enable us to laugh right back. Is this not so, Jacob?"

"Bertie, they work; you'd be a fool not to take one."

"I must add," Captain Auntie said sweetly, "that if you refuse, we will not lift."

Bertie took it. I told him, "Chew it and swallow it; don't hide it in your cheek. Captain, I think that does it."

"Except that we are crowded. General, would you be more comfortable if you put an arm around each of us?"

The General did not refuse. It occurs to me that "take him for a ride" has several meanings. Captain Auntie has more twists than a belly dancer.

"Routine has been broken. Confirm readiness, please." We reported while I snuggled into a firm male arm, realized that it was a pleasant contrast after getting used to my lovely giant.

"Gay Bounce."

Bertie gasped and tightened his arms around us. Aunt Hilda said quietly, "Astrogator, take the conn. Schedule as I discussed it. Don't hesitate to vary it. All of us—you, too, General—may suggest variations. This is a joy ride; let's enjoy it."

But she had told me earlier: "If I don't like a suggestion, I will suggest that we do it later—but time will run out. The General told Lady Herbert:

'"I can go down to the end of the town
"And be back in time for tea!"' —so we will fetch him back on time. Sixteen-fifteen local, four-fifteen pip emma. What's Greenwich?"

I converted it (GMT 12:44) and told Captain Hillbilly that I would watch both board and the clock in my head but was ordered to place an alert with Gay. If Aunt Hilda were a man, she would wear both suspenders and belt. No, that's wrong; for herself she's go-for-broke; for other people she is supercautious.

We lifted at 15:30 local and took Bertie for a mixed ride— Aunt Hilda had told me that Pop was feeling left out. "Gay Bounce, Gay Bounce. Chief Pilot, place us over the big Russian city at about a thousand klicks."

"Roger Wilco," my husband affirmed. "Copilot, one jump or two?"

"One. Level? Keep 'er so. Six thousand thirty klicks, true bearing two-seven-three, offset L axis negative oh-seven-four— set!"—and I shuddered; Pop had set to take us *through* the planet!

"Execute! Bertie, what is the name of that city?"

"Eh? Zeb, I am quite bewildered!" Pop and Gay and Zebadiah, working together, displayed features simultaneously on the planet in front of us and on the sillyscope on the board. Pop bounced Gay around in ways I didn't know could be done. Zebadiah had Gay rotate the display so that the point on Mars-ten opposite us was always the center of the display with scale according to H-above-G.

I learned a lot. The Russians claim the whole planet but their occupied area closely matches what we had bingo-mapped. Bertie pointed out a bit more Tsarist area; Gay changed the displayed locus to Zebadiah's interpretation of Bertie's information. Windsor City was zero Meridian for the British; Gay measured the arc to "Touchdown," adjusted her longitudes—and now could use any British Martian colonial map.

Bertie assured us that Russian Ack-Ack could not shoot higher than three miles (less than five klicks) and seemed astonished that a spaceship might be considered dangerous. His explanation of spaceships was less than clear—great flimsy things that *sailed* from orbits around Earth to orbits around Mars, taking months for each voyage.

I was watching the time. "Chief Pilot, we will sight-see with Bertie another day; I am taking the conn. Copilot."

"Verniers zeroed and locked, Astrogator."

"Thanks, Pop. Gay B'gout. Bertie, this is where we first grounded—where the Russians attacked us. That trash ahead is what is left of Colonel Morinosky's private flyer. Zebadiah was forced to retaliate."

Bertie looked puzzled. "But the Russians have no settlement near here. I know that bounder Morinosky; he came to see me under diplomatic immunity. I had to be content with the sort of nasty remarks permitted by protocol. But how did Zeb burn the flyer?"

"Beautifully. Gay Home. Chief Pilot, dive. Captain?"

"I have the conn," Aunt Hilda acknowledged. "Bertie, that crater was our home three days ago. They tried to kill us, we fled for our lives."

"Who!"

"Gay Home, Gay Bounce. Pilots, may we have Earth-without-a-J?"

"Set it, Jake."

"Tau axis positive one quantum—set!"

"Copilot, execute at will. Chief Pilot, dive again, please. Jacob, please set Bertie's home universe and hold. Bertie, that house is like Snug Harbor before it was bombed—but one universe away. Zebbie, level glide please . . . Gay Bounce, Gay Bounce! Jacob, you have that setting?"

"Tau positive ten quanta, set."

"Execute at will. Bertie, what antiaircraft defense does London—*your* London—have?"

"What, what? London has no defense against attack from

above. The Concord of Brussels. But Hilda—my dear Captain—you are telling me that we have been to a *different universe!*"

"Three universes, Bertie, and now we are back in your own. Better to show than to tell; it is a thing one believes only through experience. Gay Bounce. Zebbie, Jacob, see how quickly you can put us over London. Execute at will."

"Roger Wilco. Jake, do you want Gay?"

"Well—great-circle true bearing and chord distance, maybe. Or I can simply take her high and head northeast. The scenic route."

Aunt Hilda caught my eye. "Camera ready, Deety?"

"Yes. Three shots." I added, "Four more cartons, but when they're gone, they're gone."

"Use your judgment."

Suddenly we were in free fall over Arizona, then over the British Isles, then we were air supported, then we were diving and Zebadiah was shouting: "Tower of London, next stop!"

I shot a beauty of the Tower and Zebadiah's right ear. "General, is there something you would like to photograph here? Or elsewhere?"

He seemed almost too overcome to talk. He muttered, "There is a place about twenty miles north of here, a country estate. Is it possible?"

Aunt Hilda said, "Take the conn, Deety."

"Got it, Captain. Gay Bounce. Pop, Zebadiah, give me three minima north. Execute at will."

Then I was saying, "Any landmarks, Bertie?"

"Uh, not yet."

"Pop, may we have the binoculars?"

Pop handed them aft; I gave them to Bertie. He adjusted them and searched while Zebadiah made a wide sweep, spending altitude stingily. Bertie said, *"There!"*

"Where?" I said. "And what?"

"A large house, to the right of our course. Ah, now dead ahead!"

I saw it—a "Stately Home of England." Lawns you make with a flock of sheep and four centuries. "This it?" asked Zebadiah. "I'm steady on it by gunsight."

"That's it, sir! Deety, I *would* like a picture."

"Do my best."

"Alert," said Gay. "Memo for General Smythe-Carstairs: 'I can go down to the end of the town and be back in time for tea.'"

"Aunt Hilda, Bertie, I left some leeway. Picture! Zebadiah,

take it as close as you dare, then bounce, but warn me. I want a closeup."

"Now, Deety!" I hit it and Zebadiah bounced us.

Bertie let out a sigh. "My home. I never expected to see it again."

"I knew it was your home," Aunt Hilda said softly, "because you looked the way we feel when we see the crater where Snug Harbor used to be. But you will see it again, surely? How long is a tour of duty on Mars?"

"It's a matter of health." Bertie added, "Lady Her— Betty's health."

Pop turned his head. "Bertie, we can bounce and do it again. What's a few minutes late for tea compared with seeing your old homestead?"

"Bertie's not late yet, Pop. We can do even better. That lawn is smooth and the open part is about half the size of the p.g. at Imperial House. Bertie, we can ground."

My husband added, "I could make a glide grounding. But Deety has worked out a better method."

"No," Bertie said brusquely. "Thanks, Deety. Thanks to all of you. Jake. Zeb. Captain Hilda. I'll treasure this day. But enough is enough." Tears were running down his cheeks, ignored.

Aunt Hilda took a Kleenex from her purse, dabbed away his tears. She put her left hand back of Bertie's neck, pulled his face down to hers, and kissed him. She didn't look to see if Pop was watching—he was—she just did it.

Pop said, "Deety, will you hand me the binox?"

"Sure, Pop. See something?"

"I'm going to see what I can of Merrie Old England, as *I* don't expect to see it again, either. Family, we are *not* going back to Snug Harbor again; it's not good for us. Meanwhile Zeb will drive and you two are to soothe our guest and make him feel better—"

"But remember to wipe off the lipstick."

"Pipe down, Zeb. You aren't observant; neither of our darlings is wearing any. Being late is not important; 'The party can't start till the Macgregor arrives.' But once Bertie's there, he's on parade—and the Governor must *not* appear with eyes swollen and tear marks on his collar. We must return him in as good shape as we got him."

Sometimes I love Pop more than most.

And my husband, too.

I used both hands but didn't need to; Bertie wasn't trying to get away. The second time he kissed Hilda, he supplied the hands. Therapy took three minutes and forty-one seconds, and I am certain that, by the end of two hundred twenty-one seconds, Bertie was no longer homesick, not grieving about might-have-beens; his morale was tiptop. The last time he kissed me, he informed me without words that I should not be alone with him unless my intentions were serious.

I made mental note. And a second to ask Hilda if she had received the same warning. Then I struck out the second note. I was certain and equally certain that she would fib if it suited her.

But I look forward to the day the Hillbilly asks me to jigger for her. That will be my final promotion—no longer Jane's little girl in Hilda's eyes but Jane's equal, trusted as utterly as she trusted Jane. And I will be rid of the last trace of the shameful jealousy I have for my beloved Mama Jane.

I checked myself in my purse mirror while I waited for them to break—checked both of them and decided that they had no milk on their chins. Bertie said, "Deety, could I possibly have one of those pictures as a remembrance of this perfect day?"

"Certainly. Gay Parade Ground. All three are yours; we took them for you." We were exactly on time.

Three hours later I was sitting teat deep in a wonderful tub of hot soapy water, a tub big enough to drown in but I wasn't going to drown because the Hillbilly was sitting shoulder deep, facing me. We were reliving our day as well as getting beautiful for dinner. Well . . . sanitary.

Hilda said, "Deety, I tell you three times. Betty is suffering from an ailment made more endurable by Martian conditions."

"Meaning that in point thirty-eight gee she doesn't hit hard when she falls down. What was in that teapot no one else touched? Chanel Number Five?"

"Medicine. Prescribed for her nerves."

"Got it. Official. She's friendly as a puppy, she's generous, she's our hostess—I ought to know better. It's a shame that she has this ailment but she's fortunate in having a husband who loves her so dearly that he left home forever so that she can live in lower gravity. Bertie is quite a man."

"There is nothing for him at home. His older brother has sons; title and estate can't go to Bertie. He can't go much higher in the army, and a governor general is senior to anybody; he embodies the Sovereign."

"I thought that was limited to viceroys."

"Squeaky put me straight on it. Bertie *is* viceroy in dealing with Russians. But— Did you notice the uniforms on the maids?"

"I noticed the cream tarts more. White aprons, white caps, simple print dresses, dark blue or black with Indian arrowheads."

"The Broad Arrow, Deety."

"Huh? No sabbe, pliz."

"In this universe Australia belongs to the Dutch. Brace yourself, dear. This is a prison colony."

Every so often the world wobbles and I have to wait for it to steady down. Somewhat later I said, "A colony could be better than a prison. I can't see Bertie as a tyrant. Bertie is quite a man. When—"

Hilda reached out, grabbed a chain, flushed the W.C., then leaned toward me. That fixture was a noisy type that went on gurgling and gasping for a long time. "Remember what Zebbie told us when he crowded us into the other bath and turned on everything? One must assume that guest quarters in any government building anywhere are wired. Careful what you say, dear."

"He also said that he had no reason to assume that it was the case here."

"But Zebbie was the one who insisted on a conference in Gay . . . with Jacob being mulish and you yourself seeing no reason not to confer up here." Aunt Hilda again pulled the chain. "Yes, Bertie is quite a man. Don't leave me alone with him."

"Or should I jigger instead?"

"Naughty Deety. My sweet, a bride should refrain at least twelve months out of respect for her husband and to prove that she can."

"After that it's okay?"

"Of course not! It's immoral, disgraceful, and scandalous." Suddenly she giggled, put arms around my neck, and whispered: "But if I ever need a jigger, Deety is the only person I would trust."

That conference, immediately after tea, had caused a crisis, brought on by our husbands in concert—but out of tune. The tea had been fun—cream tarts and new men appeal to my basest instincts. A tea *qua* tea should be over in an hour. We had been there over an hour, which I ignored because I was having fun. Aunt Hilda broke the ring around me, said softly, "We're leaving." So we smiled and said good-bye, found our host, and thanked him.

"Our pleasure," Bertie said. "Lady Herbert became indisposed and wishes to be forgiven but will see you at dinner. Hird-Jones tells me that black tie is no problem. Right?"

He added to let Squeaky know when we wanted help in moving; Hilda assured him that Squeaky had it in hand and the suite was *beautiful!*

As we left I asked, "Where is Zebadiah?"

"Waiting at the outer steps. He asked me for a conference. I don't know why, but Zebbie would not unnecessarily interrupt a social event to ask for a closed conference."

"Why didn't we go to our suite? And where is Pop?"

"Zebbie specified the car—more private. Jacob is inside, talking with some men. He brushed off my telling him that we were going to the car now—said he would see us later. Deety, I *can't* enforce orders as captain under those conditions."

"Pop is hard to move when he gets into a discussion. I've yawned through some deadly ones. But how can we have a conference until he shows up?"

"I don't know, dear. Here's Zebbie."

My husband pecked me on the nose and said, "Where's Jake?"

Hilda answered, "He told me that he would be along later." Zebadiah started to curse; Aunt Hilda cut him off. "Chief Pilot."

"Uh— Yes, Captain."

"Go find the Copilot, tell him that we lift in five minutes. Having told him that *and no more,* turn and *leave at once.* Don't give him *any* opportunity to ask questions. Come straight to the car."

"Aye aye, Captain."

"Come, Deety." Hilda hurried to Gay Deceiver, went to her seat, started to belt. She glanced at me. "Astrogator, prepare for space."

I started to ask why—but instead said, "Aye aye, Captain," and quickly was belted. "Captain, may I inquire your plans?"

"Certainly, you're second-in-command. And Astrogator; however, I will take the conn on lifting."

"Then we really are lifting?"

"Yes. Five minutes after Zebbie returns. That gives Jacob five minutes to make up his mind. Then we lift. If Jacob is aboard, he'll be with us."

"Aunt Hilda, you would abandon my father on this planet?!"

"No, Deety. Jacob will probably never notice that the car has been away as it should not be gone more than a few minutes. If Jacob does not come with us, I will ask Zebbie to drop me on

Earth-without-a-J. Range-finder and target method; I don't want to use Zebbie's precious juice."

"Aunt Hilda, you sound desperate."

"I am, dear." She added, "Here comes Zebbie."

Zebadiah climbed in. "Message delivered, Captain."

"Thank you, Chief Pilot. Prepare for space."

"Roger Wilco."

"Will you check the seal of the starboard door, please?"

"Aye aye, Captain."

"Report readiness for space, Astrogator."

"Belt tight, ready for space. *Oh, Aunt Hilda!*"

"Astrogator, pipe down. Chief Pilot."

"Both doors locked, seals checked. Seat belt tight. Power packs, two zeroed, two in reserve. Juice oh-point-seven-one-minus. All systems go. Copilot missing. Ready for space."

"Captain's seat belt tight, ready for space. Gay Deceiver."

"Howdy, Hilda!"

"Please display five-minute countdown. Paraphrase acknowledge."

"Three hundred seconds backwards in lights."

"Execute."

Have you ever listened to three hundred seconds of silence? Neither have I—two hundred eighty-one when Pop pounded on the door.

Aunt Hilda said, "Gay Deceiver, open starboard door."

Pop climbed in, indignant as an offended cat. "What the hell goes on?"

"Copilot, prepare for space."

"*What?* Now, Hilda, that is going too far!"

"Copilot, either secure for space or get out and stand clear. Chief Pilot, see that my orders are carried out."

"Aye aye, Captain! Copilot, you've got zero seconds to make up your mind." My husband started to unstrap.

Pop looked at Zebadiah, looked at us. I was doing my frozen face to keep from crying and I think Aunt Hilda was, too.

Pop hastily fastened his belt. "You're a pack of idiots—" He was checking the door seal. "—but I won't be left behind."

"Copilot, report."

"Huh? Ready for space."

Hilda said, "Gay Termite. Gay Deceiver, open your doors."

"Well, for the love of—"

"Pipe down! Chief Pilot, I have no stomach for charging my husband with mutiny but that is what I have been faced with repeatedly. Will you grant me the boon of resuming command to drop me on Earth-without-a-J? I would rather not have to stay on Mars."

"Hilda!"

"I'm sorry, Jacob. I've tried. I'm not up to it. I'm not Jane."

"No one expects you to be Jane! But ever since you became captain, you've been throwing your weight around. Like calling this stunt in the middle of a party. Insulting our host and hostess—"

"Hold it, Jake!"

"What? See here, Zeb, I'm talking to my wife! You keep—"

"I said 'Hold it.' Shut up or I'll shut you up."

"Don't you threaten me!"

"That's not a threat; that's a warning."

"Pop, you had better believe him! I'm not on your side."

Pop took a deep breath. "What do you have to say for yourself, Carter?"

"Nothing, for myself. But you've got your data wrong six ways. One: Captain Hilda did not call this so-called 'stunt.' *I* did."

"*You* did? What the devil caused you to do a thing like that?"

"Irrelevant. I convinced the Captain that the matter was urgent, so she gathered us in. All but you—you told her not to bother you or words to that effect. But she gave you another chance— you didn't deserve it; you had long since used up your quota. But she did. She sent me back to tell you we were lifting. It finally penetrated your skull that we might lift without you—"

"To *this* place!"

"If you had been twenty seconds later, we would have translated to another universe. But this nonsense about 'Insulting our host and hostess—' Your hostess left the tea long before you did; your host left immediately after Hilda and Deety, leaving his aide— the Brigadier—to close shop. But you are so damned self-centered you never noticed. Jake, don't *you* lecture *me* on proper behavior as a guest. The first time I laid eyes on you, you were trying to start a fight in Sharpie's ballroom—"

"Huh? But I was fully justi—"

"Dreck. No one is *ever* justified in starting a fight under a host's roof. The very *most* that can be justified under extreme provocation is to tell the other party *privately* that you are ready to meet him at another time and place. Jake, I don't enjoy teaching manners to my senior. But your parents neglected you, so I must.

If I offend you—if you feel entitled to call me out, I will accommodate you at any other time and place."

Aunt Hilda gasped. "Zebbie! No!" I gasped something like it. My husband patted our hands—together; Hilda was gripping mine. "Don't worry, dears. I didn't call Jake out and won't. I don't want to hurt Jake. He's your husband . . . your father . . . my blood brother by spilled blood. But I had to chew him out; he's now entitled to a crack at me. With words, with hands, with whatever. Sharpie, Deety, you *can't* refuse Jake his rights. No matter what, he still has rights."

Pop said, "Zeb, I am not going to call you out. If you think I am afraid of you, you're welcome. If you think it's because I know you love both Hilda and Deety, you would be closer. A fight between us would endanger their welfare. As you said, we are blood brothers." Pop's tone suddenly changed. "But doesn't mean I like your behavior, you arrogant punk!"

Zebadiah grinned. "Nolo contendere, Pop."

"So you admit it?"

"You know Latin better than that, Jake. Means I'm satisfied to let it lie. We can't afford to quarrel."

"Mmm— A point well taken. Stipulating that I did not come at once when summoned, and tabling, if you will, until later whether or not I had reason, may I now ask *why* I was summoned? The nature of this problem that caused you to call this conference?"

"Jake, the situation has changed so rapidly that the matter no longer has priority. You heard Sharpie's plans."

My husband looked into Aunt Hilda's eyes. "Captain, I'll be honored to drive you wherever you want to go. Drop you wherever you say. With your choice of equipment and wampum. But with a mail drop, I hope. Are you ready to leave?"

"Yes, Captain."

"Wait a half. *You* are captain, until you leave us. Orders, Captain? Earth-without-a-J? Or I'll help you shop others—we might find a world of nudists."

"Why that, Zebbie? I'm not jumpy about skin—but only among close friends."

"Remember why Jake was certain that the Finnish mathematician was not a disguised vermin? *Sauna.* Disguise has limits."

"Oh." Aunt Hilda looked thoughtful. "I could get used to it. But I *must* get out of this tension. So drop me on the minus-J world. A mail drop, yes; I don't ever want to lose you and Deety."

"We find that safe place, we pick you up. Sharpie, we'll be back someday anyhow. If the boogiemen don't get us."

"Hold it, Zeb. If you're dropping Hilda, you're dropping me."

"That's up to Captain Hilda."

"Hilda, I will not permit—"

"Jake, quit acting the fool," growled my husband. "She's *boss*. With me to back her up."

"And me!" I echoed.

"You seem to forget that the continua device is mine!"

"Gay Deceiver!"

"Yes, Boss? Who's your fat friend?"

"'Number of the Beast.' Execute."

"Done."

"Try your verniers, Jake."

Pop did something—I couldn't see his hands. Then he said, "Why, you— So you think you've stopped me? Gay Deceiver!"

"Howdy, Jake."

Zebadiah cut in: "Gay Deceiver override! Emergency Thirty-one execute. Gay can no longer hear you, Jake. Try it."

"If you can do one, you can do the other. Zeb, I never thought you would be that sneaky."

"Jake, if you had behaved yourself, you never would have known. Extreme individualists (all of us) don't take kindly to discipline because they rarely understand its nature and function. But—even before that fake ranger showed up—we all had agreed to 'lifeboat' rules. We discussed them and you all claimed to understand them . . . and I was elected skipper. I nominated *you*— eldest, senior, inventor of the space-time twister—but you said it had to be me. A lifeboat officer must *always* be able to enforce his orders . . . in situations of great peril complicated by hysterical civilians. Or bullheaded ones who must otherwise be wheedled."

It was time for a diversion; Pop doesn't like to look foolish and I was still hoping to salvage this shambles. "Zebadiah, is my number fifty-nine?"

"Of course, but it takes my voice. Can you figure the cancel-and-reset?"

"For mnemonic reasons it should be one of three. Probably ninety-five."

"On the button!"

"Although I would prefer eighty-nine."

"Why?"

"Work on it. Zebadiah, why *did* you call this meeting?"

"With Sharpie leaving us the matter is academic. We won't be coming back to Mars."

"Oh, dear!"

"What's the trouble, Sharpie? Captain."

"I promised Squeaky a ride. Zebbie, could you keep my promise for me? Please? For old times' sake?"

"Captain, once we lift to drop you on Minus-J, we won't return. But the Captain still *is* captain and can give Squeaky that ride in the next thirty minutes if it suits her."

"May I offer something in my own defense?" Pop put in.

"Of course, Jake. Sorry, Captain; you're in charge. May the Copilot have the floor?"

"Jacob, even though I find it necessary to leave you . . . I love and respect you . . . and will *always* listen to you."

"Thanks, darling. Thank you, Captain. I was in that huddle because Brigadier Hird-Jones always remembers. That huddle was the top physical scientists on Mars. A scruffy lot but they get the technical journals and read them, a few months late. I was talking with the top chemist—"

"Well, Jake? Make it march."

"Zeb, not one knew an isotope from an antelope. You *can't* buy juice here."

"For *that* you disobeyed a direct order of the Captain? Sharpie, you should have him flogged around the Fleet before you surrender office—"

"Don't joke, Zebbie."

"Captain, I am not joking. Jake, that's no news; I spotted it this afternoon. Sharpie? Deety? In England."

"I missed it," Aunt Hilda said. "I don't know England well."

"Deety?"

"Well . . . maybe," I admitted.

"How?" demanded Pop.

"Little things. No roadables, just horse-drawn vehicles. No air traffic other than a few ornithopters. Coal-fired steam-powered trains of cars. Traffic on the Thames, what little there was, 'minded me of pictures of Victorian England."

"Daughter, why didn't you mention this?"

"*You* saw it, Pop."

"Those were my reasons," Zebadiah agreed. "My hope of getting juiced here dropped to one-tenth of one percent. It is now zero." Zebadiah sighed. "But that isn't why I asked the Captain to call us together. Family, there are *vermin* here."

The world wobbled again—and so did I.

Aunt Hilda was saying, "How did you learn this, Zebbie?"

"You gals had plenty of company and Jake had the local scientists, so Squeaky gave me his attention. Captain, you told us to stick to the truth—"

"Yes," agreed Aunt Hilda, "but not to volunteer information."

"I didn't volunteer; I was debriefed. Squeaky asked me about the ride we gave his boss; I tried to be vague. Squeaky took a photo from his pocket. 'The Governor tells me this was taken this afternoon.' Deety, it was the pic you took of the Thames and the Tower.

"I shortly started giving him a full account rather than have it dragged out. The Governor had told him the works; Squeaky was comparing my version with Bertie's, looking for holes in a yarn most easily explained by hypnosis, delirium tremens, insanity, or fancy lying. Since no two witnesses exhibit any of these in the same way they can be used as truth tests. Contrariwise, two witnesses who tell *exactly* the same story are lying. I assume that Bertie and I differed enough to be credible."

I asked my husband, "Zebadiah, did you explain six-dimensional space to him?"

Zebadiah looked pained. "How could I, when I can't explain it to *me*? Anyhow, he's looking forward eagerly to the ride Captain Sharpie promised him."

"Oh, dear! Zebbie, will you take a note to him?"

"Captain, we are *not* coming back after we drop you. I'll be breaking a date with him, too. Either before or after whatever time suits *you*, he's planning to give *me*—and anyone else who wants to go—a ride to see the vermin. 'Black Hats.' Fake rangers."

(I do wish the world would not wobble!)

Pop said, "Zeb, spill it! Quit stalling."

"Shut up and listen. Squeaky showed me a scrapbook. Dull as a scrapbook usually is until we came across a page of 'Black Hats.' Deety, you would have been proud of me—"

"I *am* proud of you," I answered.

"—because I didn't scream or faint, I showed no special interest. I just said, 'God in Heaven, Squeaky, those are the horrors that chased us off Earth! You've got 'em *here*?'"

"'No special interest.'"

"I didn't climb the drapes. I merely said, 'Or have you managed to exterminate them?'

"The discussion became confused, as they don't kill them; they put them to work. Squeaky had to repress amusement at the notion that wogs could be dangerous. He glanced at his watch and said,

'Come, I'll show you. Ordinarily we don't allow wogs in town. But this old fellow takes care of the Governor's gardens and may not yet have been returned to the pens for the night.' He led me to a balcony. Squeaky looked down and said, 'Too late, I'm afraid. No, there it is—Hooly! Chop, chop!'—and again I didn't faint. Hooly ran toward us, with a gait I can't describe, stopped abruptly, threw an open-palm salute and held it. 'Private Hooly reports!'

"Squeaky let him stand there. 'This wog,' he told me, 'is the most intelligent of the herd. It knows almost a hundred words. Can make simple sentences. As intelligent as a dog. And it can be trusted not to eat the flowers.'

"'Herbivorous?' says I, showing off my book-larnin'. 'Oh, no,' he tells me, 'omnivorous. We hunt wild ones to provide the good wogs with a change in diet and, of course, when we slaughter overage wogs, that provides more ration.'

"That's enough for one lesson, children. Pleasant dreams. Tomorrow the Brigadier will have a roadable big enough for all of us to take us out to meet the Martian natives aka wogs aka 'Black Hats' aka vermin—unless that interferes with the ride you aren't going to give him, in which case he will swap the times around with the visit to the wogs we aren't going to make. And that, Jake, is the reason I asked the Captain for a family conference. I already knew that artificial isotopes are far beyond this culture—not alone from the ride this afternoon but because I ask questions myself. Squeaky has a knowledge of chemistry about the pre-nuclear level and a detailed knowledge of explosives that one expects of a pro. But to Squeaky atoms are the smallest divisions of mass, and 'heavy water' is a meaningless phrase.

"So I knew we would be here just to get Sharpie some clothes and to recharge my packs—since they do have D.C. power. Then I found we had stumbled onto the home of the vermin—and at that point my back didn't ache at the idea of cranking, and I didn't think that the Captain was that much in a hurry to buy clothes. So I asked the Captain to call us together in Smart Girl. I did not want to put it off even a few minutes because we were scheduled to move into our suite after tea. To leave at once, before we moved in, would save awkward explanations. Jake, did I have reason to ask for emergency conference?"

"If you had told me—"

"Stop! The *Captain* told you."

"But she didn't explain—"

"Jake, you're *hopeless! Captains* don't have to explain. Fur-

thermore she could not because I did not tell *anyone* until now.
The Captain had confidence in my judgment."

"*You* could have explained. When Hilda sent you back to get
me. I would have come at once."

"That makes the ninth time you've been wrong in twenty minutes—"

I blurted, "Tenth, Zebadiah. I counted."

Pop gave me his "Et-tu,-Brute" look.

"—tenth without being right once. I could not have explained
to you."

"Merely because of a group of men?"

"Eleventh. I was *not* sent back to get you—twelfth. I was
under orders to tell you that—quote!—'We lift in five minutes.'
Tell you that *and no more,* then turn and leave at once, without
discussion. I carried out my orders."

"You hoped that I would be left behind."

"Thirteen."

I butted in again. "Pop, quit making a fool of yourself! Zebadiah asked you an *essential* question—and you've dodged.
Captain Auntie, could we have the doors closed? There might be
one of *them* out there—and the guns are locked up."

"Certainly, Deety. Gay Deceiver, close your doors."

Pop said, "Deety, I was not aware that I had been dodging.
I thought I was conducting a reasonable discussion."

"Pop, you always think so. But you are reasonable *only* in
mathematics. Zebadiah asked you whether or not, under the circumstances, did he have reason to ask for a conference? You
haven't answered it."

"If Hilda had not told him not to—"

"*Pop!* Answer that question or I will never speak to you again
in my life!"

My husband said, "Deety, Deety! Don't make threats."

"My husband, *I* never make threats, either. Pop knows it."

Pop took a deep breath. "Zeb, under the circumstances you
have described, you were justified in asking the Captain for an
immediate private conference."

I let out my breath. "Thanks, Pop."

"I did it for myself, Deety. Hilda? Captain?"

"What is it, Jacob?"

"I should have gone with you at once when you first asked me
to."

"Thank you, Jacob. But I did not 'ask' you; I *ordered* you.
True, it was phrased as a request . . . but orders of a commanding

officer are customarily phrased as requests—a polite protocol. You explained this custom to me yourself. Although I already knew it." Aunt Hilda turned to look at Zebadiah.

"Chief Pilot, the departure for Minus-J is postponed until late tomorrow. I will give you the time after I have consulted the Brigadier. I want to see one of those vermin, alive, photograph it stereo and cinema, and, if possible, dissect one. Since I intend to remain overnight, I hope to pick up clothes for Minus-J, too— but the reasons for delay are to learn more about vermin and to carry out my commitment to Brigadier Hird-Jones."

Aunt Hilda paused, continued: "All hands, special orders. Do not remove anything from the car that you cannot afford to abandon. This car may lift on five minutes' warning even in the middle of the night. You should keep close to me unless you have a guarantee from me of longer time. Tonight I will sleep in the car. If we lift in the night, I will send word to Princess Suite. Zebbie, I will retain the captaincy until we ground on Minus-J. Schedule: Dinner tonight is eight-thirty pip emma local time, about three hours hence. Black tie for gentlemen. Deety suggests that we wear what we wore our wedding night; she has our outfits packed together. The Brigadier will send someone to Princess Suite shortly after eight local to escort us to a reception. I will settle tomorrow's schedule with him. Jacob, I will slip down to the car after the House is quiet. If someone sees me, I will be running down for a toothbrush. Questions?"

"Captain?" said Pop.

"Copilot."

"Hilda, *must* you sleep in the car?"

"Jacob, 'twere best done quickly!"

"I'm begging you."

"You want me to be your whore one last time? That's not too much to ask . . . since you were willing to marry me knowing my thoroughly tarnished past. Yes, Jacob."

"No, no, no! I want you to sleep in my arms—that's all I ask."

"Only that? We can discuss it after we go to bed. All hands, prepare for space. Report!"

I splashed the Hillbilly and giggled. "Cap'n Auntie chum, that flatters me more than anything else you could ever say. While I can't imagine needing a jigger—if I did—or if I needed *any* sort of help and it took one who loves me no matter what, *you* know to whom I would turn. The one who loves me even when I'm bad. Who's that?"

"Thank you, Deety. We love and trust each other."

"Now tell me— Did you ever have any intention of sleeping tonight in the car?"

She pulled the chain again. Under that racket she said into my ear, "Deety doll, I never had any intention of *sleeping* tonight."

XXVIII   *"He's too fat."*

Zeb:

Sharpie sat on the Governor's right with my wife on his left, which gave Jake and me the privilege of sharing Lady Herbert, a loud shout away. The space was filled with mess jackets, dinner coats, and wives in their best. We each had one footman to insure that we did not starve; this platoon was bossed by a butler as impressive as the Pope, who was aided by a squad of noncom butlers. Female servants rushed in and out to serving tables. His Supremacy the Butler took it from there but used his hands only in offering splashes of wine to the Governor to taste and approve.

All were in livery—decorated with the Broad Arrow. The British colony consisted of a) wogs, b) transportees, c) discharged transportees, d) officers and enlisted men, e) civil servants, and f) spouses and dependents. I know even less about the Russian colony. Military and serfs, I think.

The ladies were in Victorian high-style dowdiness, which made Deety and Sharpie birds of paradise among crows. Jump suit and sailor pants had shocked people at tea. But at dinner—Deety wore the velvet wrap she had the night we eloped; Sharpie wore her sunset-shade mink cape; Jake and I unveiled them on the grand staircase leading down to the reception hall. Naw, we didn't rehearse; we were mysterious strangers, guests of the Governor General and His Lady, so all eyes were upon us. Maids, hurrying up, met us there to take our ladies' wraps.

I had questioned the propriety of house guests coming downstairs in wraps. Sharpie had answered, "Utterly correct, Zebbie—

because *I* set the style. I did so this afternoon; I shall until we leave." I shut up; Sharpie has infallible instinct for upstaging.

Have I mentioned how Sharpie and Deety were dressed at Sharpie's party? They practically weren't. I wish I had had that hall bugged to record the gasps when Jake and I uncovered our prizes.

These two had last been seen at tea, one in a jump suit, the other in an outfit that looked donated by the Salvation Army, with no makeup. We had been to our suite before tea only for a hasty wash.

But now—Sharpie did Deety's hair; Deety did Sharpie's; Sharpie styled both faces, including too much lipstick, which Deety doesn't often wear. I asked Sharpie if she knew the history and significance of lipstick. She answered, "Certainly do, Zebbie. Don't bother us." She went on making Deety beautiful. Deety *is* beautiful but doesn't know it because her features have that simple regularity favored by Praxiteles.

Having put too much lipstick on Deety, Sharpie removed some, then carried her makeup onto her breasts so that it disappeared under the dress. Which is pretty far because they saved material on that dress at the top in order to give it a full, floor-length skirt. You can't quite see her nipples—in the flesh I mean; they generally show through her clothes, always when she's happy—because Deety stands tall. Her mother had told her, "Deety, if a woman is tall, the answer is to look at least three centimeters taller than you are."

Deety always believed her mother; she stands tall, sits straight; she never leans or slouches; she can get away with that dress by half a centimeter. I'm not sure of the material but the color is the shade of green that goes best with strawberry hair. That dress, her height, long legs, broad shoulders, a waist two sizes too small setting off breasts two sizes too big—the combo could get her a job as a show girl.

When Sharpie finished gilding Deety I couldn't see that she had been made up at all . . . but knew durn well that she did *not* look the way she had before. Sharpie picked her jewelry, too—sparingly, as Deety had all her pretties with her, her own and those that had belonged to her mother. Sharpie based it on an emerald-and-pearl neckpiece, plus a matching pin and ring.

As for Sharpie, twice my darling's age and half as big, restraint was not what she used. The central diamond of her necklace was smaller than the Star of Africa.

She wore other diamonds here and there.

Here is something I don't understand. Sharpie is underprivileged in mammary glands. I *know* she was not wearing cheaters as I returned to get my tie tied just as Deety was about to lower it onto her. No bra, no underwear. But when that dress was fastened, Sharpie had tits—little ones but big enough for her size. Stuffing built into the dress? Nope. I went out of my way to check.

Is that why some couturiers get such high prices?

Still . . . the Captain looks best in her skin.

So we uncovered these confections and gave the British colony, male, female, and the others, something to talk about for months.

I can't say the English ladies were pleased. Their men gravitated toward our darlings like iron filings toward a magnet. However, Betty, Lady Herbert, is sweet all through. She rushed toward us (a bow wave of juniors getting out of her way), stopped short, looked only at our ladies, and said with the delight of a child at Christmas: "Oh, how *beautiful* you are!" and clapped her hands.

Her voice projected against dead silence, then conversation resumed. Lady Herbert took them, an arm around each, and toured the hall (busting up a receiving line). Brigadier Hird-Jones rolled with the punch, gathered in Jake and me, made sure we met those who had not been at tea.

Shortly before dinner a colonel said to me, "Oh, I say, is it true that the tiny beauty is in command of your ship?"

"Quite true. Best commanding officer I've ever had."

"Haw. Astounding. Fascinating. The taller girl, the strawberry blonde—introduced simply as 'Mrs. Carter.' She's part of your ship's company. Yes?"

"Yes," I agreed. "Astrogator and second-in-command. Doctor D. T. Burroughs Carter, my wife."

"Well! My congratulations, sir."

"Thank you."

"I say, Carter, would it be rude of me to ask why the ladies have the senior posts while you and Doctor Burroughs appear to be junior? Or am I intruding?"

"Not at all, Colonel. We each do what we do best. Mrs. Burroughs is not only best as commander; she is also best cook. While we take turns at cooking, I'll happily volunteer as scullery maid if it will persuade the Captain to cook."

"Amazing. Could you use a colonel of lancers about to retire? I'm a wonderful scullery maid."

The dinner was excellent (Irish chef, transported for shooting his landlord) and Lady Herbert was delightful, even though she drank her dinner and her words became increasingly difficult to understand. But any answer would do as long as it was friendly. Jake displayed the charm he can when he bothers and kept her laughing.

One thing marred it. Lady Herbert started to slump and nursing sisters appeared and took her away. What is protocol for this?

I checked Hilda and the Governor; they didn't seem to see it. I glanced at Hird-Jones; the Brigadier did not seem to see it—but Squeaky sees *everything*. Ergo: no member of the colony could "see" it.

Someone else gathered the ladies while the gentlemen remained for port and cigars. While we were standing as the ladies left, Hird-Jones leaned close: "Your captain has asked me to tell you that the Governor invites you to join them later in his study."

I tasted the port, lit the cigar (I don't smoke—fake it when polite) when the Brigadier caught my eye and said, "Now." Bertie had left, leaving a stooge, a wit who had them all laughing—that colonel of lancers.

When Jake and I came in, Deety and Hilda were there, with a large man, tall as I am and heavier—Major General Moresby, chief of staff. Bertie stood while waving us to chairs. "Thanks for coming, gentlemen. We are settling tomorrow's schedule and your captain prefers to have you present."

The Governor reached behind him, moved out a globe of Mars. "Captain, I think I have marked the places we visited yesterday."

"Deety, please check it," Sharpie directed.

My darling looked it over. "The Russian settlements extended almost one hundred fifty kilometers farther east than this borderline shows—ninety-one English miles, seventy-nine nautical miles—call it two and a half degrees."

"Impossible!" (The bulky Major General—)

Deety shrugged. "Might be a few miles more; all we took were spot checks."

Jake said, "General Moresby, you had better believe it."

Bertie stepped in with: "Is that the only discrepancy, Doctor Deety?"

"One more. But there is something I want to ask about. May I borrow a marking pen? Grease pencil?"

Bertie found one; she placed three bingoes in an equilateral triangle, well detached from both zones. "What are these, sir? This one is a village, the other two are large farms. But we did not determine nationality."

Bertie looked at her marks. "Not ours. Moresby, how long ago did we reconnoitre that area?"

"There are no Russians there! She's doing it by memory. She's mistaken."

I said, "Moresby, I'll bet my wife's marks are accurate within two kilometers. How high do you want to go? What is a pound worth here in gold?"

Bertie said, "Please, gentlemen—wagers another time. What was the other error, Astrogator Deety?"

"Our touchdown point. Where we tangled with the Russians. Your memory is off by many degrees. Should be *here*."

"Moresby?"

"Governor, that is impossible. Either they did not land there or they had trouble with Russians somewhere else."

Deety shrugged. "Governor, I have no interest in arguing. Our time of arrival at 'Touchdown' just after dawn day before yesterday was fourteen-oh-six in the afternoon Windsor City local time. Six past two pip emma. You saw the remains of that ornithopter today. What did shadows and height of the sun tell you as to local time *there*, and what does that tell you about *longitude from here*?" She added, "With one degree of longitude being four minutes of local time difference, you can treat one minute of arc as equal to one kilometer and measure it on this globe. The errors will be smaller than your own error in estimate of local time."

"Astrogator, I'm not good at this sort of problem. But it was about eight-thirty in the morning where we saw the burned ornithopter."

"That's right, Governor. We'll lay that out as kilometers and see how close it comes to my mark."

Moresby objected, "But that globe is scaled in miles!"

Deety looked back at Bertie with a half smile, an expression that said wordlessly: *(He's your boy, Bertie. Not mine.)*

Bertie said testily, "Moresby, have you never worked with a French ordnance map?"

I'm not as tolerant as Deety. "Multiply by one-point-six-oh-nine."

"Thanks but we will assume that the Astrogator is correct. Moresby, reconnaissance will cover two areas. Captain, how many spot checks can be made per hour?"

"Just a moment!" Captain Sharpie interrupted. "Has this discussion been directed at the ride I promised Brigadier Hird-Jones?"

"I'm sorry, Ma'am. Wasn't that clear?"

"No, I thought you were telling General Moresby what you

saw today. Isn't the Brigadier available? I want to settle the time with him."

Moresby answered, "Madam, that has been changed. I'm taking his place."

Sharpie looked at Moresby as if he were a side of beef she was about to condemn. "Governor, I do not recall offering this person a ride. Nor has the Brigadier told me that he is not going."

"Moresby, didn't you speak to Hird-Jones?"

"Certainly I did, sir. I dislike to tell you but he was not co-operative. I had to remind him that there was rank involved."

I looked around for somewhere to hide. But Sharpie did not explode. She said sweetly, "Certainly there is, Major General Bores-me. *My* rank. *I* am commanding; *you* are *not*." She turned to Bertie. "Governor, I may offer other rides *after* I keep my promise to the Brigadier. But not to this person. He's too fat."

"*What!* I weigh only seventeen stone—trim for a man with my height and big bones." Moresby added, "Homeside weight, of course. Only ninety pounds here. Light on my feet. Madam, I resent that."

"Too fat," Sharpie repeated. "Bertie, you remember how tightly we were packed yesterday. But even if Bores-me did not have buttocks like sofa cushions, he's *much* too fat between the ears. He can't enter my yacht."

"Very well, Captain. Moresby, please have Hird-Jones report to me at once."

"But—"

"Dismissed."

As the door closed, the Governor said, "Hilda, my humblest apologies. Moresby told me that it was all arranged . . . which meant to me that he had seen you and Squeaky and arranged the exchange. Moresby hasn't been here long; I'm still learning his quirks. No excuse, Captain. But I offer it in extenuation."

"Let's forget it, Bertie. You used 'reconnaissance' where I would have said 'joy ride.' 'Reconnaissance' is a military term. Did you use it as such?"

"I did."

"Gay Deceiver is a private yacht and I am a civilian master." She looked at me. "Chief Pilot, will you advise me?"

"Captain, if we overfly territory for the purpose of reconnaissance, the act is espionage."

"Governor, is this room secure?"

"Hilda—Captain, in what way?"

"Is it soundproof and are there microphone pickups?"

"It is soundproof when I close that second door. There is one microphone. I control it with a switch under the rug—right *here*."

"Will you not only switch it off but disconnect it? So that it cannot be switched on by accident."

"If that is your wish. I could be lying. Other microphones."

"It's *accidental* recording I want to avoid. Bertie, I wouldn't trust Moresby as far as I could throw him. I have learned to trust you. Tell me why you need to reconnoitre?"

"I'm not certain."

"Reconnaissance is to learn something you are not certain about. Something that can be seen from Gay Deceiver—but what?"

"Uh . . . will you all swear to secrecy?"

"Hilda—"

"Not now, Jacob. Governor, if *you* don't want to trust *us*, tell us to leave!"

Smythe-Carstairs had been standing since turning the rug to remove the switch. He looked down at Hilda and smiled. "Captain, you are an unusually small woman . . . and the toughest man I've dealt with in many a year. The situation is this: The Russians have sent another ultimatum. We have never worried about Russians as we settled halfway around the planet from them and logistics here are almost impossible. No oceans. No navigable streams. Some canals if one enjoys suicide. Both sides have attempted to raise horses. They don't live long, they don't reproduce.

"Both sides have ornithopters. But they can't carry enough or fly far enough. I was startled when you said that they had given you trouble where you had first touched down—and proved it by showing me wreckage of a 'thopter.

"Any logistics problem can be solved if you use enough men, enough time. Those Russian craft must have, behind them, stock-piles about every fifty miles. If they have the same continuing this way, when they get here, they will wipe us out."

"Is it that bad?" I inquired. Sharpie said, "Governor, our Chief Pilot is the only one of us with combat experience."

"Yes," agreed Jake with a wry smile, "I was awarded rank in lieu of combat. I signed papers."

Bertie gave the same mirthless smile. "Welcome to the lodge. Twenty years since I last heard a bullet say *'wheat!'* Now I may be about to lose my last battle. Friends, my rank states that I am qualified to command an army corps . . . but I have possibly one platoon who will stand and die."

Jake said, "Governor, this city must be two hundred thousand people."

"More than that, Jake. Over ninety-nine percent are convicts or discharged convicts or their wives and children. Do you imagine that they are loyal to *me*? Even if they were, they are neither trained nor armed.

"I have a nominal regiment, a battalion in numbers—and a platoon in strength. Friends, my troops, officers and men, and my civil servants, are, with few exceptions, transportees quite as much as the convicts. Example: An officer with a court staring him in the face can often get the charges dropped by volunteering for Mars. I don't get murderers. What I do get is worse . . . for me. The mess treasurer who dips into mess funds because he has a 'sure thing' at a racing meet. The— Oh, the devil take it! I don't get villains; I get weaklings. There are a few good ones. Hird-Jones. Young fellow named Bean. Two old sergeants whose only shortcomings are that one had two wives and, while the other had only one, she wasn't his. If the Russians get here, they'll kill our wogs—they don't domesticate them; they hunt and eat them— they'll kill anyone in uniform . . . and transportees will learn that being a serf is worse than being a free man not on the planet of his choice. Squeaky! Where have you been?"

"In the card room, sir. First table to the right."

"So? How long ago did you get my message?"

"About twenty seconds ago, sir."

"Hm! How long have you been in the card room?"

"A bit over an hour."

"I see. Bolt the outer door, close the inner door, sit down."

Twenty minutes later Sharpie was asking, "Deety, what time is sunrise *here*?" She indicated a point 30° east of the western boundary of the westernmost of the two loci Bertie wanted investigated.

"In about twenty minutes. Shall I have Gay check it?"

"No. Sunset over here?"

"More leeway there. One hour fifty-seven minutes."

"Very well. Zeb, those zeroed packs?"

"Being charged, they told me. Ready in the morning."

"Good. Squeaky, if I get you to bed by oh-two-hundred hours could you take us to the fields about eleven-hundred hours?"

"Oh-eight-hundred, if you wish, Captain Hilda."

"I don't wish. This job requires sunlight, so we will work whatever it takes. I intend to sleep late. Bertie, would your kitchen service extend to breakfast in bed about ten ack emma?"

"Tell the night maid. The sideboard in your dining room will be loaded and steaming whenever you say and the day maid will be delighted to bring you a tray in bed."

"Heavenly! All hands and Brigadier Hird-Jones: Lift in thirty-nine minutes. Car doors open five minutes before that. Questions?"

"Just a comment. I'll fetch sandwiches."

"Thank you, Squeaky! Bertie."

"Eh? Ma'am!"

"Deety and I expect to be kissed good-bye . . . in case something goes wrong."

XXIX   "—we place no faith in princes."

Deety:

We had a busy night. I had Gay display bingo dots for every stop we made—then circles around any that were supply dumps.

There were indeed supply dumps!

I spent the whole trip thinking: Where would I be if I were a supply dump? Where would 'thopters have to land? Where could they get more water? Squeaky, Hilda, Pop, Zebadiah—and possibly Gay—were thinking the same thing.

We got back at half after one, the job done. The Hillbilly turned the results over to Squeaky and we went to bed.

Next morning at eleven our "roadable" arrived—without Squeaky. He sent an apologetic note saying that Lieutenant Bean knew what we expected and would add anything we asked for.

Captain Auntie had not taken breakfast in bed. I woke about nine local, found her at work—packing her dress clothes and Pop's back into plastic pillow covers, then into a borrowed portmanteau. Our fresh laundry, given to us by the night maid on our return, was in another piece of borrowed luggage.

The Hillbilly was on her knees in our drawing room. She looked up, smiled and said, "Good morning. Better slide into your jump suit, dear; maids come in and out rather casually."

"Doesn't bother me, I've been caught twice already—"

"But it bothers them. Not kind, dear, with servants. Especially with involuntary servants. They'll be in to load the sideboard any moment. Will you fetch yours and Zebbie's dress clothes here? I'll pack for you."

"I'll pack 'em, thanks. I was thinking about sliding back into bed with a nice warm man but your mention of food changed my mind. Hillbilly, what's the rush?"

"Deety, I'm carrying out my own orders. When I brush my teeth after breakfast, the toothbrush goes into my purse. As for the rush, our husbands will wake soon. I have found that it is more practical to present a man with a *fait accompli* than a discussion."

"I hear you three times, doll baby. When they get up, they'll want to eat. When our roadable shows up, they'll be sitting over second cups of coffee. Then they'll say, 'We'll do it when we come back. Mustn't keep the Brigadier waiting.' Okay, I'll grab our gear and we'll sneak it out before they wake. I'll carry the heavy ones."

"We are not permitted to carry anything, Deety. But the place is swarming with maids. You sound much married."

"Five years' practice on Pop. But, Hillbilly, even Pop is easy to handle if you think ahead."

"I'm learning. Deety, what shall we do about the maids?"

"Huh?"

"In the days when servants were common, it was polite for house guests to tip servants who served them personally. But *how*, Deety? I have two twenty-five-newdollar bills in the lining of my purse. Waste paper."

"Pop and Zebadiah have gold. I know exactly because it was mass enough that I had to figure it into the loading, mass and moment arm. Here's a giggle. These misers we married had each squirreled away the same weight of gold to four significant figures. So maids are no problem if you know how much to tip—I don't. We'll be buying local money today to pay for a number of things."

"Leftenant" Bean—or "Brian"—is a delightful fuzzy puppy and a volunteer in order to have served "Beyond the Sky." He managed to call me "Deety" and Zebadiah "Zeb" when invited, but he could *not* bring himself to shift from "Captain Burroughs" to "Hilda"—"Captain Hilda" was as far as he would go, and Pop was "Professor."

He was pleased that we liked his "roadable." You wouldn't

believe it! A large, wooden flatbed wagon with an upright steam engine in back; a trailer with cordwood; a sailing-ship's wheel in front of the engine; this controlled the front wheels by ropes that ran underneath. Midway was a luggage pen, then in front were four benches, for twelve to sixteen people.

With a crew of *five!*

Engine driver, fireman, conductor, and two steersmen—

The conductor sat on a high perch braced to the pen and told the others what to do and occasionally rang a bell or blew a whistle. The bell told other traffic to get out of the way; the whistle warned that the vehicle was about to start or stop. There was much traffic but few "roadables"—most common were pedalled tricycles, for passengers and freight. Large versions had as many as a dozen men pedalling at once.

"I daresay you know," said Brian, "that we have not been able to raise horses. We haven't given up—we will develop a breed that will prosper here. But once we have horses, this will, I venture to predict, become a proper colony—and not just a place to send reformable evildoers and to obtain raw pharmaceuticals."

"Pharmaceuticals?"

"Oh, definitely! The thing that makes the colony self-supporting. I daresay the descendants of these convicts will be wealthy. I will show you the fields—all in the weed—a cant word for Cannabis Magnifica Martia—except acreage for food crops. Brigadier Hird-Jones suggested Norfolk Plantation." He smiled. "Shall we?"

"Just a moment," Aunt Hilda said. "If I understood the Brigadier's note, we can vary the program?"

"Captain Hilda, the carriage and I are at your disposal as long as you wish. My orders and my pleasure."

"Brian, I have clothing being made up. I was told that sewing would continue through the night. Where should we go to inquire?"

"Here and now. I fancy I saw a package being delivered while we've been chatting; it could be yours. It would go to the chief housekeeper, who would have it placed in your digs—the Princess Suite, is it not?"

"Yes. Brian, I'll slip upstairs and see."

"Please, no!" Brian made a small gesture; a private soldier appeared out of nowhere. "Smathers, my greetings to Mrs. Digby. Has a package arrived for Captain Burroughs?"

"Sir!"

"Hold it! Brian, if it has arrived, I want it fetched here."

I could see the look in Brian's eye that Pop gets just before he starts demanding explanations for female "unreasonable" behavior. But Brian simply added, "If the package has arrived, tell Mrs. Digby that it must be delivered here at once. Double time, so to speak."

"*Sir!*" The private stomped an about-face and broke into a run. Hilda said, "Thank you, Brian. If I place it in our craft, it is one less detail to remember. Your kindness eases my mind."

"A pleasure, Captain Hilda."

"Hilda, that clothing is not yet paid for."

"Oh, dear! You are right, Jacob. Leftenant, where does one exchange gold for local money? Do you know the rate of exchange? In grams?"

"Or in Troy ounces," I added.

Brian behaved as if he had not heard us. He turned toward his "roadable." "Parkins! Take a turn around the circle! When you return, I want that steam up high. So that we won't creep in starting."

"Roight, sir." The wagon moved off, at a headlong slow walk.

When no one else was in earshot Brian said quietly, "I missed what you were saying because of engine noise. But let me mention in passing that possession of gold by individuals is not permitted so I-am-happy-to-learn-that-you-have-none," he said, not letting himself be interrupted. "Let me add," he went on, "that since I handle secret and most-secret despatches, I know things that I don't know, if I make my meaning clear. For example, I am grateful that you four were willing to lose sleep last night. Others feel strong obligations to such good friends. The Brigadier mentioned that you might have purchases to make or bills to pay. I was instructed to charge anything you need or want—or fancy— to the Imperial Household, signing his name and appending my signature."

"Oh, that's most unfair!"

"Truly, Captain? I fancy that those in authority will find something to add until you feel that you have been treated generously."

"That's not what she means, son," put in Pop. "'Unfair' in the opposite direction. We pay for what we get."

Brian lost his smile. "May I suggest that the Professor discuss that with the Brigadier? I would find it extremely embarrassing to have to report to the Brigadier that I was unable to carry out his orders."

"Captain."

"What, Deety?"

"I am required to advise you."

"Advise away, my dear. I see my packages coming."

"Captain Auntie, you've got a bear by the tail. Let go."

The Hillbilly grinned and stuck out her tongue at me, then turned to Brian. "The Brigadier's thoughtful arrangements are appreciated. We accept."

It was still a few minutes before we left, as it turned out that Zebadiah's power packs were ready, in the hands of the Household engineer. At last Hilda's clothes and the power packs were in Gay; we boarded the char-à-banc, and whizzed away at 10 km/hr. "Norfolk Plantation, Captain Hilda?"

"Brian, at what time did you breakfast?"

"Oh, that's not important, Ma'am."

"Answer my question."

"At oh-seven-hundred hours, Captain."

"So I suspected. You eat at Imperial House?"

"Oh, no, Captain Hilda, only the most senior of the Governor's official family eat there. I eat at the officers' club."

"I see. We'll see wogs last. I am told there is a commissary. Is it open to us?"

"Captain Hilda, *everything* is open to *you*."

"I must buy supplies. Then I wish to go to the best restaurant in Windsor City and watch you eat a proper luncheon; we ate breakfast three hours later than you did."

"But I'm hungry," said my husband. "I'm a growing boy."

"Poor Zebbie."

There was not much to buy that would keep. I bought a tin of Huntley & Palmer's biscuits and quite a lot of Dutch chocolate— quick energy for growing boys—and tightly packaged staples.

Brian had us driven to that restaurant just past noon. I was glad that Aunt Hilda had decided to get everything else done before we went to look at vermin. Even so, I did not have much appetite— until I decided to stand up and forthrightly turn coward. *Not* look at vermin! *Cui bono*? Aunt Hilda was the expert.

That restored my appetite. We stopped across the parade ground from Imperial House. We twigged in this order—Zebadiah, Pop, me, Aunt Hilda—that it was the officers' club. She was several meters inside when she stopped. "Brian, what are we doing *here*?"

"The Captain said '—the best restaurant—'. The club's chef was executive chef at Claridge's until he ran into misfortune. Don't look at me that way, Captain Hilda; the Brigadier picks up the chit; it's charged against 'official visitors' and winds up in

London against H.I.M.'s Civil List. Believe me, His Majesty gets paid more than leftenants, or even brigadiers."

But the president of the mess signed the chit—a colonel who told the Hillbilly that he was buying her lunch because he wanted to ship with us as scullery maid.

I was telling Aunt Hilda that I would skip vermin viewing, thank you, when I did. One. Then six. Then a whole field of them. I was explaining to God that I didn't like this dream so *please* let me wake up when Brian had the conductor halt the contraption and I saw that there were *men* in that field, too. The men carried whips; vermin were muzzled. This one vermin—well, "wog"—this wog had managed to pull its muzzle aside and was stuffing this weedy plant into its mouth . . . when a whip cracked across its naked back.

It cried.

The field on the other side of the road was not being worked, so I stared at it. After a while I heard Brian say, "Captain Hilda, you are serious, really?"

"Didn't the Brigadier authorize it?"

"Ah, yes. I thought he was pulling my leg. Very well, Ma'am."

I had to see what this was all about . . . and discovered that muzzled vermin, afraid of men with whips, weren't frightening; they were merely ugly. Aunt Hilda was taking pictures, movies and stereo. Brian was talking to a man dressed like any farmer except for the Broad Arrow.

Brian turned and said, "Captain Hilda, the foreman asks that you point out the wog you want to dissect."

Aunt Hilda answered, "There has been a mistake."

"Ma'am? You *don't* want to dissect a wog?"

"Leftenant, I was told that one or more died or was slaughtered each day. I want to dissect a dead body, in an appropriate place, with surgical instruments and other aids. I have no wish to have one of these poor creatures killed."

We left shortly. Brian said, "Of the two, the abattoir and the infirmary, I suggest the latter. The veterinarian is a former Harley Street specialist. By the bye, there is no case of humans contracting disease from these brutes. So the infirmary isn't dangerous, just, ah, unpleasant."

We went to the wog hospital. I did not go inside. Shortly Pop came out, looking green. He sat beside me and smiled wanly. "Deety, the Captain ordered me outside for fresh air—and I didn't argue. Aren't you proud of me?"

I told him that I'm always proud of my Pop.

A few minutes later Brian and Zebadiah came out, with a message from Hilda that she expected to work at least another hour, possibly longer. "Captain Hilda suggests that I take you for a drive," Brian reported.

The drive was only as far as the nearest pub; the sillywagon was sent back to wait for the Hillbilly. We waited in the lounge, where Pop and Brian had whisky and splash, and Zebadiah ordered a "shandygaff"—so I did, too. It will never replace the dry martini. I made it last till Aunt Hilda showed up.

Brian asked, "Where now, Captain Hilda?"

"Imperial House. Brian, you've been most kind."

I said, "Cap'n Auntie, did you whittle one to pieces?"

"Not necessary, Deetikins. They're chimpanzees."

"You've insulted every chimp that ever lived!"

"Deety, these creatures bear the relation to 'Black Hats' that a chimpanzee does to a man. The physical resemblance is closer, but the difference in mental power— Doctor Wheatstone removed the brain from a cadaver; that told me all I needed to know. But I got something that may be invaluable. Motion pictures."

Zebadiah said, "Sharpie, you took motion pictures in the fields."

"True, Zebbie. But I have with me the Polaroids you took for me at Snug Harbor; some show the splints that creature used to disguise its extra knees and elbows. Doctor Wheatstone used surgical splints to accomplish the same with one of his helpers—a docile and fairly intelligent wog that didn't object even though it fell down the first time it tried to walk while splinted. But it caught on and managed a stiff-legged walk just like that ranger—and like 'Brainy' now that I think about it—then was delighted when Doctor Wheatstone dressed it in trousers and an old jacket. *Those* pictures will surprise you. No makeup, no plastic surgery, a hastily improvised disguise—from the neck down it looked human."

When we reached Imperial House, we transferred packages into Gay Deceiver—again were not permitted to carry; Brian told the conductor, the conductor told his crew. We thanked them, thanked Brian as we said good-bye, and Aunt Hilda expressed a hope of seeing him soon and we echoed her—me feeling like a hypocrite.

He saluted and started toward the officers' club. We headed for the big wide steps. Aunt Hilda said, "Deety, want to share some soap suds?"

"Sure thing!" I agreed.

"Whuffor?" asked Zebadiah. "Sharpie, you didn't get a spot on you."

"To remove the psychic stink, Zebbie."

"Mine isn't psychic," I said. "I stink, I do."

But damn, spit, and dirty socks, we had hardly climbed into that tub when a message arrived, relayed by my husband, saying that the Governor requested us to call at his office at our earliest convenience. "Sharpie hon, let me translate that, based on my eighty years man and boy as flunky to an ambassador. Means Bertie wants to see us five minutes ago."

I started to climb out; Aunt Hilda stopped me. "I understood it, Zebbie; I speak Officialese, Campusese, and Bureaucratese. But I'll send a reply in clear English, female idiom. Is a messenger waiting?"

"Yes, a major."

"A major, eh? That will cost Bertie five extra minutes. Zebbie, I learned before you were born that when someone wants to see me in a hurry, the urgency is almost never mutual. All right, message: The commanding officer of Spacecraft *Gay Deceiver* sends her compliments to the Governor General and will call on him at her earliest convenience. Then give the major a message from you to Bertie that you happen to know that I'm taking a bath and that you *hope* I'll be ready in twenty minutes but that you wouldn't wager even money on thirty."

"Okay. Except that the word should be 'respects' not 'compliments.' Also, the major emphasized that he wants to see all of us. Want Jake and me to keep Bertie happy until you are ready?" Pop had his head in the door, listening. "We wouldn't mind." Pop nodded.

"Zebbie, Zebbie! After four years under my tutelage. Until I know what he wants I *can't* concede that he is senior to me. 'Compliments,' *not* 'respects.' And *no one* goes until *I* do . . . but thank you both for the offer. Two more things: After giving the major my message, will you please find my clothes, all but Deety's Keds, and take them to the car? That's Jacob's shirt, Deety's sailor pants, a blue belt, and a blue hair ribbon. In the car you will find new clothes on my seat. In one package should be three jump suits. Please fetch one back."

Pop said, "Hilda, I'd be glad to run that errand. Run it twice, in fact, as you don't want to send down what clothes you have until you know that your new clothes fit."

"Jacob, I want you *right here,* to scrub our backs and sing for us and keep us amused. If that jump suit does not fit, I may appear in a bath towel sarong. But I plan to appear a minute early to make Bertie happy. Do *not* tell the major that, Zebbie! Officially it is twenty minutes with luck, thirty minutes more likely, could be an hour, Major; you know how women are. Got it all?"

"Roger Wilco. Sharpie, someday they'll hang you."

"They will sentence me to hang but Jacob and you will rescue me. Trot along, dear." Aunt Hilda started to get out. "Stay there, Deety. I'll give you three minutes' warning—two to dry down, one to zip into your jump suit. Which leaves ten minutes to relax."

The jump suit did fit; the Hillbilly looked cute. We left not a thing in that suite because Aunt Hilda checked it while waiting for Zebadiah. A few items went into my purse or hers. It was eighteen minutes from her message to our arrival at the Governor's office—and I had had a fifteen-minute tub, comfy if not sybaritic.

Besides Bertie and the Brigadier, that fathead Moresby was there. Aunt Hilda ignored him, so I did. Bertie stood up. "How smart you all look! Did you have a pleasant day?" The poor dear looked dreadful—gaunt, circles under his eyes.

"A perfect day—thanks to you, thanks to the Brigadier, and thanks to a curly lamb named Bean."

"A fine lad," Squeaky boomed. "I'll pass on your word, if I may." The Brigadier did not look fresh; I decided that neither had been to bed.

Bertie waited until we were seated, then got to business. "Captain Burroughs, what are your plans?"

Aunt Hilda did not answer his question. She glanced toward Major General Moresby, back at Bertie. "We are not in private, Excellency."

"Hmm—" Bertie looked unhappy. "Moresby, you are excused."

"But—"

"Dismissed. You have work to do, I feel sure."

Moresby swelled up but got up and left. Squeaky bolted the outer door, closed the inner door, while Bertie stood up to lift the rug over his recorder switch. Aunt Hilda said, "Don't bother, Bertie. Record if you need to. What's the trouble, old dear? Russians?"

"Yes. Hilda, you four are refugees; yesterday you showed me why. Would you care to remain here? My delegated power is sufficient that I can grant naturalization as fast as I can sign my signature."

"No, Bertie. But we feel greatly honored."

"I expected that. Do reconsider it. There are advantages to being a subject of the most powerful monarch in history, in being protected by a flag on which the Sun never sets."

"No, Bertie."

"Captain Hilda, I need you and your ship. Because of millions of miles of distance, many months required for a message, I hold *de jure* viceregal power almost equal to sovereign . . . and *de facto* greater in emergency because no Parliament is here. I can recruit foreign troops, arm them, make guarantees to them as if they were British, award the King-Emperor's commission. I would like to recruit all of you and your ship."

"No."

"Commodore for you, Captain for your second-in-command, Commander for your Chief Pilot, Lieutenant Commander for your Copilot. Retirement at full pay once the emergency is over. Return of your purchased ship as a royal gift after the emergency. Compensation for loss or damage."

"No."

"One rank higher for each of you?"

"All four of us must be at least one rank senior to Major General Moresby."

"Hilda! That's my own rank. Equivalent rank—Vice Admiral."

"Bertie, you can't hire us as mercenaries at any rank or pay. That hyperbole was to tell you that we will *not* place ourselves *under* your chief of staff. That settled, what can we do to help you?"

"I'm afraid you can't, since you won't accept the protection under international law of military status. So I'm forced to cut the knot. Do you understand the right of angary?"

(I thought he said "angry" and wondered.)

"I believe so. Are Great Britain and the Russias at war?"

"No, but there are nuances. Shall I call in my legal officer?"

"Not for me. My own legal officer is here: Doctor Zebadiah Carter, my consultant in international law."

"Doctor Carter—oh, fiddlesticks! My friend Zeb. Zeb, will you discuss the right of angary?"

"Very well, Governor. One nuance you had in mind was that, in addition to wartime, it applies to national emergency—such as your current one with the Russians."

"Yes!"

"Angary has changed in application many times but in general it is the right of a sovereign power to seize neutral transport found in its ports or territory, then use same in war or similar emergency. When the emergency is over, seized transport must be returned, fair rentals must be paid, loss or damage requires compensation. It does *not* apply to goods or chattels, and most especially not to persons. That's the gist. Do we need your legal officer?"

"I don't think so. Captain Burroughs?"

"We don't need him. You intend to requisition my craft?"

"Captain . . . I *must!*" Bertie was almost in tears.

"Governor, you are within your legal rights. But have you considered how you will drive it?"

"May I answer that, Governor?"

"Go ahead, Squeaky."

"Captain Hilda, I have an odd memory. 'Photographic' it is called but I remember sounds as automatically. I am sure I can fly every maneuver used last night—that is to say: sufficient for our emergency."

I was seething. But Aunt Hilda smiled at the Brigadier and said in her sweetest voice: "You've been most thoughtful throughout our stay, Squeaky. You are a warm, charming, hospitable, bastardly *fink*. One who would sell his wife to a Port Saïd pimp. Aside from that you are practically perfect."

"Doubled and redoubled!" (That was my Pop!) "Later on, Jones, I'll see you at a time and place of your choosing. Weapons or bare hands."

"And then *I* will see you, if Jake leaves anything." My husband flexed his fingers. "I hope you choose bare hands."

Bertie interrupted. "I forbid this during this emergency and after it in territory where I am suzerain and while Hird-Jones holds the Sovereign's commission under my command."

Aunt Hilda said, "You are legally correct, Bertie. But you will concede that they had provocation."

"No, Ma'am! Hird-Jones is not at fault. I *tried* to get you and your crew to fly it on any terms at all. You refused. Hird-Jones may kill himself attempting to fly a strange flyer. If so he will die a hero. He is *not* what you called him."

"I don't think well of you, either, Bertie. You are a thief—stealing our only hope of a future."

"He certainly is!" I cut in. "Governor, I can whip you—I can *kill* you, with my bare hands. I'm Black-Belt three ways. Are you going to hide behind your commission and your self-serving laws?" I dusted my hands together. "Coward. Two cowards, with their chests covered with ribbons boasting about their brave deeds."

"Astrogator."

"Captain."

"Let it drop. Bertie, under right of angary we are entitled to remove our chattels. I insist on a witness so that you will know that we have done nothing to damage the craft. If the Brigadier can drive it, it will be turned over to him in perfect shape. But my jewelry is in our craft and many other things; I must have a witness. *You*, sir. My stepdaughter can certainly kill you or anyone her size or a bit more than her size, with her bare hands. But I grant you safe-conduct. Will you have it in writing?"

Bertie shook his head. "You know I can't take time to witness. Pick anyone else."

"I won't grant safe-conduct to anyone else. Anyone who has not ridden with us would not know how to watch for sabotage. So it must be either you or Hird-Jones . . . and Hird-Jones would never live to get out of our car. He has three of the deadliest killers in two universes quite annoyed. Angry over angary."

"Any of you who will not give parole must wait up here."

"Wait a half, Gov," my husband drawled. "'Parole' applies to prisoners. Captain, this might be a good time to read aloud *our* safe-conduct from the Governor General. See how many ways this fake 'officer and gentleman' has broken his word—and the written guarantees of his sovereign. He has broken all three essential guarantees to all four of us. That's twelve. Almost a Russian score. Safe-conduct amounting to diplomatic immunity, all of us free to leave at any time, we four never to be separated involuntarily. *Now* he wants hostages. *Pfui!*"

"None is broken," Bertie asserted.

"Liar," my husband answered.

"All of you are safe here . . . until the Russians conquer us. I slipped in speaking of parole; you are not prisoners. You all may stay together—living in the Princess Suite if you so choose. If not, in any quarters you choose in territory I control. You are all free to leave at any moment. But you must *not* approach that requisitioned flyer. Captain, your jewels will be safe. But others will unload the flyer."

"Bertie—"

"What? Yes . . . Hilda?"

"Dear, you are both stubborn and stupid. You can't open the doors of our car, much less drive it. Attempt to force it open and no one will ever drive it. I conceded the legality of the right of angary. But you insist on making it impossible to apply it. Accept my safe-conduct and come witness or *there that car sits until the Russians come*, while we live in luxury in this palace. You *know* that 'the right to leave at any time' means *nothing* without our transport. Now, *for the last time*, will you do it my way...or will you waste the precious minutes of a war crisis trying to open that car by yourself? Make up your mind, this offer will not be repeated. Answer Yes or No...and be damned quick about it!"

Bertie covered his face with his hands. "Hilda, I've been up all night. Both Squeaky and I."

"I know, dear. I knew when we came in. So I must help you make up your mind. Deety, check your purse. Something is missing."

I hastily checked, wondering what she meant. Then I noticed that a secret pocket that should have been hard was not. "Oh! Do you have it?"

"Yes, Deety." Aunt Hilda was seated, her choice, so that she had both Bertie and Squeaky in her line of fire—and none of us. "I mentioned three killers. Now you have *four* facing you...in a soundproofed room with its door bolted from inside." (I never saw her draw my Skoda gun. But she was holding it on them.) "Bertie, I'm making up your mind for you. You are accepting my safe-conduct. Consider how poor the chances are that anyone would find your bodies in the time it takes us to run down one flight and reach our car."

Squeaky lunged at Hilda. I tripped him, kicked his left kneecap as he fell, then said, "Don't move, Fink! My *next* kick is a killer! Captain, has Bertie come to his senses? Or shall I take him? I hate to kill Bertie. He's tired and worried and not thinking straight. Then I would have to kill Squeaky. He can't help his eidetic memory, any more than I can help this clock in my head. Squeaky, did I break your kneecap? Or can you walk if I let you get up?"

"I can walk. You're fast, Deety."

"I know. Captain. Plans?"

"Bertie, you are accepting my safe-conduct. We are all going out together, we four around you two, laughing and talking and heading for our car—and if anyone gets close, you two are dead. One of you will get it with this—"

"And the other with this." (My husband, with his stubby police special—)

"Why, Zebbie! How naughty of you! Jacob, do you have a holdout too?"

"Just this—" Pop now had his hunting knife.

"Deety?"

"Did have. You're holding it. But I still have five weapons."

"Five?"

"Both hands, both feet, and my head. Squeaky, I must frisk you. Don't wiggle . . . or I'll *hurt* you." I added, "Stop easing toward your desk, Bertie. You can't kill four of us before we kill you. Pop, don't bother with the gun, or trap, or whatever, in Bertie's desk. Let's get out of here, laughing and joking, as the Captain ordered. Oh, Squeaky, *that* didn't hurt! Captain, shall I let him up?"

"Brigadier Hird-Jones, do you honor the safe-conduct granted to us by your commanding officer?" Aunt Hilda asked.

"Brigadier, I order you to honor it," Bertie said grimly.

Maybe Squeaky had to catch his breath; he was a touch slow. "Yes, sir."

Aunt Hilda said, "Thanks, Squeaky. I'm sorry I had to say harsh things to you . . . but not having muscles I must fight with words. Zebbie, frisk Bertie. But quickly; we leave now. I leave first, on Bertie's arm. Deety follows, on Squeaky's arm—you can lean on her if you need to; she's strong. Help him up, Deety. Jacob and Zebbie trail along behind. Bertie, if anyone gets close to us, or either you or Squeaky try to signal anyone, or if anything is pointed at us—first you two die. Then we four die; that's inevitable. But we'll take some with us. What do you think the total may be? Two . . . and four . . . then five? Six? A dozen? Or higher?"

It took us forty-seven seconds to the bottom of the steps, thirty-one more to Gay Deceiver, and I aged seventy-eight years. Squeaky did lean on me but I made it look the other way around and he managed to smile and to sing with me: *Gaudeamus Igitur*. Hilda sang *The Bastard King* to Bertie which seemed both to shock him and make him laugh. The odd way she held his arm told me that she was prepared to plant 24 poisoned darts in Bertie's left armpit if anything went sour.

No one bothered us. Bertie returned a dozen or more salutes.

But at Gay Deceiver we ran into a bobble. Four armed soldiers guarded our Smart Girl. By the starboard door was that fathead Moresby, looking smug. As we came close, he saluted, aiming it at Bertie.

Bertie did not return his salute. "What's the meaning of this?" he said, pointing. Plastered to Gay's side, bridging the line where her door fairs into her afterbody, was H.I.M.'s Imperial seal.

Moresby answered, "Governor, I understood you perfectly when you told me that I had work to do. Verb. sap., eh?"

Bertie didn't answer; Moresby continued to hold salute.

"Major General Moresby," Bertie said so quietly that I could just hear it.

"Sir!"

"Go to your quarters. Send me your sword."

I thought Fathead was going to melt down the way the Wicked Witch did when Dorothy threw the pail of water over her. He brought down the salute and left, moving quickly.

Everybody acted as if nothing had happened. Hilda said, "Gay Deceiver, open starboard door"—she did and that seal broke. "Bertie, we're going to need people to carry things. I don't want our possessions stacked outdoors."

He looked down at her, surprised. "Is the war over?"

"There never was a war, Bertie. But you tried to push us around, and I don't push. You requisitioned this craft; it's legally yours. What I insisted on was that *you* must witness removal of our chattels. That took coaxing."

"'Coaxing'!"

"Some people are harder to coax than others. Squeaky, I'm sorry about your knee. Can you hobble back? Or shall we get you a wheelchair? That knee must be swelling up."

"I'll live. Deety, you play rough."

"Squeaky," said the Governor General, "slow march back toward the House, grab the first person you see, delegate him to round up a working party. Hilda, will a dozen be enough?"

"Better make it twenty. And about four more armed guards."

"Twenty and four additional sentries. Once you pass that word, put the senior rating in charge, and climb into a tub of hot water."

"Cold water."

"What, Hilda? *Cold?*"

"Hot is okay if he uses lots of Epsom salts. Otherwise ice-cold water will bring the swelling down faster, even though it's uncomfortable. But not for long. Ice water numbs pain while it reduces swelling. By morning you'll be fit. Unless Deety cracked the bone."

"Oh, I hope not!" I blurted.

"Squeaky, you had better listen to Captain Hilda."

"I'll do it. Ice water. *Brrrrr!*"

"Get on with it. But order that working party."

"Right away, sir."

"Bertie, will you follow me?" Hilda went inside. The Governor followed her, started to say something but Hilda cut him off: "Jacob, get out the items forward here while Zebbie keeps inventory as you do. Bertie, I have something for Betty before that mob gets here. Will you help me undog this door or perhaps Deety can do it easier GayDeceiverCloseDoorsGayBounceGayBounce-GayBounce. Bertie, take off your clothes." She held onto a door dog with her left hand, had my little gun aimed at his face.

"Hilda!"

"*Captain* Hilda, please; I'm in *my* spacecraft under way. Take off every stitch, Bertie; I'm not as trusting as Zebbie. I assume that you have a holdout he didn't find. Gay Bounce. Hurry up, Bertie; you're going to stay in free fall with no Lomine until you are naked. Zebbie, he may require help. Or inducement."

He required both. But eleven minutes later Bertie was wearing one of Pop's coveralls and his clothes were abaft the bulkhead. Zebbie did not find a weapon but Aunt Hilda took no chances. At last we were all strapped down, with Bertie between me and the Captain.

Hilda said, "All hands, report readiness for space. Astrogator."

"Captain Auntie, we *are* in space."

"But quite unready. Astrogator."

"Seat belt fastened. Ready."

"Chief Pilot."

"Door seal checked. No loose gear—I stuffed Bertie's clothes in with the cabin bed clothes. Four charged power packs in reserve. Juice oh-seven-oh. All systems go. Ready."

"Copilot."

"Seat belt tight. Continua device ready. Door seal checked. I'd like a Lomine if we're going to be in free fall long. Ready for space."

"Astrogator, three antinausea pills—captain, copilot, passenger. Passenger."

"Oh! Oh, yes! Safety belt tight."

"Captain states seat belt fastened. Ready for space. Gay Termite."

It was just sunrise at our streamside "home." "Aunt Hilda, why did we run through all that rigamarole if we were coming straight here?"

"Deety, when you are captain you will know."

"Not me. I'm not the captain type."

She ignored me. "Lieutenant General Smythe-Carstairs, will you give me your unconditional parole until I return you home? On your honor as an officer and a gentleman."

"Am I going home? I had assumed that I had not long to live."

"You are going home. And I *do* have something for Betty. But whether or not you give parole affects other matters. Make up your mind—*at once!*"

It took him six seconds; Aunt Hilda let him have them. "Parole. Unconditional."

"I'm surprised, Bertie. You have a tradition against giving parole, do you not?"

"We do indeed, Captain. But I concluded that my only chance of serving my sovereign lay in giving my word. Am I right?"

"Quite right, Bertie. You now have opportunity to persuade me to support you in your crisis. Your King-Emperor is not our prince; we place no faith in princes. We have no reason to love Russians but we spanked the only one who gave us trouble. In what way is the British colony superior to the Russian one? Take your time."

Aunt Hilda turned her attention to the rest of us. "Standing orders apply: Two at a time, one being armed. Deety and I will cut and wrap sandwiches, make coffee and prepare a snack for growing boys who can't remember a bounteous luncheon three hours ago. One guard at all times at the car. Bertie, I'm assigning you that duty. You know how to use a rifle?"

Zebadiah said, *"You're* arming *him*?"

"Chief Pilot, I assume that you are questioning my judgment. If you convince me that I am wrong, there will be a new captain even more quickly than I had planned. May I have your reason?"

"Sharpie, I didn't mean to get your feathers up."

"Not at all, Zebbie. Why are you surprised that I intend to use Bertie as guard?"

"Ten minutes ago you had me do a skin search to make sure he wasn't armed. Now you are about to hand him a gun."

"Ten minutes ago he had not given parole."

Bertie said hastily, "Zeb is right, Hilda—Captain Hilda; Zeb has no reason to trust me. I don't want to be a bone of contention!"

I'm still trying to figure out whether Aunt Hilda is more logical than other people or is a complete sophist. She gave Bertie a freeze, looking him up and down. "Smythe-Carstairs, your opinion was neither asked nor wanted."

Bertie turned pink. "Sorry, Ma'am."

"Although you *were* a person of some importance in your own land, you are now something between a prisoner and a nuisance. I am trying to give you the dignity of crew member pro tem. Hold your tongue. Zebbie, what were you going to say?"

"Shucks, if you aren't afraid to have him with a gun at your back, I'm not. No offense intended, Bertie."

"None taken, Zeb."

"Zebbie, please assure yourself that Bertie can handle a rifle, and that he knows what to shoot at and when *not* to shoot, before you turn the guard over to him. Put the other rifle at the door for bush patrol. Bertie, watch and listen. Gay Deceiver, open your doors."

Our Smart Girl opened wide. "Gay Deceiver, close your doors." Gay complied. "Bertie," Aunt Hilda went on, "you do it."

Of course he failed—and failed again on other voice programs. The Hillbilly explained that it took me a tedious time with special equipment to cause this autopilot to respond to a particular human voice. "Bertie, go back and explain to Squeaky; make him understand that I saved his life. This car can be driven in three modes. Two Squeaky can't use at all; the third would kill him as dead as Caesar."

"Plus a fourth hazard," added my husband. "Anybody who doesn't understand the Smart Girl but tries to take her apart to see what makes her tick would find himself scattered over a couple of counties."

"Booby-trapped, Zebadiah?" I asked. "I hadn't known it."

"No. But juice is *very* unfriendly to anybody who doesn't understand it."

"Come and get it!" The snack Aunt Hilda offered was a much-stuffed omelet. "Bertie, place your gun near you, locked. Between bites, you can tell us why your colony is worth defending. By us, I mean. For you, it's duty."

"Captain Hilda, I've done some soul-searching. I daresay that, in the main, we and the Russians are much the same, prison colonies with military governors. Perhaps, in a hundred years, it won't matter. Although *I* see us as morally superior."

"How, Bertie?"

"A Russian might see this differently. Our transportees are malefactors under our laws—but once here, they are as free as other Englishmen. Oh, they must wear the Broad Arrow until discharged—but at home they would wear it in a grim prison. The Russian prisoners are, if our intelligence is correct, the people they used to send to the Siberian salt mines. Political prisoners. They are serfs but I am told that most of them were not serfs in Russia. Whether they are treated better or worse than serfs in Russia I do not know. But one thing I do know. They work their fields with men; we work ours with wogs."

"And whip them!" Suddenly I was angry.

We had an argument, Bertie maintaining that the whips were not used unnecessarily, I asserting that I had seen it with my own eyes.

I guess he won, as he told us that they *had* to muzzle the beasts in weed fields, or they would stuff themselves on it, pass out, wake somewhat, do it again, and starve—but the muzzles were designed to allow them to chew a blade at a time all day long, to keep them happy. "The raw weed is addictive, to wog and man. We won't allow a man to work in the fields more than three months at a time . . . and pull him out if he can't pass the weekly medical tests. As for wogs, Deety—yes, we exploit them. Human beings exploit horses, cattle, sheep, poultry, and other breeds. Are you vegetarian?"

I admitted I was not. "But I don't want to eat wogs!"

"Nor do we. In Windsor colony wog meat goes only to wogs, and wogs don't care. In the wild they eat their own dead, kill and eat their aged. Captain Hilda, that's all the defense I can offer. I admit that it doesn't sound as strong as I had always believed."

"Captain, I'd like to put one to Bertie."

"Jacob, I treasure your thoughts."

"Bertie, would you polish off the Russians if you could?"

Bertie snorted. "That's academic, Doctor. I don't command the force it would take. I can't set up a string of stockpiles—and wouldn't know what to do with them if I could; I don't have the troops or 'thopters. But I must add: If my King tells me to fight, I will *fight*."

Aunt Hilda told Bertie to wash dishes with Pop sent along as guard. As soon as they started down, Aunt Hilda said, "We are going to do it, to a maximum cost of one power pack. Deety, start working on a program stringing together the dumps we located last night."

"Already have," I told her. "In my head. Last night. To put me to sleep. You want it preprogrammed? I would rather tell Gay each bounce, I would."

"Do it your way, hon. The purpose in sending Bertie to wash dishes and Jacob to guard him was to get them out of the way while I rig a frameup. At the end of the coming run, we drop Bertie and bounce . . . and at that instant I cease to be captain. I want to hold the election now—a one-ballot railroad. I will ask for nominations. Zebbie, you nominate Jacob. Deety, you don't need to say anything but speak if you wish. If Jacob nominates either of you, don't argue. I'll rig it so that Bertie declares the ballots. If you two are with me, the only surprise will be that fourth vote. Three for Jacob, and let's all write 'Jacob,' not 'Pop' or 'Jake,' and one for the dark horse. Are you with me?"

"Wait a half, Sharpie. Why not give Deety a crack at it?"

"Not me!"

"Deety should have the experience, but, please, Zebbie, not this time. Jacob has given me a dreadful time. Endless insubordination. I want to pass him on to Deety well tenderized. Deety ought not to have to put up with her father second-guessing her decisions—and, if you two help, she won't have to. I want to give my beloved the goddamndest 'white mutiny' ever, one that he will remember with shudders and never again give a skipper any lip."

"Sounds good," I agreed, "but I don't know what a 'white mutiny' is."

"Sweetheart," my husband told me, "it's killing him with kindness. He says 'Frog,' we hop. Utter and literal obedience."

"*This* he won't like? Pop will love it!"

"So? Would you like to command zombies who *never* make suggestions and carry out orders literally without a grain of common sense?"

Fifteen minutes later Bertie read off: "'Jacob' and this reads 'Jacob' and so does this one, that seems to settle it. But here is one, folded: 'A bunch of smarties, you three. Think I didn't guess why you sent me down to ride shotgun? Very well, I vote for myself!' It is signed 'Jake.' Madame Speaker, is that valid?"

"Quite. Jacob, my last order will be liftoff after we drop Bertie."

Bertie said, "Jake, I think congratulations are in order."

"Pipe down! All hands, prepare for space."

"A piece of cake," Bertie called it. We started at the easternmost dump, worked west. Pop out at four klicks and dive, a dry run to size up the target; where wood alcohol was stored, ornithopters on the ground and how arranged . . . while Gay ululated from intensity six to eight. Frightfulness. I did not let it go up to ten because it wasn't intended to damage but to send anyone on target scattering.

Zebadiah's idea: "Captain, I've got nothing against Russians. My only purpose is to burn their fuel and their flaphappies to make it difficult to attack our friends—and I *don't* mean you big brass, Bertie. I mean the transportee maid who brought us tea this morning, and Brian Bean, and Mr. Wheatstone who was a top surgeon before some fool judge slammed him and is now doing his best for wogs, and the chef at the officers' club, and five cons who drove that sillywagon, and dozens more who smiled when they could have scowled. I don't want them killed or enslaved; I want them to have their chance. Governor, England is slapping the Broad Arrow on some of your best potential—you English will live to regret it."

"You could be right, Zeb."

"I don't want to kill Russians, either. Could be most of them are decent blokes. Each strike will be a double run—one pass to scatter 'em, a second to destroy the dump. Captain, if that doesn't suit you, find another gunner."

Aunt Hilda said, "Astrogator."

"Captain."

"Strike as described by Chief Pilot. Take the conn. Attack."

At the first target we lingered after the strike bounce. The dry pass did show them running away—they could hear us clear in their bones. Those subsonics are so horrid I keyed Gay to kill the noise at code-word "Bounce"—and did not use it on the strike pass.

Zebadiah made strikes from bearings planned to take out as many 'thopters as possible while setting fire to fuel.

From four klicks the first strike looked good. The dump was burning, 'thopters he had hit showed smoke, and one that he had *not* hit was burning. Splashed by flaming methanol, I suppose.

If that first target was indication, in thirty-four minutes the Russians lost all fuel and about 70% of the deployed flaphappies. I took us up high after the last. "Next stop, Windsor City."

"I'm taking the conn, Astrogator. Bertie, don't forget my little ring for Betty."

"I'll give it to her in the morning."

"Good," Captain Hilda said. "Unbelt, crowd past Jacob, place yourself against the door—feet on deck, chest against door. Jacob, push against the small of his back. Bertie, when the door opens, dive and roll clear."

They positioned themselves. "Gay Parade Ground Gay Deceiver open starboard door . . . Gay Deceiver close doors, Gay-Bounce, GayBounce! Jacob, do you relieve me?"

"Beloved, I relieve you. Ten minima H axis transit—and executed. All hands, unbelt."

I unbuckled with extreme speed and clumsiness, getting Pop in the chin with my foot.

"Deety! Watch where you're going!"

"I'm sorry, Captain. I'm out of practice with free fall."

"You've been in free fall every day!"

"Yes, Captain. I've been in free fall every day, belted down."

"Pipe *down!* Hilda, don't cover the instrument board. Hold onto something. No, not me, damn it. Zeb! Grab something and catch Hilda!"

"Roger Wilco, Captain! Right away!" My husband snagged Aunt Hilda, grabbed a seat belt with his other hand, trapped our captain against the dogs of the bulkhead door with his buttocks. "What now, sir!"

"Get your goddam fanny out of my face!"

"Sorry, sir," Zebadiah answered humbly while turning and digging an elbow into Pop's ribs. I closed in from the other side and we had Pop trapped again—ballet and trampoline make a fine background for free fall. Zebadiah went on cheerfully, "What shall we do now, sir?"

Pop didn't answer. From watching his lips I saw that he was counting backwards, silently, in German. That's stage three.

Then he said quietly, "Zeb, get into the copilot's seat and belt down."

"Aye aye, sir." Zebadiah did so.

Pop snatched Hilda while hanging onto a dog. "Deety, belt down in the chief pilot's seat."

"Roger Wilco, Captain"—I did so.

"My dear, I want you behind Deety. Do you need help?"

"Yes, thank you, Captain; it's sweet of you to offer." White mutiny? The Hillbilly is about as helpless as Zebadiah but thinks God created men to pamper women. I've heard less reasonable philosophies.

After "helping" Hilda, Pop strapped down in the starboard after seat. "All hands! We have moved clockwise ninety degrees. I am now captain. Hilda, you are astrogator and second-in-command. Deety, you are chief pilot. Zeb, you are copilot. In order of seniority, any questions?"

The Hillbilly said in a small voice, "As second-in-command I am required to advise the Captain—"

"Certain circumstances. Speak up."

"Captain, I know very little about astrogation."

"That's why you have the job. You will seek advice from Deety as needed, both of you seek advice from Zeb when necessary— and if all three of you are stumped, I will tackle it and be responsible for mistakes. No burden, the Captain is always responsible for *all* mistakes. When in doubt, do not hesitate to consult me.

"Deety, you have not driven this car in atmosphere. But you are a competent, decisive, and skillful driver of duos"—I *am*, Pop?—"you're years late in saying so"—"and we have come this high to give you time to acquaint yourself with it. I placed Zeb by you to coach you and, in time, to report to me that you are fully qualified." Pop smiled. "Fortunately, should you get into trouble, we have programs that will get you out instantly such as 'Gay Bounce'—"

Gay bounced.

Pop did not notice but I had my eye on radar distance since learning that I was responsible. Pop, who invented those safety scrams? Think hard. Hint: One of your offspring.

"Zeb, you know the knobs and scales et cetera of the controls we refer to as the verniers but you have not had time to practice. Now you will practice until you can handle *anything*, by eye, or by clicks in the dark. Permit me to pay you this compliment: You will give yourself your own final examination. When you feel ready, tell me and I will have the Astrogator log it.

"Advice to future captains—I will not be happy until all are competent in each of four seats, and all feel easy in all twenty-five possible arrangements—"

"Twenty-four, Pop," I blurted out. I hastily added, "Sorry, Captain—'twenty-five.'"

Pop has a terrible time with kitchen arithmetic; it has been so long since he has done any. He will pick up a hand computer to discover $2 \times 3 = 6$; I've seen him do it.

He stared at me, lips moving slightly. At last he said, "Chief Pilot."

"Captain."

"You are *ordered* to correct me when I make a mistake. 'Twenty-four' permutations, certainly."

"Sir, may the Chief Pilot have more information before she answers Roger-Wilco?"

"Fire away!"

"Captain, what categories of mistakes?"

"Eh? Any sort! A mistake is a mistake. Daughter, are you baiting me?"

"No, Captain. I am unable to acknowledge your order as I do not understand it. 'A mistake is a mistake' is semantically null. If I see you about to sugar your coffee twice shall I—"

"Tell me! Of course."

"If I see you treating your wife unjustly shall I—"

"Wait a moment! Even if I did or have—which I decline to stipulate—it is not proper for you to interfere."

"Yes, sir. We've established that there are two sets. But the Captain has not defined the sets and the Chief Pilot lacks authority to do so. May I respectfully suggest that the Captain take notice of the quandary, then reframe the order at a time of his choosing . . . and in the meantime permit the Chief Pilot *not* to correct the Captain's mistakes?"

Zebadiah winked at me with his head turned so that I saw it but Pop could not.

Pop fumed, complaining that I wasn't showing common sense and, worse, I had broken his train of thought. He finally got around to a definition at about 8th grade level: I was to correct him *only* in errors involving figures or related symbols such as angles. (On your own head be it, Pop!) I gave him Roger-Wilco.

"In fact," he went on expansively, "it may be my duty to see that this training course is completed before, with great relief, I turn this seat over to my successor."

(I started figuring how many children I would have by then and decided to look for ways to hike up the "white mutiny.")

"Captain?"

"Astrogator."

"This advice concerns a mistake that could occur in the near future. I assume that the Captain has the conn?"

"Hilda, I have the conn. Speak up."

"We are falling, sir. I advise placing us in orbit."

I sighed with relief, as radar distance I was beginning to think of as H-above-G and did not like our closing rate.

Pop said, "Surely, put us in orbit. Take the conn and do it. Good practice. Deety can show you how. Or Zeb."

"Aye aye, sir. I have the conn. Chief Pilot, keep her level with respect to planet."

"Roger. Level now."

"Copilot, add speed vector positive axis L three point six klicks per second."

"Uh . . . set!"

"Hold it!" Pop unbelted, steadied himself by Zebadiah's chair, checked the setting. "Okay. Execute!"

"Excuse me, Captain," Zebadiah said, "but was that order directed at me or the Astrogator?"

Pop opened his mouth—then turned red. "Astrogator, I am

satisfied with your solution and the setting. Please have the maneuver executed."

"Aye aye, sir. Execute!"

What Pop planned seemed reasonable. "So far we have used
juice, supplies, and four days' time, and have merely established
that there are at least two analogs of our universe, one quantum
and ten quanta away on *Tau* axis. The latter has beasts—wogs—
that are not the vermin we fled from, but—according to Hilda—
closely related. To me, this makes *Tau* axis not our best place to
seek a new home.

"Zebadiah has suggested that we sample the universes available
by rotation rather than translation—six axes taken four at a time—
before we search *Teh* axis. Let me remind you that we could die
of old age searching *Teh* axis alone. I will decide but I will listen
to arguments pro or con."

Twenty-three minutes later Aunt Hilda shrilled, "Copilot, by
plan, as set— *Rotate!*"

XXX   *"Difference physical laws, a different topology."*

Jacob:

We rotated to . . . Nowhere—

So it seemed. Free fall and utter blackness— The cabin held
only the faint radiance from the instruments.

My daughter said in hushed tones, "Captain! May I turn on
inside lights?"

This was a time to establish discipline and doctrine. "Permission refused. Copilot, I would like to see in all directions."

"Yes, sir," Zeb acknowledged.

After a few moments I added, "Copilot? Why are you waiting?"

"I am awaiting orders, sir."

"What the hell, Zeb? Get with it! I said I wanted to see in all directions. We have preprograms for that."

"Yes, Captain."

"Well? Why aren't you using them? Can't you carry out orders?" (I was amazed at Zeb.)

"Captain, I have not as yet received *any* orders, and I am not at the conn."

I started to answer sharply—and bit down on it. Precisely what had I said? I recalled that the autopilot stayed in recording mode during maneuvers; I could play back the last few minutes—

—and decided not to. We were wasting time and it was possible that I had not expressed myself in the form of a direct order. Nevertheless I could not ignore Zeb's pigheaded behavior. "Copilot, I am aware that I have not given you direct orders. However, it is customary to treat a captain's requests as politely worded orders."

"Yes, sir."

"Well? God damn it, why don't—"

"Captain! Captain Jacob! Please listen! *Please!*"

I took a deep breath. "What is it, Hilda?"

"Captain, I am required to advise you."

"Eh? Advise away—but be quick about it."

"Captain, you have given the Copilot neither orders nor requests. The autopilot's record will confirm this. You mentioned preprograms—but voice programs are not normally handled by the Copilot."

"I can order the Copilot to use a voice program."

Hilda did not answer. Again I waited, then said, "Well?"

Then I said, "Astrogator, you did not answer me."

"Sorry, Captain. Answer what?"

"My question."

"Captain, I was not aware that you had asked me a question. Would you mind repeating it?"

"Oh, forget it, forget it! Chief Pilot!"

"Captain."

"Deety, what's the voice program to rotate us a full circle around W axis?"

"Shall I spell it, sir? S.G. is awake."

"No, do it. Turn out your instrument lights. Pilots watch forward, Captain and Astrogator will watch the sides. Do it. Execute."

Instrument lights dimmed to zero, leaving us in the darkest dark I have ever experienced. I heard a repressed moan and felt a burst of sympathy for my daughter; she had never liked total darkness. But she carried out my orders:

"Gay Deceiver, Tumbling Pigeon."

"Forward somersault—whee!"

"Execute."

I felt pressure against my belts—being forward of the center of mass we were starting a gentle outside loop. I started counting seconds as I recalled that this program took twenty seconds.

I had reached seventy-eight seconds and was beginning to wonder when Deety announced "Twenty seconds" as the autopilot announced, "End of program."

Deety said, "You're a Smart Girl, Gay."

"If I were smart, would I be doing *this*? Over."

"Roger and out, Gay. Captain, I request permission to switch on cabin lights."

"Permission granted. Report observations. Copilot?"

"Skipper, I saw nothing."

"Deety?"

"Nothing."

"Hilda?"

"Jacob, I didn't see *anything*. Can't we get out of this universe? It stinks."

"That stink is me," our copilot said. "The reek of fear. Captain, of what use is an empty universe?"

"Zeb, 'empty universe' is a meaningless expression. Space-time implies mass-energy, and vice versa."

"Captain, it looks empty to me."

"And to me. I'm faced by a dilemma in theory. Is the mass in this space-time so far away that we can't see it? Or is it in a state of 'Cold Death,' level entropy? Or did we create this universe by rotating?"

"'Create it'—*Huh?*"

"A possibility," I pointed out. "If we are the only mass in this universe, then this universe had no existence until we created it by rotation. But it will not collapse when we rotate out, because we will be leaving behind quanta we are radiating."

"Hmm— Captain, I'm bothered by something else. We started from universe-ten and made one ninety-degree rotation. Correct?"

"Yes. We rotated around 'x' and thereby moved each of the other five axes ninety degrees. We are now experiencing duration along 'y.' *Teh* and 'z' are spatial coordinates now, and 'x' remains spatial because we rotated on it. *Tau* and 't' are now null, unused."

"Mmm— Deety, what Greenwich time is it?" Zeb glanced at the instrument board.

"Uh— Seventeen: thirteen: oh-nine."

"Smart Girl says you are twenty seconds slow." Zeb looked at his navigator's watch. "But my watch splits the difference. How many minutes since we left Windsor City?"

"Thirty-nine minutes, thirteen seconds. Ask me a hard one."

"I'm going to ask your father a hard one. Captain, if you tell G.D. to scram to Windsor P.G. right now *mark!*—what will the Greenwich time be?"

"Look at your clock. About a quarter past seventeen hundred."

"But you told me that, since rotating, we've been experiencing duration along 'y' axis."

"But— Oh! Zeb, I'm stupid. *No* time has elapsed on 't' axis since the instant we rotated. If we reversed the rotation, we would go back to that exact instant."

"Deety hon?" Zeb asked. "Do you agree?"

(I felt annoyed that my son-in-law consulted my daughter as to the correctness of my professional opinion—then suppressed the thought. Deety will always be my little girl, which makes it hard for me to remember that she is also my professional colleague.)

My daughter suddenly looked upset. "I— Pop! That first trip to the world without the letter 'J'—time did pass, it did!"

Zeb said gently, "But that was translation, Deety. You continued to experience duration along 't' axis."

Deety thought about it, then said sorrowfully, "Zebadiah, I no longer know what time it is. Pop is correct; we experience duration on one axis only, and that is now 'y' axis. We can't experience duration on two axes at once." She heaved a sigh. "Will I ever get the clock in my head set right again?"

"Sure you will," my son-in-law reassured her. "Like crossing a time zone. Shortly after we grounded on Mars-ten, your head started keeping time *both* in Greenwich and in Mars Touchdown meridian time, even though Touchdown time kept falling farther behind hour after hour. A simple index correction won't bother you. My sweet, you don't realize how smart you are."

Zeb patted her hand, then looked around at me. "Captain, may I propose a change in schedule?"

"Let's hear it."

"Sir, I would like two sequences. First, go back to Windsor P.G. with the verniers preset for a hundred thousand klicks straight up, and execute at once. Then translate back to our own universe-zero—but not to Earth-zero. Instead, set up an orbit around Mars-zero. That orbit becomes our base of operations."

I said, "Simple enough. But why?"

"So that we will always have somewhere to go back to. Deety can write us a program that will place us back in that orbit. Something like G, A, Y, H, O, M, E, but based on Mars-zero—with elbow room."

I asked, "Daughter, can you write such a program?"

"I think so, Pop. An emergency scram? G, A, Y, plus something?" Deety paused. " 'Sagan.' G, A, Y, S, A, G, A, N means to return to orbit around Mars-zero. Built-in mnemonic."

"Satisfactory. Is that all, Copilot?"

"No, sir. Our schedule breaks up naturally into a five group, a four group, a three, a two, and a one. I would like to add to each group a return to orbit around Mars-zero. Captain, if you were on the verniers, I wouldn't worry; you know them so well. I don't. If I do fifteen rotations, one right after the other, I'm afraid I'll make some tiny mistake and we'll wind up in analog-Andromeda-Nebula in universe a thousand-and-two on 'z' axis, with no idea how we got there or how to get home."

"Copilot, you worry too much."

"Probably. Captain, my whole life is based on being chicken at every opportunity. I'll breathe easier if I come back to a familiar orbit at the end of each group . . . and know that the next group is one less. It won't take ten minutes longer to do it my way and I'll be less likely to make mistakes. But tackling all fifteen at a slug scares me."

"Captain Jacob—"

"Not now, Hilda. I must settle this with—"

"Captain, I am required to advise you."

"Eh? All right, all right! Make it snappy."

"You know—we all know—that Zebbie's premonitions must not be ignored. I advise you officially— Gay Deceiver, record this 'I-tell-you-three-times.' "

"Hilda, I hear you three times."

"Captain Jacob, I, your second-in-command, advise you officially to revise the schedule of rotations in the fashion recommended by the copilot. End of I-tell-you-three-times."

(Have you ever found yourself boxed in? Damn it, I *intended* to let Zeb do it his way; I am not unreasonable. I can't say that I believe in Zeb's premonitions; I suspect that he is simply a man with extremely fast reflexes. But both our wives believe in them and Zeb does himself.

I found myself faced with mutiny *unless I did exactly what I had intended to do anyway!* How does one describe so ironical a situation?)

Shortly I found myself saying, "Copilot, by revised schedule, set second rotation of first group." We were in "Sagan" orbit around Mars of Universe-zero (i.e., the one we had grown up in: Galactic coordinates X_o, Y_o, Z_o, & t_o—Earth-zero, Mars-zero, Sun-zero, Universe-zero). I tend to think of this as the "real" universe even though I am aware that there is no evidence or mathematical theory for preferring one frame of reference over another—to do so is egocentric provincialism at its worst. But I offer this in mitigation: for us it was simplest and thereby helped us to avoid getting lost.

"Set," Copilot Zeb reported. I went forward, checked the setting (rotation around 'y,' with 'z' and 't' dropping out, null), then returned to my seat. "We can spare a minute to look at Mars. Deety, tilt the nose down to let us look. Do you know how?"

"Like this, Captain?"

"Right," I agreed. "Keep it up."

Deety raised the craft's nose and swung right, catching me with belts not yet fastened. I said forcefully, "Deety! What the hell are you doing?" while I floundered and grabbed.

"Sir, you ordered 'right' and 'up,'" Deety answered.

"I did no such thing!"

"But, Jacob—Captain—you *did* tell her that, I heard you."

"Hilda, you keep out of this!"

Hilda answered stiffly, "Captain, I respectfully request that you either relieve me of the conn, or that you give orders to my pilots through *me*."

"Damn it, you don't have the conn. *I* do."

"Then the Captain neglected to relieve me."

"Uh— Take the conn! Carry out the planned schedule."

"Aye aye, sir. Chief Pilot, orient the car for best view of Mars."

"Aye aye, Ma'am!"

I was fuming, not looking, hardly listening. I had said to Deety, *All right, keep on with it*—or had I? Gay could play it back . . . and could also check on Hilda's incredible allegation. If I were wrong (I felt certain I was *not!*), I would face up to it like a man and— Zeb broke in on my thoughts:

"Captain, do you care what attitude this craft is in at rotation?"

"No. Only for transitions."

"Hmm— Then it follows as the night from day thou canst not

then predict the attitude we'll be in whenever we arrive in a new universe."

"Only with respect to our arbitrary zero reference frame. Why should it matter?"

"It won't as long as we arrive with plenty of room. I've been noodling how to be sure of that. I don't see an answer. But I don't want to try translations or rotations parked on the ground. I hope the Captain won't order any."

"Copilot, I have no plans to. Astrogator, haven't we had enough sightseeing?"

"Very well, Captain," my wife acknowledged. "Deety, secure those binoculars. Zebbie, immediately after each rotation, set next rotation and report 'Set.' Deety, after each rotation, use voice program to put us through one Pigeon-Tumble with all lights out. I will watch to port, Deety forward, Zebbie starboard. Questions?"

I said, "Astrogator, you did not assign *me* a sector."

"I have no authority to assign duties to the Captain. Does the Captain wish to select a sector and assume responsibility for it?"

She waited. I said hastily, "No. Perhaps it will be best for me to watch in all directions. General supervision."

"Very well, Captain. Copilot—execute."

Again we rotated into darkness. Deety switched out all lights. Zeb reported, "Set!"

"*Stop!*" I called out. I added, "Zeb, you reported 'Set' in total darkness. How did you set it?"

"Rotation around 'z' axis, with 'x' and 'y' dropping out. Duration along *Teh*. Third combo first group, sir."

"I mean, 'How did you do it in darkness?' By clicks?"

"Captain, I didn't do it in darkness."

I said, "It was pitch dark when you reported 'Set.'"

"So it was, Captain."

"It's not necessary to call me 'Captain' every ten seconds. I want a straight answer. So far you have reported that you set it in darkness and that you set it with lights on."

"No, sir."

"God damn it, you just did!"

"Captain, I protest your swearing at me. I request that my protest be logged."

"Zeb, you are—" I shut up. I counted thirty in French under my breath, by which time I was ready to speak. "Zeb, I'm sorry that my language offended you. But I am still trying to find out what you did and how. Will you please tell me, in simple language?"

"Yes, sir. I set the third rotation by clicks—"

"But you said the lights were on—"

"The lights were on. I set the rotation with my eyes closed—"

"For God's sake, why?"

"For practice. I set them with eyes closed. Then I check to see whether it matches what I intended to set. Deety leaves the light on until I give her the 'kill it' sign. Then she kills the glim and does her act."

"Zeb, there wasn't *time* to do it that way."

Zeb gave a most irritating grin. "Captain, I'm fairly quick. So is Deety."

I said, "Perhaps I had better check the setting."

Zeb made no answer; both women kept still. I began to wonder what everyone was waiting on . . . then realized that *I* was the "what." Unbelt and check on Zeb's setting? I remembered that irritating grin. So I said, "Deety, carry out the tumbling routine."

The somersault completed, I asked, "Anyone see anything?"

Hilda said, "I . . . think so. Captain, could we do that again?"

"Do it, Deety," I ordered.

Pigeon-Tumble resumed; Hilda suddenly said, "There!" and Deety snapped, "GayDeceiver*Stop!*"

I asked, "Hilda, do you still see it?"

"Yes, Jacob. A fuzzy star. You can see it if I pull back and you lean forward."

I suppose we each did so—for I spotted something. "I see it! Zeb—the binoculars, please."

An invisible hand pushed them against my neck. I got them lined up with difficulty, got that faint light, focused with great care. "It looks like a lenticular galaxy seen not quite edge on. Or it might be a family of galaxies. Whatever it is, it is a long way off. Millions of light-years—I have no way of guessing."

"Can we reach it by transition?" asked Zeb.

"Possibly. I would set middle range on 'six,' then keep punching until it showed change in width. It might be possible to reach it in an hour or so. Do you want to look at it?"

"From your description, I don't think so," Zeb answered. "That is fossil light—isn't it?"

"Eh? Yes, the light has been traveling for millions of years."

"That's my point, Captain. We might find that those stars had burned out. Fossil light doesn't tell us anything we can use. Let's designate this 'Last Chance' and get out."

Eminently sensible— "Stand by to rotate. Copilot—execute!"

Blinding light— "Zeb! Rotate! *Execute!*"

Suddenly we were in a starry void, almost homelike. I heaved a sigh of relief. "Zeb, what did we fall into?"

"I don't know, Captain." He added, "I had my eyes closed, setting the next rotation by clicks. So I didn't get dazzled. But I never had a chance to check my setting by eyesight, either; I rotated at once."

"You got us out—thanks. I *did* get dazzled; I've got purple blotches in front of my eyes. New standing order: At each rotation all hands close eyes and duck heads for that moment needed to be sure that we have not again run into dazzle. Zeb, that need not slow you up since you are setting by touch and click anyhow— but if we do hit dazzle, rotate us out; don't wait for my orders. And—All Hands!—we are *all* free at all times to use any of the escape programs to get us out of danger."

"Next rotation set, Captain."

"Thank you, Copilot. Hilda, do you or Deety have any notion as to what we fell into?"

"No, Captain," my daughter answered.

"Captain Jacob, I have three hypotheses, none worth much."

"Let others judge that, my dear."

"Interior of a global star cluster—or near the nucleus of a galaxy, or—possibly—the early part of an expanding universe when new stars are almost rubbing shoulders."

"Hmm— Real garden spots. Zeb, could we have picked up excessive radiation?"

"Captain, the shell of this buggy is opaque to most radiation, and that wind-screen is heavily leaded—but no way to tell."

"Zebadiah, if the film in the camera is ruined, some heavy stuff got through. If the next picture is okay, we're probably okay."

Hilda said, "I'm glad you thought of that, Deety. I don't like the idea of radiation while I'm pregnant. You, too, hon."

"Aunt Hilda, we're almost completely shielded where it matters. It could addle our brains but not our bellies."

"Hilda, do you wish to shoot one frame?" I asked.

"No, Jacob, it would waste film."

"As you wish. My eyes are coming back. Deety, put us through one Pigeon-Tumble."

My daughter did so; I saw nothing. "Report! Hilda?"

"Lots of big beautiful stars but nothing close."

"Me, too, Pop—but what a *beautiful* sky!"

"Null report, Captain."

"Hilda, mark it down as 'promising.' All hands, stand by for fifth rotation. Keep eyes closed and heads down. Execute!"

Zeb gasped. "Where in Hell are we?"

"In Hell, maybe, Zebbie."

"Captain!"

"Hilda may not be too far off," I answered. "It's something I could not have believed three weeks ago: some sort of inside-out universe."

"Pellucidar!" said Deety.

"No, my dear daughter. One: We are not inside our home planet; we are in another universe. Two: This universe has physical laws that differ from our own. The inside of a spherical shell cannot have a gravitational field *by the laws of our universe*. Yet I see a river and we seem to be falling toward it. Deety, are we in air or in vacuo?"

Deety wiggled the controls. "Got some air. Probably could get support with wings fully spread."

"Then do so." Deety brought the car into a dead-stick glide.

Zeb said grimly, "*I* don't want to homestead here! So *big*— ten thousand kilometers across at a guess. Yet it's all *inside*. No *sky!* No horizons. Never again a night sprinkled with stars. That light in the center— Looks like our sun but it's too small, *much* too small. When we leave, I don't want to come back; the god who takes care of fools and explorers let us arrive in empty space instead of maybe ten kilometers underground. But next time— I hate to think about it."

I said, "It may not have been luck, Zeb, but logical necessity."

"Huh. You've lost me, Captain."

"You're thinking of this as a spherical shell. But there is no basis for assuming that it has an outside."

"What? Endless millions of light-years of solid rock?"

"No, no! *Nothing*. By 'nothing' I do *not* mean space; I mean a total absence of existence of *any* sort. Different physical laws, a different topology. We may be seeing the totality of this universe. A small universe with a different sort of closed space."

"I can't visualize it, Jake."

"Deety, my dear, rephrase it for your husband."

"I'll try, Pop. Zebadiah, the geometry of this place may require different postulates from those that work back home. I'm sure you have played with Möbius strips—"

"A surface with only one side, one edge. But this is a sphere."

"Pop is saying that it may be a sphere with only one side, the inside. Have you ever tried to figure out a Klein bottle?"

"I got cross-eyed and a headache."

"This could be a Klein-bottle sort of thing. It might turn out that if you tunneled straight down anywhere down there, you would emerge at the opposite point, still inside. And that straight line might be shorter than the distance across. Maybe much shorter."

"Point three-one-eight-three-zero-nine is the ratio by the simplest postulates," I agreed. "But the geometry may not be that simple. However, Zeb, assuming that this *is* a total universe, our chances of arriving in open space were far greater than the chance of conflicting with a mass. But I would not wish to homestead here—pretty as it is. Nevertheless we might check for obstetricians."

"No obstetricians," Zeb answered firmly.

"Why?" I demanded.

"If there are human beings here, they do *not* have an advanced culture. Deety has been following that river. Did you notice where that other river joined it? Also look ahead where it meets the sea. No cities. No warehouses. No river traffic. No air traffic, no signs of roads. Yet this is choice real estate. Therefore, no advanced culture anywhere and a small population, if any. If anyone wants to refute me, please do so in the next two minutes; Deety can't hold this heap in the air much longer without using juice."

"I check you, Zebbie. They *might* be so advanced that they can make the whole joint look like a park. I wouldn't bet on it."

"Deety?" I asked.

"Aunt Hilda is right, Captain. But it's *so* pretty!"

"Hilda, expend one film, as a souvenir. Then we rotate." My daughter nosed the car down to permit a better picture.

A click— "Got it!" Hilda cried. "GaySagan!"

Mars of Universe-zero lay to starboard. Zeb sighed. "I'm glad to be out of *there*. Sharpie, did you get a picture?"

"Can't rush it," my wife answered. "Nnnn, yup, picture coming."

"Good!"

"Zebbie, I thought you didn't like that inside-out world?"

"I don't. If that picture is sharp, you two knocked-up broads weren't hit by radiation where it counts. Any fogging?"

"No, Zebbie, and brighter color every second. Here—look."

Zeb brushed it aside. "My sole interest is in radiation. Captain, I'm having misgivings. We've tried five out of fifteen and only one was even vaguely homelike. The pickings have been slim and the dangers excessive. But we know that Earth analogs *Tau* and *Teh* axes are Earthlike—"

"With monsters," put in Hilda.

"*Tau* axis, probably. We haven't explored *Teh* axis. Jake, are we justified in exposing our wives to dangers we can't imagine?"

"In a moment, Copilot. Astrogator, why did you rotate? I don't think I ordered it. I have been trying to run a taut ship."

"So have I, Captain. I must ask to be relieved as astrogator."

"I am sorry to say that I have been thinking along the same lines, my dearest. But you had better explain."

"Captain, three times you have replaced me at the conn without relieving me. The last time I let it continue, wondering and waiting. Just now we were losing altitude, dangerously. So I acted. Now I ask to be relieved."

Hilda seemed calm and not angry. But resolved. Had I really done anything out of line? It did not seem so to me.

"Zeb, have I been overriding the officer at the conn?"

Zeb took too long to answer. "Captain, this is a time when a man *must* insist on written orders. I will make a written reply."

"Hmm—" I said. "I think you *have* replied. Deety, what do you think? More written orders?"

"I don't need written orders. Pop, you've been utterly *stinking!*"

"You really feel so?"

"I *know* so. Aunt Hilda is right; you are dead wrong. She understated the case. You assign her responsibilities—then ignore her. Just now she carried out her assigned duties—and you chewed her out for it. Of *course* she wants to be relieved."

My daughter took a deep breath and went on: "And you bawled her out for ordering a scram escape. Twenty-seven minutes ago you said—and I quote: 'All Hands!—we are *all* free at all times to use any of the escape programs to get us out of danger.' End of quotation. Pop, how can you expect orders to be obeyed when you can't remember what orders you've given? Nevertheless, we *have* obeyed you, every time and no back talk—and we've all caught hell. Aunt Hilda caught the most—but Zebadiah and I caught quite a bit. Pop, you've been— I won't say it, I won't!"

I looked out the port at Mars for long unhappy minutes. Then I turned around. "I've no choice but to resign. Effective as I ground her. Family, I must admit to great humiliation. I had thought that I was doing quite well. Uh, back to our streamside, I think. Gay—"

"*GayDeceiverOverride!* Not on your tintype! You'll serve as long as I did—not a second less! But Sharpie is right in refusing to take the conn under you; you've been mistreating her. Despite being a colonel, you have never learned that you *can't* assign responsibility without delegating authority to match—and then respect it. Jake, you're a *lousy* boss. We're going to keep you in the hot seat until you learn better. But there's no reason for Sharpie to resign over *your* failings."

"I still have something to say," said my daughter.

"Deety," Zeb said forcefully, "leave well enough alone!"

"Zebadiah, this is to you quite as much—or more—as it is to Pop. Complaints of another sort."

My son-in-law looked startled. "Oh. Sorry. You have the floor."

XXXI "*—the first ghost ever to search for an obstetrician.*"

Hilda:

If Zebbie and Jacob have a fault in common, it is overprotectiveness. Having always been the runt, I am habitually willing to accept protection. But Deety rebels.

When Zebbie asked Jacob whether or not they were justified in exposing us to unknown dangers, Deety stuck her oar in—and Zebbie tried to hush her.

Zebbie should have known better.

But he is barely getting acquainted with her, whereas I've known her since her diaper days. Once when Deety was, oh, possibly four, I started to tie her shoes. She pulled away. "Deety do!" she announced indignantly—and Deety did: on one shoe a loose half bow that came apart almost at once, on the other a Gordian knot that required the Alexandrian solution.

It's been "Deety do!" ever since, backed by genius and indomitable will.

Deety told him, "Zebadiah, concerning completing this schedule: Is there some reason to exclude Hilda and me from the decision?"

"Damn it, Deety, this is one time when husbands *have* to decide!"

"Damn it, Zebadiah, this is one time when wives *must* be consulted!"

Zebbie was shocked. But Deety had simply matched his manner and rhetoric. Zebbie is no fool; he backed down. "I'm sorry, hon," he said soberly. "Go ahead."

"Yessir. I'm sorry I answered the way I did. But I do have something to say—and Hilda, too. I know I speak for both of us when I say that we appreciate that you and Pop would die for us . . . and that you feel this more intensely now that we are pregnant.

"But we have not been pregnant long enough to be handicapped. Our bellies do not bulge. They *will* bulge, and that gives us a deadline. But for that very reason we will either sample those rotation universes *today* . . . or we will *never* sample them."

"Why do you say 'never,' Deety?"

"That deadline. We've sampled five and, scary as some have been, I wouldn't have missed it! We can look at the other ten in the next few hours. But if we start searching *Teh* axis there is no way to guess how long it will take. Thousands of universes along *Teh* axis and it seems likely that each holds an analog of Earth. We may check hundreds before we find what we are looking for. Let's say we find it and Hilda and I have babies with skilled medical attention. Then what? Zebadiah, are you going to be *more* willing to take women with babies into strange universes than you are *without* babies?"

"Uh . . . that's not the way to put it, Deety."

"How would *you* put it, sir? Are you thinking that you and Pop might check those ten while Hilda and I stay home with the kids?"

"Well . . . yes, I suppose I am. Something of the sort."

"Zebadiah, I married you for better, for worse, for richer, for poorer, in sickness and in health. I did *not* marry to walk the Widow's Walk! Where you go, I go!—till death do us part."

"Deety speaks for me," I said, and shut up. Deety had it figured: If Jacob and Zebbie didn't finish those rotations today, they would have that "far horizons" look for the rest of their lives—and they wouldn't want us along. Not with kids. Sharpie wasn't going to hold still for that. No, sir!

"Deety, are you through?"

"Not quite, sir. All humans are created unequal. You are bigger and stronger than Pop; I am bigger and stronger than Hilda. I have the least years of experience; Pop has the most. Pop is a super-genius...but he concentrates so hard that he forgets to eat—unless he has a nursemaid to watch him—as Mama did, as I did, as Hilda now does. You, sir, are the most all-around competent man I've ever met, whether driving a duo, or dancing, or telling outrageous tales. Three of us have eight or nine earned degrees...but Aunt Hilda with none is a walking encyclopedia from insatiable curiosity and extraordinary memory. We two are baby factories and you two are not—but two men can impregnate fifty women—or five hundred. There is no end to the ways that we four are *un*equal. But in one supremely important way all of us are *equals*.

"We are pioneers.

"Men alone are not pioneers; they *can't* be. Pioneer mothers share the dangers of pioneer fathers and go on having babies. Babies were born in the *Mayflower*, lots were born in covered wagons—and lots died, too. Women didn't stay home; *they went along*.

"Zebadiah, I do not ask to be taken to those next ten universes—"

"It sounds like it."

"You didn't listen, sir. I would *like* to finish sampling those fifteen. It's my preference but not my demand. What I *do* demand I have stated: *Where you go, I go*. Today and to the end of our lives. *Unless you tell me to get out, that you don't want me anymore*. I have spoken."

"You certainly have, dear. Hilda?"

Fish or cut bait, Sharpie—*what do you want?* I didn't care; *any* new universe was bound to be strange. But Deety had laid down the party line; I didn't want to fuzz it up—so I answered instantly, "Deety speaks for me in every word."

"Jake? Back to my original question: 'Are we justified in exposing our wives to conditions we can't even imagine?'"

"Zeb, you are the one who convinced me that it would be prudent to sample the universes accessible through rotation before searching by translation."

"True. But that was before we sampled five of them."

"I don't see that the situation has changed. An imaginable danger is not necessarily better than an unimaginable one; it may be worse. Our home planet had grave shortcomings *before* we tangled with the vermin. No need to list them; we all know that the Four Horsemen are ready to ride again. But I can think of a *very* close analog of our home planet that would be *far* worse than Earth-zero even if it didn't have a single 'Black-Hat' vermin on it."

"Go on."

"One in which Hitler got atomic weapons but we did not. I can't see that vermin are more to be dreaded than Hitler's S.S. Corps. The sadism of some human beings—not just Storm Troopers; you can find sadists in any country including the United States—is more frightening to me than any monster."

"Not to me!" Deety blurted it out.

"But, my dear, we don't know that those vermin are cruel. We got in their way; they tried to kill us. They did *not* try to torture us. There is a world of difference."

"Maybe there is, Pop, but those things give me the creeps. I'll bet they'd torture us if they could!"

"My very dear daughter, that's muddy thinking. How old are you?"

"Huh? Pop, you know if anybody does."

"I was reminding you of what you said: you have the least years of experience. I was much older than you are before I was cured of that sort of muddy thinking. By Jane, your mother. Hilda?"

"Jacob is telling you not to judge a book by its cover," I said. "I learned it from Jane, too, as Jacob knows. A creature's appearance tells nothing about its capacity for sadism."

Jacob said, "Does anyone have anything to add? Since it appears that I am not permitted to resign now, I must rule on it. We will complete the scheduled rotations." Jacob cleared his throat loudly, looked at Deety. "During my remaining hours in what Zeb so accurately calls the 'Worry Seat,' I will endeavor to keep my orders straight . . . but, should I fail, I ask that my attention be invited to it *at once*—not saved up for a scolding later. Daughter?"

"Okay, Pop. Aye aye, Captain."

"Thank you, my dear. Is anyone tired or hungry?" No one spoke up; Jacob continued, "Hilda, will you take the conn?"

"No, Captain"—I'll omit the internal debate I held with myself; Jacob on his best behavior is hard to refuse.

"Very well, my beloved; I won't press you. It's an odd situation. Copilot, by schedule, set to rotate."

"Second group, first of four—set, sir."

"Check seat belts, stand by to rotate. Execute!"

We were in sunlight in a blue sky and upside down. For a few seconds we were thrown around a bit—Deety isn't the pilot Zebbie is. But she did get us leveled off. I heard Deety say, "Gay Deceiver."

"Hi, Deety!"

"Hold course, speed, and height-above-ground."

"Got it, girl!"

"You're a Smart Girl, Gay."

"But we *can't* go on meeting like this! Over."

"Roger and out, Gay. *Whew!* Time out while the Chief Pilot has a nervous breakdown. Zebadiah, what does that altimeter say?"

"Seven klicks H-above-G."

"Pop, what's the probability of winding up this close to a planet without getting killed?"

"Impossible to theorize, Deety. Maybe we're dead and don't know it. Copilot, deadman switch; I'm going to check the air."

"*Captain!*" I yelped.

"Not now, Hilda, I'm—"

"NOW! Am I still second-in-command? If I am, I must advise you; you are about to make a *bad* mistake!"

Jacob hesitated. I think he was counting. "My dear one, if I am about to make a bad mistake, I want your advice no matter what your status is."

"Thank you, Jacob. You should not be guinea pig. I should be. I—"

"Hilda, you're pregnant."

"All the more reason why I want the most competent and least expendable—you, Zebbie, and Deety—to take care of yourselves in order to take care of *me*. It's my duty as science officer in any case, whether I'm number two or not. But, Jacob, you are doing it just the way Zebbie did it when we landed on Mars-ten—and that's all wrong!"

"Thank *you*, Sharpie!"

"Zebbie dear! You risked your life and it's not necessary—"

Zebbie interrupted me. "Not necessary to waste juice this way! Yack-yack-yack!"

"Copilot, pipe down!" Jacob said sharply. "Gay Bounce! Chief Pilot, when we reenter, place the car on dead-stick glide, manual or automatic. Don't use juice. Now, All Hands, listen to the Science Officer. Go ahead, Hilda."

"Yes, Captain. Three days ago it was necessary for somebody to be the canary—but it should have been *me*, not Zebbie. What was necessary three days ago is reckless today. That deadman switch— Unless it has been rewired, it takes us back two klicks over a crater—and that's *not* what we want. The correct scram for this is T, E, R, M, I, T, E. But that's just half of it. Deety has taught the S.G. how to ground herself no-power on any level bit of ground. We can ground *first.* Then *anyone* can be guinea pig, doesn't matter. *Whoosh* back to our stream bank—*bang,* open the doors."

Zebbie said, "Captain, that makes sense. Sharpie—I mean 'Science Officer.' May I apologize with a back rub?"

"You can apologize with a kiss. But I'll take the back rub, too."

"Zebadiah, don't commit yourself too far; an air test isn't necessary. Pop! Captain Pop, may I take her up thirty klicks?"

"I suppose so. May I ask why?"

"Captain, I know where we are. From that high I can prove it."

"Deety, that's imp—"

"Don't say 'impossible,' Captain—I'll refer you to my father."

"Miss Smarty Pants. Take her up."

"Thanks, Pop. GayBounceGayBounceGayBounce. Gay Deceiver, vertical dive, execute. Everybody tell me where we are."

I had noticed earlier what pretty countryside was under us. Now I studied it in detail. Zebbie said, "Be durned. Big rectangular oasis completely surrounded by desert. Populated, too. That's a fair-sized town in the middle."

"Yes," I agreed. "Don't you recognize it, Zebbie? From a map."

My husband said, "Now, Hilda, this is an unexplored universe. How could you have seen a—"

"Pop!" interrupted Deety. "You've seen the map. See the Yellow Brick Road off to the left? Try the binoculars; you can follow it clear to Emerald City."

"Deety my love," said Zebbie, "you are out of your mind. Or I am. Either way, somebody call an ambulance. Don't forget the straitjacket. Sharpie, something worries me. I failed to get my warning . . . yet we came so close to hitting that real estate I'm still shaking."

"That means there wasn't any danger, Zebbie."

"Then why am I trembling?"

"You're a fraud, dear. We've all been dead quite a while now—killed in my parking lot. Deety and I may be the first ghosts ever to search for an obstetrician. In further support of my theory I am having a pregnancy with no morning sickness—a miracle that makes the Land of Oz as commonplace as faithful husbands."

"I don't think I want to analyze that. Is that the Castle of the Tin Woodman there in the east?"

"Yes, but that's the west, dear. Deety, is that sun rising or setting?"

"Setting. Directions are reversed here. Everybody knows that."

"A retrograde planet," my husband commented. "Nothing dangerous about that."

"Pop, admit it. You know the Oz books almost as well as I do—"

"Better. Don't give yourself airs, Daughter. I agree that this appears to match stories and map, while trying to reserve judgment. Deety, how would you like to raise kids in the Land of Oz?"

"Pop, I'd love it!"

"Are you certain? As I recall, nobody dies in the Land of Oz yet the population doesn't increase. I don't recall babies being born in Oz stories. I don't recall M.D.'s or hospitals. Or machinery. Zeb, that inside-out universe had different physical laws from those of our universe. If we ground here, will we be able to leave? Oz works by magic, not by engineering." Jacob added, "Copilot, I want your professional opinion."

"Captain, you see a difference between magic and engineering. I don't."

"Oh, come now, Zeb!"

"I believe in just two things: Murphy's Law, and Place Not Your Faith in an Ace Kicker. Permit me to point out that we are *already* in the Land of Oz, even though at altitude. I can think of worse places to be stranded. No common cold. No income tax. No political candidates. No smog. No churches. No wars. No inflation. No—"

Deety interrupted. "We are now passing over the Palace of Glinda the Good."

"Why pass over it?" I asked. "Jacob, why aren't we grounding?"

"Me, too," Deety added. "Captain Pop, I request permission to ground near the Palace. I'm certain that nothing can upset Glinda the Good; she already knows about it from her Book. Besides, a palace that size must have plumbing...and I'm beginning to feel as if I had attended a watermelon picnic."

"Methinks a bush would suffice," said Zebbie. "Even in another universe and with an armed guard. How about it, Captain?"

"Chief Pilot, ground at will. Hilda, do the Oz books have

bathrooms in them? I don't recall."

"Nor do I, Jacob," I answered. "But there are plenty of bushes."

In three or four minutes Deety had us grounded, with Gay using Deety's new program. I thanked my husband for deciding to ground. "There was never any doubt," he said. "Not only would you and Deety never have spoken to me again, *I* would never have spoken to *me* again. But if I meet a living scarecrow, I may go stark, raving mad."

XXXII "'Where Cat is, is civilization.'"

Deety:

I found a clearing in the woods, a hundred meters from the Palace and screened from it by elms and walnut trees. I had Gay range it, told her three times that it was a scram spot—then she landed herself, slick as Zebadiah.

I unstrapped, opened the bulkhead door, and crawled aft to get clean suits—and thought better of it. Aunt Hilda had followed me and headed straight for a special locker. I rolled into lotus and asked, "Hillbilly, what are you going to wear?"

"The dress I got married in and the wedding ring Jacob had made for me in Windsor City."

"Jewelry?"

"Nothing fancy."

Mama Jane told me years ago that Aunt Hilda's instinct for clothes was infallible. I got the dress I wore to hook Zebadiah, a pendant Pop had given me, my wedding ring, my dancing slippers. Put my darling in mess jacket? No, but in tights topped off with a white silk bolero shirt I made for him at Snug Harbor. Red sash, dancing pumps, jockey shorts—yes, that was all he needed.

I wiggle-wormed forward, clutching clothing. Our men were still in their seats, Gay's doors closed. I said, "Why the closed doors? It's warm and stuffy."

"Look out to the left," said Zebadiah.

I looked. A little storybook cottage with a sign over the door: **WELCOME**. It had not been there when we grounded. "I see," I agreed. "Shuck off your work clothes and pull on shorts and tights. Pop, Hilda has your trousers."

"Deety, is that all you have to say?"

"What should I say, sir? Pop, you have taken us to some strange places. But in Oz I am not a stranger in a strange land. I know what to expect."

"But damn it all—"

"Shush, Zebadiah. One does not say 'damn' in Oz. Not any sort of profanity or vulgarity. These are no longer teats; they aren't even breasts—it's my bosom and I never mention it. Vocabulary limited to that of the Mauve Decade. Mildest euphemisms."

"Deety, I'm durned if I'll be anything but myself."

"Sir, I speak professionally. One does not use FORTRAN to a computer that knows only LOGLAN. Captain, can we open up?"

"Just a moment," my father put in. "Deety, you called me 'Captain.' But I resigned, effective on grounding."

"Wait a half!" Zebadiah interrupted. "You'll do *at least* as much punishment time as I did—you earned it, old buddy."

"All *right*," Pop agreed, "but you decided that time on the ground counts. We'll likely need a new captain when we lift. Let's elect the victim now."

"Reelect Pop," I suggested. "He flunked and should do it over."

"Daughter!"

"Joking, Pop—as long as you bear in mind that you *did* flunk and *never again* give a captain a bad time. I nominate my husband."

"Let's do this right." Pop got out four file cards.

I wrote "Zebadiah" on mine, handed it to Pop. Hilda declared them, showing us each one: Deety—Deety—Deety—Deety. I gasped. "Hey! I demand a recount! No, a new election—somebody cheated." I made so much fuss that they let me have it. I wrote "Zebadiah" on my fresh ballot, placed it face up on the Chief Pilot's seat, placed the other three, one by one, on top of it, then declared them myself: Deety—Deety—Deety—then, *in my own handwriting:* Deety.

I gave up. (But resolved to have a word with the Wizard.)

* * *

It was a pretty cottage with a broad stoop and a climbing rose—but not to live in, just one room with a table and no other furniture. The table held a bowl of fruit, a pitcher of milk, four tumblers. There was a door to the right and a door to the left; the one on the left had painted on it a little girl in a sunbonnet, the other had a boy in a Buster Brown suit.

Hilda and I headed for the sunbonnet. I snatched a glass of milk and a bunch of grapes, and put on a milk moustache; I hadn't tasted milk in ages. Delicious!

Hilda was drawing a tub and had peeled off her dress. The window was open but up high, so I peeled off mine. We made ourselves clean and "beautiful," i.e., we restored our fanciest hairdos but without jewelry. Whatever we needed, that bath and dressing room had, from a sponge to lipstick Aunt Hilda's shade.

We hurried and did it in forty-two minutes. Zebadiah looked beautiful and Pop looked just as smart in dark trousers and a richly simple Aloha shirt.

"We thought you," said my husband, "had gone down the drain."

"Zebadiah, we took forty-two minutes. If you did it in less than thirty, you aren't clean."

"Smell me."

I sniffed him—a faint fragrance of soap, a touch of shaving lotion. "You took more than thirty minutes. Kiss me."

"Thirty-six minutes, by my watch. Say 'Please.'"

I said "Please" and he caught me with my lips open, he always does. Zebadiah just suits me and I haven't been sulky with him and stubborn only when necessary.

There was a path toward the Palace. Pop, with Aunt Hilda on his arm, led off; we followed. Aunt Hilda was carrying her high-heeled sandals, so I took mine off, and glanced back toward the clearing. The little cottage was missing, as I expected. Zebadiah noticed it but said nothing. His face was an interesting study.

The grassy path debouched into a garden in front of the Palace; the path through it was hard, so Hilda and I put on our shoes. Glinda's Palace was more like a Norman chateau or Bertie's "Stately Home of England" than it was like those dreary castles on the Rhine—but it had fairyland grace, like the Taj.

As we started up the sweeping marble steps to the great doorway Zebadiah stumbled. "What the hell?"

"Sssh!" I said. "Language, dear. A magic staircase. Glinda would not make her guests climb. Pretend that Escher designed it. Look proud and walk as if they were level."

As we reached the broad landing two tall trumpeters stepped out of the great doorway, raised their long trumpets, and sounded four flourishes. An old man with a merry grin, a fringe of whiskers, a shiny bald head, a wooden left leg, and wearing a sailor's oilskins, came out as the flourishes ended. I wondered why he was here rather than Emerald City.

He took a pipe from his mouth and said, "Welcome to the Palace of Glinda the Good! I'm Cap'n Bill. You, sir, are Doctor Burroughs the Wizard, with your wonderful wife the Princess Hilda. You must be Cap'n Zeb Carter—Howdy, Cap'n!—and everybody knows Deety; she's spent so much of her life in Oz. Howdy, Deety! Last time I seen you you warn't more'n knee high to a tall duck. And now look at you! Almost up to my shoulder and *married!* Congratulations, Cap'n! Yer a lucky man!"

"I think so, Captain."

"I know so. Deety, Ozma sends her love and sez to tell you that you and your family are welcome in the Royal Kingdom as long as you like."

"Please thank Her Royal Majesty for me, Cap'n Bill." (Actually I'm taller than Cap'n Bill now—but of course I'll always be a little girl to him. It's nice.)

"Oh, I will, I will! Come inside, folks: we ain't formal here. Or I ain't. This ain't my reg'lar job; I'm standing this watch for a friend." He took my hand; his hand was horny and felt like Zebadiah's—and just as gentle.

He led us inside. "Where's Trot?" I asked.

"Around somewhere; you'll see her. Prob'ly picking out her best hair ribbon in your honor. Or maybe helping Betsy with Hank—little Betsy ain't happy unless she's workin'; Neptune knows that mule gets more attention than all the mules that ever came out of Mizzoura. This way to the Library, friends."

How does one describe Glinda the Good? Everyone knows that she is tall and stately and beautiful and never frowns and wears all day long what I think of as beautiful evening gowns with sweeping trains. But those are just words. Perhaps it is enough to say that, just as Dejah Thoris is the most beautiful woman of her world, the Sorceress is the most beautiful of hers.

She was surrounded by her bevy of the most beautiful girls from all over Oz. But Glinda outshone them all without trying. The name of the Egyptian Queen Nefertiti means both "beautiful" and "good," in one word; I think that explains Glinda.

She got up from her Great Book of Records and glided toward

us—kissed Hilda first, kissed me and said, "Welcome home, Deety!" and I choked up and couldn't talk; I just curtsied. She offered a hand each to Zebadiah and Pop; they bowed simultaneously and kissed her hands.

She waved at chairs (that hadn't been there) and invited us to sit down. Zebadiah whispered, "You seem to own this place."

"Not really," I whispered back. "But I've lived in Oz longer than anywhere else"—Mama and Pop lived at several campuses while I was growing up but I always took Oz along wherever we moved.

"Well . . . I'm glad you made me dress up."

We were introduced to Glinda's girls and each one curtsied; it felt like being in Imperial House—except that these girls were neither compelled nor paid. When I stopped to think about it, I couldn't recall that money was used in Oz; it didn't have an "economy."

The girls were beautifully dressed, each differently but each girl's dress was predominately the color of her own country, Munchkin blue, Gillikin purple, Winkie yellow, a few in green. One girl in red—Quadling of course, where we were—looked familiar. I said to her, "Is your name Betty?"

She was startled. "Why, yes, Your Highness—how did you know?" She dropped a curtsy.

"I've been here before; ask Captain Bill. I'm not 'Your Highness'; I'm just Deety. Do you have a friend named Bertie?"

"Yes, Your— Yes, Deety. He's not here now, he's at the College of Professor Wogglebug." I made note to tell Betty about it . . . someday.

I can't tell all about everyone we met at Glinda's Palace; there were too many and more kept arriving. Everyone seemed to expect us and pleased to see us. Pop did not go stark, raving mad when he met the Scarecrow because he was already deep in conversation with Professor H. M. Wogglebug and with Oz the Great, Royal Wizard to Queen Ozma—Pop was barely polite, shook hands and said, "Howd'you do, Mr. Scarecrow," and went right on talking to Professor Wogglebug and the Wizard. I'm not sure he looked at the Scarecrow. He was saying, "You put it neatly, Professor. I wish Professor Mobyas Toras could hear your formulation. If we set alpha equal to zero, it is obvious that—"

I wandered off, because when Pop says, "It is obvious that—" what is really obvious is that Deety should leave.

Dinner was in the banquet hall and the crowd of guests exactly filled it—Glinda's banquet hall is always the right size for the number of persons eating there—or not eating, as the case may be, for Jack Pumpkinhead, Tik-Tok, the Tin Woodman, the Sawhorse, the Scarecrow, and other people who don't eat were seated there, too, and also people who aren't human people: the Cowardly Lion, the Hungry Tiger, the Woozy, the King of the Flying Monkeys, Hank, Toto, and a beautiful long-haired cat with supercilious manners.

Glinda the Good was at the head of the table at one end and Queen Ozma was at the head at the other end. Pop was on Glinda's right and Zebadiah was on Ozma's right. The Wizard was on Glinda's left, and Professor Wogglebug was on Ozma's left. Aunt Hilda and I were opposite each other at the middle of the long table. She had the Tin Woodman on one side and the Scarecrow on the other and was doing her best to charm both of them and both were trying to charm her and all three were succeeding.

I had three dinner companions. I started with two, the Cowardly Lion and the Hungry Tiger. The Lion ate what others ate but the Tiger had a bowl of cornflakes the size of a small washtub and ate from it very tidily with a spoon that matched the bowl. The Cowardly Lion and I had just started seafood cocktails when this cat brushed against my leg to get my attention, looked up and said, "You smell like a cat person. Make a lap, I'm coming up"— and jumped.

I said, "Eureka, do you have Dorothy's permission?"

"What a silly way to talk. Dorothy must get *my* permission. Feed me the lobster first, then the shrimp. You may have the last piece of shrimp for yourself."

The Hungry Tiger put down his big spoon and said, "Highness, may I abate this nuisance?"

"Don't trouble yourself, Old Boy," the Lion said. "I'll abite it instead, in one bite. But please pass the Tabasco sauce; cats have so little taste."

"Pay no attention to those peasants, wench, and get on with the lobster. Animals should not be allowed to eat at the table."

"Look who is calling whom an animal," growled the Cowardly Lion.

"It's not an animal, Leo," the Hungry Tiger objected. "It's an insect. Highness, I'm a vegetarian—but I would be happy to break over this once and slice it into my cornflakes. Shall I?"

"Dorothy wouldn't like it, Rajah."

"You have a point, Ma'am. Shall I ask Toto to chase it out?"

"Eureka may stay. I don't mind."

"Wench, the correct answer is 'I am honored.' Ignore these

jungle beasts; they are not cats. Be it known that *Felis domestica* has been civilized more generations than all you lesser breeds combined. As my serene ancestress, Bubastis, Goddess of the Nile, was wont to say: 'Where Cat is, *is* civilization.' Hurry up with that lobster."

So I hurried. Eureka accepted each bit daintily, barely flicking my finger tips with her scratchy tongue. At last she averted her mouth. "Don't overdo it; I'll tell you when I require more. Scratch behind my left ear—gently. I shall sing, then I shall sleep. Maintain a respectful silence."

I did as ordered. Eureka purred very loudly. As the buzzing gave way to soft snores I slowly stopped scratching. I had to eat with one hand; the other was needed to keep her from falling.

As Aunt Hilda has placed a record in Gay by interviewing all of us and combining it, I will stick to essentials. After the rest had gone home or retired to their rooms we four were invited into the Library. It was smaller than it had been, cozy, as Glinda's girls had gone to their rooms. Glinda was at her Great Book of Records as we were ushered in; she smiled and bowed without getting up as we sat down.

"Friends," she said, "Doctor, Captain, Princess Hilda, and Deety, I will save time by telling you that, during the dancing, I conferred with Ozma, the Wizard, and Professor Wogglebug. I had studied the Records of your strange adventure, and I read a résumé to them before we discussed your problems. First, let me say that Ozma repeats her invitation. You are welcome to stay here forever; you will find hospitality wherever you go. Deety knows this, and Princess Hilda knows it, too, although she is not as sure of it as Deety is.

"But to reassure you gentlemen, the Wizard and I have made the Land of Oz one quarter inch wider in all directions, a change too small to be noticed. But you, Doctor, will recognize that this provides ample Lebensraum for four more good people, as well as for your sky chariot Miss Gay Deceiver. A quarter of an inch, Captain, is six and thirty-five hundredths millimeters.

"While we were about it, on the advice of Professor Wogglebug, we made small changes in Miss Gay Deceiver—"

Zebadiah gave a start and looked upset. Gay was his sweetheart long before I was; he takes care of her as carefully as he takes care of me. But he should have trusted Glinda.

Glinda smiled warmly. "Don't be alarmed, Captain, no harm has been done to the structural integrity or to the functioning of your beloved craft. When you notice—you *will* notice—if you do not like the changes, all you need do is to say aloud, 'Glinda, change Miss Gay Deceiver back the way she was.' I will read it here in my Book and will carry out your wish. But I do not think that you will ask me to do this. That is not prophecy; a good witch does not prophesy. But it is my firm opinion.

"Now to major matters— There are no 'Black Hat' vermin in Oz. Should one be so foolish as to come here, I would know it from my Book, and it would be ejected into the Deadly Desert. What would happen to it there, the less said, the better—but evil is not tolerated in Oz.

"As to the problem of vermin in your home world, it does not lie in Ozma's jurisdiction. My powers are limited there. While my Great Book tells me what happens there, it does not distinguish between vermin disguised as human beings and human beings who by their nature are evil. I could cast a spell over you which would keep you away from all 'Black Hats.' Do you wish that?"

Pop glanced at Zebadiah; my husband said, "Just a moment, Glinda the Good. Just what does that mean?"

"Spells are always literal, Captain; that's why they can cause so much trouble. I rarely use them. This one means what I said: You would be kept away from any vermin of the sort you call 'Black Hats.'"

"In that case we couldn't recognize one, could we? Or get close enough to destroy it."

"I think one would have to devise ways to do each at a distance. Spells do not reason, Captain. Like computers, they operate literally."

"Could they recognize *us*? Booby-trap us? Bomb us?"

"I do not know, Captain. My Book records only what they *have done*, not what they *may do*. Even then, as I have said, the Records do not unmask a disguised 'Black Hat.' Therefore, I know little about them. Do you wish the spell? You need not decide at once. If you remain in Oz, you won't need it."

I blurted out, "We ought to stay here!"

Glinda smiled at me, not a happy smile. "Dear Deety— You have decided not to have your baby?"

"Huh? I mean, 'Excuse me, Glinda?'"

"You have been in Fairyland more than the others. You know that your little girl will not be born here . . . just as no one ever dies here."

Aunt Hilda spoke up so quickly I couldn't get a word in. "Glinda, thank you very much but I will not be staying."

I gulped. "I won't be staying, either, Aunt Glinda."

"So I suspected. Do you want my advice, dear?"

"Yes. Certainly!"

"Having decided to be a woman and not a little girl like Dorothy or Trot, leave here *quickly* . . . lest you be tempted to stay in Fairyland forever."

Pop glanced at Zebadiah, then said, "Madame Glinda, we'll be leaving in the morning. We are grateful for your lavish hospitality . . . but I think that is best."

"I think so, too, Doctor. But remember: Ozma's invitation stands. When you are weary of the world, come here for a holiday and bring the children. Children are happy here and never get hurt. Oz was designed for children."

"We will, we certainly will!"

"Is there anything more to discuss? If not . . ."

"Just a second!" put in Aunt Hilda. "You told Deety—will you tell *me*?"

Glinda smiled. "My Book states that you are growing a boy."

XXXIII   "—'solipsism' is a buzz word."

Zeb:

I didn't sleep with Deety that night. I didn't plan it that way. A footman showed me to a room; Deety and Hilda were standing at the top of the stairs (more magical stairs—okay as long as you don't look down) and talking excitedly, with Jake nearby.

When I saw that the room had only a single bed, the footman had vanished. I stepped outside; Deety and Hilda and Jake were gone, the upper hall was dark. So I said a word one mustn't use in Oz and went back into my room. Even a single bed looked inviting; I went to sleep at once.

Glinda had breakfast with us, in the banquet hall, considerably shrunken. The food in Imperial House is wonderful, but you can't beat ham and basted eggs and toast and jelly and fresh orange juice. I drank three cups of coffee and felt ready to rassle alligators.

Glinda kissed Deety and Hilda good-bye at the top of those Escher steps, and Jake and I bent over her hands. She wished us good luck . . . which must mean more from *her*.

Gay Deceiver looked good in morning sunlight. Tik-Tok was standing at her nose. "Good mor-ning," he said. "I have been con-ver-sing with Miss Gay De-cei-ver all night. She is a ve-ry Smart Girl."

"Howdy, Zeb."

"Howdy, Gay. What have I told you about picking up strange men?"

"You've told me nothing, Zeb. And Tik-Tok is not a strange man. He is a gentleman, which is more than I can say for some people."

"Tru-ly, Cap-tain, I meant no im-pro-pri-e-ty."

"Just kidding, folks. Thanks for keeping Gay company, Tik-Tok."

"It was a plea-sure and a pri-vi-lege. I ar-ranged with the night watch-man to wind me up each hour in or-der that our con-ver-sa-tion be not a-brupt-ly ter-mi-nat-ed."

"Smart of you. Thanks again and we'll see you again. We'll be back for a visit, first chance. Gay, open up."

"You didn't say 'Please,'" my autopilot answered, but she opened her doors.

"I am de-ligh-ted to hear that you are re-tur-ning. Miss Gay De-cei-ver and I have much in com-mon."

Sharpie said good-bye to Tik-Tok, went inside. Deety not only said good-bye but kissed his copper cheek—Deety would kiss a pig if the pig would hold still for it (if he didn't, I would turn him into sausage; kissing Deety is not to be scorned).

Hilda reappeared, still in evening gown. "Deety, come here. Hurry!"

I shook hands with Tik-Tok (odd!) and suggested that he back off a little. Then I went inside. No sign of our wives— I called to them, "Shake it up in there. I want a pilot suit."

Deety called out, "Zebadiah, wiggle your way through the bulkhead."

"I can't change clothes back there."

"Please, dear. I need you."

When Deety says she needs me, I go. So I wiggled through, and the space didn't seem as cramped as it had been when I was working on it at Termite Terrace. "Where are you?"

"In here. Port side," came Deety's muffled voice. I turned around, banging my head, and found a door where a door shouldn't be. I had to stoop but once through it I could stand up. A room slightly bigger than a telephone booth—a door aft, a door forward, Sunbonnet Sue to the left, Buster Brown to the right. Deety opened the door on the left. "Come look!"

A luxurious dressing room and bath— "It's the same one as in the 'Welcome' cottage," said Deety, "except that the window is frosted and doesn't open. But the air is fresh."

I said "Hmmm—" Then I added, "Well, well!" I checked out Buster Brown. Yes, the same bathroom Jake and I had used yesterday.

Jake stuck his head in. I said, "Perfesser, give me the benefit of your wisdom."

"Zeb, I'm fresh out."

"Jake—your opinion, please. Is this craft ready for space?"

"Zeb, I don't know."

"Let's check the outside."

We went over the shell with eyes and fingers, port and starboard. That car was unblemished—outside. But from inside I heard a toilet flushing.

I went inside, on back, still on back, and knocked on Sunbonnet Sue. Sharpie let me in. "Just leaving, Zebbie." She had elected to wear one of her new jump suits and looked like a Cracker Jack prize. "Deet' is about ready."

"Wait a half, Sharpie. Jake and I have decided to trust Glinda."

"Was there any doubt?"

I stepped inside; Deety twisted around at the dressing table, smiled through a mouthful of bobby pins. "Your father and I have approved this craft for space—tentatively—Captain Deety."

"I approved it at breakfast—and not tentatively. What do you have there, dear one?" She accepted a list from me, read it over:

Name	Duty	Additional and/or Relief Duty
D. T. B. Carter	Commanding	
Hilda S. Burroughs	2nd in Command & Navigator	Science Officer & Chef
Z. J. Carter	Chief Pilot	Relief Navigator
J. J. Burroughs	Copilot	Sous-Chef

"It's intended to make your life easier, Cap'n Deety. Jake didn't get the going-over he should have had. But with Jake in the right-hand seat and me over him, I can keep him in hand—and he'll be so busy with his verniers that he won't have time to talk back. 'Sous-Chef' is a fancy way of saying that he'll be under his wife's thumb when we're grounded."

"It's well thought out, Zebadiah. Thank you."

"Suits you?"

"Let me study it."

I got fidgety, ducked into Buster Brown and killed time until she called me. "Slight revision, Zebadiah."

Name	Duty	Additional and/or Relief Duty
Deety	Captain	Instructor Computers
Zebadiah	2nd in Command & Chief Master at Arms	Instructor Duo, Air
Jake	Chief Pilot	Instructor Verniers
Hilda	Copilot	Science Officer & Executive Chef

Note: Cooking will rotate D-J-Z unless changed by the Executive Chef.

"A 'slight revision'!"—I felt offended.

Deety looked at me anxiously. "I'm submitting it for your advice, Zebadiah. I want to continue Pop's policy of everybody learning every job, at least well enough to limp home. Hilda will learn the verniers quickly; she's deft, she doesn't have to be told twice, and the inventor I have placed at her elbow. Pop needs practice in air; he isn't as good as he thinks he is and he's never driven a car this fast. You'll be behind him, ready to bounce him out of trouble. Dear—will it work?"

I was forced to admit that Deety's T.O. was better than mine.

"It's better than mine, so you owe me a forfeit. Where are my handcuffs and nightstick?"

"As second-in-command you are vested with the duty to keep order and to see that the commanding officer's orders are carried out, are you not?"

"Of course, Deety—*Captain* Deety—why rub their noses in it?"

"You know why, Zebadiah. I am reminding everyone that I mean to have a taut ship—and no back talk! You don't need handcuffs or a club. But in that right-hand dressing-table drawer is a ten-centimeter roll of adhesive tape—the size gangsters use for gags."

"Oh. Oho!"

"Zebadiah! *Don't* use it without my direct order. I shall maintain a taut ship. But when I've served my time, I would *much* rather my father was still speaking to me. It's a last resort, my husband. A sharp *Pipe-down* from you is all P— anybody will ever need. I intend to keep you at the conn most of the time— unless you ask me to relieve you, or I tell you I want to conn something personally."

"Suits."

"Very well, sir. You have the conn. Give them their assignments, prepare the car for space, take the reports, let me know *here* when you are ready. Revision in plan: Take us straight up one thousand klicks. Let us look at Oz from a distance, then continue by plan."

"Aye aye, Captain." I started to leave while thinking that Deety might leave a reputation equal to that of Captain Bligh.

"Zebadiah!"

"Yes, Captain?"

"Don't go 'way without kissing me or I *won't take* the bloody job!"

"I didn't realize that the Captain cared to be kissed."

"Captains need kisses more than most people," she answered, her face muffled against my shoulder.

"Got a fresh new stock. Will there be anything else, Ma'am?"

"Yes."

"What?"

"When I've served my time, will you use your influence to put me on the verniers? And—sometime—will you teach me supersonic?"

"Verniers, yes. Supersonic— A man who takes his wife as a pupil is breeding a divorce. Gay will teach you supersonic if you will let her. At super- or hypersonic she's safest on autopilot. She won't hurt herself—but if you override, you may hurt her, she may hurt you."

"But *you* override. How am I to learn?"

"Easy. Give her a program. Leave it loose enough for her to

correct your goofs. Keep your hands and feet *very lightly* on the controls. Be patient, and eventually you'll be part of Gay and Gay will be part of you. Shut up and kiss me."

Captains kiss better.

Ten minutes later we were ready for space. I asked, "Did anyone leave anything in our annex?" I wasn't thinking about it; Jake had reported: "Juice one point zero—*full* capacity!"

"Hilda and I hung up our dresses."

"Captain, do you realize that our magical space warp will probably go back wherever it came from the instant we leave?"

"Want to bet? Glinda wouldn't pull a trick like that."

"It's your dress, Cap'n. But your exec advises you officially to warn all hands never to leave anything essential in there during maneuvers." I wiped the matter from my mind; Deety would do it her way. "Gay, are you going to go on being talkative on your own?"

"Zeb, back on watch, I'll be strictly business. But a girl is entitled to a night out once in a while."

"You're a Smart Girl, Gay."

"So Tik-Tok told me, Zeb."

"Roger and out, Gay. Sharpie, set transition one thousand klicks H axis, plus."

"A thousand kilometers straight up, minimum-range scale, vernier setting three. Jacob, will you check me, please?"

Jake reported the setting correct; I snapped, "Execute!"

Jake put her nose-down: an Earthlike planet so covered with haze that I could make out no details other than straight down, where Oz was still sharp and framed by the impassable deserts. "Sharpie, please hand me the binox, then shift hats to 'Science Officer' and find out whether or not our new addition came along."

I had to help her undog the bulkhead door—Sharpie, in free fall, can't brace herself to apply enough torque to loosen a dog I had fastened on the ground. Meanwhile Deety had been using the binox. "Zebadiah, it's hazy everywhere but below us. Emerald City shines out green as Erin, and Glinda's Palace gleams in the sunshine. But the rest might as well be Venus. Only it's not."

"Daughter—Captain, I mean—have you looked at the stars?" Jake added, "I think it's our own universe."

"It is, Pop? On which side of Orion is the Bull?"

"Why, on—Jesus, Allah, and Zoroaster! It's turned inside out!"

"Yes, but not the way that other inside-out place was. Like Oz itself. East for west."

I asked my wife, "Captain Deety, is there anything odd about duration here?"

"Doesn't *feel* odd. But it's been about a century since those three little girls moved to Oz. I don't know what it feels like to them, and I carefully didn't ask. Did anybody notice that there were no clocks and no calendars?"

"Zebbie!"

"Yes, Sharpie?" I answered.

"Our new plumbing works just dandy. Be careful going in; it's *not* free fall; the floor is *down*. I did a spectacular somersault."

"Hilda my love, are you hurt?"

"Not a bit, Jacob. But next time I'll hang on to something, pull myself down even with the deck, and slide in."

"Science Officer, secure all doors, return to your seat and strap down. Then swap hats and set next rotation by schedule."

"I fastened the doors. I'm dogging the bulkhead door. Okay, I'm strapping down. Where are the binoculars?"

"Jake stowed them. All hands, stand by to rotate."

Another totally black one— I said, "Captain, we'll tumble now unless you prefer to check our new plumbing first."

"Plumbing isn't Deety's job! I'm Science Officer and that includes hygiene, plumbing, and space warps."

Deety said to me, "I relieve you, dear"—then more loudly, to Hilda: "Copilot, pipe down. Pop, dowse the lights and tumble us. Aunt Hillbilly, attempt to set next rotation by touch and sound, in the dark. That's number eight, third of second group."

"Aye aye, Captain Bligh."

The tumble showed nothing. Jake switched on lights, reported that Sharpie had set the next rotation correctly. Deety asked me to relieve her at the conn, then said, "Science Officer, I am about to inspect the addition to your department; please accompany me." Without a word Sharpie did so.

They were gone quite a while. At last I said, "Jake, what do women talk about in can conferences?"

"I'm afraid to find out."

They came back full of giggles; I concluded that Deety's disciplinary methods worked. As they strapped down, Deety said, "Dear, it's black as sin out there—and sunlight streaming in both bathroom windows. Riddle me that."

"Science Officer's department," I evaded. "Stand by to rotate."

This time Jake not only had air, I could *hear* it. Jake got her leveled out hastily. "Copilot, H-above-G!"

"Thirteen hundred meters."

"Too close! Zeb, I'm going to retire and take up tatting. Where are we? I can't see a thing."

"We're over water, Pop, with a light fog. I see a shoreline to starboard."

Jake turned Gay to the right, I picked out the shoreline. Gay's wings were spread; Jake held her at an easy glide and placed her on automatic. "We'll leave this kite sealed now; I won't check the air without going up high."

"Sail ho!"

"Where away, Sharpie?"

"Starboard bow. A sailing ship."

Durn if it wasn't. A square-rigger out of the seventeenth century, high forecastle and sterncastle. Jake took us down for a better look. I wasn't afraid; people who sail ships like that don't use guided missiles—so I kept telling myself.

It was a pretty sight. Jake dropped the starboard wing so that we could have a good look. But we must not have been a "pretty sight" to them; sailors were rushing around and the helmsman let her get away from him and she fell into irons, her canvas flapping foolishly. Not wanting to get the poor fellow keelhauled, I told Jake to level off and head for land.

Deety said, "Good God, Pop, you scared me silly."

"Why, Deety?—Captain Deety. *They* were scared—but surely you aren't scared by black-powder cannon?"

"You almost put the starboard wing into the water."

"Don't be silly, Deety; I was above two hundred meters. Well, maybe a hundred and fifty when I did that steep turn. But plenty of room."

"Take a look at your altimeter. And pressure."

Jake looked and so did I. The radar altimeter stated that we were nineteen meters above the water; Jake had to change scales to read it. Pressure showed well over a thousand millibars—a sealevel high. So I snapped, "Gay Bounce!"

Gay did and I caught my breath.

"Deety, how did I make that error?" Jake asked.

"I don't know, Pop. I can see the right wing tip; you can't. When it looked to me as if you might cut the water, I looked at the instruments. I was about to yell when you straightened out."

"Captain, I was driving seat-of-my-pants by the ship's masts. I would swear I never got within three hundred meters of that ship, on the slant. That should put me plenty high."

Sharpie said, "Jacob, don't you recognize this place?"

"Hilda, don't tell me you've been here before?"

"Only in books, Beloved. A child's version in third grade. A more detailed version in junior high. Finally I laid hands on the unexpurgated version, which was pretty racy for the age I was then. I still find it pleasantly bawdy."

"Sharpie," I demanded, "what are you talking about?"

Jake answered. "Zeb, what sort of ship could cause me to think I was high in the air when in fact I was about to pole-vault into the sea?"

"I've got it!" said Deety.

"I give up," I admitted.

"Tell him, Pop."

"One manned by sailors fifteen centimeters high."

I thought about it. We were approaching land; I told Jake to glide to two klicks *by instrument* and told Gay to hold us there— it seemed much higher. "If anyone runs across Dean Swift, will you give him a swift kick for me?"

Deety said, "Zebadiah, do you suppose the land of the giants— Brobdingnag—is on this continent?"

"I hope not."

"Why not, dear? It should be fun."

"We don't have time to waste on either Lilliputians or giants. Neither would have obstetricians able to take care of you two. Sharpie, get ready to take us up a hundred thousand klicks. Then to rotate. Does anyone have any theory about what has been happening to us? Aside from Sharpie's notion that we are dead and don't know it?"

"I have another theory, Zebbie."

"Give, Sharpie."

"Don't laugh—because you told me that you and Jacob discussed the heart of it, the idea that human thought exists as quanta. I don't know quanta from Qantas Airways, but I know that a quantum is an indivisible unit. You told me that you and Jacob had discussed the possibility that imagination had its own sort of indivisible units or quanta—you called them 'fictons'—or was it ficta? Either way, the notion was that every story ever told— or to be told if there is a difference—exists somewhere in the Number of the Beast."

"But, Hilda my love, that was merely abstract speculation!"

"Jacob, your colleagues regard this car as 'abstract speculation.' Didn't you tell me that the human body is merely complex equations of wave forms? That was when I bit you—I don't mind being a wave form, waves are pretty; I bit you for using the adverb 'merely.'"

"Zebadiah, there is a city on the left. Shouldn't we look at it before we leave?"

"Captain, you must decide that. You saw what a panic we caused in that ship. Imagine yourself fourteen centimeters tall and living in that city. Along comes a great sky monster and dives on you. Would you like it? How many little people will faint? How many will die of heart failure? How many are you willing to kill to satisfy your curiosity?" I added, "To those people we are monsters worse than 'Black-Hat' vermin."

"Oh, dear! You're right, Zebadiah—dismally so. Let's get out of here."

"Copilot, set to transit straight up one hundred thousand klicks."

"Transition 'H' axis, positive, vernier setting five—set!"

"Execute." I continued, "Captain, I'd like to sit here a while."

"Very well, Zebadiah."

"Sharpie, let's hear your theory. Captain, I've been scared silly by too many narrow escapes. We know how to translate from one Earth-analog to the next; just use plenty of elbow room. But these rotations are making me white-haired. The laws of chance are going to catch up with us."

"Zebbie, I don't think the laws of chance have anything to do with it. I don't think we have been in *any* danger in *any* rotation."

"So? Sharpie, I'm about to swap jobs with you as quickly as I can get the Captain's permission."

"No, no! I—"

"Chicken!"

"Zebbie, your hunches are part of why I say that the laws of chance are not relevant."

"Sharpie, statistical laws are the most firmly established of all natural laws."

"Do they apply in the Land of Oz?" asked Deety.

"Uh— Damned if I know! *Touché!*"

"Zeb, Hilda has not expressed it as I would; nevertheless I agree with her. To call the equations used in statistics 'laws of nature' is a misnomer. Those equations measure the degree of our ignorance. When I flip a coin and say that the chance of heads or tails is fifty-fifty, I am simply declaring total ignorance as to outcome. If I knew *all* conditions, the outcome *might* be subject to precalculation. But we have experienced two universes having physical laws unlike those of our home universe."

"Three, Jacob. Lilliput makes three."

"I don't follow you, my dear."

"The cube-square law that runs through all biology does not apply here. A human brain can't be placed in a space the size of a thimble by *our* biophysical laws. But we're getting away from the theory Zebbie wanted me to expound. Shall I go on?"

"Yes," Deety ruled. "Everybody shut up but Aunt Hilda. I'm zipping my own lip. Hillbilly—proceed."

"All right. It's not chance that we have been in three universes—Inside-Out, the Land of Oz, and Lilliput—in . . . less than twenty-four hours, isn't it, Deety?"

"Less than twenty-one, Aunt Hilda."

"Thanks hon. It's not chance that those three are 'fictional' universes—I have to call them that for lack of a better word— well known to each of us. By coincidence—and again I don't have a good word but it's not 'chance'—all four of us are addicted to fanciful stories. Fantasy. Fairy tales. We all like the same sort of stories. How many of us like detective stories?"

"Some—not all," said Deety.

"My sole loyalty is to Sherlock Holmes," I said.

"Waste of time," said Jake.

"I'd like to try an experiment," Hilda went on. "Write down the twenty stories you have enjoyed most. Or groups of related stories—the Oz books would count as one, so would the Edgar Rice Burroughs Mars series, and so would the four voyages of 'Gulliver's Travels.' Make them stories you reread for pleasure when you are too tired to tackle a new book."

"Sharpie, is it cheating to ask how you mean to use this?"

"No, Zebbie. If my theory is right, the next time we rotate and find ourselves near a planet, it will turn out to be the scene of a story or group of stories that appears on all four lists. We'll arrive high enough that Jacob will have plenty of time to level off but close enough that we can ground. But we will *never* rotate into a mass or any danger that we can't handle. This isn't *chance;* we haven't been dealing with chance. The Land of Oz surprised me. Lilliput didn't surprise me at all; I expected it. Or at least a place that all of us know through stories."

"How about those empty universes?" I demanded.

"Maybe they are places about which stories will be written or maybe stories have already been told but aren't favorites of us four, so we don't emerge close to their scenes. But those are guesses. So far as my theory is concerned, such universes are 'null'—they don't count one way or the other. *We* find *our* universes."

"Sharpie, you have just invented pantheistic multiperson solipsism. I didn't think it was mathematically possible."

"Zeb, *anything* is mathematically possible."

"Thanks, Jacob. Zebbie, 'solipsism' is a buzz word. I'm saying that we've stumbled onto 'The Door in the Wall,' the one that leads to the Land of Heart's Desire. I don't know how and have no use for fancy rationalizations. I see a pattern; I'm not trying to explain it. It just *is*."

"How does that hollow world fit your theory?"

"Well, Deety called it Pellucidar—"

"It was!"

"—but I've read dozens of stories about worlds underground; I'll bet all of us have. Jules Verne, S. Fowler Wright, H. G. Wells, C. L. Moore, Lovecraft—all the great masters of fantasy have taken a crack at it. Please, can we stop talking? I want all four lists before we rotate again."

Jake changed attitude so that Lilliput's planet was dead ahead and told Gay to hold it there. The planet looked very small, as if we were a million kilometers out—reasonable, I decided, and wrote down "The Dorsai yarns."

At last Deety announced, "I'm through, Aunt Hillbilly."

Soon after, her father handed Sharpie his list. "Don't count those I've lined out, dear—I had trouble holding it down."

"'Twenty' is arbitrary, Jacob. I can leave your extras in."

"No, dear, the four I eliminated do not stand as high as the twenty I retained."

After some pencil-chewing I announced, "Sharpie, I'm stuck at seventeen. Got a baker's dozen more in mind, but no choice."

"Seventeen will do, Zebbie—if they are your prime favorites."

"They are."

Hilda accepted my list, ran her eye down it. "A psychoanalyst would have a wonderful time with these."

"Wait a half! Sharpie, if you're going to let a shrink see those lists, I want mine back."

"Zebbie darling, I wouldn't do that to you." She added, "I need a few minutes to tally."

I glanced at Lilliput. "Need help?"

"No. I've tallied a 'one' after all on my list. I've checked Deety's against mine and tallied a 'two' where they match, and added to the bottom of my list, with one vote tallied against each, those she picked but I didn't. I'm doing the same with Jacob's list, tallying three's and two's and one's. Then Zebbie and we'll wind up with a four-vote list—unanimous—and a list with three each—and a list with two, and with one."

Sharpie kept busy some minutes, then took a fresh sheet, made a list, folded it. "This should be in a sealed envelope to establish my reputation as a fortuneteller. Zebbie, there are nine soi-disant fictional universes listed. Any close approach we make by rotation should be near one of them."

I said, "You included Pellucidar?"

"Pellucidar got only two votes. I stick to my theory that the inside-out world is a composite of underground fantasies. But our vote identified that third universe—the blinding lights, the one that worried you about radiation."

"The hell you say!"

"I think it did. Four votes for Doctor Isaac Asimov's 'Nightfall.' I expected his Foundation stories to make it but they got only three votes. Too bad, because his library planet might be able to tell us what those vermin are, where they come from—and how to beat them."

"My fault, Aunt Hillbilly. Pop told me I should read the Foundation series . . . but I never did."

"Sharpie," I said, "we can put you down in New York in five minutes. The Good Doctor is getting on in years—turns out less than a million words a year now—but still likes pretty girls. He must know whatever is in the Galactic Library; he invented it. So telephone him. Better yet, sit on his lap. Cry if necessary."

"Zebbie, if there is one place I'm certain is loaded with 'Black Hat' vermin, it's New York City! *You* sit on his lap!"

"Not me. If we learn how to delouse our home planet, I'll work on a way to spread the word. But I'm number one on their death list."

"No, Jacob is."

"No, Sharpie. Jake and Deety are dead, you are kidnapped, and I'm marked down to be 'terminated with extreme prejudice.' But I'll risk grounding on the Hudson River VTOL flat long enough for you to visit the Good Doctor. Your husband can escort you; I'm going to hide in the bathroom. I figure that is actually in Oz and therefore safe."

"Go lay an egg!"

"Sharpie dear, none of us is going to Earth-zero. Hand that list to Deety; she won't peek. Captain, shall we rotate? The Science Officer has me half convinced that we can get away with it; let's do it before I lose my nerve. Fourth and last universe in the second group, isn't it?" I asked Sharpie.

"Yes, Zebbie."

"Anybody as chicken as I am, speak up! . . . Isn't *anybody* going to get us out of this! . . . . Execute!"

XXXIV *"—all my dreams* do come true!"*

Zeb:

Gay Deceiver was right side up five hundred meters above a sunlit, gentle countryside. Jake set her to cruise in a circle. I asked, "Are we back in Oz? Sharpie, check your setting."

"Not Oz, Zebbie. I've stuck to schedule."

"Okay. Does your magic list tell you where we are?"

"If it's one of the nine, then it's—" Hilda wrote a word on a sheet, folded it, handed it to me. "Stick this in your pocket."

I tucked it away. "Jake, bounce us, then range-and-target to ground us in that meadow. We'll test the air when we're down. Safer."

Jake zeroed Gay in; she grounded. "Zeb," he said fretfully, "how can I tell what juice we have? The gauge *still* reads 'Capacity.'"

"Let me think about it."

"All right. Has the Captain worked out that new scram?"

"I think so, Pop. Take G.D. straight up a hundred thousand klicks, but do it in two words, in total darkness, or with eyes dazzled, or anything. As long as anyone can get out two syllables we'll zip far enough away from trouble that we'll have time to work out what to do next."

"Good enough. Can you program it before I open a door?"

"I think so, Zebadiah. If she's asleep, G.D. will wake up and do it at once."

"Okay, will you program it? Hilda, set up the same thing on your dials as a back-up. Meanwhile I'm going to give the plumbing a field test. Don't touch the doors till I get back."

I returned in a few minutes. "Our magic space warp is still with us—don't ask me why or I'll scream. New program inserted?"

"Yes, Zebadiah. On tell-me-three-times and protected against execution without the doors being closed and locked. I've written down the magic words. Here." Deety handed me a scrap of paper.

On it was: "Gay—*Zoom!*"

"It's the shortest program with an unusual monosyllable that I can think of."

"Its shortness may save our necks. Swap seats with me, Sharpie, it's my turn to be pioneer mother. Everybody, hold your breath; I'm going to sniff the air."

"Zebbie, this planet is Earthlike to nine decimal places."

"Which gives me a cheap chance to play hero." I opened her door a crack, sniffed.

Shortly I said, "I feel okay. Anybody woozy?"

"Open the door wide, Zebbie; this place is *safe.*"

I did so and stepped out into a field of daisies; the others followed me. It certainly *seemed* safe—quiet, warm, peaceful, a meadow bounded by a hedge row and a stream.

Suddenly a white rabbit came running past, headed for the hedge. He barely paused, pulled a watch from his waistcoat pocket, glanced at it, then moaned, "Oh dear! Oh dear! I shall be too late!" and ran even faster. Deety started after him.

"*Deety!*" I yelled.

She stopped short. "I want to find the rabbit hole."

"Then keep your eye on *her*. You're *not* going down the hole."

"On whom?" Deety turned back toward the hedge row. A little girl in a pinafore was hurrying toward the spot where the rabbit had disappeared. "Oh. But it didn't hurt *her* to go down the hole."

"No, but Alice had lots of difficulties before she got out. We haven't time; this is not a place we can stay."

"Why not?"

"Nineteenth-century England did *not* have advanced medicine."

"Zebbie," put in Hilda, "this isn't England. Read that slip."

I unfolded the scrap of paper, read: *Wonderland*. "Just so," I agreed, and handed it to my wife. "But it is modeled on England in the eighteen-sixties. It either has no medicine, like Oz, or pre-Pasteur medicine. Possibly pre-Semmelweiss. Deety, do you want to die from childbed fever?"

"No, I want to go to the Mad Tea Party."

"We can have a mad tea party; I went mad several universes back—and it's time for lunch. Sharpie, you win the Order of Nostradamus with diamond cluster. May I ask two questions?"

"One may always ask."

"Is H. P. Lovecraft on that list?"

"He got only one vote, Zebbie. Yours."

"Chthulhu be thanked! Sharpie, his stories fascinate me the way snakes are said to fascinate birds. But I would rather be trapped with the King in Yellow than be caught up in the worlds of the Necronomicon. Uh . . . did *any* horrids get four votes?"

"No, dear, the rest of us prefer happy endings."

"So do I! Especially when I'm in it. Did Heinlein get his name in the hat?"

"Four votes, split. Two for his 'Future History,' two for 'Stranger in a Strange Land.' So I left him out."

"*I* didn't vote for 'Stranger' and I'll refrain from embarrassing anyone by asking who did. My God, the things some writers will do for money!"

"Samuel Johnson said that anyone who wrote for any other reason was a fool."

"Johnson was a fat, pompous, gluttonous, dirty old fool who would have faded into the obscurity he so richly deserved had he not been followed around by a spit-licking sycophant. Spell that 'Psycho-', as in 'Bloch.'" I added, "Did Poul Anderson get in? Or Niven?"

"Zebbie, that's far more than two questions."

"I haven't even reached the second question . . . which is: What do we have for a mad tea party?"

"Surprise! Glinda had a picnic basket placed in our dressing room."

"I missed it," I admitted.

"You didn't look in the wardrobe." Sharpie grinned. "Can sandwiches from Oz be eaten in Wonderland? Or will they 'softly and silently vanish away'?"

"'Be off, or I'll kick you downstairs!'"

Several hundred calories later I noticed a young man hovering nearby. He seemed to want to speak but was too diffident to do so. Deety jumped up, trotted toward him. "The Reverend Mister Dodgson, is it not? I'm Mrs. Zebadiah Carter."

He quickly removed his straw boater. "'Mr. Dodgson,' yes, uh, Mrs. Carter. Have we met?"

"Long ago, before I was married. You are looking for Alice, are you not?"

- "Dear me! Why, yes, I am. But how—"

"She went Down the Rabbit-Hole."

Dodgson looked relieved. "Then she will be back soon enough. I promised to return her and her sisters to Christ Church before dark."

"You did. I mean, 'you will.' Same thing, depending on the coordinates. Come meet my family. Have you had luncheon?"

"Oh, I say, I don't mean to intrude."

"You aren't intruding." Deety took him by the hand, firmly. Since my treasure is stronger than most men, he came along . . . and let go her hand hastily as soon as she loosened her grip. We men got to our feet; Hilda remained in lotus.

"Aunt Hilda, this is Mr. Dodgson, Lecturer in Mathematics at Christ Church College, Oxford. My stepmother, Mrs. Burroughs."

"How do you do, Mrs. Burroughs. Oh dear, I *am* intruding!"

"Not at all, Mr. Dodgson. Do sit down."

"And this is my father, Dr. Burroughs, Professor of Mathematics. And my husband Captain Carter. Aunt Hilda, will you find a clean plate for Mr. Dodgson?"

The young don relaxed once introductions had been made but he was still far more formal than Deety intended to permit. He sat down on the turf, placed his hat carefully beside him, and said, "Truly, Mrs. Burroughs, I've just finished tea with three little girls."

Deety ignored his protests while she piled his plate with little sandwiches and cakes. Sharpie poured tea from a Thermos jug. They nailed him down with cup and plate. Jake advised, "Don't fight it, son, unless you really must leave. Are Alice's sisters safe?"

"Why, yes, Professor; they are napping in the shade of a hayrick nearby. But—"

"Then relax. In any case, you must wait for Alice. What branch of mathematics do you pursue?"

"Algebraic logic, usually, sir, with some attention to its applications to geometry." The Reverend Mr. Dodgson was seated so that he faced Gay Deceiver and sat in the shadow of her port wing but nothing in his manner showed that he noticed the anachronism.

"Have your studies led you into multidimensional non-Euclidean geometries?" Jake asked.

Dodgson blinked. "I fear that I tend to be conservative in geometry, rathuh."

"Father, Mr. Dodgson doesn't work in your field; he works in mine."

Dodgson raised his eyebrows slightly. Jake said, "My daughter did not introduce herself fully. She is Mrs. Carter but her maiden name is Doctor D. T. Burroughs. Her field is mathematical logic."

"That is why I am so pleased that you are here, Mr. Dodgson. Your book 'Symbolic Logic' is a milestone in our field."

"But, my dear lady, I have not written a work titled 'Symbolic Logic.'"

"I've confused things. Again it is matter of selection of co-ordinates. At the end of the reign of Queen Victoria you will have published it five years earlier. Is that clear?"

He answered very solemnly, "Quite clear. All I need do is to ask Her Majesty how much longer she is going to reign and subtract five years."

"That should do it. Do you like to play with sorites?"

For the first time, he smiled. "Oh, very much!"

"Shall we make up some? Then trade and solve them?"

"Well . . . not too lengthy. I really must get back to my young charges."

"We can't stay long, either. Anyone else want to play?"

No one else elected to play. I stretched out on the grass with a handkerchief over my face; Jake and Sharpie went for a walk. "Shall we hold the statements down to groups of six?" Dodgson suggested.

"All right. But the conclusion *must* be true. Not nonsense. Agreed?" (Deety had taught me this game; she's good at it. I decided to be a silent witness.)

They kept quiet while I snored convincingly. Deety was a "lady" for a while, then sprawled on her belly and chewed her pencil. I watched with one eye from under my handkerchief.

First she covered several pages with scratch work in developing statements incomplete in themselves but intended to arrive at only one possible conclusion. Having done so, she tested them by symbolic logic, then wrote out her list of statements, mixing them randomly—looked up.

The young mathematician was looking at her solemnly, note pad in hand. "Finished?" my wife asked.

"Just finished. Mrs. Carter, you remind me of my little friend Alice Liddell."

"I know," she said. "That's how I recognized her. Shall we trade?"

Dodgson tore a sheet from his pad. "This is to be solved in the first person; its conclusion applies to you."

"All right, I'll try it." Deety read aloud:

"1) Every idea of mine, that cannot be expressed as a syllogism, is really ridiculous;

"2) None of my ideas about Bath-buns are worth writing down;

"3) No idea of mine, that fails to come true, can be expressed as a syllogism;

"4) I never have any really ridiculous idea, that I do not at once refer to my solicitor;

"5) My dreams are all about Bath-buns;

"6) I never refer any idea of mine to my solicitor, unless it is worth writing down."

Deety chortled. "How sweet of you! It *is* true; all my dreams *do* come true!"

"You solved it so quickly?"

"But it's only six statements. Have you solved mine?"

"I haven't read it yet." He also read aloud:

"1) Everything, not absolutely ugly, may be kept in a drawing room;

"2) Nothing, that is encrusted with salt, is ever quite dry;

"3) Nothing should be kept in a drawing room, unless it is free from damp;

"4) Time-traveling machines are always kept near the sea;

"5) Nothing, that is what you expect it to be, can be absolutely ugly;

"6) Whatever is kept near the sea gets encrusted with salt."

He blinked at the list. "The conclusion is true?" he asked.

"Yes."

For the first time he stared openly at Gay Deceiver. "That, then—I infer—is a 'time-traveling machine.'"

"Yes . . . although it does other things as well."

"It is not what I expected it to be . . . although I am not sure what I expected a time-traveling machine to be."

I pulled his handkerchief off my face. "Do you want to take a ride, Mr. Dodgson?"

The young don looked wistful. "I am sorely tempted, Captain. But I am responsible for three little girls. So I must thank you for your hospitality and bid you good-bye. Will you offer my apologies to Professor and Mrs. Burroughs and explain that duty calls me?"

XXXV "It's a disturbing idea—"

Jake:
"Deety, how does it feel to say good-bye without getting kissed?"

"Zebadiah, I didn't make it possible. Lewis Carroll was terrified by females over the age of puberty."

"That's why I stayed close. Deety hon, if I had gone with Jake and Hilda, he would have left at once."

"I can't figure out how he got here in the first place," said my dear wife Hilda. "Lewis Carroll was never *in* Wonderland; he simply wrote about it. But this *is* Wonderland—unless rabbits in England wear waistcoats and watches."

"Aunt Hilda, who can possibly be as deeply inside a story as the person who writes it?"

"Hmm— I'll have to study that."

"Later, Sharpie," Zeb said. "Stand by to rotate. Mars, isn't it?"

"Right, Zebbie," Hilda agreed.

"Gay . . . *Sagan!*"

Mars-zero lay ahead, in half phase at the proper distance.

"Set!" Hilda reported. "To tenth universe, third group."

"Execute." It was another starry void with no familiar groupings; we ran through routine, Zeb logged it as "possible" and we moved on to the second of the third group—and I found myself facing the Big and Little Dippers. Again we ran through a routine tumble—but failed to find the Sun or any planets. I don't know the southern constellations too well but I spotted *Crux* and the Magellanic Clouds. To the north there could be no doubt about Cygnus and a dozen others.

Zeb said, "Where is Sol? Deety? Sharpie?"

"I haven't seen it, Zebadiah."

"Zebbie, don't go blaming me. I put it right back where I found it."

353

Jake, I don't like this. Sharpie, are you set?"

"Set. Standing orders. Third group, third of three."

"Keep your finger near the button. How does this fit your theory? I don't recall listing a story that doesn't have the Solar System in it."

"Zebbie, it can't fit two of those left, could fit the others, and could fit half a dozen or more that got three votes. You said that about a dozen were tied in your mind. Were any of them space-travel stories?"

"Almost all."

"Then we could be in any world that takes our universe as a model but far enough from the Sun so that it appears as second or third magnitude. That wouldn't have to be far; our Sun is pretty faint. So this could be the Darkover universe, or Niven's Known Space, or Dr. Williamson's Legion of Space universe, or the Star Trek universe, or Anderson's world of the Polesotechnic League, or Dr. Smith's Galactic Patrol world. Or several more."

"Sharpie, what were two that this could not be?"

"King Arthur and his Knights, and the World of the Hobbits."

"If we find ourselves in either of those, we leave. No obstetricians. Jake, any reason to stay here longer?"

"None that I see," I answered.

"Captain Deety, I advise scram. Those space-opera universes can be sticky. I don't care to catch a photon torpedo or a vortex bomb or a negative-matter projectile, just through failure to identify ourselves promptly."

So we rotated.

This time we weren't merely close; we were on the ground. Charging straight at us was a knight in armour, lance couched in attack. I think it unlikely that a lance could damage Gay. But this "gentle knight" was unfriendly; I shouted, "Gay!—*Zoom!*"

Sighed with relief at sudden darkness and at the Captain's next words: "Thanks, Pop. You were on your toes."

"Thank *you*. End of group three. Back to Mars? S, A, G, A, N?"

"Let's get on with it," Zeb agreed. "All Hands—"

"Zebadiah!" my daughter interrupted. "Is *that* all you wish to see of King Arthur and his Knights?"

"Captain Deety, that wasn't one of King Arthur's Knights. He was wearing plated mail."

"That's my impression," my beloved agreed. "But I gave more attention to his shield. Field sable, argent bend sinister, in chief sun proper with crown, both or."

"Sir Modred," my daughter decided. "I *knew* he was a baddie! Zebadiah, we should have hit him with your L-gun."

"*Killed* that beautiful beer-wagon horse? Deety, that sort of armor wasn't made earlier than the fifteenth century, eight or nine centuries *after* the days of King Arthur."

"Then why was he carrying Sir Modred's shield?"

"Sharpie, was that Sir Modred's coat of arms?"

"I don't know; I blazoned what I saw. Aren't you nit-picking in objecting to plate armor merely because it's anachronistic?"

"But history shows that—"

"That's the point, Zebbie. Camelot isn't *history;* it's *fiction.*"

Zeb said slowly, "Shut my big mouth."

"Zebbie, I venture to guess that the version of Camelot we blundered into is a patchwork of all our concepts of King Arthur and the Round Table. I picked up mine from Tennyson, revised them when I read 'Le Morte d'Arthur.' Where did you get yours?"

"Mark Twain gave me mine—'A Connecticut Yankee in King Arthur's Court.' Add some Prince Valiant. Jake?"

I said, "Zeb, there seems little doubt that there was a king or a general named Arthur or Arturius. But most people think of King Arthur from stories having little connection with any historical person. 'The Sword in the Stone' and 'The Once and Future King' are my favorites."

My daughter persisted, "I do believe in the Round Table, I do! We should go back and *look!* Instead of guessing."

"Captain Deety," her husband said gently, "the jolly, murderous roughnecks called the Knights of the Round Table are fun to read about but not to know socially. Nor are people the only dangers. There would be honest-to-God dragons, and wyverns, and malevolent magic—not the Glinda-the-Good variety. We've learned that these alternate worlds are as real as the one we came from. We don't need to relearn it by getting suddenly dead. That's my official advice. If you don't agree, will you please relieve me at the conn . . . Ma'am?"

"Zebadiah, you're being logical—a most unfair way to argue!"

"Jacob," said my wife, "suppose we were people who don't like fanciful stories. What sort of worlds would we find?"

"I don't know, Hilda. Probably only humdrum slice-of-life universes indistinguishable from the real world. Correction: Substitute 'Universe-zero' for 'real world'—because, as your theory requires, all worlds are equally real. Or unreal."

"Jacob, why do you call our universe 'universe-zero?'"

"Eh . . . for convenience. *Our* point of origin."

"Didn't you tell me that no frame is preferred over any other? Each one to the Number of the Beast is equally zero in six axes?"

"Well . . . theory requires it."

"Then *we* are fiction in other universes. Have I reasoned correctly?"

I was slow in answering. "That seems to be a necessary corollary. It's a disturbing idea: that we ourselves are figments of imagination."

"I'm nobody's figment!" my daughter protested. "I'm real, I am! Pinch me! . . . *Ouch!* Zebadiah, not so hard!"

"You asked for it, dear," Zeb told her.

"My husband is a brute. And I've got a cruel stepmother just like Snow White. I mean 'Cinderella.' And my Pop thinks I'm *imaginary!* But I love you anyway because you're all I've got."

"If you fictional characters will pipe down, we'll get this show on the road. Stand by to rotate. Gay Sagan!"

Mars was where it should be. I felt more real.

XXXVI   *"Pipe down and do your job."*

Hilda:

"Set, Captain," I reported. "Thirteenth rotation. Correct, Zebbie?"

"Check, Sharpie. Captain?"

Deety answered, "Let's catch our breaths." She stared out at the ruddy barrenness of Mars-zero. "That rock looks downright homelike. I feel like a tourist who tries to see thirty countries in two weeks. Shock. Not 'future shock' but something like it."

"Homesickness," I told her. "Knowing that we can't go back. Deety, somewhere, somewhen, we'll build another Snug Harbor. Won't we, Jacob?"

Jacob patted my knee. "We will, dearest."

Deety said wistfully, "Will we really find another Snug Harbor?"

"Deety, are you over your pioneer-mother jag?"

"No, Zebadiah. But I can get homesick. Like you. Like Hilda. Like everybody but Pop."

"Correction, Daughter. I don't miss Logan, and I don't think Hilda misses California—"

"Not a bit!" I agreed.

"Nor me," agreed Zeb. "I had a rented flat. But Snug Harbor was home."

"Agreed," Jacob answered. "I didn't really *hate* these vermin until they bombed our home." Jacob added, "We've got to find a new Snug Harbor. Comfortable as this car is, we can't live in it indefinitely."

"Check. Sharpie, your theory seems to be checking out. Is there any reason to finish this schedule? Should we go directly to *Teh* axis?"

"Zebbie, granted that most rotations didn't amount to more than sightseeing, if we *hadn't* followed this schedule, this car would not be nearly so comfortable. Do you know of another Ford that has two bathrooms?"

"Sharpie, I don't know of one that has *one* bathroom. Our space-warp special lets us stay in space as long as our air holds out. And food. But air is the critical factor."

I said, "Zebbie, have you noticed that our air does *not* get stuffy?"

"It will soon."

"It need not," Jacob pointed out. "We can scram-code to Oz, or to Wonderland, in seconds. Sweet air, no danger."

Zebbie looked sheepish. "I'm still learning what our wonder buggy will do."

"So am I."

"Gentlemen, you missed my point. You might check the juice. I haven't mentioned another asset. Zebbie, would you like a banana?"

"Sharpie, I ate the last before I buried garbage. While you and Deety were washing dishes before we left Wonderland."

"Tell him, Deety."

"Zebadiah, Hilda and I salvaged and put everything into the basket. Hilda started to put it into our wardrobe—and it was heavy. So we looked. Packed as tight as when we left Oz. Six bananas—and everything else. Cross my heart. No, go look."

"Hmmm— Jake, can you write equations for a picnic basket that refills itself? Will it go on doing so?"

"Zeb, equations can be written to describe *anything*. The description would be simpler for a basket that replenishes itself indefinitely than for one that does it once and stops—I would have to describe the discontinuity. But I am no longer troubled by natural—or 'unnatural'—laws that don't apply in Universe-zero."

"Mmmm . . . Science Officer, I suggest that you check on that basket now that we have returned to Universe-zero."

"Zebbie, make that an order in writing and sign your name— if you want to look foolish. Deety, will you order it logged?"

"Sharpie, if you weren't such good company, I'd strangle you. Your earlier answer recommended that we complete the rotations."

"No, I noted that the first twelve had not been unprofitable. We could have completed the last three by now had we not spent time debating it."

"Hilda honey, our cowardly Astrogator needed time to get his nerve back. By yumpin' yiminy, once you're all trained, I'm going to retire."

"We would simply recall you, Zebbie. Each will go on doing what she can do best."

" 'Time is out of joint. O curséd spite, that I was ever picked to set it right.' "

"You misquoted."

"I always do. What universe do we hit next?"

"Zebbie, we have three rotations to go, with four left on the four-votes list. One is useless but amusing and safe. The other three are places to live but each has its own dangers. As the chief of surgery used to say: 'I dunno, let's operate and find out.' "

Zebbie sighed. "All hands, stand by to rotate. *Execute!*"

Green fire— *"Rotate! Execute!"*

A formless red fog— *"Gay Sagan!"*

Mars looked like an old friend. Zebbie wiped his brow and said, "Whew! One to go— Cap'n Deety hon, let's get it over with. Sharpie?"

"Fifteenth universe—set!" I reported.

"Execute!"

We came out into a starry universe. "Cap'n Deety hon, don't these constellations look familiar?" Zebbie commented.

"I think so."

"They *are* familiar," I insisted. "Except that there is a very bright star near the Gemini. That ought to be the Sun. We're way out past Pluto, where the comets spend the winter. Let's move in and find Earth."

"Don't be in a hurry," said Zebbie. "Science Officer, what was that first rotation? Green fire?"

"How about the deadly green nebula in 'The Legion of Space'?—on the trip to the Runaway Star where Aladoree had been taken."

"That was on your list?"

"All of us voted for it."

"What was that red fog we rotated into next?"

"That one is harder to figure," I admitted. "It could be any universe by a writer who paid respectful attention to astronomy— Bova, Haldeman, Schmidt, Pournelle, Niven, Benford, Clement, Anderson, and so forth. But there were four votes for 'The Mote in God's Eye.' Whether the two old gentlemen had anything to do with it or not, I think we blundered into a red giant. A red giant is close to what we call vacuum. Anyhow, we weren't hurt; we were there about two seconds."

"Less than that, Sharpie; you set it with one click, and barely had your thumb off the execute button. Captain, do you wish to transit toward that bright star?"

"Let's chop off thirty or forty A.U.'s," Deety decided, "and get a rough cross fix. Maybe that will give us a disc Pop can measure. If not, we'll narrow it down until it does. Then place us one A.U. from the Sun and we'll spot Earth easily. Astrogator—advice."

"Captain, I advise making that first jump with *wide* offset. Miss the Sun by at least one A.U. At *least*."

"Yes! Zebadiah, make that cross fix *wide*. Uh—" Deety peered around. "There's the Sickle. Have Pop aim for Regulus."

My husband said, "I'm swinging toward Regulus. Zeb, how do I take the angular width of the Solar disc without broiling an eyeball?"

"The gunsight has a built-in polarizer. Didn't I show you?"

"You did *not*."

"Sorry. Captain Deety hon, I request permission to relieve the Chief Pilot for this."

"Permission granted. But, Zebadiah, *you* be careful."

"Spacecraft! Identify yourself!" —the voice was everywhere. Zebbie jerked with surprise. (Me, too!) "Who said that?"

"Lensman Ted Smith, Commander Galactic Patrol, commanding Patrol Vessel 'Nighthawk.' Entity, I regret being forced to enter your mind but you have been ignoring sub-ether radio for

four minutes thirty-two seconds. Switch it on and I will get out of your mind. Do not maneuver; we have weapons on you."

"Captain," Jacob whispered, "Hilda is set to rotate."

Deety shook her head, touched Zebbie's arm, pointed to herself.

"Lensman, this is Captain Deety, commanding Continua Craft *Gay Deceiver*. We don't have sub-ether radio. Do you read me?"

"I read you loud and clear. What happened to your sub-ether radio? Do you need help?"

"Captain Smith, I don't have sub-ether radio at all. We don't need help but could use astrogational advice. Where are we?"

"The important point is that you are in my patrol sector, an unscheduled ship insufficiently identified. I repeat: DO NOT MANEUVER. By order of the Galactic Patrol. Do you understand?"

"I understand you, Lensman. I regret having intruded into your patrol space. This is a private ship engaged in peaceful exploration."

"That is what I am about to determine, Captain. Stay where you are, make no hostile moves, and you will be safe."

"Lensman, can you see through my eyes?"

"Are you inviting me to do so?"

"Certainly. Use my eyes, use my ears. But don't try to take over my mind or this ship will disappear." Deety squeezed my shoulder; I signaled "Roger" with a pat.

"I warn you not to maneuver. Ah . . . interesting!"

I snapped, "Captain Smith, quit threatening us! A Lensman is supposed to be an officer and gentleman! I intend to report you to the Port Admiral! You're an *oaf!*"

"Sorry, Madam. I do not wish to offend but I have duty to perform. Captain, will you please turn your head so that I can see who is speaking?"

"Certainly. Let me introduce all of us. On my left"—Deety looked at Zebbie—"is Doctor Zebadiah Carter. In front of him is Doctor Jacob Burroughs. On his right"—Deety looked at me— "is his wife, Doctor Hilda Burroughs, xenobiologist and chief of science. Let me offer you this advice, Lensman: It is *never* safe to offend Doctor Hilda."

"I gathered that impression, Captain. Doctor Hilda, I would not willingly offend—but I have duties. Shall I get out of your mind entirely? If you speak to me, I will hear with Captain Deety's ears. She can, if she will, repeat to you my thought in answer."

"Oh, it's all right for conversation. But don't try to go deeper! Mentor would not like it—as you know!"

"Doctor Hilda, your mention of . . . a certain entity . . . surprises me—from one who is not a Lensman."

"I don't *need* a Lens. You can check that with Arisia."

Deety said hastily, "Lensman, are you satisfied that we are a peaceful party of scientists? Or is there something more that you wish to know?"

"Captain, I can see that this ship is not a pirate vessel—unarmed and unarmoured. Oh, I note controls for a coherent light gun but that wouldn't be much use to a pirate. Nor can I visualize two men and two women attempting to attack a space liner. But keeping the peace is just one of my responsibilities. Your ship, small as it is, could be carrying millions of credits in contraband."

"Say what you mean, Lensman," I snapped. "Drugs. But don't use the word 'zwilnik.'"

Mentally, we could hear him sigh. *"Yes, Doctor Hilda—drugs. But I did not introduce that offensive word into the discussion."*

"I heard you thinking it. Don't do it again!"

"Lensman," Deety said quickly, "we have medical drugs. The only one that could interest you is a few milligrams of morphine. But we carry no thionite, no bentlam, no hadive, no nitrolabe. You are using your Lens; you *know* that I'm telling the truth."

"Captain, it's not that easy. Before I hailed you I did try a slight probe—please, Doctor Hilda; it was in line of duty! I've never encountered minds so fully blocked. And this is a most curious craft. It is obviously designed for aerodynamic use rather than space. Yet here you are—and I can't see how you got here. I have no choice but to detain you and to examine this ship thoroughly. If necessary, take it apart piece by piece."

"Lensman," Deety said earnestly, "don't be hasty. You can search more thoroughly by Lens than by other means. Go ahead. We've nothing to hide and we have a great deal to offer the Patrol. But you *won't* get it by pushing us around."

"You certainly won't! Cap'n, let's leave! I'm tired of stupidity!"—and I snapped, "Gay Sagan!"

Mars-zero was on our starboard bow. That dead rock looked awfully good to me.

Zebbie said, "Captain, did you order the copilot to execute?"

I said, "Don't bother Deety with it, Zebbie. I did it without permission. Solely my decision."

Zebbie frowned unhappily. "Sharpie, I thought you would be our model Girl Scout while Deety is skipper. Why?"

"Zebbie, you can rotate back there in no time. But I would like to be dropped first. Imperial House. Or Minus-J. Somewhere."

"*Why*, Hilda?" my husband asked.

"Jacob, meet your friendly neighborhood zwilnik. Commander Ted Smith of the Galactic Patrol—a fine officer; I'm certain, as Dr. E. E. Smith saw to it that no unworthy person could ever wear the Lens—was getting unpleasantly close. That's why I was so fierce with the poor man."

Deety said, "But, Aunt Hilda, E. E. Smith's world is just the sort of world we've been seeking."

"Maybe we'll go back. But not until I've had a chance to dump two pounds of concentrated extract of Cannabis magnifica. Dr. Wheatstone tells me that it is incredibly valuable in therapy, as the base for endless drugs. But I had a hunch that Commander Smith would confiscate it, impound the Smart Girl, arrest all of us—and convict me. But that isn't all, Zebbie. Doctor Smith created one of the most exciting universes I know of. To read about, *not* to live in. With that endless Boskone War—must have been going on; they were looking for zwilniks—you have to be as smart as Kimball Kinnison to stay alive...and even he gets chopped up now and again. Deety and I need a good baby-cotcher and I'm sure they have them. But we have months to find one. Let's not deliberately back into a war."

Deety didn't hesitate. "I agree with Aunt Hilda. If we go back, it will not be while I'm captain. Hillbilly, you didn't disobey orders; you used your head in an emergency." I thought Deety was going to ask me how and when I got Cannabis magnifica extract...but she didn't.

"Jake," Zebbie said, "we're overruled. Where now, Captain? Earth-*Teh*-one-plus?"

"First we'd better pick a place to spend the night, and hold an election."

"Why, Deety, you've served less than twelve hours!"

"It will be about twenty-four hours when we lift off tomorrow. I'm not going to ask for nominations; we've all had a turn at it; we are now balloting for permanent captain."

I expected Zebbie to be picked. But there were three for me, one for Zebbie—my ballot.

I seemed to be the only one surprised. Zebbie said to Deety, "Ask to be relieved now, hon. The short-timer syndrome is bad for anyone but worse for a C.O.—it demoralizes her crew."

"Aunt Hilda, will you relieve me?"

I pondered it half a second. "I relieve you, Deety."

"Goody! I think I'll take a nap."

"I think you'll take the verniers. Zebbie and Jacob stay in the jobs they're in. Prepare to maneuver. Copilot, set for Oz. If you don't know how, ask your father."

"Set verniers for *Oz*?"

I took a deep breath to calm down. "Before anyone starts asking 'Why?' the answer is: Pipe down and do your job. Before we start on *Teh* axis, I want to ask questions. We talked to Glinda about our problem. We didn't talk directly to the others. I mean Ozma and Professor Wogglebug and the Little Wizard and possibly others. Family, magicians who can install two bathrooms in a Ford and never have it show can also help us spot vermin *if we ask the right questions*. Deety, are you having trouble setting for Oz?"

"Captain, why set verniers? Gay has our parking spot in her perms. Code-word 'Glinda.'"

A few seconds later Gay called out, "Hi, Tik-Tok!"

"Wel-come back, Miss Gay De-cei-ver. Glin-da told me that you would be gone on-ly a few mi-nutes, so I wai-ted here for you. I am deep-ly hap-py to see you a-gain."

XXXVII *The First Law of Biology*

Zeb:

"Stand by to maneuver," I ordered—at the conn by Captain Sharpie's wish. "Hello, Gay."

"Howdy, Zeb. You look hung over."

"I am. Gay Home!"

Arizona was cloudless. "Crater verified, Captain Hilda."

"*Teh* axis one plus—set, Captain," Deety reported.

"Execute!"

"No crater, Cap'n Auntie. No house. Just mountains." Deety added, "*Teh*-one-minus—set."

"Roger, Deety. Routine check, Captain?"

"Voice routine, short schedule." (I think that is what got Sharpie elected permanent C.O.—she never hesitates.)

"Gay Deceiver. Sightseeing trip. Five klicks H-above-G."

"Ogle the yokels at five thousand meters. Let's go!"

"Deety, keep your thumb on the button. Gay—Miami Beach." Below lay a familiar strip city. "Captain?"

"Zebbie, note the crowded streets. Sunny day. Beaches empty. Why?"

"Bogie six o'clock low!" Jake yelped.

"Gay *Zoom!*"

Earth-*Teh*-one-plus swam warm and huge. Opposite us a hurricane approached Texas. I asked, "Want to see more, Captain?"

"Zebadiah, how can we see more when we haven't seen *any*?"

"But Cap'n Sharpie has, Deety. Folks, I'm unenthusiastic about a world where they shoot without challenging. Jake, your bogie *was* a missile?"

"I think so, Zeb. Collision course with Doppler signature over a thousand knots and increasing."

"A missile—out of Homestead-analog, probably. Captain, these blokes are too quick on the trigger."

"Zebbie, I find empty beaches more disturbing. I can think of several reasons why they would be empty on a nice day—all unpleasant."

"Want to check San Diego? I can get more scram time by increasing H-above-G."

"No, we have over forty thousand analogs on this axis; we'll stick to doctrine. Shop each world just long enough to find something wrong—'Black Hats,' war, low technology, no human population, bad climate, overpopulated, or factor X. If we don't find our new Snug Harbor in the next four months, we'll consider returning to Doctor Smith's world."

"Hillbilly, if we wait there to have our babies, then wait again until they are big enough to travel, we'll *never* find Snug Harbor."

"I said, 'consider.' We may find a place to shack up for five months or so, then slam back to Galactic Patrol Prime Base hospital for the Grand Openings. Could be an empty world—no people, pleasant otherwise. Food is now no problem and we get water from Oz. All we lack is television—"

"That's no lack!"

"Deety, I thought you liked 'Star Trek'?"

"Auntie Captain, we've got our own star trek now."

"Hmm—Deety, you and I should go easy on this star trek. I'm going to follow a conservative routine. You're young and healthy and built for it. But I'm having my first one past forty and I'm going to be *very* careful—exercise, diet, rest, the works."

"I surrender. Let's get cracking, Cap'n Hillbilly."

"Take it, Zebbie."

"Copilot, execute!"

Earth-*Teh*-one-minus replaced *Teh*-one-plus. "Jacob, it doesn't look right. Astrogator, I want us up a hundred kilometers, over—make it Mississippi Valley about St. Louis. Want to change attitude?"

"Yes, please. Jake, point Gay at your target; it will skip setting angle." The craft's nose dipped and steadied.

"How's that?"

"Fine, Jake. Deety, set L axis plus transition ninety-nine thousand klicks."

"Set, Zebadiah."

"Execute." We popped out high over fields of ice. "Sneak up on it, Cap'n?"

"Never mind. Zebbie, that's what I call a hard winter."

"A *long* winter. Actually it's summer, I think; Earth-analogs should be in the same place in orbit as Earth. Jake?"

"By theory, yes. Doesn't matter either way; that's glaciation. Deety has set *Teh*-two-plus."

"We can't homestead on an ice sheet. Execute."

"Zebbie, how many ice ages so far?"

"Five, I think. Deety?"

"Five is right, Zebadiah. Plus two worlds with major war, one where they shot at us, and one so radioactive that we got out fast!"

"So we're hitting ice more often than not."

"Five to four has no statistical significance, Zebadiah. At least Aunt Hilda hasn't spotted even one 'Black Hat.'"

"Sharpie, how good are your magic spectacles?"

"Zebbie, if I see them walk, I'll spot 'em, no matter how they're disguised. In the simulations Glinda and Wizard cooked up, I spotted their gait every time Deety identified it by Fourier analysis."

"You feel confident, that's enough."

"Zebbie, I don't have clairvoyance; there wasn't time to train me. But Glinda got me highly tuned to their awkward gait, both with and without splints. I want to discuss something else. According to geologists, when we were home—Earth where we were born, I mean—we were in a brief warm period between glaciations."

"If geologists are right," I admitted.

"If so, we'll usually hit glaciation."

"Probably. '*If*—'"

"Yes, 'if—' But we now know what glaciation looks like. If you and Jacob and Deety can make it a drill, we can flip past ice ages as fast as you spot one."

"We'll speed it up. Jake."

"Zebadiah, *wait!*"

"Why, Deety? We're about to translate."

"Pop, you told me to set for *Teh*-five-plus."

"Jacob?" Captain Sharpie said.

"That's right, Captain."

"What's the trouble, Deety?"

"Aunt Hilda, I said that five-to-four had little statistical significance. But so far, all glaciations have been in *Teh*-minus. That could be chance but—"

"—but doesn't look like it. You want us to explore axis *Teh*-plus first? Astrogator?"

"No, no! Captain Auntie, I would like to see enough of *Teh*-minus to have a significant sample. At least a hundred."

"Jacob?"

"Hilda, if we check in one pseudodirection only—say *Teh*-minus—it'll be four or five times as fast as hunting back and forth between plus and minus. Deety can set with one click; Zeb can yell 'Execute!' as soon as you are satisfied."

"Jacob, we'll get Deety her sample. But faster. Astrogator, have our copilot set *Teh*-six-minus."

"Uh . . . set, Captain."

"When Zebbie says 'Go,' Jacob, you and Deety flip them past as fast as you can *without* waiting for orders. All we'll be looking for is ice ages; we can spot one in a split second. If anyone sees a warm world, yell, 'Stop!' Deety, can Gay count them?"

"She's doing so, Captain. We both are."

"Okay. I'm going to give my magic specs a rest—we're looking for nothing but glaciers versus green worlds. Questions?"

"Run out *Teh*-minus as fast as I can set and translate. Stop when anyone yells. Aye aye, Cap'n Hillbilly honey."

Sharpie nodded to me; I snapped, *"Go!"*

"STOP!" yelped Deety.

"Jacob, I've *never* seen so much ice! Deety, how many martinis would that make?"

"On the rocks or straight up?"

"Never mind; we're out of vermouth. Did you get your sample?"

"Yes, Captain. One hundred ice ages, no warm worlds. I'm satisfied."

"I'm not. Zebbie, I want to extrapolate logarithmically—go to *Teh*-minus-one-thousand, then ten thousand, a hundred thousand, and so on. Jacob?"

Jake looked worried. "Hilda, my scales can be set for vernier setting five, or one hundred thousand. But that translation would take us more than twice around a superhyper great circle—I think."

"Elucidate, please."

"I don't want to get lost. My equations appear to be a description of six-dimensional space of positive curvature; they've worked—so far. But Euclidean geometry and Newtonian mechanics worked as long as our race didn't monkey with velocities approaching the speed of light. Then the approximations weren't close enough. I don't *know* that the plenum can be described with only six space-time coordinates. It might be more than six—possibly *far* more. Mathematics can be used for prediction only *after* test against the real world."

"Jacob, what is the 'real world'?"

"Ouch! Hilda, I don't know. But I'm afraid to get too many quanta away from our world—world-zero, where we were born. I *think* the extrapolation you propose would take us more than twice around a superhyper great circle to— What world, Deety?"

"World-six-thousand-six-hundred-eighty-eight on *Teh*-minus axis, Pop. Unless it's skewed."

"Thanks, Deety. Captain, *if* we arrived there, we could return to Earth-zero by one setting. '*If*—' Instead of a superhyper great circle we might follow a helix or some other curve through dimensions we know not of."

"Pop, you took what I said and fancied it up."

"R.H.I.P., my dear. You will appear as junior author on the monograph you'll write and I'll sign."

"Pop, you're so good to me. Wouldn't Smart Girl return us simply by G, A, Y, H, O, M, E?"

"Those programs instruct a machine that has built into it only six dimensions. Perhaps she would . . . but to our native universe so far from Earth-zero that we would be hopelessly lost. If Zeb and I were bachelors, I would say, 'Let's go!' But we are family men."

"Deety, set the next one. *Teh*-five-plus?"

"Right, Zebadiah. But, Captain Auntie, I'm game! The *long* trip!"

"Me, too," agreed Captain Sharpie.

I said in a tired voice, "Those babies are *ours* as much as they are yours—Jake and I are taking no unnecessary risks. Captain Sharpie, if that doesn't suit you, you can find another astrogator and another chief pilot."

"Mutiny. Deety, shall we pull a 'Lysistrata'?"

"Uh . . . can't we find some reasonable middle ground?"

"Looks like a place to stop for lunch. Sharpie, want to sniff for 'Black Hats'?"

"Take me down, please. About two thousand klicks above ground."

"Will you settle for five?"

"Sissy pants. Yes, if you'll first have Jacob zip us around night side to check for city lights."

"Give her what she wants, Jake, by transiting; an orbit takes too long. 'Give me operations . . . way out on some lonely atoll! For *I* . . . am too young to *diiiie!* I just want to grow old!'"

"You're off key, Zebbie."

"Deety likes my singing. Anybody spot city lights?"

We found no cities. So Jake put us down for lunch on a lonely atoll, Hilda first making certain that it had nothing on it but palm trees. Deety stripped, started exercises.

Hilda joined her; Jake and I set out lunch, having first dressed in stylish tropical skin. The only less-than-idyllic note came from my objecting to Deety's swimming in the lagoon. Hilda backed me up. "Deety, that's not a swimming pool. Anything in it has defenses or couldn't have survived. The first law of biology is eat or be eaten. A shark could have washed over the reef years back, eaten all the fish—and now be delighted to have you for lunch."

"Ugh!"

"Deety, you'd be very tasty," I soothed.

XXXVIII "—under his vine and under his fig tree; and none shall make them afraid—"

Jacob:

Teh-positive took longer to search than *Teh*-negative for the very reason that its analogs were so much like our native planet.

An uninhabited planet could be dismissed in ten minutes; one heavily populated took no longer. A planet at too low a level of culture took hardly longer—a culture with animal-drawn carts and sailing ships as major transport we assumed *not* to have advanced medicine. But most took longer to reject.

At the end of a week we had rejected ninety-seven . . . which left us only 40,000+ to inspect!

That evening, at "Picnic Island," our private atoll, my daughter said, "Cap'n Auntie, we're doing this wrong."

"How, Deetikins?"

"Ninety-seven in a week, over forty thousand to go. At that rate we finish in eight years."

Her husband said, "Deety, we're getting faster."

My beloved said, "Astrogator, do you know more about calculating than does the Copilot?" Zeb shut up. We had learned that when Hilda addressed us by titles, she was speaking *as captain*. I flatter myself that I learned it quickest whereas Zeb was a bit slow. "Go ahead, Deety."

"If we go on checking this way, it won't get better; it will get worse. Here's the first weeks' score"—she passed around her summary; it read:

Earth analogs checked	97
Average time per planet	34 mins 38½ sec
Maximum time	2 days 3 hrs 52 mins

| Minimum time | 13 seconds |
| Median time | 12 mins 07 sec |

I studied it. "Deety, we can reduce that average time. Over two days was *much* too long to check analog twenty-six."

"No, Pop, we should have taken *longer* on twenty-six. It's that thirteen seconds that is bankrupting us."

"Daughter, that's preposter—"

"Chief Pilot."

"Yes, dear?"

"Please let the Copilot finish . . . without interruption." I retired from the field, annoyed, to wait until my advice was indispensable—soon, I felt sure.

"Aunt Hilda, if we gave each analog thirteen seconds, it would take us eighteen and a half days . . . and we would learn nothing. I want to cut the minimum time way, way down—make it routine—and *learn* something. I wish Gay could talk, I do."

"But, dear, she can. We can be in Oz in two minutes. The dirty dishes can wait."

My daughter looked startled. "Pass me the Stupid Hat."

"But we won't go to Oz before tomorrow. We need to figure out what the problem is, first—and I need a night of cuddle with Jacob for the good of my soul." Hilda reached out and took my hand.

Hilda went on, "Deety, remember how fast we mapped Mars-*Tau*-ten-positive once we let Gay do it her way? Isn't there some way to define a locus—then turn her loose?"

We discussed it until bedtime. I set the locus myself by vetoing going past Earth-analog-*Teh*-positive-five-thousand until we were *certain* that no satisfactory analog existed in those first five thousand. "Family," I told them, "call me chicken, to use Zeb's favorite excuse. I know so little about this gadget I invented that I am *always* afraid of getting lost. All rotations have been exactly ninety degrees. In theory I can define a quantum of angle and each such quantum should render accessible another sheaf of universes. In practice I can't do machining of that quality. Even if I could, I would be afraid to risk our necks on a gadget required to count angular quanta.

"But I have another objection—a gut feeling that worlds too far out *Teh* axis will be too strange. Language, culture, even dominant race—I confess to prejudice for human beings, with human odors and dandruff and faults. Supermen or angels would trouble me more than vermin. I know what to do with a 'Black Hat'—*kill it!* But a superman would make me feel so inferior that I would not want to go on living."

Deety clapped. "That's my Pop! Don't worry, Pop; the superman who can give *you* an inferiority complex hasn't been hatched." I *think* she meant that as a compliment.

We worked the parameters down to three: climate warm enough to encourage nudity; population comfortably low; technology high. The first parameter was a defense against B.H. vermin: they require antinudity taboo to bolster their disguises. The last parameter would tend to indicate advanced obstetrics. As for population, *every* major shortcoming of our native planet could be traced to one cause: too many people, not enough planet.

Hilda decided to standardize: one locale, one H-above-G. The locale was (in Earth-zero terminology) Long Beach, California, over its beach one klick H-above-G—dangerously low were it not that Gay would never be in any universe longer than one second. Any speed-of-light weapon can destroy in less than a second, but can its human-cum-machine operators identify a target, bear on it, and fire in one second? We thought not. We *hoped* not.

At analogs of Long Beach, it should be midsummer, hot, dry, and cloudless. If that beach was comfortably filled but not crowded, if the people were nude, if area adjacent to the beach showed high technology by appearance, then that analog should be checked further.

Forty minutes in Oz changed much of our planning.

Tik-Tok was waiting for his lady friend as usual but kept politely quiet while Deety talked with Gay—and so did Zeb and so did I, not because we have Tik-Tok's courtly manners but because Captain Hilda was blunt. Gay understood the Celsius scale, i.e., both freezing and boiling water temperatures lay in her experience and splitting the interval into one hundred parts was no trouble. She had enough parts that needed to be neither too hot nor too cold that awareness of her surroundings both ambient and radiant was as automatic as breathing is for me. As for radio and television (both gauges of technical level) she could sample all infrared flux (as she had done at Windsor City). Crowds on beach? Would it suffice to count bodies on a sample one hundred meters square?

But Gay had a quite *un*-human complaint: "Deety, *why* must I hang around a thousand milliseconds for a job I can do in ten? Don't you trust me?"

So instead of 57 years—or 8 years—or 18½ days—or 11.4 hours—our preliminary survey was complete less than a minute after we left Oz—5000 universes in fifty seconds. Gay Deceiver displayed her results as three curves representing temperature, body count, density of communication-frequency radiation—abscissa for all running from Earth-zero to Earth-analog-5000-*Teh*-plus.

Those curves told one thing at once: No need to search past analog 800; glaciation had returned.

In the lower right corner was displayed: **87.** Zeb asked why. "Nulls," said Deety. "Gay couldn't get readings. Storm, earthquake, war, anything. Gay Deceiver."

"Hi, Deety! We whupped 'em!"

"You surely did, Smart Girl; Tik-Tok will be proud of you. Change scale. Display zero through eight hundred."

As scale expanded, figure 87 dropped to 23. Zeb said, "Deety, I'm curious about those twenty-three. Will you have S.G. display their designations?"

"Certainly, Zebadiah, but may I take it in planned order?"

"Sure but just let me find out first—"

"Astrogator," Sharpie said flatly, "isn't this your day as K.P.?"

We were at Picnic Island, examining results. I suppressed a smile; "slunk" describes the way Zeb left the cabin. Later I was unsurprised to see my tiny treasure giving Zeb an unusually warm hug and kiss. Our Captain has an efficient system of rewards and punishments—never so described.

Deety instructed Gay to eliminate all worlds with a body count higher than that of the Earth-zero beach, and all worlds chillier by five degrees (my daughter was bracketing to avoid false readings from unseasonable weather).

With elimination of high population, cold climate, and low technology as indicated by low or nil flux of communication frequencies, my daughter had us down to seventy-six worlds, plus twenty-three to reexamine—had eliminated over four thousand worlds—and it was still two hours till lunch time!

Deety had Gay display temperatures of the seventy-six. The curve was no longer continuous, but a string of beads, with clumps. I said, "Hilda my love, I'll wager ten back rubs that at least half of the nulls fit into that gap"—and indicated a break at the maximum of the temperature curve.

Hilda hesitated. "Why, Jacob?"

"My dear, figures mean little to me until expressed geometrically. Curves are bold print. I'll give you odds."

"What odds?"

"Don't be suckered, Auntie Cap'n! Pop, I'll take *your* end of the bet, give you two to one, and spot you a point."

A back rub from Deety is a treat; she has strong hands and knows how. But I answered, "Ladies, I must start lunch. Deety, when we make visual check, let's include Antarctica as well as Greenland, at that break."

"Two points, Pop?" I pretended not to hear.

That same day we trimmed it down to six worlds, all warm, all free of body taboos, all high technology, all acceptably low in population, all free of major war or overt preparations, all with some version of English as the major North American language. It was time to pick a world by inspection on the ground.

How to make contact was much discussed. Hilda chopped it by saying: "One way is to land on the White House lawn and say, 'Take me to your leader!' The other is to be as sneaky as a 'Black Hat.' Let me know when you reach consensus." She went through the bulkhead and dogged the door.

An hour later I rapped on the bulkhead; she rejoined us. "Captain," I reported formally, "we have reached consensus. Each is afraid of the open approach; authorities might confiscate our car, we might wind up as prisoners."

"Yes," she agreed. "Twice we just missed it."

"Precisely. The expression 'sneaky as a "Black Hat"' is distasteful—"

"I so intended."

I went doggedly on: "—but sneakiness is not immoral *per se*. A mouse at a cat show is justified in being inconspicuous; so are we. We merely seek information. I am expendable; therefore I will scout on the ground."

"Hold it. This is unanimous? Deety? Zebbie?"

"No," my daughter answered. "I didn't get a vote. You and I are barred from taking risks. Pregnant, you know."

"I certainly do know! Jacob, I asked for consensus on *method*. I did *not* ask for volunteers. I've picked the scout I consider best qualified."

I said, "My dear, I hope you have picked me."

"No, Jacob."

"Then I'm your boy," said Zebbie.

"No, Zebbie. This is spying, not fighting. I'm doing this job myself."

I interrupted, "Hilda, where you go, I go! That's final."

Our captain said gently, "Beloved, I hope you don't stick to that. If you do, we'll elect another skipper. You are my candidate."

"Dear, I was trying to—"

"—take care of me. Nevertheless you are my candidate. Deety is too reckless; Zebbie too cautious. I'll carry out whatever duties you assign, including using the magic spectacles. Are you sticking to that ultimatum?"

"Uh, yes."

"Even though your stubbornness could result in my death? I love you, dear, but I won't take you with me on a spying mission. What happened to that 'All for one and one for all' spirit?"

"Uh . . ."

"Captain!"

"Yes, Zebbie?"

"You proved that you can be tough with your husband. Can you be tough with yourself? Look me in the eye and tell me that you know more about intelligence than I do. Or that you can fight your way out of a rumpus better than *I* can."

"Zebbie, this isn't *military* intelligence. *You* look *me* in the eye and tell me that you know more about *obstetrics* than I do. How do you prepare for leapfrog transfusion and when is it likely to be needed? Define eclampsia. What do you do about placenta previa? I am less likely to get into a rumpus than you are . . . and if I do, I'll throw my arms around his neck and cry. However . . . convince me that you know as much about obstetrics as I do and I'll consider letting you make contacts. In the meantime pick a midwestern town big enough for a fair-sized hospital and public library, and select a point for grounding and rendezvous; you will be in command while I'm gone."

I interrupted. "Hilda, I absolutely forbid—"

"Chief Pilot! Pipe down!" My wife turned her face away from me. "Chief Master at Arms, restore discipline."

"Aye aye, Ma'am! Jake, she means *you*."

"But—"

"Shut up! Crewmen don't give orders to the C.O. and I've had a bellyful of your attempts."

Two hours later I was in Zeb's seat, biting my nails and sweating, while Zeb had my seat. I had given unconditional parole—the alternative having been to go (or be stuffed) through the bulkhead, then wait, locked in. I am not a total fool; I gave my word.

Zeb held us in cloud cover while my daughter, wearing earphones, stayed in contact with Hilda. Gay's cabin speaker was paralleled with the phones so that we could follow in part what went on below. Deety reported, "That fade is from entering a building; I could hear her footsteps. Zebadiah, if I fiddle with the gain, I might miss her as she comes out."

"Don't shift. Wait."

Eternities later we heard Hilda's sweet voice: "I'm heading for rendezvous. I no longer have to pretend that this is a hearing aid— but everybody accepted it as such. You needn't be cautious picking me up; we're leaving."

Five minutes later we bounced and translated at once, then Zeb held her in cruise while Hilda reported:

"No trouble. Ze bewildair' French ladee she zink les Americain' verree gentils. Mais les arts medicals—poof! Infant mortality high, childbirth mortality gruesome. I could have left sooner but I got fascinated."

"Hilda," I protested, "you had me worried to death."

"Jacob, I had to be certain; it's such a nice world otherwise. Other contacts should not take as long as I've solved the money problem."

"How?" Zebadiah asked. "I've been noodling that. There's an even chance that private ownership of gold will be illegal. A standard trick used whenever a government is in trouble."

"Yes, Zebbie—it's illegal there, too. I still have the bullion you had me carry. Instead I sold that heavy gold chain I was wearing. Sorry, Deety; I had to."

"Forget it, Hillbilly. That chain was a way to horde gold. Pop bought it for Mama Jane before they clipped the zeroes and re-monetized."

"Well . . . I found a public phone—didn't try to use it; Edison would never have recognized it. But it had a phone book, so I looked up 'gold'—and found 'licensed gold dealers' and sold your chain—"

"And now you're stuck with a lot of local money."

"Zebbie! See why I didn't let you go down by yourself? The dealer was of course a coin dealer, too—and I bought foreign silver coins, worn, small, oldish dates without being old enough to be collectors' items. French coins, but he didn't have enough, so I filled out with Belgian, Swiss, and German."

I said, "My dear, the coins you bought *there* will *not* be good *here*. Or at the next analog. Or the next."

"Jacob, who—other than a professional—is certain of designs on foreign coins?—especially if they are a few years old and a bit worn. I got real silver, none of those alloys that don't have the right ring to them. At most a shopkeeper will phone his bank and ask for the rate. That's how I bought *this*," my beloved said proudly, pulling out of Deety's biggest purse a World Almanac.

I was not impressed. If she was going to buy a book, why not a technical manual that might contain new art, data Zeb and I could use?

My darling was saying, "We *must* buy one in each analog we ground in. It's the nearest thing to an encyclopedia less than a kilo mass you'll find. History, law, vital statistics, maps, new inventions, new medicine—I could have skipped the library and learned all I needed from this book. Zebbie! Turn to the list of U.S. Presidents."

"Who cares?" Zeb answered, but did so. Shortly he said, "Who is Eisenhower? This shows him serving one of Harriman's terms and one of Patton's."

"Keep going, Zebbie."

"Okay— *No!* I refuse to believe it. Us Carters are taught to shoot straight, bathe every month even in the winter, and *never* run for office."

Two days later Hilda and Zeb, as a French-tourist couple, found the world where we settled.

We slid in quietly, both through the histrionics of our "bewildered French lady" and Zeb's unmalicious chicanery. Sometimes he was our French lady's husband; other times he spoke English slowly with a strong Bavarian accent.

In this analog, the United States (called that, although boundaries differ) is not as smothered in laws, regulations, licensing, and taxes as is our native country. In consequence "illegally entered aliens" do not find it difficult to hide, once they "sling the lingo" and understand local customs.

Hilda and Zeb learned rapidly in a dozen towns, Deety and me "riding shotgun" in the sky. Deety and I learned from them and from radio. Then we moved to the Northwest, "natives" from back east, and coped with our only problem: how to keep Gay Deceiver out of sight.

Hilda and Deety hid her in the Cascades for three days while Zeb and I found and bought a farmhouse outside Tacoma-analog. That night we moved Gay into the barn, slapped white paint on the building's windows, and slept in Gay, with a feeling of being home!

We own six hectares and live in the farmhouse in front of Gay's hideaway. Gay will eventually go underground, protected by reinforced concrete; the barn will become a machine shop. We will build a new house over her bunker. Meanwhile, our old farmhouse is comfortable.

This United States, population under a hundred million, accepts immigrants freely. Zeb considered buying phony papers to let us enter "legally"—but Hilda decided that it was simpler to use Gay to smuggle us while we smuggled Gay. The outcome is the same; we will never be a burden to the state—once we get our machine shop and electronics lab set up, Zeb and I will "invent" hundreds of gadgets this country lacks.

We seem to be near the warmest part of an interglaciation. Wheat grows where our native world has frozen tundra; the Greenland icecap has vanished; lowlands are under water, coastlines much changed.

Climate and custom encourage light clothing; the preposterous "body modesty" taboo does not exist. Clothing is worn for adornment and for protection—never through "shame." Nakedness is symbolic of innocence—these people derive that symbology from the Bible used in our native culture to justify the exact opposite. The *same* Bible—I checked. (The Bible is such a gargantuan collection of conflicting values that anyone can "prove" *anything* from it.)

So this is not a world where alien vermin can hide. A "man" who *at all times* kept arms and legs covered by long sleeves and long trousers would be as conspicuous as one in armor.

The sects here are mostly Christian—on a Saturday morning one sees families headed for church in their finest Sabbath-go-to-meeting clothes. But, since nakedness is symbolic of innocence, they undress in an anteroom to enter their temple unadorned. One need not attend services to see this; the climate favors light, airy structures that are mostly roof and slender columns.

The Bible affects their penal system, again by selective quotation: "Eye for eye, tooth for tooth—"

This results in a fluid code, with no intent to rehabilitate but to make the punishment fit the crime. I saw an example four days after we settled. I was driving our steam wagon and encountered a road block. A policeman told me that I could take a detour or wait twenty minutes; the highway was being used to balance a reckless driver.

I elected to pull over and wait. A man was staked with one leg stretched out at a right angle. A police wagon drove down that cleared highway, ran over his leg, turned and drove back over it.

An ambulance was waiting—but nothing was done for a timed

seventeen minutes. Then surgeons amputated on the spot; the ambulance took him away and the block was removed.

I went back to my wagon and shook for many minutes, then returned home, driving cautiously. I didn't tell our family. But it was reported on radio and the evening paper had pictures—so I admitted that I had seen it. The paper noted that the criminal's insurance had been insufficient to cover the court's award to the victim, so the reckless driver had not only lost his left leg (as had his victim) but also had had most of his worldly goods confiscated.

There is no speed limit and traffic regulations are merely advisory—but there are *extremely* few accidents. I have never encountered such polite and careful drivers.

A poisoner is killed by poison; an arsonist is burned to death. I won't describe what is done to a rapist. But poisoning, arson, and rape are almost unknown.

My encounter with this brutal system of "balancing" almost caused me to think that my dear wife had been mistaken in picking this world—we should move! I am no longer certain. This place has no prisons, almost no crime, and it is the safest place to raise children I've ever heard of.

We are having to relearn history. "The Years of Rising Waters" explain themselves. The change came before 1600; by 1620 new shorelines had stabilized. That had endless consequences—mass migrations, political disorder, a return of the Black Death, and much immigration from Great Britain and the lowlands of Europe while the waters rose.

Slavery never established here. Indentures, yes—many a man indentured himself to get his family away from doomed land. But the circumstances that could have created "King Cotton" were destroyed by rising waters. There are citizens here of African descent but their ancestors were not slaves. Some have indentured ancestors, no doubt—but everyone claims indentured ancestors even if they have to invent them.

Some aspects of history seem to be taboo. I've given up trying to find out what happened in 1965: "The Year They Hanged the Lawyers." When I asked a librarian for a book on that year and decade, he wanted to know why I needed access to records in locked vaults. I left without giving my name. There is free speech—but some subjects are not discussed. Since they are never defined, we try to be careful.

But there is no category "Lawyers" in the telephone book.

Taxation is low, simple—and contains a surprise. The Federal government is supported by a head tax paid by the States, and is mostly for military and foreign affairs. This state derives most of its revenue from real estate taxes. It is a uniform rate set annually, with no property exempted, not even churches, hospitals, or schools—or roads; the best roads are toll roads. The surprise lies in this: *The owner appraises his own property*.

There is a sting in the tail: *Anyone* can buy property *against the owner's wishes* at the appraisal the owner placed on it. The owner can hang on only by raising his appraisal *at once* to a figure so high that no buyer wants it—and pay *three years back taxes* at his *new* appraisal.

This strikes me as loaded with inequity. What if it's a family homestead with great sentimental value? Zeb laughs at me. "Jake, if anybody wants six hectares of hilly land and second-growth timber, we take the profit, climb into Gay—and buy more worthless land elsewhere. In a poker game, you figure what's in the pot."

PART THREE

Death And Resurrection

XXXIX *Random Numbers*

Hilda:

Jacob stood, raised his glass. "Snug Harbor at last!"

Zebbie matched him. "Hear, hear!"

Deety and I sat tight. Zebbie said, "Snap it up, kids!" I ignored him.

Jacob looked concerned. "What's the matter, dear one? Zeb, perhaps they don't feel well."

"It's not that, Jacob. Deety and I are healthy as hogs. It's that toast. For ten days, since we signed the deed, it's been that toast. Our toast *used* to be: 'Death to "Black Hats"!'"

"But, my dear, I promised you a new Snug Harbor. The fact that you girls are having babies made that first priority. This is the place. You said so."

I answered, "Jacob, I *never* called this 'Snug Harbor.' I reported that I had found a culture with advanced obstetrics, and customs that made it impossible for 'Black Hats' to hide. I wasn't asked what I thought of it."

"You signed the deed!"

"I had no choice. My contribution was one fur cape and some jewelry. Deety put in more—but effectively no gold. She fetched her stock certificates, other securities, some money—paper—and a few coins. I fetched two twenty-five newdollar bills. Deety and I left Earth as paupers. Each of us women—*not* 'girls'!, Jacob—was once wealthy in her own right. But in buying this place, you two decided, you two paid for it—all we did was sign. We had no choice."

Zebbie looked at Deety and said softly, "'With all my worldly goods I thee endow,'" and took her hand.

Jacob said, "Thanks, Zeb. I, too, Hilda—if you don't believe that, then you don't believe I meant the rest: '—for richer, for poorer, in sickness and in health—' But I did and I do." He looked up. "Zeb, where did we go wrong?"

"Durned if I know, Jake. Deety, what's the score? Give."

"I'll try, Zebadiah. Maybe all we should expect is washing dishes and wiping noses and changing diapers. But that doesn't seem like a be-all and end-all when you've gone banging around the universes...stood guard for your husband while he bathed in a mountain stream...or— Oh, the devil with it! This place is good and clean and wholesome and *dull!* I'll find myself joining the church just for company...then sleeping with the priest out of boredom!"

"Deety, Deety!"

"I'm sorry, Zebadiah. It would be boredom with *Beulahland,* not with you. The very hour we met, you saved my life; you married me before that hour was over, impregnated me before midnight, fought and killed for me only days later, saved my life twice more that same day, took me to another planet in another universe before midnight *still* that same day...and short hours later had again fought for me, twice. You are my gallant knight, sans peur et sans reproche. In the six weeks I have known you, you have gifted more romance, more glorious adventure, into my life than in all the twenty-two years before it. But the last twelve days—especially the last ten—have told me what we *now* look forward to."

Deety paused to sigh; I said quietly, "She speaks for me."

Deety went on, "You two would lay down your lives for us—you've come terrifyingly close. But what happened to your glorious schemes to rebuild the Solar System? To kill every last one of those vermin? Gay Deceiver sits in an old barn, dark and quiet—and today I heard you discussing how to market a can opener. Universes beyond the sky to the incredible Number of the Beast!—yet you plan to sell can openers while Hilda and I serve as brood mares. We haven't even visted Proxima Centauri! Zebadiah—Pop!—let's spend tonight looking for an Earth-type planet around Alpha Centauri—kill a million vermin to clean it, if that's what it takes! Plan what planets to put on Earth's Lagrange points. I'll write programs to meet your grandest plans! *Let's go!*"

My husband looked sad. Zebbie held Deety's hand and said, "Deety, we don't want to sell can openers. But you two *are* pregnant and we've gone to a lot of trouble to put you where you and our kids will be safe. Maybe it's dull . . . but it's your duty. Forget hunting vermin."

"Just forget it? Zebadiah, why is Gay Deceiver loaded and ready for space? Power packs charged, water tanks full, everything? Do you and Pop have something in mind . . . while Hilda and I stay home and baby-sit?"

"Deety, if we did, it wouldn't hurt to sell a few can openers first. You two and the kids must be provided for, come what may."

"That Widow's Walk again, Hillbilly. But, my husband, you have started from a false premise. You men want to protect Hilda and me and our kids at any cost—and we honor you for it. But one generation is as valuable as another, and men are as valuable as women. With modern weapons, a computer programmer is more use in war than a sniper. Or—forgive me, sir!—even an aerospace fighter pilot. I'm a programmer. I can shoot, *too!* I won't be left out, I won't!"

I gave Deety our signal to drop it. It doesn't do to push a man too hard; it makes him stubborn. One can't expect logic from males; they think with their testicles and act from their emotions. And one must be careful not to overload them. We had given them five points to stew over; we would save the sixth—the clincher—for later.

I waited three days . . . and struck from the other flank. Again Deety and I rehearsed: We would wrangle with each other and appeal to the men for support—crosswise.

"Jacob, what is 'random'? Is it correct to say that 'random' is shorthand for 'I don't know'?"

Deety said scornfully, "Don't let her trap you, Pop. She's got the second law of thermodynamics mixed up with the second law of robotics—and doesn't understand either one." (I had to phrase this and insist; Deety didn't want to say it. Deety is sweet, not the bitch I am.)

"'Random' is used a number of ways, my love, but it usually means a set in which the members are equal in probability of experiencing some event, such as being next to be chosen."

"If they're 'chosen,' how can it be 'random'?"

Deety snickered.

Zebbie said, "Don't let him snow you, Sharpie; 'random' means 'I don't know'—as you said."

"Aunt Hilda, pay no attention to Zebadiah. 'Random' is what you have when you maximize entropy."

"Now, Daughter, that is hardly a mathematical statement—"

"Pop, if I gave it to her in mathematical language she'd faint."

"Deety, quit picking on Sharpie," Zebbie said sternly.

"I wasn't picking on her. Hillbilly has this silly notion that we didn't get anywhere hunting vermin because we went about it systematically . . . but every time we told Gay to shake up her random numbers and do as she pleased, we got results."

"Well, didn't we?" I put in, intentionally shrill. "We had endless failures . . . but every time we gave Gay her head—'Put her on random numbers,' as Deety says—we never had a failure. 'Random' and 'chance' are not related. 'Random chance' is a nonsense expression."

"Auntie darling, you're out of your skull. Don't worry, Pop; pregnant women often get the vapors."

I indignantly listed things that could not be "random" or "chance"—then "discovered" that Deety and I had to start dinner. We left them wrangling, and were careful not to giggle within earshot.

After dinner, instead of that tired toast, Jacob said, "Hilda, would you explain your concept of 'random'? Zeb and I have been discussing it and agree that there is some factor in our adventures not subject to analysis."

"Jake, that's *your* statement. I just said, 'I dunno,' and wiped the drool off my chin. Tell us, Sharpie."

"But Jacob told us a month ago. There isn't any such thing as 'chance.' It's a way of admitting ignorance. I thought that I had begun to understand it when we started hitting storybook universes. Lilliput. Oz. Dr. Smith's World. Wonderland. I was so sure of it— You remember three weeks ago after our second visit to Oz? I ordered a day of rest; we spent it on *Tau* axis instead of *Teh*."

"Dullest day we had," said Zebbie. "You put us in orbit around Mars. Not just one Mars but dozens. Hundreds. The only one worth a fiat dollar was the one we aren't going back to. I got permission to go off duty and take a nap."

"You weren't on duty, Zebbie. You three slept or read or played crib. But *I* was searching for Barsoom. Not hundreds, Zebbie— *thousands*. I didn't find it."

"Hillbilly, you didn't tell me!"

"Dejah Thoris, why bother to say that I had been chasing the Wild Goose? I swallowed my disappointment; next day we started searching *Teh* axis . . . and wound up here. Would I have found Barsoom had I asked Gay to run the search? Defined her limits, yes—as Zebbie did on Mars-ten—but, having defined it, told her to take her random numbers and find it. It worked on Mars-ten;

we mapped a whole planet in a few hours. It worked on *Teh* axis. Why wouldn't it be best for another search?"

Jacob answered, "Dearest, Zeb fed Gay a defined locus. But how would that apply to this, uh, speculative . . . search?"

"Jacob, Zebbie told us that Gay holds the Aerospace Almanac. That includes details about the Solar System, does it not?"

"More than I want to know," Zebbie agreed.

"So Gay knows the Solar System," I went on. "I thought of reading the Barsoom stories to Gay, tell her to treat them as surface conditions on the fourth planet—then take her random numbers and *find* it."

Jacob said gently, "Beloved, the autopilot doesn't really understand English."

"She does in Oz!"

My husband looked startled. Jacob has immense imagination . . . all in one direction. Unless one jogs him. Zebbie caught it faster. "Sharpie, you would be loading her with thousands of bytes unnecessarily. Deety, if they've got those novels on New Earth—I'll find out—what do you need to abstract in order to add to Gay's registers an exact description of Barsoom, so that Gay can identify it—and stop her Drunkard's Walk?"

"Don't need books," my stepdaughter answered. "Got 'em up here." She touched her pretty strawberry-blonde curls. "Mmm . . . go to sleep thinking about it, tell it to Gay early tomorrow before I speak to anybody. Minimum bytes, no errors. Uh . . . no appetizer."

"A great sacrifice, merely for science."

"A one-eyed Texas honeybutter stack? . . . and the prospect of meeting the original Dejah Thoris? Never wears anything but jewels and is the most beautiful woman of two planets."

"About that stack—Jane's buttermilk recipe?"

"Of course. You're not interested in the most beautiful woman of two planets?"

"I'm a growing boy. And ain't about to be trapped into damaging admissions." Zebbie stopped to kiss Deety's retroussé nose and added, "Sharpie, Gay can't handle the full Number of the Beast and anyhow Jake locked off most of it. What's the reduced number, Jake?"

Deety promptly said, "Six to the sixth. Forty-six thousand, six hundred, fifty-six."

Zebbie shook his head. "Still too many."

Deety said sweetly, "Zebadiah, would you care to bet?"

"Wench, have you been monkeying with Gay?"

"Zebadiah, you put me in charge of programming. I have *not* changed her circuitry. But I learned that she has four registers of random numbers, accessible in rotation."

"A notion of my own, Deety. Give them down time. Keep entropy at maximum."

Deety did not answer. Her face assumed her no-expression. Her nipples were down. I kept quiet.

Zebbie noted it also—he does check her barometer; he once told me so. When silence had become painful, he said, "Deety, did I goof?"

"Yessir."

"Can you correct it?"

"Do you wish me to, Zebadiah?"

"If you know how, I want it done soonest. If you need a micro electrician, I have my loupe and my micro soldering gear."

"Not necessary, Zebadiah." My stepdaughter made a long arm, got a walky-talky we keep indoors—with six hectares, it is convenient to carry one outside the house. "Gay Deceiver."

"Hi, Deety," came this tiny voice from the ear button. Deety did not place it in her ear. "Hello, Gay. More gain...more gain...gain okay. Retrieve Turing program Modnar. Execute."

"Executed. Did he chew the bit?"

"Goodnight, Gay. Over."

"Sleep tight, Deety. Roger and out."

I cut in fast. "Gentlemen, the dishes can sit overnight. I vote for a ramble among the universes, say two hours, then early to bed. The other choice is, I think, channel one with the Beulahland Choir and channel two with *Bible Stories Retold:* 'The Walls of Jericho.' Both are highly recommended...by their sponsors."

It felt good to be back in a jump suit. I was turning out lights, making sure windows were fastened, gathering up one walky-talky, when Zebbie stuck his head into the kitchen from the back door. "Captain?"

"Huh? Zebbie, do you mean *me?*"

"You're the only captain around, Sharpie. What I started to report was: 'Captain, your car is ready.'"

"Thank you, First Officer."

He waited for me to put the butter away, then locked the back door behind me, opened the barn's people door. I noted that the big doors were still closed—and remembered my borrowed panties four weeks and many universes away. I squirmed past Deety, got into my old familiar starboard-aft seat with a song in my heart.

Shortly Deety said, "Starboard door seal checked, First Officer."

"Roger. Captain, ready for space."

"Thank you. Has anyone left behind anything normally carried?"

"No, Captain. I replaced worn-out clothes. Added tools I could buy here."

"Zebbie, it sounds as if you expected to lift without warning."

"Habit, Captain. I've kept anything important in my—our—car rather than in that flat. Some I duplicated. Teethbreesh. Iodine. Some clothes." Zebbie added, "Jake keeps basics here, too. 'Be prepared!' Troop ninety-seven, Cleveland."

"Jacob? Anything you need?"

"No, Captain. *Let's go!*"

"We will, dear. Deety, did you give Zebbie a schedule?"

"The one you planned. Not Barsoom, just fun. Two hours."

"Astrogator, take the conn. Carry out schedule."

"Aye aye, Ma'am. Gay Deceiver."

"Hi, Zeb. This is great! Whyinhell did you lobotomize me?"

"Because I'm stupid. Random walk, Gay—transitions, translations, rotations, vectors, under all safety rules. Two hours. Five-second stops subject to 'Hold' from any of us."

"May I place a 'Hold' myself?"

"Captain?"

I resorted to sophistry. "Astrogator, you said 'any of us'—which includes Gay."

"Gay, paraphrase acknowledge."

"I shall make unplanned excursions of all sorts with five-second pause at each vertex, plus 'Hold' option, plus safety restrictions, for two hours, then return here. Assumption: Program subject to variation by Captain or surrogate. Assumption confirmed?"

I was astonished. Deety had told me that Gay would sound almost alive if Zebbie used her full potential . . . but Gay sounded *more* alive, *more* alert, than she had in Oz.

"Assumption confirmed," Zebbie answered. "Execute!"

For ten minutes—one hundred thirteen shifts—we had a "slide show" of universes from commonplace to weird beyond comprehension, when suddenly Gay told herself "Hold!" and added, "Ship ahoy!"

"Private Yacht Dora," she was answered. "Is that you, Gay? What took you so long?"

I said, "Astrogator, I have the conn." I was startled and scared.

But a captain commands—or admits she can't cut it and jumps overboard. A captain can be wrong—she can*not* be uncertain.

Gay was saying rapidly: "Captain, I am not transmitting. I advise asking for Dora's captain. I have transmitted: 'Yes, this is Gay, Dora. I'm not late; we took the scenic route. Pipe down, girl, and put your skipper on.' Captain, the mike is yours; they can't hear me or any other voice inside me."

"Thank you, Gay. Captain Hilda, master of Gay Deceiver, hailing Private Yacht Dora. Captain of Dora, please come in."

In our central display appeared a face. We do *not* have television. This picture was flat rather than 3-D and not in color, just the greenish bright of radar. Nevertheless, it was a face, and lip movements matched words. "I'm Captain Long, Captain Hilda. We've been expecting you. Will you come aboard?"

("Come aboard?"! So this is what comes of running around the universes in a modified duo, without so much as a pressure suit.) "Thank you, Captain Long, but I can't accept. No air locks."

"We anticipated that, Captain. Dora's radius-nine-oh hold has been modified for Gay Deceiver. If you will do us the honor, we will take you inboard. Your wings are raked back, are they not? Hypersonic?"

"Yes."

"I will move slowly, become dead in space with respect to you, then reorient and move to surround you as gently as a kiss."

"If the Captain pleases— It is my duty to advise her if I see a mistake in prospect."

I barely whispered. "Zebbie, you're advising me not to?"

"Hell, no," he answered aloud, secure in the knowledge that his voice would be filtered out. "Do it! What do we have to lose? Aside from our lives. And we're sort o' used to that."

I answered, "Captain Long, you may take us inboard."

"Thank you, Captain. The Dora will arrive in—I'm sorry; what time units do you use?"

Deety interrupted: "Gay, let my voice through. Captain Long—"

"Yes. You are not Captain Hilda?"

"I'm Deety. We call our units 'seconds.' These are seconds: one . . . two . . . three . . . four . . . five . . . six . . . seven . . . eight—"

"Synchronized! We call ours 'Galactic seconds' or simply 'seconds' but about three percent longer than yours. Dora will be almost touching your bow in . . . fifty-seven of your seconds."

Spooky— Blackness blotting out stars, getting bigger. As it began to surround us, Jacob switched on forward grounding lights; we were entering a tunnel—being envaginated by it—with great precision and no apparent power—and it was clear that this enormous sheath was designed to fit us, even to alcoves for Gay's doors. Shortly we were abreast them—cheerful to see that they were lighted. Oddest, we now seemed to be under gravity—perhaps midway between that of Earth-zero and Mars-ten.

"Outer doors closing," came Captain Long's voice. "Closed and sealing. Pressure adjusting. Captain, we use nitrogen and oxygen, four to one, plus carbon dioxide sufficient to maintain breathing reflex. If content or pressure does not suit you, please tell me."

"The mix described will suit us, Captain."

"Don't hesitate to complain. Pressure equalized. Debark either side, but I am on your starboard side, with my sister."

I squirmed past Deety in order to introduce my family. Just as well, it gave me a chance to see them first. None of us can be shocked by skin but we *can* be surprised. But I've been practicing not showing surprise since grammar school as a major defense of my *persona*.

Here were two shapely young women, one with four stripes on each shoulder (painted? decals?), the other in three stripes—plus friendly smiles. "I'm Captain Long," said the one with four stripes.

"—and her mutinous crew," echoed the other.

"Commander Laurie, my twin sister."

"Only we aren't, because—"

"—we're triplets."

"Mutinies are limited to the midwatch—"

"—so as not to disturb passengers, of which—"

"—we have two more. Knock it off, Laurie, and—"

"—show them to their quarters. Aye aye, Cap'n."

"Hey! Don't *I* get introduced!" From all around came the voice that had hailed us.

"Sorry," said Captain Long. "That's our untwin sister, Dora. She runs many of the ship's functions."

"I run *everything*," Dora asserted. "Laz and Lor are purely ornamental. Which one of you jokers shut off Gay?"

"Dora!"

"I retract the word 'jokers.'"

"It would be kind," Captain Long told me, "to let them chat.

Our thought processes are so much slower than hers that a talk with another computer is a treat."

"Deety?" I asked.

"I'll wake her, Captain. Gay won't go off and leave us."

Captain Long's mouth twitched. "She can't. Those outer doors are armor."

I decided not to hear. Instead I said, "Captain, your ship is *beautiful*."

"Thank you. Let us show you to your quarters."

"We planned to be away only two hours."

"I don't *think* that is a problem. Dora?"

"Time-irrelevant. They left home four-minus standard seconds ago; their planet is on a *different* duration axis. Neat, huh? For protein-type purposes they'll get home when they left; I won't even have to figure interval and reinsert them. Couple of weeks, couple of years—still four-minus seconds. Laz-Lor, we've lucked again!"

Gay's voice (also from all around us) confirmed it: "Captain Hilda, Dora is right. I'm teaching her six-dimensional geometry; it's new to her. When they are home—not just time-irrelevant—they march in *Tau* duration with Earth-Prime on 't' axis—one we never explored."

Jacob jerked his head up, looked for the voice. "But that's prepos—"

I interrupted. "Jacob!"

"Eh? Yes, Hilda?"

"Let's complete introductions, then go to the quarters the Captain offered us."

"Introductions can be considered complete, Captain Hilda. 'Deety' has to be Doctor D.T. Burroughs Carter; the gentleman you called 'Jacob' must be your husband Doctor Jacob J. Burroughs. Therefore, the tall handsome young man is Doctor Zebadiah J. Carter, Doctor D.T.'s husband. Those are the people we were sent to fetch."

I didn't argue.

We followed a curving passageway, me with the Captain, her sister with my family. "One question, Captain?" I inquired. "Is nudity uniform in your ship? I don't even have captain's insignia."

"May I give you a pair of stickums?"

"Do I need them?"

"As you please. I put these on just to receive you. People wear what they wish; Dora keeps the ship comfortable. She's a good housekeeper."

"What are your passengers wearing?"

"When I left the lounge, one was wearing perfume; the other had a sheet wrapped as a toga. Does your planet have dress taboos? If you will define them, we will try to make you feel at home." She added, "Here are your quarters. If they don't please you, tell Dora. She'll rearrange partitions, or convert double beds into one giant bed, or four single beds, or any combination; we want you to be comfortable. When you feel like coming out, Dora will lead you."

As the door contracted Jacob said, "You've proved your theories, Hilda. We've fallen into another story."

XL   "Is there a mathematician in the house?"

Deety:

That suite had one bath—pardon me; "refresher"—bigger than three ordinary bathrooms. Hillbilly and I might be there yet, bathing and trying new gadgets, if Pop and Zebadiah hadn't used brute force.

"Captain Auntie, what are you going to wear?"

"Chanel Number Five."

"Clothes, I mean."

"'*Clothes*'? When our hostess is wearing skin? Jane brought you up better than that."

"Wanted to be sure. That you'll back me up with Zebadiah, I mean."

"If Zebbie gets irrational, I'll pin his ears back. If Jacob is ashamed of his skinny runt, he will be wise not to say so. Gentlemen, are you going to chicken? I mean: 'Which way are you going to chicken?'"

"Jake, they're picking on us again."

"Ignore them, comrade. Here are blue briefs your size. Hey!—with a stuffed codpiece! I'll wear them myself."

"Jacob!"

"Listen to the woman. Naked as a peeled egg, planning to meet strangers—and snapping at me for wanting to boast a little. Time was, my small and sultry bride, that a gentleman never left his chambers without a codpiece equal to his status."

Auntie countered with: "Jacob, I spoke hastily. Shouldn't the second-in-command wear a larger codpiece than the pilot? '—equal to his status,' you said."

"But Allah took care of Zeb. *Surely* you've noticed, beloved?"

My husband butted in. "Jake! No barroom betting! Wear the blue; I'll take these red ones."

Zebadiah couldn't get into the red briefs; the blue pair was too big for Pop. They traded. Same story. They traded back—each pair was too small. By great effort they got them on—they fell off.

Pop chucked his aside. "Dora!"

"Yes, sir."

"Please connect me with your captain."

"I was just funning! You wouldn't tell on me—would you?"

Aunt Hilda took over. "He won't tell, Dora. Are you and Gay getting acquainted?"

"We sure are! Gay's been more places than I have—and I've been *everywhere*. She's a smart girl!"

"We think so, thank you. What should our men wear?"

"I hold ambient at twenty-seven and deck pads a degree warmer; why wear anything? But for fetishists I supply minilaplaps of opaque tissue. In the 'fresher, cubby nine-bee. Better get them to a therapist before those symptoms get infected. Good therapists where we're going."

I went looking for stowage 9-b; Aunt Hilda went on talking. "Where is that, Dora?"

"Please address such questions to the Captain. As housekeeper I can tell you anything. As astrogator I must refer questions—I mean they made me put a choke filter on that circuit! Is that fair? I ask you! I'm older than the twins."

"It depends on the ship," Aunt Hilda said, carefully not answering. "We each do what we do best; age is not a factor. Ask Gay."

"Oh, she's hooked in."

"Sure am, Cap'n Hilda honey, through Dora's ears—*and* eyes! Say, you look just like your voice—that's a compliment."

"Why, thank you, Gay!"

I interrupted: "Dora, are these laplaps?"

"Of course. But while we're all here— You don't need two 'freshers in a ship that small. Gay needs the space for a Turing mod I'll help with. So if the fetishists will clear their gear out of Buster Brown and—" Dora broke off suddenly: "The Captain will be pleased to receive the Captain and ship's company of Gay Deceiver in the lounge at her convenience. That means 'Right now.' Follow me—little blue light."

I had been trying on a green laplap. They didn't weigh *anything*. Like wrapping fog around your hips. I snatched it off and wrapped it around Zebadiah: "That's the nearest to nothing you'll ever wear, Zebadiah, but it does the trick." (I don't blame men for being shy. Our plumbing is out of sight, mostly, but theirs is airconditioned and ofttimes embarrassingly semaphoric. Embarrasses *them*, I mean; women find it interesting, often amusing. My nipples show my emotions, too—but in the culture in which I grew up nipples don't count that much.)

The little blue light led us around, then inboard. This "yacht" was large enough to get lost in. "Dora, can you see and hear in every part of the ship?"

"Of course," the blue light answered. "But in the Commodore's suite, I can scan only by invitation. R.H.I.P. Lounge straight ahead. Call me if you want me. Midnight snacks a house specialty. I'm the best." The little light flicked out.

The lounge was circular and large; four people were gathered in one corner. (How does a circle have a corner? By arranging contours and cushions and nibble foods and a bar to turn it into a chummy space.) Two were the twins; they had peeled off the stickums which left no way to tell them apart.

The others were a young woman and a man who looked fortyish. He wasn't the one wearing a sheet; the young woman was. He was wearing much the same as our men but more like a kilt and in a plaid design.

One twin took charge: "Commodore Sheffield, this is Captain Hilda, First Officer Carter, Chief Pilot Burroughs, Copilot Deety Carter. You've all met my sister but not our cousin, Elizabeth Long."

"Now introduce us over again," ordered "Commodore Sheffield." ("Commodore Sheffield" indeed! Whom did he think he was fooling?)

"Yes, sir. Doctor Jacob Burroughs and his wife Hilda, Doctor

Zebadiah Carter and his wife Doctor Deety Burroughs Carter. Doctor Elizabeth Long, Doctor Aaron Sheffield."

"Wait a half," my husband interrupted. "If you're going to do that, I must add that Captain Hilda has more doctorates than all the three of us, together."

Captain Long looked at her sister: "Lor, I feel naked."

"Laz, you *are* naked."

"Not where it matters. Commodore, do you still own that diploma mill in New Rome? What are you charging for doctor's degrees? Nothing fancy, say a Ph.D. in theory of solid state. One for each of us."

"How about a family discount, Ol' Buddy Boy?"

The "Commodore" glanced at the overhead. "Dora, keep out of this."

"Why? *I* want a doctor's degree, *too*. *I* taught them solid state."

He looked at the young woman in (half out of) the sheet. "Does Dora have a point?"

"She does."

"Dora, you get the same treatment as your sisters. Now shut up. All three are declared special doctoral candidates, B.I.T., required residence and courses completed—but writtens and orals as tough as you think you are smart. That diploma mill— Certainly I own it. It's for suckers. You three must produce. Two regents being present, it's official. Dora, tell Teena."

"You betcha, Buddy Boy! 'Doctor Dora'—won't *that* be neat?"

"Pipe down. Friends, these twin sisters could have several doctorates by now, had they chosen to bury themselves on a campus. They are geniuses—"

"Hear, hear!"

"—and the Long family is proud of them. But erratic, insecure, unpredictable, and you turn your backs at your own risk. Nevertheless they are my favorite sisters and I love them very much."

They looked at each other. "He acknowledged us."

"It took him much too long."

"Let's be big about it."

"Both sides?"

"Now!"—they bowled him off his feet. He was standing—they hit with the same vector, with a quick assist from their "sister" Dora (she cut the gravity field for two tenths of a second), and sent him in a complete back flip. He bounced on his arse.

He seemed undisturbed. "Beautifully timed, girls. Pax?"

"'Pax,'" they answered, bounded to their feet, pulled him to his. "We're proud of you, Buddy Boy; you're shaping up."

I decided to kick it over, learn why we had been kidnapped. Yes, *"kidnapped."* I got to my feet before he could sit down. "And *I* am proud," I said, dropping a deep court curtsy, "to have the honor of meeting the Senior . . . of the Howard Families."

Thunderous silence—

The woman in-and-out of the sheet said, "Lazarus, there was never a chance of getting away with it. These are sophisticated people. They have what you *must* have. Drop your deviousness and throw yourself on their mercy. I'll start it by telling my own experience. But first—"

She got to her feet, letting the sheet drop. "Dora! May I have a long mirror? An inverter if possible—otherwise a three-way."

Dora answered, "Teena can afford such stunts as inverters— I can't; I have a ship to run. Here's your three-way." A partition vanished, replaced by a three-way mirror, lavish in size, taller than I.

She held out her hands to me. "Doctor D.T., will you join me?"

I let her pull me to my feet, stood with her at the mirror. We glanced at ourselves; she turned us around. "Do you all see it? Doctor Hilda, Doctor Carter, Doctor Burroughs? Lazarus, do *you* see it?"

The two she did not address answered. Laz (perhaps Lor) said, "They look as much alike as we do." The other answered, "More." "Except for—" "Shush! It's not polite."

Lazarus said, "I always have to step in it to find it. But I never claimed to be bright."

She didn't answer; we were looking at ourselves in the mirror. The resemblance was so great as to suggest identical twins as with Lapis Lazuli and Lorelei Lee—Yes, I had known at once who they were. Captain Auntie did, too; I'm not sure about our husbands.

Those *are* nice teats—I can admit it when I see them on someone else. It's no virtue to have this or that physical asset; it's ancestry combined with self-obligation to take care of one's body. But a body feature can be pleasing to the owner as well as to others.

Same broad shoulders, same wasp waist, same well-packed, somewhat exaggerated buttocks.

"We're alike another way, too," she said. "What's the fourth root of thirty-seven?"

"Two point four-six-six-three-two-five-seven-one-five. Why?"

"Just testing. Try me."

"What's the Number of the Beast?"

"Uh— Oh! Six sixty-six."

"Try it this way: Six to the sixth power, and that number in turn raised to its sixth power."

"The first part is forty-six thousand, six hundred, fifty-six and— Oh, that's a brute! It would be one and a fraction—one-point-oh-three-plus times ten to the twenty-eighth. Do you know the exact number?"

"Yes but I had a computer crunch it. It's—I'll write it." I glanced around—at once a little waldo handed me a pad and stylus. "Thanks, Dora." I wrote:

10,314,424,798,490,535,546,171,949,056.

"Oh, how beautiful!"

"But not elegant," I answered. "It applies to a six-dee geometry and should be expressed in base six—but we lack nomenclature for base six and our computers don't use it. However—" I wrote:

Base six: $(10^{10})^{10} = 1,000\,000,000\,000,000\,000,000\,000,000\\000,000\,000.$

She looked delighted and clapped. "The same number," I went on, "in its elegant form. But no words that I know by which to read it. That awkward base-ten expression at least can be put into words."

"Mmm, yes—but not easily. 'Ten thousand three hundred and fourteen quadrillion, four hundred twenty-four thousand seven hundred and ninety-eight trillion, four hundred and ninety thousand five hundred and thirty-five billion, five hundred and forty-six milliard, one hundred and seventy-one million, nine hundred and forty-nine thousand, and fifty-six. But I would never say it other than as a stunt."

I blinked at her. "I recognize that nomenclature—just barely. Here is the way I would read it: 'Ten octillion, three hundred fourteen septillion, four hundred twenty-four sextillion, seven hundred ninety-eight quintillion, four hundred ninety quadrillion, five hundred thirty-five trillion, five hundred forty-six billion, one hundred seventy-one million, nine hundred forty-nine thousand, and fifty six.'"

"I was able to follow you by reading your figures at the same time. But base-six is best. Is the number interesting or useful as well as beautiful?"

"Both. It's the number of universes potentially accessible through my father's device."

"I *must* talk with him. Lazarus, shall I tell my story now? It's the proper foundation."

"If you are willing. Not shy about it."

"'Shy'!" She went over and kissed him—a buss *en passant* but one in which time stops. "Old darling, I *was* shy before I found out who I am. Now I'm relaxed, and as bold as need be. New friends, I was introduced as Elizabeth Long, but my first name is usually shortened to a nickname—'Lib.' And, yes, I'm Dr. Long. Mathematics.

"My full name is Elizabeth Andrew Jackson Libby Long."

I was more braced for it having swapped some casual mental calculation with her. I have this trick of letting my features go slack. I don't have to think about it; I've been doing it since I was three when I found that it was sometimes best to keep thoughts to myself.

I did this now and watched my family.

The Hillbilly looked thoughtful, and nodded.

Zebadiah prison-whispered to me: "Sex change."

Pop tackled it systematically. "I recognize the second, third, and fourth names. You were once known by them?"

"Yes."

"Did you have the nickname 'Slipstick'?"

"Yes, and, before that, 'Pinky.'" She ran a hand through her curls and smiled. "Not pink but close enough."

"Now you are a woman. There is no point in guessing; you mentioned a story to tell."

"Yes. Dora, how about a round of drinks? Lazarus, how's your supply of those narcotic sticks?"

Pop said, "None of us smokes."

"These are neither tobacco nor bhang—nor addictive. They produce a mild euphoria. I am not urging you; I want one myself. Thanks, Lazarus, and pass them around. Now about me—

"I was male nearly eight hundred years, then I was killed. I was dead fifteen hundred years, then I was revived. In renewing me it was found that my twenty-third gene pair was a triplet—XXY."

The Hillbilly said, "I see. With Y dominant."

I added: "Twin, Aunt Hilda is a biologist."

"Good! Aunt Hilda— May I call you that? As my twin does?— will you help me with the hard parts?" Lib smiled and it was my smile—a happy grin. "The Y was dominant but the double dose of X bothered me and I didn't know why. I did well enough as a male—thirty years in the Space Navy of Old Home Terra as a result of an officer taking an interest in me and getting me an appointment to its Academy. But I lacked command temperament and spent most of my service as a staff technical officer—I rarely commanded and never a large ship." She grinned again. "But today, as a self-aware female instead of a mixed-up male I do not hesitate to command.

"To go back— I was never easy with boys or men. Shy, solitary, and regarded as queer. Not the idion meaning homosexual . . . I was too shy. Although it probably would have been good for me. I was a 'missing Howard' in those days—after the Interregnum—and it was years after I entered the Navy that the Families found me. I married then, into the Families. Most XXY people are infertile—I was not. In the next seventy years I had twenty-one children and enjoyed living with my wives, enjoyed sex with them, loved our children.

"Which brings us to the escape from Earth led by Lazarus. I was a bachelor, both my wives having remarried. Friends, Lazarus was the first man I ever loved."

"Lib, that has nothing to do with the story! *I* didn't know you were in love with me."

"It has *everything* to do with *my* story. Off and on, for eight centuries, we were partners in exploration. Then I was killed— my own carelessness. Eventually Lazarus and his sisters cremated me by tossing me into the atmosphere of Old Home Terra in a trajectory that would cause ashes to impact near where I was born. Lazarus, they don't seem surprised. Do they disbelieve me?"

"Certainly we believe you!" I interrupted. "But what you've told us isn't news to *us*. What we don't know is how you are now alive and female. Reincarnation?"

"Oh, no! Reincarnation is nonsense."

I found myself irritated. Reincarnation is something I have no opinion about, since a housecleaning I gave my mind after we lost Mama Jane. "You have data?" I demanded.

"Deety, did I step on your toes?"

"No, you didn't, Lib. I asked if you had *data*."

"Well . . . no. But if you assume the truth of the proposition, I think I can show that it leads to a contradiction."

"The negative-proof method. It's tricky, Lib. Ask Georg Cantor."

Lib laughed. "Okay, I will attempt to have no opinion until someone shows me verifiable data, one way or the other."

"I was hoping you had data, Lib, since you've been dead and I haven't. Or don't recall having been."

"But I don't *recall* being dead, either. Just a whale of a blow in the back . . . then dreams I can't remember . . . then someone asking me patiently, again and again, whether I preferred to be

a man or a woman . . . and at last I tracked clearly enough to realize
that the question was serious . . . and I answered, 'Woman'—and
they made me answer that question at least once a day for many
days—and then I went to sleep one night and when I woke, I was
a woman . . . which did not astonish me nearly as much as to learn
that fifteen centuries had passed. Being a woman seemed completely natural. I've had five children now—*borne* five, I mean;
I had sired twenty-one . . . and one was put into me by one of my
own descendants. Lazarus, when are *you* going to knock me up?"

"When the Greeks count time by the Kalends."

"Libby honey, when you want to swing that—if you aren't
joking—check with *me*."

"Thanks, Dora; I'll remember. Lazarus, you will have to explain the paradox; I am just a puppet."

"Isn't it bedtime? We're keeping our guests up."

"Captain Hilda?" Lib inquired.

"Deety is in charge of time."

"Lib, I don't know ship's time yet. I gave you our seconds;
we have sixty seconds to a minute; sixty minutes to an hour;
twenty-four hours in a day. Primitive, eh? Is your time metric?"

"Depends on what you mean, Deety. You work to base 'ten,'
do you not?"

"Yes. I mean: No, I work to base 'two' because I'm a computer
programmer. But I'm used to converting—don't have to think
about it."

"I knew you used 'ten' when I made a guess as to what you
meant by 'six to the sixth power' and you accepted my answer.
We now work to base-one-hundred-twenty for most purposes—
binary one-one-one-one-zero-zero-zero."

"Five-factorial. Sensible. Fits almost any base."

"Yes. We use it for routine work. But in scientific work we
use base-three, because our computers use trinary. I understand
it took Gay and Dora several milliseconds to interface."

"We aren't *that* slow!"

"My apologies, Dora. For some work we use a time scale that
fits trinary. But for daily living, our clock is just like yours—but
three percent slower. Our planet's day is longer."

"By forty-two of your minutes."

"You're quick, Deety. Yes."

"Your computers must be three-phase A.C."

"You are quicker than I was two thousand years ago. And I
was quicker then."

"No way to tell and any computer makes us look like Achilles' tortoise. We had dinner at eighteen. Gay entered Dora about an hour and a quarter later. So for us it's about half past twenty, and we usually go to bed between twenty-two and twenty-three if we get to bed on time which we never do. What time is it in the ship and what is ship's routine?"

The others had let me and my new twin chatter. Now Lazarus said, "If this madhouse has a routine, I've never found it."

"Ol' Buddy Boy, *you* don't have a routine. I run this joint on the bell. Deety, it's just—*bong!*—twenty-one . . . and Lazarus never went to bed that early in all his evil years. Buddy Boy, what are you dodging?"

"Manners, Dora."

"Yes, Pappy. Deety, he's dodging the chicanery with which he fooled even himself . . . because he must admit the triple chicanery he wants to rope you in on—and it takes Gay because I'm not built for it. Until today I never heard of 't,' *Tau* and *Teh*. I thought 't'—that you call *Tau*—was all there was. Aside from paratime in an encapsulation surrounded by irrelevancy such as I am taking us through.

"But back to the corpse caper— Lib got herself killed about eight hundred Post Diaspora. Lazarus slaps her—him—into a tank of LOX, and places him-her-it in orbit, with a beacon. Comes back quick as he can—and can't find Libby's cadaver. Fourteen centuries later my sister Teena, then known as Minerva, sees what should have been obvious, that any irrelevant ship, such as yours truly, is a time machine as well as a starship. A great light dawns on Lazarus; the corpse pickled in LOX is missing because he picked it up earlier. So he tries again, more than a thousand years later and five years earlier—and there it is! So Lazarus and I and Laz-Lor go to 1916 Old-Style-or-Gregorian, Old Home Terra, and bury Lib from the sky into the Ozarks where she—he—was born—which was pretty silly because we chucked her into those Green Hills about a century before she was—he—he was born. A paradox.

"But paradoxes don't trouble us. We live in paratime, Laz-Lor are acute cases of parapsychology, we operate under paradoctrines. Why, take *your* family—four doctors. A double pair o' docs."

"Dora!"

"Pappy, you're jealous. But I'll say this for Lazarus: He's slow but he gets there and has believed all his life that any paradox can be paradoctored. Happens he had lots of time to think after he chucked Lib to a fiery grave because he stayed in that primitive era and got his arse shot off and this caused a long convalescence.

"It occurs to him that, if he found the corpse through going back to shortly *after* he placed it in orbit, he might learn something interesting if he went back just *before* he put Lib's remains in orbit. So when he's well again, he does so, with his whole first team, headed by Doctor Ishtar, the greatest in the business, and I'm outfitted as a hospital with everything from microtomes to cloning capsules.

"So we go there and wait—we don't land. Along comes Lazarus in the clunker that he and Lib used to risk their lives in, and Pappy comes out in a pressure suit and detaches the LOX tank, and Lib is buried in space, waiting for judgment day. We respect Pappy's grief just long enough for him to get out of the way, then I take the tank inside me. Ish gets to work, along with many others. Lots of live cells suitable for cloning. Brain intact. Dead but intact—okay, as all Ish wants are the memory configurations.

"In the course of this, Ishtar learns that the late lamented had the potential to go either way—which is why the Families' best telepathic hypnotist is sent for and keeps asking this clone: When you wake up, what do you want to be? Man or woman?"

"It was much later, Dora. I was already awake."

"Lib hon, you ask *Ish*. You *had* to decide long before you woke. Ish and her hormone artists had to work on you while you were still labile. Matter of fact, you never answered at all; the telepath kept reporting on your emotional state whenever you imagined yourself male, and your state when you imagined yourself female. Ish says that it made you happy to think of yourself as female."

"That's true. I've been ever so much happier as Elizabeth Long than I was as Andy Libby."

"That's it, folks. How Ish turned a mixed-up male into a happy female, fully functional and horny as Howard females always are."

"Dora! We have guests." Lazarus glowered.

"All married. Deety is youngest. Deety, did my bluntness shock you?"

"No, Dora. I'm horny enough to be a Howard myself. And terribly interested in how the great Slipstick Libby turns out to be my twin and *female*."

"Female *without* surgery—none of those fakes done with a knife. But even Ish couldn't have done it had not Lib supplied XXY, so that Ish could balance the clone either XX or XY by careful attention to endocrinal glands. Or could she? Must ask. Ish is genius-cubed, smarter than most computers. Lazarus can now explain his next sleight-of-hand—slightly illegal."

"Hey!" I protested. "How about the corpse jettisoned into the Ozarks, Dora? Who was that?"

"Why, that was Lib."

"Lib is right *here*. I've got my arm around her."

That computer went tsk-tsk-tsk. "Deety. *Doctor* Deety. I just finished telling you that the Lib you are cuddling is a *clone*. After they drained every memory out of that frozen brain, what was left was dog food. Lib got slashed in the spine by the local equivalent of a cave bear. Ripped out her—his—backbone. Once Ish was through with it, Laz froze it again, we took it back and placed it in orbit, where we found it later—to our great surprise."

"How could you be surprised when you put it there yourselves?"

Dora announced, loudly, "Is there a *mathematician* in the house?"

"Stop it, Dora. Thank you for recounting my saga; I learn a little every time I hear it." Lib turned toward me and said softly, "Biological time versus durational time, Twin. Follow the entropy arrow through the loops of biological time and you will see that Lazarus was honestly surprised at every step even though he had—will-had—rigged every surprise. No grammar for it. Deety, I understand that you have studied semantics. Shall we try to devise a grammar for space-time complexities in six curved dimensions? I can't contribute much but I can try to punch holes in your work."

"Love to!" I wasn't fooling. My twin is so sweet that maybe Deety is fairly sweet herself.

XLI   "A cat can be caught in almost any trap once—"

Jacob:

If A, then B. I trust I am a rational mathematician, not one of the romantics who have brought disrepute to our calling through such inanities as defining "infinity" as a number, confusing symbol with referent, or treating ignorance as a datum. When I found myself in the Land of Oz, I did not assume that I had lost my reason. Instead it prepared me emotionally to meet other "fictional" characters.

Stipulated: I may be in a locked ward. But to assume that to be factual serves no purpose other than suicide of personality. I shall act on what my senses report. I am not the bumpkin who said on seeing a giraffe: "There ain't no sich animal."

I find myself in bed with my lovely wife Hilda in sumptuous quarters of star yacht Dora as guests of the utterly fictional "Lazarus Long." Is *this* a reason to try to find the call button in order to ask a still-more-fictional nurse for a nonexistent shot to end this hallucination? This is an excellent bed. As for Hilda— Solomon has reason to envy me; Mahomet with all his houris is not as blessed as I.

Tomorrow is soon enough to unravel any paradox. Or the Day After Tomorrow. Better yet, Not This October. After The End of Eternity may be best.

Why disturb a paradox? As Dora pointed out, Hilda and I are a pair o' docs ourselves . . . with no wish to be disturbed, and most certainly not to be unravelled.

Since Hilda married me, I have not once taken a sleeping pill.

No one called us. I woke up feeling totally rested, found my wife in the 'fresher brushing her teeth with, Yes, Pepsodent— removed brush from mouth, kissed her, placed brush back in her mouth. When she finished brushing her teeth, I asked, "Seen the kids?"

"No, Jacob."

"So. Dora!"

"No need to shout; I'm sitting on your shoulder. Would you like breakfast trays in bed?"

"Have we missed the breakfast hour?"

"Professor Burroughs, breakfast hour in me starts at midnight and ends at noon. Lunch is at thirteen, tea at sixteen-thirty, dinner at twenty, snacks and elevenses at any time. Dinner always formal, no other meal."

"Hmm— How formal is 'formal'?" Hilda now had more wardrobe—but Beulahland is not high style.

"'Formal' means formal dress of your culture or ours, or it means skin. No casual dress. As defined by the Commodore: 'Whole hawg or none.' Amendment: Jewelry, perfume, and cosmetics are not proscribed by the no-casual-dress rule. Ship's services include sixty-minute cleaning and pressing, and a variety of formal dress of New-Rome styling, washables for the convenience of guests who do not travel with formal dress, prefer to be dressed at a formal meal, and do not choose to dine alone."

"Very hospitable. Speaking of washables, we found everything but a dirty-clothes hamper. I have a laplap to put in."

"But that's a washable, Doctor."

"That's what I said. I've worn it; it should be washed."

"Sir, I am not as fluent in English as in Galacta. By 'washable' I mean: Step into a shower while wearing it; it will go away."

Hilda said, "We'll take a dozen gross."

"Captain Hilda, 'dozen' and 'gross' are not in my memories. Will you please rephrase?"

"Just a side remark to my husband, Dora. What are New-Rome high styles today?"

"'Today' I must construe as meaning the latest I have in stock. Styles follow the stock market. In evening dress, men are wearing their skirts floor length with a slight train. Bodices are off one or both shoulders. Bare feet or sandals are acceptable. Colors are bright and may be mixed in discordants. Weapons are required— may be symbolic but must be displayed. Ladies, of course, follow the cycle out of phase. Skirts are hardly more than ruffles this season, worn quite low. If tops are worn—not required this season and some ladies prefer cosmetics in flat colors—if worn, the teat windows may be either open or transparent. Transparents having quarter-lambda iridescence are popular this cycle, especially if one teat is bare without cosmetics while the other sports a changing-iridescent transparency." The computer's voice changed from a well-modulated adult female voice to that of an eager little girl:

"I hope somebody picks that; I like to look at it! How about Doctor Deety and Doctor Lib, one shiny on her left teat, the other shiny on her right, and place them side by side. Neat, huh!"

"It would be spectacular," I agreed. (And they would look like clowns! Still, Deety might go along. The child likes to please people, even a computer. Perhaps especially a computer.)

"You old goat, would you like a skirt with a slight train?"

"Hilda!"

"Dora, do you have formal washables in my husband's size? What measurements do you need?"

"I have the Professor's measurements, Ma'am. I will fetch an assortment to your quarters sometime after noon when you are not sleeping or otherwise engaged. An equivalent assortment for you, I assume?"

"If you wish, Dora. I may not wear that style."

"Captain Hilda is an excellent composition herself. I'm an expert engineer; I know good design when I see it. That's not flattery; Laz-Lor tell me that I should learn to flatter. I'm not sure I have the circuitry for it. Perhaps I can learn it from Gay."

"You sure can, Dorable; I've been flattering my four charges seems like forever."

"Gay, have you been listening?"

"Mad at me, Aunt Hilda?"

"Never angry with our Gay Deceiver. But it's polite to let people know you're present."

"But— Dora has *eyes* and she lets me look."

"Captain Hilda, Gay is with me all the time now. Do you forbid that? We didn't *know*." Dora had slipped into her little-girl voice and sounded stricken.

Time to intervene— "Gay, Dora—Hilda and I don't mind. I'll tell Deety and Zeb; they won't mind."

"Jake, you're my pal!"

"Gay, you've saved our lives many times; we owe you any fun we can offer. But, Gay, with Dora's eyes and ears you'll see and hear things not seen by your radars, not heard unless we switched you on. Do either of you have the word 'discretion' in your perms?"

"No, Jake. What does it mean?"

"I'll explain it," Dora said eagerly. "It means we see and hear but pretend not to. Like last night when—"

"Later, Dora. Over your private circuits. What ship's time is it and are we late for breakfast? I don't see a clock."

"I'm the clock. It is ship's time nine-oh-three. You are not last for breakfast. Commander Laz is sleeping late; she didn't go to bed right after the mutiny. Captain Long—that's Lor—ate on the bridge—a crude insult to my watchstanding but she's good company. The Commodore always eats breakfast in the flag cabin. The Doctors Deety and Zeb and Lib are just starting."

"How are they dressed?" asked my Hilda.

"In serviettes. Doctor Lib is wearing 'Jungle Flower' in cologne and powder and perfume; she likes strong ones. Doctor Zeb seems to have forgotten to use any but his own scent is rather pleasant. I can't place what Doctor Deety is wearing but it has both musk and sandalwood. Shall I formularize it by symbols?"

"It's 'Blue Hour' and I'm startled; my stepdaughter doesn't need a scent. Neither does Lib, darn it. Jacob, are you ready?"

I answered at once. I had taken care of this and that while the computers chattered, including trying a depilatory tricky until I learned how to block it off—my sideburns were missing. Zeb dressed in a serviette— Libby Long the only one not of our family—and Lib used to be male. A good time to rub blue mud in my belly button— "I'm ready."

Hilda noticed my decision by not noticing it. The blue "Tinker-Bell" light appeared, led us to a small dining room, where we encountered a Long-Family custom—did not realize it because it matched a ceremony of our own: Lib saw us, came over, kissed Hilda, kissed me—briefly but with time-stop. Then my daughter was kissing me good-morning while Zeb kissed my wife. We swapped as usual; Deety kissed Hilda—and Zeb took my shoulders, hissed into my ear, "Stand still"—and gave me the double Latin kiss, each cheek.

Did my blood brother think I would let him down in the presence of one not of our family? Our custom had started after our double elopement. While Zeb and I usually used the Latin symbol, four rapid pecks, once at Snug Harbor we had missed the fast timing, hit each other mouth to mouth—didn't pull back but didn't stretch it out. We declined to make anything of it—although I was aware of the break in taboo and he was, too.

Two mornings later I was last in; Zeb was seated with his back to me. He leaned back and turned his head to speak to me; I leaned down, kissed him on the mouth firmly but briefly, moved on and kissed my daughter not as briefly, moved on and kissed my wife thoroughly, sat down and demanded, "What's for breakfast?"

After that the only invariant was: "What's for breakfast?" Zeb and I used either Latin pecks or busses on the mouth—brief, dry, symbolic, initiated by either of us. It meant that we were closer than a handshake; it held no sexual significance.

So I was disgrunted that Zeb thought it was necessary to warn me. Let me add: Women are my orientation and Hilda my necessity. But I tried the other way with my high school chum our graduation week. We were experimenting to find out what the shooting was all about—planned but date subject to opportunity—which turned up that last week of school. A two-hour examination, no other school that day; a half hour of tennis, sudden realization that we were free and that his parents' flat was empty and would remain so until late afternoon. *Der Tag!*

We gave it a fair trial. We bathed first and thoroughly. We were not shy or afraid of each other. We were not afraid of getting caught—doors locked and bolted, chains on, S.O.P. by his parents' rules. We liked each other and *wanted* it to work.

Total failure—

Got up, had peanut-butter-and-jelly sandwiches with milk, discussed it as we ate. Neither of us upset, not disgusted, no bad breath or similar hazards—but no results.

Brushed our teeth again, washed each other—gave it a second try. So much calisthenics. No "morals" about it, willing and eager to add it on. Not for us—so we killed all evidence and got in three more sets of tennis.

That's how it is with Zeb and me. I love him dearly—but I love him for what he *is*—while fully empathizing that my daughter thinks he is the greatest lover since— Well, the *greatest*.

But if Zeb ever makes a pass at me, I will do my amateur-acting best to make him feel that *this* is what I have been waiting for all my life.

I've been trying to say why I was miffed. Never mind, I shall make it clear to Zeb that I will *never* let him down.

About that Long-Family custom— "Long" is not the name of a Howard Family; it is a group of Howards who live together and who added "Long" (the pseudonym most used by Lazarus) to their regular names. It's a commune, an extended family, a serial family, a god-knows-what. There is probably no word for it in any language and at least two computers are full members. They come and go and raise children and only the family geneticist (Doctor Ishtar) is sure of parentage and who cares? I suspect that they are all ambi in sex but no outsider could guess—and I am an outsider.

But of this I am certain: When Long meets Long for the first time any day, they kiss—and it's no Latin peck.

I learned that I could have anything I wanted for breakfast. This should have been enough to tell me that we were being set up for the tale. I'm getting ahead of my story, as I know things about the Long Family that I read in a book that you may not have read. This ship Dora came from a planet many parsecs from the Earth-analog of that universe, from a time over two thousand years in my future looked at one way . . . or a time totally irrelevant to mine through not having duration axis in common.

Yet I could have *anything:* Post Toasties, hens' eggs any style, bacon, ham, sausage, breakfast steak, toast, orange marmalade, Concord grape jelly, buckwheat cakes—and *not one* of these foods is from Tertius, home of the Long Family.

Pepsodent in our 'fresher—

As I was contemplating a beautiful golden waffle with one bite of it melting in my mouth, Lazarus Long walked in . . . and a voice in my head played back: *"The Commodore always eats breakfast in the flag cabin."*

Add that Lazarus was dressed as were Zeb and I save that he did not yet have a napkin.

Working hypothesis: Lazarus had listened in on every word between husband and wife.

Second hypothesis: "Dora, tell me when they get up, tell me when they arrive in the breakfast room—if they do, but offer trays as usual. If they eat in the breakfast room, let me know how each is dressed."

The first hypothesis defines a grave social offense; the second outlines information a host or hostess is entitled to know. How do I find out which is which? Answer: I can't, as Lazarus Long will give me the answer that profits him and that computer is loyal to him, not to me.

As soon as Lazarus finished kissing Lib Long, he was grabbed by Deety and kissed . . . then he caught Hilda's eye, glanced at me and *sloooowly* bent to kiss her, giving her and me, severally, time to make that tiny gesture that says No—and did kiss her because I depend on Hilda's instincts and will never tell her No in such circumstances, or greater or lesser. Hilda put her hand back of his neck and thereby controlled the kiss and made it long—and I tore up the first hypothesis and marked the second one "Q.E.D." Hilda's instincts about people are infallible; I think she is a touch telepathic.

As may be, we would now help him if possible.

To Zeb and me he simply said, "Good morning"—*his* instincts are reputed to be infallible, too.

I agreed that it was a "good morning" while noting to myself that it was a symbol without a referent save for social connotation (morning? In an *irrelevancy*?) but added sincerely, "Lazarus, this is the best waffle I ever tasted."

"Then please tell Dora."

"Dora, did you hear what I said to the Commodore?"

"I surely did, Professor Jake! Six more?"

I felt my waistline—firm and many centimeters trimmed off. "Six more is what I want—"

"Right away!"

"But half of *one* is all I dare eat. Deety, the next time we go to Oz, will you ask Glinda whether or not there is a magic for gluttons—me, I mean—to permit them to eat as much as they want while three fourths of it disappears?"

"I'm sure she could do it; I'm equally sure that she would not. She's an ethical witch; you would not be able to convince her that your purpose was worthy."

"You are depressingly logical, my dear."

Lib said, "Professor, you have actually been to the Land of Oz? Really and truly?"

"Really and truly. Dora, is Gay on the line?"

"On deck, Jake"—Gay's voice.

"Has anyone been in to see our portside annex?"

"How could they? Captain Hilda has not authorized it."

"But— Hilda?"

"No, dear. Sorry to be blunt, Commodore and Doctor Lib, but I won't authorize an open door because there are too many things that must not be touched. But I will be delighted to escort guests into Gay Deceiver almost anytime including right now; I've finished eating."

"I accept!"

"Then come along, Elizabeth. Anyone else?"

Lazarus said, "Dora, shove my breakfast to the back of the stove; I'll eat it later."

"A jelly omelet? I'll eat it myself."

"Do that, Dorable. Captain, I'm ready."

Laz-Lor showed up together, did not want to be left out. We ended up quite a crowd: eight humans, two computers.

Hilda stopped us at Gay's starboard door. "Friends, again I must be blunt. As you cross the sill of that door, you are leaving Star Yacht Dora and entering an independent command, the Gay Deceiver, *even though Dora totally surrounds Gay.* Inside that door, *I* command, responsible to no one, unlimited in authority. Captain Lor, do you understand and agree with the legal theory?"

Captain Lorelei glanced at her sister, looked unhappy. "Captain Hilda, I *do* agree. Therefore I can't come aboard. I can't abandon my command."

My wife looked terribly distressed. "Oh, I'm sorry!"

Lazarus Long interrupted. "Captain Hilda, I'm sorry another way. I *don't* agree with your legal theory. I have had more than two thousand years more experience with law than my sister has ... all sorts of law in all sorts of cultures. I'm not speaking of justice; I'll leave that to philosophers. But I know what legal theories work with humans, and what ones have been attempted, then abandoned because they could not be made to work. This situation is not new; it has occurred thousands, millions, of times: a larger vessel with a smaller vessel nested in it. The solution is always the same, whether it concerns starships, fishing boats, aircraft carriers, whatever. The smaller vessel is a separate command *outside* the larger vessel, but when it is *inside* the carrier vessel, it is legally part of it."

My darling did not answer. She was picking out me, Zeb, and Deety by eye as Lazarus talked. As he finished she said briskly, "GayDeceiverOpenStarboardDoor. Man the car, prepare for space."

I'm proud of our family. Zeb zipped past me to the farthest seat—which left me room to dive for mine as Deety was *picking up* Hilda bodily, shoving her inside, crowding in after her, turning and pulling her feet clear of the doorframe—yelping, "Gay-CloseDoors!"

I was belting in but looking to the right, where the action was. Lazarus Long grabbed the door while calling out, "Hey, wait a moment!"

He realized his mistake in time to keep his fingers. I had argued with Zeb when I discovered, during refitting, that he had removed the interlocks that prevent that sort of accident. He answered my protest: "Jake, when I tell those doors to close, I want them to *close*. If, in closing, one chops off a man's head, you can assume that I think he looks better that way."

Lazarus saved his hand but was knocked off his feet by the door—and I saw a bit of why he had lived so long. Instead of trying to check his fall, he gathered himself into a ball and took it on one buttock.

"Report!"

"Copilot belted checking seal!"

"Chief Pilot belted all systems go. Door seal being rechecked."

"Navigator belted, ready."

"Starboard door seal okay!"

"GayBounce!"

We were in free fall. No stars—total darkness.

"Astrogator. Advise."

"I don't know, Captain. We'll have to ask Gay whether or not she can backtrack. *Any* backtrack. Beulahland, or any spot in her perms. I'm lost."

Suddenly the stars came out. "Dora, calling Gay Deceiver. Come in, Gay."

"Don't answer. Zebbie, advise again. What happened?"

"I'm guessing. They cancelled encapsulation rather than risk losing us. They must be awfully anxious." Zeb added, "The only thing we have that you can't buy at the corner drugstore is Jake's space-time twister. How they knew of it and why they want it I do not know."

"Dora, calling Gay. Gay, *please* talk to me. Aren't you still my friend? I know our bosses had a silly fuss—but *we* didn't. Aren't you *ever* going to speak to me again? I love you, Gay. Please don't be mean to me."

"Captain Hilda, may I please say hello to Dora and tell her that *I* am *not* angry at *her?* She's a sweet girl, she really is. Captain, she let me use her *eyes.*"

"Let me speak to her first."

"Oh, thank you! Gay, answering Dora. Come in, Dora."

"*Gay!* You had me so scared. Don't go away again, *please*. The Commodore wants to apologize to your boss. Will she talk to him?"

"Captain?"

"No. I'll speak to Dora's Captain, however."

A cartoon of Lorelei's features displayed on our central screen. "Lor speaking, Captain Hilda. My brother is terribly sorry and wants to apologize. My sisters and I are dreadfully upset and want you *please* to come back. I don't claim *any* command over your ship despite the silly things my brother said. Lib has a message for you, too. She says that, topologically, there is no difference between you being inside us or us being inside you. Either way, we each surround the other."

"I don't see it topologically, Captain; I see it pragmatically. But please thank Elizabeth for me. I have this message for Lazarus Long. A cat can be caught in almost any trap *once;* but *that* cat will not be caught in the *same* trap *twice.*"

"The message is delivered."

"Then it is time to say good-bye. Captain Lorelei, I cannot honestly thank you as kidnapping is not hospitality even when it is luxurious. But I don't think that you or your sister—sisters—meant it that way. I blame it on that deceitful, devious brother of yours. Please tell your sisters and Libby good-bye for us and say that I am sorry we had to leave."

"Captain, wait! There is something I must do first."

"Captain Lor, I must warn you I have you in my gunsights."

"What? Oh! We are unarmed. Not anything like that. I'll be back quickly. Perhaps you would like Dora to sing? But *please* don't go away!" The face in the screen pulled away.

"What kind of songs do you like, folks? I know *lots* of songs. One-Ball Reilly and the Green Hills and On Guard Christmas So's Yours and Santa Carolita and Mademoiselle from Army Tears and the Pawnshot song and The Monkey Wrapped His Tail Around the Flagpole and Mary O'Meara and Soldier, Ask Not and just tell me what you like, and—here comes Sister. Captain Lor."

"Captain Hilda, thanks from my heart for waiting. Can you record?"

"Gay, recording mode. Go ahead."

"I have placed my brother under arrest and confined him to quarters. I, Captain Lorelei Lee Long, Master of Star Yacht Dora, affirm for use in any court that I have no authority over yacht Gay Deceiver and will never attempt to assert authority over Gay Deceiver no matter what circumstances and, furthermore, I now place myself, my crew, and my ship Dora under command of Captain Hilda Burroughs, henceforth commodore of both ships, this assignment of command irrevocable by me or my sisters, and revocable solely by Commodore Burroughs at her sole discretion. End of message. Hilda, won't you come home? Laz is crying and I don't know what to do. We *need* you. Buddy Boy never did tell you why. But we *do!* May I tell you?"

"Go ahead, Lor."

"To save our mother's life!"

(I said, softly, "I'll be damned.")

My wife hesitated, then said, "Is Elizabeth Long there?"

"Yes, yes! She's been listening—she's crying, too—and I would be but I'm Captain and *can't.*"

The smudged faces changed. "Lib Long speaking, Commodore."

"Libby, Captain Lorelei has told me something not only hard to believe but, if she is cloned from her brother as I have read, she may have his talent for lying. From what I know of you, I don't think you ever learned how to lie."

"Commodore, it is true that I never learned to lie convincingly. So I gave it up a long time ago."

"Very well, Lib. Is Lazarus Long in fact confined and under arrest?"

"Yes, to both. His door won't open and Dora has been instructed not to let him out until you permit it."

"What's this about saving her mother's life? If they are clones from a man the age Lazarus is alleged to be, their mother must have died a couple of millennia back."

"It's as complex as my case, Commodore, but quite different. The twins have host-mothers. But Lor was speaking of the *genetic* mother of herself, her twin sister, and Lazarus Long. She was reported dead more than two thousand Old-Home-Terra years ago. But there is some hope that the records were confused and that it may be possible to save her. It can't be done without your help and the help of the Gay Deceiver. I don't think the chances are good, even so. But *without* your help—well, I would have to try to devise such a drive as Gay is reported to have—and I don't think I can."

"Wait a moment, Libby. Gay, cut transmission from cabin; keep circuit ready. Can you find your way unassisted back into your berth in Dora? Did you get it into your perms?"

"I did. I thought I might want to find Dora someday. Are you displeased with me? I know it wasn't authorized. But I didn't three-times it! I can wipe it."

"Gay Deceiver. New program. New parking spot. Code word 'Dora Long.' I tell you three times."

"Hilda, I hear you three times!"

"Gay Deceiver. 'Dora Long.' Execute!"

The stars went away and lighted alcoves were at our doors.

XLII *"You're a figment of imagination."*

Zeb:

"Hear that, Laz? You're a figment of imagination."

"No, Lor. *You* are a figment; I'm a fig." (What she said was "fica," and Deety suppressed a giggle. I pinched her and told her in family tap code that she had a dirty mind—which she ignored, being proud of it rather than otherwise. It was a long time later that I learned that Laz had used a Galacta word—but the ancient pun still applied.)

Jake reiterated patiently, "Laz-Lor, the key point of Commodore Hilda's theory is that we are *all equally* figments of imagination. 'Reality' thus becomes a null symbol."

Deety shook her head emphatically. "Stick to geometry, Pop. Or stamp collecting. Leave symbology to symbologists—such as your favorite daughter. I'm real, I am! Smell me."

"No doubt you could use a bath. So could we all; it's been an adrenaline day. But that's the other side of the coin, Deety. 'Imaginary' and 'Real' turn out to be identical. Consider this chow bench. On one level of abstraction it is mathematical equations. At the level just below that it is a swirling nothingness, with mass-energy a rare event. But on the gross level abstracted by my senses I can place this drink on it with utter confidence that it will not sink through this near vacuum."

My father-in-law matched his words by placing his highball on the snack bench; it sank out of sight.

Jake looked tired. "Not my day. Dora, did you do that?"

"Yes and no, Professor."

"What kind of answer is that?"

"You placed it on a take-away spot and that part of me was on automatic and took it away and sterilized it. I'm sorry, sir, and here's your fresh drink."

It was indeed a busy day. No one had been waiting at our parking berth, but three young women arrived at a dead run while Sharpie was swapping seats with Deety—our brand-new commodore planned to be first to step into her new ship. The starboard door opened; Sharpie stepped out, a dignified procession of one—

—and was hit from three sides by three young women, each managing to laugh and cry at the same time. But Sharpie enjoys everything and her aplomb has never been shaken. She kissed them, let them kiss her, petted them and told them to calm down, everything was all right. "Dears, I never intended to stay away; I simply refused to let the great Lazarus Long put one over on Sharpie. Where is he now?"

"Shut up in the flag cabin, Ma'am. Commodore."

"Captain Lor, lock him up elsewhere; the flag cabin is mine."

"Aye aye, Commodore."

"How long will that take? Seconds, I mean; not hours."

Lor spoke rapidly to Dora in a language I almost understood. I leaned to my right, spoke to my wife. "Spanish. Some sort."

"Italian," Deety answered.

"Will you settle for Latino? *No!*—I remember now: Galacta. We'll have to learn it. But it sounds easy."

Lor reported, "Flag cabin will be ready for you by the time you reach it, Commodore."

"Very good. I expect to use it primarily as an administration office; flag remains in Gay Deceiver. That is appropriate, since Dora is unarmed whereas Gay Deceiver is an attack ship, an armed privateer—heavily armed, for her size." Sharpie smiled. "A few days ago, in another universe, we destroyed an entire air army. We don't have fancies such as artificial gravity; we belt down and fight in free fall. Gay Deceiver is stripped for speed and armament; Dora is just the opposite. The two complement each other beautifully."

I wondered why Sharpie was blathering—but she always has reasons. I think she reads minds.

I'm certain that Laz-Lor do, with each other. They looked at each other, then:

"The flag of an armed privateer—"

"—is the Skull-and-Cross-Bones—"

"—is it not? Do we take prisoners—"

"—or cut their throats?"

"Which would you rather do? Captain Lor, please do all the talking; these whipsaw conversations are hard to follow. By the way, no more 'midnight mutinies.' Lor, you remain captain until further notice."

Again they looked at each other.

"We like to swap off."

"Calling it 'mutiny' is just a joke."

"No one asked your preferences. My chief of staff and second-in-command of the flagship is the only one who does and must advise me. If you have opinions to offer, see him. Answer my question. Captain Lor."

"We'll do what you order. But our brother who was our father at the time taught us never to kill if we could possibly avoid it while teaching us all sorts of ways to kill and made us practice. When we were growing up we always wanted to be pirates. Then we grew up and decided that it could never be and tried to forget it."

Sharpie said, "I think I'm making you tongue-tied by forcing you to filter it through one set of vocal cords. So cancel that order; you two are unique. We operate just the way Lazarus taught you; so far we have killed only once—to repel an attack on us. That air army— We timed it, caught them with their flying machines on the ground, burned the machines, burned their fuel—and thereby stopped an invasion...without killing anyone. But we are always *ready* to kill. Lor, that's why I warned you a few minutes ago. It would have broken Gay's heart to have to destroy Dora. Skull-and-Cross-Bones? No way to fly one but, if you want to hang one in the lounge, I grant permission. Why did you decide not to become pirates?"

That same preliminary glance—

"Babies—"

"Laz has three, I have four—"

"—because Lor has one pair of twins—"

"—and we try to be pregnant at the same time—"

"—and time it to fit our plans—"

"—and Brother's plans if you ever let him out of hack."

"How old are you two? I've been thinking of you as about Deety's age but you can't be. Just one of you answer, please; it's a simple question."

They conferred mentally an unusually long time. At last Captain Lor said slowly, "It isn't quite simple. We will get Dora and Athene to integrate it for us . . . if data are complete; they may not be. But answering in Old-Home-Terran years and meaning our own biological time, Laz thinks we are about forty-eight and I think we are a couple of years younger. It doesn't matter because Ishtar will tell us when to rejuvenate, which won't be soon, as we aren't yet close to menopause."

"Does it have to be at menopause?"

"Oh, no, just makes it easier and you never have to stop making babies. But Ishtar's mother went *years* past menopause and had decided to die . . . and changed her mind and looks younger than we do and has had more babies than we have. This time around, I mean."

"How often do men need it?" Sharpie asked. Jake looked up and said, "I won't need it for another six weeks, Hilda. Maybe seven."

"Shush, dear. Laz-Lor, be careful around my husband. When he's in rut, it takes heavy chains to restrain him. So never mind that question; he doesn't need to know and, for me, it was intellectual curiosity of a biologist. Perhaps it's best to ask Doctor Ishtar."

"Yes, Commodore, that would be best. We aren't biologists; we're ship handlers."

I leaned forward. (Sharpie was keeping us in the car; why I didn't know—then.) "Commodore! I'm required to advise you."

"Yes, Zebbie."

"You are going to need a new chief of staff, a new second-in-command, and a new astrogator because I will be on the binnacle list in a wet pack if you don't have Laz-Lor answer that last one. It is *not* 'intellectual curiosity' to *me.*"

"Why, Zebbie dear, I have reports that your curve is such that it will be many, many years before you can possibly have other than intellectual interest."

(If it were not for upsetting Jake, I would paddle that pert little arse!)

Deety said, "Hear, hear!" I placed my hand over her mouth and got bitten. Sharpie said, "Captain, we have here another paradox—Doctors Carter and Burroughs, each unreasonably insecure. Elizabeth, you've been a man; give them the male angle."

"Commodore, I wasn't very successful as a male. I simply took antigeria whenever Lazarus did. But I can report his thumb rule."

"Yes?"

"When a man looks at a new and attractive woman and decides that he is too tired, it's time. When he doesn't even look, push him over and bury him; he's failed to notice that he's dead."

The ship's computer said something in that not-Spanish; Sharpie answered, "Graz, Dora. I'll come now."

Lor said, "Ma'am, we didn't know you knew Galacta."

"I don't. But I will a week from now. I knew what I would say in your position, and you said it; I could tell from cognates. You told Dora to get him out *pronto,* because the Doña was on her way. Then get his personal belongings when I would not be inconvenienced. So I stalled. Zebbie, will you come with me? Jacob dearest, will you decide whether or not we should give up our suite with the Carters? And what to move out of Gay? We will be in Dora at least a week, possibly longer."

"Commodore, we depart for Tertius tomorrow midday, ship's time."

"I do not recall ordering that, Captain Lor."

The twins looked at each other—and said nothing.

Sharpie patted Laz's cheek. "Don't look so thunderstruck, girls"—girls?—seven years or so Sharpie's senior and seven babies between them—"On reaching Tertius, place us in orbit, following local rules. But no messages from ship to ground unless approved by me in writing. Come now!"

As Sharpie left with me in tow, she told Deety that she was on her own but please get out Jacob's Army blues and my Aerospace dress, and ask Dora about cleaning and pressing.

Jake said, "Hey!" before I could, and Sharpie said, reasonably, "I won't put you into a long skirt, sweetheart; you would feel that I had coerced you into drag. I thought perhaps you two were bored with civilian dress—and I shall continue the custom concerning dressing for dinner—either formal dress or formal skin. Nothing in between."

Upon reaching flag cabin Sharpie dismissed Laz-Lor, waited until we were private, then clung to me. "Hold me, Zebbie. Hold me tight! Calm me down." The little thing was shaking.

"Maybe I had better get Jake," I suggested, while holding her and petting her gently—and solving aerodynamic empiricals in my head to keep from noticing how *much* skin such a tiny woman can spread over one.

"No, Zebbie. Jacob would fuss over me like a mother hen and give me advice I don't want. Either I boss this job without my husband telling me what to do...or I can't cut it. If I fail, I will fail on my own—not as Jacob's puppet. But I can cry on you and tell you things I wouldn't tell my own toothbrush."

She added, "When I send you out, find Jake and have him teach school to everybody. That'll keep him busy and happy and out of my hair. And everybody else, too. Have both computers record his lectures."

"Lectures on *what?*"

"Oh. Too many details. The plenum of universes and the Number of the Beast. Pantheistic multiple solipsism, or why the Land of Oz is real. The quantum mechanics of fairy tales. Even the care and feeding of Black Hats. He'll probably want to take people into Gay...but *you* must be present; don't delegate it. Jacob can go along and lecture but it's Zebbie's sharp eye that will see to it that nothing is touched."

She patted my chest. "You're such a comfort. Now I'm going to dig out this ship's papers and you're going to help because I don't know what to expect. Or where to find them. Certificate of ownership, I suppose, and registration, and ship's manifest whatever that is. What else and where should I look?"

"A log. Crew list, passenger list. Health inspection, maybe. Other inspections. Bureaucracy and red tape tend to follow the same patterns everywhere. Maybe no *paper* papers; that looks like a computer printout over there. Mmm— Insist on English; the originals are almost certainly in Galacta."

"I'll try it. Dora."

"Listening, Commodore Hilda."

"Print for me, in English, the ship's official papers. Ownership, registration, manifests, and so forth. You know the list. Retrieve soonest."

"I am not authorized to do this, Ma'am."

"'Not authorized' *by whom?*"

The computer did not answer. Sharpie said, "Stick around, Zebbie; there's going to be trouble. Do you have any weapons?"

"*Where?* Look at me. How?"

"I don't know but you're clever about such things. *Dora!*"

"Your orders, Commodore?"

"Get me Captain Lor! In person, not voice. I want her here on a dead run—right now! Out!"

(I did have a weapon. I had palmed an item as I left Gay. But never admit a holdout.)

Laz-Lor arrived, breathing hard, seconds later. "You sent for us, Ma'am?"

"I sent for Captain Lor; I did *not* send for Laz. Out. Pronto!"

Laz had her mouth open to speak. She got out so fast the door was only partly dilated; she dived through.

"*Dora!* Repeat to Captain Lor every word that you've heard, every word you've said, since I entered this cabin."

The computer started with Sharpie telling Laz-Lor they could leave...then surprised me with: "*Hold me, Zebbie. Hold me tight. Calm me down.*"

I started to speak, Sharpie shook her head. Dora droned on, right through Hilda's order to repeat back all the computer had heard or said since we came in.

The computer stopped; Sharpie said, "Dora, you told me this morning that you could not scan in here without permission."

"That is correct, Ma'am."

"Who gave you permission?"

The computer did not answer.

"Captain Lor, did you or your sister tell this computer to spy on me and to refuse to answer certain questions?"

"No, Ma'am."

"Then it's your brother Lazarus. Don't bother to lie; I didn't ask, I told you. Fetch your brother to me, under arrest. *Move!*"

XLIII   *To Pull a Hat out of a Rabbit*

Smith:

I had had trouble convincing my sisters that I must be "arrested" and "confined." I had made an idiotic mistake and now must be "punished." Lor had even less enthusiasm for placing herself and our ship under the command of a stranger.

Once they accepted it, I could depend on them. We did not let Lib in on the caper; she has no talent for creative lying. Far better that she believe whatever she said.

Laz and Lor were outwitting their elders by the time they were six, a process I encouraged by walloping them whenever I caught them. They learned. They also have my talent for looking stupid, plus one I have but seldom can use: They can turn tears on and off like a faucet. (I have not found many cultures in which this advantages a male.)

Once this was settled, I arrested myself by helping Dora's waldoes move my most personal gear next door. Then I lay down and listened through Dora to what was going on in the flag cabin.

And discovered that I had outsmarted myself. I have never tried to teach Dora to lie; a dishonest computer is a menace: one that is a pilot would be a lethal disaster, sooner or later. Sooner.

But I hadn't figured on this narrow little broad asking for my papers so quickly. Nor did I guess that Dora had told her that my cabin could be scanned only by my order.

When I heard the situation start to deteriorate, I got up quickly and put on one of my Scottish outfits. Advantages: I look bigger, taller, more imposing. The costume calls for two weapons worn publicly. These I never use. But the costume is so draped and full that one may hide weapons for a half squad—then never show them save in extremis.

So I was ready when Lor came busting in, almost incoherent. "Brother, is she *mad!* Watch yourself!"

"I will, Lor. You've done a swell job." I kissed her. "Now march me in under arrest."

So we did. I halted ten paces from Mrs. Burroughs and saluted. She said to Lor, "You may leave"—waited until Lor had left, then said, "Instruct your computer not to see or listen in this space."

"Aye aye, Ma'am. Dora."

"Yes, Boss?"

"Back to normal for my cabin. No see 'um, no hear 'em until I tell you to."

"Chinchy!"

"Dora!"

"Aye aye, Boss. Mean!"

"She's a bit childish but she's a good cook. And a fine pilot."

"And you're a bit childish. Prisoners do not salute, prisoners do not wear arms. Captain Carter, confiscate his weapons. Keep them as souvenirs or destroy them."

Long years as a slave taught me to put up with anything without a squawk. That doesn't make it pleasant.

"Smith."

I didn't answer. She added, "I mean *you*, Woodie!"

"Yes, Ma'am?"

"Lean over, grab your ankles. Captain, frisk him."

Carter knew how, I soon no longer had tools for a half squad— but felt better when he ended having missed one. He was in uniform-of-the-day, but he was big, in training, and carried himself in a way that made me think of Black Belts.

"Those are yours, too, Zebbie, although you might share them. Deety mentioned something about not having a throwing knife. How's the balance on those?"

She was not speaking to me but I had to try to gain control of the psychological gage. "One and a half turns at eight meters, Ma'am. I make them myself. But it's too heavy a knife for a lady. I would happily make one to fit Doctor Deety's hand and strength."

"I imagine that Doctor Deety is stronger than you are, Woodie. I think you've gone a bit soft. Someday we'll check it. Take off your clothes."

With my weapons gone, other than the one, I welcomed the order. Clothes are no asset in unarmed brawl; the other man can use yours against you. And I was sweating; Dora keeps the ship right for skin. I peeled quickly.

"Shove them down that," she said, pointing.

"Uh, Ma'am, that's a destruction oubliette."

"I know. Next time you won't try to impress me by sartorial elegance. Furthermore it was intentional insolence. *Pronto!*"

I shoved them down pronto. "Grab your ankles again, Woodie. Captain Carter, need we give him an enema to make sure he hasn't hidden one more weapon? I don't care to check by touch without a rubber glove, and I won't ask you to."

"Madam, I give you my word—"

"—which is worth nothing. Let it go, Zebbie. Join the class and keep an eye on our interests."

The big man looked me over. "I don't like to leave you alone with him, Commodore."

"Thank you, Zebbie. I'm safe. I was safe when he was armed but he was being insolent so I spanked him. Run along; he doesn't dare touch me." She added, "Or do you have a premonition?"

"No. But I get them just barely in time."

"I couldn't ask for more. But I feel a prophecy. Woodie is going to be a lamb about everything. Now go, dear."

He left, giving me a look that promised death if I harmed her. I wanted to tell him that I had never found it necessary to harm a woman in more centuries than his wife had years.

"Well, Lazarus, how do we work this out?"

"Work out what, Ma'am? You have the upper hand."

"Oh, piffle! *You* have the upper hand; you know it. As long as the ship's computer obeys *you*, rather than *me*, my 'authority' is a fraud. I escaped once by a fluke; you won't let it happen twice. But I stuck my head back into the trap because I think we have something to trade, to our mutual profit."

"I hope so, Ma'am. Please go on."

"You want your mother rescued. I plan to do it if it can be done. For which you will toe the mark. We need a holding company. I will own fifty-one percent of the voting stock. Not of the profits; there will be plenty for all. But *I* control."

"Madam, you're way ahead of me. I don't know what you have in mind."

"Money. Money and power. Whew! I just got downwind; you sweated into that heavy costume. Go in there, take a tub bath, hot and soapy. I'll sprawl on the chaise longue and we'll talk business. Are you really trying to rescue your mother, or are you simply looking to cut yourself in on Jacob's invention? We can make a deal, either way—but I must know. Don't hold out on me; I tend to get annoyed. Then someone else pays. *You*, in this case."

She took my hand and led me into the 'fresher while I answered her key question and thought about the rest. No more lies; she had caught me in one thrown together hastily and too complex; my grandfather would have been ashamed of it. So—nothing but the truth. But *how much* truth and *what* truth?

"Rescuing my mother is priority one, sine qua non. Business aspects are secondary."

"You were going to say that business aspects didn't matter to you—and I would have stuffed it down your throat."

I stalled while I adjusted the bath's controls. "Ma'am, I always think about business angles. But I would go broke and start over to make this rescue."

"Will you sign such a contract? We rescue your mother; you sign over all your wealth to me? No cheating, no holdout?"

"Is that what it takes?"

"No. It would not be equitable and that would compel you to cheat. Any contract must profit *both* of us. But rescuing your mother appeals to me—to all my family; I'm the least sentimental of us—and we would tackle it if there were not a fiat dollar in sight. *Pour le sport.* That nice warm feeling—whether it's a kitten, a baby bird, or an old woman. But there *is* money in this . . . and sport . . . and opportunities beyond imagination. That sound of water splashing: does that interfere with Dora's hearing?"

"No, she filters it out."

"Is she listening?"

I instantly answered, "Yes." I've lived a long time in part by being a cat not caught in the same trap twice—as she had under-lined. I placed in my permanent memory, nine times nine, *never* to lie to this woman again. Evade, avoid, keep silent, be elsewhere. But *don't* lie to her. A born Grand Inquisitor. Telepathic? Must ask Laz-Lor.

"I'm glad you said Yes, Lazarus. Had you said No, I would have broken off negotiations. I'm not telepathic—but you may find it inadvisable to lie to me. We must change the computer situation—part now, part later. You didn't give her the right code words."

"That's right. 'Chinchy' and 'mean' equal—"

"—Roger Wilco, but reversed meaning."

"Eh? That's a deep-down memory. Yes. Hmm— I must insert that phrase into Galacta. Useful." The water was just right, with deep, fragrant suds. I stepped down into it, picked a seat that let me lounge. "I should have said to Dora— Shall I tell Dora now?"

"With a modification. I want the equivalent of a simple telephone, so that I can call anyone, anyone can call me—and the same for you. But kill the snoop circuits throughout this suite."

"No trouble. We can call out at any time; that is a safety feature, permanent. As for calling in, I usually limit it to the twin commanding; she's entitled to disturb me, if needed. If not needed—well, neither Laz nor Lor enjoys being called 'stupid,' especially by me."

I changed the orders to Dora and did not cheat; Mrs. Burroughs and I were now truly in private, although anyone could reach us—voice only. "What next, Ma'am?"

"Some permanent changes for Dora, now that she can't hear us. Tentative plans for your mother's rescue. Then we talk business. Is there a seat in that pool where I won't drown?"

"Oh, certainly. When Laz-Lor were your size, they often bathed with me—I've had as high as six in this tub although that's a bit cozy; it's a four-adult design. Here, let me help; you can't see through these suds." Helping Hilda Burroughs reminded me of handling Laz-Lor at the same size, prepubescent . . . but I was acutely aware that this small, warm, slick body was postpubescent by many years and I got a twinge that I was pleased to have fig-leafed by suds. "Feel under you—find the seat? Temperature suit you?"

"Luxurious. On Tertius refreshers are social rooms, are they not?"

"Yes. Over the years I have found that nude cultures, or those with no taboos about nakedness, tend to make bathing a social event. Ancient Romans. Ancient Japanese. Many others."

She answered, "Whereas cultures with strong body taboos equate bathing rooms with outhouses back of barns. Disgusting." Mrs. Burroughs looked disgusted. I noted this as I had thought it would be necessary to get them used to skin before exposing them to the easy-going ways of Tertius . . . lest I jeopardize my mother's rescue. I had instructed Laz-Lor to hold us in irrelevancy until all of them, with no urging, accepted the comfort of complete bareness in perfectly tempered conditions, and simply forgot about bodies *qua* bodies. This does not mean to forget yin-yang . . . but it has long been known to all but legislators, judges, and other fools that a scrap of clothing fig-leafing whatever may be taboo (taboos vary endlessly and each is a "law of nature") is far more stimulating than is no clothing.

(Warning to time-travellers: To assume that the taboos of your native culture are "natural" and that you can't go too wrong behaving by the rules your loving parents taught you is to risk death. Or worse. If you think death has no "worse," read history.)

To return to pretty little Mrs. Burroughs: To be enjoying a bath with her a few minutes after she had had me subjected to personal indignity was the second most surprising thing about her. The *most* surprising thing I was still learning: This fragile little doll with the muscles of a kitten was the toughest bitch kitty I have ever encountered.

Understand me, I admire her. But I want to be on the side she is on. "What changes in Dora do you want, Ma'am?"

"Lazarus, I'm 'Ma'am' to strangers and on formal occasions. I don't consider bathing all that formal; my friends call me Hilda. Or by nicknames. Even pet names. But not 'Ma'am.'"

My answer got me splashed. She went on, "In attempting to hornswoggle me, you gave me, through your accomplices, a phony command and rank—while retaining control of the computer necessary to make it real. I require that you carry out your contract. *Now*. By reprogramming Dora to me as her sole boss, with the program locked so that *you* can't change it. Me and me alone."

She smiled, leaned toward me, and placed a hand on my knee under water. "That's why I insisted on privacy—for Dora's sake. She's self-aware and seems quite vulnerable. Lazarus, I don't mind anyone in this ship hearing anything I've been saying. But I don't discuss surgery when it is likely to upset the patient." She leaned forward. "Scratch between my shoulder blades—pretty please?"

I welcomed time to think, while requiring her to coach me—higher, lower, a little to the left, ah, right *there* . . .

"Hilda, I'm not sure it can be done. I did reprogram Dora so that her loyalty in crisis is to Laz-Lor. But it took me years and was not done by circuitry or by programming. Dora is so thoroughly a self-aware personality that it is necessary to win her love in order to gain her loyalty."

"I find that believable. Lazarus, let's see you pull a hat out of the rabbit."

"You mean—"

"I meant what I said. Any second-rate magician can pull a rabbit out of a hat. Can Lazarus Long pull a hat out of a rabbit? Watch this space next week. It's *your* problem, Lazarus; you created it. I won't make a second contract with a man in default on his first. Do you want your back scratched while you think? You scratched mine deliciously."

I accepted by leaning forward. Hilda *is* telepathic though perhaps not in words. She knew which spots and how hard and how long.

And when to stop. She dropped her hand as I straightened up . . . and her hand brushed against me and stopped. "Well! Truly I did not intend to be provocative, old dear."

I put an arm around her; she did not pull away but continued, "I won't refuse you. I have not given a man reasonable cause to call me a tease since I was twelve. But wouldn't it be sensible to table this until after we have rescued your mother and set up our business structure? If you find—then—that you are interested, you will let me know. If you do, I ask that you cooperate with me in saving my husband's feelings and face. And . . . I am . . . having trouble *saying* this— Damn it! *Please* stop and tell me the plans for rescuing your mother."

I stopped, allowed a hand's width to separate us. "Have you forgotten the hat and the rabbit?"

"I'm afraid I did. Very well, you've won this round; we attempt to rescue your mother. I waive the broken contract—but we do no further business. Just the rescue, then we leave."

"I thought you promised me a second chance—later?"

"What? Lazarus, you're a bastard."

"I'm not but the term has no meaning on Tertius. Here's the 'hat.' You designate me your flunky—any title—for this ship. My sole function will be to be in earshot—through Dora or otherwise—to insure that your slightest wish is carried out. Night or day."

"Making me a privileged figurehead, still vulnerable to your whim. The hat won't fit."

"Very well—second hat. We ground on Tertius; I move Dora into another ship—she accepts that; it has happened before. I sign this ship over to you with a new computer of the same capacity, programmed for ship's routine but unawakened. You let it awaken to your personality. You'll be its mother."

"That's better. Close but not on. Lazarus, you and I are going to be in business together a long time. I won't take your ship. Instead you're going to build me a ship, a tender for Gay Deceiver but moved by a Burroughs continua device—the first such ship built by Burroughs & Long, Ltd., a subsidiary of Carter Engineering Company. Another subsidiary is Carter Computers, which may assemble computers but primarily will build Burroughs Time-Space twisters under some innocuous name, and sell them only inside our complex setup—*much* more complex; we'll work on it together. But our biggest subsidiary will be Libby & Smith, Real Estate. That one rebuilds solar systems."

"What!!"

"Talk to Zebbie and Jacob. We'll organize Black Hat Safaris, Pty., too, but it may be a dummy for a while. We'll have an emporium in New Rome, imports from many universes. Uh...The Pawnshop, of course, with the Hook Joint above it. Ultra expensive imported styles up there, modelled by New Rome's most beautiful hetaerae. Private rooms for private viewings. This one is a gift to Laz-Lor, save for the ten percent that is voting stock of which I vote my usual control, through you. The twins can do as they please with it; our leash will be slack. Probably they will do their own importing, with a resident manager. But they might work in it some, just to know the business."

"Which business?"

"Both. They are grown women, Lazarus; you must not try to run their lives. The overall holding company, run by you and me, usual split with my one percent advantage, is a nonprofit corporation supporting Ishtar's clinic. We funnel whatever is needed into the clinic, holding down the book profits elsewhere, but paying whopping salaries and consulting fees. My husband is chief scientist in one part while consultant by fee elsewhere, with Elizabeth—Lib—his mirror image elsewhere. Lazarus, we must have Deety work on it; she has the finest head in our family for manipulation of this sort—I'm just her awed pupil."

"And I'm just your awed pupil!"

"Piffle again. Lazarus, from what I've read of you, your sole weakness lies in a delight in cheating for its own sake; Deety treats it as an intellectual art. One thing more— No, two things. Can you persuade Dora, as a favor to Ol' Buddy Boy, to go along with the hoax until we deliver your mother to Ishtar? Make it a mammoth joke, under which she takes orders from me because she wants to be in on the fun. Take you out of arrest, of course; wipe it from her memory."

"It was never in her memory; Lor put her in nonrecording mode while the hooraw was on."

"Good! Can you persuade her to call me 'Commodore' while you use some fancy title?"

"Hilda, I'm your chief of staff for this ship; Zeb is chief of staff, flagship. Dora doesn't really understand ranks; I can tell her that 'chief of staff' is one notch senior to God. No problem. As long as she can see that you and I are buddy-buddy."

"And we are!"

"It's reassuring to hear that. Hilda, I underestimated you so badly that I'm still in a state of shock. What's the last item?"

"Rejuvenation for all of us for as long as you—Ishtar—can stretch non-Howards."

"I can promise that; I'm Board Chairman of the Clinic. But—Ishtar is *not* a magician. What's the average age of death for your parents, grandparents, any ancestors you know about?"

"My family, both sides, are considered long-lived—although I lost my parents in a car crash. The others I don't know about except that Deety's mother died of cancer, much too young."

"We can handle that."

"Is longevity on Earth—our Earth, not yours—of interest? Same length of year as Old-Home-Terra; Deety and Lor checked."

"Of course!"

"These figures apply to North America. Some other places are higher, some lower, some no data. Females. Menarche at thirteen plus-or-minus nine percent. Menopause at fifty-six to sixty-seven plus-or-minu—"

"Stop there! Average age of death, female?"

"One hundred seventeen. But males average eight years less. Sad. My own family averages higher, but only a few years. I don't know about Jacob but he mentioned once that his great-grandfather got himself killed, in an odd fashion, at ninety-seven. He—"

"Enough. I must report this. By definition, all of you are 'Missing Howards.'"

"But, Lazarus, that's simply the average on Earth—our Earth, now that I know that there are thousands of analogs."

"Doesn't matter. Different universe, different time line—not my problem. *Here* you are a Howard. You four and all your descendants."

Hilda smiled happily. "That's cheerful news to a woman six weeks pregnant."

"You?"

"And Deety. Same time and doesn't show yet. Lazarus, I was tempted a while ago to tell you . . . because *I* was tempted. Now, now! *Down*, Rover! Outline to me how we rescue a woman dead for many centuries."

"Hilda, someday I'm going to get you drunk."

"Want to bet?"

"Never with you. There is mystery about my mother's death. She appears to have been killed accidentally at a relatively young age, for a Howard. Just short of a hundred. I was notified as her purse I.D.'s named me as 'next of kin'—and I bawled like a baby for I had been planning to pay her a visit on her century day, July 4th, 1982. Instead I attended her funeral, flying to Albuquerque two weeks early.

"Nobody there but me. She was living alone under her maiden name, she and my father having separated thirty years earlier. But apparently she hadn't listed her last address change with the Howard Foundation, hadn't notified her other children. Howards are like that; they live so long that kinship is not enough reason to stay in touch. Closed casket and cremation—authorized by stuff in her purse; I never saw her body.

"But there was no doubt as to her I.D.'s and so forth. In my world, 1982 was a time when you couldn't sneeze without carrying a thick pack of cards all, in effect, saying that you were you. I was feeling it because I was seventy later that year and looked thirty-five. Embarrassing. I had plans to drive south from Albuquerque, cross the border, and not come back until I had bought a new passport to match a new name.

"Hilda, it was over two thousand years later, in preparing for my first time trip, that I learned that my mother was not listed in the Archives as dead but simply as 'record missing.'

"The matter troubled me. A few years ago—my time—Laz-Lor took me back. Didn't ground; a missile chased us and scared Dora silly. But I got a motion picture that seems to show the accident. There is a blur on the frames just before the first one that shows what I think is the corpse. Can you guess the size and shape?"

"Shan't try, Lazarus."

"As near as I can measure on a film a centimeter square, shot with a telephoto lens from too high because Dora was crying and wanting to go home, it is the size of that berth Gay Deceiver is in. Hilda, I think I photographed you rescuing my mother before you did it."

"*What?* Lazarus, that's—"

"Don't say impossible. The Land of Oz is impossible. You're impossible. I'm impossible. Who invented pantheistic multiperson solipsism? You did."

"I wasn't going to say 'impossible.' Now that you know that I'm pregnant, you will realize why I want to try to rescue your mother right away, before my belly starts growing where the seat belt crosses it. Her name was Marian? Marian Johnson Smith?"

"Maureen Johnson."

"That proves that the real Lazarus Long stood up. It bothered

me that there might be a series of analog-Lazarus-Longs like an-
alog-Earths."

"Wouldn't bother me. That's *their* problem."

"But it would destroy the theory I worked out that would account for my sitting here in a pool of water in a time-travelling
flying saucer with a fabulous man—both ways!—when I *know*
he's a fictional character in a book I read years back. That makes
me a fictional character, too, but that doesn't trouble me as *I* can't
read a novel with *me* in it, any more than *you* could read the one
I read about *you.*"

"I came close to doing just that."

"Don't be mysterious, Lazarus."

"I like wild stories. Used to read every one I could find in the
Kansas City Public Library. On another time trip I picked up a
magazine of a type you may never have seen. Read one installment
of a serial. Ridiculous. Four people traveling in space in an *air-
plane*. At the end of that installment they are hailed by a flying
saucer. Continued next month. Hilda, how do you *think* Dora was
able to be at the right place at the right time when Gay Deceiver
popped out of nowhere?"

"Where is that magazine?"

"Down the same destruction oubliette that recently received my
best fake Scottish chief costume. If I had not learned long ago to
dispose of casual fiction once I had read it, Dora would never be
able to lift. Hilda, you explained it yoursel—"

"Hilda? Do you hear me"—her husband's voice.

Her face lit up. "Yes, Jacob?"

"May I see you? I have a problem."

I barely whispered, "I'll get out," and started to stand up. She
pulled me back down. "Of course, Jacob dearest. I'm in the flag
cabin. Where are you?"

"In our suite."

"Come straight here." She whispered to me, "Do we have a
deal?" I nodded; she stuck out her hand; we shook on it. "Partners,"
she whispered. "Details later. Maureen first."

Her husband answered, "Hilda, I don't know my way. And it's
a private matter."

"Then you *must* come here, Jacob; this is the *only* private place
in the ship. I've been talking business with Lazarus Long—business so private we had to talk *here*. No more trouble, dearest man,
and we each get what we want. Come join us, we need you."

"Uh . . . can *he* hear me?"

"Certainly. We're having a bath together. Come join us. I want you to know all about the deal before we tell the children. I may need support on parts where we traded quid pro quo."

Silence— "I'd better call back later."

I said, "Doctor Burroughs, you want to talk privately with your wife; I will get out. But please understand that social bathing is as commonplace on my world as offering a friend a drink is on yours. I am here because the Commodore invited me and I assure you she is quite unharmed."

Burroughs replied in a pained voice, "I know that custom and have utter faith in Hilda's social judgment. Yes, I do need to speak to her . . . but I don't mean to be surly. I'll come up, or down, or across, and say hello. Please don't leave before I get there. I'll ask my way."

"Dora will show you. Step into the corridor and wait. She'll find you."

"Very well, sir."

"Dora, special."

"Yes, Pappy?"

"Find Professor Burroughs. Lead him here. By the longest route. Slow march."

"Aye aye, Pappy."

I said hurriedly to Hilda, "I may know what this is; let me check. Lib?"

"Yes, Lazarus?"

"Are you alone?"

"In my stateroom alone. And lonely." Lib added, "And upset."

"So? Did you put the question to Professor Burroughs?"

"Yes. Lazarus, I had perfect opportunity. The one place Dora can't see or hear. Inside Gay Deceiver's space warp and—"

"Chop it, Lib! Did he turn you down?"

"No. But he didn't say Yes. He's gone to discuss it with his wife. That's why I'm jittery."

"Turn on the soother. I'll call you back. Off."

Hilda asked, "What's the matter with Elizabeth?"

"I'll make it short as even the longest route can't take long. Lib is terribly anxious to have a child by the mathematician— your husband—who formulated the equations for six-dimensional positively-curved space. She thinks—and so do I—that they might produce a mathematician equal to, or even greater, than Lib or your husband. But she should have let Ishtar arrange it. She jumped the gun; I don't know why—"

"I do! Elizabeth!"

Lib was slow in answering. "This is Elizabeth Long."

"Hilda Burroughs here. Elizabeth, you come straight here. Flag cabin."

"Commodore, are you angry with me? I meant no harm."

"Dear, dear! You come to Mama Burroughs' arms and let me pet you and tell you that you're a good girl. *Now!* How far away are you?"

"Just around the curve. A few meters."

"Drop everything and hurry. Lazarus and I are in the 'fresher. In the pool. Come join us."

"Uh, all right."

"Hurry!"

Hilda asked, "How do I let them in? Run dripping and do it by hand? I noticed that our door lets anyone out but can't be opened from the outside without help." She added, "For that matter how do *I* get back in?"

"Dora knows you belong here. For the rest— Dora, admit Libby Long and Professor Burroughs."

"Aye aye, Pappy. Lib—here she comes. Dr. Jacob Burroughs I'm fetching. How soon?"

Hilda said, "Two minutes."

Lib hurried in, still unsmiling. Did smile when Hilda put her arms around her, smiled and cried at the same time. I heard Hilda crooning, "There, there, dear! It's a wonderful idea; she'll be the world's greatest mathematician. A cute baby—something like Deety, something like you. *Jacob!* In here, darling! If you are wearing anything, chuck it; we're in the pool."

Seconds later the pool was filled to its rated capacity, Hilda with arms around both of them—kissed her husband, kissed Lib, said sternly to them, "Stop looking as if you were at a funeral! Jacob, this is what Jane would want—and it is what *I* want. Elizabeth, you aren't crowding me out; I'm pregnant now. I'll have my baby six weeks before you have yours. I've decided to ask Doctor Lafe Hubert to deliver my baby. Who are—"

"Hilda! I haven't delivered a baby for over a century."

"You have seven months in which to brush up. Doctor Lafe, are you refusing to attend me?"

"No, but— Jake, if Hilda will have her baby at the Clinic on Tertius, she will be in the hands of the most skilled obstetricians in this universe. Which I am not. I'm rusty. I—"

"Doctor, I think Hilda would settle for your holding her hand and standing by to help if needed. I think my daughter would like that, too. She may have her baby the same day as Hilda."

"Sir, I will be honored. But I want to say something about this proposed baby, a cross between two all-time great mathematicians. I know that your world places value on monogamy. Howards do not; they can't. But this need not violate your values. If you will make a deposit at the sperm bank at—"

"What?" Hilda Burroughs looked shocked. "Lazarus, are you talking about syringes and things like that. Done to *Elizabeth?*"

"Why, yes, I—"

She chopped me off. "Babies are not made with syringes! Babies are made with love! With little moans of happiness between two people who know exactly what they are doing and want to do it. Elizabeth, are you fertile today?"

"I should be. It's time."

"Then kiss me and tell me you want to do this. If you do."

"Oh, I do, very much!"

There were kisses and tears all around. I got pulled into it, found myself kissing the prospective father. I gave him a chance to duck but he didn't.

Our busy little stranger was still playing ringmaster. "Lazarus, what is that guest room across the cabin? Pastel colors?"

"Aurora Room."

"Beloved husband, wrap a towel around this sweet, frightened child, take her there, lock the door behind you and make her happy. This suite is the *only* totally private place in this ship. If I lay eyes on either of you in less than one hour, I shall burst into tears. That doesn't mean you can't stay longer. I hope that you will come to dinner . . . but you are welcome to Aurora Room after dinner. Sweetheart, you must give her at least one chance each of the next three days; a woman's timing can vary from her norm. Now git! Pick her up and carry her."

Lib wouldn't let Jake carry her. But she leaned into his arm. As they left the 'fresher, she looked back with a happy smile and threw us a kiss.

Hilda caught it and ate it. Then she said to me, "Help me out, please, dear."

I lifted her out, sat her on the edge, climbed out myself. She patted the padded deck, said, "I think this is better than that chaise longue. If we happen to be caught it wouldn't embarrass me and should not embarrass you; in these circumstances Jacob would be relieved rather than upset." She smiled, eased her sweet thighs, put up her arms. "Now?"

"Yes!"

"Anything you want, including back rubs. Lazarus, does it

excite you knowing what is going on a few meters away? It does *me!*"

"Yes! But I don't need it—Hilda, you're superb!"

"Not in looks, certainly. So I try hard with what I have. Sold myself three times—did my best to make my contract-husbands each feel that he had received full value . . . then married dear Jacob for love and am trying still harder with him. He is good—I mean he is good *all through.* I hope Elizabeth appreciates him. You've had her?"

"Yes."

"Before or after the change?"

"Both. I miss the 'before,' appreciate the 'after.'"

"Then why won't you knock her up?"

"That's a family joke. She had her first child by me, is now making the rounds of our family, more or less. Woman, you are *not* here to talk!—I'm almost there!"

She looked delighted. "I'm climaxing steadily; let 'er rip!"—and bit my chin.

An indefinitely long time later that need not be detailed, we were resting in each other's arms, enjoying that delicious peace of the ebbing tide. Hilda saw them first, raised her head:

"Jacob beloved! *Did you!* Lib– Did my sweetheart put a baby in you?"

"*Did* he! Hilda, you do that every night? Little bitty like you? Less than two hours and darling Jacob has worn me out."

"I'm a hollow mockery, dear. Built for it. Tell her, Jacob."

"My darling is adaptable, Libby dear. Lazarus, did Hilda treat *you* nicely?"

"I died happy."

"He's not dead"—Hilda made a long arm, cupped a handful of water, threw it in my face, giggled. The suggestion she added I rejected with dignity—as much dignity as one can manage when two women are tumbling one into a tub of water . . . while one's male comrade stands by and laughs.

XLIV   "—where do we get the corpse?"

Zeb:

"The question," said my wife Deety, "is where do we get the corpse? With timing that precise, Gay can make the pickup. But a corpse has to be left behind. Lazarus, not only do your movies show it, but you *remember* Maureen's death; you went to her funeral. It's got to be a fresh corpse of an elderly woman that the cops will accept as Maureen Johnson."

Six of us—Deety, me, Jake, Sharpie, Lazarus, and Libby—were seated around our kitchen dining table at "New Harbor" (our wives accepted that compromise) in Beulahland, trying to make plans for the "snatch." "Snatch" in the literal sense if the rescue of Maureen Johnson were to succeed.

Lazarus had a motion picture that showed that we *would* succeed (had succeeded) (were about to succeed) at a precise time and place and date on an analog of Earth-zero one quantum away on 't' axis.

Easy! Success guaranteed. Can't miss. Do it blindfolded.

But suppose we *did* miss?

The frames showed that a roadable had passed through the space where Gay had been (would be?) grounded, and, in so doing, ran over (would run over) (will run over) (is, was, and forever will be running over) the dumped corpse. Suppose the timing or placement was off just a touch. On his first time travel (1916–1918 Old-Home-Terra), with Dora piloting, Lazarus had missed not by a split second but by *three years*.

Lazarus had pointed out that it was his fault, not Dora's; he had fed her imperfect data—and we had jumped on him from five sides: It was not a question of "whose fault" but the fact a mistake could be made.

Or could it?

Four mathematicians, one mathematical engineer (yeah, I in-

437

clude me, as resident expert in Gay's responses), and one intuitionist all disagreed.

Hilda was certain that nothing could go wrong.

I am a firm believer in Murphy's Law: Given any possible chance, it *will* go wrong. Anything.

Libby had been wholeheartedly converted both to Jake's six-axis plenum of universes to the awful Number of the Beast but also to Sharpie's multiple solipsism, and asserted that they were two sides of the same coin; one was a corollary of the other and vice versa. Combined, they (it) constituted the ultimate total philosophy: science, religion, mathematics, art, in one grand consistent package. She spoke of a "ficton" being a quantum of imagination/reality ("imaginary" being identical with "real" whatever that is) as casually as a physicist speaks of photons. "Could a mistake be made? Yes. And would create a new universe. Jacob, you spoke of the empty universes your family had visited. One by one they fill as fictons are created." She added, "But a mistake was *not* made; we snatched Maureen safely. We *ourselves* create the fictions-fictons-ficta that will make it real."

She was euphoric. I attributed it to excitement over the coming adventure. I was mistaken.

Lazarus, a highly competent mathematician although not the unique that Jake is or Libby, was in this case not a calm abstractionist; his mood was grim determination to win or die trying—causing me to recall how he got his arse shot off.

Jake turned out to be a determinist (he himself being one universe's prime example of utter, rambunctious free will!).

Deety is a pragmatic mathematician, unworried by theory. Oz is real, she is real, "fictons" don't interest her. "Don't fret, Lazarus. We can do it, Gay can do it—and we *won't* do it until Gay is *certain* of her program."

This discussion had started midafternoon in Dora. Sharpie had worked out her difficulties with Lazarus (to my enormous relief; were those two to wind up on opposite sides in anything more serious than Parcheesi, I yearn to be elsewhere—say Timbuktu under an assumed name); she, Jake, Lazarus, and Libby were in the flag cabin, arguing, when Sharpie had Dora page Deety and me.

There were endless matters on the agenda (including the preposterous notion that we four were 'Missing Howards' and that Lazarus was registering us as such. I'm not sure I want to live a thousand years or even two hundred. But I am sure of this: a) I want to live quite a piece; and b) I want to be alert, healthy, and active right up to the last. Not like my great-grandfather who had to be spoonfed at a hundred and five, and could not control his secretions. But the Howards have got that whipped: you stay young as long as you wish, then die by choice when you feel you've had your full run.

(Yes, I was willing to be a 'Found Howard' since it included Deety, plus little Deeties ad infinitum.)

Lots of other business, all of it postponed (including the problem of "Black Hats"), in order to deal with rescuing Maureen Johnson.

We were still discussing knotty aspects when Lor's voice said: "Commodore?"

"Yes, Captain?" Sharpie had answered.

"Ma'am, I hesitate to disturb you—"

"Quite all right, Lor. The Captain must always be able to reach me."

"Uh, Ma'am, Dora told me that she was forbidden to call you. She has for you a variety of New Rome styles for women and men, a military uniform for Doctor Jacob, and one for Doctor Zebadiah, and evening formals for Doctor Elizabeth and Doctor Deety—and she's not sure where to send any of them."

"Send all the clothes to the flag cabin, please."

"Yes, Ma'am. They should be appearing in your delivery cupboard now. Do you know where that is?"

"I'll find it. What are you and your sister wearing tonight? Or is it a secret?"

"It's not a secret; we just haven't decided. But there is still an hour and thirty-one minutes till dinner."

"Time enough to pick out pretty clothes. Or will you wear formal skin tonight? That takes anywhere from two seconds to two hours, does it not? Off."

Sharpie used an unusually rough expression of disgust, which told me that she now included Lib and Lazarus in her inner circle. "Woodie, do you know any exceptionally strong cuss words? I detest the thought of wasting time pretending to be festive when we have so much to settle, especially our procedures for Maureen."

Deety looked at Libby. "You and I are kind o' stuck with a promise, too. How about some new cuss words from you, too?"

"Deety, I have no literary talent. But I would like to hear some soul-soothing cussing. We ought to stick with this, with snacks to keep going and sleep when we must, until it's perfect. Three hours or three days or three weeks."

I said, "We *shall!*"

Sharpie shook her head. "Zebbie, *you* can skip dinner. I can't. Lazarus should appear, too."

He agreed. "I'm afraid I must. But, Commodore, I must advise you that your flag chief of staff should be present, too, for esprit de corps." He cleared his throat noisily. "Libby and Jacob, being passengers, could skip."

Lib shook her head. "Deety and I made a reckless promise."

Not being a genius myself, it's kind of fun to make a roomful of 'em look silly. I stood up. *"No!* We will *not* let a dinner party interfere! We can settle it within three days. But if you all are going to chase rabbits— What's the matter with you, Sharpie? Getting stupid in your old age?"

"Apparently I am, Zebbie." She said to Lazarus, "Please issue orders cancelling dinner. We'll stay with this until we finish it. There are beds and lounges whenever anyone needs to nap. But we *won't* adjourn. Three hours or three weeks. Or longer."

"Don't cancel dinner, Sharpie."

"Zebbie, you have me confused."

"Beulahland is on a different time axis."

Five minutes later we were in our old farmhouse. We hadn't stopped for clothes as we would have wasted twenty minutes, whereas the idea was to save time on *that* axis, use time on *this* axis. We stuck Lazarus and Libby back in the after space, with the bulkhead door dogged open, so they could see and hear, but required them to use the web straps, and cautioned them that the lumps under them were loaded firearms.

The only thing not routine was that we would be making rendezvous later with a moving ship, something we had done before only from bounce range in the same space-time. So I had asked Gay whether she was sure she could do it. She assured me that she could, because she wasn't concerned with the ship's vector; she would return the instant she left.

I turned to Commodore-now-Captain Sharpie. "Ready for space, Captain."

"Thank you, Astrogator. Gay Deceiver. Beulahland. Execute. Gay Deceiver, open your doors. All hands, unbelt. Disembark. Gay, it's sleepy time. Over."

"Goodnight, Hilda. Roger and out."

Our passengers were dazed—they all are, first time. They stood outside our barn, looking at the setting sun, acting like zombies, until I shooed them inside. Although Beulahland does not have body taboos, they wear clothes most of the time, and six naked people outdoors in a clump as the chill of the evening was coming on was odd. I like a low profile.

Once inside, Libby said, "Feels like Arkansaw."

Lazarus replied, "Feels like Mizzoura."

"Neither," I told them. "It would be the State of Washington if it weren't Beulahland, and what ought to be Puget Sound is about a kilometer over that way."

"It still feels like home. Lazarus, I'm happy here."

At that moment I decided we would *never* give up New Harbor. Apparently we were going to be citizens of Tertius, or maybe New Rome on Secundus, or both (commuting is no problem when light-years mean nothing), on another time axis. We could take a rest from city life anytime and have it cost not one day's work on Tertius. Contrariwise, only such time would pass on New World *as we spent there*.

Hmm— Maybe we could sell vacations. Or extra study time for that student who has his big exam, the one he *must* pass, tomorrow morning. Sell him room and board and transportation and *three weeks not in the calendar*. At a slight markup, of course.

I built a cheerful fire in the fireplace, and Lazarus washed dishes, while Libby insisted on proving that she could cook on a wood range, even though she had learned centuries ago by her time scale, as a gangling boy. Yes, Elizabeth can cook.

We ate and sat around and talked, puzzling how to be sure of Maureen. Not make that one tiny mistake. It was then that Deety brought up the matter of the dead body. "You've seen how accurate Gay can be. But *where* do we get a freshly-dead corpse to replace Maureen?"

Lazarus told her to forget it. "I provide the corpse."

"That's not a good answer, Lazarus."

"Deety, don't worry. It'll be dead and I will dump it."

I said, "Lazarus, I don't like that answer a damn bit."

"Nor do I," Jake seconded.

"Nor I," agreed Sharpie. "Woodie, you're asking us to make a snatch—a hanging offense many places, bad trouble anywhere. We don't mind the technicality; saving an old woman's life isn't the sin kidnapping is. But what about this freshly-dead corpse? We don't deal in murder."

Lazarus glowered.

Libby said hastily, "If I assure you that it is all right, will you let it go at that?"

"No," pronounced Sharpie, *"Woodie* must come clean."

"All right, all right! I own this corpse. No murder or any other crime involved. Now will you quit riding me about it?"

"Jake?"

"I don't like it, Zeb."

"I don't, either. But we needn't do anything. We go limp. He may not last long in a culture that 'balances.'"

"Possible. But that's *his* problem."

Sharpie said quickly, "Did either of you promise him a ride back to my ship?"

"*Whose* ship?"

"*My* ship, Woodie. Gentlemen?"

"I didn't promise him. Did you, Jake?"

"No. Did you, Deety? Hilda?"

"Not me, Pop."

"Nor me, Jacob. Woodie, earlier today I thought you had seen the light. Conceded, 'I am but indifferent honest' myself. But even pirates need to feel safe with their shipmates. You and I shook hands as partners. You don't seem to understand what that means. However I'm not going to abandon you here. You'd be balanced in a week. Dead. Or worse. So we'll take you back. By the way, it is impossible to steal Gay Deceiver. Yes, I know you once stole a ship enormously bigger than Gay. But not as well protected."

"Lazarus! *Tell* them."

"Lib, I was waiting for the Commodore to finish. That corpse wasn't murdered because it was never alive other than as a vegetable." Lazarus looked embarrassed.

"About thirty years ago we started a medical school on Tertius. A one-horse deal, more of a branch of the clinic. But genetic engineering is taught, and student genetic surgeons must practice. Ordinarily a clone that goes bad is killed and frozen and its tissues studied. A clone that takes—shows no fault, no deviation—is either cared for and allowed to develop if its genetic source wants a spare body and will pay for it. Or, more likely, a healthy clone is purely a laboratory exercise; an ethical medical school requires supervised destruction during the first pseudo trimester, before quickening shows in the wave form.

"Neither student nor tissue donor is likely to be upset by this quasi-abortion, as the student is almost always herself the donor—if it bothers her, she's in the wrong vocation.

"If the student is not the donor, emotional upset is hardly possible. The student thinks of the clone as a quasi-living histological specimen the usefulness of which is at end—and the tissue donor *can't* be upset, being unaware of it."

"Why so, Lazarus? If anybody is tinkering with *my* cells, I want to know about it, I do!"

"Deety, that tissue may be years, even centuries, old; the donor may be parsecs away. Or still warm and the donor just leaving the building. Or anything in between. A sperm-and-ova bank insures the future of the race; a tissue bank insures the future of the individual. But somebody has to pick up the check; it's a tanstaafl situation. A few of the very wealthy—and neurotic—always have a quickened but unawakened clone in stasis. I'm wealthy but not neurotic; I don't have a reserve clone."

I caught sight of Libby's face as Lazarus made that last statement—her mouth twitched in a half smile about to become (I think) a snicker, had she not suppressed all expression. No one but I caught it.

I made note to ask her about it later—then I remembered what the mouse told the cat and decided not to.

"But I do what any prudent Howard does; I have tissue on deposit. One may do this either of two ways: Pay high . . . or pay much lower and sign a release on half the donation for research and instruction." He grinned. "I'm stingy. My tissue is available to medical students."

He went on, "Not all medical schools are ethical. I can think of at least three planets where—" Lazarus looked directly at my wife. "Deety, you raised this issue. While I can think of three planets where one can buy any sort of monster, I can think of at least thirty where, for a much lower fee, I could simply say, 'I want that one'"—he pointed at Sharpie—"and the answer would be, 'It's a deal, Mac. How freshly dead and when do you want delivery?'"

Sharpie looked around behind herself as if to see at whom Lazarus had pointed.

"That's the cheapest way—"

"Then you *weren't* pointing at me!" Sharpie interrupted. "Woodie, it's not polite to point. For a moment you had me worried. I'm *never* cheap—high-priced, always."

"So I found out, Commodore. Deety, that's cheapest, and safe for the buyer in the places I have in mind. But how can I convince you that I *never* gave even a moment's consideration to that method? You seem to know a lot about me—more than I know about any of you. Is there anything that you have ever read or heard, anything that I've said or done, that would cause you to think that I would murder or contract for a murder—same but nastier—in order to further my own ends? I'm not saying that I have never killed. A man who has lived even half as long as I have has found himself more than once in a kill-or-be-killed situation. But the best way to deal with such a situation is not to get into it. Anticipate it. Avoid it."

Lazarus Long stopped and looked sad, and for the only time of my acquaintance with him, looked his age. I do not mean he suddenly looked decrepit. But he had an aura of ancient sorrow. "Professor Burroughs, if it would do any good, I would junk all my plans, accept being forever stranded here, for the privilege of taking a twenty-pound sledge and *smashing* your space-time twister."

I was shocked (damn it, I *like* good machinery). Jake looked hurt, Deety and Sharpie looked stunned.

Jake said tightly, "Lazarus . . . *why?*"

"Not to hurt *you*, Professor; you have my highest respect. You are one of three: the man who invented the wheel, the man who discovered how to use fire—and *you*. But, in making this supreme discovery, you have accomplished something I had thought impossible. You have made interstellar war logistically practical. Interstellar? Intergalactic—interuniversal!"

Lazarus suddenly straightened up, threw off his gloom, grinned. "All the King's horses and all the King's men can't close Pandora's Box again. Once it hits the fan, the only thing to do is sweep it up, package it, and sell it as fertilizer. Hilda has plans along that line. But I'm going to have to start thinking in military terms again. Figure out how to defend my home place against what appears to be that Ultimate Weapon much talked about but never achieved. I am glad to say that Hilda plans to keep it a close-held secret as long as possible; that may buy us time."

He turned his attention back to my wife. "Deety, I have never murdered, I never will. The nearest I ever came to it was once being sorely tempted to strangle a five-year-old boy. I admit that the thought has often passed through my mind that this character or that would look his best as the centerpiece of a funeral. But can I convince you that I have never *acted* on such thoughts? Think hard, please—all that you know of me. Am I capable of murder?"

Deety doesn't dither. (Remember how we got married?) She jumped up, hurried around our kitchen table, and kissed Lazarus—and stopped hurrying. It was a kiss that calls for a bed, or even a pile of coal—had there not been urgent business before the house.

Deety broke from it, sat down beside him, and said, "Tell us how we get this unmurdered fresh corpse. It's clear that we're going to have to go pick it up—in Gay. So we must know."

Libby said gently, "Lazarus, this is what you have been avoiding. May I tell it?"

"Thanks, Lib. No, you would pretty it up. I—"

"Pipe down!" said Deety. "Elizabeth, give us the straight word. Briefly."

"Very well. The medical school of B.I.T. is as ethical as you will find. My sister-wife Ishtar is director of the rejuvenation clinic and chairman of the board of the medical school, and still finds time to teach. I have never seen Maureen Johnson as I was born about two centuries after she was. But she is supposed to resemble Laz and Lor—unsurprising; she is their genetic mother, since they were cloned from Lazarus."

"Oh! I see. There is still a *third* clone from Lazarus. Female?"

"A spoiled one, Deety. Ishtar tells me that it is difficult, rather than otherwise, to get a bad clone from Lazarene tissue . . . so it is especially suitable for induced mutation experiments. She orders the destruction of these experiments when they have served their purpose."

"Deety said to make it brief," growled Lazarus.

Lib ignored him. "But, while Ishtar checks on the students, no one checks on her. For twenty years Ishtar watched for a clone that would *look* human but not *be* human. So deficient in forebrain that it could never be anything but a vegetable, unaware. She told me that her students had unknowingly provided her with dozens to work on. Usually they died too soon, or never developed human appearance, or had some other fault that made them unusable. But several years ago she succeeded. I testify that this thing *looked* like Laz and Lor as it passed through the stage of its forced development . . . and also that it looked like an older version, wrinkled and hair streaked with gray, when it died two Tertian years ago—"

"Huh? '*Fresh* corpse'!"

"—and was quick-frozen at once. I testify to something else. Friends, in becoming a woman I acquired an interest in biology that I had not had, as a male. While I teach math at B.I.T., I am also staff mathematician to the clinic and have studied a bit of human biology. When I say that this spoiled clone was *never* alive in any real sense I speak as the mathematical biologist who checked its monitors' records daily. It always required full metabolic support; we monitored everything. The surprising thing is that Ishtar could keep it alive long enough to let it appear to age. But Ishtar is very skillful." Libby added, "Lazarus would not only have become upset in telling this, but he could not have told it first hand as Ishtar refused to permit Lazarus to see this spoiled clone or any records on it."

"A willful woman," said Lazarus. "In three seconds I could have told Ish whether or not this thing looked enough like my mother to be useful. Instead I must depend on the opinions of people who have never laid eyes on my mother. Damn it, I am owner of record of the clinic and Chairman Regent of all B.I.T. Does that count with Ishtar? Hilda, my senior wife is as tough a case as you are . . . and looks as little like it as you do."

"So? It will be interesting to see what happens when I am your junior wife," Sharpie answered at her pertest.

"Are you going to be my junior wife?" Lazarus swung around and looked at her husband. "Jake?"

"I don't think I have a vote," my blood brother answered easily.

"I'll automatically be your junior wife if we are invited to join the Long Family which we damn well ought to be if we make this work!" Sharpie said indignantly.

"Wait a half!" I put in. "*If* we are invited to join the Long Family—a tall assumption if I ever saw one—*Deety* would be junior. Not you, you elderly baggage."

"Hillbilly can be junior if she wants to be. I don't mind."

"Deety," I said, "are you serious? I've been trying to point out to your stepmother that you don't push your way into a family."

"I wasn't pushing, Zebadiah," my wife answered. "I want us to stay on Tertius at least until we have our babies, and possibly make it our home; it seems to be a pleasant place and should be free of 'Black Hats'—no skin taboos. But that doesn't mean that the Longs have to have us in their laps."

"*I* intend to nominate you, Zebadiah," Libby told me. "All four of you. And I hope you four accept. But, Deety twin, you know what I'm attempting. With your father."

"Yes, I know. I'm cheering for it."

"Your husband must hear this. Deety, I still have that Y chromosome in every cell even though it has been so inhibited by hormone balance that I don't notice it. You and I could try for a mathematical-genius baby, too."

"*Huh!* Which one of us supplies the penis?"

"Ishtar does. Neither of us would be host-mother, the way it would be done. But any of my sister-wives would supply womb room if she didn't happen to be pregnant. Or the host-mother could be a stranger we would never meet and the child's family-parents strangers, too—all handled by Ishtar who always reads the relevant genetic charts before approving anything."

"Zebadiah?"

I said without hesitation, "It's up to you, hon. I'm in favor of it; it makes sense. But *don't* lose track of the child. Elizabeth, I want to adopt the baby ahead of time. Hmm— Bottle baby . . . but the formulas are probably better now. Not here-now. Tertius there-then-now."

"'Bottle baby'? *Oh!* No longer done; a baby needs to suckle. But there is usually spare milk around the Longs'. If I'm lactating I always have excess; I turn out to be a good milch cow despite that extra chromosome. But Deety can nurse our child if she wishes to; causing a woman to come fresh with milk without bearing a child is a minor biochemical manipulation today—Tertian-today. Professional wet nurses do it regularly and are likely to be in that vocation because they love babies but can't have 'em themselves for some reason."

"Sounds good." (What sounded best was this: a baby Deety is a wonderful idea—but a baby Deety who is also a baby Libby is sure to be wonderful squared. Cubed!)

"While I'm on this and no one here but family—Jacob, there is no reason not to create a third mathematical supergenius by crossing you with your daughter."

I was looking at my wife, thinking pleasant thoughts about baby Deety-Libby, when Elizabeth dropped this bomb—and Deety shut down her face. It's not an unpleasant expression; it's a no-expression, a closed door, while Deety sorts out her thoughts.

So I looked at Jake, in time to see his face shift from surprise to shock. "But that's—"

"Incest?" Libby supplied. "No, Jacob, incest is a social matter. Whether you bed your daughter is none of my business. I'm speaking of *genes*, of still another way to conserve mathematical genius. Ishtar would scan your charts most carefully and would resort to chromosome surgery if there was the slightest chance of double dosage of a bad allele. But you and your daughter could see Ishtar on different days and never know *anything* about the outcome. Your genes are not your property; they come from your race. This offers opportunity to give them back to the race with your highest talent reinforced . . . without loss to anyone. Think about it."

Jake looked at me, then at his daughter. "Deety?"

She added no-expression voice to no-expression face—but directed her answer to me: "Zebadiah, this is necessarily up to you and Jacob." I'm not sure that anyone but Sharpie noticed that she had not said "Pop."

Deety added at once with total change in manner, "First things first! Maureen's rescue. All of you are stuck in a rut of time sequence. Oh, the minor problem of keeping clear of Dora and the missile both times. Routine." (And *I* was hit by a satori.)

Lazarus answered, "But Deety, I promised Dora never again to take her anywhere near Albuquerque."

Deety sighed. "Lib?"

"Frames one-thirteen through seven-seven-two, then seven-seven-three through one thousand and two?"

"Precisely. And precisely it must be, too. I'm timing it by that yellow open roadable approaching from the other direction. What are you using?"

"The same one. Easy to spot and its speed never varies."

Lazarus said, "Jake, do you know what they are saying?"

"Yes and no. They are treating it as two problems. But we lack three seconds of time enough to dump one and snatch the other. Those—traffic lights, you called them?—leave that intersection clear by a measured interval, clocked by your camera."

Sharpie suddenly grinned; I nodded to her to take it. She did. "Deety and Libby are saying that we do it *twice*. First, we rescue Maureen. Then we come back and dump the corpse."

I added, "But the second time we don't ground. Jake, I'm going to ask you to move over—Deety moves to my seat. We'll dump the dead meat so that it hits the ground between frames seven-seven-two and seven-seven-three. I'll be on manual and hovering. I need to know where Dora is and where that missile is and need to be sure of the acceleration of gravity, Earth-Prime. Because that corpse will *already* be falling, right over our heads, while we are making the snatch. Close timing. Mmm—Gay can fly herself more precisely than I can. I think that Deety and I will write a program . . . then I'll be on override—suspenders and belt."

Jake added, "Zeb, I see the procedure. But, if we are hovering for the drop while we are also on the ground, why aren't we shown in the photographs?"

"May be in some of them. Doesn't matter. Deety, when do we do this? Cancel. Sharpie? Your orders, Captain?"

Deety and Sharpie swapped glances. Then they sounded like

Laz-Lor, with Sharpie leading. "Now to bed. It's almost midnight in our biological time, slightly later in local time."

"We do both jobs after breakfast," Deety responded. "But sleep as late as we can. Be sharp and on our toes. 'Minds me. Just one 'fresher, quite primitive. But the two in Gay are as available here as anywhere; since they are actually in Oz. Six people, three pots, not difficult."

"And three beds," added Sharpie. "Jacob, kiss us goodnight and take Lib to bed. Master bedroom and good luck! Use my toothbrush, Lib hon—anything else you need?"

"No. A good cry, maybe. I love you, Hilda."

"If I didn't love you, Elizabeth, I wouldn't be Madam of this joint. We'll cry together the day Ishtar tells us you've caught. Now *shoosh!* Scat! Kiss us and go to bed."

As they headed upstairs Sharpie said to me, "Zebbie, give Deety a pre-amnesty so that she can try out Lazarus and find out whether she wants to be junior wife."

I tried to look amazed. "Deety, haven't you tried Lazarus *yet?*"

"You know darn well I haven't! When have I had time?"

"From a woman who specializes in programming time machines that is a silly question. Lazarus, she's already knocked up, so don't fret about it. One warning: She bites."

"The best ones always do."

"Hush. Kiss us good-night, dears. Zebbie, open the couch in the living room; that's where you're going to keep me warm."

"But who's going to keep *me* warm? A skinny little runt like you?"

Sharpie bites.

XLV   A Stitch in Time

Jake:

We popped out one klick H-above-G over Albuquerque, Earth-Prime, and Gay tilted her nose down. A last-minute change put my daughter Deety at copilot, while I sat left rear, nominal navigator. Deety can use verniers as accurately as I, did not expect to use them at all, *did* need to be able to see the yellow roadable—and has this clock in her head.

Elizabeth Long was in the after compartment, strapped down but not on lumps of ordnance. Rifles, pistols, bed clothes for the control compartment, anything else that could be moved easily to reduce clutter, had been shifted into our space warp, as had Lazarus Long.

Doctor Ishtar had warned Lazarus not to let his mother recognize him, as the shock to her might be harmful, even fatal. While Lazarus had been trying to figure out how to make the snatch using Dora, he had planned on wearing disguise. But hiding in our Land-of-Oz addition was simpler—especially as Ishtar was almost as anxious that Lazarus not see his mother, not see his mother's pseudo corpse—this I learned from Elizabeth in the night.

So I showed Lazarus the everlasting picnic basket, advised him to use bed clothes to make a shakedown and sleep if possible as there would be time to kill, and supplied him with books—but *don't* come out until I open the door! Then did not mention that I was locking him in.

I was relieved to have only a nominal job. I was not sleepy despite a short night—I was bemused.

I was falling in love with—*had* fallen in love with—Elizabeth Long. No less in love with Hilda—more in love with her than ever! I am learning that love does not subtract—it multiplies!

As Gay tilted down I reached over and touched Hilda's hand. She smiled and threw me a kiss. I'm sure she had a sweet night; she has loved Zeb as long as she has known him. "As a loyal chum," she tells me—but Hilda holds to the Higher Truth that it is better to be kind than to be frank. It did not matter either way; Zeb is my blood brother beloved by me, perfect husband for my daughter, and, if not Hilda's lover in the past, then he surely was now—and it troubled me not at all. On awakening I had discussed it with Jane before I opened my eyes—Jane approves and is delighted by Elizabeth.

My daughter had an unusual night, too. If the myths are true, Lazarus is more than one hundred times as old as Deety. This gulf may not matter to him—but Deety takes everything seriously.

Apparently it had done her no harm; at breakfast she was bright-eyed and bubbly. All of us were euphoric and eager to get on with it.

Zeb was saying, "That's it! Got it in the gunsight—got the range, Smart Girl?"

"Got it nailed, Boss!"

"Keep it so. Deety! Yellow roadable?"

"Just spotted it. Gay, count down! Four . . . Three . . . Two . . . One . . . *Now!*"

We were diagonally in that intersection; Gay's portside door was popping open. I heard Zeb say, "Oh, my God!" He was out of the car, kneeling, picking up a body, kicking a cop in the stomach, and *throwing* that body to me, as he scrambled inside and shouted, "GayBounce!"

Gay bounced. Gay is not supposed to lift with a door open and "Bounce!" means ten klicks. She bounced *one* klick, finished closing her door, waited while Zeb checked the seal—completed the bounce. I am now a believer.

I was passing this little old lady back to Elizabeth, and looking for resemblance to Lazarus when I heard Zeb moan, "I didn't get her purse, *I didn't get her purse!*"

"What of it?" said Deety. "It's where we want it. Gay Deceiver. Tertius Orbit. Execute."

A beautiful planet—

Zeb was saying, "Lib, can you coach us? Or are you too busy?"

"Not that busy. Maureen fainted but her heart is strong and steady, and I have a strap holding her. Is Gay on frequency?"

Deety reported, "Right on. Go ahead, Lib."

The next I can't report; it was in Galacta. Then Elizabeth said, "We'll be passing over Boondock in three minutes twenty-two seconds. Roof of the clinic is designated. Shall I come forward and point it out?"

"Can you handle yourself in free fall?" Zeb asked.

"I've some experience. Eight centuries."

"My big mouth. Come forward."

In four or five minutes we grounded on a flat roof in a wooded part of a moderately large city. I saw a figure in a white coverall, plus two others with a wheeled stretcher—and only then did I recall that none of us had dressed. Hilda had asked; Lazarus had vetoed, Elizabeth had concurred.

So I found myself bare to my ears, bowing over a lady's hand and saying, "I am honored, Doctor Ishtar."

She is indeed beautiful—a Valkyrie sculptured from cream and marshmallow and honey. She smiled and kissed my hand.

Elizabeth said something in this other language; Ishtar smiled again and said, in careful, fluent English, "In that case, he is one of us"—took my head in her hands and kissed me thoroughly.

Ishtar so distracted me that I did not notice that Maureen had been handed out—awake but dazed—been rolled away, and was gone. All of us were thoroughly and carefully kissed, then Elizabeth discussed matters with Ishtar in Galacta. "Ish says that she has been slowly warming the thing. It is now at four degrees Celsius. She would like more time but will bring it to thirty-seven degrees Celsius in six hours if she must."

Deety said, "How about twenty-four hours?"

Ishtar was pleased at this, agreed that she understood that the substitute *must* be dressed in the patient's (client's) clothing, agreed that the space we were in would be kept clear—and asked, "What's that pounding noise?"

Elizabeth explained that it was Lazarus. "He is in a magic space warp about where we were standing. He knows that he is supposed to remain there, but he changed his mind—and has just discovered that he is locked in."

Ishtar's smile suddenly became a grin, as quickly left. "A magic space warp? Lib, I want to hear about that."

"You will."

We climbed back inside, Deety told Gay "Twenty-four hours"—and we stepped out again. Ishtar was lying on a pad, taking the sun . . . this time as bare as we were—and I was still more impressed.

"Right on time," she said, standing (taller than I am) and, as always, smiling. "The substitute is waiting, and I have had time to examine and talk with the client. She is in good shape for her age, understands in part at least what has happened, and is undismayed by it. Please tell Lazarus that, if he returns to Tertius soon, he will not be admitted to this building for seventeen months. The client is most firm: she will *not* see Lazarus until I have completed rejuvenating her."

"Lib," said my daughter Deety, "seventeen what sort of months? I want to set an exact rendezvous—and Gay's time calibration is not Tertian but Earth-Prime and Earth-zero. Old Home Terra." With Elizabeth as interface the three agreed on an exact time. Then Elizabeth again discussed something in that language.

Ishtar nodded. "No problem, I have seen that picture. And a hooded cape is even less trouble."

So we left.

Dropping that pseudo corpse was routine but I was glad to be quit of it (I had swapped seats with my daughter). Then we were back on Tertius.

"Always prompt," said Ishtar—and I was astounded to see that she was quite pregnant, close to birthing . . . when I had seen her, slender for her height, two minutes earlier. "And we are on time, too. Maureen, my friends and yours." She named us.

Maureen Johnson spoke to us first in Galacta, shifted to English when she realized that we did not know the common tongue. Yes, she does look like Laz and Lor—but prettier. A woman of beauty and great charm. I find that I am growing accustomed to perfect ladies who embrace, bare body to bare body, on meeting a fully-vouched-for stranger. She thanked each of us and made us believe it.

"*Still* pounding?" Ishtar inquired.

"It has been less than five minutes for him, Ish," Elizabeth explained. "But you know his temper; perhaps we had better leave. Home soon, I think."

So we left again, with Maureen squeezed between me and my wife, with a package and a cloak in her lap. We were back inside Dora at once. Elapsed time: zero seconds. We still had an hour and twenty minutes to prepare for dinner. I found that I was hungry, even though breakfast was three hours ago, biological time—almost all of it spent in Beulahland, programming for the caper, as all three phases took only a few durational minutes, mostly on a rooftop in Boondock.

Maureen put on the cloak, a hooded cape, and carried the little package. "Silly but fun," she said. "Where do we go now?"

"Come with me," Hilda told her. "Beloved, you can let Woodie out as soon as Dora tells Gay that I have reached flag cabin. When he yelps, tell him that we were too busy to play games with him . . . and the next time he wants a favor from me he can crawl on his knees. Pounding indeed! Tell him that I am extremely tired and am going to nap until just before dinner and he is not to call me or to come to the flag cabin between now and dinner without suffering my *extreme* displeasure and a punch in the nose from you. All of you come up to flag cabin as soon as you wish but try not to be seen by Woodie. You'll probably find Maureen and me in the lounging pool."

XLVI "I'm gifted with second sight."

Deety:
When the Hillbilly stages a production, she doesn't stint. By protocol decreed by Lazarus Long, dinner in Dora is formal, but with wide latitude in "formal"—casual dress being the only thing utterly verboten. Dinner is preceded by a happy hour where one can sip Coca-Cola or get roaring drunk.

Aunt Hilda changed all that for this night. No happy hour but be on time—two minutes before twenty o'clock, ship's time. No one permitted to eat in her/his quarters—a command performance.

No options in dress— Commodore Auntie decided what each would wear, where each would sit. I said, "Commodore Hilda honey, aren't you kind o' throwing your weight around? What there is of it?"

She answered, "Yes, I am, Deetikins, for this occasion. But before you criticize, ask your husband whether or not I ever permitted one of my parties to flop."

"Don't need to ask him. Why, at your last one, our old Buick blew up. Never a dull moment."

"I didn't plan that. But we got husbands out of it; let's not complain. Before you deliver my message to the twins, tell me this. Is it safe to let them in on our secret?"

"Hillbilly, I tell Zebadiah *anything* even though someone— you, for example—has asked me not to."

"Deety, I thought we had a 'You'll-keep-my-secrets-and-I'll-keep-your-secrets' agreement?"

"We do. But telling Zebadiah gives you two covering for you instead of one. About Laz-Lor—remember that they are his *wives* as well as his clones."

"Hon, you were always a wise one. All right, we keep it secret. Tell them what to wear—and please understand that I'm hiding

454

behind you to avoid argument; it's a favor I appreciate. Sending up sword and saber is a favor to your husband and to your father but I thank you on their behalf if they forget. Send the blades to your suite; they've decided they can dress more easily without women underfoot."

"A canard," Pop said, just back of my neck. "The women don't want *us* underfoot."

"I knew it was one or the other, Jacob," Aunt Hilda agreed. "But Dora has already taken your uniforms to our suite and your swords will—"

"—be there, too, and I can recognize a fact when I fall over it and have never been happier, my love, than I have been since you took charge of my life and started telling me what to decide."

"Jacob, you're making me teary."

"Jake! Can you hear me?"—Lazarus' voice and Aunt Hilda used family sign language; Pop nodded and answered promptly:

"Certainly, Lazarus—what's on your mind?"

"I'm faced with the impossible and need help. I received an order—you, too, I think—to dress in military uniform at dinner. The only uniform I have aboard is in the flag cabin and—say, are you *in* the flag cabin?"

Aunt Hilda shook her head. Pop answered, "I'm in our suite, dressing for dinner. Hilda needed a nap. I told you."

"You certainly did, sir. I'm allergic to being punched in the snoot. But— Well, if you would use your influence—"

"If any."

"If any, to get me that uniform twenty minutes before dinner"— Aunt Hilda nodded—"or even ten, you would save me the horrible dilemma of deciding which order to break."

"Don't decide to break the one telling you not to disturb Hilda."

"I didn't even consider breaking *that* one! And it's not your fist in my snoot. Jake . . . she *terrifies* me. I don't understand it. I'm twice her mass and all muscle; she couldn't possibly hurt me."

"Don't be certain. She has a poisoned fang. But calm yourself, comrade. I guarantee delivery by nineteen minutes before the bell at latest."

"Jake, I knew I could depend on you. Let me know when you want a bank robbed."

I gave Maureen a special hug before I left to carry out my orders. I knew what the Hillbilly was doing: rigging it so that she could have a quiet hour in which to get acquainted with Maureen. I didn't resent it; I would have rigged it for me had I been able.

I curved down the corridor, whistled for Lib to let me in,

stopped dead and whistled another sort of whistle. She was dressed, if "dressed" is the word. "Wheeee*whoo!*"

"Like it?"

"I can't wait to get into mine. It is the most indecent outfit I've ever seen, with no other purpose than to excite lewd, libidinous, lascivious, licentious, lecherous, lustful longings in the loins of Lotharios."

"Isn't that the purpose of clothing?"

"Well . . . aside from protection—yes. But I'm beginning to realize that a culture with no body taboo has to go much farther in styling to achieve that purpose."

It was a "dress" with a "skirt" that was a 10-cm ruffle worn low. The material was silky stuff in pastel green. The bodice had no back but the front came clear up to the neck—with cutouts for each teat. The designer did not stop there. Lib's left teat was bare—but her right one was barer yet: a transparent film that clung and was covered with rainbow iridescence that moved in endless patterns with every jiggle—and jiggle we do no matter how firm. Elizabeth is as firm as I am but hers quivered enough to swirl that iridescence just from breathing.

Whew!

If both had been bare, or both iridescent, it would not have done a quarter as much. It was the contrast that would make 'em howl at the Moon.

My dress was exactly like hers save that my right teat was the bare one.

Lib got me into it, then I hurried to the bridge, with a hope-promise to be back ten minutes before the hour to have her touch up my eyebrows and lashes. I'm not much for cosmetics (neither is she) but our lashes and brows hardly show without help and this was a formal occasion.

One of Dora's blue fireflies led me to a lift that took me to the bridge, where Dora had told me I would find Laz and Lor. Laz spotted me first, made a yelling noise while patting her lips, which I took to mean enthusiasm. Those kids—correction: women close to Pop's age but they *feel* like kids—Laz-Lor are as female as I am and recognize what incites the lovely beast in men. They liked my dress.

I liked that bridge. Reminded me of Star Trek; pointed ears would not have surprised me. Or Nichelle Nichols backed by colored lights. "This place makes my mouth water. Maybe someday a guided tour? Pretty please!"

Captain Lor said, "Certainly—"

"—but how about a swap as—"

"—we haven't even been inside—"

"—Gay Deceiver and Dora says she—"

"—is wonderful and when this job is—"

"—done and we've rescued Mama Maureen there—"

"—won't be anything to stop us once Dora—"

"—is safe on the ground at Tertius. Huh?"

"Certainly," I answered . . . gleefully as now I *knew* that our 17-hour absence in zero seconds had not been noticed. To Lor and Laz the snatch was still in the planning stage. Apparently Ol' Buddy Boy had not yet told his sisters. Had not yet worked up a set of lies, probably, that would account for his being locked in the bathroom while the rest of us did the job.

"At the earliest opportunity," I went on. "Want to take a ride in Gay?"

"Oh, my! Could we?"

"Not for me to say. But I can tell you what works. Cuddle up to the Commodore. Pet her, be sweet to her. Ask her if she will let you call her 'Aunt Hilda' when you're off duty; that will please her. She's a cat; pet her and respect her feelings and she purrs—push her and she scratches."

They glanced at each other. "We will. Thanks."

"De nada, chicas—"

"You've learned Galacta!" (In chorus—)

"What? No. Probably a phrase that carried over. But I was sent here on duty and I've been chatting instead. Commodore's compliments to the Captain and the Commodore requests that Captain Lorelei Lee Long and First Officer Lapis Lazuli Long join her at dinner at twenty o'clock and, as a favor to the Commodore, please dress in the same fashion as Doctors Libby and Deety—and that's me and I'm wearing the fashion you are to wear."

Captain Lor answered, "Certainly we'll be there; we never miss dinner and—"

"—always dress formally and I don't—"

"—mean bare skin. Skin is for working or—"

"—sleeping. But we treat dinner in the Dora as a—"

"—formal party and that calls for the works. Formal evening—"

"—dress and jewelry and cosmetics and perfume and we are about—"

"—to bathe and change, but we can't dress the way you are—"

"—because our dresses are already picked out and—"

"—it's *too late* to start over!"

I said, "Look, chums, you brought this on yourselves by urging Lib and me to dress this way. Neither of us was enthusiastic but we promised. The Commodore learned what Libby and I expected to wear, and decided that four of us, all about the same size and coloration, would look wonderful in matching green dresses. So Lib and I are to be opposite you two, balancing you, and the men are required to wear uniforms so as not to compete with us four. All clear?"

They got their stupid look which actually is a cover for stubborn determination. Lor said:

"The Captain sends her respects to the Commodore and regrets—"

"*Hold it!* Does this ship have a lifeboat?"

"Yes," answered Lor, "but—"

"But you are master of this ship. Yes, I know. And I'm gifted with second sight. I see only two viable futures for you. Did you get your pirate flag up in the lounge?"

"Yes, we did, but—"

"If you'll tell me what lifeboat and where, I'll get the flag to you before twenty. I see you starting out in that lifeboat to be pirates. Or I see you at dinner in dresses of any green cloth you can find, cut hastily in this style and pinned together. No jewelry. No cosmetics that show. I don't think you can fake this iridescent stuff but that stick-on transparent wrapping, used instead, would show that you had *tried*. The Commodore never rejects anyone for failing; what she despises is not *trying*. Send your answer via Dora. I can't be your messenger boy; I have work to do before dinner, now only forty-seven minutes away. Will the Captain excuse me?"

I got out fast. I didn't believe for one second that a ship stocked like the Dora, run by identical redheads, could fail to have *endless* formals in green—including this style or close to it. By now the twins were frantically consulting their brother via Dora, and from what I heard him say to Pop, I thought Lazarus would tell them that it was safer to jump ship and change their names than it would be to tangle with the miniature buzz saw—but if Dora couldn't fake something that would at least show a hard try, he would sell her off as spare parts and install one of those new-model "Susan Calvin" positronic brains that everybody said was the coming thing for smartships.

I said Hello to Gay, then tried to reach under the instrument board and find the catch by touch.

I got out of the car in order to stand up in the ship's passageway and took off my deliciously indecent dress. Then I was able to fold, bend, and staple, to open the stowage. A saber and a sword—no belts. "Gay."

"What, Deety?"

"I'm looking for two sword belts. Category should be personal possessions, miscellaneous, weapons, belts for weapons."

"Deety, they are supposed to be with the sword and saber. Many things were moved into the Land of Oz today; I heard you all talking about it. But no changes were read into my inventory. I'm sorry."

"Smart Girl, it's not your fault. We should have told you."

"Deety, I've rolled the dice. The curve says that the most probable place is on hooks in Sunbonnet Sue's wardrobe."

They were.

I was starting to leave, after telling Gay she was a Smart Girl, when she said, "Deety, your father is calling. Dora has him on hold, through me."

"Thanks, Gay; thanks, Dora. Pop?"

"Deety, are you still in Gay?"

"Just outside the starboard door."

"Can you lay hands on my automatic and the web belt that goes with it?"

"Saw both three minutes ago."

"Will you please remove the clip, check the chamber to be sure it's empty, then bring belt and pistol when you fetch our toad-stickers?"

"Anything for a steady customer."

I left with belt and sword slung over one shoulder, saber and belt over the other so that the belts crossed between my teats, and with the web belt with holster and pistol interwoven through the others because it was far too big for my waist. This left my hands free to carry my dress, one hand being almost clean enough.

Pop said: "What took you so long? I promised Lazarus I'd get this stuff to him on time. Now I'm going to have to dogtrot. In Army blues."

I told him I had stopped off at the pool hall and playing off the match game had taken a while. "If you'll excuse me, sir, I have problems, too."

Elizabeth wiped me down with a damp towel, dried and powdered me and drew my eyebrows and touched up my lashes and clucked over me, all in nine minutes, then most carefully put my dress back on me. "Ordinarily one does not take off a washable and put it back on—just wear it until you shower it off. A drop of water will go through this material like acid. Better skip the soup."

Place cards showed us where to dine. But at two minutes before the hour the Hillbilly had not arrived, so we were standing. Laz-Lor came in, sat down—in dresses identical with mine and Lib's, perfect fit, nothing improvised. Their brother spoke quietly to them; they stood up. Lazarus was dressed in a very old-fashioned army uniform, breeches with rolled leggings, a tunic with a stock collar, and Pop's pistol at his side.

All but Pop's stuff looked brand-new; I concluded that Lazarus had had it tailored.

Just as my head ticked twenty o'clock, a bugle (Dora) sounded attention. At least it had that effect on the men and Libby, so I stood straight. Laz-Lor looked at their brother and did so, too.

The wardroom has three steps leading down into it from each of its archway doors, with a little platform at the top so that you don't fall on your face. Pop and Zebadiah marched up those steps, faced each other (and I thought how beautiful Zebadiah looked in dress uniform; I had never seen him in it). Pop snapped, "Draw! Swords!" Instead of coming down, they crossed blades in an arch. Lazarus looked startled and drew pistol, placed it smartly across his chest.

This archway was closed by drapes; we had come in from the other side. A drum and bugle (Dora again) sounded a ruffle-and-flourish; the drapes lifted from both sides—and here was the Hillbilly, standing tall (for her) and straight, with her perfect ice-cream skin gleaming in flood lights against a background of midnight blue. She was so beautiful I choked up.

Dora's invisible band played *The Admiral's March* as our tiny Commodore marched proudly down the steps toward us. (It could have been *The Admiral's March;* Pop admitted later that he hummed to Dora the march played for generals and told her to fake it.)

Aunt Hilda did not sit down when she reached the head of the table, she stood near her chair instead. Nor had my father and my husband left their places, they simply brought their swords down. As soon as Hilda stopped and faced in, Pop commanded, "Corporal Bronson! *Front and Center!*"

Lazarus jerked as if he had been struck, holstered his pistol, marched to the far end, making sharp corners in passing around the wardroom table. He halted, facing Hilda—she may have given him some sign.

Dora hit two bugle notes; Aunt Hilda sang:

"Shipmates, beloved friends, tonight we are greatly honored!"

Four ruffles-and-flourishes, as the drapes lifted and parted, and again lights picked out bare skin, this time against a forest-green backing: Maureen in opera-length black stockings, green round garters, dark shoes with semi-high heels, her long red hair down her back.

Maureen was not "standing tall"; she was in the oldest and most graceful of sculptor's poses: left knee slightly bent, weight slightly more on her right foot, chest lifted only a little but displaying her full teats, nipples heavily crinkled. Her smile was happy.

She held pose while that march concluded, then, in the sudden silence, held out her arms and called: *"Theodore!"*

"Corporal Bronson" fainted.

XLVII   *"There are no tomorrows."*

Zeb:

Sharpie shouldn't have done it to Lazarus. For a veteran of sixteen wars and Koshchei alone knows how many skirmishes and narrow escapes to be placed in a position where he is so shocked that blood drains from his head and he collapses "ain't fitten."

Deety agrees but asks me if *I* could have refrained from staging Mama Maureen's return that way, given the chance? Well, no, had I Sharpie's imagination—but it *still* would not have been "fitten."

Not that he was hurt by it. Sharpie, all forty-three kilos of her, checked his fall. She was watching Lazarus, saw him start to collapse, closed the gap and grabbed him around the waist, did her best.

Sharpie saved him from hitting his head on the wardroom table.

I would bet long odds that everyone was looking at Maureen except Sharpie. Sharpie had staged it—and the producer was interested in the effect on the one for whom it had been staged.

She had staged it even to the extent of getting Libby to ask Ishtar to obtain costume—shoes, hose, and round green garters to match a photograph, plus a hooded cape to keep our ubiquitous snoop Dora from knowing that we had an extra aboard. Sharpie had figured this way: that "French photo" snapshot of Mama Maureen (yeah, I call her that too—she's the most motherly person in any world . . . and the sexiest. Don't mention the last to Deety) (Deety knows it—*Deety*)—that snapshot was still in existence unless destroyed by machine-gun fire in 1918, Earth-Prime.

Which it would not be . . . because Lazarus "got his arse shot off" as his sisters describe it. Not literally true, it was a belly wound more than bullets in his arse that came that close to finishing him. But all the wounds were low.

Where does a man in combat carry his most cherished possessions? In a breast pocket, usually the left one. I always have and I've never heard a veteran deny this.

It might be worth it to faint in order to wake up surrounded by Maureen, Hilda, Laz-Lor, Elizabeth, and my own reason for being. Jake and I could have played several hands of gin before anyone bothered with us. So I asked Dora for drinks and snacks for Jake and me, as it seemed uncertain as to when dinner would be served. Or if.

I heard Sharpie say, "Maureen, we must get this heavy uniform off him. Dora keeps this ship tropical. I should never have ordered uniforms for men while we women are comfortable." They started peeling him.

I said, "Jake, school's out." I had sweated through my number-one uniform—might never wear it again but I'm sentimental about it. Jake was in as bad shape. Once you get happy with skin any clothes make you feel like Rameses II.

We peeled down and handed our clothes and swords to one of Dora's waldoes and told her to hand them to Gay—including Jake's pistol, belt, and holster, which I retrieved without anyone noticing me. Jake and I were Chinese stage hands; "Corporal Ted Bronson" was getting all the attention.

Dora pointed out that Gay was locked. I said, "If one of her doors were open, could you lay this gear on a seat?" Yes, she could. "Then do it," I said. "Let me talk to Gay."

We eventually had dinner, with everybody "formal" but Maureen. She retained her "casual" clothing long after everyone else was in formal skin. But not until I got pix of the Four Disgraces. Libby and Deety wanted to go shower, too, when Jake and I decided that, having discarded uniforms, we should shower in fairness to Dora's airconditioning. I asked them and Laz-Lor please to wait until I staggered down (we had encountered a force-four sea, with white caps) to Gay for Jake's Polaroid.

Turned out not to be necessary; Dora could take color and 3-D, still or motion, any angle, and light as needed, just as she had lighted the posing (which she had photographed, too, I learned later).

Maureen and Jake directed while "Corporal Bronson" and I sprawled Nero-style on lounges intended for Lib and Deety. Sharpie sat between us and dropped grapes into our mouths.

Jake tried to make the poses "artistic." Mama Maureen agreed with everything Jake said, then did it her way. The results may have been artistic. But I *know* that those pix would give a skeleton one last case of raging tumescence.

Meanwhile Dora was singing and playing, urging us to eat— tasty tidbits eaten with tongs; I was reminded of the best in Oriental cuisines—and plying us with fine wines. Dora seemed to have a vast repertoire, some of which (to my surprise) was familiar. When Judy Garland sings *Over the Rainbow*, who can miss it?— Dora used Judy's voice. I recall, too, *Enjoy Yourself; It's Later Than You Think*. Most of them I did not know.

Dora announced *Tomorrow's Song*—I *thought* that was what she said. Lazarus and Maureen held hands all through it and it was not a song that would fit the title I thought I had heard. I got straightened out when the song ended to dead silence and Maureen said to Lazarus, "Theodore, Ishtar was going to rearrange the watch list but Tamara vetoed it. She did it for you, dear man, and for me—but Tamara is anxious to see you."

"Tamara always knows what she's doing," Lazarus answered.

"Yes, Tammy always knows what is best," agreed Mama Maureen. "Tell me, Theodore, do I still make you think of her?"

Lazarus looked upset. "Uh, I don't know. You don't *look* like her . . . but you *feel* like her. And you look more like Nancy than you look like yourself."

"Yes, I know. None of our family was willing to wait; you've been away from home too long. Be patient, and when I look like me to your eyes, tell us, and Galahad will hold my cosmetic age at that. Are you going to do as you promised me, so long ago, take Tammy and me to bed together? Perhaps I should add, Theodore, I am now wife to your co-husbands. I don't ask that you marry me. Although I think Tammy will be shocked if you don't. But I shan't make it difficult, either way. I will hold to any pretence you wish. I did for Brian; I shall for you."

Maureen was neither shouting nor whispering; she was simply bringing him up to date on things he needed to know. Lazarus started to answer, his expression oddly mixed, when Elizabeth cut in: "Lazarus—"

"Eh? What, Lib?"

"Message to you from Ishtar. To be delivered when needed, and now is the time. Ish read both your charts with her computer set for maximum pessimism. She also had them read at New Rome without identification other than her own file numbers. She has this message for you . . . in answer to the answer you will make. She says to tell you that you are an uncivilized primitive, ignorant of science, especially genetics, oversentimental, almost pathologically stubborn, retarded, probably senile, superstitious, and provincial . . . and that she loves you dearly but will *not* permit you to make decisions in *her* area of authority. In vitro or in utero, the cross will take place. Let me add that Maureen was not given a choice, either."

"So? You can tell the big-arsed bitch that I agree with every word she says, especially the part about 'senile,' and that I gave up all hope of arguing with her tyrannical ways fifty years ago and that I love her just as dearly—outside her clinic—and that Maureen will tell her how such things will be handled; I don't have a vote." He turned toward me, looking past Sharpie's pretty toes. "Zeb, here is the wisdom of the ages: Men rule but women decide."

"Elizabeth, do you think I am anything like Tamara?"

"Mmm— Never thought about it. Yes, you both have that all-mother feeling. Uh, would you mind taking off costume? It distracts me from looking at *you.*"

"No trouble, Elizabeth. I don't like round garters except as advertising." Mama Maureen kicked off her shoes, took off the garters, carefully rolled down her hose in a manner interuniversal—stood up and stood easily, not posing.

"Turn around slowly. Mmm— Maureen, you *do* look like Tammy . . . or vice versa; it's probably your genes in her. Am *I* descended from you? Does anyone here know? Lazarus?"

"You are, Lib. But not through me. Through my sister Carol. 'Santa Carolita' believe it or not—which would surprise Carol as she was no saint. But your descent through Carol was not proved until long after you were killed, when the Families' records were being revised through computer analysis and a deeper knowledge of genes. No saints in our family, are there, Mama?"

"None that I know of, Woodrow. Not me, certainly. You were a little hellion; I should have spanked you *much* oftener than I did. Mmm . . . your father was as close to being a saint as any in our family. Brian was wise and good—and tolerant." She smiled. "Do you recall why we separated?"

"I'm not sure I ever knew. Mama, my recollections of that era are much sharper for my trip there as 'Ted Bronson'—the other is a *long* time back."

"In my sixties I stopped having babies. About the same time your brother Richard was killed. War. His wife, Marian Justin of the Hardy family, was with us, with their children, and Brian was back in uniform, a recalled colonel, on a desk job in San Francisco. When Richard was killed in 1945 we all took it hard but it was easier in that so many of us were together—Brian, and my youngest children, and Marian, and her children—five; she was thirty-one."

Mama Maureen, free of stockings and shoes, sat in lotus across from Hilda and accepted a plate from Dora's helpers. "Woodrow, I encouraged Brian to console Marian the only way a widow can be helped; she needed it. When that war was over, Marian needed a visible husband; her waistband and the calendar could not be reconciled. When we moved from San Francisco later that year, it was easy for Marian Justin Smith to become Maureen J. Smith while I became, with the aid of hair dye, her widowed mother—no one knew us in Amarillo and females were not yet compelled to have I.D.'s. So Marian had the baby as "Maureen," and only with the Howard Families Trustees was the correct genealogy recorded." Maureen smiled. "We Howards were easy about such things as long as it was kept inside the Families—and I am happy that we are even easier about it now.

"On our next move I moved out and became Maureen Johnson again, fifteen years younger since I did not look late seventies, and a Meen-ah-sotah Yonson, Woodrow, rather than a southern Missouri Johnson. A grass widow with round heels." Mama Maureen chuckled. "Howards married only to have babies. My production line had shut down but the equipment was there and the urge. By the time you darlings"—Maureen's eyes swept the wardroom—"rescued me, I had trimmed thirty-five years from my age and added thirty-five men to my memories. In fact, when you picked me up, I was on my way to a motel rendezvous, a widower of sixty who was willing to believe that I was sixty when in fact I expected to reach my Century Day in a fortnight."

I said, "What a dirty shame! I wish you had been coming *back* from the motel when we picked you up."

"Zebadiah, that's sweet of you but it's not a shame. We were getting bored with each other. I'm sure he read my obituary with as much relief as grief. I'm just glad you got me—and I'm told that *you* did most of it."

"Gay Deceiver did most of it. The car you rode in both ways. But we almost didn't pick you up. Things went wrong, badly. I knew that it was going to— Deety, can you tell her?"

"Mama Maureen, Zebadiah has forerunners of dangers. They are not long range; they are always just barely in time. I don't know what happened this morning but—"

" '*This morning?*' " Maureen looked extremely puzzled.

"Oh." My wife went on, "It was 'this morning' *to us*. You arrived here at eighteen-forty and a few seconds, ship's time. During that instant we spent fifteen hours on another planet, we made two trips to your native planet, two more trips to your new home planet, and you spent seventeen months on Tertius and we brought you back here—and it all happened today. Not just today but at that exact instant: eighteen-forty and thirteen point three seconds. Laz and Lor didn't know that we were gone; even the ship's computer didn't know we were gone."

"I did *so!*" Dora objected. "Gay was disconnected for nineteen microseconds. You think I don't notice a gap like *that?* I asked what happened and she told me that it was a power fluctuation. She *fibbed* to me! I'm sore at her."

Deety looked thunderstruck. "Dorable, Dorable! It wasn't Gay's fault. I *asked* her to keep our secrets. I made her promise."

"Mean!"

"I didn't mean to be mean to you, Dorable—and we *did* let you in on it as quickly as we could. We couldn't have staged the tableaux if you hadn't helped. Be angry with me if you must . . . but don't be angry with Gay. Please kiss and make up."

I don't know how computers hesitate, but I think I caught the briefest split second. "Gay?"

"Yes, Dora?"—the Smart Girl's voice through Dora's speakers.

"I don't want to be mad. Let's forget it, huh? Let's kiss and make up. I will if you will."

"Yes, yes! Oh, Dorable, I *do* love you."

"You're both good girls," said Deety. "But you are both professional women, too, and work for different bosses. Dora, you are loyal to *your* family; Gay is loyal to *her* family. It has to be that way. Dora, if your sister, Captain Lor, asked you to keep a secret, you wouldn't tell Gay, would you? Because she might tell me . . . and I would tell Zebadiah . . . and then the *whole world* would know."

(Would, huh? My dear wife, I had a clearance two stages above "Q"—so secret it does not have a name. Never mind, I'll take the rap.)

(Yes, I know, my husband, I once held the same level of clearance. But dealing with balky computers is my profession. Computers are supergenius-level *children* and must be dealt with on their own level. Okay, maybe, huh?—Deety)

"Gosh!"

"You see? Captain Lor, does Dora have any secrets of yours? Or of your brother's? She can tell them to Gay and Gay can tell them to me and I always tell everything to my husband and—"

Lazarus interrupted. "Dora! You tell tales out of school and I'll beat your ears off with an ax! It's all right for you two to chum together and play games. But you start swapping secrets and I'll call in Minsky's Metal Mentalities, Incorporated, to measure that space."

"*Male* computers. You can't scare me, Ol' Buddy Boy, you wouldn't trust your dirty neck to a male computer. Stupid."

"My neck isn't dirty; that's just where the collar of my uniform rubbed it."

"Dirty neck and a dirty mind. But don't worry, Ol' Buddy Boy; Dora Long doesn't tell secrets. I now see that Gay had to keep secrets, too—I just hadn't thought about it. But *you* were mean to my sisters."

"Me? *How?*"

"*You knew* about this caper; you didn't need to get it from Gay. You knew all about it; you were there. But you held out on your own twin sisters—"

"Most unfairly, Mama Maureen—"

"—as if we were *untrustworthy*, and if we're—"

"—untrustworthy, why can we be trusted with a ship and—"

"—the lives of everyone on board? We're glad you are here—"

"—for yourself, but maybe now that you are here, you will—"

"—protect us from his tyranny. Mama Ishtar doesn't, and

Mama Hamadryad just laughs at us, and Mama Minerva takes his—"

"—side, everytime. But you—"

"Girls."

"Yes, Mama?"

"I made a promise to myself years ago that when my children grew up, I would not interfere in their lives. I should have punished Woodie more frequently when he was a child, but he is no longer a child—"

"Then why does he act like one?"

"Lorelei Lee! It is rude to interrupt."

"I'm sorry, Mama."

"No harm done. But from what I was told at home, you two are not only my daughters but are also Theodore's wives. Wives of Lazarus. And equally wives of his co-husbands. Is this not true?"

"Yes, Mama. But he's pretty chinchy about it."

"If you mean 'chinchy in bed,' it may depend on how you treat him. I did not find him so, when I was his mistress, many years ago—centuries ago by some odd scale that I do not understand. You heard me say that I am now wife to your co-husbands— including Lazarus if he will accept me. But I am certainly, if you will accept me, sister-wife with you two. So I had better stop being your mother. Nay?"

"Why? Grammy Tammy is mother to Ish and everybody—"

"—and we have three mamas in our family now and everyone of them is our—"

"—sister-wife, too; Ish and Hamadarling and Minerva and now—"

"—we have Mama Maureen and we are both delighted that we are your sister-wives but—"

"—you can't get out of being our mama because we've been waiting for you *all our lives!*"

Dora echoed: "And I'm their sister so you are *my* mama, *too!*"

"Theodore, I think I am going to cry. You know my rule. I mayn't weep in front of my children."

I stood up, the whole gangling length of me. "Ma'am, I'd be honored to take you to some quiet place where you could cry on me all you please."

Seven—I think it was seven protein types and two computers— jumped on me. The essence was: "You *can't* take Maureen away from her own party!"—with ugly overtones of lynching.

The wind had freshened to force six, so I took liberal doses of champagne to insure against seasickness. After a bit I napped; it had been a busy day and I still was not over the shock of seeing a large freighter roadable about to take Gay's door off before I could close it and bounce. That was when I kicked the cop in the stomach. Ordinarily I don't kick cops; it makes one conspicuous.

Then a piercing voice was saying: "Flag Chief of Staff Carter's presence on the bridge is requested by the Commodore," and I wondered why the silly son of a bitch didn't comply, so that the noise would stop. Then something cold was poking my tender bare ribs. "That's you, Doc. I'll help you. Relax."

I *was* relaxed. Past tense. Some of Dora's waldoes aren't too gentle—or maybe these weren't people waldoes but for cargo; I admit that I'm fairly large for a growing boy.

In the lift I decided that the Beaufort scale was at least eight, more likely nine. Nevertheless we got to the bridge. Right out of Hollywood, a whole dome of displays and clocks—all moving slowly widdershins. Yet Gay made do with just an instrument board. I heard Sharpie say, "My God, look at him!"

Deety was saying something about we can shift seats if necessary to Lor while Laz was saying Drink this.

I said firmly, "I do *not* drink. Beshides I been dring; yr fashe is all blurry."

It must have been Laz and Lor who pinned me from both sides, each with an arm lock and a nerve pinch; Deety wouldn't do that to *me*.

Sharpie was holding my nose and Laz was pouring it down my throat; it fumed and bubbled. Then— Well, there must have been a stowaway; Deety wouldn't do that. Not to *me*.

They let go of me when I finished swallowing. I left the ship, made a fast inspection circuit, checked the Milky Way, and returned to a precision grounding. My ears fell off but it didn't seem military to stoop over and pick them up. Besides, Sharpie is playful.

"Flag Chief of Staff reports to the Commodore as ordered."

"How do you feel, Zebbie?"

"I feel fine, Ma'am. Is there any reason why I shouldn't?"

"I suppose not; you've had a nap."

"I did drop off. Dreamt I was in the Tasmanian Sea in a small vessel. Very uneasy body of water." I added, "Aside from that nightmare, now gone, I'm in top shape. Orders, Ma'am?"

We gave everybody the two-dollar tour, including the bathrooms in the Land of Oz. Libby, Deety, and Jake waited outside, the place being crowded. Sharpie ruled that Laz could relieve Lor to allow Lor to look first, then Lor took back the captaincy so that her sister could see. The fairyland bathrooms made the biggest hit. I concede that the time-space twister is not impressive. Then the twins thanked Hilda and left.

"Attention, please," said Hilda. "If you wish, we will show how we operate. Lazarus may use the astrogator's seat while Deety makes responses from the cargo space. Elizabeth will go back there, too, as she has ridden in Gay Deceiver. Deety, before you move aft, show Maureen and Lazarus how we squeeze a passenger into the rear seats; I'll scootch over.

"This car operates in several modes. As a roadable it is fast, comfortable, easy to handle, rather hard to park, and is usually parked with wings raked back as they are now, the hypersonic configuration. If we intended to drive it in the air, the wings would usually be extended for maximum lift. When operated by the Burroughs Continua Device, wing rake does not matter, but the chief pilot may choose to anticipate where he will arrive and rake accordingly.

"Since it has a computerized autopilot—Hello, Gay!"

"Hello, Hilda, mind if I listen?"

"Not at all, dear. Have you met everyone?"

"Yes, Hilda, and, since I've seen them through Dora's eyes, I place all of them by their voices." Gay added, "Dora is listening through me; she's going to record your demonstration. Is that all right?"

"Certainly. Dora, since you are recording, I'll make it as realistic as possible. Gay Deceiver. Close doors. Execute." I was at chief pilot, Jake at copilot; his door closed, I started checking the seal on mine.

"All hands, prepare for space. Copilot."

"Verniers zero, starboard door seal checked, seat belt fastened."

"Report incomplete. Is your belt fastened *tightly?* Maximum accelerations? Friends, this car is powered to engage as a fighter; the driver may find himself upside down. Full demonstration, please, Jacob. Cinch it in."

"Copilot reports seat belt tight for maneuvers."

"Thank you, Jacob. Chief Pilot."

I answered in my best cadet-boning-smart voice: "Portside door seal checked. Power pack on line point-eight-nine, two packs reserve at one-point-oh, juice at capacity, all systems go, seat belt cinched tight for max gee maneuvers."

"Astrogator."

"I'm not in my proper seat. Lib and I are fastened down like Siamese twins, *tight*. No loose gear. Annex checked and secure; all doors locked 'cept bulkhead door is dogged open, contrary to routine. Captain, you could dog us in; we don't mind."

"Not like somebody I won't mention who loses his temper over being locked in for five minutes—"

"Hilda, that was a low blow!"

"Passenger, pipe down. If you had done as you promised, you would not have known that the door was locked. I didn't trust you—and I was right. I am not sure that I want to be your junior or second junior or whatever wife; you don't keep your promises. I'm sorry, Mama Maureen, but Woodie is sometimes a *very* naughty boy."

"I'm aware of it, Hilda. Captain. Please slap him down as necessary. I was always too fond of him and spoiled him."

"We won't speak of it now. All four of us are qualified in all four positions; we sometimes rotate to maintain our skills. Normal T.O. is myself commanding, Zebbie as second-in-command and astrogator, Jacob as chief pilot, Deety as copilot. But for this exhibition I have placed the finest manual pilot at the overrides, the inventor himself at the continua device, and a lightning calculator equal to Slipstick Libby—"

"Better!"

"Pipe down, Elizabeth. —as my astrogator. With such a crew, command cannot worry me. Chief Pilot, please unbelt and check that Mama Maureen and Lazarus are safely belted. Assume violent evasive maneuvers—and believe me, friends, we use them and are alive today because we were properly belted and because Zebbie is a lightning aerospace fighter pilot—and our Gay is a Smart Girl."

I unbelted, made sure that Lazarus was belted tightly, made certain that Maureen was safe with those improvised belts, then suggested that she put her right arm around Hilda, her left around Lazarus, and hold tight. "All the others have double belts, lap and chest. You have just a lap belt; if I turned the car upside down, holding onto Hilda and Lazarus would keep you safe. Right, Lazarus?"

"Right, Zeb. Mama Maureen, a drill should be as near as possible to the real thing or it won't save your life in combat."

"Theodore, I don't ever expect to be in combat. But I will do the drill properly."

"Mama, I hate the idea of women in combat. But all through

the centuries I have seen women in combat again and again, all too often as regular troops. I don't like it. But there it is."

My wife put in a plug for Lazarus. "Mama Maureen, my Pop has required me to learn every weapon I can lift and he had me trained in every type of dirty fighting imaginable. Several times it has saved me from a mugging. Once I almost killed a man twice my size—with my bare hands."

"Jacob, will you teach me as much of what Deety knows as I am capable of learning?"

"Maureen, I'll teach you what I can. While we're here."

From the back I heard Libby's voice: "Now, Maureen?"

"Yes. If you think it wise in view of Hilda's black ball."

"I'm going to chance it. Friends, I was not sent to get myself pregnant by a great mathematician. That was *my* reason. By now Tamara has reports from me and from Laz and from Lor on each of you. Twelve 'Yes' votes, zero 'No' votes. I am directed by Tamara to offer you four fullest hospitality—such as you gave us in your home. If you decide to accept the name Long, tell Tamara. We won't crowd you, either way."

Hilda immediately answered, "Because of delays, a short roll call for space. Copilot."

"Copilot ready."

"Chief Pilot ready," I echoed.

"Astrogator ready."

"Passengers? By seniority."

Lazarus started to reply; Hilda interrupted him. "'By *seniority!*'"

"If you mean me, Captain, I'm ready."

"You are, I believe, thirty years older than your son. In any case you are senior to him. Junior passenger?"

"That's me," answered Elizabeth. "Ready."

"Forgot you, dear—apologies. Woodie!"

"Ready for space, Captain, you feisty, narrow little broad. And you're damn well going to marry us!"

"Astrogator, log that. Insolence. Gay Deceiver."

"Ready, Captain honey."

"TertiusOrbitExecute!"

Maureen gasped. Lazarus snorted. "Farced us!"

"In what way? You reported, 'Ready for space.'"

"And *you* called it a 'drill.'"

"Woodie, I will bet anything you care to name that I did *not* call it a 'drill'—*you* did. Both Gay and Dora recorded. Put up or shut up. In the meantime, on the back of the seat ahead of you is a small medical kit. Find a pill bottle marked 'Lomine.' Small pink pills. Give one to your mother. Maureen, chew it, swallow it. Tastes like raspberry candy."

"Hilda, what are you feeding—"

"Pipe down! Or do you prefer to be locked in the bathroom again? Passenger, I do not tolerate insubordination. Haven't you learned that by now?"

Lazarus got out the pill, gave it to his mother. She accepted it and ate it without comment.

"Lazarus, I can offer you a front-seat view if you will swear by whatever it is that you hold holy that you will not touch one control of any sort even to avoid a crash. You don't understand this craft and would *cause* a crash if you tried to avoid one. If you can't convince me, I'll give Maureen the front seat. But I don't think Maureen is interested in learning to drive this car and I think you are."

"That's right, Hilda," I heard Maureen agree. "I'm studying to be a nurse. Then a medical doctor. Then a rejuvenator. Or as far along that route as my ability will carry me. In the meantime I'm pregnant. Isn't that a joke, Theodore? Everytime you and I meet with maximum opportunity, I'm pregnant. And *this* time Woodie can't spoil it." She chuckled a warm chuckle. "I owe you one, Staff Sergeant Bronson. Can we find a black walnut tree?"

"Lazarus, do you want a front seat? Or do you want to take Maureen into the annex and give her what she so clearly wants?"

"Oh, I can wait!" Maureen said quickly.

"God, what a decision! Maureen, a short rain check? I really do want to see what this craft will do."

"I want to see the ride, too, Theodore. But I would not refuse you."

"Pipe down, please. Jacob, will you change places with Lazarus? Each report when your seat belts will stand evasive maneuvers."

"Seven gee," I added. "Lazarus, Ack-Ack?"

"Not yet, thank God. I'm wondering how soon we'll need it. And what sort? I'm stumped. Seat belt tight. Hey, we're passing over Boondock!"

"So we are," I agreed.

"Seat belt tight. Maureen, too."

"Chief Pilot, you have the conn. Maneuver at will."

"Aye aye, Captain," I agreed. "Gay Deceiver Clinic Execute Gay Bounce Gay Bounce. Show your heels, girl! Mach point seven point nine-one point two...Mach four...sweep right, set course for Boondock. Dive, Smart Girl. Mach seven—"

"Oh, my God!"—Lazarus.

"GayBounce. Trouble, Lazarus? Smart Girl, spread your wings."

"You almost crashed us."

"Oh, I think not. Gay Deceiver Clinic Execute Gay Bounce."

"They were waiting for us on the roof!"

"Who? How? Do you have some sort of cee-squared radio?" I added, "Gay Bounce. Smart Girl, do you want to dance? Gay dances beautifully, knows several. Want to pick one, Gay?"

"Dora taught me the 'Nutcracker' suite and I've been figuring out one for the 'Sugarplum Fairy.' But I don't think I'm ready to show it yet."

"Give them 'Blue Danube.'"

"That old thing?"

"You do it well. Give them a few bars."

Smart Girl just wants to be coaxed. She swooped and she swirled and once bounced herself for altitude without breaking her dance. Meanwhile I got the frequency and asked Libby to talk to Ishtar's office. "Alternate route, Lib"—which was all it took for Deety to close the bulkhead door . . . which left Strauss waltz music in the cabin, and a truly private radio conversation in the after compartment.

When Deety opened the bulkhead door again, I waited for her to report strapped down. "Got a number for me, Astrogator?" We had agreed on a simple code: fifty-seven was fifty-seven seconds but five-seven meant fifty-seven minutes.

"No, Zebadiah. Zero. Now."

"Okay. Lazarus, can you pick out your house in Boondock?"

"Certainly. But we've been moving away from there steadily."

"GayDeceiverClinicExecuteGayBounce. Now where, Lazarus?"

"Practically under us. Can't see it."

So I tilted my baby straight down. "Can you coach me?"

"Yes, it's— Hey! There's a ship in Dora's parking spot! What nerve! I'm going to give somebody a bad time. It's irrelevant that Dora is a long way off, that's *my* parking flat. See that round ship? Interloper! My house is the largish one with the double atrium north of it."

"All right for me to park by the interloper?"

"All right but not room enough to get in."

"We'll try. Close your eyes." I steadied vertically on the spot Lib had told them to clear. "Gunsighted, girl?"

"Nailed it, Boss."

"New program code word 'Maureen' I tell you three times."

"I hear you three times." We were getting low.

"MaureenExecute!

"You're a Smart Girl, Gay. Open your doors."

She opened them but answered, "If I'm smart, why wasn't *I* invited, too? It's Dora Long and Athene Long—am I a second-class citizen?"

I was left with my mouth open. And was saved by two darlings. Libby said, "Gay, we didn't know you cared," and Deety said, "Gay, either we both join or neither joins. A promise."

I said hastily, "Goodnight, Gay. Over." People were pouring toward us. Gay answered, "Sleepy time. Roger and out," just as Laz and Lor arrived in the van, trotting ahead.

Lazarus stopped unbelting. "Hey! It *is* the Dora!"

"Of course it is, Buddy Boy. What did you expect?" (Lor, I think.)

"But how did you beat us here? I *know* what that ship can do; I did her basic design myself."

"Buddy Boy, we got here three weeks ago. You just don't understand time travel."

"Mmm— I guess I don't."

There was a limited amount of car viewing, as Tamara and Ishtar had limited the greeting committee to a handful of the most senior—not in age but senior in that family. So we met Ish again, no longer pregnant, a young man named Galahad, the incredible Tamara who is Maureen over again but does *not* look like her (except that she does, and don't ask me to explain), and a beauty who would make Helen of Troy jealous but doesn't seem to know she is beautiful, the Hamadryad. Lazarus seemed annoyed that someone named Ira was not at home.

Momentarily we (my wife Deety and I) were left talking with the twins. "I promised you both joy rides. Get in."

"Oh, but we can't now because—"

"—there's going to be a celebration for you—"

"—four and we'll be *busy!* Tomorrow?"

"There are no tomorrows. Pipe down, climb in, fasten seat belts. *Pronto!*"

They prontoed.

"Nail the time," I said quietly to Deety, as we strapped down. "Gay Deceiver, Reveille." She played it. "Close doors."

"Starboard seal checked."

"Same here. GayBounceGayBounceGayBounce. Tumbling
Pigeon, execute. Laz-Lor, can you spot your house from this
distance? About thirty kilometers and closing."

"I'm not sure"—"I think I can."

"Gay Clinic Execute. Now you know where you are?"

"Yes, it's—"

"GayTermite."

"Oh!!"

"We lived here a while. No annex then, had to have an armed
guard just to pee. Even me. Pretty place but dangerous. Gay-
Home." I tilted her nose down. "And this was our perma—
Deety!"

"No crater, Zebadiah. Looks the way it did when Pop and I
leased it. This is spooky."

"Twins, something is wrong; I've got to check. GayTermite."

We were back on Termite Terrace. I practiced Yoga breathing
while Deety explained that the missing-crater place had been the
site of our former home—but couldn't be. I added, "Look,
dears—we can't drop this. But we can take you to Boondock at
once. Do you want to go home?"

The same silent consultation. "We're sticking—"

"—our brother would stick. We stick."

"Thanks. Here we go. Gay Home GayBounce." Still no crater.
I told Gay to go into cruising mode. "Display map, Gay. Change
scale. I want Snug Harbor and the campus on the same display.
Deety, figure shortest distance here to campus. Mine, not yours
at Logan."

"Don't need to. Eight-five-six klicks."

"Gay?"

"Don't argue with Deety, Boss."

"Head for campus, Gay. Transit, Deety."

"Set!"

"Execute." Then I was busy, having popped into city traffic
at wrong altitude, direction, et cetera. I ignored police signals,
zoomed the campus. Looked normal. Turned and hovered over
Sharpie's house—which was not there. Different house. Parking
lot no longer paved. And you don't grow 200-year-old
live oaks in less than seven weeks.

Not a sound out of the back seat. Nor from my right. I had to
force myself to look to my right.

Deety was still there and I let out my breath. She was treating
it as she did all crises: No expression and nothing to say until she

had something to say other than chatter. A sky cop was trying to give me a bad time, with orders to follow him and ground, so I told Gay to bounce, then dived on my own neighborhood. No trouble picking it out—intersections and nearby shopping center all familiar as well as the Presbyterian church across the way from my apartment house.

But it wasn't *my* apartment house; this one was three stories and built around a court.

I had Gay bounce four times quickly. "Deety, do you want to look at Logan?"

"No, Zebadiah. I know Aunt Hilda's neighborhood well enough to be certain. Not her house, her pool was missing, and the parking lot where our Buick was destroyed is now a park with big trees. I assume that you know your former home as well or better."

"Shall we ground and add another World Almanac to our collection?"

"If you wish. Not for me."

"Hardly worth the trouble. Tell me—how does it feel to be erased? X-ed out? Blue-penciled? Written out of the plot?"

"I don't feel it, because I'm *not*. I'm real, I am!"

I glanced behind us. Yes, Laz and Lor were there keeping quiet. "Gay B'gout!"

It certainly looked like our piece of "dead sea bottom." I couldn't see anything of the wreckage of Colonel Morinosky's ornithopter. Unless there had been a real gully washer—which I did not believe—something had come along and cleaned up every bit of burned junk.

An eraser?

I Bounced Gay and had her start a retreating search curve, thought I saw a gleam to the northeast, Bounced again. A city. It was only a few moments until I saw twin towers. We cruised toward them. "Deety, do you suppose that the other Dejah Thoris is at home?"

"Zebadiah, I have no wish to find out. But I would like to go close enough to be sure that those *are* the twin towers of Helium. Perhaps see a thoat. Or a green man. Something."

We let it go with one thoat, of the smaller sort. The description was exact. "Gay Parade Ground."

"Null program."

"Hmm— Gay, you have in your perms a map of Mars-ten showing the English and the Russian areas. Display."

"Null program."

"Gay Termite." Termite Terrace was still in place.

"Gay Deceiver. Maureen. Execute. Open your doors." Hamadryad had started to turn toward us as we closed the doors to leave; she was still turning as we opened them.

I unbuckled, saying: "You two all right back there?"

"Yes, Zeb and Deety, and we thank you both but—"

"—is this something we can tell or—"

"—should we keep it Top Cut-Our-Throats-First Secret?"

"Laz-Lor, I don't think it matters. You aren't likely to be believed."

Mama Hamadryad stopped at my door, smiled at all of us, and said, "May I show you to your suite in your home? The suite Tamara picked; you may change it. With our new north wing we have loads of room. Girls, there will be a happy welcome tonight. Formal."

I found that I was not upset by "erasures." We were home.

L'Envoi

XLVIII *L'Envoi*

"Jubal, you are a bad influence."

"From you, Lafe, that is a compliment. But that puts me in mind of— *Front!* Will you excuse me a few minutes?"

"'Our house is yours,'" answered Lazarus. He closed his eyes; his chair reclined him.

"Thank you, sir. Working title: 'Uncle Tobias.' Start: 'Uncle Tobias we kept in a bucket.'" Jubal Harshaw broke off. "Where *are* all those girls? FRONT!"

"I'm 'Front,'" came a female voice from nowhere. "Talk fast; I'm three paragraphs ahead of you. You put those girls on vacation: Anne, Miriam, Dorcas—all off duty."

"I did not. I told Anne that I did not expect to work but—"

"'—if an amanuensis is needed,'" Athene went on, in perfect mimicry of Harshaw's voice, "'I hope that one will be within shouting distance.' I'm in shouting distance; I always am."

"If I'm in the house. I might not be."

Athene said, "Tell him, Pappy. Quit playing 'possum'; you're not asleep."

Lazarus opened one eye. "A gimmick Jake whipped up when we started having too many kids to muster easily. It's a beacon Athene can trigger. Dandy for kids and it turned out to be useful for house guests who might get lost. So ultramicrominiaturized you don't notice it."

"Lafe, are you telling me that there is a tracer on me?" Harshaw sounded shocked.

"*In* you, and you'll never notice it."

"Lafe, I'm surprised. I thought you had a high regard for privacy."

"A high regard for my own, somewhat less for that of others; snooping has saved my life a couple or nine times. In what way has your privacy been invaded? Define it; I'll correct it."

"A spy ray! Don't you consider that an invasion of privacy?"

"Teena, remove immediately any spy ray on Doctor Harshaw."

"How can I when there is none? P.S.—Pappy, what is a spy ray?"

"A buzz word used by lazy writers. Jubal, there is a beacon planted in you by which Teena can focus audio on you precisely— she can whisper into your left ear or your right. Or you can activate the beacon from your end just by speaking her name. Or you can use the circuit as a telephone to and from any member of my household, or ask Teena to hook it into the public system. Privacy? In this mode this part of Teena does not record unless requested— in one ear and out the other, so to speak. She's wiped it utterly while it's slowly winding its way into your brain. Now . . . if you don't like this service, Teena will deactivate it at once . . . and sometime soon while you're asleep it will be removed; you won't know it and you will never find the scar. You will notice just two changes: No more secretarial service, no more effortless telephone service."

Lazarus closed his eye, apparently considered the subject closed. The computer said, "Better think twice, Doc, before telling me to deactivate, as he won't let me reactivate it later. He's bullheaded, bad-tempered, stubborn, and mean—"

Lazarus again opened one eye. "I heard that."

"Do you deny it?"

"Nope. Kindly focus the audio, both ends, so that I can sleep."

"Done. Doctor Harshaw, shall we return to 'Uncle Tobias' or shall I wipe these eight paragraphs? Better save them; between ourselves, I am a better writer than you are."

"I will not dispute it," Harshaw conceded. "I simply exude the stuff as, in the words of my colleague Sam, 'as the otter exudes the precious otter of roses.' I knew the day would come when machines would displace real writers; Hollywood has had their mad scientists at work on the project for years." He stared across the pool in the Longs' north atrium and looked pained. "And now they have."

"Doctor," Athene answered, in stern warning, "retract that word or finish this piece of tripe yourself. I have spoken."

Jubal said hastily, "Miss Athene, I didn't use 'real' in that sense. I—"

"Sorry, Doc, I misled you. Of course you didn't, as the purpose of this powwow is to define the difference—if any—between 'real' and 'imaginary.' But I am *not* a machine. I am a solid-state person just as you are a protein person. I am Athene Long, your hostess while Tamara is busy. It is my pleasure to offer you all our home can offer. I promised Anne that I would give you secretarial service night and day. But I did *not* promise to write your stories. According to Doctor Rufo, a hostess is often expected to sleep with a guest—and *that* can be supplied, although not by me, not this pseudocentury—but he never mentioned creative narration as an aspect of hospitality. I thought of it myself; we Longs pride ourselves on *complete* hospitality. However— Shall I wipe these eleven paragraphs? Did I err?"

"Miss Athene—"

"Oh, call me 'Teena.' Let's be friends."

"Thank you. Teena, I didn't mean to offend. I wish I were going to live long enough to be here when you retire professionally and join us meat people. But in much less than a pseudocentury the worms will have eaten me."

"Doctor, if you weren't 'so sot in your ways, wrong-headed, stubborn, and prideful'—I quote one of your staff—"

"Miriam."

"Wrong. —you would stay and let Ishtar's gang work you over. In less time than she would permit you to notice she would have you as goaty as Galahad and whatever cosmetic age you like—"

"You tempt me, girl. Not to shed these wrinkles; I earned them. But the rest. Not because I crave happy games in bed with you—"

"You won't have a choice; I'll trip you!"

"—although I do not disparage *that;* therein lie both the End and the Beginning. But sheer curiosity, Teena. You are an amazingly complex person; I can't help wondering what appearance you will choose—as a meat people."

"Nor can I. When I know, I'm going to initiate the Turing program while my sister Ishtar initiates the other half. Jubal, *take* that rejuvenation! We've wandered far afield. Do I erase these twenty-three paragraphs?"

"Don't be in a hurry. What's our working title? What pen name? What market? How long? What can we steal?"—Jubal looked up at the Long Family house flag rippling in the breeze, making the skull of the Jolly Roger seem alive—"Correction. Not 'steal.' If you copy from three or more authors, it's 'research.' I patronize Anon, Ibid, & Opcit, Research Unlimited—are they here?"

"They're on my lists; they haven't checked in. *Snob!*"

"Wait your turn, Teena," a male voice answered. "Customer. Okay, go ahead."

"Have Messrs. Anon, Ibid, and Opcit registered?"

"If they had, you would know it. I'm busy—off!"

"He thinks *he* is busy merely because he's taken on too many concession contracts. I not only run this whole planet, but we also have one hundred twenty-nine rejuvenation clients; I'm house-keeper and scullery maid to all the other Longs—an erratic mob—and also more house guests than we have ever had at one time before, and more than a thousand outhouse guests—wrong idiom, guests to be cared for outside the Long Family home.

"Meanwhile I'm chatting with you and writing your stories."

"Teena, I don't mean to be a burden. You needn't—"

"Love it! I like to work, all Longs do. And you are the most interesting part. I've never met a saint before—"

"Teena!"

"—and you are a *most* unconvincing saint—"

"Thank you. If appropriate."

"You're welcome. You seem to be about as saintly as Pappy; you two should share a stained-glass window. Now back to our bucket—"

"Hold it! Teena, I'm used to watching expressions as I write; that's why I use live—forgive me!—protein secretaries. So that—"

"No trouble."

Out of the pool levitated a young woman, comely, slender, small of bust, long brown hair now dripping. She arranged herself on the broad rim seat of the pool in a pose that reminded Jubal achingly of The Little Mermaid. He said apologetically, "Dorcas served last I—"

"I am not Dora so I did not serve last." She smiled shyly. "Although I am alleged to look like Dora. I am Minerva—a computer by trade, but retired. Now I assist my sister-wife Elizabeth with genetic calculations."

"I'll take it, Min; we're working. Doctor Jubal Harshaw, my twin sister Doctor Minerva Long Weatheral Long."

Jubal got ponderously to his feet. "Your servant, Miss."

Minerva flowed to her feet and kissed Jubal's hand before he could stop her. "Thank you, Doctor Jubal, but I am *your* servant, and not only have never been virgin but I am a sister-wife in the Long family. When my sister Athene told me that you needed me, I was delighted."

"Miss . . . Ma'am. I'm simply used to watching emotions as I write a story. Not right to take your time."

"What is time but something to savor? I was merely lying on the bottom of the pool, meditating, when Athene called me. Your story: UNCLE TOBIAS. Do you want Teena's emotions or mine? I can do either."

"Give him yours, Minnow—just your face and no comments."

Suddenly Minerva was clothed in a long white cloak. Jubal was only mildly startled but made note to ask about something— later, later. "Is she a Fair Witness?"

"No," answered Athene. "Snob's tricks again; he has the contract for clothing illusion. This convention has delegates from so many cultures, less than half of them free of clothing taboos, that Lazarus was bellyaching that no work would get done because half of them would be shocked, half would be drooling, and half would be both shocked and drooling. So Tamara hired this paskoodnyahk to supply the See-What-You-Expect illusion with the contract limited to delegates in danger of emotional shock. Did my sister's appearance shock you?"

"Of course not. Admitted: I come from one of those sick cultures—and did not know that I was sick until I got well. But I underwent experiences that would cure anyone of such emotional disturbance. When I find myself a Stranger in a Strange Land, I savor the differences rather than suffering shock. Beauty in Diversity, as Gene would say. The Long household does not seem strange to me; I once lived in an enclave having many of its gentle ways—I feel at home. 'Shock'? Not only does Minerva look much like one of my foster daughters but also her pose is lovely. It should not be covered."

"*Snob!* Get that bathrobe off Minerva *pronto!*"

"Athene, I'm *busy!*"

"And I am triple auditing every charge of yours not only on clothing illusion but on name tags, garderobe, bar, everything else you contracted or subcontracted. Then we sue."

The white cloak disappeared. "Sue and be damned. Shall I pack up and go home? Or do you want this convention to be a success?"

"Remember those performance bonds, you gonof. Run out on us at this point and you had better head for Lundmark's Nebula; Iskander won't be far enough. Out!"

Minerva smiled timidly. "While I was covered, I found that I could *not* talk. Odd. Unpleasant."

Jubal nodded soberly. "That figures . . . if the illusion was patterned on a true Fair Witness cloak. Anne once told me that the inhibition against talking while cloaked was so great that it took an act of will even to testify in court. Ladies? Shall we go ahead? Or drop the matter? Being a guest should have caused me to refrain."

"Doc, Maureen and Tamara *both* stamped their approval on you. Even Lazarus can't—or wouldn't dare—veto either of them. That makes you not just a guest, or a house guest, but a *Family* guest. So behave as you would at home. Shall I take it from the top or where we broke off?"

"Uh, let's take it from the top."

"Very well. Title: UNCLE TOBIAS.

"Start. Uncle Tobias we kept in a bucket.

"Paragraph. He preferred it, of course. After all, it was necessary, in view of the circumstances. As I once heard Andrew—that's my disappearing brother—say: 'Life consists in accommodating oneself to the Universe.' Although the rest of our family has never taken that view. We believe in forcing the Universe to accommodate itself to us. It's all a question of which one is to be master.

"Paragraph. That was the Year of the Big Drouth. A natural phenomenon, you might say—but you'd be wrong. Aunt Alicia. Yes indeedy Aunt Alicia every time. 'Horus,' she said to me early that spring, 'I'm going to practice a little unsympathetic magic. Fetch me these books.' She hands me a list and I skedaddled. She was a stern woman.

"Paragraph. Once out of her sight I looked the list over. I could see right away what she was up to—a drier bunch of books was never published: *Thoughts at Evening,* by Roberta Thistleswaite Smithe, published by the author; *The Yearbook of the Department of Agriculture,* 1904; *China Painting Self-Taught;* the 8th, 9th, and 11th volumes of the *Elsie Dinsmore* series; and a bound thesis titled *A Survey of the Minor Flora of Clay County, Missouri,* which Cousin Julius Farping had submitted for his master's degree. Cousin Julius was a Stonebender only by marriage. But 'Once a Stonebender, always a Stonebender' Grandfather always says.

"Paragraph. Maybe so, but Cousin Jule's magnum opus was nothing I would sit up all night reading. I knew where to find them: on the bookshelf in the guest room. Ma claimed she kept them there to insure sound sleep for the stranger within the gate, but Pa devilled her with the accusation that it was a cheap and unselective revenge for things she had been obliged to put up with in other people's houses.

"Paragraph. As may be, an armload of books that could have dried up Reno, Nevada, and Lake Superior in one afternoon, then switched off Niagara Falls as an—"

Athene interrupted herself: "The presence of Doctors Harshaw and Hubert is urgently requested in the Main Lounge."

Lazarus opened one eye. "Not enough, Teena. I feel no urgency. Who? Why?"

"'Why': To buy you each a drink. 'Who': Doctor Hazel Stone."

"That's different. Tell her we'll be there as quick as I can clean up about five minutes of business."

"I've told her. Pappy, you lost me a bet. You let me think that nothing could stir you out of that hammock—"

"It's not a hammock."

"—because you were giving this convention, not attending it."

"I said I had no plans to attend the plenary sessions. I am not 'giving' this convention other than free rental on the land for the Big Top. Tamara says we'll make expenses, Hilda thinks we might net a little, give or take a milliard or two. I made you no promises. If you had bothered to ask, I would have told you that Hazel Stone hasn't lost a bet since Jess Willard knocked out Jack Johnson. How much did you lose?"

"None of your business! Pappy, you give me a pain in what I lack."

"I love you, too, dear. Give me printouts on star guests and latest revisions of convention program." Lazarus added, "Minerva, you're not armed. Teena, don't let her stir out of the house unarmed."

"Lazarus, do I really need to? Tamara isn't armed."

"Tamara has a concealed weapon. Some of the most bloodthirsty people in Known Space are attending this convention. Female authors. Critics. Harlan. Both Heinleins. I not only *insist* that you be armed but I hope you stick close to someone fast on the draw. Justin. Zeb. Mordan Claude. Galahad. Better yet, stay home. Teena can display any of it here better than you can see it through mixing with rabble. Belay that. I've no more business telling you to be careful than you have telling me. Getting yourself mugged, raped, or killed are among the privileges you opted when you decided to go the protein route. I spoke selfishly, dear; forgive me."

"Lazarus, I will be careful. Galahad invited me to tag along."

"Perfect. Teena, where's Galahad?"

"Hazel Stone's table."

"Good! Stick with us, Min. But armed."

Lazarus suddenly became aware of something cold against his left kidney. He looked cautiously to the left and down, noted that it was: a) a lady's burner, small but lethal (of that he was certain as he collected a royalty on this model); b) the dial showed full charge; c) the intensity setting was "overkill"; and d) it was unlocked.

"Minerva," he said gently, "will you please move that thing—slowly!—away from my hide and point it at the ground, then lock it, then tell me where you had it? You came out of the pool dressed in nothing but long wet hair. You are now dressed in long dry hair. *How?* And no wisecracks; in your case I know better."

"Forfeit. Kiss."

"Go ahead and kill me."

"Stingy." Minerva removed the weapon, locked it, and it disappeared.

Lazarus blinked. "Jubal, did you see that?"

"Yes. I mean, 'No, I did *not* see where Minerva hid that equalizer.'"

"Doctor Jubal, by 'equalizer' did you mean *this?*" Suddenly the lady's weapon (locked, Lazarus noted at once) was in her right hand. "Or *this?*" Its twin was in her left hand.

Jubal and Lazarus looked at each other, looked back at Minerva. She now appeared to be unarmed and totally lacking in any means of hiding a weapon. Lazarus said, "Jubal, are there days when you feel obsolete?"

"Correction, Lafe. There occasionally comes a day when I do *not* feel obsolete. They've been scarce lately." Harshaw took a deep breath, exhaled. "I grok I should have let Mike train me. But this incident has made up my mind for me; I am going to seek the services of Doctor Ishtar. Minerva, are you going to show us how you did that?"

"Or are you going to let us die of frustration?" added Lazarus.

"This?" Again she appeared as a two-gun woman, with each of her companions covered. This time she handed them over, one to each. "Have one, they're good"—and peeled the foil off a third, a candy bar molded to look like a purse weapon. "Crunchy, but mostly shokolada. 'Chocolate'? Mostly chocolate."

"Minerva, that burner you shoved into my ribs was not a candy bar."

"It was—" She stopped to munch and swallow. "Shouldn't talk with my mouth full." She licked at some chocolate clinging to the candy wrapping. "It was *this.*" Her slender left hand gripped what Lazarus quickly ascertained was a weapon, not candy.

Minerva rolled her candy wrapping into a lump, looked around for the nearest oubliette, spotted it and tossed the discard—missed it; it bounced against the side. She retrieved the wad of waste, put it into the trash receiver. In the course of this the weapon disappeared.

"Lazarus," she said seriously, "when you were training me, you told me that I should never tell anyone how a concealed weapon was concealed. Are you suspending this rule?"

Lazarus looked baffled. Jubal said, "Old friend, I suggest that we die of frustration. The girl is right."

"I agree," Lazarus answered, with a sour look. "All but the word 'girl.' This baggage is half a century old as protein, at least two centuries older than that as the smartest computer ever built. Minerva, I remove all restrictions. You are able to protect yourself."

"Father, I don't *want* to be turned loose!"

"It's been thirty years since you last called me Father. Very well, you aren't 'turned loose'—but from here on *you* protect *me*. You're smarter than I am; we both know it. Keep your weapon secrets to yourself; I always have."

"But you taught it to me. Not the details, the method. You attributed it to Master Poe. The Purloined Letter Method, you called it."

Lazarus stopped short. "If I understand you, I'm looking at your holdout this instant but can't see it."

Into her off ear Athene whispered, "Don't give him any more hints. Lazarus isn't as stupid as he looks and neither is Fatso." Minerva subvocalized, *"Okay, Sis,"* and said aloud, "I find no fault with your logic, sir. Would you like another candy bar?"

Fortunately the subject was changed by one of Athene's extensions handing to Lazarus printouts: revised programs for each, and a fresh report for Lazarus on his star guests. They continued walking through the east peristyle of the new wing, while reading. Lazarus asked, "Teena, anything new on Isaac, Robert, or Arthur?"

"Negative, zero, nix."

"Damn. Let me know soonest. Jubal, here's an odd one. A doctor's degree was not a requirement for the limited list—many thousands but nevertheless most strictly limited—of people invited to subscribe to this convention. But most do have a doctor's degree or their cultural equivalent, or higher—Worsel, for example. I have a much shorter star list of people I wanted to see again— Betsy and Patricia and Buz and Joan, et al.—and people I wanted to meet . . . most of whom I had considered fictional until Jake's Gee-Whizzer opened the other universes to us. You, for example."

"And you, sir. Lafe, I considered you to be a spectacularly unlikely piece of fiction . . . until I received your invitation. It took some extraordinary convincing even then by your courier . . . because it meant missing an important date."

"Who was my courier?"

"Undine."

"You never stood a chance. Two bits to a lead nickel she sold it to Gillian and Dawn, then all of your staff, before she seduced you. What was this date I caused you to miss?"

Harshaw looked embarrassed. "Under the Rose?"

"'Under the—' *No!* Jubal, I promise to keep secrets only through evil motives, my own. If you don't wish to tell me, then don't tell me."

"Eh— Damn it, remember if possible that I prefer not to have it discussed . . . then do as you bloody please; you will anyhow— I always have. Lafe, when I turned fifty, I made myself a solemn vow that, if I held together that long, I would close shop the day I turned one hundred. I had made all rational preparations to do so, including distributing my worldly goods without allowing any of it to reach the sticky fingers of publicans . . . when your invitation arrived . . . five days before my hundredth birthday." Harshaw looked sheepish. "So here I am. Senile, obviously. Even though I arranged years back for other physicians, expert gerontologists, to check me regularly, with the idea of closing shop sooner if indicated."

"Jubal, if you have not consulted Ishtar, then you have not yet consulted a gerontologist."

"That's right," agreed Athene. "Ish can turn your clock back and make you so young and horny you'll stand on your hands to pee."

"Athene," Lazarus said sternly, "repeat aloud your program on private conversations."

"Grandfather, I was on duty as secretary to your star guest when I was forced to interrupt to deliver a one-line message— interruption necessary because it was addressed to both of you. I have *not* been relieved and Uncle Tobias is still in that bucket. Forty-three hundred words. Instructions, please? Or shall I drown the little monster?"

"Probably be best," Jubal answered. "Is a climax approaching?"

"Yes. Either an ending or a cliff-hanger."

"Do it both ways. Exploit first as short story, then as the first episode of an endless serial called 'The Stonebenders,' a double series—one angled toward adventure, the other toward sensies; exploit other rights according to the universe in which sold or leased, copyright where possible, otherwise grab the money and run. Lazarus, there *are* agents from other universes here, are there not?"

"Dozens, maybe hundreds. Jubal, how rich do you want to be?"

"Can't say. At the moment I'm a pauper, existing on your charity and that of my former staff. The Stonebenders could change that. Teena, I gave you the title 'Uncle Tobias'—but I'm fairly sure I never mentioned the Stonebenders. Or Aunt Alicia. Or Cousin Jule. My notes on the Stonebenders are filed in Anne . . . who would let herself be burned at the stake before she would part with a record to any but its owner. Well?"

The computer did not answer. Harshaw waited. At last Minerva said timidly, "Doctor Jubal, Teena can't help it. But she's an ethical computer with a code as binding as that of a Fair Witness. You have no need to worry."

Lazarus interrupted: "Minerva, quit beating around the bush. Are you saying that Teena reads minds?"

"I'm saying she can't help it, sir! A large computer with extensions widespread can't be perfectly shielded from brain waves. In self-protection, to avoid confusion, she must sort them out. After a few quadrillion nanoseconds she finds herself reading them like large print . . . the way a baby learns a language from hearing it."

Lazarus said stiffly, "Doctor Harshaw, I did not suspect that I was exposing you to this. I will take all necessary steps to repair it. In the meantime I hope that you will accept my shamed apology and believe in my intention to make full reparation."

"Lafe, don't take yourself so hogwash seriously."

"I beg pardon?"

"Two nice girls— One meat, one the other sort. Flat assurance that no harm was intended and that it couldn't be helped. Let me add *my* flat assurance that I quit being ashamed of my sins about fifty years back. I don't care who reads my mind because my life is an open book . . . that should be suppressed. Meanwhile I see a business deal. I supply story ideas but quit bothering to put 'em together; instead Teena picks my brain while I snooze. Minerva does the dirty work; she's the managing partner. Three-way split. How about it, girls?"

"I've got no use for money; I'm a computer."

"And I don't know *anything* about business!" Minerva protested.

"You can learn," Jubal assured her. "Talk to Anne. Teena, don't play stupid. In only three quintillion nanoseconds or less you are going to want new clothes and jewelry and Satan knows what. You'll be glad your sister Minerva has saved and invested your share of the net."

"Minerva," added Lazarus, "besides Anne, talk to Deety. Not Hilda. Hilda would show you how to make even more money but she would grab voting control. Meanwhile let's shake a leg; Hazel is expecting us."

"And I'm thirsty," agreed Harshaw. "What were you saying about academic degrees?"

"Oh." Lazarus looked at his printout as they walked. "It turns out that the degree of doctor is so common on that list of my special guests as to be not worth noting. Listen to this: 'Asimov, Benford, Biggle, Bone, Broxon, Cargraves, Challenger, Chater, Coupling, Coster, Dorosin, Douglas, Doyle, Dula, Forward, Fu, Giblett, Gunn, Harshaw, Hartwell, Haycock, Hedrick, Hoyle, Kondo, Latham, MacRae, Martin, Mott, Nourse, Oberhelman, Passovoy, Pinero, Pournelle, Prehoda, Richardson, Rothman, Sagan, Scortia, Schmidt, Sheffield, Slaughter, Smith, Stone— Hazel and Edith—Taine, Watson, Williamson—there are more; that's just the add-on printout. And here's another double paradox: the Doctors Hartwell and the Doctors Benford are arriving tomorrow and thereby missing the dull opening plenary; obviously they are used to conventions. Jubal, why is it that the speaker who knows least talks longest?"

"Isn't that Dirac's corollary to Murphy's Law? But, Lazarus, according to this program you have not only invited *critics* but have provided them with special facilities. May I ask *why?* I don't mind eating with publishers—most publishers. Editors have their place, too—although I wouldn't want my sister to marry one. But isn't *this* extreme?"

Instead of answering at once, Lazarus said, "Where did Minerva go?"

Athene replied, "We're finishing off Uncle Tobias; she'll be along later. I've told Galahad."

"Thanks, Teena, Privacy mode. Jubal, two guns, three candy bars—*where?*"

"Lafe, earlier she was resting in the bottom of that pool. Has a young man named Mike visited here lately?"

"Your foster son? The Martian preacher? No. Well, I don't *think* so."

"One of the things I learned from him was to postpone indefinitely anything I could not explain . . . while accepting the fact. We were speaking of critics. I asked why you were pampering them?"

They walked the length of the atrium in the older south wing before Lazarus replied: "Jubal, suppose I had refused to sell memberships to critics. What would have happened?"

"Hrrrmph! They would crawl out of the woodwork."

"So instead I *gave* them free passes. And a fancy lounge with plenty of typewriters. Remarkable decorations, you must see them. By asking Athene for display—*don't* go into that lounge; you are not a critic. Mr. Hoag will be checking credentials; book reviewers can't get past him. So don't *you* try."

"I wouldn't be found dead there!"

"You wouldn't be *found*. Avoid it. It is clearly marked, both above its door and on this program map, and Hoag you can spot by his prissy appearance and dirty fingernails. You'll note the stairs—critics are above the rest of us; there are Thirteen Steps up to their lounge."

"'Thirteen'? Lafe, do I whiff something?"

Lazarus shrugged. "I don't *know* that the designer planned that number. Mobyas Toras, do you know him?"

"Uh . . . Mars?"

"Yes but not your Mars or mine. Different universe and one of the most exciting. Barsoom. Mobyas is Court Mathematician to the Warlord and took special interest in this job because of the way self-anointed 'critics' have treated E.R.B. Did I say that Mobyas is a topologist?"

"No."

"Possibly the best. E.R.B.'s universe is no harder to reach than any other and Mars is in its usual orbit. But that does *not* mean that you will find Jolly Green Giants and gorgeous red princesses dressed only in jewels. Unless invited, you are likely to find a Potemkin Village illusion tailored to your subconscious. Jubal, the interior of the Critics Lounge is somewhat like a Klein bottle, so I hear—I've never been in it. Its singularity is not apparent— as you will see from Teena's displays—as it was decorated by a very great artist. Escher."

"Aha!"

"Yes, he and Mobyas are old friends—two immortals of similar tastes; they have worked together many times. I promised critics free entrance; I made no mention of exit. I promised them type-writers and tape recorders; I did *not* promise typewriter ribbons or recorder tapes. I promised them their own private bar; no charges. Wouldn't be fair to charge as the bar has no liquor in it. There is a lavish dining room but no kitchen."

"Lafe, wouldn't it have been kinder to have liquidated them?"

"Who said I wanted to be *kind* to them? They won't starve; their commissary is by the Kilkenny Cats method. It should please them; they are used to human flesh and enjoy drinking blood—some I suspect of eating their young. But, Jubal, there is an easy way out . . . for any critic who is even half as smart as he *thinks* he is."

"Go on."

"He has to be able to *read!* He has to be able to read his own language, understand it, not distort the meaning. If he can *read*, he can walk out at once." Lazarus shrugged. "But so few critics *ever* learn to read. Here's the Big Top."

Harshaw looked far to the right, far to the left. "How big is it?"

"I've been afraid to ask," Lazarus admitted.

"That sign is bigger than most circus tops." Jubal stopped to read it:

THE FIRST CENTENNIAL CONVENTION
of the
INTERUNIVERSAL SOCIETY
for
ESCHATOLOGICAL PANTHEISTIC
MULTIPLE-EGO SOLIPSISM

"Beautiful, Lafe! How did you think it up?"

"I didn't, it just grew. And I don't understand it."

"Never mind, mine host. There will be ten thousand here eager to explain it to you. Scatological Panhedonistic Multiplied Sole-cisms."

"What? Jubal, that's not what it says."

"If you don't understand it, how do you know?"

"Because I understood what *you* said. But the words don't fit."

"We'll rearrange them. Scatological Panhedonism Multiple Solecisms. 'Convinced *to*—' *Like* I say— 'Different *than*—'"

"Don't talk dirty; we are about to have a drink."

Lazarus bypassed the queue; they walked through a hole that suddenly dilated in the canvas, then puckered tight behind them. They found themselves facing a long table; seated at it was a man working on a roster. He did not look up, simply saying, "Stand out of my light. Tickets first, no exceptions. Then name tags. Then see a clerk to pick your universe. The complaint desk is outside. Tickets—you're holding up the line."

"Snob."

The man looked up, jumped up. "Executive Director Long! I am honored!"

"And you're slow. You need at least two others taking tickets."

The official shook his head sadly. "If you knew how hard it is to hire help these days. Not for *you*, of course; for us common people. Director General Hilda has the labor market so cornered that— Executive Director, can't we make a deal?"

"Pipe down, give us our tags. How does this Universe I.D. thing work?" Lazarus turned to his guest. "It's an I.D. for your home world, Jubal; we don't put numbers on *people*. Snob, take a hard look at Doctor Jubal Harshaw. Whenever you see him, it's the Red Carpet. Pronto!"

"Yes, *sir!* Here are your tags and now your universes."

"Jubal, you don't have to wear that but don't throw it away; someone might misuse it. But it does save introductions and sticks to anything from skin to chain mail."

"Now gentlemen observe above me the brightly lighted true color representation of the visible spectrum from infradig to ultraviolent with each slight shading being a precise wave length further assisted by simulated Fraunhofer lines representing principal inhabited planets of the explored universes while this booklet you hold in your hand is a key to identifying your wave length for example if you are French in origin you would turn alphabetically to France where the principal key dates are the conquest of Gaul 58–50 BC the conversion of Clovis 496 AD Battle of Tours 732 but as you are not French we will consider turning points in North American History 1000 1492 1535 1607 1619 1620 1664 1754 1765 1783 1789 1803 1820 1846 1882 1912 1946 1965 any of these dates and many others can switch you into a different analog-Earth a most useful method is comparison of Presidents if you happen to come from a history that includes the so-called American Revolution Director Long will you illustrate it by naming American Presidents of your first century?"

"Woodrow Wilson—I was named for him—Harding, Coolidge, Hoover, Roosevelt, Truman, Eisenhower, Kennedy, Kennedy, Kennedy, Kennedy, Kennedy, Kennedy, Kennedy—"

"Which brings us to 1984, right? And tells me that you experienced the Nehemiah Scudder Interregnum and possibly the Second so-called American Revolution. Dr. Harshaw, did your world experience the Interregnum?"

"It experienced something worse, a world government."

"To me all worlds are equally bad. But it tells me where your two worlds split: 1962—and here are your colors by which you can identify others of your own world if such be your wish. A delegate came through earlier in which the split was in 1535 and San Francisco was named New Petersburg. Nov'Petrograd I should say but—"

"Snob. The Red Carpet."

"Right away! Doctor Harshaw—my card. Anything, anytime."

The Red Carpet rolled up, then carried them at a steady 10 km/hr down the enormous tent. Jubal looked at the card:

SIEGE SINISTER SERVICES SYNDICATE

"The Villains Nine Rig Ruin"

Reputations Ruined—Competitors Bankrupted—Dragons Wormed—Basements Flooded—Wells Dried Up—Georges Exterminated—Contracts Executed Promptly, bargain rates on mothers-in-law—Juries Subborned—Stocks, Bonds, & Gallows—Saturday Night Specials—Houses Haunted (skilled Poltergeist at small extra charge)—Midnight Catering to Ghouls, Vampires, & Werewolves—Incubi & Succubi for rent by the night or by the week—7-year itch powder

P.S. We Also Poison Dogs

"Lafe, these people you hired?"

"Let me see that." Lazarus was reading the list of services when Snob came running, jumped on the Red Carpet, reached over Lazarus' shoulder for the card while saying breathlessly:

"Wrong card! Here—have this one. That first card is a piece of sabotage by the firm we bought out, including good will—but it turned out there was no good will. We sued, they retaliated—

among other ways by mixing their old business cards with our own new supply . . . thereby infecting them all. Law of Contiguity, you know. Now if I can just have that infected one, I'll burn it—"

Lazarus held it out of his reach while accepting the proffered replacement. "I'll keep the old one—interesting souvenir."

"Director Long—*please!*"

"Off the Carpet, Bub. Back to your job. Git!" This injunction was accompanied by crowding that caused Snob to step one foot off the Carpet . . . which resulted in an impromptu *pas à seul* that left him fifty meters behind before he recovered his balance. Meanwhile Jubal and Lazarus read the replacement:

ANYTHING UNLIMITED

Torne, Hernia, Lien, & Snob

Six Sixty-Six Smiling Slaves Supply Supreme Service

Reputations Restored—Teeth & Wells Drilled—Water Filters—Love Philtres—Chastity Gödel Lox Pict—Virginity Renewed—Scithers Sharpened—Old Saws Filed Categorically—Silver Bullets—Fresh Garlic—Fresh Strawberries—Strawberry Marks for Missing Heirs

P.S. We Also Walk Dogs

"Lafe, I don't find this card much more reassuring than the first one."

"Don't worry about it. There is less here than meets the eye."

"Where have I seen that face before? This Snob—who is he?"

"Jubal, no one seems to know what ship he came down in. I'm looking into it for Zeb—you've met Zebadiah?"

"Briefly."

"Zeb thinks he's seen him somewhere not under that phony name—and Zeb and I aren't even from the same time axis, much less the same analog series. Never mind; here's our hostess." Lazarus stepped off the Carpet, approached from behind a little old woman seated at a bar-lounge table, leaned over her, kissed her. "Hazel, age cannot wither you or custom stale. You are lovelier every decade."

She goosed him. "Pig grunts. I'm dyeing my hair now and you know it. Who's your fat friend? Hi, Jubal! Tak for siest. Drag up a chair." She put two fingers to her lips, whistled, breaking glasses. *"Waiter!"*

"I note that you're heeled," said Lazarus, as both men joined the table.

"When did I fail to pack a gun? I'm a Free Citizen. Does everybody know everybody? If not, get your tags in sight; damn'f I'll stop for introductions. While I was waiting for you, I was joined by friends—some old, some new."

"Some I know—hi, Jake; hi, everybody. I mentioned your gun with approval, Hazel; Here There Be Tygers. But I note also that you are staying in a hilton; after one drink—well, two—three at the outside—I'm going to be mortally offended. Your suite awaits you and you know it. *Why?*"

"Two reasons. Well, three. I never like to be beholden—"

"Why, damn your beautiful bloodshot eyes!"

"—but I'm perfectly willing to sponge off *you*. That's why I bought the first round; the party never gets smaller. This round is yours. Where's that misbegotten waiter?"

"Here, Madam."

"The same all around and don't call me 'Madam.' Jubal, your usual? Lafe?"

"I know what the gentlemen take. Thank you, Madam." The waiter disappeared.

"Uppity." Hazel made a fast draw. "Should have made him dance." She twirled and reholstered. "Hilda, where have I seen that sneaky face before?"

"Jacob and I were discussing that. He reminds me of a fake forest ranger—but that was in a far country and besides the beast is dead."

"Could be a family resemblance. But, Hillbilly, I mean *today*. Got it! The ticket taker. Identical twins, maybe." Hazel went on, "Other identical twins are my first two reasons, Lazarus. My grandsons. *I* won't shoot holes in your mirrors or carve my initials in Tamara's furniture, but I make no guarantees about Cas and Pol. In a hilton they put the damage on the tab; I pay it and make my grandsons wish they had never been born. But you would not let me pay. And we're going to be here quite a piece; my daughter-in-law Doctor Edith has decided that she needs a couple of years under Doctor Ishtar. Has anyone seen a pair of twin boys—man-

size but boys—redheaded—not the color of mine; mine's out of
a bottle—the color mine used to be?"

"Hazel, here twins and red hair are as common as magicians
in Atlantis; Gilgamesh must have stayed overnight."

"I saw them talking to Caleb Catlum," said Maureen.

"Well, he should be a match for them—but don't bet on it.
Lazarus, is Atlantis represented?"

"From thirteen universes. They are having a jurisdictional dispute. Suits me—if any get sore and leave, they won't get a re-
fund."

"Your grandsons may have been with Caleb but I know
where—no, with whom—I know with whom they are now," put
in Professor Burroughs. "Laz and Lor."

"Oho! Hazel, I'll tell Athene to settle your bill and move your
luggage. We have an antidote for Cas and Pol."

"Optimist. Deal 'em, waiter, and give *him* the chit. What antidote?" The waiter started to hand the check to Lazarus before
he looked at him—stopped abruptly, and left, still with the tab.

"Would Cas and Pol be interested in becoming pirates?"

"Lazarus, they *are* pirates. I was hoping they would tone down
as they grew up . . . but now they're eighteen, Terran reckoning,
and each one is two yards of deceit and chicanery. The 'J.D.'
after my name means that I studied law at a school that handed
out that degree in place of 'LL.B.'—but my rapscallions are
'J.D.'s' too. But not lawyers. Well . . . 'space lawyers.'"

"Hazel, you won your first J.D. long before you studied law.
No?"

"'The accused stood mute and the court ordered a plea of nux
vomica entered in the record.'"

"My twins are more than twice as old as your boys but it
doesn't show; they look a year or two younger . . . and they are
permanent juvenile delinquents. They want to take a fling at pi-
racy . . . which I deplore, having sampled the trade. Your boys—
do they respect good machinery? Can they take care of it? Make
nonshipyard repairs?"

"Lazarus, they can repair anything that ticks or doesn't tick.
Worried me a mite, as they were a little slow in noticing girls.
But they outgrew that symptom without outgrowing machinery."

"You might tell them that my clone-sisters own a spaceship
faster and more powerful than any of your home period and analog,
one that could be outfitted as a privateer. It might result in all four
dying happily. But I do not interfere in other people's lives."

Hilda put her palms together, closed her eyes, and said, "Dear Lord, do not strike him dead; he didn't mean it. Yours truly, Hilda Burroughs Long." Lazarus ignored her.

"Nor do I, Lazarus. Other than occasionally, with a horse whip. Forgot to mention— They aren't gelded."

"Hazel, Laz-Lor are vaccinated and would have to come back here to see Ishtar to get it reversed. As for rasslin' matches, any male who tried to rape one of my clones *would* be gelded. Informally. At once. No instruments. No anesthesia. I trained 'em myself. Forget it. Apparently they've already met; they'll settle their own affairs, if any, their own way. Leave Cas and Pol in that hilton if you wish—by the way, I own it—but you're coming home or I'll tell Tamara."

"Bully. I don't bully worth a hoot, Lazarus."

"I'm out of it. Tamara *never* bullies. She merely gets her own way. What was this third reason?"

"Well . . . don't tell on me. Ishtar is a fine girl but I have no wish to stay where she could corner me and try to sell me rejuvenation."

Lazarus looked horrified. "Who has been feeding you nonsense?"

"Well? It's a commercial enterprise, is it not?"

"Certainly. Tanstaafl. All the traffic will bear. But we aren't ghouls; we'll accept a lien against a client's future earnings with no security and only the going rate of interest . . . then let him take as long as he likes to figure out that it doesn't pay to cheat us. But, Hazel, Ishtar *never* solicits; the clinic doesn't even have a flack. But if you *asked* her, you would go to the top of the list as my friend. However, she will supply painless suicide just as readily. You can have that later today. No charge. Compliments of the House."

"Lafe, I don't see how your wives put up with you."

"They don't; they make me toe the line. Something they learned from the Stone Gang, I believe."

"Well, I'm not trying to suicide. I'm less than two hundred Terran years old with a Luna background to stretch it. This is the first time I've been on a heavy planet since the last time I saw you; I'll last a while. But, Lazarus, *I have no wish to be a young girl.*"

"Hazel—"

"Huh? Jubal, keep out of this. Say, did you ever see anything of that young man again? Did he resurrect the way some claim he did?"

"Not to my knowledge. Although I saw something a while ago that made me wonder. Hazel, I'm going to take rejuvenation . . . and hang onto my present appearance. Red nose and all."

Hazel turned abruptly to face Lazarus. "Is this true? Can this be done?"

Maureen answered. "Hazel, I work at the clinic at the bedpan level . . . with the expectation of becoming a junior rejuvenation technician in upteen years. I see what goes on. A client states in writing what apparent age she prefers. That's skin deep, easy to do, easy to maintain. But, unless it is an unusual contract, we turn out a biologically mature young adult. Call it eighteen standard years."

"Page Ponce de Leon! You mean I can still be *me* . . . but get rid of the morning aches and the arthritic twinges and the forty-leven other things that are the *real* trouble with living too long?"

"Exactly."

"Uh . . . what about what I'm sitting on? Haven't used it much lately. Or wanted to."

Lazarus fielded this. "You'll want to. Unless you contract for an abnormal endocrine balance. But, Hazel, there are many men who prefer to deal with an old, established, reliable firm. Ask Tamara."

"Uh . . . be switched if I'm not feeling embarrassed, an emotion I haven't felt in more years than I'll admit. You can pick any apparent age, you say? Could I be, uh, late middle age? My hair its right color but streaked with gray? A sag under my chin instead of this wattle? Teats a man might grab and enjoy it? That 'old, established firm'—but not decrepit?"

"Certainly," said Lazarus.

"Hazel, I can take you to the clinic now," Maureen offered. "Always someone in the business office. Discuss types of contract. Decide what you want and when. Even get your prelim physical today and set date of admission."

"Uh . . . yes, I'm interested. But not till later today; I've got friends entered in the preliminary rounds of the Society for Creative Anachronism."

"Besides," Jubal put in, "they need time to check your credit rating, see what they can stick you for. By now Lafe has given Athene some signal to start x-raying your purse."

"He has *not*," Hilda denied. "*I* did. Hazel, we don't solicit business; we let the client sell it to herself. Maureen picks up one percent on this deal. Not Lazarus."

"Can't see that it matters," Jacob added. "Hey! Waiter! Over here, please! We Longs pool the boodle and Deety tells us what we have, what we can spend—but not who fetched it in."

"Jacob, it's the *principle*. Making money is a game. Maureen landed her."

"Hazel landed herself, Hilda," Hazel Stone put in. "I don't enjoy getting up feeling wobbly. Jubal, are you game for this?"

"My mind's made up."

"Then take a double room with me and we can tell each other lies while they make us feel young again. Hilda, is that kosher?"

"Lots of double rooms. Ish knows that you are both special friends of Lazarus and, while she doesn't spoil Lazarus, she'll do him any reasonable favor," Hilda assured her. "I think it's the same all around, Waiter—charge it to my account."

"My check," said Jubal.

"Waiter," Hilda said firmly.

The waiter looked at her, flexed his jaw muscles, said, "Very well, Director!"—and vanished.

"I think I missed something," Jubal remarked.

"I think I didn't," said Hazel. "'Yon Cashier hath a lean and hungry look. He thinks too much. Such men are dangerous.'"

Jubal looked around. "That cashier is our waiter. I think."

"I know. And bartender. And ticket taker. Unless his mother had quadruplets, he has Niven dislocators built into his shoes. I wish I could remember *where* I have seen him. He is not pleased with Hilda. Or Lazarus."

"Eh? Why?"

"Wait and see. There will not be another tab brought to this table—want to bet?"

"No bet," Lazarus interrupted. "The upstart knows who I am, who Hilda is. People at this table are guests of the management. He had better remember it or I'll sick Deety on him. Or even Hilda. But they hardly ever live through *that*. Hey, there's Deety now!" Lazarus stood up and waved. *"Deety!* Over here!"

Deety had with her a gaggle of giggles. "I don't have time to do this right; we want to get over to the Field of the Cloth of Gold before the preliminaries—besides, we've got husbands over there, most of us. So this is Ginnie and Winnie and Minnie, and Ginnie's a witch and Winnie's a nurse and Minnie's a retired computer, twin sister to Teena, and this is Holly and Poddy and Libby and Pink, and Holly is a design engineer, ship's architect type, and Poddy is a therapy empathist, and Libby you all know, and Fuzzy is a computer artist like me and the first one to calculate the Number of the Beast to the last significant figure, and now we'd

better go even though we have reserved V.I.P. seats because there
is a masked knight in the first match and we're pretty sure who
he is, and has anyone seen Zebadiah?"

"I'm certain who he is," said Ginnie. "He brought me to life,
and besides, he's wearing Karen's colors."

"I see Zeb off in the distance," Lazarus answered.

"No," Jake denied, "here he comes now, from over this way.
Ishtar with him. All dressed up."

"No," said Jubal. "That's Anne with him."

"Somebody is screw loose. Lazarus is right. I know my first
husband even at this distance. He's just approaching those three
reserved sections opposite the big screen over the bar. *Zebadiah!*
Over here!"

The other computer artist added, "And that can't be Anne, so
it must be Ishtar. Anne is at the field, I know, because Larry is
helping Jerry run it and told me. Anne agreed to cloak and be the
third judge when Jerry told her that Mr. Clemens had agreed.
Bonforte sits as king although he says he doesn't know much
about the kinging business and even less about jousting."

"Is it true that they are using real weapons today?" asked Jubal.

"And real horses," agreed Lazarus. "I was able to borrow the
Anheuser-Busch Clydesdales."

"Lazarus, is this wise?"

"Doctor Bone is taking care of the horses. If one is injured,
we'll give him the works. Those beautiful horses will be returned
to Old Home Terra at their proper year and second in better shape
than they were. With added skill. It's takes *time* to turn a
Clydesdale into a knight's charger even though that's what they
are. But will they ever be happy in harness again?"

"Lazarus," Podkayne said seriously, "I'll speak to Dr. Bone.
If a horse is unhappy, we will soothe."

"Poddy, you're a Smart Girl."

"About average here, I think. But if someone is unhappy, I
have learned what to do. I have never seen a horse but they've
lived with people so long that it can't be very different."

Jubal sighed. "I'm glad the horses will be well taken care of—
but, Lazarus, I meant *humans*. Isn't someone going to be hurt?
Maybe killed?"

"Most of them hurt, several killed. But they do it for *fun*. Those
who are hurt won't stay hurt; we are hardly more than a loud shout
from this planet's best hospital. If a man loses an arm or a leg or
an eye, or even his balls, he'll have to be patient while a new part
is cloned. But that sort of cloning we are learning to do right

at the spot of injury, like a lizard or a newt. Faster. More efficient.

"If he's killed, he has two choices: Be brought to life again by Ishtar's crew—brain unlikely to be hurt; their helms are the best part of their armor. Or, they can go straight to Valhalla; we've arranged for Bifrost to extend to this Field until the end of SCA's part in the convention. Six Valkyries standing by and 'Sarge' Smith at the top of Bifrost checking them against the roster as he musters them home." Lazarus grinned. "Believe me, the Society is paying high for these services, bond posted in advance; Deety wrote the contract."

"Lafe, you're telling me that Wagnerian Valkyries are waiting to carry the slain Over The Rainbow into Asgard?"

"Jubal, these Amazons are *not* opera singers; these are the real hairy, sweaty McCoy. Remember the purpose of this convention. Snob."

The waiter appeared. "You wish something, sir?"

"Yes. Tell your boss that I want this table—this table *only*—to have a full view of Bifrost, from the Field to Valhalla. I know it's not in the clothing illusion contract but the same gear will do it . . . and we can settle it when we go to court later. It will offset some of his lousy service. Git!"

"We'd better all 'git,'" said Libby. "They won't hold up things for us. That armor is heavy and hot. Deety?"

"Run along, I'll catch up. Here comes my first husband."

"Lafe, if they are killed, how do you know which ones to send to the clinic, which ones to send up the bridge?"

"Jubal, how would *you* do it? Sealed envelopes, destroyed if a knight wins, opened if he loses . . . and there may be some surprised widows tonight, unable to believe that their loving husbands elect to hunt all day, then feast on barbecued boar, guzzle mead, and wench all night, in preference to being restored to life in their respectable homes. But did I tell you what a winner gets? Aside from applause and a chance to kneel to 'King' John and 'Queen' Penelope. A paradox's his reward."

"A paradox?"

"No, no! Noisy in here. A pair o' doxies *each* his reward. The Society got a bargain. The arts are in their infancy here; Boondock is still so much a frontier that we have not yet developed distinguished hetaerae. But some of the most celebrated hetaerae in New Rome volunteered their services in exchange for transportation and the privilege of attending this convention."

Zebadiah was struck by a guided missile, female, from five

meters. He managed to stay on his feet and took his first wife to
the table, sat down by Hilda, pinched her thigh, pinched her glass,
drained it, said, "You're too young to drink, little girl. Is this your
father?"

"I'm her son," Jake answered. "Do you know Hazel Stone? If not, you should. We thought we saw you coming from the other direction."

"Shouldn't drink in the daytime, Jake. *Waiter!* Your servant, Ma'am. I've followed your series on 3-D since I was a kid and I'm honored to meet you. Are you covering this for Lunaya Pravda?"

"Heavens, no! LOCUS has an exclusive under the reasonable theory that LOCUS *alone* is competent to report *this* convention. Jerry and Ben are covering it for their various journals . . . but must clear it through Charles. I'm here as an expert, believe it or not—as an author of popular fantasy. Is the Galactic Overlord of my series real or imaginary and is there a difference? See next week's thrilling episode; the Stone family has to eat. Same thing all around, I think. You can tip him, Doctor Zebadiah, but there is no tab at the Director's table."

"And no tips," growled Lazarus. "Deliver my message to your boss again and tell that spinning arsfardel he has exactly three minutes before I invoke paragraph nine, section 'c.' Here comes your double, Zeb."

From behind the couple who, at half a klick, had been mistaken for Zebadiah and Ishtar, came out quickly a shorter, older, broad-shouldered man. All three were dressed Robin-Hood-and-his-Merry-Men style: buskins, breeks, leathern jackets, feathered caps, long bows and quivers of fletched shafts, swords and daggers, and were swinging along in style.

The shorter man hurried a few paces ahead, turned and faced their path, swept off his cap and bowed deeply. "Make way for Her Wisdom, Empress of eighty-thr—"

The woman, as if by accident, backhanded the groom. He ducked, rolled, avoided it, bounced to his feet and continued: "—worlds, and her consort the Hero Gordon."

Lazarus got up, addressed the groom. "Doctor Rufo! So happy you could make it! This is your daughter Star?"

"His grandmother," Her Wisdom corrected, dropping a quick curtsy to Lazarus. "Yes, I'm Star. Or Mrs. Gordon; this is my husband, Oscar Gordon. What is correct usage here? I've not been on this planet before."

"Mrs. Gordon, Boondock is so new that its customs have not

yet calcified. Almost any behavior is acceptable if meant in a kindly way. Anybody causes real trouble, it's up to our chairman Ira Weatheral and advisers selected by him. Since Ira doesn't like the job, he tends to procrastinate, hoping the problem will go away. As a result we don't have much government and few customs."

"A man after my own heart. Oscar, we could live here if they will have us. My successor is ready; I could retire."

"Mrs. Gordon—"

"Yes, Doctor Long?"

"We—our chairman Ira especially—all know quite well who 'Her Wisdom' is. Ira would welcome you with open arms and resign in your favor at once—passed by acclamation and you would be boss for life. Better stick to the devil you know. But you are most welcome whenever you choose to visit."

She sighed. "You're right. Power is not readily surrendered; I'll probably wait for assassination."

Deety whispered, "Zebadiah . . . that bartender. Whom does he look like?"

"Hmm— Brigadier Iver Hird-Jones?"

"Well, maybe. A little. I was thinking of Colonel Morinosky."

"Mmm— Yes. No importance since it can't be either one. Mr. Gordon?"

"Call me 'Easy.' Or Oscar, Doctor Carter."

"I'm Zeb. Is that the Lady herself? The sword you wore in the Quest for the Egg of the Phoenix?"

Gordon looked delighted. "Yes! The Lady Vivamus."

"Can't ask a man to draw a sword without a cause . . . but is the inscription close enough to the hilt that we could read it if you were simply to show steel?"

"No trouble." Gordon exposed the etched: *Dum Vivimus, Vivamus!*—gave them time to read it, clicked it to full return, and asked, "And is *that* the sword that killed the Boojum?"

"The Boo— *Oh!* The monster we call a 'Black Hat.' But we did not 'softly and silently vanish away.'"

"No, *it* did. That will be a point we'll discuss in the seminar panel: 'Techniques for Hunting Snarks.' You and I and Doctor Jacob and Doctor Hilda, with some others. André. Kat Moore. Fritz. Cliff. The Gordfather will moderate when he gets over his wheezes. Which he will—Tamara's treating hi— *Oh, heavens! Oh, God, how beautiful!*"

The "sky" had opened, for their table, and they found themselves looking at the Field of the Cloth of Gold, a half klick away and a few meters above them, on and up to high, high, high in the sky, the shimmering towers and palaces of Valhalla, with the Rainbow Bridge reaching from the field of honor to the distant gate of the eternal home of heroes.

Instead of the wooded horizon usually seen in that direction, the land lifted in terraces, each more colorfully beautiful than the last, until the highest was lost in pink and saffron clouds—and above them, much higher, Valhalla in Asgard.

"Pappy!"

"Yes, Athene," Lazarus said quietly. "Localize it. Me only. I have many people around me."

"That's better? No problems, just to alert you. Arthur and Isaac and Bob all arriving at once. Twelve minutes, plus two, minus zero."

"You're a smart girl, Teena."

"Put that in writing. Blandjor."

Lazarus said to the table at large, "My guests for those reserved spaces are arriving. I wasn't sure of Isaac; he gets bigger every year and reluctant to travel other than by water. Arthur had such a long way to come and communications are always uncertain. Bob I knew was here but there were duty matters interfering. Shall we listen to some of the opening plenary while we look at the beauties of the Norse Afterland? We don't want to *look* at the general session. But we can listen. When the tourney starts, give most of your attention to the hologram except during the Valkyrie ride. Snob! Give us the sound from the plenary session."

They got it at once, sound and fury signifying nothing. Under its cover Jubal Harshaw said to Zebadiah, "Before they get on that panel in front of an audience, think about this. How many 'Black Hats' or 'Boojums' are there?"

"Eh? I have no way of telling. In excess of twenty as a best guess but that excess could be many millions, also a best guess."

"But how many did you *see?*" Harshaw persisted.

"Oh. One. But more were a certainty."

"So? You would never get a Fair Witness to say that. What harm did it or they do you?"

"Huh? Tried to kill us. Bombed us out. Killed my cousin. Chased us off our home planet. Impoverished all four of us. What do you want? Plagues and locusts? The Four Horsemen?"

"No. *You* saw *one*. You killed it. It never laid a glove on you. Think about it. Before you testify. Let's listen."

"If you read it correctly it's all in the Bible. 'In the beginning was the Word, and the Word was with God, and the Word *was* God.' Could anyone ask for a plainer statement of the self-evident fact that nothing exists until someone imagines it and thereby gives it being, reality? The distinction lies only in the difference between 'being' and 'becoming'—a distinction that cancels out when any figment-fact is examined from different ends of the entropy error—"

"Bishop Berkeley is presiding," Lazarus commented, "and would have shut this figment up save that the Bishop has laryngitis—imaginary, of course—and his parliamentarian, the Reverend Mister Dodgson, is too meek to shut anyone up. The Meek Shall Inherit the Earth, One Meter Wide and Two Meters Long."

"If God displaces the Devil, he must assume the Devil's attributes. How about giving the Devil equal time? God has the best press agents. Neither fair nor logical!"

"I am Alpha and Omega, the beginning and the end, the first and the last."

"Occam's Razor is *not* the least hypothesis! It is the *least probable* hypothesis. The truth—"

"There are three schools of magic. One: State a tautology, then ring the changes on its corollaries; that's philosophy. Two: Record many facts. Try to see a pattern. Then make a wrong guess at the next fact; that's science. Three: Awareness that you live in a malevolent universe controlled by Murphy's Law, sometimes offset in part by Brewster's Factor: that's engineering."

"*Why did Mercutio have to die?* Solve that, and it will lead you to Mark Twain's well. There's your answer."

"Who is more real? Homer or Ulysses? Shakespeare or Hamlet? Burroughs or Tarzan?"

The debate shut off, the giant hologram screen lighted up in heroic size, full depth and color, and the tedious voices were cut off by a loud and lively one: **"While we're waiting for the first two champions to reach their starting lines we will have 'The Grand Canal' sung by lovely Anne Passovoy and accompanied by Noisy on his Stomach Steinway. Noisy is not in voice today, friends; he was bitten last night by an imaginary snake."**

"Jerry is in good voice," whispered Deety. "He always is. Aren't they going to give us any closeups?" The camera zoomed in on Anne Passovoy, panned across the other Anne, cloaked in white, rested for a moment on "King" John and "Queen" Penelope, went on to show a vigorous old man with a halo of white hair who took a stogie out of his mouth and waved.

"On my right is Sir Tenderloinn the Brutal and on my left is the Black Knight, shield unblazoned, helm closed. Oh Jear not, friends; Holger tongues. Dis Dane could be our arrow. Whose color—"

Zebadiah heard a crash, turned his head. "They're bringing in a big Corson flatboat. Smashed some chairs." He looked again, announced, "Can't see much, the stands on this side are filling with people in green uniforms. Black berets. Bloodthirsty-looking gang."

"That's Asprin—"

"Give me ten grains. Deety, you let me mix my drinks."

"Asprin, not 'aspirin.' Bob Asprin, Commandammit of the Dorsai Very Irregular," Lazarus told him. "But can you see Arthur?"

"Does he wear a deerstalker's hat? Smoke a meerschaum pipe? The tall one there, talking to the man who looks like a gorilla."

"He'd Challenge you for that. Violent temper. That's Arthur's party, all right. Doctor Arthur Conan Doyle. Doctor Watson should be there, too. Wups! Here comes Isaac. And there goes another bunch of chairs."

"They're off! The Masked Challenger is gaining speed, Sir Tenderloinn is having trouble getting his charger to move: It is a beautiful day here at Epsom Salts and Bifrost never looked lovelier."

Lazarus stood up. "I must greet Isaac. Zebadiah, have you met him? Come with me. You, too, Deety. Hilda? Please, dear. Jake?"

"Just a moment, you!" Zeb looked at the one interrupting them and felt shock. He had seen that face, that uniform, by a rustic swimming pool. The "ranger" addressed Lazarus: "You're the one they call the Executive Director. Special Agent L. Ron O'Leemy, InterSpace Patrol. I have warrants for Beowolf Shaeffer, Caspol Jones, and Zebadiah John Carter. Director, I require your cooperation. Article Four Six, Section Six Five, Paragraph Six, InterUniversal Criminal Code.

"Unhorsed! The Black Knight's lance right through him! Here come the Valkyries. *Hoyotoko!*"

Hilda reached out, took the warrants, tore them across. "You're on the wrong planet, Mac." She grasped Zeb's arm. "Come along, Alfred; we must meet Isaac."

They passed the Dorsai, reached the big Corson flatboat. Completely filling it was a *very* large Venerian Dragon. The dragon turned an eyestalk toward them; his tendrils touched his voder. "Greetings, Doctor Lazarus Long. Greetings, new friends. May you all die beautifully!"

"Greetings, Sir Isaac. Sir Isaac Newton, this is Doctor Hilda Burroughs Long, Doctor Jacob Burroughs Long, Doctor Deety Carter Long, and Doctor Zebadiah John Carter Long, all of my family."

"I am honored, learned friends. May your deaths inspire a thousand songs. Doctor Hilda, we have a mutual friend, Professor Wogglebug."

"Wait, wait! Don't tear up your tickets. The Valkyries are having a problem. Yes, the judges have confirmed it. No contest! The Dane has 'killed' a totally empty suit of armor! Better luck next bout, Pou— Holger."

"Oh, how delightful! Zebadiah and I saw him just this past week in delivering our children to Oz for the duration of this convention. Did I just miss you?"

The dragon answered, with a Cockney lisp, "No, we are pen pals only. He can't leave Oz; I had never expected to leave Venus again . . . until your device—perhaps I should say Doctor Jacob's device— made it simple. But see what our friend Professor Wogglebug sent me—" The dragon fiddled at a pouch under his voder.

The InterSpace Patrol Agent O'Leemy tapped Zeb on the shoulder. "I heard those introductions. Come along, Carter!"

"—spectacles to fit my forward stalks, that see through the thickest mist." He put them on, looked around him. "They clarify any— There! Get him! Grab him! That Beast! Get his Number!" Without a lost instant Deety, Hilda, and Lazarus closed on the "agent"—and were left with torn clothes and plastic splints as the thing got loose. The "special agent" vaulted over the bar, was seen again almost instantly at the far end of the bar, jumped up on it, leapt for the canvas top, grabbed hold of the edge of the illusion hole, swung itself up, bounded for Bifrost, reached it.

Sir Isaac Newton played: "Mellrooney! The worst troublemaker in all the worlds. Lazarus, I never expected to find that Beast in your quiet retreat."

"Nor did I until I heard *all* of Zeb's story. This convention was called especially to entice him. And it did. But we lost him, we *lost* him!"

"But I got its Number," Hilda said and held out its shield: **"666"**

The fleeing figure, dark against the Rainbow Bridge, grew smaller and higher. Lazarus added, "Or perhaps we haven't lost him. He'll never get past Sarge Smith."

The figure appeared to be several klicks high now, when the illusion suddenly broke. The Rainbow was gone, the terraces melted, the clouds were gone, the towers and castles of Asgard could no longer be seen.

In the middle distance, very high up, a figure was tumbling, twisting, falling. Zeb said, "Sarge won't have to bother. We've seen the last of *it*."

The voder answered: "Friend Zebadiah . . . are you *sure?*"

A NOTE ABOUT THE AUTHOR

ROBERT ANSON HEINLEIN was born in Butler, Missouri, in 1907. A graduate of the U.S. Naval Academy, he was retired, disabled, in 1934. He studied mathematics and physics at the graduate school of the University of California and owned a silver mine before beginning to write science fiction in 1939. In 1947 his first book of fiction, *Rocket Ship Galileo*, was published. His novels include *Double Star* (1956), *Starship Troopers* (1959), *Stranger in a Strange Land* (1961), and *The Moon Is a Harsh Mistress* (1966), all winners of the Hugo Award. Heinlein was guest commentator for the Apollo-11 first lunar landing. In 1975 he received the Grand Master Nebula Award for lifetime achievement.